OF LOVE AND LIFE

OF LOVE AND LIFE

Three novels selected and condensed
by Reader's Digest

The Reader's Digest Association Limited, London

The Reader's Digest Association Limited
11 Westferry Circus, Canary Wharf, London E14 4HE

www.readersdigest.co.uk

ISBN 0-276-42870-6

For information as to ownership of copyright in the material of this book, and acknowledgments, see last page.

CONTENTS

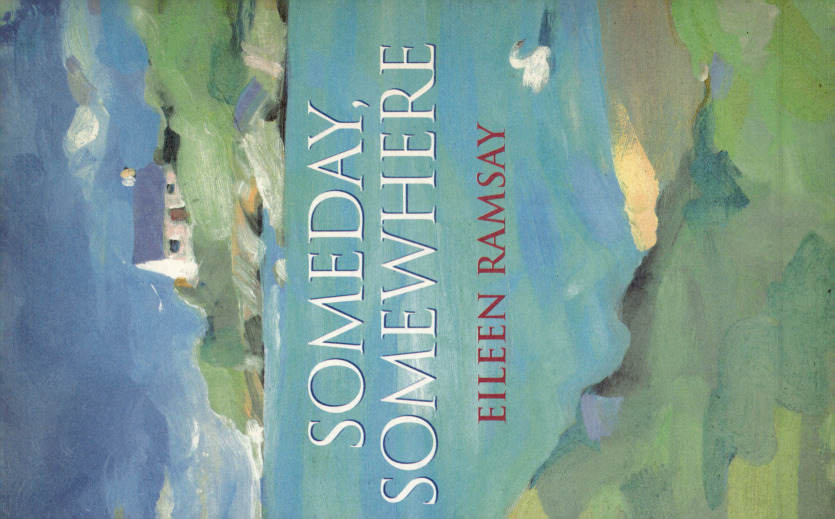

Someday, Somewhere

Eileen Ramsay

Idyllic summers spent with her reclusive and artistic Aunt Tony at her cottage in Scotland are some of Holly Noble's most precious childhood memories. When Tony dies and Holly returns to the cottage to claim her inheritance, it feels like coming home. But what she discovers there leads her to question both her past—and her future.

CHAPTER ONE
TORRY BAY, 1998

Everything, darling Holly, that you find in the cottage is yours to do with as you think best. I made a pact—but no one is alive now who cares one way or the other.

HOLLY LOOKED UP at the cottage that she had once considered her second home. Aunt Tony was dead—the awful news was beginning to sink in—and now this cottage, where she had had so many wonderful holidays, was hers, but it would never be the same, not without Tony, her ghastly cigarettes, her far from fashionable clothes and her boyish haircut.

The building was as it had always been, a small squat structure that looked as if it had been set down in the bay and then patted firmly on the head by a kind but giant hand, so that the base seemed to have spread out slightly further than the edges of the roof. It was, it seemed to say, there to stay and would withstand the storms that raged around it during the winter months and would bask in the heat of the sun that played on its white walls in the summer. The petunias in the window boxes suffered no matter the weather, but on the few days when everything was perfect they rewarded the careless gardener with an almost embarrassing exuberance of colour.

A scrabbling sound on the roof distracted her and she looked up. A young seagull had landed on the incongruity of the large window that Tony had had inserted into the roof so that there was some light in her attic studio. Holly half laughed, half sobbed as the young bird scrambled wildly to keep his balance as he slid inexorably down the sheet of glass. Just before he reached the base he obviously remembered that he could fly and took off into the air with an angry squawk. Young birds had been doing that almost as long as Holly could remember.

She sighed and took the keys out of her handbag. Keeping the cottage was out of the question, no matter how it called to her. Glasgow was where she worked and she did not earn enough to keep two places going. The cottage would have to go, but first she would take away one or two of the things she had loved as a child. The old armchair where Tony had died would be first on the list. A thousand happy memories were in that chair. It would go into her bedroom in her thoroughly modern apartment. One day soon it would be a feature in her home, hers and John's.

Holly turned the key in the lock and, pushing back a sob, opened the door and stood in the doorway waiting just as she had always waited, looking, listening, smelling, assessing. The past, with all its happy memories, drifted out with the dust sprites to meet her. To the left was the main room, the living room that doubled as a dining room; ahead of her the almost perpendicular staircase leading to the bedrooms and the bathroom that huddled together beside Tony's attic studio under the roof. To the right of the front door was the tiny kitchen. Some time in the last twenty years Tony had had a wall knocked through to the old wash-house so that she would no longer have to challenge the elements to do her washing.

All mod cons, darling girl.

But no, there was no time to wallow. The school had been so kind about giving her a few days to go off to Argyll to arrange the funeral but it would not be too happy if this second visit to close the cottage extended into another week. She would be ruthlessly efficient. Her flat was too small to take many of the loved items; after all, some of John's things would be coming soon too. John loathed what he called 'old tat'. She would look round and, no matter how forcibly her heart told her to keep and cherish some valueless treasures, she would dispose of them. John, however, would understand that she had to have some souvenirs; he loved her, didn't he, and would want her to be happy. She would make quick decisions; pack the items she just must keep before going back to the city. That's where her life was, no matter how unsatisfactory.

We write our own scripts, darling girl.

The voice was so clear that she started. Tony might have been standing at her elbow, just as she had been so many times for over thirty years. Holly smiled and closed the door behind her. The living room of the cottage was just as it had always been: two huge shabby armchairs in front of the fire, another in the window looking not at the fire but out to the beach, a table with two chairs . . . Two? One for Tony and one for Holly. As far back as she could remember there had only ever been two people in the cottage, herself and Tony. Don't be childish, Holly, she scolded herself. Tony must have had friends from the village.

Of course. Mrs Fraser from the shop. She would have to go up to the village to see her, to ask her if she would like some memento. Who else? Canon Gemmell? How real he was and yet he was dead now, had been dead a long time, although he would live for ever in the magnificent portraits that Tony had painted of him.

Tony had learned to drive some time in the sixties and had always met her waif of a niece at the station in Glasgow. For me, Holly had thought with childish satisfaction, she learned to drive for me.

I know there are closer stations, darling girl, but we are so privileged to be able to drive through Argyll.

Holly had loved those drives in that ancient car. What kept it going? Prayers probably, more than science, but what joy those drives had been, what fun they had had, talking and singing and stopping abruptly to drink in a view.

Holly, look at the light on the sea.

So blue, isn't it?

No, it's not, see—it's lilac . . . and pink. Look with all your senses, Holly, not just your eyes.

Sometimes, if the weather was right, they would stop for a picnic on a bank of purple heather. How that heather scratched, but views like those were worth a little discomfort; Tony never remembered clever things like blankets.

Holly went back to her inventory. There, against the wall, was the settee that was never used, the bookcase with its eclectic collection of books under the window, the ornaments, the vases and the oil lamps. For the first time she realised that the lamps had Tiffany shades. That would please John. She sighed. John: John who was the major part of her unsatisfactory life. She would not think about him now. There was too much to do and too little time in which to do it.

Instinctively she looked at the mantelpiece and smiled with relief. The clock was still there, the beautiful gilded girl holding up her pendulum, as she had held it all through Holly's childhood. The pendulum was motionless, but Holly remembered a time when she had eaten something that disagreed with her and Tony had carried the clock upstairs to the little room under the eaves where the young Holly had gone to sleep, lulled by the swinging pendulum and the soft tick-tock. The adult Holly looked at the clock with John's eyes and saw that it was valuable, but she would not sell it, she would keep it. Perhaps, one day, if they didn't wait too long, there would be a little John to soothe to sleep.

She picked up her overnight bag and went upstairs. Her room was just as she had left it. Damn, damn, damn. When had she last spent more than an afternoon in this cottage? John did not want to 'waste time in the wilds of Scotland', and so for almost five years she had made little effort to see the person who meant more to her than anyone else in the world. She lay down on the bed under the window and wept, as copiously as the child Holly had wept, but with a woman's damaged heart. Had she known Tony was failing she would have come. John would have come; he was not so selfish. But Tony had never complained.

'Young people in love, darling girl. I know all about that. Don't worry about me. Come when you can. This is your home, you know.'

She had meant to make the journey but she never had. Tony, who knew nothing whatsoever about being madly in love with the most unsatisfactory person, who knew nothing about love at all, had absolved her niece of all guilt.

Holly slept and, when she woke in the dark room, for a moment she did not remember where she was. John expected her to be away for only one night and now, stupidly and childishly, she had slept hours away. She would get something to eat and then continue her inventory. He missed her when she was not there, he said. She refused to question how John could miss her if he was often too busy to see her when she was there. He is working hard so that we can marry soon, she told herself.

Downstairs she lit the oil lamps, because they were so much friendlier than the electric light that Tony had installed in the seventies, and then made instant coffee and ate bread and cheese and fruit, while sitting at the table looking out onto the beach. The moon was high and it played on the soft surface of the sea. Sometimes its beams darted in the window and doused the stones and shells on the window ledge with soft pale light. The stones. The shells. Every holiday they had collected them and one had been selected to sit on the window ledge.

Holly 1966 . . . Holly 1970.

The dates went on. None had been thrown away as soon as the child Holly had been taken back to Glasgow and put on the train or the plane that would take her to be deposited once again in her boarding school, or with her rather overwhelmed parents.

Holly piled her cup and plates into the sink and went back upstairs. She would choose some things from the bedrooms. If she kept the chair and the Tiffany lamp, the clock, some books, an ornament or two, things that whispered 'Tony', perhaps her flat would remind her of Achahoish and Torry Bay.

The main bedroom was just as it had always been. It held the large comfortable bed with its pile of pillows, the chair, the wardrobe with Tony's clothes, and her dressing table. Holly stared at the dressing table that was so neat when Tony had been so unbelievably untidy. What was it that was so different about this dressing table? That was it. Every other dressing table she had ever seen had at least one photograph on it, but Tony had no framed photographs.

'The people I love are in my heart, Holly. I don't need photographs.'

'People? But there aren't people, Tony. There's only me.' She heard again her jealous childish voice and she saw again Tony's smile.

'Of course there's you, darling girl,' Tony had said, lighting a cigarette. 'Now don't tell Iron Girder that I'm still smoking like an old chimney.'

The young Holly had laughed guiltily because, really, Aunt Tony must not call Mummy 'Iron Girder'. Her name was Gilda. She had forgotten that Tony had not agreed that there were no other people in her heart. But they were all dead now: Daddy, Mummy, and Tony herself.

One by one she opened the drawers. There would be nothing that she would want to keep here. Tony had been small and dainty. Beside her, Holly had sometimes felt large and ungainly although she was barely five foot five herself. All Tony had ever worn were her oversized shirts and paint-marked jeans and occasionally a flamboyant flowing skirt. Holly would take everything to a charity shop in Glasgow. She no longer knew anyone here in Achahoish. Tony's old friends, whom she had met from time to time, were all dead, except for the doctor who had retired to Spain and had felt too old and too sad to come to the service. Maybe one day she would write to him or go to see him, but what would she say? 'Do you remember me? I used to visit my aunt. You took a fish-hook out of my ear once.'

No, he would not care. Why should he?

She was faintly surprised to find a lovely evening stole and she held its soft fabric against her. It smelt slightly of very expensive perfume, Tony's 'special day' perfume. Perhaps she might keep just this one personal possession although she had never seen Tony wear it. In the bottom of a drawer filled with sketchbooks was a large box tied up with string, and on top was a sealed envelope with 'Holly' written on it in Tony's elegant hand. She picked it up, opened it, and a large, old-fashioned key fell out.

Darling girl,

Everything in the boxes is for you. Enjoy them. The key is to the attic and that's where I keep the work that I never wanted to sell in my life-time. But, as I stated in my will, do what you like with them now. I hope you will keep one or two to remember.

Yours, with all love, Tony

Her work, Tony had been a painter; one, moreover, who sold what she painted. Holly's father had never quite come to terms with having a painter for a sister, so bohemian. But Holly knew that her aunt had trained at a world-famous art school in London and had had several shows until the seventies, when she had stopped exhibiting. Her shows were the only times she left Torry Bay. She put her beautiful landscapes, the odd portrait of a local worthy, into the trunk of her funny old car, drove to London or Glasgow or Edinburgh, handed over the work, and returned as soon as she could get away.

That stole must have been what she wore to openings. Her one bit of glam. I can just hear them: 'Here comes old Tony Noble in her ancient stole, poor old thing.'

But this note was saying that there was other work.

Holly put the large box to one side—she would look at it later—and went out onto the landing. There were four doors at the top of the stairs: Tony's room, Holly's room, the bathroom and the attic studio.

It was as if the lock had not been turned in some time, for it was difficult to turn the key, but eventually the door opened and again Holly was assailed by memories. The air in the dimly lit room was stale; above all it smelt of paint. Memories of a pigtailed Holly standing in a swimsuit daubing paint on a canvas, while Tony stood beside her and made wonderful swirls of blue and pink and grey that somehow metamorphosed into hills and the sea and the village over there across the bay, flooded back. There was only one easel there now. Tony had long ago agreed that Holly's genius, if it existed at all, did not lie in paint pots.

'But there is something, darling girl, and we'll find it. Don't listen to those teachers. What do they know?'

The teachers had known and Tony had not. There was no genius lurking in Holly Noble. Antonia Noble was the family genius.

Holly smiled as again she saw her aunt in her jeans and her oversized shirt, cigarette (often unlit) hanging from her lip, painting, painting, painting. She looked around at the bare walls and the huge window that Tony had had put into the roof. During the day or on a bright starry night the electric light was hardly necessary and, by the light of the moon, Holly saw bulky sheet-wrapped shapes that had to be the canvases mentioned in the letter. They were everywhere. She walked over to those directly under the window and knelt beside them.

The work that I never wanted to sell in my lifetime.

They must be of me. But she couldn't have painted . . . Holly looked around wildly; there were canvases everywhere . . . thirty, forty paintings of me? She gave them to Mummy, anyway, didn't she? Holly drew back the sheet that covered the pile beside which she was kneeling. The paintings still mocked her. Their faces were turned modestly away from the prying eyes of their public. She stood up and turned the first one over. For a second she was relieved. It was one of Tony's wonderful seascapes, that was all. What had she expected?

Not this, not this stunning vision of a sea such as she, Holly, had never seen and, in the middle, a boy, a youth, a satyr, difficult to tell. His green eyes gleamed at her from his perch on the back of a whale. The youth's face was vaguely familiar. No, it could not possibly be . . . Holly turned on the light and blinked.

Damn this light. Damn this room; it was so small. This was a large painting and she had to see it better. Holly manhandled the painting down the stairs and into the living room where she propped it against the dresser. She went round the room turning on every lamp and then she stood back and looked again at the painting. Yes, a seascape, and a mythological story; an old, often told story, 'The Boy on a Dolphin'. The boy's eyes smiled at her out of a tanned face of almost amazing beauty. A working title was written on the back in Tony's flamboyant hand: *Sea Sprite*, London 1937.

Holly sat back on her heels and looked at the painting. How beautiful he was, how wicked his smile. It couldn't be, of course; not that she had seen too many paintings of him, or photographs. Besides, it was impossible. *Sea Sprite*, 1937. Where was Tony in 1937? At the Slade. And he, the boy, the sea sprite? 'No,' she said loudly this time so that there could be no doubt. But it was.

Tentatively Holly reached out a shaking hand but she did not touch the picture.

Oil on your fingers, darling girl.

She pulled herself up as if she were an old woman and climbed the stairs to the studio. The paintings were still there; they had not been a dream or a nightmare. She turned a second, a third, and she gasped. They were, for the most part, large canvases, and yes, the child Holly was in several of them. But she did not dominate the paintings. Each and every one of the paintings she uncovered featured one man. In turn he was thoughtful, joyful, desolate, mischievous: he was Blaise Fougère, indubitably the greatest tenor France had ever produced, and possibly the greatest French singer of all time.

With a cry of pain Holly turned off the lights and, locking and closing the door behind her, ran back downstairs. It was still there: *Sea Sprite*, and the beautiful eyes, mocking, looked straight at her.

. . . as near as I can get to where I want to be.

Holly had almost forgotten that throwaway line. She looked across at the sideboard where she had put the casket that she had carried with her from Glasgow. No, said Holly, and again, no. She loved me and she loved Torry Bay. This is where she wanted to be buried.

'Tomorrow, Tony, I'll take your ashes up to the little headland and I'll scatter them. That's what you wanted.' She spoke directly to the urn.

Tony, vibrant, wonderful Tony, reduced to a few handfuls of dust.

Sea Sprite, 1937. Just before the war. Did they worry about war? Did he, this sprite? The sea was so real she could almost smell the tang. If she touched the painting the spray would dampen her hand. She looked into the green eyes. They did not mock. They were smiling at the artist. What did they say?

'I know you. I love you.'

For a moment Holly felt like a voyeur, as if she were looking at something private and holy, and she had no right, no right at all.

'There's only me, Tony.'

The painting told her that part of her life was a lie. Tony might have been everything to her but she was not everything to Tony. Antonia Noble, beloved spinster aunt, who had lived alone in this cottage, happy to wait for visits from her niece, had had another very different life. How well that secret had been kept. Holly had lived with her on and off all her life, because her parents, missionaries, had been overseas. There had never been anyone else there, never, ever, and certainly not this man.

Holly looked at the kneeling figure and he looked back at her.

Hollyberry.

Who spoke, who spoke?

She was my aunt, she was adamant: I would have known. She would have told me. Holly looked at her watch. This was madness. It was after midnight but she had to see them, had to find out. She went back to the studio and one by one she unwrapped as many of the paintings as she could reach easily and, to her, it was obvious that these were not the paintings of a diseased mind. These were not a lonely, frustrated, sex-starved old woman's paintings of the man on whom she had an unhealthy and secret crush. These were named and dated. *Blaise, Kensington Gardens*, 1938; *Blaise, Paris*, 1954; *Blaise, Torry Bay*, 1969; *Blaise*, 1990. Blaise, Blaise, Blaise.

She knew little of opera singers, but he had been so famous—a household name—and so the world knew that 1990 was just before his death. Holly looked at the paintings in which she featured. In one he was holding her hand and she was dancing into the sea beside him, at ease,

SOMEDAY, SOMEWHERE

content. She had met him, known him, and she did not remember.

With a stifled cry Holly threw the sheets over the brilliant images. She had to get away from them. She locked the door and stood leaning against it for a moment with her heart thumping madly against her ribs. Tony and Blaise Fougère.

The people I love are in my heart.

Tony Noble and Blaise Fougère had known each other for over fifty years; the paintings showed an intimacy; knowledge. They were paintings of a man by a woman who loved him and, from the light in his eyes in the paintings, who had been loved by him. A secret life. How could Tony Noble have known Blaise Fougère so intimately for so long and no one had known? It was impossible. Fougère was world famous. For a time so had Tony been. The press would have ferreted it out, would have emblazoned their love across the tabloids.

But the pictures were not lying. They were too . . . intimate to be fantasy. Holly retreated downstairs. There she curled up in the big armchair by the window—he had been painted relaxing in it—and she looked out over the water to the hills beyond. The moon laid a carpet of silver from the sky to the sea and then across the surface of the sea to the beach.

The fairy's path.

How Tony had loved that view and how she had loved to tease her brother, Holly's father, the Reverend Frederick Noble.

"'I to the hills will lift mine eyes,'" she had managed to quote at least once on each of the few occasions that her brother had visited her.

"'From whence will come mine aid.'"

'Really, Antonia, how many times must I tell you that it's a question. "From whence will come mine aid?" The hills are full of bandits.'

'Not these ones,' Tony had retorted.

Now, thinking of them, one whom she had loved so dearly and the other whom she had tried so hard to respect and love, Holly sighed. They were both dead: her father aware too late that he had never really known his own daughter, and Tony, who Holly thought she had known so well and had never known at all.

Blaise Fougère? I knew Tony liked opera. She introduced me to it. She played records—did she play Fougère's? She went to the opera in London or Glasgow when she was showing, but this . . .? I knew him when I was small and obviously liked him. But did I? There is no memory. Yes. Tony would never lie.

Her life was a lie.

Was he the reason why, when I was older, my visits had to be rearranged sometimes? He wouldn't want me to see him if they were keeping their relationship a secret, but why? Why didn't they marry? He was French. Was he Catholic? Tony never worried about labels. Perhaps he did. He was married to someone else? But why didn't he get a divorce? The Catholic business, I suppose. This painting is dated 1937. Did people care more about divorce in those days?

Holly got up and made herself another cup of coffee. She could barely assimilate what she had learned. Never ever had she thought of a man in connection with her aunt. Even when her parents had muttered things about wishing Antonia would find someone nice and stop living such an unconventional life, she had reflected complacently that Tony loved her, Holly, and therefore had absolutely no need of anyone else. And all the time Tony had been in love with Blaise Fougère.

No, that could not be. An affair? Tony? Eccentric Aunt Tony had had a relationship with a world-famous man. Possible? No, they could never have kept it a secret. But those paintings? Even examined by moonlight they showed a man who loved the artist who was painting him. Holly knew enough about art to know that. She took her coffee and went back upstairs. Perhaps the boxes would yield some clues.

She opened them on the bed and was glad that she was sitting; her knees would never have stood up to this new shock. Tiffany's windows were nothing. The boxes contained jewellery; expensive, custom-made jewellery: diamonds, emeralds, sapphires and gold. There was a note:

He was a very naive man in many ways, Holly. He could not believe that some women don't like jewellery. He was incredibly generous to everyone—charities, of course, but he loved giving and when he made money he spent it on presents. I gave up arguing with him and wore the jewellery when I was with him. The rubies are my favourites: they look fabulous with jeans! No pearls. Pearls are tears. He did not want to give me tears.

Holly picked up the necklace and bracelet made of rubies. The precious stones formed the centres of tiny gold flowers and were surprisingly delicate.

'But not with jeans, Tony,' she said as she held them for a moment close against her heart, and incidentally against her one piece of good jewellery: the pearls John had given her on their fifth anniversary.

The rubies, whatever John said, she would keep.

What on earth was she going to do? She had faced the prospect of losing the cottage and had accepted that. Life moved on and one had to leave people and places behind. But now there were the paintings that had to be worth something and the jewellery and even the furniture that her child's eye had not recognised as anything special.

I suppose that I am now a rich woman. John will be pleased.

But thoughts of John's pleasure did not thrill Holly. She almost wished she had not found Tony's letter and that she wasn't mentioned in her will. She did not want Blaise Fougère's jewels or his paintings.

Do what you like with them.

But what do you want me to do with them, Tony? You say that you hope I'll keep a few. I will but I can't house all of them and . . . they're important, aren't they? You were a more than respected painter and he was, well, he was who he was. John will be very practical and say things like, 'This will make a great deal of difference to our plans: we won't have to wait now.' But I wanted to marry him yesterday when we had nothing. By my standards I am now wealthy. What would the Director of Education say if I resigned?

But she could not do that. She loved children. Oh, how much she had grown to love other people's children. But now . . . no, too much to think about. One step at a time. It was now so late that the only sensible thing to do was to go to bed. The paintings had waited—some of them—for many years. They could wait another night.

Holly woke very early next morning and was aware of a feeling of deep happiness. She stretched her hand out for John but met the edge of the bed and, for a moment, was disappointed. Then she remembered: she was at Torry Bay. 'Perfect, perfect.'

No, it was not perfect, for she was here only because Tony was dead. Tony, her wonderful aunt, who had made total joy out of an unsatisfactory childhood, was gone for ever. This place was full of her. She could call 'Tony', and a voice would answer 'In the studio, darling girl'. There she would be painting, painting, her cigarette hanging unlit from her lip. Unlit. Of course it was unlit. She loved a singer, a tenor, for God's sake, the most delicate plant in the operatic garden.

And I never guessed. What a self-absorbed little snot.

Holly lay and looked at the ceiling and, as dawn came up, light began to stretch across the room. Her lovely perfect room where she had always been so happy. But nothing is perfect. There was a damp patch in the corner. It would be better to get the roof mended before putting the cottage on the market.

Then she remembered that she need not sell the cottage if she did not want to. She could keep it. She and John could come here. She could hear herself selling him the idea.

It will be a perfect place to get away from it all, John.

John wanted to go into local and then national politics. Holly lay and painted a rosy picture of Mr and Mrs Robertson with their daughter, no, their son, their son and daughter. She groaned and turned into the pillow, her whole body aching for John—or was she aching for the baby John could give her? She thought too much in this place, felt too much.

Please, John, there are so few years left for babies.

It was over two years since she had spoken of a marriage date and the prospect of a family because John had been hurt and angry when she had tentatively suggested a legalisation of their position. She had apologised, of course. She had agreed with him that, no, she did not need children to prove that she was worthwhile and a fully functioning woman. No, she did not see him merely as a carrier and then a donor of sperm. She loved him, adored him. She just had this picture of a happy family—father, mother, child—all loving, caring, functioning together and apart, and, yes, she was prepared to wait for that until the time was right.

That had been the beginning of the doubts that attacked her in the middle of lonely nights. How long had it taken her to appreciate that she had done nothing for years but work and minister to John's needs? But people liked their politicians married and with children. Everything would be all right, thanks to Tony and her unexpected generosity.

It will be perfect. Holly smiled. And I'll teach the children to swim and sail right here at Achahoish.

The future looked as rosy as the sky. Holly jumped out of bed and her bare toes met the cold floor. Carpeting. She began her list. Next chore—no, it wasn't a chore—was to ring John on her mobile phone and bring him up to date.

He sounded as if he were in the next room. 'How are things, Holly? Have you talked to an estate agent yet? I hoped you would be on your way home.'

She wrapped a blanket round her. September in Scotland might look nice but it was cold. 'No, I haven't seen anyone yet. I fell asleep.' She waited for the explosion but it did not come.

'Get someone in today, and get the place on the market.' He stopped talking and she could see him, mastering himself, trying hard to be supportive. 'Did you find anything you want to keep?'

'I want a chair.'

There was silence while his quick mind surveyed his memories of the cottage furniture. 'You have got to be kidding! A chair? Come home. My bed looks so empty.'

'John, maybe I won't bring the chair—' she began. She had to tell him she wanted to . . . intended to keep the cottage.

SOMEDAY, SOMEWHERE

'Great,' he interrupted. 'I mean the furniture was lovely, but not for our dream flat.'

'You're right, so I'll leave it and we'll enjoy it here.'

Now he did explode. 'Damn it to hell, Holly! I've told you a thousand times we have to watch every penny. One day we'll have a beach house but at the right beach.'

Her turn to interrupt. 'John, I can afford the cottage. Tony left some paintings in her studio. Remember the landscape I sold when my parents died?' She did not mean to say it, but out it came. 'The one that I used to help with your down payment; ten thousand pounds? That was five years ago. There are maybe forty paintings.'

His voice was excited. 'Ten times forty? Four hundred thousand pounds. Christ.' He was quiet, stunned, perhaps, as he tried to assimilate the news. 'No, they can't be worth that, Holly. Grow up, for God's sake. They're the ones she couldn't sell.'

'I can't hear you. My battery's shot,' said Holly and disconnected.

She had never hung up on him before. In fact she had never hung up on anyone before.

It's the air.

Holly was laughing as she hurried downstairs. By the time she had had two cups of coffee she was ashamed of herself, but consoled herself by thinking that she could ring John when he got back from the office. It had not been a great idea to ring him early. He was never at his best on a weekday morning. She rinsed her cup out and went upstairs to shower and dress.

No shower.

The list again. Carpet. Shower.

She had to get back to school. Other people's children. There is nothing wrong with wanting children before my biological clock cuts off, and no, I do not have to have a child to fulfil myself as a woman.

So there.

She needed to find out about the paintings. She went to Tony's room and opened the drawer again, the one that held the boxes of jewellery and the sketchbooks. Tony had made notes on some of her sketches. She did not particularly relish the one on a sketch of her and John.

When will she learn?

She didn't like it and it made her mad, mad as hell. How dare Tony who knew zilch . . .

But Tony had known.

She leafed through the sketchbooks and laughed and cried as she saw her parents, herself, and Blaise, Blaise, Blaise. Canon Gemmell, who had been Tony's friend and who she had painted; the doctor, the old woman who used to run the village shop, her swans, horrible birds—swans, lovely to look at but . . .

Faithful unto death.

Was she hearing things? Who had said that? It had to be something she had read somewhere, she supposed. She put the books back and closed the drawer. Downstairs again she went through Tony's drawers. She needed the number of an art gallery that Tony had dealt with. An expert would have to come to value the paintings. Then there was the jewellery; she would have that valued before she sold it.

Otto von Emler. There was the name in Tony's address book. It rang a bell; possibly she had heard Tony speak about her agent. He, of all people, would know the value of Antonia Noble's paintings. Holly panicked. It was too soon. She would leave the paintings here while she came to terms with their existence. As for the jewellery, the lawyer would have a place to keep it until she arranged for it to be sold. The rubies. She would keep the rubies.

Holly ran upstairs and got out the jewel boxes. The rubies winked and cajoled her. With shaking hands she put them on.

Where could Tony Noble and a world-famous French tenor have met? Where?

Sea Sprite
LONDON, 1937

London was incomparable among world cities—she said this even although it was the only one she had ever seen—and in May, well, quite simply, it was breathtakingly beautiful. The streets were hazy with a magical light that turned the buildings to pink or blue or lilac. The trees were in full leaf and the tones of green on London's streets dazzled the eye. In Regent's Park swans and ducks glided majestically over the water, then lost their dignity when they waddled up onto the grass.

'Oh, silly, silly swan,' Antonia Noble addressed the rather malevolent eye of a great white bird, 'you really must stay in your element if you want to hide your weaknesses from your admiring public. On dry land, my dear, you look like Uncle Thomas's daily. In a minute you will take a cigarette from under your wing and start puffing it defiantly.'

The swan hissed at her and waddled away.

Tony, who had become Tony as soon as her train from the country had arrived in London, laughed. She was eighteen years old, and studying art in London. Her parents had been absolutely astounded that she had wanted to go to art school. Painting was for bohemians; it was certainly not for the daughter of a village schoolmaster. Their son was destined for the Church and their daughter should become a schoolteacher.

But they had capitulated because she had refused point-blank to do anything else. Frederick, thank God for Frederick who could hardly wait to get into college to study Divinity. Then he was determined to go off and find some heathens to convert.

'Poor unhappy heathens,' mused Antonia.

She walked on happily, swinging her satchel. She would eat her lunch when she found a quiet seat in the sun.

There was an iron seat on the path. Automatically Tony dusted the seat and sat down. She opened her satchel and savoured the smell of bread and cheese and apple. Mrs Lumsden, her landlady, baked her own bread and was generous with butter and cheese. Tony was just about to bite into her sandwich when she became aware of the man.

He was lying on his stomach on the grass, reading a book as he propped himself up on very tanned, slim arms. He was so engrossed in the book that he had not heard her approach across the grass. She saw his face and knew, without a doubt, that it would haunt her for the rest of her life if she did not sketch it immediately. He was beautiful, with deep-set eyes—she wished she could see them; they would be blue—a straight nose, a high forehead on which black curls tumbled as if they had been artistically arranged, and a well-shaped and sensuous mouth, spoilt by the grass he was chewing, but she could leave that out.

She took one healthy bite of her sandwich, put it down, pulled out her charcoal and began, swiftly, to draw. He was a perfect subject because he did not move. She caught the face, then sketched the hand that was holding the book. What a wonderful shape, the fingers long and delicate, the nails clean and well cut. Perhaps he was a pianist: it was a book of music. No, he was only a boy, but she would know better if she could just see those deep blue eyes.

They were green. A surprise, but immediately she knew that green was just right. He was a sea creature, thrown up by the waves. In another life he had ridden on the backs of whales. That's how she would paint him with his sea-green eyes and his black curls: mystical creature.

'You have permission?' he asked suddenly and she jumped because she had not expected him to talk. He had been so still, a still life in Regent's Park.

'Permission?' she asked stupidly.

'To make my portrait?' he asked again. His voice was strongly accented, French, she thought, but the English was good, if a little archaic.

'No,' she said and knew that she sounded even more stupid.

'Then I will have to examine and decide.' He got up in one quick, lithe movement, and she realised that he was tall, too. He towered over her as those beautiful hands held themselves out waiting for the surrender of her sketchbook. She looked at them—she would have to sculpt them—and wordlessly handed him the book.

He sat down again, crosslegged on the grass. He really was incredibly fit. Perhaps he was an athlete, because the body was a very good shape: broad shoulders, deep chest and slender hips above those long legs. She stifled a sudden and frightening desire to touch him.

He looked through her sketchbook slowly, methodically. She would learn that he always worked that way.

When he was finished he handed the book back to her and smiled. How powerful that smile was. It was electric.

'Bien.' He nodded his consent. 'You may proceed, but first I shall eat the rest of your sandwich for payment.'

She was floundering. He smiled at her again. 'You may have the apple,' he said magnanimously, 'but this bread, the smell came to me across the grass. English bread is without taste, you understand, but this?'

'My landlady bakes it herself.'

'Does she take male students?' He pulled the sandwich into two unequal parts and handed her the smaller part out of which she had taken a bite. 'There, I will not be greedy. I will give you back half.'

Tony looked at her share. His mathematics was not so good as his English. 'No. I mean, thank you for the sandwich and no, it's a hostel for females.'

'Go on,' he said. 'I arrange myself.'

She laughed at him. He wanted to be sketched: he was delighted that she had acknowledged his beauty. None of the boys in the village would have reacted the way this young man did. Already he was folding himself back onto the grass with the book. Could he be a student and live in a hotel? He would have to be wealthy. She had never met anyone who was wealthy.

'Why do you laugh?' He did not move, did not turn.

'Your ego.'

'Me, I am in a small hotel on the Marylebone Road'—he pronounced it Mary Le Bone—'and everything I have ever heard about the cooking of England was written in this hotel.' He had demolished her sandwich. A hotel? He was on holiday and he would go away and she would never see him again. The world was suddenly bleak.

He sat up quickly and looked at her, astonishment in his eyes. 'But the ego is necessary. Why do you say it with the disdain? You must have the ego too, or you will never be a great painter.'

'Oh, yes I will. I'm going to be the greatest.'

He nodded seriously. *Bien.* That is correct. Without the ego you will not struggle. You say, "I am great", *et voilà*, before you know, you are great, and, more important, the world admits too.'

'Lie down again,' she said, and blushed at his wicked smile. 'I don't have too much time.'

He arranged himself and she began sketching again.

What could she say to him? How could she keep him here? How could she keep him? She did not understand but with one glance from those wicked eyes he had enslaved her. Was it terribly rude to ask intimate questions such as, 'Who are you, how long are you going to be in London, will you please stay for ever and ever?'

'What is your book?' she asked lamely.

'It is not, strictly speaking, a book. It is a score, *Lohengrin.*'

She had no idea what he was talking about.

'Wagner,' he said impatiently. 'You have heard of Wagner?'

Of course she had heard of Wagner. 'He's awfully German.'

He threw down the book . . . score. *Mon Dieu!* He is a composer. What does it matter how German he is, whatever that means? You, mam'selle, are *awfully* English.'

She laughed. *Touché.*'

He sat up again and smiled. It was a relief to see him smiling; she thought she had infuriated him.

'You speak French?'

'No, *touché* is about it.'

'I will teach you. It is a very civilised language. And now I must go or I will be late for my class.' He gestured vaguely towards the Royal Academy of Music.

He was going. Stunned, she sat and watched him walk with long strides across the grass. He was going. He was . . . turning. 'Tomorrow,' he called. 'Bring more bread.'

She stood watching until he had disappeared and then she made her own way out of the park. She too had a class. She walked to her bus stop and got on a bus to Gower Street, to the Slade.

Only that morning, being a student at that most prestigious school had been the most important thing in her life. Now, nothing was relevant, nothing but a boy with green eyes and beautiful hands who had eaten her sandwich and who she would probably never see again.

Next morning she asked Mrs Lumsden if she might have two sandwiches. Her landlady, who had tried to serve her some filling porridge, smiled. "'Course you can, love, but don't I keep telling you that if you starts the day with a nice plate of porridge, you'll last through till your dinner time?'

Tony sat down and poured herself a cup of tea. 'You're right, of course, Mrs Lumsden, that is exactly what my mother always says and I am quite determined to do things my way. Besides, I loathe porridge. One understands about the Scots when one sees porridge. It either looks completely dead or as if it's a bubbling volcano.'

The landlady folded her arms across her massive but shapeless bosom. 'Whatever will you say next, Miss Noble? Better not let any of my Scotch ladies hear you.'

'It'll be our little secret, dear Mrs Lumsden. And I may have two sandwiches today, large ones?' She looked winningly up at her landlady, who shook her head and went off into the kitchen to make sandwiches. Her young ladies were well fed and if they chose to eat nothing at breakfast and two huge sandwiches for their lunch that was their prerogative.

Ten minutes later she handed Tony a large packet. 'And take two pieces of fruit from the sideboard,' she suggested. 'You mustn't get so fired up with lessons that you neglect your health.'

Tony smiled as she obeyed. Later it would occur to her that it was not strictly ethical to have her landlady feed . . . whoever he was, even if she herself skimped on breakfast to make up. But for now all she could think of was getting through the morning.

Her lecturer's magic wove its usual spell though. He was opinionated but Tony was willing to listen and then make up her own mind.

'Reason tells me and everyone else with a perfect eye that Turner is the greatest of all British painters. But if you really want to paint, not just make some pretty daubs of oil on a canvas, study Titian. Go to Italy. Go by bus—a few pounds will take you there. Titian manipulated paint as no one else has ever done. His blues and reds sing. Your red, Miss Noble, is crying out in agony. Relieve its pain.'

She tried to put her red out of its misery, but since she could see nothing wrong with it, except that it did not sing, she failed to please the master. She decided not to ask her father for 'a few pounds'. Titian and Italy would have to wait as she waited now for the lunch break.

And then she was out and the sky was overcast. He would not be there. Dejectedly she sat on the park bench.

He was there. She had expected yesterday's open-necked short-sleeved shirt but he was bundled up in a heavy dark green sweater.

SOMEDAY, SOMEWHERE

'You look like a fisherman,' she said and she tried to speak calmly although her heart was beating rapidly as if she had just run for a bus. 'Yesterday I thought you resembled a sea sprite.'

He looked down at his legs. 'I am with too long legs for a sprite, I think,' he said judiciously. 'Have you bring some bread?'

Wordlessly she reached into her bag and took out his sandwich.

'Such a waste of good bread,' he scolded as he spread open the sandwich and scraped off the cheese. He produced a package and when it was opened Tony smelt unknown but tantalising delights. 'I have bring sausage and real cheese,' he said. 'Now throw the inside of yours to these hungry little birds and eat. I have wine also.'

'Wine?' Wine, ginger wine, was something Tony's family had every Christmas. This was not the same thing at all. It was red and smooth and slipped down Tony's throat so easily.

'The civilised way to eat,' he said. 'Bread, sausage, cheese and a glass of wine. Fruit we should have also but all I could find was wrinkled.'

'I brought an apple and a pear.'

He examined them critically. '*Bien.* And now I think we should be introduce, don't you think? Who will introduce us? This little sparrow? Monsieur, will you introduce Blaise Fougère to this great artist?'

'How do you do, Mr Fougère,' said Tony gravely.

'And you, mam'selle. You will allow Monsieur Sparrow to make the introduction?'

'Antonia Noble,' she said.

'Antoinette. How perfect,' he said.

'Actually, I have begun to call myself Tony. I think it sounds like an artist, don't you?'

'I think it sounds like a man, but it is your name, Tony, and Tony you will be.'

'And you are Blaise?'

'Yes. The patron saint of the throat, but it is a coincidence, or again, maybe it is not. My parents are not thinking that their child will be a singer; they are thinking he will be a lawyer like his papa.'

'A singer?' She remembered the score, *Lohengrin.* 'An opera singer? Goodness, I have never met an opera singer before.'

'I am not an opera singer. I am a student. I study voice and one day, maybe, I will sing.'

'I would love to hear you sing,' she said shyly.

He shrugged. 'One day. Now, Miss Tony, tell me about Antoinette. Why is she a painter?'

'I'm not, and I think my teachers believe I never will be one. My favourite tutor told me today that my reds don't sing. That was rather demoralising.'

'I think I understand him. Reds should shout, "Look at me". You will learn. You must study the masters. We learn from the magnificent dead, Tony, and maybe, one day, Beethoven would be please with how I sing his Florestan—'

He broke off and looked at her. 'You know Beethoven?'

She nodded.

'But not Florestan?'

She shook her head in shame.

He hugged her. How very French of him. She rather thought she might have some French blood somewhere because she wanted to hug him back, but already he was reaching out his hand to pull her up.

'What fun we are going to have, Toinette,' he said, already forgetting that he had promised to call her Tony. 'You will teach me about painting and I will teach you about music. But for now, I have a class and the maestro will say, "Go back to France. You sound like a pig caught in a drain." I do not really understand the pig and the drain but I will hang my head and beg for another chance because I have hear that he says this to everyone. And one day he will say in the Crush Bar at Covent Garden, "Fougère, I taught him all he knows", and you will make my portrait as Lohengrin to hang in Paris.'

She believed him. It would happen. There was nothing they could not do. They were young. They were in London and a dazzling future spread itself out before them. But first she would learn how to make red hum a little and she would paint him on the back of a whale.

CHAPTER TWO

TORRY BAY, 1998. GLASGOW, 1998

DECISIONS HAD TO BE MADE. The paintings would have to be valued and the best person to do that was undoubtedly Tony's agent, Otto von Emler. Did he even know that she was dead? No one except Holly, John, the lawyer and Mrs Fraser from the shop had been at the funeral. Tony had wanted no fuss, and no publicity.

The ashes. Tony's last wish.

SOMEDAY, SOMEWHERE

As near as I can get to where I want to be . . .

Holly put her list down on the table. Later she would add, *phone lawyer, phone agent*, but first she would carry out Tony's last instructions. She picked up the casket containing her aunt's ashes. Outside it was cold and clear and the sea around Torry Bay was calm. Several swans floated on the water, rising and falling with the tide. That was why Tony had painted swans—they were there. 'God, I can't think of a prayer. Forgive me.'

Lohengrin.

'That was not a prayer. A whisper. Silly Holly, there is no one here to whisper.'

Hollyberry.

She shook her head and wiped tears from her eyes. 'Tony, dearest aunt, dearest friend, here we are together for the last time. No, that's not right. You'll always be with me. Where are you now? If God is just, Tony, and I always thought He was, you're with Blaise. I'm wearing your rubies. I must say they feel a bit odd, but they were your favourites and they'll give me courage. I wish you were here so that you could be at the exhibition, for that's what I'm going to do. Next year some time there will be an exhibition of your glorious paintings that will stun the art world. I won't say goodbye.'

She opened the casket and scattered the ashes.

Damn it, damn, she could see nothing because of tears and the September sun on the water. She closed her eyes for a moment and was aware of the powerful smell of the sea.

'I only just decided about the exhibition, Tony. Is that what you want?'

Hollyberry.

Who spoke, who spoke?

'Did you tell me that one hears better with one's eyes closed, Tony? I hear the sea, a kind of slurping sound, and I can smell it and I can smell the funny coconutty smell of gorse, and if I was anywhere else in the world and closed my eyes I think I could conjure up Achahoish and Torry Bay and you, darling Tony. Paint, every time I smell paint I will be here with you in the studio. Remember what fun we had, you with your glorious swirls and me with my splodges. How generous you were to live with such ghastly paintings.'

The child Holly had taken it for granted that her paintings should hang side by side with Tony's. She had been fourteen before she had been able to convince Tony that she would not be traumatised to have them put—where they belonged—in the bin.

She was sobbing now, loud, harsh, uncontrolled sobs that made her nose run. She had no hankie and drew her hand across her nose like a child. A hymn; there should be a hymn.

I should have been better prepared for you, dearest Tony.

She opened her eyes and all that was before her was the softly sighing sea and the swans still rising and falling at the whim of the waves. 'Goodbye.' There, she had said it after all.

She turned and ran back to the cottage. She washed the dishes, took the sheets off the bed and bundled them into her suitcase, and turned off the electricity. The paintings and the jewellery were back where she had found them. They had been there for years. Surely they would be safe until she had spoken to Otto von Emler.

She stood in the doorway for a moment, aware of how much she wanted to stay. This is my home, the nearest to a real home that I have ever had. Its magic tugs at me wherever I am. Then she smiled, for, thanks to Tony, it was hers and she could stay for ever if she so chose.

She drove slowly back to Glasgow and was unaware of the distance because her mind was busy. The paintings would have to be sold. Their sheer size meant that they could not be housed in a normal home and, more importantly, they were, taken together, a valuable historical document and should be seen by millions.

But first I want to look at them quietly by myself, learn their secrets because they have secrets, and then I want the world to acknowledge that Tony Noble was a genius.

Stopped at a traffic light, she closed her eyes and conjured up John's face. A warm glow suffused her . . . everything was going to be all right. This, not Torry Bay, was home. Of course it was. The past, all of it, had to be allowed to stay in the past: no point in being selective.

Back inside her flat, Holly had a shower, changed the sheets on her bed, and then looked in the refrigerator.

You are wasting time, Holly Noble. Ring John.

But she wanted to think about her legacy and make her decisions before she talked to him. There was a pizza in the freezer. She put it in the microwave on defrost and dialled his number.

'You have reached John Robertson. I can't take your call just now but if you leave your . . .'

You couldn't really expect him to be in, sitting by the phone, waiting for your call.

Yes, I could. What would be great would be if he was rushing to see me, or even better, if he had been waiting in the flat.

How could he, when he didn't know for sure that you were coming?

SOMEDAY, SOMEWHERE

Would it have made any difference?

The bell on the microwave answered her. She had forgotten to heat up the pizza in the oven, but she turned it on and sat at the table with a notebook and pencil while she waited for the pizza to cook.

Question: What am I going to do with the paintings, the jewellery and the cottage?

Answer/solutions: Keep them all. Impossible. Sell everything or keep some, sell some; but how do I choose?

What to do with the rest of my life?

Have some pizza, unpack and go to bed. You have to teach tomorrow. That's good enough for now.

It was difficult to get to sleep. She was tired but her body did not yearn for sleep; it yearned for John. She tossed and turned, then almost jumped out of her nightgown when the strident ringing of the telephone shattered the stillness of the night.

'Holly, it was you. Why didn't you leave a message?'

'Where were you?'

'It's Sunday. My parents. Remember?'

'I wish you were here.'

'Why didn't you come here, silly girl? Are you working tomorrow?'

'Of course. I'm not sure what to do yet.'

'About what? Look, I'll come over and sleep at your place and we'll talk about it.'

'I'm tired, John.' Suddenly she was, very tired.

He laughed. 'No one is ever that tired.'

He hung up. She looked at the electric clock beside her bed. It was only just after midnight.

Should she open wine?

Don't be stupid. That's seduction.

Coffee, coffee was the answer. First she took the box containing the rubies from under her winter woollies and slipped the necklace on under her nightie.

Grow up, Holly.

But she left them on.

While waiting for John, she thought about the paintings. She would have an exhibition; they would sell to collectors, to galleries. Otto von Emler would help with that and he could be paid from the proceeds. The jewellery could be sold, probably at auction. She could leave that to Tony's lawyer. The cottage? She would keep the cottage—at least for a year or two. If she could get John there again he would love it, she knew he would, and then it could be their summer home.

At last she heard a car drive up to the front of the building and there was John. Oh, she loved the look of him; the way his hair flopped forward over his brow, his slight stoop, his funny snub nose. She went into his arms as soon as he opened the door and he dropped his overnight bag and hugged her to him. She walked backwards as he half carried, half pushed her towards the bedroom.

'John, wait.'

'Why?'

Why indeed. She wanted it too, didn't she? Wanted him, not it. It was not quite as she had imagined but it was good. Such a build-up of tension and then that wonderful release. When it was over she realised that he hadn't even seen the rubies.

'John, how could you miss these?' she said, sitting up.

He lay looking up at her, at the delicate red stones snuggling between her breasts. 'Wow, where did you . . . are they real?'

'What do you think?'

'I think you should always dress just like that.' He laughed.

Holly laughed too. Was that what Tony had meant? 'Perfect with jeans.'

'They are real. They're rubies but they're good stones; they were Tony's favourites.' She looked up at him. His eyes were on the stones. 'I want to keep them.' She spilled out the history of the boxes of jewels, the gifts to Tony from her one true love.

'Of course, but'—he hesitated—'a gift from some man to your aunt. We could sell them and then you could choose something . . .'

She could read his mind. Fougère had been Tony's lover; ergo, there was something faintly distasteful about his expensive trinkets.

'Tony loved Blaise Fougère, not some man, all her life. I'm sure she thought of herself as his wife. She hoped I would enjoy some of her jewellery and these were her favourites.'

He reached out his hand. 'Keep it, if you like it. Makes my pearls look insipid though.'

'I promise never to wear them together.'

Why didn't you call in sick and get the whole thing done while you were there?'

Holly had showered, and they were drinking coffee in the kitchen.

'Now you will have to go back to get the paintings valued, two opinions probably,' he went on. 'Sell the jewellery at auction, and put the cottage on the market.'

'I won't sell.'

He slammed his mug down on the table with such force that coffee slopped over the edge. 'No one has a cottage in Argyll, for God's sake. The South of France, Holly, or Tuscany or Spain.'

'I'm too tired to talk about it just now. It's getting late, John,' said Holly as she stood up. She walked to the sink for a cloth and wiped up the spilt coffee. 'It's left a mark.'

John ignored the stain. 'I've had a thought. All the paintings have this opera singer in them?'

'Right.'

'Does he have a family?'

Family? Did Fougère have a family? 'I have no idea. If there is family they might have some feelings.'

'Strong feelings. Look, I'll see what I can find out, and you should talk to Tony's lawyer and find out what he knows.'

'If Tony was right and no one is left alive who cares, then it'll be easier to decide what to do with the paintings.'

'Great. Now that's settled I'd like a fresh look at those rubies.'

But for some reason, Holly was in no mood. 'I'm already showered, John, and we have work to go to in a few hours.'

They lay without touching until the alarm clock woke them at six. Fences to mend. 'You have the bathroom first, John.'

'I'm sorry about this morning, Holly. Did I sound selfish? I didn't mean to, and I do try to understand how much that little cottage means to you. But it's not right for us, Holly, and when we can afford a second home—God, we're keeping two apartments as it is—I want somewhere in the sun.'

'We have two apartments, John, because you won't set a wedding date and because your parents don't approve of hanky-panky.'

'I can't hurt them.' Suddenly he grabbed her and held her close. 'It's different now, Holly. With your little nest egg perhaps we could think dates. Life was too unsure before, but I have some news for you too. I have a chance of being selected as a candidate at the next election. It takes money, Holly, and now we have it. It's the beginning for us, Holly. We'll talk about it tonight. Come over to my flat after school; we'll have dinner and make plans.'

Then there was no time to think until the school bell rang at three thirty. Holly stuffed papers into her briefcase and caught the under-ground train to Hillhead. When John arrived just after seven a chicken was roasting, the table was ready, and she and her list were in a chair beside the window. 'Much better view from the cottage at Torry Bay,' she said with a smile as he bent to kiss her.

'I'll open some wine.'

A few minutes later he handed her a glass. 'Holly, I was thinking, and I have come to the conclusion that you should take a leave of absence and get this business settled. We could go up together this weekend, if you like. Perhaps we should bring the jewellery and the paintings here.'

Holly stood up. 'The chicken,' she said.

He followed her into the kitchen. 'They could be stolen or the cottage could be burned down.'

'It could be hit by a meteorite, John, but I thought I would leave everything there until I have decided what to do. I can't make up my mind. I love my job and don't particularly want to give it up.'

He put his arms round her and she leaned against him. 'No one wants you to resign. I said, for the moment, you should take a leave of absence.'

'It will take me weeks to clean up the mess my supply teacher leaves. If ten per cent of what the children say is true—'

'For heaven's sake, Holly. They're not your children; you owe them nothing. If these jewels are real and if these paintings are valuable, then you just can't leave them in an empty house. They've been there for years, certainly, but Tony was there, and she's dead, Holly. Sweetheart, I don't want to be a bully but you must see that I'm right. Unless we can do everything this weekend. Could we get the paintings into two cars?'

She shook her head.

'We can bring the best ones, surely?'

'I don't know which they are, John. I haven't seen all of them. They're stacked five, six deep against the walls.'

'I'll hire a van.'

'And where do you suggest we leave forty valuable paintings? They're safer in Achahoish than they would be in Glasgow.'

He pushed her away from him so roughly that she almost fell. 'Do you want my help, Holly, or am I going to be put away in a drawer with my pearls while you run around in some poncey soprano's rubies?'

Holly looked at him. Who was he?

She picked up her briefcase. 'The chicken has about thirty seconds left before total meltdown. The same might be said of our engagement.'

He grabbed her before she reached the door. 'Sweetheart, sweetheart, please. Forgive me. I didn't mean to push you.'

She forced herself out of his grasp. 'I need space, John. I have to have time to think, to evaluate. He was a tenor. One of the greatest the world has ever known. I looked him up on the Internet at school.'

For someone who had just told her fiancé to get lost, she felt remarkably well. She could feel the rubies inside her well-cut and totally dull blue cotton shirt, and she smiled. Perhaps she was different since she had begun to wear the 'poncey sopranos' rubies.

By the time she had reached her flat she had decided to apply for a leave of absence to begin as soon as the school district could find a suitable replacement. She had also decided to go to Torry Bay every weekend possible. Perhaps Mr von Emler would consider coming one weekend since it was imperative that an accredited expert should see the paintings without delay.

John did not ring her. She had not expected him to do so. He was sulking and these sulks always took a day or two. She was glad because it gave her time to reflect. Too often she had damped down her longing for Torry Bay and Tony because of John. Now, although it was too late for Tony, she could respond to those faint tugs at her heartstrings.

The next day she forfeited her lunch break, discussed her situation at length with her head teacher and then applied for a leave of absence. When school was over, she hurried home in time to ring either the lawyer or the agent before the close of office hours.

By the time she had reached her flat she had decided that the number one priority was the paintings and so she took a deep breath, sat down at the kitchen table with a mug of lemon and ginger tea and rang Otto von Emler.

He had not known of Tony's death and was shocked. 'I knew Tony Noble almost all my life, Miss Noble. I think I may safely say that I was responsible for much of what was good in her life. That she left no instructions to tell me—', He broke off, obviously quite distressed.

'There was no one at the funeral, Mr von Emler, only old Mrs Fraser from the shop at Torry Bay, who found my aunt, and my aunt's lawyer. You may understand more when you see what Tony has left in her cottage.'

His voice changed. He had sounded old and tired but now the tone was that of a young, vibrant man. 'A painting.' He almost breathed the words. 'Tony has left a new painting? So often she hinted and half promised and for years, nothing,'

'There is an attic full of paintings, Mr von Emler.'

She could hear him blowing his nose resoundingly.

'May I see them?'

'Your name was in my aunt's address book. Since you know her work better than anyone, I hoped that you would consider flying up to Scotland to see them, perhaps to value them.'

'I hate to fly and I have other painters. Had you waited one more week, Miss Noble, you would have had to wait until the spring. No one goes to Scotland after October, didn't you know that?'

She ignored that and had the feeling that he had expected her to ignore him or at least to pay little attention to anything he said that had nothing to do with art, that is Art with a capital A, the life force that motivated him.

'This weekend, Mr von Emler?'

'I'll fly to Glasgow, Miss Noble. Meet me there.'

She did. He said very little on the way to Torry Bay. 'I prefer cities,' he said as they drove into the magnificence of Scotland's west coast. There was really nothing to say to that. She had a sneaky feeling he was starring in a script he wrote for himself, for fun.

When they reached Achahoish he sat forward on the edge of his seat, as full of anticipation as Holly herself used to be, and as they headed down to Torry Bay all his affectations slid away like melting snow off a warm roof.

'Her bay,' he said and his voice was quiet, as in church. He said nothing as she parked and opened the door to the cottage.

Hollyberry. Welcome home.

'If I could see the paintings, Miss Noble.'

He spent hours in the attic. Holly offered him tea, coffee, whatever, and he behaved as if he did not hear her.

'Damn it all, I am starving,' she said at nine in the evening and went storming up to the studio. He was sitting on the floor in his Armani suit—it was Armani if it didn't have a collar, wasn't it?—just looking at two paintings.

'So young,' he whispered as she walked in. 'So full of joy, of promise.' *Les Dents de Lion.* Blaise, dressed only in shorts, was rolling in a field of glorious golden dandelions.

The Performing Bear. What did it mean? It was of Blaise but he was wearing a clown's costume and there was a chain round his neck. It was a disturbing picture and Holly shivered.

'Yes, I like that one,' she said, pointing to the dandelions.

'Like, Miss Noble? You do not *like* a painting. You are possessed or you walk away.'

'I am possessed,' said Holly quietly, and went back downstairs to scramble some eggs. This odd little man would obviously be there all night.

Holly ate her eggs on warm buttered toast while she sat by the window and watched the supreme artist paint the bay. First He tried the effect of dark brooding purples and then He made the sea dance with joy as He coloured it gold. The sky He streaked with red and pink and all with a dusting of gold left over from the sea.

She took Otto coffee and a sandwich before she went to bed, and told him that the main bedroom was prepared for him. But in the morning he was still in the studio.

He came down while she was making coffee. 'A major exhibition, with your permission, Miss Noble,' he said. 'I always hoped, but still, now they are here and they are her finest paintings. One or two I have seen before but she would not sell them.'

'And now you know why?'

'No, I don't even pretend to understand and I am too exhausted to think. Will you drive me to the airport?'

'Of course.'

'And you will trust me?'

'My aunt trusted you.'

'Yes, she did. I will take this legacy and together we will give Tony Noble the place she deserves. The first thing is to have the paintings shipped to my London gallery. There I can study them at leisure and value them. Only then will we decide what to do.'

'When, Mr von Emler?'

'Otto,' he said almost automatically. 'First I have a major show in London to deal with. I expect all the paintings will sell, and when they are gone I will bring Tony's work down. If God is good they will be out of here before winter.'

'Mr von . . . Otto, do you know anything about Mr Fougère?'

He almost buried his nose in his coffee. 'I'm so tired, Miss Noble.'

Holly smiled. She felt he was playing for time. 'Holly,' she said, and it was his turn to smile.

'Holly. Yes, I know about Mr Fougère but I have no permission to share such knowledge. I suggest you ring Tony's lawyer. If she told him nothing then I will reconsider what I know.'

He accepted some toast but ate it absent-mindedly. The sandwich was still on the floor and so, as far as she knew, he had eaten nothing for almost twenty-four hours. 'When I have mounted this exhibition, Holly, I can die. Do you understand that? I have watched her since I was six-teen years old and I knew, I knew Tony had to paint. Oh, not the pic-tures she did for the tourists, the swans at Torry Bay, flowers sometimes, all with merit, you understand—she was too fine, too good, ever to do less than her best—but the paintings with her blood in them. I knew. I knew,' he said again and his whole small body was tense with passion.

'And at last I have seen them and I will not sleep a wink until they are properly mounted and hanging where the world can come to pay homage.' He looked up at her. 'Thank you, Holly, for the most wonderful night of my life.'

Les Dents de Lion
GODALMING, 1938

They swept round the corner on their hired bicycles. Suddenly Tony uttered a cry and screeched to a halt. 'Look, Blaise, have you ever seen anything so beautiful?'

His heart thudding painfully—she had yelled so loudly that he had been sure that she was hurt—Blaise looked. 'I see fields,' he said cautiously. He could see nothing that merited such spectacular braking. 'And many weeds on the verges.'

'Crétin,' she said. 'Weeds are flowers that someone doesn't like.'

He nodded judiciously. 'My father would not like these. Look at the heads; in a few weeks there will be seed heads blowing all over the fields to bring a thousand times as many next year. They should be cut down.'

Her hand slipped into his. 'They're beautiful, Blaise. Look again.'

And he looked, but this time he looked with Tony's eyes and he saw hundreds of brilliant golden heads flying atop strong green stalks. The meadow rose in a slight incline and some dandelions marched along the skyline, outlined against the clearest of blue skies. Blaise laughed. 'Yes, Tony, ma mie, they are very beautiful.'

They left their bicycles under the hedge by the side of the road and climbed into the meadow. Hand in hand they wandered up to the skyline and saw more of the field laid out before them. It too was ablaze with dandelions.

'Les Dents de Lion,' said Blaise. 'They are the teeth of the lion.'

'Les Dents de Lion, dandelion. I never knew that,' said Tony. 'Aren't they beautiful?' She laughed like a little girl, lay down in the lush grass and rolled down to the bottom of the incline.

What could he do? He shouted with laughter and followed her example, and when he bumped into her at the bottom of the slope it was only natural that he should begin to kiss her greedily, hungrily, and then his body blotted out the sky and the field and the dandelions and Tony moaned and pulled him closer until all she saw was his face with its beautiful green eyes gazing into hers. At last he collapsed on top of her and made as if to roll away, but she held him with surprisingly strong arms and they lay together until they began to feel cold.

SOMEDAY, SOMEWHERE

'That was quite something,' she said, as without embarrassment they searched for discarded clothing.

Blaise said nothing.

Tony looked at him. 'I wondered what it would be like and I wanted the first time to be wonderful and it was. It wasn't the first time for you though, Blaise, was it?'

'No,' he said sadly, 'and it should have been. I want to share everything with you. I should have waited and then we could have discovered it together.'

'Was it wonderful, the first time, for you? Was she very special?'

'At the time she was. She was my mother's maid and twice my age. She was very kind to a young boy and did not laugh.'

'Good. Come on. We had best find our bikes or we'll miss the train back to London. I hope your parents didn't fire her.'

'Fire? Oh, to dismiss. No. Perhaps they were glad it was someone . . . clean. I was always falling in love, Toinette, and with the most unsuitable people.'

'But you didn't *love* them?'

'No. Most of them terrified me. The friends of my parents were, how you say . . . racy, some of them.'

'What bliss,' said Tony as they clambered back through the hedge. 'To know racy people, I mean. I have led such a *dull* life, Blaise.'

He looked down at her serious little face and his heart contracted. 'Oh, madame is so old and still so inexperienced.'

'My parents are such worthy people. And so dull.'

He looked at her questioningly as he methodically rebuttoned her blouse. She had done it up any old way. 'Is worthiness dull?'

'No, of course not, but they manage to make it sound dull so that one always wants to do the exact opposite of what they suggest.'

She laughed up at him and as always when she laughed her plain little face changed, becoming animated and elf-like, and he caught his breath.

'I know nineteen isn't old, but if I am to become a great artist I must have lots of experiences.'

His heart, which a second before had been so exultantly beating, checked in its mad thumping. 'So, I am an experience.'

She stopped. 'No,' she said seriously. 'You are life.'

He caught her to him. 'And you are my eyes, Toinette. You will show me the beauty in simple things and you will make me stop and look and be aware of something outside my voice.'

'If you want me to be.'

'I will need you, Antonia Noble, all my life, to keep my feet on the ground, to show me the difference between weeds and flowers.'

She kissed his throat. 'There is no difference, Blaise. You must look at everything with wonderment and love.'

'You will have to teach me.'

'I will be there, *ma mie*,' she said, stealing his endearment. 'Always.'

They put their bikes on the train and went back to London, holding hands and without talking, each of them aware that everything was changed between them. Tony looked at him and smiled as she relived their moments in the field. So that's it, she thought. I'm not a virgin: I'm a woman, Blaise's woman.

For almost twelve months they had been inseparable; meeting after classes, cycling south from Tony's boarding house, crossing and recrossing the bridges of the Thames as Blaise looked for '*un appartement*,' touring the museums and art galleries and spending evening after evening in the gods at Covent Garden. Blaise could afford good tickets but Tony could not, and, since she would not allow him to pay for her, he swallowed his pride and climbed the steps with her. He had not realised, he said, that he was in training to climb Mont Blanc. They sat in teashops drinking tea and eating scones, and they talked and talked. They discussed art and music. They spoke about their families.

Blaise adored his parents, especially his beautiful, sophisticated mother, and he loved his baby sister, Nicole. He told Tony of their country house in the Lot—'There is a village there called Fougère'—and of his home in Paris.

'Paris is part of every artist's education, Tony. *En effet*, you must return to Paris with me in the vacation. I will take you to see the Bois de Boulogne. I went to school nearby. And on Thursdays my nurse or sometimes Maman, would take me to . . . *guignol* . . .' He looked puzzled. '*Guignol* is . . . *les marionnettes*, puppets, very famous, and after we would cross the river and go to Angelina, a café on the rue de Rivoli.' He sniffed the air. 'Almost from here, I can smell their hot chocolate. Oh, yes, *ma Toinette*, you must come to Paris.'

'I should like that,' she said seriously, and her heart was heavy in her breast because she could hear her father.

'French? A French boy? You will come home where we can look after you, my girl. Isn't it enough that we have to sit here and worry while you're at your art school meeting who knows what kind of bohemian, smoking and drinking?'

Blaise had introduced her to wine and now she decided that as soon as she could she would start to smoke. What bliss. Super-sophistication, and now sex.

They looked at one another as they approached Tony's residence. They did not want to part.

'I will take you to dinner, *chérie*, a proper meal, not a "Blaise, this is ridiculously expensive", meal. Go, I will return for you at eight o'clock.'

They went in a taxi to the Ritz—'but, of course the Ritz, Toinette'—and because Blaise was a Frenchman they spent a great deal of time discussing what they would eat. But afterwards Tony could remember only a haze of smells and tastes and his green eyes smiling at her.

The summer evening was perfect and so they walked back to his hotel. Other lovers strolled through Green Park and they smiled at one another in understanding. At last they were there and with their arms round one another they went slowly upstairs and she was in his bedroom and knew that it was the right place for her to be. They kissed and undressed one another, not with feverish haste, but with slow deliberation, uncovering each delight in turn and worshipping at its shrine until they could bear no more. He lifted her in his arms and stood for a moment, looking out at the moon as if he were offering a sacrifice, and then he laid her gently on the bed and taught her all she wanted to know.

'I love you,' she gasped as dawn broke.

Je t'aime,' he whispered. 'And I will love you all my life.'

They were very practical.

'It is not the time for marriage, *ma mie*,' Blaise said. 'We have too much studying to do.'

'We could be terribly modern and just not get married.'

He was shocked and sat straight up in the bed. 'But this is nonsense. Of course we will marry. It is the right, the only thing to do. I regard you as my wife now and one day we will marry before the mayor and before the priest, but for now I must sing and you must paint.'

'I can paint anywhere,' she said as she memorised the curve of the muscles of his arm. 'I shall paint you while you sing.'

'If you would allow me to buy a decent ticket for the opera you would see that that is impossible. I am very ugly, me, when I sing. There is so much hard work, so much—how you say *déformation?*—distortion, strain on the muscles, the jaws, and neither do I stand still. How can you capture the pain of singing?'

'I shall try. I shall paint the joy and perhaps when I am very good, the pain. The pain doesn't hurt, Blaise?' she asked anxiously, sitting up.

'No, I cannot explain. Only a singer would understand. It is like to run very fast; to sing well exhausts. That is the pain but also the joy.'

She sighed happily and lay back down, her arms behind her head. He looked down at her and desire stirred again. 'Tony, there must not be babies. I know what to do. Next time I will be . . . prepared. I am too greedy tonight and we must hope.' She was inexperienced. He was the one who should have thought. He shrugged. He would handle it. Now he needed sleep.

'Go to sleep, Toinette. We have classes tomorrow and you will ask your parents if you can visit my family in the *vacances*.'

But, held in his arms, she was already asleep.

Her mother was torn between worry that some nameless harm would come to her daughter in France, and gratification that that same daughter should have found favour with a young man like Blaise. His parents owned two houses. Think of it! She wondered if they had different sets of bed linen or did they carry their blankets from house to house?

'This young man's family. Do you think they have two sets of everything?' she said out loud to her husband.

'I will not have my daughter adopt a hedonistic lifestyle. She will not go to France under the protection of this young man. A singing student? Only one in a million is any good and their morals are extremely dicey, to say the least. And he's French!' Charles Noble almost shuddered. Everyone knew they ate frogs. What kind of civilisation bred men who ate frogs? 'He'll get nowhere, Judith. Opera, if it has to be sung at all, should be sung by Italians. So much less embarrassing for everyone.'

'We could invite him here, Dad.' Tony's brother, Frederick, raised his head from his battle with logarithms. 'There must be decent French people, and if Antonia likes this chap he must be fairly nice. Let us see him before you let Antonia travel abroad. Let him see that she comes from a respectable family and so, if her being an art student has given him any ideas, he'll see the error of his ways.'

The parents looked at their prodigy. Did the Bible not say, 'Out of the mouths of babes?'

Therefore Tony received a letter that told her that although they could not, at this juncture, countenance a visit to a foreign country in the company of a young man of whom they knew only what she had told them, they would be delighted to welcome Mr Fougère for a weekend visit.

'The summons,' Blaise laughed when she had told him. 'I am fill with terror.'

'You'll be bored to tears,' mourned Tony. 'We'll have fish on Friday evening. On Saturday we'll go to the tennis club to watch Freddie—

that's my brother—and my father play father–son doubles. The tea is good. We'll have dinner and play bridge. On Sunday we'll go to church and have lunch at the inn. Oh God, you're a Catholic.'

'You need not say it as if it was the same as "You're a leper". Don't worry. I am also French and will compromise.'

'And Blaise, dearest, darling, sweetest Blaise, you know you can't come into my bedroom.'

He drew himself up to his full height and glowered down at her. 'Madame, you insult. I am a gentleman.' Then he dropped down beside her on the bed and his hands began their searching. 'And I will be the perfect guest, but for now I will be very not perfect.'

'Imperfect,' she tried to say, but it was muffled by his lips.

The visit was quite as bad as Tony had expected. She tried hard not to be caught looking at Blaise. Her eyes would give her away. But her father knew, she was quite sure. He was cold and studiously polite, but then he was always like that with strangers, wasn't he? Besides, not only was Blaise a stranger, he was a foreigner.

Her mother was worse. She gushed. 'A singer. How nice. You must sing for us. "One Fine Day". I do so adore that. French, Antonia tells me. How clever of you to speak English.'

And then the horrifying nightmare of the hostess. 'I hope you can eat English food.'

Freddie behaved like a missionary out to convert the heathen even if Blaise was not a heathen but a baptised Catholic. Perhaps for the Freddies of this world that was even worse.

Blaise was naughty and called Freddie the Archbishop ever after.

Tony lay tossing in bed, thinking of Blaise in a room just two doors away and hoping and praying that he would forget that he was a gentle-man. He did not and being a practical Frenchman had gone to sleep as soon as his head had touched the pillow.

He had worked hard to avoid having to sing.

'I am not warmed up,' he had told Mrs Noble, who had hurriedly put another log on the fire.

'His voice, Judith, his voice,' Tony's father had said tetchily and Blaise had taken pity on her and asked her if once again she would show him the garden that reminded him of his father's. It did not. His father's rose garden was a masterpiece that covered over six acres but, as he reminded Tony as their train chuntered them back to London, 'I am a gentleman and gentlemen always try to put other people at their ease. Courtesy, *ma mie*, costs nothing.'

CHAPTER THREE

SCOTLAND, 1998. LONDON, 1998

A DOZEN RED ROSES were delivered to Holly at school. She took them to her classroom where they stood looking incongruous all afternoon but still filling her with delight each time she looked at them.

Once home, and with the flowers carefully arranged in her best vase, she rang John's office.

'I'm sorry too,' she said after she had listened to John's breast-beating. 'Look, John, Tony's agent came up to the cottage and had a preliminary look at the paintings. He thinks they're good. On Saturday I'm seeing Mr Gilbert again.'

'Great, I'll go with you.'

She hesitated. 'That would be lovely, John, except—it's just that he's taking me to his club on Princes Street for lunch. No office hours on a Saturday. He's doing me a big favour and I'm grateful and can hardly ask if I may bring a guest.'

'Is it the New Club?' he asked.

'Yes.'

'Very nice. I'll be here afterwards if you want to talk. I love you, Hol. I miss you.'

'Me too,' said Holly and, after she had hung up, wondered if she had told the truth.

Henry Gilbert, Tony's Edinburgh-based lawyer, had spoken to Holly at the funeral but she remembered nothing at all about him. She met him in the elegant foyer of the New Club, that sacred bastion of legal men that sits on Princes Street and stares balefully out at passers-by, and he guided her through to the dining room. He resembled nothing so much as a very merry garden gnome. He was small and bouncy, with a completely bald head but a delightful soft white beard, and his eyes twinkled. They sat down at a table by the window, and he watched Holly as she gazed in awe at the view of Edinburgh Castle.

'Next time you must bring your camera.' Twinkling eyes or no, Henry Gilbert was also extremely astute.

'You have had time to look at your legacy, Miss Noble?'

'Yes, and there are questions.'

'You are now a wealthy woman, and I congratulate you. Your aunt loved you very much and we discussed her will several times. You have her jewellery?'

'Yes, but of course I couldn't keep it.'

'If you wish to sell the jewellery then I can help you with that, although I believe she did hope you would keep some of her favourite pieces. She thought you might suit the rubies and then the diamond earrings—she was sure you wore earrings.' He looked at her shrewdly. 'It's insured for almost a million.'

Her stomach had dropped on the floor. 'A million . . . whats?'

'Pounds naturally,' he said almost severely. 'Are you all right? Good heavens, you do look peculiar. Let me get you a brandy.'

'No, I'm all right. It's just that . . . Mr Gilbert, almost all the jewellery is in my handbag and I have just walked here from the parking lot under the castle.'

The waiter came to take their orders, and when he had gone Henry Gilbert spoke to her severely. 'You have been highly irregular and very foolhardy, Miss Noble. But it was also foolish of your aunt to leave it at the cottage. Never mind, I was aware of the jewels and their approximate value. I did not know, however, about the paintings. And there Miss Noble made a mistake, if I may say so—most unsatisfactory—but I have had some people tell me, and this without their seeing them, of their probable worth. If they are genuine, as I'm sure they are, they are very valuable. Miss Noble was one of the most respected painters of her day. You probably know that in the years just after the war she became quite a cult figure in London society. Everyone who was anyone wanted her to paint him or her: a bit like Sargent or Raeburn.'

'I should have asked you about this when I spoke with you, Mr Gilbert, but did you know of my aunt's relationship with Blaise Fougère, the French tenor? The paintings in the attic are portraits of him.'

'I was your aunt's lawyer, Miss Noble, not her confidant. I know, however, that she painted Blaise Fougère for the Paris Opera House in 1952 and for the City Opera in New York in 1949. That, by the way, was later gifted to Covent Garden. New York commissioned a second portrait in 1960 but she never delivered it. After 1960 she painted less and less and almost always landscapes or seascapes.'

'She loved Turner's paintings,' Holly contributed, a catch in her voice. She said that looking at *Ancient Rome: Agrippina Landing with the Ashes of Germanicus* and *Venice: Storm at Sunset* was worth an entire term of lectures on colour and light.'

He coughed and fiddled with his glass. He did not understand colour and light. The law, now, that was easy to understand. 'If,' he began sternly, 'as I said before, the paintings are what we think they are, and I see no reason why they should not be,' he added hurriedly as he correctly interpreted her quick look of anger, 'they will be much sought after. Perhaps the agent knows the provenance of each work. All I can say is that I am told that the Fougère Foundation is connected with the Hartman Corporation and I will research further if you wish.'

A waiter arrived with their order and Holly picked up her fork. 'The Hartman Corporation? Sounds like money.'

Henry Gilbert supervised the pouring of the wine before he spoke. 'The usual term, I believe, is filthy rich.'

'The name means nothing to me, Mr Gilbert, but I would like to inform any relative of the existence of the paintings. The subject matter must be of interest. I could arrange for someone to view the paintings, perhaps even to donate one to the foundation or whatever it is.'

The lawyer looked somewhat startled. 'You are under no obligation, Miss Noble, and I'm not sure that this isn't highly irregular. I said I was not Miss Noble's confidant. That is true to an extent. She did, however, speak to me of her hopes for you. She was very proud when you decided to work for that charity in Africa, but she worried that, like your father, you were cutting yourself off from other young people. He married, rather late in life, I believe, and she hoped that you would—' he stopped and smiled—'meet a nice young man, fall in love and marry.'

'I did,' said Holly wryly. 'Twice. Fall in love,' she added as he looked a little surprised. 'As for Africa—I loved every minute. I do not regret the years I spent there.'

'Good, now let us enjoy this delicious monkfish, and after lunch I will take the jewellery, by taxi, and lock it in the vault at my office.'

H Holly strolled through Princes Street Gardens to the parking lot where she had left her car. Her heart as well as her bag was lighter. She drove home and rang Otto at his gallery.

He prevaricated. 'One assumed, Holly, I have already told you and I can say no more than that.'

Holly was deeply disappointed. She had been so sure that if anyone could tell her anything about Blaise Fougère and his place in Tony's life it would be Tony's agent. 'You've seen the paintings. They tell the whole story of their love for one another, Otto. Do you know anything about Fougère, why they never married? If they loved one another as much as these paintings show that they did, why were they not together?'

'Fougère married just after the war, I think.'

SOMEDAY, SOMEWHERE

'And there are no paintings during the war years.' Holly was excited. 'I saw 1937 and then the sixties or was there one in the fifties?'

'There were paintings, Holly. We sold landscapes for her, some portraits, and her swans.'

'I believe Mr Fougère had no children?'

'No.'

Holly held the receiver and listened attentively but heard nothing but air. Why was he finding it difficult to speak?

'Holly, there's a nephew.' He cleared his throat and began again. 'There is a nephew from the marriage of Fougère's sister, Nicole, to an American, Bradley Hartman, a member of a wealthy Pennsylvania family. Started in mines, earned enough to go into politics, and diversified. Nowadays there are more strands to the Hartman money than there are paintings in my gallery. The senator died about eight years ago but there is the son, Taylor Fougère Hartman. He'll be in his early forties I would say, and is certainly one of the richest men in America, having inherited everything from his father's family, his uncle, and his French grandparents.'

'I know, filthy rich, according to Mr Gilbert.' Holly sighed. She had no interest in Taylor Hartman or his money, but since he appeared to be Blaise Fougère's only living relative he should be told about the paintings. 'I feel we should tell him of the existence of the paintings; the subject matter must be of interest to him. Wouldn't it be nice if he could tell me something about Tony and Blaise, and perhaps there's a painting he would like to own. I could give him one.'

'Give Hartman a painting?' He was stunned. 'Holly, I have, as it happens, met him and I can give you a number for his office in New York. But he can afford to buy. Don't be hasty. Don't worry about the Hartmans, they can take care of themselves.'

'My aunt loved Blaise Fougère. I'm sure she knew, what's his name, Taylor. Otto, Tony would want him to see the paintings.' She could feel an inner frisson of excitement. The paintings were becoming more than just a legacy. 'Apart from their artistic value, they're a social document. Don't you see it? They tell a great deal about a famous man during a long life. He's so happy in some of them but he's so unhappy and almost disillusioned in others. It will be fascinating to research his life with Mr Hartman.'

Later she was to feel that this was the understatement of the entire twentieth century. It took weeks even to approach the inner sanctum where Taylor Hartman reigned supreme. His secretaries' secretaries had secretaries, and not one would allow Holly anywhere near him.

Holly told John of her frustrations. He had taken her to dinner at Rogano, her favourite restaurant, and they were relaxing with their after-dinner coffee. Holly was torn: she felt that she was drifting, like one of the swans at Torry Bay, in no particular direction but at the whim of the tide; in this case, John's stronger personality. On the other hand, there was her considerable investment in the relationship over the past five years. She could not abandon that on what might turn out to be merely caprice.

They were, therefore, no longer at ease with one another, and John was on his best behaviour. He was the perfect date: charming, courteous, attentive but not pushy, and he very carefully said nothing at all about Holly's inheritance until she brought it up.

'If you found that there was a horde of unseen masterpieces featuring someone in your family, John, wouldn't you want to see them, possibly to have one as a special memento?'

John held his brandy glass in the palm of his hand and inhaled the aroma. 'Part of my brain says that the very rich Mr Hartman has all the mementos he wants and so why does he want or need a painting, especially as a gift from you. He's not one of your waifs and strays, Hol.'

'That's not the point.' She leaned forward and he saw the excitement in her eyes. 'It's not a painting, John; it's a Tony Noble.'

'Wish I could excite you as much as this corporate executive does.'

She put her hands on his. 'Oh, John darling, it's not him; it's the paintings.'

'You're different, Hol.'

She sat back, astonished. 'I'm not. Try to understand. It's not the money. Never ever did I think Aunt Tony had any money. It's, oh, darling, don't sneer, but I just feel something in the cottage, some atmosphere. It's as if I've been given a sacred duty.'

'And a million quid's worth of jewels.'

'I never think of them. One day I will, I suppose, and it'll dawn on me that they are real. I just can't come to terms with all this. Fougère has a foundation. Maybe there should be a Tony Noble Foundation for artistically talented children who are too poor for lessons.'

'How about the Holly Noble Foundation for indigent lawyers who want to get into politics to do something for everybody's children?'

She looked at him over the rim of her coffee cup, and then sipped slowly. 'John, the money is not relevant. Of course you have my full support, you have always had that, but I have to do this; see it through for Tony. Then I can think about money and investments and all that kind of lawyer-speak.'

'I thought I was speaking fiancé-speak.'

Was she being unfair? Serenely floating swans, if she remembered correctly, were paddling away like mad under the calm, unruffled surface of the water. That's what she was, paddling furiously, trying to keep her head above water.

'Don't pressure me, John. I have so much on my mind, especially guilt. She was there for me, John, all through my childhood when my parents didn't really want to be bothered. She was my support through university and first boyfriends, and I just didn't bother to spend any time with her lately.'

He signalled for the waiter. 'And that's my fault, I suppose.'

'No, it's mine. I'm responsible for me and for my actions, and I'm not too happy with myself. I owe her.'

'Because she left you her Lothario's presents.'

At that her eyes widened in shock and he spoke quickly. 'I'm sorry, I'm sorry, Hol, but I'm having a hard time here too.'

Holly walked quickly before him out of the restaurant and waited while he paid the bill. 'I'm going home, John. I need time to think.'

'Don't think too much, Holly,' he said, and, turning on his heel, he left her in the middle of the pavement.

Shrewd and more worldly-wise than Holly, John had decided that Hartman himself had decreed that he had no interest in Miss Holly Noble. He waited three days and then sent Holly more flowers and followed up with a visit.

'I hoped you'd let me drive up to Torry Bay with you this weekend.'

Holly stared at him. Torry Bay and John. She buried her face in the flowers to give herself time to recover from the disloyal feeling that she did not want John at the cottage.

'I don't know, John. It's kind of you but—'

'We're both tense, sweetheart, and I think it's this Hartman fellow who's at the bottom of it. Once you've told him about the exhibition, you'll be relaxed.'

'He refuses to return my calls.'

'Tell one of the minions that you plan to run a story in a tabloid about the affair.'

Holly was shocked. 'But that's unethical and dishonest. I want him to see the paintings and have first choice, but if he expresses no interest then I intend to show and sell them—apart from the ones I shall keep.'

He laughed. 'All the ones that have you in them, I suppose. I bet you were the sweetest little girl.'

Holly jerked away from his teasing fingers. 'I might keep a painting called *Uncle Fire* but not the others. There are some sad ones that I like. I'll have to think.'

What is wrong with me? This is my fiancé. We have been practically living together for five years and now I feel I can hardly bear to have him touch me. Get a grip, get a grip.

She turned into his arms and relaxed against him. 'You're right. I'm too tense. Let's drive up, just for the afternoon'—she did not want to sleep with him in the cottage—'and I'll show you some of the paintings.'

The following week an account of the discovery of the paintings was printed in the *Daily Mail*. Within hours of its publication Taylor Hartman was on the line from New York. To say that he was furious would be a gross understatement.

Holly, unfortunately, had absolutely no idea what he was talking about and was shocked when he told her. She asked herself, who could have sold such a story? Someone in Mr Gilbert's office? In Otto's?

'Mr Hartman,' she quavered, glad that the width of the Atlantic prevented him from seeing her knocking knees, 'you must believe me—I did not give that paper this story and I have no idea who did. The only people who know about the paintings are of the highest—'

He interrupted. 'At least one isn't, Miss Noble. Demand a retraction and an apology immediately. These paintings, if there are paintings, are certainly not of Blaise Fougère. The idea is preposterous.'

Holly's knees were beginning to behave and her tongue had unstuck itself from the roof of her mouth. She would not be bullied. 'Kindly listen—' she began, but he was already talking.

'Do you have any idea of the number of women who claimed to have had an affair with my uncle in his lifetime, Miss Noble?' The voice was full of repressed anger. 'And every one of them proved a liar. The opera world is full of sick groupies who create fantasies for themselves. Blaise Fougère was a gentleman. He was devoted to my aunt and would never have done anything to hurt her.'

'Antonia Noble was an eminent British painter,' said Holly. 'There are two famous paintings by her of Blaise Fougère—'

'Yes, yes, I know,' he said impatiently. 'Chocolate-box covers, both of them, sickly sentimental. *Lohengrin* in Paris and an absolutely nauseating *des Grieux* now in London. You should go see it—it stinks.'

'No doubt you are also a renowned art critic, Mr Hartman.' Holly was now quite calm; Tony had never been sentimental or sickly sweet. She loathed Taylor Hartman. 'The point is there are over forty canvases of

SOMEDAY, SOMEWHERE

Mr Fougère in my cottage in Scotland. They are signed and dated and none of them is a costumed portrait. They are pictures of a great singer *en vacances*, as it were. The first one was painted in 1937 and the last in 1990.'

'An obsession,' he said after a pause. 'A diseased mind. Opera singers, especially the few really great tenors, attract them.'

'There is some fabulous jewellery too, Mr Hartman. My aunt's lawyer assures me that it's valuable. As to the paintings, I am in several of them and my aunt would never have put me in a fantasy. These are genuine and the world deserves to see them.'

There was silence for a while and Holly let the wires hum while he thought of his next strategy. 'You're going to tell me you knew him well, that he held you on his knee?' The voice was sarcastic, full of loathing and, surprisingly, of hurt.

'I remember nothing about him at all, Mr Hartman.'

'Where are they?'

Holly laughed. 'They're in a place called Torry Bay which is near Achahoish in Argyll.'

She thought she heard a gasp before he swore fluently but quietly in French. 'That's so godawful it has to be true,' he said at last in English. 'Have you photographed them?'

That had never occurred to her. 'No.'

He swore again but in English and obviously in exasperation. 'Well, do it, Miss Noble, and then call me at this number and I'll meet you in London. I can be there in three hours . . .'

'I work for a living, Mr Hartman, and I can't just drop everything.'

'I'm dropping everything to suit you and your cartoons, Miss Noble. Call me.'

She rang John to tell him of her surprise phone call. 'Out of the blue, John. After all the trouble I have taken to contact him, the phone rings, I pick it up and it's a very angry Taylor Hartman. He says his British lawyer told him there was what he termed "an inflammatory article" in the *Daily Mail*. "Paintings prove love nest", or something like that. But how could there have been anything? Surely Mr Gilbert . . . Otto . . .'

'Agents, Holly. A bit of sensation and the price goes up.'

'I can't believe that of Otto. He was so . . . moved by the paintings.' She stopped talking, for the thought that wanted to come into her head was too awful to express or even to contemplate. She shook her head as if to chase it away. 'Hartman is prepared to fly in to London to see photographs of the paintings although he seems to think there's no credibility in my story. He says other women claimed to have . . . known Blaise Fougère.'

'Perhaps they did.'

'Blaise Fougère loved my aunt.'

'Oh, come on, your aunt never left a tiny cottage in Argyll. It's fantasy, Holly. Hartman knows it and you won't accept it. You cannot argue with the Hartmans of this world. If he tells the press you're a sensationalist, he'll make a fool of you and your aunt and of me, Holly, and my chances of getting into politics will go right down the tube. Sweetheart, sell the damned cottage and the paintings and let's get married.'

Holly stared at the phone as if she could not understand what she had heard. Married. How often during their relationship had she longed to hear those words? How many times had he sweet-talked her into agreeing to postpone it?

'I'll go to London, John. While I'm there, I'll see Otto. Now, if you'll excuse me, I'm off to buy a Polaroid.'

Two weeks later she telephoned Taylor Hartman and this time was put straight through. She told him she had photographs of the paintings and they arranged to meet the following Saturday.

He had a suite in the Park Lane Hotel and Holly visited him there.

'I meant a professional photographer, Miss Noble,' he said after sitting for several minutes looking through the photographs and handing them back. 'I'll have to view them. I can see they are of my uncle but the photography is so amateurish that it's impossible to judge the quality.'

Holly tried not to be insulted. She was considered a fair photographer but she had never photographed paintings before. She would not allow this man to annoy her. She had been stunned to see how much he resembled his uncle. The body was leaner but he was just as tall. The face was harder, perhaps, but still very handsome. She would not permit herself to be attracted to him, though. He must be so used to being courted. Life, and Miss Holly Noble, had a nice little surprise in store for him.

'As I told you, the paintings are stored in an attic in my aunt's cottage in Argyll. I intend to sell some; unfortunately I cannot keep all of them.'

'There are letters in my uncle's hand? Some real proof?'

'No. My aunt had obviously cleared out what she did not want to be found. She left me a letter that led to the paintings. If it makes you feel any better, I do not intend to make an issue of the relationship that undoubtedly existed between Mr Fougère and Miss Noble.'

He looked at her shrewdly. 'The inflammatory article was just a ploy to get my attention?'

'I did not sanction the release of that story, Mr Hartman. I told you that I know nothing about it.' She took a deep breath and smothered the suspicion that kept popping up. 'Now, if you would like to see the paintings, I am in Achahoish almost every weekend and can meet you at Torry Bay.'

He stood up abruptly and she had the distinct feeling that it was to prevent himself from strangling her. Mr Hartman was not used to being thwarted.

'Miss Noble. Concorde brought me here. I had intended to fly back this evening; I have a very important meeting in Washington tomorrow.'

'Have a pleasant flight,' Holly said and picked up her bag. She could feel him drawing himself together.

'Miss Noble.' Was he speaking through gritted teeth? She dared not look. 'I will postpone my meeting and fly to this godforsaken place with you.'

Should she tell him that she was in London so seldom that she had hoped to go to the theatre, an art gallery? Better not.

'I had a return flight booked for tomorrow.'

He smiled. 'Allow me to make the arrangements. I can't wait for scheduled flights. You had better check out of your hotel so we can fly up as soon as possible, view the paintings and make some decisions. Where may I contact you?'

She gave him the number of her hotel and, feeling as if she had been steamrollered, hurried from his suite.

Later that afternoon Taylor's private secretary, Chandler North, telephoned her. His car would pick her up in exactly thirty-five minutes. They would proceed to the airport where they would board a private plane that would fly them to Argyll. A car would be waiting to transport them to Torry Bay.

'Do you always travel by private plane, Mr Hartman?' she asked as they approached the airport.

'No,' he said shortly, and then, as if ashamed of his abrupt answer, he elaborated. 'Concorde isn't private but it's the quickest way of getting from New York to London. My time is valuable, and usually a private plane allows me to work with my secretaries without interruption. And sometimes, Miss Noble, if I keep the minions' noses to the grindstone while they are in the air, I allow them some free time to see the sights when we set down. Are there sights in Argyll?'

'None that I think will interest you.'

'You know absolutely nothing about what interests me, Miss Noble.' That was such a well-deserved put-down that she stayed down until they were in the air. She had always liked flying, but to be in a privately chartered plane was exciting. She tried, and failed, not to show it.

'The ground looks just the same from the window of British Airways,' he said with a smile and she found herself for one moment prepared to like him.

She laughed and sat back. 'I know, but I just can't get over the fact that a plane gets into the air in the first place.'

They did not fly to Glasgow, as Holly had assumed they would, but to a small private airstrip near Oban. A car was waiting. For the Taylor Hartmans of this world a car would always be waiting.

'Ever been on a bus?' Holly asked unkindly but he did not think her remark worthy of comment. Quite right too, she decided.

Hartman was looking at a map and discussing the route with the car's original driver. 'He's not coming with us?' Holly had been ushered into the passenger seat—she had assumed because she knew the way—and now Hartman was trying to find enough room for his long legs in the space behind the wheel.

He glanced over at her. 'Your virtue is quite safe.'

Holly flushed and subsided. She almost wished that she had never decided he had some right to see the pictures. They drove for an hour in a sun-warmed silence. Autumn in Argyll was on its best behaviour.

Hartman broke the silence with an exclamation. 'Do you mind?' he asked and before she could say anything he had stopped the car and was getting out. 'Ancient stones,' he said as he closed the door.

Intrigued, she followed him as far as a low stone wall that bordered a field where a circle of great quiet sentinels stood waiting for someone to discover their secrets. Hartman, oblivious to the damp ground and the dried grass that pulled at his expensively tailored trousers, was walking round the stones, touching them. He turned and saw her at the wall and smiled. He was very attractive. She would not smile back.

'Blaise was here,' she called across the field. 'Tony has . . . had several books about Pictish stones. They're at the cottage.'

She went back to the car and several minutes later he joined her.

'Can we call a truce for the rest of the day?' he said. 'I'm starving and I want to eat at that little inn back there. Would you care to join me?'

They retraced their steps to the small hotel and Holly was surprised by the quality of the food in such an out-of-the-way place. Hartman was not. 'I always look for places like this. Sometimes you get a real bummer of a meal, but most times it's great regional cooking. Now I feel much more ready to fight you over the paintings.'

'I didn't have to tell you about them,' Holly said, but without rancour.

SOMEDAY, SOMEWHERE

Something in their relationship had changed subtly. Was it the breaking of bread together?

They talked about the stones and of the Picts—that ancient people who had lived in the area and carved their strange messages on the great stones—until they were almost in sight of the cottage. The road meandered up and around the glen and then it stopped for a moment at the top of the hill before plunging breathlessly down to the bay.

'Achahoish,' said Holly, her heart full of its beauty and its association, 'and there's Torry Bay.'

Hartman stopped the car, looked at her quickly and then away again. 'Merde,' he said, and then he was quiet.

Holly looked too and tried to see the view as Taylor Hartman had seen it, completely unknown, but she could see nothing that could cause such a response. She smiled with happiness as she saw the few houses snuggling into the valley and the purple and green of the hillsides. She saw the sea curling round as if holding the bay in its arms.

He said nothing as they drove to the wall of rhododendrons that made a huge arc round the cottage and its garden.

'Sometimes the sea meets each wing of the rhodies. It can be quite bleak but it's absolutely glorious in the spring, a wall of pink and lilac.'

Still he was silent. She left him with his own thoughts and went to open the front door.

'It's quite small,' she said when she found him at her side. 'Look round if you like. I'll open the studio where the paintings are. You might want to bring some of them downstairs to the living room.'

She went upstairs and unlocked the attic door. The paintings still stood, their faces turned to the wall, and then Hartman was there, bending his head to enter. He reminded her of something.

You cannot expect me to stand up in here, ma mie. This is for little sprites, like you and my Hollyberry.

She looked round, but the ghost—if ghost it had been—was gone, and Hartman had heard obviously nothing. He went to the first painting and turned it from the wall. He said nothing but just stood, and then he looked at a second painting, and Holly left him and went downstairs to sit in the chair by the window and look at the sea.

She heard him moving around, cursing as he bumped his head, and then she heard him on the stairs.

'Holly?' he shouted. When had she become Holly?

'Turn right,' she called and soon he was in the room, his size and the large painting filling it up alarmingly.

'We can't leave these paintings here,' he said. 'There could be a fire or a burglary.' He propped the canvas against the table. It was of Blaise sitting in a field of dandelions. 'What's Godalming?'

'A little town in Surrey near London.'

'I like this,' he said. 'My uncle very rarely let himself be seen so at ease. The painting is quite crude, of course. The gold is a little harsh.'

'It looks just fine to me.'

He laughed and was gone, leaping up the old oak staircase and returning more slowly with another of Tony's paintings.

By nine in the evening Holly was beginning to grow rather nervous. Hartman was as gripped as Otto had been and seemed unaware of the time, and it was at least two hours back to Glasgow. She went upstairs and found him sitting crosslegged on the floor. 'It's getting late.'

'Got anything to eat in the freezer?'

He seemed astonished to discover that there was neither food nor freezer. Holly went to the kitchen to see what she could find. 'There's a farmhouse near the village just across the bay. I'll see if they'll sell me some eggs.'

'Great,' he said. 'If you fix us something to eat, I'll spend some more time on the pictures, and then I'll make some calls and find a hotel. You don't mind staying over one night? Use my cellphone if there's someone who'll be worried.'

'There's no hotel for miles.'

He was unperturbed. 'I wonder if there's an old razor or a toothbrush in the bathroom. Won't matter. Chandler, my secretary did tell me to be ready for anything. He'll be so pleased to be able to say, "I told you so."'

Holly shrugged, changed into some flat shoes and walked off to visit their neighbours. She was not afraid to spend the night in a remote cottage with a complete stranger. It just wasn't done though. When she returned to the cottage, she wondered what he would say when she told him that.

'Good heavens! How medieval! Now, I've checked the bedrooms and you may have the little one. If you object to being turfed out of the main bedroom feel free to share.'

'Very funny,' said Holly, with an attempt at lightness.

'Come on, Holly, I'm too tall for that sweet little bed. What did you manage to rustle up?'

'Rustle is about the right verb. We have some eggs, some venison sausages and some home-cured ham.'

'Sounds wonderful. Any time you're ready.'

'I can't cook,' said Holly angrily. That was not strictly true, but he was used to fine dining in first-class hotels. She could not cook for him.

'Believe me, you have got to be better than me. Look, I'll fix the table and wash up after. How's that for equality?'

The sausages were just a little too well cooked but he did not complain about that or the instant coffee.

He pushed himself away from the table and leaned back in his chair. 'I could get used to the simple life.'

She did not rise to that bait so he began to talk about the pictures.

'Thank you for allowing me to see them. I'm not admitting that my uncle posed for any of them but they are extremely good paintings and if you are agreeable I would like one or two for my private collection.'

'They're real: the relationship was a reality and very important to each of them. Admit it.'

He looked towards the window. The sky outside was lilac and pink. 'I knew him all my life. I would have known,' he said bleakly.

She said nothing. Had she not felt exactly the same herself? 'They're genuine. Choose your favourite. I have my own almost decided.'

'I won't fight about that,' he said at last. 'It's what to do with the bulk. Would you consider storing them properly until I can do some research . . . and come to terms with what they're telling me?'

'That shouldn't be a problem.'

'I'll make some calls,' he said.

'I have already made perfectly good arrangements, Taylor.'

He smiled. 'Taylor,' he said. 'I wondered when you would use my name. To show us that we're equal.'

'Where the paintings are concerned, I am in absolute control.'

'I'm not going to steal them, for God's sake, but I want them properly stored and professionally researched and valued.'

Until that moment, no matter what John had said, Holly had never seriously considered their actual monetary value. To her they were a long letter from Tony. 'To me they are absolutely priceless, Mr Hartman, but you wouldn't understand that.' She walked past him to the stairs. 'There's some washing-up liquid under the sink. Good night.'

The Performing Bear
LONDON, 1939

'Love me, Toinette, love me.'

He was undoing her blouse and she gave herself up to the magic of his hands, his lips. 'I adore you, Blaise. I will always adore you.'

Later she sat wrapped in his bathrobe and listened to his humming while he prepared them a meal. 'I have never heard you sing, Blaise,' she said reflectively. They had been together for nearly two years but never had she heard him sing.

He stopped whisking his eggs. He was surprised. 'But I sing all the time, *ma mie*. I was singing now.'

'You were humming; and sometimes you warm up, but that's just like gargling or water going down the drain.'

Omelette pan in hand, he bowed low as if for a compliment. 'I sing on the bicycle.'

'To yourself, or sometimes you shout, "En passant par la Lorraine avec mes sabots", but that's not singing, singing.'

'It is my most favourite song and I, Blaise Marie Fougère,' he said, again bowing to her grandly, 'never shout. I am a tenor, from *tenir*, to hold, not some word for to shout.'

She examined her toenails critically and decided to paint each one a different colour. 'You told me that already; when may I hear you sing?'

'It is better that I make you sing,' he said, slipping his hands under the robe and running them over her warm, responsive body.

'The omelette,' she said, before it was too late.

He laughed and released her.

The omelette and the salad of fresh herbs were delicious. Blaise had moved into a small, inexpensive flat on the other side of the river at the end of his first year of study. It meant that they could stay together without feeling guilty. He could make omelettes, he could concoct salads, and he made the most delicious coffee. Tony could cook nothing palatable. All her creativity was expended on her canvases—or in loving Blaise. All week she lived at the students' residence for which her father paid, but from Friday evening until Sunday evening she stayed with Blaise. She knew that she would have to tell her parents, but since she was well aware that they, and her brother, would disapprove, she kept putting it off.

'You haven't answered me,' she said as she watched him walk around the tiny kitchen area. She loved watching him.

'What I loved most about her,' he said looking at an empty chair instead of at Tony, 'was that in all our life together she never asked me to sing.' He laughed. 'All my public life I will meet people who will treat me like an automaton. You know: drop in the penny and the performing bear performs. Every song I sing, I will sing for you, Toinette, but I cannot sing in this little apartment because I will wake the babies and the old people.'

'But it's as if you are keeping something from me. I show you my paintings: that's laying bare my soul, Blaise. I need to see your soul.'

SOMEDAY, SOMEWHERE

'Such melodrama. Are you sure you are not French, my Antoinette? No, no,' he said, holding her tightly as she tried to pull away from him. 'I am wicked to tease. Come on, put on some clothes. We will go to find a place where I can sing for you.'

They crossed the river and went to Hyde Park, which Blaise knew closed at midnight. They were going to hide in the park after the gates had closed. At this stage in his career an empty, locked London park was the only place he could find where they would be undisturbed.

As innocently as possible they managed to slip behind the bandstand, and there they sat until they were quite sure that the park was empty. Then he stood up. He bowed to her. 'You wish?'

She nodded and he walked lightly up the steps to the bandstand and stood in the moonlight while he listened to the orchestra playing in his head. He began to sing.

Nothing had prepared Tony for this first experience. He sang in French, *Je Crois Entendre Encore*, the delicate tenor aria from Bizet's *Les Pêcheurs de Perles*, the pearl fishers. The words poured in a golden stream into the silver night. She did not know that he still had much to learn of technique, that the power and purity for which he was to become world famous were still in their infancy. It did not matter.

One aria over, he began another, this time in Italian: *'Una Furtiva Lagrima'* from Donizetti's comic opera, *L'Elisir d'Amore*. As it rose to its climax in one great long breath she began to cry. She knew so very definitely that he was not and never would be hers. He would never belong entirely to her. He belonged to the world and she knew that there would be weeks, months, when she would sit and wait to receive whatever he had left to give her. But something deep inside told her that he would need her to be there. For his sanity he would need to know, without question, that she would be waiting always, ready to give and give again.

He stopped singing in some consternation and jumped down. *'Ma mie,* that is a happy song. I have sing it badly. You cannot see that I smile in the moonlight. See me smile.' He was beside her on the grass, holding her, kissing her eyes, her hair.

'I know. I was crying because it was so beautiful,' she lied. 'I feel almost as though you are not real, Blaise, not a human being at all, and I have touched something almost mystical.'

He snorted with anger as only a Frenchman can. 'Shall I show you how human I am, my Tony? Who better than you knows that I am just a man with needs like other men?'

Plus a once-in-a-lifetime talent. She thought it but did not say it. For her he must be Blaise the friend, the lover, not Fougère the tenor.

Suddenly there was strong torchlight shining on his face and a large policeman was holding the torch.

'What do you think you're doing? How did you both get in here?'

'Officer, how wonderful to see you,' said Tony, fluttering her eyelashes. 'I can't think how we got locked in. We were trying to get someone's attention.'

'Very unusual way if I may say so, miss. Your friend, foreign is he?' 'French.'

'Ah, well then,' he said, as if Blaise's nationality explained everything. 'Come along. You ought to be had up but I won't report you this time.'

'Thank you.' Tony watched him lock the gates behind them. 'Come along, Blaise,' she said and, without a word, he followed her.

'Tell your friend he could make a nice little bit down the pub of a Friday night if he learned somethin' in English.'

Blaise laughed. 'See, if my professors are in the right and I have no future, I can make a nice bit down the pub. We will not starve.'

She threw her arms round him, binding her eagle to her while he was still unaware of the true power of his wings. 'You will be the best, Blaise. Millions of people will pay anything to hear you sing.'

'Funny little Tony. I have so much to learn before I will be allowed onto a stage. But, Toinette, when I am there, I will need you with me. You fill all my senses. Without your love I will sing with technique but without heart. Love me, Toinette, always.'

'With my last breath I will tell of my love for you, Blaise Fougère.'

'My woman,' he said and she exalted in her power as she heard the passion in his voice.

She was painting the sun and the moon into a background of a portrait of Blaise when she heard that Germany had invaded Poland. Blaise had been muttering things about German aggression for over a year now, but Tony had soothed and comforted him and made him think only of his studies or of her.

He had not heard the broadcast. There was a pile of open books and scores on the desk in front of him and he was concentrating. His powers of concentration fascinated her. He would sit there, making notes, humming lines, until severe stomach pains told him that he was hungry. Tony was almost the same when she was painting.

She turned off the radio and that, of course, since she did not want it to do so, disturbed him.

'Is it time for dinner, Toinette?' he asked, his eyes still on the score. She decided not to tell him. She would keep him here for ever. Never again would she switch on the radio. She would be happy here, with him, for ever and ever, Amen.

But he would not be happy. And that was all that mattered.

She went over and pulled his head back against her stomach. 'Germany has invaded Poland.'

He stayed, his head against her belly, for some time.

'Bastards,' he said in English and then a long stream of fluent and, thankfully, incomprehensible French. 'There will be war, Toinette, another world war that will make the war to end all wars like a squabble among children.' He jumped up. 'Come. I must talk with my papa.'

He held her hand and pulled her along through crowded September streets that somehow seemed tense and sad. The world was waiting.

He found a telephone box. She watched him shovel coins into the box and then talk and laugh and talk and cry.

When he put the receiver back he stood for a moment, weeping, and then he pulled her to him and cried into her hair and she was terrified and cried too.

They went back to the flat and he closed the door and she turned into his arms and quickly, methodically, he took off first her clothes and then his own, and he took her to the bed and they made love until they cried out together in mingled ecstasy and pain. Never had he been so rough; never had he been so gentle; and Tony tried to match his passion, his grief, his love, his regret. Afterwards they slept, and when they woke it was Sunday morning and it was dark.

He sighed. 'It is fact, Toinette. Papa is sure that France is about to declare war on Germany. He wants me to stay here but I must go back to France and fight for my country.'

She threw herself into his arms. 'No, no. I will not let you go. You are too valuable. Civilisation needs the arts, Blaise. Your voice will heal wounds.'

He held her and rocked her as if she were a baby. 'But how could I live with my own wounds? Try to understand, *ma mie*, the more fast I go, the more fast I will come back. In two or three years I will be more mature, my body and my voice, I mean. This will not stop my career.'

'Unless you're killed. Don't go, Blaise,' she begged, all pride forgotten, clutching him. 'Your father is rich and important; he can keep you out of it. The war machine doesn't need you and I do, I do.'

'I will return, Toinette, and I will sing Florestan for you, and Alfredo and Rodolfo, and one day Parsifal and Otello and even Tristan. We will conquer the world together, *ma mie*, you with your painting, me with my singing, and the world will be a nicer place because we were in it.'

He took off his signet ring with its deeply carved B.M.F. and put it into her hand. 'Tomorrow I will buy a gold chain for you to wear this round your neck. When the war is over, I will ask for it back and I will replace it with a wedding ring, and then there will be babies, *ma mie*, lots of fat little babies who will sing as they paint. Is that not a glorious picture to hold in your head?'

'I will hold it in my heart,' she said.

CHAPTER FOUR
TORRY BAY, 1998. GLASGOW, 1998

TAYLOR HAD BEEN perfectly amiable in Argyll. He had woken her at the crack of dawn and driven her down roads where mist lingered to the airport. They were in Glasgow before eight o'clock. 'I go direct from here to Washington,' he said. 'You have my New York number. Ask for Chandler North; he will tell you where I am.' He looked round to where a uniformed driver was waiting. 'The car will take you home.'

She was absolutely exhausted and sat down at her kitchen table to catch her breath. Without the overwhelming strength of Taylor's size and personality she had time to think.

Damn. Otto. She had intended to see him while she was in London, at least see his gallery.

A very groggy voice answered on the ninth ring. 'Miss Noble, it is not yet nine o'clock on a Sunday morning. I went to bed at three.'

'I'm so sorry, Otto. It's just that Taylor has been here.'

'Taylor. Wait. I can't think without my glasses. You said Taylor as in the Hartman Corporation?'

'The very same.'

'Tell me.'

'He rang me. Seemingly there was a rather lurid article in a newspaper.' She did not ask if he knew about it; she was sure he would not stoop to such actions. 'He asked me to photograph the paintings and meet him in London—you know these jet-setters, fly in fly out? Next thing, I am on a private jet flying back to Argyll! The important thing, however, is that he has seen the paintings and I think he wants one or two.'

'What did he say about their authenticity?'

'I take it you're asking if he believes in the relationship? He asked if there were letters. There are none.'

'Are you sure, Holly? Have you searched?'

'I found a letter addressed to me in the bottom of a drawer full of Tony's sketchbooks. Inside the envelope was a key to her attic studio, where I found all the paintings. But there were no other letters. Otto, are you free yet to pack and appraise the paintings?'

'I will make myself free. I want them out of Scotland before the winter. Are you able to join me?'

She thought of school, where they had still not found a replacement for her and she thought of John. No, she was not free. 'Whenever you can come, Otto, will be fine.'

'I'll ring you in a few days.'

The unseen but all-powerful Chandler had been informed of their progress. London in March was impossible. Mr Hartman had to be in Japan. May perhaps. Would Miss Noble agree to a private showing with no publicity? The family were anxious to avoid any scandal. Scandal? That made Holly really angry. Tony had not been ashamed of her love for Blaise Fougère. Each of them, Tony and Blaise, had kept quiet about their relationship for their own reasons. If Blaise was anything at all like his arrogant nephew, he was the one who had wished to keep the affair such a well-kept secret. He was the one who had allowed all the publicity that said he was a devoted husband whose eyes never strayed. That pose was a lie as the paintings showed. She was so angry about the word 'scandal' that the word 'family' failed to register.

'Chandler, I think I should talk to Mr Hartman.'

Taylor had telephoned sounding cold and remote and they had had a real argument. 'Look, Holly, not every artist has a relationship with her subject. No one has ever associated Blaise with her, even though she was commissioned to paint him . . . he was the nicest guy in the world; maybe they were friends.'

Holly interrupted. 'Don't be silly. Friends? They were lovers and you know it. Your pride just won't let you accept it.' She would not join the hundreds of people who allowed Taylor Hartman to browbeat them.

'I will not have my uncle a subject for gossips. He spent his life protecting my aunt, and his own privacy. His will asked me to protect his reputation; it's a sacred trust. He still has an enormous following.'

'Of people who loved to hear him sing. Do you think they're suddenly going to stop buying discs if they hear he had a . . .?' She had been about to say mistress but that was not Tony's role.

'Holly, you don't understand—' he began.

'I understand being patronised, Mr Hartman. I'll remind you again that I had no legal obligation to show you the paintings and I will show and sell them when I feel the time is right.'

Several weeks later Chandler contacted her. Mr Hartman would prefer that the paintings be shown in New York. He would be most grateful. Would he indeed? Holly's initial response was to say no and Otto had agreed. 'I smell deviousness, Holly. The same international buyers would come if I hung them in the kitchen at Torry Bay.'

'I would like Tony to have an international reputation . . . but as a painter, Otto, not as a mistress. I am right? The paintings are good?'

'Some of them are great, darling girl.'

She almost wept but, glad that Otto could not see her eyes, spoke briskly. 'Good. Now let us arrange a date for the opening. The Hartman Corporation will be informed like any other prospective customer.'

That conversation over, it was time to deal with John. 'How are you?'

He answered her question with one of his own. 'Where are you, Holly? Achahoish?'

'No, still here at the flat.' She stopped and then rushed on. 'I could make us some dinner and we could talk.' She hated begging, but surely there should be no false pride where love was. She had promised to marry John; they could work this out. Compared with Taylor Hartman and his faults and failings, John was a paragon among men.

'I have some work to finish. Say eight.' He sounded so cold, so dismissive. Then he said, 'I've missed you, Holly.'

Her heart swelled with relief. They would work it out.

The telephone rang again almost immediately.

'How are you, Holly?'

Holly sat down, almost clutching at the table for support. What on earth did he want? 'I'm quite well, Taylor. What do you want?'

'Want? Why do you always have to yell at me? I called to say hi.'

'I can't be blamed if your reputation precedes you. Naturally when I heard your voice—so unexpectedly, no wonderful Chandler smoothing the way—I assumed you either had bad news for me or you wanted something. Why did you ring?'

He was quiet for so long that she began to think he had disconnected.

'God knows,' he said at last. 'I guess I got to feeling bad about my attitude, thought maybe I should have tried to explain my position better.'

'Perhaps you should,' she agreed sweetly.

'Goddamn it, Holly. I'm not used to grovelling.'

'Then get used to it. It suits you.'

And naturally he slammed down his receiver.

Holly sat for a minute not feeling particularly pleased with herself. He had behaved, for once, like a normal human being, and she had ruined it for him. Strangely that made her feel rather excited.

'Damn. I'm thinking about a man I do not like in the slightest when I should be involved in preparing a meal for the man I . . . love.'

She took great care with the preparation of the meal and the table. They would come to an understanding, she was sure of it. John was not Taylor and she was not a meek female who could be dictated to by either of them. She and John would reach an agreement or the engagement would go no further.

He was over an hour late. She refused to think that he was teaching her a lesson. He was a lawyer and often worked late.

'Holly, I'm sorry,' he said, enfolding her in his arms. 'Those damn papers had to be read. Forgive me?'

'Of course.' Holly smiled as she took the wine he had brought and carried it to the sideboard. 'I have tuna steaks marinating, so if you open the wine we can have a glass while it's cooking.'

'Tell me about your progress,' he said as he obeyed her.

'I have resigned as from Friday. That was such a difficult decision to make. When this is all over I might need a job and good teaching jobs don't grow on trees.' If she had expected him to say something reassuring she was disappointed and went on, 'Otto is coming on Monday to start packing the paintings. Earlier this evening I spoke to Taylor who is making grumbly spoilt millionaire noises.'

He gulped his wine and refilled his glass. 'Why?'

Carefully Holly turned the fish. 'Because a newspaper columnist is saying that there was a *relationship* between Tony and Blaise Fougère and Fougère's publicity people had created the myth that he was as pure as the driven snow. Their carefully constructed idyll is crumbling around his family's ears and they don't like it.'

'Can't you just deny a relationship? Say that it was professional, artist–subject?'

'Let's eat this while it's perfect,' said Holly, putting two blue glass plates on the table. She had brought them from the cottage and there was a slight catch in her throat when she continued. 'I have ambivalent feelings about everything now. Tony seems to be telling me that she wants her paintings exhibited; she wants her story told. She kept her relationship with Fougère a secret but not because she was ashamed. I believe she pandered to his paranoia, his wish for privacy.'

'What's paranoid about wanting one's private life to be private?'

This from the man who had probably hinted at scandal to the newspapers. Challenge him. Did you do it, John? Ask him, damn it.

She took a deep breath and tried. 'That's rich coming from you.' She hated herself for being unable to ask outright. What a weakling. This is no basis for happy marriage. 'John, if I share something with you in complete confidence can I rely on you to keep it that way?'

'Good God, Holly, I'm a lawyer. I deal with client confidentiality all the time.' He sounded angry.

'I'm not a client, John,' said Holly quietly.

'No, you're my fiancée, the woman who will marry me. You trust me enough to sleep with me but not to confide in me.'

Holly could see the pretty picture she had painted of her future dissolving before her eyes. 'It was you who told the press the subject of the portraits, wasn't it?'

He threw down his fork and stood up. 'Sure, it was easy. Hartman would have ignored you. You'll never learn how to manipulate people.'

'Because I wouldn't want to learn. How could you do something that you should have known is completely against my principles?'

'Don't be so naive. When you're ready to grow up, you know where to reach me.'

Did he expect her to run after him, to beg, to say she was sorry? Her knees were trembling and she felt sick but she would not do it and he reached the door, picked up his raincoat and left.

Relief was the strongest emotion she felt.

She sighed and then laughed. Her fiancé had just walked out and she felt more relief than regret. A showdown had been coming for months now. Had that been a showdown or merely a skirmish before the big deciding battle? 'Damn you, John,' she swore softly. 'You know you were wrong and I'm damned if I'm going to let you ruin a very expensive piece of fish.' She would eat, then she would open some of the boxes of letters—family archives brought from her parents' home and so far totally ignored—and tomorrow she would go back to Torry Bay to see what it told her of the love between her aunt and Blaise Fougère.

But the letters revealed nothing. That is, they told her nothing about the love affair. Instead, Holly read of her father's doubts when Tony sank her savings into buying the cottage from her landlord. She read interminable accounts of her own progress in painting, swimming and later, sailing. No child, it would appear, had ever constructed a finer sandcastle.

What a prodigy I was, Holly thought as she wiped away tears. She had taken that devoted love for granted all her life and had been too busy, too determined to be in love with John, even to visit her aunt. How could I have done that? How could I let one man take me over to that extent, to where I was an automaton doing his bidding?

She drove to Argyll, to Achahoish, and on to Torry Bay and the cottage, her cottage, the cottage she knew now that nothing would persuade her to sacrifice. I'll live here, possibly do supply teaching or volunteer work. When I sell some of the jewels I'll put in central heating. Add state-of-the-art television set and video to the 'must-have' list.

How had Tony managed through all those bleak and lonely winters? She had never seemed to feel the cold, out walking every day up to that little headland she had painted so often. Holly felt an urge to go up there, but it was dark and cold, so she unloaded the car, promising herself that she would visit the headland first thing in the morning. She went upstairs to Tony's bedroom, the room that she had shared with Blaise Fougère.

'I suppose I should sleep here now,' Holly said out loud, but she could not bring herself to put her things there. She opened the wardrobe and began to sort through Tony's clothes, clothes for two lives. Tony had not stayed a recluse in Torry Bay. She had visited Edinburgh, London and Glasgow for her own art shows and she must have visited other countries with Blaise. At least it appeared that she had been with him in Paris, Milan, Bayreuth and even New York and San Francisco, because several of her major canvases were set in these cities. Holly resolved to study Tony's passport.

She took out a huge pile of heavily beaded cocktail dresses and threw them on the bed. So much for her naive idea that Tony had lived a quiet life. A few carefully packed outfits had been concealed among the dresses. Holly opened the bags to reveal sweaters, slacks and shirts. She recognised the bulky, dark blue Guernsey. Blaise Fougère was wearing it in the painting called *Grief*. That brown shirt he was wearing in *Uncle Fire*. Holly held the sweater against her face and a faint smell of soap and shaving cream came to her. Tony had not washed the sweater after he had worn it for the last time: she had wrapped it up carefully and put it in the deepest recess of her wardrobe.

'She loved you so much,' she told the ghost who had worn the sweater. 'Did you love her or did you merely use her?' She looked down at an evening gown. Its glitter reminded Holly of the valuable jewels hiding in Mr Gilbert's safe. If she looked at them again, what would they tell her? She was afraid they would speak only of a rich man's ability to assuage his guilt. A memory tried to push itself forward. There was a jewel that Tony wore always and with anything, but what was it?' Holly could not remember . . . it was not Tony's favourite rubies . . . well, if the memory was important, it would return.

Back downstairs she sat in the big chair by the window, looking at the moon playing on the surface of the bay. Tony must have sat here day after day, night after night; Blaise Fougère too. They had loved here in this room. She could feel their presence; sense their love. And suddenly she knew that the love was for her too. They loved her; they approved of what she was doing.

'I want the world to know that Tony was a superb painter, Blaise. She kept these magnificent portraits hidden to protect you, to protect your wife, but you are dead now, all of you. You will not be hurt by the story the paintings tell. The millions who revere the memory of Blaise Fougère, the tenor, will not abandon you because you needed the love and support that Tony gave you all your life. She was here, patiently waiting, sublimating her phenomenal talent to foster yours. It's her turn now and you want her to have it, don't you?

Hollyberry.

'I won't let either of you down, I promise.'

It was after eleven, so only just after six in New York. Thank God for mobile phones. She would have a permanent line installed, together with the central heating.

'Hello, Taylor. It's Holly.' She spoke as if they had not had a recent fight. 'I'm at Torry Bay. His clothes are here. He loved her; he's told me that . . .'

'My uncle has been dead for years. When did he tell you?'

He would laugh her to scorn but she did not care. 'Just a few minutes ago. I feel his presence here, hers too. They want me to fight you, Taylor. I will show the paintings to the world.'

'I guess you're at the cottage. Don't get rid of anything till I get there.'

She panicked. 'I don't want you here. I was merely letting you know my plans.'

'I'm letting you know mine. Give me your mobile number in case I need to call you. I'll leave New York as soon as I can get clearance.'

He arrived less than forty-eight hours later when she was up at the headland. She had found a little hollow that protected her from the wind but which still allowed her to see the glorious view.

'Love me, Toinette, love me.'

'I do, mon ange, I do. But we are so near the cottage.'

He was undoing her shirt, one of his that he had left on his last visit. 'I can't wait,' he said.

Tony and Blaise were there with her. Holly sat down and looked at the view spread out before her. It could have changed very little since her aunt had first seen this delightful place. It had to be the peace, the atmosphere that had drawn them both back again and again. Here there was no stress, here there was acceptance and deep love. That's what I want.

She heard his voice and stood up. I'm talking of peace and acceptance and love and what do I get? Taylor Hartman—and there's still no food in the place.

'Here,' she shouted.

He had parked his rented car at the door and was standing watching her as she walked back from the headland.

'Why did you come, Taylor?' she asked aggressively. 'There is nothing for you here.'

He laughed. 'Chandler ordered a hamper from Fortnum and Mason's. It was waiting at the airport.'

'I wasn't talking about food as you jolly well know.'

'As you jolly well know,' he mocked. 'Holly, Miss Noble, I would like to see what you tell me are my uncle's effects. Pretty please.'

Holly pushed past him and opened the door. 'You may look at the things in the wardrobe, Taylor, but only because you have come such a long way, which, by the way, is an obscene waste of money . . .'

He grabbed her and turned her towards him. 'Not that it is any of your business, I loved Blaise Fougère—I thought more than anybody. And not that it's any of your business, I thought he loved me best too.'

He took a deep breath. 'Damn it all, I can't deal with you when I'm tired. I would like to see his things,' he finished almost humbly.

'The bedroom.'

He was quite some time and his face was very white when he eventually rejoined her.

'May I see the notes your aunt left, and the jewels, Holly?'

She retrieved her precious letters and handed them to him. 'The jewellery is in a vault.'

The letters he read over and over. 'She sounds nice, your aunt. I'll get the food,' he said, 'and then I'll drive back to Glasgow.'

'Taylor.'

He stopped.

'You may use the bedroom tonight. You must be tired.'

His back was to her. 'I don't think I can, Holly, but thank you. There's just too much to take in.'

When he came back with the hamper it was obvious that he did not want to talk about Blaise or Tony or the paintings. But she had to ask before he left.

'The clothes, Taylor?'

'Give them to charity. See you sometime, Holly.'

She watched him drive away, and as she walked back to the cottage she asked herself whether that was a threat or a promise. She opened the door slowly and whispers on a sigh reached her.

Darling girl.

Hollyberry.

LONDON, 1939

Extract from Exhibition Catalogue

We have no paintings from this period in the artist's life. Three paintings of Canon Gemmell—see p. 60—were painted during this time and we believe this was when the first of her famous *Lohengrin* series of swans was painted.

Britain declared war on Germany on September 3, 1939. For two days Tony had waited, hoping against hope that somehow everything would be all right. There could not be war. Blaise could not abandon his career to become a soldier. If he left her she would die. She knew it. He was more important to her than the air she breathed, the food she ate. Even her painting came second to her need for him.

'Paint, Toinette,' he ordered her. 'Paint my babies, our babies, five, I think, two boys for you and three little girls for me to spoil.'

To please him she made sketches of plump little cherubs with streaks of paint on their dimpled little behinds.

'This one is going to be world famous,' Blaise told her seriously as he pointed to a singing cherub. 'She has the voice of an angel. What a Tosca she will be, and when she is between roles she will paint masterpieces.'

But Tony cried and he held and comforted her.

'It mustn't happen,' she said—but it did.

He did not leave immediately. Tear-stained letters from his mother forced him to remain, much against his wishes, at the Academy.

The year 1940 came and on June 14, German troops entered the French capital. Blaise was filled with despair and Tony tried hard to forget her own terror and to think only of what it must be like to know that your parents and sister are living in a city that has been invaded. She did not know how to reach him. Sometimes Blaise sat for hours staring at something she could not see. Then one day she returned to his flat and he was gone. There was a letter that she could not read because her eyes filled with tears. He had gone to join the Free French movement and would contact her if and when he could. In the meantime his father had paid the rent on the flat for two years and so, if Tony would enjoy it, she could use it whenever she chose.

For the next year Tony lived two lives. During the week she was Tony Noble, art student. She attended classes and lectures in one of the most beautiful cities in the world—the Slade had moved to Ruskin College, Oxford—and she did not see its beauty. She returned to London as often as she could, at first by train, then bus, and sometimes even perched on the top of a lorry load of vegetables.

Today there will be a letter. I just know it.

Next weekend there will be a letter, I can feel it.

If there was a letter, and occasionally there was—a few fragile tissues signed *Je t'aime, ma mié*—she would stay for a night. The paper was fragile, but the message was strong. He will come back and, in the meantime, I will learn to paint.

There was one teacher who terrified her. He would look at her work, scream vitriol at her, and then take the brush from her hand and show her. It took weeks for her to accept that this meant that he thought she was worth bothering about, but she never recovered from her fear of sudden noises.

'What the hell are you painting? A man, or the Decline and Fall of bluidy Civilisation? Study the Florentines, for Christ's sake, and be *precise.* Your painting starts long before you touch the fucking canvas.'

Her upbringing had not prepared her for anything like this and, without Blaise's arms to support her, she considered fleeing back to staidness, quietness, dullness.

'What are you painting with, Miss Noble? What are you trying to convey? A photographic likeness? Go and buy a bluidy box camera and stop wasting my time. Oh, ho, the mouse has spirit. She doesn't like that. Good. Good. Paint with your guts, Miss Noble.'

At night she painted the babies she and Blaise would have: she painted them on clouds floating in a blue sky. She opened all the little mouths and let the golden notes fly. She could not paint Blaise. How she missed him. When her pain seemed unbearable, she missed classes and hitched to London where she felt close to him.

She was at the apartment on the August night when the boarding house where she had first lived received a direct hit. Mrs Lumsden was killed, the first person to die whom Tony had actually known, and she tried to mourn, but her heart was too aware of its own suffering to make room for that of anyone else.

She heard that General de Gaulle was fighting from London for a free France. Was Blaise with him? Was he near her? Marshall Pétain became head of state in 1940 and headed the pro-German government of unoccupied Vichy France, and then that same government broke off diplomatic relations with Britain.

Nothing mattered except Blaise.

Tony took her paintings and the several prestigious awards conferred on her at graduation by her college, locked them in the attic at her parents' home in Surrey and then, against her mother's wishes, returned to London where she did war work and painted . . . nothing.

How can I create anything when I am dead inside myself?

The rent was paid until the end of June but Tony could not consider taking over the lease; her feeble earnings could not begin to cover the cost of the flat. She would leave London. Perhaps, in the circumstances, it would be better to go far away to wait until the war was over and Blaise returned. She wrote to him, but he did not answer, and at the beginning of May, when pink and white blossom waved defiantly from trees all over London, she packed up his few belongings and her own and, without contacting her parents, she went to King's Cross Station to find a train, any train, going as far from London as possible.

That night there was one leaving that would eventually reach Glasgow, a city that was as familiar as Timbuktu, but it did not matter where she was. Several times on that interminable journey she wondered if she was not a little mad, but at last, cold, stiff and incredibly weary, she stumbled from the train at its final destination. She later sketched, but never painted, the NAAFI canteen where she got a cup of tea. Holding the mug for warmth, she looked at a dilapidated poster and found an idyllic background for a perfect painting. She could not pronounce its name, and neither could the ticket clerk, but between them they found the most direct route to Achahoish.

Blaise was on a mission to London that May night. He had successfully delivered the waterproof packet that he had carried from France. His work done, his mind was free to think of Tony. He imagined the exquisite joy of seeing her for just one moment, or of hearing her voice, but his orders were clear: return immediately. He was almost ashamed when he heard the air-raid warning. He could not now attempt the return journey; no one would expect it. He could walk through the streets to find her. She was his life, his sanity. In all the time that they had been apart he had received only three letters from her; letters that showed they were a small part of a great rainforest of letters, in which she spilled out her love, her longing, and he had answered them but had no way of knowing if his letters ever reached her. It did not matter. His Toinette knew that he would come back.

But finding a specific street in an air raid is not easy, especially since London had changed. Great areas of the city had completely disappeared in the horrifying raids of the previous September: streets that he had known so well were no longer there. He had lost his way and he turned, looking desperately for a marker. The river and St Paul's should be behind him. 'If I keep them there, I will know where I am.'

Then Blaise stood stock still and watched as the front wall of an entire building dissolved in front of him. One moment there was a huge looming shadow, then a ball of flame that showed an old man making a hot drink, a baby in a crib, silent furniture, and then they were all sucked into a hell on earth and he thought he would be drawn in there too. The fire services, the air-raid wardens, the ambulances were already there, and he joined in automatically.

There was no fear, no time for fear. One saw, one acted. Then, at last, someone said, 'There's no more you can do here, lad. Here, get this inside you.' A warden, his face dirty, his clothes torn and smoke-grimed, pushed a tin mug into Blaise's shaking hands. 'Bloody Bomber's Moon tonight, lad. Bastards are peppering all round the Elephant and Castle with incendiaries. Fires are spreading.'

Blaise did not answer. He nodded his thanks. For almost three years he had spoken very little English and he did not want to risk having to waste time explaining. I am more alert than I thought, he decided, if I can think about that. Suddenly he was terrified. What was he doing, drinking tea and wasting time? Their London was being obliterated around him and Toinette was in the midst of it. He knew the Elephant and Castle: it was their pub.

He began walking again, and his heart knew a second of joy as he turned, he thought, into his own street. His mind refused to accept what he saw. Where the street had been there was a huge smoking crater, and there were ants scurrying around everywhere. As he reached them the ants metamorphosed into ARP wardens and fire-fighters. Blaise stopped one, an old man with a face grey from exhaustion.

'Where is the street?' he asked desperately. 'Where is the street?

'In that 'ole, Frenchie.' The warden looked at him, compassion on his dirty face. 'No survivors, lad, if you was looking for someone.'

'My wife.'

73

Blaise looked into the crater and was amazed at how calmly he was behaving. Toinette was somewhere in that crater. She was dead and, therefore, since she was his heart, he was dead too. That was why he was so calm. He was dead.

Blaise turned and walked away, his mind full of Tony. Tony as he had first seen her, when, pretending to be absorbed in *Lohengrin*, he had watched her walk across the grass and begin to sketch him; Tony in the dandelions when he had first loved her; Tony sitting crosslegged on the bed in his apartment. Tony, Tony, Tony.

I too am dead, my Toinette, but what is left will love you for ever.

CHAPTER FIVE
LONDON, 1999

'A GALLERY IN BAYREUTH has asked for an option on all the swans, Holly.'

'Why? They must have some connection with Blaise but a very nebulous one and, besides, there are many swan pictures out there.'

Otto was not really listening. 'We'll call them the *Lohengrin* series,'

'But he seldom sang Lohengrin. It's hardly a role associated with him like Cavaradossi or des Grieux.'

They were relaxing after an excellent lunch in Otto's magnificent London flat. Holly thought the drawing room was the most subtly beautiful one that she had ever seen in her life, then she thought of Torry Bay. 'This is very different to Tony's cottage.'

'I wish I had visited her there, too stupid, but she was so private about it.' Otto smiled at her. 'I hear that even the elegant Taylor enjoyed his little stay. What did you do to make one of the richest men in the world happy in a teeny-weeny pied-à-terre?' he added wickedly.

Holly decided to ignore the innuendo. 'Why, Otto, I gave him sausages for supper and made him wash up.'

He choked on his coffee. 'How very bourgeois of you, Holly.' He looked at her measuringly as she sipped her coffee innocently. 'No matter. The paintings aren't from the Fougère series—she painted hundreds of swans—but they were in the attic studio. We can still cash in.'

Holly stood up. 'I hate it when you talk like that.'

'Holly, I am a businessman. For Tony I want worldwide acclaim; for you I want as much money as possible and no, I will not give my cut to your little foundation, whatever it is. The paintings are good. They are fine examples of her style, her incredible facility with light, colour. Do you want to consider selling them as a series?'

'Mr Hartman to see if you are at home, sir.'

They had not heard the manservant, Phil, open the door. Holly had not seen Taylor since he had left her in Argyll. Her raging pulse told her that she was looking forward to seeing him again.

'Show Mr Hartman in. Well, this is an unexpected pleasure. Another cup, Phil, please. Taylor, you know Miss Noble?'

Holly could tell that Taylor was as surprised to see her as she was to see him, but he recovered more quickly. 'Hello, Holly.'

'Taylor.'

He turned back to Otto who waved him to a sofa. 'You are just too frightening when you tower over one, Taylor, and I will not be intimidated in my own sitting room.'

Taylor smiled and sat down. 'Holly, I'm glad you are here. There must be some way of contacting you at the cottage. You gave Chandler your Glasgow number but not your cellphone.'

Holly found herself teasing him again. 'They'll take a message at the shop.' It had worked for Blaise. But Taylor was not Blaise and Holly was not Tony. Blaise had loved Tony and she had loved him. Holly did not love Taylor, she did not even like him, and he disliked her too.

There, she had admitted it and it did not hurt at all.

'Cellphones, Holly, the Internet, email, et cetera. That journalist, no, sorry, legal-eagle boyfriend of yours surely doesn't like you to be so incommunicado. I would be worried sick. If I loved someone,' he added hastily. He was embarrassed, not a condition with which he was familiar and he did not like it.

Holly was enjoying his predicament so it was left to Otto to help his unexpected guest. 'I was just telling Holly that a gallery has asked for an option on the *Lohengrin* series.'

'One question. Does Holly make more money if they are sold separately at auction or as a job lot?'

He sounded like John. Money, money, money.

'There are other considerations, Mr Hartman.'

He almost groaned. 'Mr Hartman again. Holly, only people with no money make holier-than-thou statements like that. Surely you spent enough time sweating in Africa to know that the more money a true philanthropist has, the more he can do for humanity. You want maximum cover?'

Holly was confused. One part of her wanted to know how he had found out about her work in Africa; another part ached to argue, 'I am not a philanthropist,' but that was what she wanted to be, basically, wasn't it? She finally said only, 'Of course.'

He was looking at her, an expression she could not read on his handsome face. 'Then make sure you get it off to a great start. This is a one-off, Holly.'

Holly stood up. She was furious. He knew she was annoyed. 'I must be off, Otto. You and Mr Hartman have great deals to do, I'm sure.'

Taylor ignored Otto. 'Miss Noble? Happy now? I stopped by Otto's apartment to see if he knew a way of contacting you. We need to talk about having the paintings valued and shipped.'

Otto coughed. 'Dear boy, all is in order.' He reeled off the names of three world-renowned authorities. 'Every one a masterwork, according to them. We decided to bring the paintings straight here before having them valued. They were unpacked a week ago and the last valuation was carried out today. They are hanging in my storerooms.'

'I expected to have been told,' said Taylor stiffly.

'Why?' asked Holly. 'Their value has nothing to do with you.'

'You must be the first to see them, dear boy,' Otto said swiftly. 'In fact, we could go to the storerooms right now. Remember though, Taylor, a storeroom is just that, merely four walls, and the lighting is not right. They have not been *hung*.'

'I know what you mean and I would still like to see them. Do I have your permission, Miss Noble?'

Holly decided to be gracious. 'Of course, and you may even choose the one you would like me to give you.'

She smiled sweetly as she saw his jaw clamp shut, and turned, still smiling, to Otto. 'I'll come too. We'll have to decide whether to hang them chronologically, the unfolding of the love story, as it were. Have you finished your coffee, Taylor?'

She smiled again as she heard the delicate cup clatter against its saucer and decided to behave; she had goaded him enough.

Since Taylor's car was outside they took that and drove to the great warehouses where Otto stored works that were awaiting showing or shipment. Holly felt her excitement grow as she prepared to see the paintings again. Almost every one was too big to show to advantage in the cottage at Torry Bay but here, in these huge rooms with the stark white walls, the explosion of colour and light was tangible.

'Look at them,' she breathed. 'They're beautiful.'

'Magnificent,' Otto agreed.

Taylor said nothing. He began to walk slowly down the room, familiarising himself with the work. He had not seen all of them before; that had been impossible in the cramped conditions at the cottage. Holly forgot that she did not like him and went with him, exclaiming, pointing out things that she had not noticed before and that he too might not have seen.

'Look, Taylor, at the rainbow . . . do you see, how clever.'

'Why is there a chain round his neck? The title is so strange too.'

'Oh, the swan, look at the swan; she's writing messages.'

The paintings were in no particular order: 1978 following 1990, 1947 side by side with 1982, Torry Bay nestling against Bayreuth, Vienna giving elbow room to New York, a very young Blaise in a bandstand beside a more mature Blaise in a field of clover.

'It's mind-blowing,' said Taylor at last.

Holly turned to him, face radiant, eyes sparkling. He agreed with her. They're breathtaking, aren't they?'

'They're obscene,' he said. 'A sick mind. I knew him better than anyone except my mother and she . . .' He stopped and turned to Otto. 'We would have known. If you don't want to take a cab, come now.'

'We'll find a taxi, dear boy.'

Taylor said nothing. He walked out.

Holly was incredulous and furious. 'He called them obscene.' She almost choked with anger. 'What a swine he is, Otto.'

'Holly, let Uncle Otto tell you something about the male species. They become extremely miffed if their little balloons get burst. Taylor Fougère Hartman assumed he was the only person his uncle cared about, and voilà, an entire series of paintings that shows a hidden life: people and places of whom Taylor knew nothing.'

'How childish,' said Holly, and then remembered guiltily that she too had been surprised and not a little hurt to find that she had not been the only love of her aunt's life. Naturally she said nothing of this to Otto.

'We might as well enjoy them while they're our secret, Holly.'

Holly looked, really for the first time, at paintings of Blaise Fougère his fans would hardly recognise but would love. Blaise pensive. Blaise laughing. Blaise in his beloved Paris, in London, in Torry Bay. The Lohengrin pictures . . . some, Holly saw at once, now that she really looked, were merely paintings of swans, but others were pictures of the swan prince sailing across the sea, carrying, it was to be hoped, the maiden's longed-for lover on his broad back.

'Look, Otto.' And she showed Otto what she had been excited to show Taylor. 'If you have very good eyesight and peer very closely you can see that this is not a smudge but a golden crown. He was on his way back to her in the end, I know it.'

'We'll put them all in together then, shall we, darling girl?'

'Otto, you have no soul.'

'Such a nuisance in business.'

A few days later, Holly and Otto met to select the photographs that might be used to illustrate the catalogue for the exhibition.

'There is such a big gap over the war years and beyond.'

'We know he was a soldier.'

'Yes, but the war was over in 1945. Even if we allow several months for combatants to return, there are no paintings, in this collection, of Blaise until 1953. You would think if he loved her, really loved her, he would have gone to her as soon as Paris was liberated.'

'We must assume that they lost touch during the war. He was working undercover for de Gaulle and for some reason she went to Scotland. If she loved him, surely she would have left a forwarding address?'

'Why, Otto?' Holly turned over the photographs. 'Look at his face. He adores her. Why didn't he go looking for her?'

'He may have thought she was dead. Didn't I read somewhere that his apartment block in London was razed to the ground before his eyes?'

'He didn't check that she really was dead?' John would come looking for her, wouldn't he? He would turn up on her doorstep as often as Hartman seemed able to do, wouldn't he? 'It's the appalling waste that gets to me. Waste of her life, her child-bearing years. She loved children. What about that and then her potential to succeed as an artist? She deliberately kept her greatest work hidden. He went swanning around the globe leading this double life and she stayed in a tiny cottage in Argyll when she could have been world famous. Why did she do that?'

'Maybe he met Eleanor during the war, had a relationship with her, got married, and then when the marriage went wrong he decided to resurrect his first real love. The date of the first personal postwar painting is 1953. Yes, it would take a few years for the gilt to wear off.'

Holly scooped the pictures up and thrust them back into the envelope. 'Except, if he thought she was dead, as you were saying a few minutes ago, how did he find her?'

'Why? Why did he marry someone else when he was in love with Tony?'

'Love.'

'Very one-sided.'

'He was married.'

'Why? Why did he marry someone else when he was in love with Tony?'

SOMEDAY, SOMEWHERE

'Where are you going?'

'Covent Garden. I want to look at the *des Grieux* and you are the only person I know who can tell me how good or bad it is.'

'I would adore to be seen going into the Opera House with a beautiful young woman but I have a gallery to run and, besides, it is not a matinée. Who would be there to see me?'

She looked at him sadly. 'You're an old fraud, Otto. Come on.'

Less than half an hour later they were standing in the Royal Opera House.

'Was he really that pretty or did she just gild the lily a little?'

Otto looked critically at the painting. 'His physical appearance was out of the ordinary; indeed, interest in his looks rather than, as he saw it, in his voice, was one of the things that drove him to hide himself. He felt that his voice was the only thing about him that should even remotely concern his audiences. A little naive, I think.'

Holly nodded. 'We had better go, Otto. Can't stand here admiring pecs all day.'

'I can,' said Otto, but he was smiling. 'Now, tell me what seeing this painting has to do with Tony.'

'The date, Otto: 1949. According to the archivist, Eleanor's family commissioned and donated the painting. Did my aunt paint him knowing he was married and, if she did, why did she paint him? She must have known,' she went on, answering her own question. 'But why did he marry Eleanor and not Tony?'

TORRY BAY, 1942. SURREY, 1942

She looked from the window on to a field. Her gaze ran across it until it reached the sea. Grey water bounded in the first instance by grey rocks and then, further out, by grey clouds. Grey, grey, grey, like her spirit. As she watched, however, slowly, slowly the grey clouds began to dissipate and she saw pink and pale blue.

Her breath caught in her throat as she saw him, his head held high as he sailed towards her across the bay.

Still in her pyjamas, she ran down to the beach. 'Hail, my Lord Lohengrin,' she said as she reached the shingle.

The swan dipped his head in the silver-grey water, pulled it out again and a shower of water diamonds flew around him as he sailed. She barely breathed, willing him not to leave, and at last he stopped and settled in the water a few feet from the shore.

'I'll feed you,' she whispered to him. 'In the bad weather you'll be able to trust me, I promise.' She was cold, her pyjamas were damp, and she was painfully aware of her bare feet. 'Please don't go,' she pleaded, but when she reached her bedroom window and looked out the swan had gone.

'He'll come back,' she whispered. 'He must.' Her heart was light because she knew she had done the right thing. This was her place, her nest. Here she would wait.

She realised that she would starve to death if she did not earn some money. She had one marketable skill: her painting. Ergo, she must paint and she must sell. She would paint the swan and she would sell him.

She walked up to the village. If she was going to live here for ever then she must get to know her neighbours.

The village was no more than a street that wandered haphazardly around the bay. There were a few houses, a village shop combined with post office, and a slightly grander house with a brass plate that said, DOCTOR'S SURGERY. She went in.

'Hello. What can I do for you?'

The resident doctor presumably. 'Nothing,' she said, holding out her hand. 'I'm Tony Noble and I've just rented the cottage at Torry Bay.'

He looked disappointed for a moment. 'Good lord. You don't look like a lunatic. The entire village is talking about the eccentric millionaire who has moved into Torry Bay. I had hoped you were a patient. I'm Simon McRae, the new doctor.'

He had to be about her own age, early twenties. He was smallish, thin, and badly in need of a decent haircut. Suddenly he reminded her of Blaise. Blaise who was tall, handsome, sophisticated.

'It's your eyes,' she said with a smile. 'They're kind.'

He blushed a flaming red that did nothing for his appearance. 'Sorry?'

'Don't mind me, Dr McRae. I assure you, if I ever need a doctor, I shall yell, loudly.'

'Please, Miss . . . Noble, was it? Won't you come in? I was about to have a cup of tea and some toast. I should sign you up as a patient if you are going to be staying long.'

'The rest of my life, I should think,' said Tony, and her voice was sad and burdened by acceptance. 'I was living in London, wanted out. I saw a poster and the word Achahoish, which I did not pronounce properly. I got on a train and here I am.'

'I'm sure we are all very glad. London must have been hell.'

He saw her animated face grow bleak.

'Hell,' she echoed.

'But it couldn't be worse than . . . that . . . place you're renting.'

Tony smiled. 'It's not the Ritz. I got a lift on a lorry and the driver took me to a farm where they let me sleep on the sofa, very scratchy. Horsehair. But they, the farmer and his wife, own the cottage and they've let me have it and I'll do odd jobs on the farm till the war's over.'

He took her into the tiny living room. 'Everything comes with the surgery,' he explained as Holly looked round. 'It's my uncle's. Would you believe they took him and he's forty-three. They wouldn't take me because, well, my eyesight's not too good and Uncle Henry gave me this practice to keep for him while he sorts out the enemy. Very good at sorting things, Uncle Henry.'

'I should loathe your Uncle Henry,' said Tony as she demolished a raspberry jam tart. 'Why did you want to go?'

'A man does,' he said after some thought. 'You want to be counted.'

'What makes you think your bit has to be done "over there"? I . . . know someone, a Frenchman. He needed to be counted, but perhaps, like you, his skills are more needed somewhere else, or when it's all over and all the wounds still have to be healed.'

His face brightened. 'He's a doctor?'

'A singer. The greatest tenor the world may never hear.'

'A different kind of medicine man,' he said and Tony knew she had found her first friend.

'I need a job.'

He seemed perplexed. 'This isn't exactly a hotbed of industry, not out here. You might get something on the land.' He looked at her. 'You don't look as if you could sling a sack of feed around.'

'No brawn,' she agreed. 'I'm a painter.'

'Everyone does their own here,' he said gloomily. 'Oh, you mean a real painter. I say, how marvellous. I can't draw a straight line.'

She laughed. 'I was looking for something menial. I thought I might clean house or wait tables.'

Suddenly Tony realised the enormous foolhardiness of what she had done. She should have gone back to her parents and tried to earn a living from home . . .

She *was* home. Now, with certainty, she knew that. Something had spoken to her as she had seen the remote peninsula on the poster, it had cried out to her when she had found the cottage, and it had soothed her quietly this morning when she had seen the swan.

Lohengrin had come to her across the water. If she stayed here, Blaise would come. If he was still alive, he would find her.

She smiled and Simon McRae's heart contracted in the most unmedical way. When she smiled she became beautiful.

81

'I inherited Jessie from Uncle Henry,' he said, 'or I'd hire you like a shot. Mrs Douglas—she who baked those raspberry tarts—used to have a girl before the war to help sell sweets and ice creams to holidaymakers, but there haven't been many tourists lately.' He stood up and opened a door. 'Come on,' he said. 'I've an idea.'

She followed him into a narrow stone passageway and through a door that opened onto a formal and very gloomy sitting room.

'You don't paint pictures like these, I hope?' he asked.

'Good heavens, no.' The walls were covered with dark brooding paintings of mountains, gullies, dying Highlanders or dying deer. 'I never sit in here: all that blood and all those eyes. I don't suppose you'd—' he began and got no further.

Tony was walking round looking at the heavy pictures in their heavy frames. 'You poor thing. Never mind, I shall lend you one or two of mine until I can paint you something bright. My cottage is much too small for some of my canvases.'

He almost whooped with joy. 'I was trying to ask you to paint something for me—wasn't quite sure what to say.'

Tony smiled at him. 'Silly you. Now I must go and speak to . . . Mrs Douglas, was it?'

When she had gone he saw that the sitting room was even darker and gloomier since her light had left it.

Chrissie Douglas had tearooms near the harbour. She laughed with wonderful warm Glasgow humour when Tony asked her if she needed help. 'I need a bloody miracle, hen. Here I am, the best baker in the whole of Scotland, and the last paying customer in here was in 1940. What brought you up here?'

'I'm a painter, an artist. I've rented the cottage on the point.'

'My God. Highway robbery. That place is falling down and should be pulled down. You've been done, lassie.'

'The view is incredible.'

Chrissie Douglas looked at her pityingly. Her home had an insecure roof but nice views: an artist, right enough. 'The view won't keep you warm in the winter. We'll have to think of something.'

'I'm going to paint. Maybe you'll be good enough to let me show some of my work in the tearooms?'

'Aye, the two of us can admire it, and the canon when he comes in for a cup of tea, and Dr McRae.'

'That's three more than are admiring it just now,' said Tony lightly. Everything would be all right. She would paint, the war would end, the tourists would come back and one day she would hear from Blaise.

SOMEDAY, SOMEWHERE

The war went on but at last the tide was turning. In September 1944 Tony read that the Allies had captured Paris in August. Was Blaise there? Was he even alive? Yes, of course he was. She would feel it if he were dead. She wanted to stay at Torry Bay for Christmas but a feeling of duty, not of love, caused her to repeat the dreadful experience of that spring. The train was colder and even more crowded than the one that had brought her north more than two years before. It did not help when her parents and Frederick threw up their hands in horror at her appearance.

'When did you last eat, Antonia?' her mother wept over her.

'Mummy, I eat well at Torry Bay and I'm working and selling.'

She did not say that her single sale was to a travelling salesman from Liverpool and had earned her ten whole shillings.

She did eat well, even if her meals were repetitive and simple, and she was warm enough. There was plenty of driftwood for the fire and seaweed used cleverly helped her keep the kitchen fire going all night.

'Your hands, Antonia? What are you doing with your hands?'

'Painting, Mummy, and collecting wood, stripping walls and furniture, all sorts of things. Gardening even.'

'Do tell us more about this doctor?'

She could smell the hope from her mother.

'He's a good friend, Mummy, like Chrissie Douglas and Canon Gemmell.' Whoops, she should not have mentioned the canon.

Her father swelled with disapproval. 'A Catholic? You're not going to his church?'

'No,' was all she said, but Freddie looked at her disapprovingly.

'Whatever happened to your Frenchman?' he asked.

'He went back to France to fight,' she managed to say steadily. 'I haven't heard from him for years.'

'Just as well, dear,' soothed her mother. 'No future in singing, I shouldn't think. A doctor now . . . oh, he's not Scotch, is he?'

'Of course Simon is a Scot.'

Her mother offered her more potatoes. 'Well, it could be worse, dear.'

Stifled, Tony stood up. 'Yes, he could be a French singer. I'm tired; I'll go to bed.'

She was aware of their hurt, anxious faces but she had to get out of that room. How had she ever thought she could go back, even for such a time as Christmas? She should have stayed at Torry Bay. She should have spent Christmas with Chrissie and gone to Midnight Mass at the canon's tiny chapel. Everything about Torry Bay was refreshing. Simon, Chrissie and Canon Gemmell were her friends and one or other of them had found a way to the cottage at least once a week to see how she was, to admire or wonder at her paintings, to lend a hand when she was working. She, of course, did the same for them.

She had painted views of the village and the bay for Simon and had loaned him *Sea Sprite* for a time. Chrissie had paid her ten shillings to wait tables and wash up after the Scottish Women's Rural Institute Christmas lunches.

Two local tradesmen had come down to do major work on the cottage and she painted what she called 'chocolate-box covers' for their wives, and that led to a few commissions that would keep her from starvation until the war was over.

Canon Gemmell had studied at The Scots College in Rome. He was a cultured man and Tony found herself wondering why the Church had sent a multilingual academic to minister to a few crofters and fishermen.

'That's a snobbish viewpoint, my dear Tony. There are intellectuals among the crofters, men and women too, very knowledgeable about the arts. There isn't much to do here in the winters besides reading and listening to the wireless.'

He never pried, never asked her why she had chosen to live in Achahoish. She was there. That was enough. And he let it be known that he was there, if needed. He did realise that she was a trained artist and they spoke together about London and its galleries, for he had travelled and seen great paintings in most of the European capitals.

'This is not a good place for someone without an income, Tony. You will have to exhibit. Let me take *Sea Sprite* to Glasgow, to show him.'

'No.' She smiled to soften her rejection of his kindness. 'You can take *Lohengrin* when he's finished.'

'Lohengrin? Wagner's Lohengrin?'

'Mine. He's a swan in the bay. I look for him first thing in the morning and last thing at night. Silly to be dependent on a swan, but, when I see him, I just feel that everything is going to be all right.'

'Is that Lohengrin?' He gestured to her easel.

'No, you'll recognise him when you see him. This is a chocolate-box picture for my parents' Christmas present.'

'Have a lovely holiday with your family, Tony.'

But she did not have a lovely holiday. It seemed to Tony, as yet another train groaned its way back to Argyll, that the relationship with her parents, with her brother, worked better when she stayed away from them. Perhaps if *Lohengrin* sold, if she received some kind of recognition . . . But would they still be suggesting, as they had suggested several times during the holidays, 'Isn't it time you got a proper job, Antonia, or married a nice young man?'

'As far as I'm concerned, I am married,' she had told them baldly, 'I was living with Blaise and even to look at anyone else would be unfaithful.'

Her mother had cried. Her father had gone white with anger. 'Living in sin? Our daughter? And your brother about to be ordained. You are selfish and self-centred, Antonia. You always were. You have ruined your chances of a good marriage, and for what? To give yourself to a bloody frog who had his way and then discarded you . . .'

'He's dead,' her mother had sobbed. 'He has to be dead.'

Dead? Discarded? No. She would know if he was dead and he would never discard her. One day he would sail back across the waters that divided them on the back of a swan. She had to believe that.

CHAPTER SIX
LONDON, 1999

GUESTS STARTED ARRIVING unfashionably early; so many rumours had been circulating about this major showing of previously unseen works by Tony Noble. Holly looked around the huge gallery, at the white walls on which Tony's lifelong love story was hung, and sighed. 'I hope this is the right thing to do, Otto.'

Otto took her arm. 'Just think of all the lovely money for good causes. Now, come and have a drink—champagne, *naturellement.*'

Holly took a last look at the walls and went with him. He was right. Of course he was right. This was what Tony had wanted. Wasn't it?

Marcelline Sandhurst was the first art critic to arrive. She stood in the glass doorway, as still as if she herself were one of the exhibits, and took one long measuring look at the walls.

'Holy shit,' said the urbane Marcy and reached for her mobile phone.

Gleefully Otto clinked his glass with Holly's. 'Didn't I tell you, my angel? It's started. That was not a comment on the skill of the artist.'

Holly put down her wine. 'She can't be calling in her critique?'

'She's ringing Amy Rosenthal. They are such good chums.'

Holly grimaced. Amy Rosenthal was a notorious gossip columnist. 'I don't think I can bear it.'

'We went into all that. The questions will start and the speculation will go on and on and the paintings will sell and sell.'

'I'd prefer that they sold because Tony is a wonderful artist.'

'Of course that's why they'll sell. But when the punters see the subject, the object of a life's work, they'll understand why so few paintings were exhibited in the artist's lifetime and that adds an extra frisson of excitement. It also explains the prices I'm asking for the works of a painter most of the world has forgotten.'

She did not want to ask but she did. 'Has Taylor accepted the invitation?'

'The Taylor Hartmans of this world don't accept or reject invitations. They come if the mood takes them. Why? Were you hoping to see him? He's not for you, darling girl. He would eat you for supper and spit out your little bones. You're too naïve, Holly, too trusting, and while we're on the subject, you don't make nearly enough of the canvas you were given.' He looked at her to see what effect his words were having and saw the clear eyes merely watching, waiting for him to finish. He shrugged. 'Hartman has the pick of the world's rich and famous, Holly, women who give as good as they get. Spoilt from the moment he was born. His uncle absolutely adored him, the son he never had.'

'Spare me.' Holly winced and gulped some of her wine. Thinking about Taylor, which she did far more often than she wanted to, or talking about him, was a certain way to ruin a pleasant evening. 'I think I'll stay in your office for a while, Otto. You go and say the right things.'

'Coward,' he said, but he was smiling.

'Not a coward, Otto,' Holly said to his retreating back. 'Just not my scene.' She looked in the mirror quickly and had to agree with Otto. High time she had a decent haircut. She looked out into the salon. She could clearly see the expressions on the faces of the people walking around. They were impressed, surprised. Was it surprise at the subject or surprise at the talent?

The telephone on the desk beside her rang loudly and she looked for guidance to Otto. Otto was waving to her, gesticulating. She nodded and picked up the receiver. She recognised the voice, having heard it—usually raised in anger—several times before. Taylor Hartman.

'Get me Otto,' he ordered.

'I'm afraid Mr von Emler is in the middle of a private showing.'

'He can be in the middle of anything he wants,' said the voice. 'Tell him to come to the telephone, now.'

There it was again, that damned annoying fluttering low in her stomach. Nausea, that was what it was, plain old nausea. 'You are the rudest person I have ever had the great misfortune to meet, Mr Hartman. I will see if Mr von Emler can answer the master's summons,' and she pressed the hold button so hard that she broke a carefully nurtured fingernail.

She went out into the hordes of people who were drinking, eating the amazing canapés, and talking, talking, talking about the magnificent portraits. Holly managed to catch Otto's eye.

'Taylor Hartman is on the telephone. He wants to speak to you, now.'

Otto excused himself from a very wealthy socialite—my, the pull of an even wealthier one—and hurried to his office. He spoke for some minutes, listened for even longer, and then hung up the receiver. Then, like a man about to make a very important announcement, he went to the wine table and tapped a crystal glass with a tiny pickle fork.

He wiped his perfectly dry brow with a silk handkerchief and then was ready to speak. 'Ladies and gentlemen, an anonymous buyer has just called in with a bid of'—he paused, until he was sure that every eye was on him—'five million dollars, American, for the entire collection.'

There was uproar and more mobile phones than Holly had ever seen at one time were pulled out of handbags and pockets.

'Anonymous, hell. Five gets you ten it's . . . .'

'Hugo, I just have to have the dandelion one. I have to have it. Outbid. Do something . . .'

Holly could hear parts of frantic conversations and, in the middle of all the bedlam, she saw Otto walking around, calming, cajoling. She went to him.

'Otto, they are not all in the sale.'

He was almost dancing with excitement. 'I know, Holly. Isn't this fun?'

Holly was frantic. 'Why does he want them? He can't want all of them.'

'He did say something about putting the lot in the incinerator.'

Holly gasped. 'You haven't sold them to him?'

'Dear, dear Miss Noble, I can't sell without your authorisation. Calm yourself. You are about to make an absolute fortune.'

He left her and went round soothing his guests, promising who knows what, until everyone had left. Holly and Otto found themselves alone in the great studio, when the door opened and there was Taylor Hartman, looking for his prey. He saw it where it faltered, shaking.

'Hello, Taylor,' Holly managed. 'How nice of you to come. You're wasting your time though. You can't have them. I reject your bid.'

She turned and walked into Otto's office and almost fell into a chair. Taylor followed her as quietly as a big man, who was also very angry, could.

'Why I came to talk to either of you I do not know. I should have had the opening cancelled. I asked you for a discreet private showing—carefully vetted, selected art lovers. You would make the same amount of money but no, you want this . . . this flagrant display. The thought of gossip columnists gawping at my family turns my stomach. Take the damn cheque. You're giving most of it to charity anyway so you should be pleased. These paintings will not be shown and my family will not be flavour of the month in the world's gossip columns. I could take out an interdict or injunction or whatever it's called here.'

The nausea was gone. She was herself again; ready to deal with Taylor. 'To do what? Make the paintings even more interesting? Besides, Taylor . . .' Here Holly, surer of her ground, stood up. A bad move. He seemed even bigger and more threatening when she was standing trembling in front of him. 'Oh, do sit down. You're cutting out all the light.'

He sat down, smiling, aware of her discomfort. She guessed he was probably aware of his effect on people. 'You were saying?' he asked politely.

'No court would issue an injunction. I own the paintings outright and have the artist's authority to do exactly as I please with them.' She was right, wasn't she? Tony's letter said so, didn't it?

'Otto, explain the facts of life to our little ingénue. And you, Holly, I hope you read the contract this crook has written. Make sure he gets only that to which he is entitled.' He walked out and the vast gallery that had seemed so full now felt empty.

'Unkind,' breathed Otto, 'but he is upset.' He smiled and turned to Holly. 'Let me take you to dinner and we'll discuss this little contretemps. But, not a word about dear Taylor until we have ordered. All I will say at this juncture is that it never pays to spoil children.'

Despite her size, Holly had a formidable appetite, and Otto, who ate barely enough to feed the proverbial sparrow, laughed as she tucked in. 'Now,' he said when at last she sat back to enjoy her coffee, 'let us examine the offer from Taylor.'

'He can't have them to destroy them, Otto. That would be sacrilege.'

'He is hot-blooded and hot-tempered and does not like to be crossed, but he is also aware of the intrinsic value of these paintings. He will not burn them. The paintings should be seen, not because of what they tell us of Mr Perfect Husband'—Holly winced—'but because they are great art. She was a genius, Holly. Her paintings have stood too long wrapped in old sheets. Taylor will keep them locked away somewhere and that is cruel. They should be enjoyed.'

'Otto, what if he takes out an injunction?'

Otto frowned. 'He'll try. Pity we had so little warning. You had spoken to him.' It was not a question.

'I haven't seen him since he was with us in the storerooms. Naturally I was in touch with Chandler North. Taylor and his "discreet, private showing". How dare he handpick buyers for Tony's work? It was not "a sordid little affair". Nineteen thirty-seven, Otto, was the date of the first painting, and Blaise was still visiting her just before he died. They must have loved one another very much.'

He knew the answer but still he kept hoping. 'She left no letters, no diaries? They, together with the paintings, would be priceless.'

She shook her head. No one should ever see the sketchbooks with their sometimes acerbic comments. 'Anyway, the paintings tell the whole story.'

'But paintings don't talk,' Otto argued bitterly.

Holly laughed. 'What a very strange remark for a world authority on painting to make.'

His smile was rueful. 'You deliberately misunderstand me. They do speak to us, but if they could talk, really talk, what a story they would tell. Holly, dear, have you searched the cottage thoroughly?'

Holly looked at him. 'Otto, has it occurred to you that I have a home and commitments and a . . . relationship?'

'An unsatisfactory relationship, my dear. Why isn't John here with you? If he loved you . . .'

'You have no right, Otto. How dare you judge John? He had a court case. He's not like Taylor . . .'

'He's too like Taylor: selfish, self-centred, used to getting his own way. I bet he's not happy with your plans.'

She did not want to admit that he was right. She was still wearing John's ring, unable somehow to take it off and return it. That was so final, so frightening. John was displeased with the amount of time she had spent away from Glasgow over the past few months and he was not ecstatically happy that she planned a scholarship in Tony's name, but he was not like Hartman. Not in the slightest.

John, dear John. Naturally he missed her; he needed her. Perfectly natural too that, after all their years of hard work, he should feel that her unexpected inheritance should help them achieve their ambitions.

'There's enough, John,' she had cajoled him, 'enough for everything: your plans, Tony's memorial. You'll see.'

'My private life is my own concern, Otto,' she said now. 'I offered you these paintings because you were Tony's agent. Don't make me change my mind.'

'You can't. We have a contract.'

Why did a man always have to have the last word?

As soon as Otto had dropped her off at her hotel, Holly rang John.

Again her fingers were crossed, but this time it was so that John would react as she hoped he would and not as she was sure he would.

'Five million dollars. I can't believe it! My God, Holly, even in sterling that's incredible. You sold them.'

'No.'

Silence. And then, 'Clever little Holly. He'll go higher.'

'I won't sell them to him.'

At that he had shouted so loudly that he had almost no need of a connection. 'Why not, for God's sake?'

She had wanted to cry. How could she love someone so much who was so different from everything she believed in? Desperation? Was that really what kept her in this relationship? Apathy, acceptance, fear? 'He's threatening to burn them.'

'What do we care? Keep your favourite ones. Be quite a talking point in the future—and it will up their value, so what does it matter what he does with them?'

Her heart sank like a stone dropping into a pool. It was over. Stupid, stupid Holly. What a wonderful judge of men you are, to be sure. John would never understand. Tony, her beloved Tony, spoke to her from every painting. In every canvas she laid bare her heart, her soul. She had entrusted her life, her love for Blaise Fougère to Holly. Why? Surely because she knew that, basically, Holly was like her. Holly would understand what the paintings meant. Holly would cherish her legacy.

'Goodbye, John,' was all she said. She wanted to add, 'For ever,' but felt that smacked of melodrama. She faced the fact that she had given her heart—and everything else—to John too quickly and that she had sublimated herself to his driving ambition. Everything was a mess: her private life and now her hopes for Tony dashed, almost before they had had a chance to blossom. She would not cry and she would not cave in. A little setback, Tony, but we'll do it. We'll show these paintings and we'll make Taylor acknowledge you. Just you wait.

TORRY BAY, 1945. LONDON, 1946. SURREY, 1947.

The war was over and the letter never came. 'Either he is dead or he no longer wants me. If he has forgotten his promises I will not beg and plead. I have my pride.'

Tony was not the first woman to find pride a very uncomfortable bedfellow. She finished throwing bread to the swans, took a deep breath and just enjoyed looking around her, marvelling at the way the purple-grey of the hills met the blue-green-grey of the water. 'I will try to paint that but first I will discover if he is alive and not in any kind of need.' She knew that if she found Blaise in a hospital, in a mental home, wounded mentally or physically, she would care for him. He was her husband, her life. It was as simple as that.

She went to see Canon Gemmell. 'This has got to be the most inhospitable garden in Argyll, Canon,' she said as she saw him kneeling down on his arthriticky old knees, scrabbling at the stony earth that grudgingly gave him a few cabbages every winter.

'Oh, one of these days I'll grow a rose, my dear. Help me up and tell me what I can do for you.'

She told him that she had decided to paint seriously. His ascetic face lit up with joy. 'My dear child, you are prepared to exhibit?'

She nodded.

'Then you must go to London. There is an Austrian refugee making quite a name for himself. Gallery owner, agent, von Emler, Klaus, I think. I saw his gallery a year or so ago when I was visiting in London. What can you show him?'

'Some of the swans are perhaps good enough, and some landscapes.'

He looked at her with his gentle, understanding eyes. 'Your best work is *Sea Sprite*.'

Tony looked back at him and her broken heart looked out of her eyes and he saw it. 'I'm sorry, my dear, you know best.'

'There are others,' she said, thinking of *Les Dents de Lion* and *Les Bébés qui Chantent*—still in her parents' attic—in particular, 'but there is a good reason why I'm not ready to exhibit them. You have a very fine face, Canon. I hoped I might do you and then Chrissie, the aristocrat and the peasant, but don't tell her I said that.'

She painted two portraits of Canon Gemmell during the winter of 1945. In one he was wearing his robes, and in the other he was wearing his oldest clothes and digging his garden. Chrissie she painted in her apron and her pink fluffy slippers, and these two paintings became the yardstick by which all her commissions—and there were many of those—were judged.

'No,' stressed the great and the good, 'a camera can catch me like that. I want the real me like that old chap in his garden.'

But before that Tony had to paint the portraits and show them to this new dealer. It took her almost a year.

She travelled to London with three portraits, two small landscapes and one of her swans. At von Emler's small gallery Tony met two people who were to affect her life almost more than any other except Blaise himself. Klaus von Emler did not live up to his aristocratic name but looked more like Tony's idea of an old grandfather. His sixteen-year-old son, Otto, would one day look exactly like everyone's idea of what an art dealer should look like. He was small and slim and very blond with rather lovely blue eyes. At this first meeting he smiled at her shyly and said nothing as his father examined the paintings.

'You have talent, Miss Noble,' said Klaus at last.

'Oh, Papa, she's a genius,' said young Otto before he could stop himself, and the father laughed.

'Such a poor businessman,' he teased his son, 'but already he knows more about paintings than I do. We will be honoured to arrange a show for you, Miss Noble, but it will take some time.'

Tony gave him her address at Torry Bay and Canon Gemmell's telephone number and then she took the train to Surrey. The visit home was not a success. She was thin—her mother called her scrawny—her clothes were not only too loose but out of fashion, and her hair had not benefited from a hairdresser's care in several years.

'And while we are talking, Antonia,' said her father—Were they talking? Had they ever?—'I would like to know how you have been living for the past few years.'

Good heavens. Did he think she was on the street, on the game? 'I sell paintings, Daddy. You spent a great deal of money to send me to the finest art school in the world. Now, at last I am going to have an exhibition in London. You will come?'

'That man? The singer.'

The pain struck her again just behind the breastbone. 'A casualty of the war.'

Her father had the grace to look slightly discomfited. 'Antonia, we only want what's best for you,' he pleaded.

'No, Daddy, you have always wanted what you decided was best for me. Now, tell me about Freddie.'

Thank God for Freddie. They could go on about him all day. They asked nothing about the exhibition and since she knew nothing, she said nothing. She told them she had to go back to Scotland and went back for a day to London. She went to Covent Garden. During the war it had been used as a dance hall. Would it ever reopen as an opera house? She went to the Slade. The students would soon return from exile in Oxford. Some of her classmates must have died in the war but some must be painting somewhere. She would find out. She went to Blaise's flat, but she could not find it. The area near the Elephant and Castle that they had loved so much was either no longer there or totally unfamiliar. Had I not left London, I would have been killed, Tony thought. That awful fate seemed remote. She could not get worked up about the girl who had waited in that flat for her lover. She seemed to have nothing at all in common with the Tony Noble who looked at the rubble where her heart had been.

Mrs Lumsden? A cold hand seemed to squeeze her heart. Mrs Lumsden was dead, and the secret of her wonderful bread with her. When it happened I was too lost in my own misery to react properly. I will mourn now, dear Mrs Lumsden.

She wished she could push the train home to Torry Bay. It seemed to groan and moan at every incline. She did not see the fields and shattered towns of England; she saw Mrs Lumsden's body in the ruins of her house and she pictured Blaise Fougère's body in the ruins of their flat. Had he come back to find her, gone to the flat and been killed? One sad story among a hundred, a thousand, a million like it? When she came back for the exhibition she would try again to find him.

She was on a train heading back to London for Freddie's ordination, which would follow the opening of her first exhibition, when her mother had a telephone call.

'Mrs Noble, I do not know if you remember me. My name is Blaise Fougère.'

Judith Noble listened, saying nothing, but thinking, thinking. She has come through. She has a chance to do well, to be famous, and here comes that Frenchman who turned her against us, ruined her life. And Freddie's ordination on Saturday.

'Mrs Noble, you are hearing me? I'm sorry if it has been a shock but I lost touch during the war and I saw our *appartement* and they said everyone was dead, but I keep hope. I am going to be in London soon and I think, I will try one more time.'

Judith steeled herself. It was for the best. 'You were wrong to hope, Mr Fougère. You saw the street?'

His heart plummeted. 'Yes.' He could never speak of what he had felt . . . experienced . . . as he had seen the hole where his life had been.

'They told you then?' Oh, he had to help her. She did not want to tell an outright lie. Her son was going to be ordained on Saturday.

'No survivors, they said, but I kept hoping, praying . . .'

'Let her go, Mr Fougère. I'm so sorry to hurt you.' She was not lying. She did not want to hurt him and she had never actually said that Tony was . . . she could not even think the word. 'Goodbye, Mr Fougère.'

His sister found him with the receiver still clasped in his hand. 'What's wrong, Blaise?'

'Nothing, *chérie*. I had hoped to meet an old friend when we go to London, but she is . . . not there.'

Nicole laughed. She was too young to remember her brother's phone calls telling his family all about the miracle of true love. 'Then you can spend more time with that lovely American girl. She's crazy about you.'

He could not think of Eleanor Ridgeway and her flattering adoration. Toinette was dead. Her mother had confirmed it. And when Blaise Fougère made his debut at Covent Garden, his parents, his young sister and a very wealthy American family were in the audience.

CHAPTER SEVEN

LONDON, 1999. GLASGOW, 1999

WITHOUT THE NOISE AND BUSTLE of the opening night, the gallery was almost like a cathedral. There was a breathless hush that was almost solemn. Holly began to wander around. Every so often she stopped and allowed a painting to invade her heart and mind completely.

Tony created this, Tony, and I never knew, never suspected her brilliance. *Sea Sprite*, 1937. The sprite's wicked green eyes smiled at her from the whale's back. Would she keep it? No, she would have the *Dandelions* just to spite Taylor.

The bell on the locked front doors rang as if it resented the force with which it was being pushed.

'Good heavens,' said Otto. 'Dear dear, Mr Hartman, the poor bell may never ring again.'

'So sue me. My solicitors are on their way with an injunction. Right now I want to speak to Miss Noble.'

Holly's heart, which had been behaving very oddly, now took complete fright and seemed to flip over. 'You are a bully, Taylor, and I will not be bullied. Your lawyers have no grounds for an injunction. The paintings are mine.'

'Holly, in my uncle's will he specifically charges me with guarding his privacy. I have been granted a temporary sympathetic injunction; it's what they call an equitable remedy. You can't show the paintings while I'm collecting the information that proves they hurt . . . Blaise's family.'

Holly looked at him but could no longer see his eyes. He's avoiding me; he has something to hide. 'Nonsense. These pictures can't hurt his reputation and they will certainly enhance my aunt's.'

Taylor threw some newspapers on Otto's immaculate desk. They opened as they fell. She read one of the headlines and tried not to wince: THE ARTIST, THE SINGER AND THE SOCIALITE.

Taylor was still talking. 'My mother is elderly and she adored her brother. I won't have her memories sullied; and there's my aunt. Life treated her so badly and he went to great lengths to protect her. She deserves to be left alone.'

This was too much. 'She was treated badly? By your uncle, I suppose. He married her when he was already in love with someone else. Why, Taylor? Rich, was she? Did he need her money to finance his career?' Holly gasped at her cattiness. What a terrible thing to say. 'She clung on to someone who was in love with another woman. Vindictiveness must run in the family.'

He looked down at her and he sighed, and it was as if all his anger left him. 'How well he kept her secret. Tony told you nothing of her?'

She shook her head.

'Eleanor Ridgeway Fougère was insane, Holly. She died in a secure asylum a few weeks before Blaise died. She had been hospitalised for nearly fifty years. My uncle adored her and never once contemplated divorcing her. That's real love, Holly. He gave all the time and received nothing in return but still he stayed faithful. I cannot . . . I will not believe these paintings were painted from life. I'm sorry. Tony Noble met Blaise Fougère in New York—once, only once. The *des Grieux* and the *Lohengrin* have different dates but they were painted at the same time.' He looked into the gallery and threw out his hands in an all-encompassing gesture. 'This, this is fantasy, a fabrication. My uncle loved his wife and protected her. I have to do the same—for both of them. These paintings will not be exhibited.'

She could say nothing, do nothing. By the time her brain began to function again he was out of the office.

She could not look at Otto. Her stomach was churning with the horror, the tragedy of it. 'Did you know? Did you know about his aunt?'

He did not look at her directly. 'The world's best-kept secret. She was . . . reclusive. There were rumours, you know: alcohol, drugs. For the first few years they were seen everywhere, all the smart parties. The golden voice married to America's golden girl, and then it all went wrong. She lost a baby. Then she disappeared and he hid from his public, didn't give interviews. All that did was to make him more popular than ever. The mystery combined with that glorious voice and the body. Even when he stopped singing, still they hunted him. Can you imagine what it must have been like? He left the theatre and there were hundreds of screaming women, and photographers, waiting to catch him, Mr Perfect being imperfect, being human.'

'Tell me you didn't know about his wife.' Holly stood up. She was going to be violently ill all over Otto's minimalist desk in a moment.

'I've told you all I know—and what I know I read in the newspaper.' But Holly had run for the bathroom. When she came out she went straight back to her hotel. If it was true, and it probably was, then it was tragic. But what about Tony?

No one is alive now who cares one way or the other.

But you're wrong, Tony darling, Taylor cares very much. Tony had allowed her career to take second place to Blaise's career—because she had loved him. In her last note to her niece was she not hinting that she would like the paintings exhibited? Holly had been told that she could do what she wanted with them. They were hers to sell or to keep, and selling meant showing. There were gaps in Tony's painting career: she would have to look carefully at the dates on the paintings and the places in which they had been set and then go through family papers to see if they told her anything. She would go back to Scotland to look through the rest of the crates she had not cared enough about to open when her parents had died in that stupid, senseless accident on a narrow Himalayan road. Maybe, a little voice whispered, she would rake through her feelings about John. Maybe. First things first. She would put Tony first. Tony had always . . . No. She had thought that she, Holly, had always been first with Tony but all the time there had been this secret, more important, more powerful love.

But I can't have Otto's gallery closed for weeks while I fight the Hartman empire in court. No way can I afford that. I'm sorry about poor Eleanor but she's dead and nothing can hurt her.

She rang Otto.

'It's been bedlam here all day, Holly. Every paper in the country seems to have been on the telephone. Any reporter I have ever informed of a launch wants a scoop. I have been offered money,' he added with distaste in his voice. 'This temporary whatever it's called is exactly that—temporary. The judge will throw him out of court. Tony's paintings will go all over the world.'

'I'm going back to Scotland, Otto.'

'Don't tell me you are running away from Taylor. My lawyers are fighting back. In a week or two, with all this lovely free publicity, I will be able to sell anything. Not that I would, *naturellement*. One has taste, one has standards. But everyone will want me to represent him or her.'

She took a deep breath. 'I'm going to Torry Bay, Otto, to live.'

'Holly, my dear, you can't leave. It's just beginning to get exciting and I can't make decisions without you.'

'I'm taking the paintings off the market until I've done some research. Pack them up and send them back to Achahoish, if you like.'

'I would adore to be free to send them anywhere. I'm afraid, too, that you can't just take them off the market. They are literally wards of court. No one, including you, their rightful owner, can do anything with them without the permission of the court.'

'So I can't sell them but Taylor can't buy them either and that makes me feel absolutely wonderful.'

She caught the first train back to Glasgow. It was clean, well staffed and ran on time. Bliss.

On the way north she mused that she had been a drifter all her life. Damn it. I'm thirty-seven years old, and still drifting, looking for the perfect man who will help me build the perfect home, the perfect family, breed the perfect babies.

Torry Bay, she realised, had never been her second home. It had been, quite simply, her home, the one place in the world where she had always felt completely welcome—and safe. She would stop blaming her parents for their inadequacies, their inability to show her that they had loved her. She would accept that she had in fact inherited a few good qualities from them. Why would she have spent her first few years after university teaching in children's homes in Africa if they had not taught her to care about those who were less well off? If they had also taught her to worry incessantly about what constituted a real family, a real home, well, that was something she would have to learn to deal with. She would ring John and tell him about her concerns and worries. Weakly, she allowed herself to remember and tally all John's good points. It was a formidable list.

I'm crazy. Why am I even thinking of giving all this up?

She reviewed in her mind some of the paintings: Fougère in a field of clover, under a rainbow, desolate in a rowing boat, and a Fougère, who could never have been a romantic fantasy, helping a little girl to make a walkway of shells while Tony dozed against a rock.

Toinette, ma mie. Hollyberry, Hollyberry.

The voice in her head was as real as if he were sitting beside her.

Refuge from the Storm.

What strength there was in that painting. The storm raged around the couple on the headland, that little headland from where she had thrown

Tony's ashes. Did you want me to do that, Tony?

Darling girl.

For the rest of the journey she looked out of the window and tried to see nothing but the landscape before her.

She heard her telephone ringing as she let herself into her flat. It was John. 'I read about it in the papers. I should have been there for you; I'm sorry. Can't we talk, Holly? I don't want to throw five lovely years away because of some silly arguments.'

'John . . .' she began.

'No sex. Just talk. Please, Holly.'

They agreed to meet in a little Italian restaurant they liked near the Theatre Royal. 'Tell me more about the exhibition,' he said after they had ordered.

'It was a madhouse; so many people turned up. Everything was going along swimmingly and then Taylor phoned and ruined everything.'

'Have you thought about his offer? Should you reconsider?'

'He knew I wouldn't agree. I don't want his money.'

'What exactly do you want?' John asked aggressively.

'Recognition of Tony's genius. If her greatest paintings are hidden away or destroyed, her greatness is merely hearsay.'

'I can't believe it. It could be our future. That's what you're throwing in the river.'

Was it the wine, the satisfying flavours of perfectly cooked food? Holly knew for a certainty that she had no future with John. She put down her glass. 'I'm selling my flat, John, and moving to the cottage. I'm not running away; I'm not Tony. I need civilisation and I'll come back—some time—but right now I need Torry Bay.'

'You're out of your mind. What's happened to you, Holly?'

'Looking at Tony's incredible paintings has opened my eyes.' She stood up and handed him her engagement ring. 'I'll send the pearls back tomorrow.'

Pearls are tears. Fougère was right.

Des Grieux
TORRY BAY, 1949. NEW YORK, 1949

'I'm sorry, Klaus. Who did you say? It's such a bad line.'

Tony was in Canon Gemmell's hall trying to understand a telephone call from her agent, Klaus von Emler. Klaus's accent and the poor connection were making every second or third word disappear.

'It's a wonderful opportunity, Tony. They will send you to New York which is where he is for the winter; well, November and December.'

'Who is in New York, Klaus? I'm not sure that I heard you properly.' Tony's hand was shaking and she sat down on the wooden chair.

'Fougère, Tony. He is a singer, a very great one and the opera house wants you to paint him as des Grieux. That's a character in an opera.'

Tony did not reply. Des Grieux, the tenor role in Puccini's *Manon Lescaut*. She had seen the opera with Blaise before the war.

'Blaise Fougère?' she managed at last. 'He wants to commission me?'

'Some rich family is donating it to the opera house. Have you heard of Fougère? I took Otto to hear him in *Rigoletto* a few years ago, about the time of your first exhibition. Yes, when the Garden opened again after the war. Such a voice. Tony, can you hear?'

'Yes, I hear.' He was alive; he was singing and he had forgotten her. Her parents were right. He had used her when he needed her and then dropped her. She could not take in what Klaus was saying.

'I'm too busy, Klaus,' she said and hung up because she could no longer speak. All the tamped-down pain was pushing its way to the surface. She had to get away. She could not scream with pain and disillusionment in the canon's front hall. She closed the front door as quietly as possible and hurried down the lane and onto the path that led to the bay. When she was out of sight she began to run and run until she was sobbing for breath and there was a stitch in her side.

The swans were in the bay. They disregarded her. They're swans, she told herself, not disguised princes and no knight in shining armour is going to come sailing across the sea on the back of one of them. What a fool I have been. Did I make any effort to keep in touch with him? I wrote a few letters that he never answered. I had no address for his parents, but when the war ended I could have gone to Paris and looked at telephone directories and I could have written to every Fougère who was a lawyer. That's what he said, 'My father is with the law.' I could have fought but I sat up here like a romantic fool and waited for a bloody swan.

His ring. Oh, God, I thought this was my wedding ring. How could I have been so naive? She lifted the gold chain over her head and threw the ring as far as she could into the sea. She was humiliated to see it plop into the water just a few feet from the shore. She began to wade in. She was going to throw it far, far . . . No, she wanted it back. She found herself panicking as the waves refused to give up her treasure.

'Please, God, let me find it. Oh, help me, please help.'

The swans hissed at her angrily and paddled off to calmer water as she walked up and down searching methodically. Her skirt and her shoes were soaked. At last she saw the chain lying on a stone almost at her feet. She picked it up and slipped it over her head again.

I didn't fight hard enough. Did I believe, deep down, that I wasn't good enough, special enough for him? His first letter said: 'Trust me.' But I did trust you, Blaise. I waited . . . dear God Almighty, I waited for a bloody swan, and he told me, many times, that he was just a man.

Canon Gemmell was waiting for her at the cottage and her heart contracted as she saw how he had aged. 'Hello, my dear. Klaus rang back.' He said nothing at all about her wet clothes.

'Come in and have a cup of tea, Canon. Give me a second to change.'

He followed her into the cottage and when she came downstairs she found he had already put the water on to boil.

'I owe you an explanation,' she began, but he interrupted her.

'You owe me nothing, my dear, except a cup of tea. Klaus worried that you did not understand the importance of this commission.'

'I understand. I was . . . afraid.'

'Forgivable, understandable even, but remember, Tony, that you are the one who is being sought out now. You have a reputation: no need to be afraid of the rich and famous or of your own talent. That's a very insidious fear. Many geniuses have it.'

'I'm not a genius,' she began and remembered Blaise's voice. *You must have the ego.* 'I'm good, Canon, and maybe I will go to New York and paint Mr Fougère.'

'So will you come back with me and ring Klaus?'

It appeared, according to Klaus, that a wealthy sponsor in New York wanted to donate a portrait of Blaise Fougère to the city opera house. The opera company and the wealthy family, which was one of its major sponsors, wanted Fougère to make New York his base. The portrait was only one of the little inducements being thrown his way.

'The Ridgeways saw your portrait of Lord Butterstone and were extremely impressed.'

'Klaus. Does Fougère know the name of the artist?' She could hardly bear to know the answer.

'I really don't know. I believe it's to be a surprise gift for him.'

It will be a surprise all right, thought Tony.

She decided to go. She tried not to let her heart hope that he still loved her, that there had been some horrid misunderstanding, but if there was any way to fight for what she wanted she would fight. She was sick all the way across the Atlantic.

If he had wanted you, he would have found you years ago.

Blaise stood, stunned, in the middle of the drawing room of the Ridgeways' magnificent mansion. He could not believe it. It was a joke in bad taste, a nightmare—insanity.

Sarah Ridgeway had expected her protégé to show some gratitude. The painter was fairly expensive, even though she was quite new. 'We hoped you'd be pleased, dearest.'

He looked desperately at his brand-new secretary, Stefan Lazlo, who didn't understand his reaction either. 'Noble, you say, Tony Noble. It can't be a woman.'

Henderson Ridgeway laughed heartily. 'Don't tell me you don't like women artists. She's the up-and-coming portrait painter.'

'You're just darling in the des Grieux costume, Blaise dear,' said Sarah Ridgeway, 'and I just bet it will cheer up our little Eleanor.'

Eleanor. My God, Eleanor. 'Yes, I must go to see her at once.'

'No, don't be hurt, honey, but she really doesn't want to see you yet. Dr Kermaly is taking care of her. A little rest and she'll be fine. You and Stefan here have so much work to do. Henderson and I will take Miss Noble to dinner and we'll set up an initial sitting.'

As soon as the door had closed behind them he turned to Stefan. 'Find out where Miss Noble is staying and get me a car.'

'She's at the Carlisle, monsieur.'

'You are definitely going to be indispensable, Stefan.'

He was as nervous as the night he had made his debut. No, more nervous. Then, what was the worst that could happen? He might forget the words; he could crack on a note. But this, this. He was still having difficulty believing that it was true; that all this time she had been alive.

'Miss Noble's room, please,' he asked the receptionist and waited for the few seconds that it took her to connect him with the room.

'Hello.' Her voice was just the same.

He tried to speak but no sound came. He tried again and this time the voice obeyed him. 'Tony? Toinette? Is it you?'

He heard her gasp and then there was silence.

'May I come up?'

Again there was silence and then quietly, slowly, she gave him the number of her room.

The lift seemed to crawl. His pulse was racing, his heart was pounding. At last, at last he was on the seventh floor.

The door opened and Tony stood there. For a soundless lifetime they stood looking at one another and then with a groan, almost of pain, he opened his arms and she ran into them.

'She told me you were dead,' he said, and kicked the door closed.

CHAPTER EIGHT

GLASGOW, 1999. TORRY BAY, 1999

THE NEXT AFTERNOON, Holly went to see a local estate agent and arranged to put her flat on the market. It had not, in the end, been such a difficult decision. Torry Bay called to her and, without her job that she had loved, and John, whom she had thought she loved, Glasgow meant little. On the way back to her flat she posted the pearls and stopped in at several shops to buy some odds and ends to tide her over at Torry Bay.

A very small blue car was parked outside her building and Taylor was leaning against it. Her stomach churned with what? Fear, excitement, some animal instinct she refused to call simple lust? He looked . . . good, standing there.

'What do you want now?' she asked crossly.

'Nice to see you too,' he said as he straightened up.

She flushed. 'Why are you here, Taylor? You've changed your mind and you're sorry you made such a fuss about nothing?'

'Protecting the people you love is not nothing, Holly. May I join you for coffee?'

'I have tea at this time of day.'

'For God's sake, Holly. Anything but vitriol would be fine.'

She looked at his tired face and she heard her shrewish voice. What changes there were in her; she was no longer overawed or intimidated by Taylor Hartman. 'I'm sorry. Of course you can have coffee.'

He followed her into her flat. 'This is nice but the walls aren't big enough.' He did not say 'for Tony's canvases'.

'I'm moving,' she said casually as she filled the percolator. 'I'm going back to the cottage. I'm going to sit on that headland and think.'

'I hope Tony left you a fur coat.'

She laughed and he laughed too. If she didn't dislike him so much she could quite like him. 'I can make you a sandwich.'

He sat at the table in the kitchen while she sliced bread and avocado. 'My mother wants to see the paintings, to meet you.'

Surprised, she looked down into his eyes as she put the blue plates from Torry Bay on the simple blue checked cotton tablecloth. They were green. 'Damn,' she said and blushed. It was such an insufferable cliché.

She had looked into his eyes and felt she was drowning. She pulled her head above the water. 'Why?'

'She said she owed it to her brother.'

No one is alive now who cares one way or the other.

Nicole Fougère Hartman. She would know for sure, if anyone did.

'Did she know—about her brother and Tony?'

He put the sandwich down untasted. 'There was no Blaise and Tony.' She stood up abruptly and moved away.

'There are things I have to do at Torry Bay. Have her talk to Otto.'

He left the table and stood, towering over her. He made no effort to distance himself from her and she could see a pulse beating in his throat. 'Thanks for the sandwich,' he said and he was gone. She heard the car door slam and the low sound of the engine as it moved away.

She stood in the kitchen and lifted the mug he had been using, then slammed it down hard so that the coffee slopped onto the tablecloth. 'Damn, damn, damn, he's eaten my supplies.'

Holly was filled with urgency to get away. She could not think in Glasgow. There were too many intrusions. She almost ran around in her haste to pack the few things she would need. From the kitchen window a yellow primula reminded her that spring was on the way. She could not leave it to die. A few hours later, even after stopping to restock her provisions, she put the plant between some stones on the windowsill at Torry Bay. Holly 1970 . . . Holly 1972.

The morning after her arrival Holly walked down to the cove and sat watching the swans. Soon the bay would be full of brown cygnets. She would stay for the cygnets and she would stay for the light, so soft, so gentle. She would stay for the air which was cool and clear. She would stay for the peace which came 'dropping slow'. How peaceful it was without the worry of John and their relationship.

'Can I love someone if I am relieved to be away from him?' she asked the swans who, in their serenity, ignored her and so she answered herself. 'No, I do not love him, not as Tony loved Blaise.'

Tony had never been at real peace without Blaise. The paintings told Holly that. The letters were less communicative. Those from Holly's father in answer to Tony's were full of domesticity and church matters. Sometimes they dealt with the child Holly.

You know how difficult it is for us to have Holly here. It was quite thoughtless of you, my dearest sister, to arrange a show at her school holiday time. Now we will be forced to ask the headmistress to find someone to look after the child.

Just one of many letters from parents who found their 'flock' easier to deal with than their only child. Holly had felt even worse about the letter when she had checked the dates with the schedule of Tony's exhibitions and found that none had taken place at the times suggested in the letter. Tony had not wanted her; it was as simple as that. She tried to banish the hurt as easily as she had banished Taylor. Blaise had been there and his needs came first. What would it be like to be so in love, so loved that no one and nothing mattered but the beloved? If John had loved me the way Tony loved Blaise . . . if I had loved him . . .

She did not know where the hours went. The days were getting longer and the evenings stretched beautifully out to the bay. She woke early and tidied the cottage, cleaning out the fireplace, a task she remembered sharing with joy when she had stayed with Tony. Then she laid a new fire—the evenings were chilly yet—and went out. She walked and walked and spent a great deal of time looking for the tiny yellow primroses that hid among the roots of trees, or sitting watching the play of light on the water.

She watched the swans, aware that Tony had watched them. Darling Tony, how could you wait for him so faithfully? You knew the story of Lohengrin was a myth; but still you believed Blaise would come back. Sometimes she thought she heard a loving, laughing voice.

When it's right, you'll know it, darling girl, and you'll wait till the end of time if need be.

Holly was too practical for such nonsense. She knew she was not hearing voices and if she were then she would seek help, probably from a psychiatrist. Still, it was a joy to curl up in Blaise's chair before the fire in the evenings and look through Tony's sketchbooks, laughing sometimes, smiling often and too often reduced to tears.

A sketch of Blaise in a rowing boat and the words 'such pain'. Two figures, unrecognisable, on the point. The man tall and broad, the woman sheltered in his arms, tiny. The words 'peace, shelter'. She remembered that painting from the aborted exhibition. The child Holly with a doll. Joy. Whose was the joy, Tony, yours or mine? I hope both.

But it could not last for ever. Letters came from John, from Taylor and even from Otto. How dare they disturb her peace?

Forgive me, Holly. I love you and need you and will try to understand about the cottage. Please come home. It will soon be time for the nominations.

Would she feel differently if, instead of writing a letter, John had driven out to Torry Bay, carrying her engagement ring?

*Darling Taylor has been here twice, in person, so terrifying. I am very
skilfully—and tastefully—keeping the story in the public's fickle beady
little eye. You'll thank me but you can't thank me from the wilderness.*

She ignored them all and restudied the family letters. None of Tony's
relatives or friends ever alluded to her relationship with Blaise Fougère.
Did they know he existed? Where was Blaise during the war? Why did
they never marry?

Disillusion

NEW YORK, 1949. TORRY BAY, 1949. SURREY, 1949

Tony had not wanted, sought, to have an affair with a married man. He
had not said, when she let him into her room, that he was married. They
had been capable of no rational thought. Years of frustration and heart-
breaking sorrow had disappeared for a while under the surging tide of
desire. When he had told her about Eleanor she had been furious, not
that he had married but that he should have come to her and loved her.
'Get out, get out,' she had screamed. 'You have made me a whore.'

Her anger frightened him and he imprisoned her hands. 'No, oh no,
ma mie, never, never. Listen, Toinette,' he had beseeched desperately.
'Listen to me, please. You never wrote; the building was destroyed. She
told me you were dead. Obliterated. All that was left of you was in my
heart, in my blood, under my skin. I mourned my wife, my wife.'

'So you jumped into bed with someone else?'

She knew the look of pain that crossed his sensitive face was because
of her crude language.

He went on, feverishly, the words spilling out, trying to make her
understand. 'I met Eleanor in Paris after the war. I believed that you
were dead and so I stayed in Paris and resumed my studies. The
Ridgeways were making a tour and they heard me sing. I was invited to
New York. Eleanor fell in love, maybe with my voice, and I was lonely,
Toinette. I thought you were dead. I had tried to find you. Did you try to
find me?'

What could she say? 'I waited for a knight in shining armour to sail
across the sea on the back of a swan'? She prevaricated. 'I wrote to every
address you gave me; you never answered.'

The telephone rang. It was the front desk.

'Mr Ridgeway is coming to take you to dinner.'

Tony looked in horror at the receiver. 'I've got to get out of here.'
Wildly she began to throw things back into her suitcase.

'Tony, I'm sorry, stay, paint the picture.'

'I'd rather die.'

'Tony, it's a job, nothing more. Paint the picture. A tenor in a fancy costume, no more. Then you can leave my life and I will leave yours, I promise, if that's what you want.'

'How dare you. Of course I want.' She looked at him and her eyes were full of contempt. 'You make me feel dirty. Get out.'

He stumbled backwards to the door, his hand held out before him as if to protect himself from her hatred.

The next day Blaise began his sittings with Tony. It was her least successful portrait and the Ridgeways were disappointed.

'It's not you, Blaise. The eyes are . . . calculating.'

'It's a painting of des Grieux.' He tried to defend her.

'Then you should have told her that des Grieux is a young man blinded by his love for an unsuitable woman.'

He said no more. He did not say that Tony had refused to speak to him during the sittings and had not explained why she had decided to complete the assignment.

Later she told him that his father-in-law had told her a little of Eleanor's story and that she had feared to add to the young woman's grief by refusing to paint her husband. She too was unhappy with the painting because to her it resembled neither Blaise nor des Grieux. She had not liked the expression in the eyes of the portrait because it was not the expression she had seen as she worked. Those eyes were sad. She wanted to paint what she saw but her fingers refused to do what she told them to do.

After she left New York he wrote to her and Klaus forwarded the letters but she did not read them and burnt each one as it arrived. It was the boy, Otto, who gave Blaise the address of the cottage, a sin for which he refused to ask his father's forgiveness.

'They love one another, Papa. I want her to be happy.'

Blaise knew better than to write to Tony again. He waited until he had a few days between performances at Covent Garden. Stefan booked the trains. He said nothing, but Blaise could tell that his secretary thought he was out of his mind.

It was his last chance. He had to explain, make her understand. He could not bear that she should hate him. He refused to admit that he wanted her to love him as he loved her.

As the train lumbered through the hills and valleys he wondered what could have made her mother let him believe such a terrible untruth, but he could come to no rational conclusion. He decided not to think about it any more. Eleanor was stable. Perhaps, if she got really well . . . no, he would not think about anything at all. He would take refuge in music: in Beethoven, in Mozart. The music filled his head.

It was raining when he arrived in Argyll and he took a taxi from the station to the village. The rain had stopped, obligingly, and he saw, for the first time, the incredible beauty of Scotland after rain. The light was so soft and beautiful that he felt his heart, heavy for such a long time, lighten. Above him a rainbow arched across the sky and he saw that at the rainbow's end was a cottage, small and square and bulky, with a blue door and blue windowsills, where fat pots of petunias lifted drenched heads to the emerging sun.

The blue door opened and a woman came out. She walked away from him towards the sea and he saw the swans.

Dare he? Dare he? "*Mein lieber Schwan.*" He began to sing the delicate melody that Lohengrin sings off stage to the bewitched swan.

Slowly, as if she could not believe what she was hearing, she turned. The rainbow seemed to frame her. He stopped walking and only his voice went towards her and then she smiled.

'You had better come in,' she said. 'You've come such a long way.'

He did not try to touch her. They sat at the kitchen table for hours and they talked, and the next day he was gone.

She smiled. She had not promised him but she had promised herself. She would see him again.

No one in New York had had any idea that she was painting two pictures: the one the Ridgeways wanted and were paying for, and the other painting, her secret painting. During the hours when Blaise had sat for her she had painted the stiff figure of des Grieux and she had not been able to get him right. She hated the painting and would have destroyed it but the Ridgeways wanted des Grieux.

At night she had painted Lohengrin and the earnest young face that had emerged from the canvas was otherworldly. It was better to see Blaise only as a mythical creature, unreal. The re-creating of the legend exhausted the artist who, when the commissioned painting was finished, limped back home to recuperate. The second painting, unfinished, was rolled up in her flight bag.

As her body had rested and recharged its batteries, her mind had gone over and over her talk with Blaise and she had remembered some words she had forgotten: 'She told me you were dead.'

Her life was ruined—as was Blaise's—because 'she' had said that Tony was dead. Who was 'she'?

It was time that *Les Bébés qui Chantent* and *Les Dents de Lion* were brought home, and there was money at last to transport them. She wrote a brief note to her mother.

Her father met her at the station in Godalming. She was surprised when he asked, 'What's happened? You look different somehow.'

'It's the New York experience,' she tried to joke. 'It's an amazing place.' At home, her mother was over-jovial. 'Here comes the world traveller.' She smiled but the smile, or so it seemed to Tony, was uneasy, unnatural.

They ate dinner and her mother chatted vivaciously about Freddie and all the doings in the village and everything except Blaise Fougère.

'Blaise is married,' she broke in to the nonstop chatter. 'Why, Mother, why would you tell him such a thing?'

Judith began to whimper. 'It was for the best, dear,' she whispered.

So it *had* been her own mother who had betrayed her. Tony stood up carefully, like a frail old woman. 'I love Blaise Fougère with every atom of my being. I will never ever forgive you.'

She walked out of the room leaving her mother weeping at the table. She carried on upstairs to pack her paintings. When that was done she went to her old room and lay down fully dressed on the bed.

Her father knocked on the door around ten in the evening. 'He'd heard you were killed, Antonia. Mummy thought you were doing so well with your paintings, better not to start things up again. She did what she thought was best for you. That's all we have ever tried to do.'

Tony sat up in the bed and looked at him and he flushed. 'You have always done what you have wanted to be the best for me. You have never considered what I thought was best for me.'

He was angry now. 'We let you go to that arty, crafty school.'

'Yes, you did, and I will always be grateful for that. Pity you are so embarrassed by the swan the school created, Daddy. You never really believed in me. I can just hear the conversations. "We'll let her go, Judith, get it out of her system. Then she'll come back, settle down with a nice chap from the village." Isn't that right?'

Her words were so accurate that he coloured furiously.

Tony lay down again. 'Good night,' she said dismissively.

She was gone before they woke in the morning and she never saw either of her parents again. She was in Vienna with Blaise when her father died of pneumonia. Two days later her mother died peacefully in her sleep. The broken-hearted Freddie knew no way to reach her, and the funeral was over before his sister returned to Torry Bay. As usual she took refuge on the headland. They were dead and she had never forgiven them. Instead she grieved for them, for Freddie and for the 'might have been'. She knew that Blaise would never be her husband, the singing babies would never be born, but Lohengrin had returned to find her waiting. So he would always find her.

CHAPTER NINE
TORRY BAY, 1999. LONDON, 1999

'You will never guess who rang me this morning: Nicole Fougère Hartman. She has invited you for lunch.'

Holly said nothing and in the silence she could hear rain lashing against the window and the wind howling because it was caught in the old chimney. She would have to find someone to look at that.

'You have fallen off the planet?' Otto's mild voice brought her mind back from her domestic problems.

'Sorry, Otto, there is a gale blowing here. Has Mrs Hartman deigned to tell you where I am to have lunch?'

'Naughty, naughty. No, she rang from Paris to ask for your telephone number; she has an enchanting apartment on the Ile Saint Louis. Blaise used to take her to a puppet show when she was a little girl and they'd walk across a bridge near the island to have pastries and hot chocolate at a special café. She said, "I told him I would live there when I grew up, and he promised to buy me an *appartement*—and he did." Generous man, Blaise Fougère.' Otto sighed, no doubt remembering the beauty of Madame's apartment. 'I thought I'd get in first and warn you.'

As it happened, Nicole Fougère Hartman waited until evening to ring and although she was expecting the call, Holly jumped nervously.

'Were you expecting my call, Miss Noble, or may I call you Holly? I plan to return to the States soon but will stay in London for a few days first. I would like to see these paintings and to meet you.'

What to say, what to do? How to react? With charm, with honesty? 'Mrs Hartman, did you know my aunt?' she asked abruptly.

Mrs Hartman sounded surprised when she answered. 'No, my dear, but I knew of her. We can talk if you will be so kind as to meet me in London. So clichéd, but I stay at the Ritz; Blaise always stayed there when he was in London.'

Holly tried again. 'Can you at least tell me what you know of the relationship between your brother and my aunt because it was real, wasn't it, and Taylor knows?'

'So many questions. So much more pleasant to speak face to face,' Holly admitted defeat and agreed to travel to London because her father had phoned the Royal Overseas League in London because her father had always stayed there in his later years, and because it was within walking distance of Mrs Hartman's hotel. She was assured that a room would be waiting for her and so, with some reluctance, she packed for a few days away from Torry Bay.

Blaise had stayed here. Had Tony? Had this beautifully appointed hotel been one of her special places? No, too public. Poor Tony. While Blaise Fougère relaxed in pampered seclusion at the Ritz, and hotels like it in other parts of the world, Tony had lived in a cottage at Torry Bay and . . . died alone.

Tears pricked at Holly's eyelids. Did you love her, Blaise Fougère? *Love never dies, Hollyberry. I had to go ahead but I waited for her.*
Did you love her?
'*Ma mie.*'

Holly looked round. A woman in a glorious green silk dress was looking at her questioningly.

Now I'm talking to myself in public places. Holly walked towards some display cases of jewellery.

'Miss Noble?' A porter was beside her. 'Mrs Hartman wonders if you would join her?'

Holly had not expected to feel quite so nervous when she was ushered into the sitting room of Taylor's mother's suite. Her first coherent thought was that the Fougère genes were very strong; Taylor's mother resembled both her brother and her son, although she was small-boned and fragile but not frail.

She kissed Holly first on the left cheek and then on the right. She had lived in America for nearly fifty years but she was undeniably French.

'Toinette's niece. I am happy to meet you at last, little Hollyberry. Come, do sit down and we will have some coffee.'

Holly did as she was bid and took the cup that was handed to her. She set it down on the table and said very deliberately, 'Mrs Hartman, I want to be civilised but I have travelled a long way to meet you. You knew Blaise's name for me and I think that fact alone proves the authenticity of the paintings and the relationship. I would like to know when Taylor will lift the injunction or whatever it is that one does with bans.'

'I would like to see the paintings, Holly. What did you call him, Blaise, I mean, so sweet, like a child . . . Uncle Fire?'

'He told you that?'

'*Bien sûr.*'

Holly felt sad. 'I don't remember him at all.'

Nicole waited for a moment to give Holly time to compose herself. 'The coffee, it is all right?' She waited while Holly picked up the cup and saucer again. 'He told me everything. He had to have someone to talk to; *ça va sans dire.* Everyone needs someone.'

'Then will you tell me why Taylor doesn't know, or pretends that he doesn't know?'

'But he did not know.' She shrugged expressively. 'I did not tell my son, Holly, because I did not at first know of your inheritance. Taylor thought to protect me from worry.' She looked at Holly from over the top of her cup and smiled. 'He is a thoughtful man, *n'est-ce pas?* He worshipped Blaise and has worked hard to protect his reputation and to keep his sad secret.'

'I'm sorry about your sister-in-law, Mrs Hartman, but Taylor is rich and powerful and will fight for her. Tony has only me. She sacrificed herself for your brother and he abandoned her in an isolated cottage— and I did too. She died alone, Mrs Hartman, and I can't forgive your precious Blaise, or myself, for that.' Holly sat back, embarrassed, but feeling she might as well finish. 'The paintings show that he loved Tony. Your son does not believe my aunt and your brother were lifelong lovers. You know the whole story, don't you, and you must tell Taylor.'

Nicole Hartman smiled again. 'Taylor does not *want* to believe it but in his heart he knows. *Sûrement,* my dear, you have lived long enough to know that life is not simple. For Blaise, Tony was *un coup de foudre,* a lightning bolt. He remained in love with Toinette until the day he died.'

'But you never met her.'

'No. She never visited us but he went to see your . . . grandparents, it would be and met . . . Frederick?'

'My father. He has been dead for a long time, madame. But, please, why then did Blaise marry Eleanor?'

Nicole shrugged. 'He thought Tony was dead. He went to London in the war and found the hole where his apartment had been. Oh, *quelle douleur,* what grief. He was a madman, scrabbling in the dirt for his Antoinette . . . I was a child and he did not tell me all, but later . . .' She sat still, thinking, remembering, and at last Holly became impatient.

'Please, Mrs Hartman, if you know, please tell me why he married someone else. The paintings . . .'

'Ah, yes, I would like very much to see all the paintings, without Otto, or Taylor. He is so disturbing, Taylor, so energetic and exhausting, but I have sent him to San Francisco on business.'

Holly was having a hard time picturing Taylor as someone who could be sent anywhere by anyone. 'But—madame, my aunt moved to Scotland during the war. Why did Blaise not try to find her? Surely . . .'

'But she told him she was dead, chérie. Who would doubt the word of a mother?'

No, it could not be. Holly gasped. 'My grandmother told him?'

'Her parents did not like a French singer, a Catholic, any more than my parents would have liked Tony, a penniless art student.'

'But to lie.'

'Who knows? Let the dead sleep. Holly. My brother married poor Eleanor, mainly I think because he was too tired to say no.' Nicole Hartman sighed. 'He wanted a home and children. Toinette was dead. He was distraught, unable to train, to function even. Eleanor adored him; her family were influential at a time when we wanted out of Europe. The war changed him as it changed so many. Before he used to say, "To be great you must believe in yourself", but then all those years without music, without practice . . . If, peut-être, without his Toinette he could have believed in his own greatness, maybe he would have taken another route, but he married Eleanor and he loved her till the end. He was faithful to her you know, until he met Tony again.'

'But why didn't he divorce her and marry Tony?'

'Because she is . . . because she was insane.'

'I know and that's terrible but, forgive me, Mrs Hartman, it doesn't really answer my question.'

'He felt guilty.'

'Why? Because she lost a baby?'

Nicole nodded sadly. 'Babies. Blaise felt that the pregnancies were his fault and so he vowed to protect Eleanor and to keep the press away from her, for her sake not his own. Poor chivalrous Blaise, the knight in shining armour. His princess understood nothing. In the last years of his life she did not even know who he was and yet he continued having her clothes made just as she liked them when she was young and beautiful; he continued to visit her at least once a month, and Tony stayed in her cottage painting those magnificent pictures waiting for him. She was the breath in his body, his heartbeat, that is what he meant by ma mie.'

Holly tried to remember Uncle Fire, the big man who had walked with her into the sea, and at last she saw his face as he had looked back at Tony. 'I know,' she said quietly.

'I hope she knew he was on his way to her when he was killed. I believe he had finally made up his mind to make a life with Tony. He changed all his plans and flew to Britain when he was not due there for six months. What else could he have been doing but going to Tony?'

'Would you have been angry if your brother had divorced Eleanor?'

Mrs Hartman signalled for the maid to take away the coffee. 'Shall we go downstairs for lunch and we can continue to talk.'

They went down into the opulent dining room with its splendid draperies and exquisite floral arrangements.

'Frankly,' Nicole continued, 'I would have welcomed it. It was Blaise who would not consider divorce. Not that he did not love Tony but . . . men can be so stupid sometimes. His honour would not let him divorce Eleanor. Had she been mentally stable he would have divorced her *immédiatement*, like a shot . . . *pauvre* Taylor,' she added.

Poor Taylor? 'Mrs Hartman, if you will forgive me, it's the last adjective I would use to describe him.'

Nicole laughed. 'But, like Blaise, he too is wasting his life, Holly. I should not tell you but maybe it will help. In college he loved a girl who loved his greenbacks, more than she loved his green eyes. He is looking for a woman like Eleanor to love chastely and devotedly when he should be looking for another Tony who will love him as fiercely as he loves her. It was . . . difficult to make him believe in my brother's love for your aunt. Discretion can be such a nuisance.'

Holly assured herself that she had no interest in Taylor Hartman or his aborted love life. 'Discretion? Another word, if you'll forgive me, that I wouldn't use in connection with your son.'

Mrs Hartman laughed. 'Not Taylor, *chérie*, Blaise. He was almost paranoid about privacy, you know, for himself, for Eleanor, for me—and yes, he wanted privacy for his beloved Toinette. He did not want his problems gossiped over and, besides, he was sure that the miscarriages were the cause of Eleanor's condition although, frankly, I'm sure she was unstable before they were married.'

Holly thought of her own longing for a child. 'Did he want a child badly?'

'He would have enjoyed being a father; he adored Taylor and from his expression in some of those catalogue photographs, he was fond of you too. But it was not a compelling force. You have no children?'

'No,' answered Holly shortly. This was something she would not discuss with a woman she had only just met.

Mrs Hartman recognised her stress. 'What an astonishing amount of feeling can go into such a little syllable, Holly.'

When they had finished their meal Nicole rose. 'Come, we will have coffee in my sitting room. I want you to tell me more about yourself, and the paintings.'

'They will go to galleries all over the world. If you would like to choose one . . .'

'My dear, you do not plan to give me a painting.'

'If you would like to have one . . .'

Nicole shook her head sadly but she was smiling. 'Taylor was right in one regard. He said, "She is giving me a painting out of goodness, not because she wants anything from me." You have no head for business, *chérie*. Even from the photographs I can see that there are several pictures I would give anything to own and I have a great deal of *anything*. Will you show them to me now, today?'

'I'm not sure that I can. They are wards of court.'

'You cannot sell them until the court decides their fate but they are still in the gallery, no?'

'Yes.'

'Then we will call dear Otto and tell him to open the door. He knows how to be quiet, Otto, not like my Taylor who must always charge in head first. Otto is like me, subtle. You watch how we get our own way.'

'Doesn't Taylor usually get his own way?'

'Of course and especially with women. His tactics are . . . different. Be warned.'

Holly fumed over that last remark all the way to the gallery, where Otto greeted one of his best customers in French and then remembered Holly.

'I thought you were German, Otto.'

'Unkind. You know perfectly well I am Austrian, but, unlike the British, we real Europeans speak more than one language.'

'Children,' admonished Mrs Hartman.

Later Holly would ask Otto why he had never told her that he knew Nicole Hartman well.

'Mrs Hartman would like to view the paintings of her brother, Otto.'

'Of course, dear ladies.'

He opened the door and ushered his visitors into the cathedral-like rooms where Tony's passionate paintings still graced the walls. They bombarded the senses with their colours, their phenomenal use of light, their messages. He loves her; he loves her not; he loves her.

Nicole Fougère Hartman walked slowly along through the galleries looking at a part of her beloved brother's life. She said little but would stop often and gaze at the images, occasionally sighing or even laughing, and smiling often. *Sea Sprite, Les Dents de Lion, Uncle Fire* . . . Then she came to a large canvas. It was called *Rainbows* and was, of course, of Blaise, who stood on the point at Torry Bay. Behind him the sky was aflame with several rainbows.

'I should like to have this one, if I may, Holly.' Nicole's eyes were wet with tears. 'I feel like a voyeur, you know, to see so much intimacy. I am falling in love with a painting.'

Holly looked at her, at the expensive couturier suit, the handmade shoes, at the tears on her cheeks.

'That is exactly how I feel about the paintings. They called to me.'

'And Blaise, does he call to you? He is very beautiful, no, and such a talent. My son is very like him', said Mrs Hartman enigmatically.

Holly refused to say anything.

Grief
TORRY BAY, 1957

Tony was sick with excitement and then she was sick with fear. But most of all she was sick because she was pregnant. How had it happened? They had been careful, hadn't they? She had been in London for the whole of June and almost every night Blaise had managed to steal away to be with her. It had been wonderful, just like being married. He went out to work and then he came home; they ate supper and went to bed. There, he would talk of work and pleasure, and he would make her sing, and then they would lie pleasantly exhausted listening to London waking up.

'It's not waking up, *mon cher*. London never sleeps.'

'Thank God it dozes a little, like Paris. But Parisians wake to the smell of bread and flowers, and Londoners wake to petrol fumes and smog. I wish we could go to Torry Bay and smell the sea.'

'When we are old, we will wake every morning in Torry Bay, Blaise.'

With the sound of the sea in their ears and the smell of the sea in their nostrils they would sleep at last, until it was time for Blaise to dress and go to his hotel to pretend that he had been there all night.

Blaise's secretary, Stefan, was their ally. Did he approve, disapprove? Tony did not know and Stefan said nothing, never showed his feelings. All that was sure was his unquestioning loyalty to his employer.

There had been no time to go to Scotland. Blaise had gone from Covent Garden to Bayreuth to sing Wagner for the first time and Tony had gone to Torry Bay to wait for him; and now she was not alone in her waiting. On one of those magical nights a baby had been conceived.

Would it become the soprano who would set the musical world on its ears with her Tosca?

Suddenly Tony felt cold. She was pregnant but she could not have this baby. For a few minutes she had indulged in daydreams. Blaise would be thrilled. He would see that the only thing to do was to divorce his wife and marry the mother of his child.

'I can never divorce her, Toinette. Her inability to give me a living child destroyed her mind. I will never leave her.'

But his baby, my baby, is more important. Eleanor will never know, never understand.

Her family will suffer.

They are suffering already.

She argued with herself over and over.

If they really love Blaise, they will be happy for him.

Frighteningly she found that she was beginning to hate Eleanor and even once wailed, 'Why won't she die?'

Blaise wrote from Bayreuth. Wagner's *Tannhäuser* was an unbelievable challenge. He was finding it so difficult.

I can't give him another major problem when he has so many already, but I can't wait until the end of the run.

She went to see Simon McRae.

The young doctor did not judge. 'You are at least two months pregnant, Tony. What has the father to say?' For a second she saw deep disappointment.

Tony did not try to explain. 'I haven't told him. I have decided on termination.'

The words tried to float out of the window but they were too heavy and ugly. They hung for a moment and then fell into the silence.

He took her hands, hands that were cold with fear. 'Tony, that's a human being inside you. A real, live human being. I heard a story once about this woman. She'd had several children, all of them handicapped in some way, and then she found herself pregnant yet again. "Get rid of it. You can't afford it." She refused. "It's God's gift," she told them. "Do you know the name of the baby who was born, Tony?"

She covered her ears with her hands.

'Beethoven, Antonia. Ludwig von Beethoven.'

'Shut up! Tell me the medical options, *Doctor*, nothing else.'

'There are no options in this office, Tony. I promised to respect life, not to destroy it.'

She got up and walked out. She did not speak to Simon for months. Termination, abortion. Abortion, termination. To abort. To terminate.

Dear God, forgive me. Baby, forgive me. She must not think of a baby, not a real baby. If she imagined a real live baby with his father's looks and his beautiful voice floating around inside her, she would go mad. *Les Bébés qui Chantent*. Singing babies. Which one are you? This naughty one on the cloud who is spoiling his sister's painting? This serene little one who is putting paint on the clouds instead of her canvas?

Tony packed a suitcase, locked up the cottage, and left. Two months later she came back. She went to Chrissie's for milk and bread.

Chrissie had always known when to pry and when not.

'You look a bit peaky, Tony, tired like. That's the trouble with holidays. I always need a holiday to get over my holiday.'

She tried to smile, to answer. 'That's it. Too much sun and late-night restaurants. A few days at Torry Bay will put me right.'

'I'm here, Tony, like always.'

'My friend,' said Tony.

She reached the haven of her cottage and in the following weeks tried to decide whether or not she should tell Blaise; triumphant Blaise who had confounded the critics and forced the Germans to accept him in a Wagner role. She examined her body and hated it because it gave no sign. It was still slender but unmarked and somewhere, surely, it should say, 'A baby was aborted from this womb.' But it said nothing.

I must tell him. He has a right to know.

Don't be stupid. He did not want the baby. Remember how careful he was.

Do I want him to grieve with me, to share my suffering?

Possibly, probably and you have no right to such indulgence.

Bayreuth. Next stop Vienna, her favourite city. Then it was Tokyo and after that Australia and home to New York for Christmas.

'Come, Toinette. I miss you so. You love Vienna. Come to see the city.'

'I have an exhibition in Glasgow. I'm too busy.'

'From Tokyo I will go to Sydney and then to New York. Come to New York, *ma mie*. I cannot live without you.'

How could she tell him that she was too afraid? At night she lay longing for him or dreaming of him. During the day she painted like a madwoman: babies that she scraped away with her palette-knife before falling weeping onto her bed.

Please, God, forgive me. I made a terrible mistake.

Mistakes could be rectified. Her mother had told her so.

Sorry. Sorry. Sorry. I will never do it again.

Too late. Too late.

He arrived on December 16 and she was so happy to see him that she fell into his arms without thinking.

'*Ma mie, ma mie*, you are so thin. You have lose too much weight. You are working too hard, Toinette.'

She forgot everything but her love, her need. She responded to his desire, his passion, clinging to him with her arms, her legs. Together they climaxed and fell asleep exhausted.

Later his fingers traced her breasts, her stomach. 'How you are thin, Toinette. We will go to New York for Christmas and get fat together.'

'I had an abortion.'

The words came out of their own volition. The air grew cold around them. His hands that had been holding her dropped to his sides and he lay still. She lay beside him wishing the words back.

He got up from the bed like an old man and walked to the window. There he stood looking out at the storm that was broiling itself up in the bay. It echoed his anger and, he realised, his overpowering grief.

'You killed our baby. How could you do it?'

Never in her wildest imaginings had she dreamed that he would say anything quite so cruel. The anger that she did not know that she had been suppressing for so long boiled up and spewed itself out. 'Our baby?' she asked. 'It was my baby. You were just there for the conception. You come here when it suits you; you screw me out of my mind for two or three days and then you leave. I don't hear from you, sometimes for weeks, and you have the audacity to say "our baby".'

'Sometimes your lack of real breeding shows, Antonia.'

He began to pull on his discarded clothes. When he was dressed he ran downstairs and went out into the storm.

Where was he going? What was he going to do? Blaise. Blaise. Blaise. She followed him downstairs and out into the wind. It caught her and tried to push her back into the cottage. 'Blaise,' she screamed. 'Blaise, forgive me. Come back, please come back,' but if he heard he paid no heed and she turned back to the cottage.

She almost crawled up the staircase to their room and crept into bed. She wept and, weeping, fell asleep, and so she did not hear him return. She did not hear him stoke up the fire in the kitchen. Nor did she hear him cry for his dead child.

When the outside storm was over he went out and down to the sea. Their rowing boat was there, high above the water line and he pulled it down the shingle to the water. Then he began to row, out, out, until he was exhausted and then he shipped the oars and sat there until the tide drew the boat back to the shore, where Tony found him.

She would never forget his face, never, even if she never saw him again and she was so horribly sure that she never would. He hated her.

He would never be able to understand her desperate action. He pulled the boat up the shingle, and only then did he turn to her.

'It is over, Antonia. I am going away and I will not be back.'

She would not beg. She would not throw herself down and clutch at his legs to be dragged screaming up the shingle to the cottage. If she had believed for one second that such tactics would have been successful she would have resorted to them.

He turned and went back to the cottage, and when he had gone inside she ran up the little hill beside it, where she waited until she heard his car start up, and then she watched him drive out of her life.

Tony did not weep. Some grief is too deep for tears. When she had aborted the baby she had thought that she could experience no greater pain, but the pain that ravaged her now tore at her belly and her entrails just as the abortion had done. She prayed that she might die from such pain but she did not die.

It was weeks before she painted. She had thought to paint her own grief, but the painting that came was that of a man sitting in a rowing boat, staring helplessly out at what was and what might have been.

When the lawyer's letter came with the cheque in it that would keep her comfortably for the rest of her life, she almost destroyed the painting. Such appalling anger struck at her.

'How could he?' she moaned, and she raised the palette-knife to gut the painting, to destroy his grief, but she could not and instead she did her best to tear the cheque into as many pieces as possible.

Before she sent the pieces back to his lawyer she put the painting with its face to the wall in the attic and never looked at it again.

CHAPTER TEN
LONDON, 1999. PARIS, 1999. SCOTLAND, 1999

HOLLY DECIDED TO UNDRESS, wrap herself in one of the Royal Overseas League's bathrobes and order room service: a steak sandwich, a glass of red wine and coffee. An evening of absolute bliss beckoned.

The room telephone disturbed her before the first bite. Who, apart from Nicole and Otto, knew that she was in London?

'How did you know I was here?'

'It's lovely to talk to you too. My mother actually. Maybe this call wasn't such a great idea.'

'I'm sorry, Taylor, but you can't expect me to be thrilled to hear from you; unless you're calling to say you're lifting the ban.'

'No. I'm on my way to Paris.'

He stopped talking but she was full of a sense of disappointment and, strangely, of betrayal.

'And?' she prompted.

'I thought you might like to meet me.'

'Where? Paris?'

'Of course, Paris. It's a few hours, at most, from London. Get a single. I'll fly you back when I go pick up my mother.'

'Do you want us to meet so that we can discuss what your mother has told me?'

'Never occurred to me. I actually thought you might like to see the *Lohengrin*; definitely a girl's painting.'

She hung up and immediately snatched the receiver up again, but the connection was terminated.

Double damn. You are your own worst enemy, Holly Noble, but he is arrogant, believing that I would just jump to see him.

She heard the telephone again while she was in the bath and, telling herself that she was convinced it was Otto with important information, she got out, wrapped her towel around her and went to answer it.

'Hanging up is so rude, Holly.'

Holly stood there, telephone receiver in one wet hand, and laughed.

'Taylor, what's the hidden agenda here?'

There was silence for a while. 'Damned if I know,' he said at last. 'Maybe I just like you, Holly Noble. You're so . . . you're real, Holly.' Not beautiful, fascinating, intellectually challenging. Damn him.

'And you are impossible and I am going to hang up on you again. It gave me tremendous pleasure to cut you off,' she lied. 'You will thank me one day for pointing out, a little brutally perhaps, that you and your singing uncle are mere men.'

'Was,' he interrupted. 'He was a mere man. He just had to walk into a room for everyone to fall silent. In a restaurant other diners would stand when he walked in and clap until he sat down. He hated it but I couldn't breathe for excitement.' He stopped as if aware that he was giving too much of himself away. 'I was calling, politely, to ask you if you would like me to arrange for you to be allowed to see the painting.'

'Oh, the temptation. To see the only painting of Blaise Fougère as Lohengrin, painted by Tony at the beginning of his amazing career.'

She booked a return flight. The indispensable and unfailingly efficient Chandler met her and drove her to the opera house. He gave her a handwritten note from Taylor:

Have dinner with me this evening. We can compare notes on the undoubted quality of the painting.

Naturally she wanted to refuse but, just as naturally, since the note was deliberately written to annoy her, she accepted.

France was proud of Blaise Fougère. The painting had been moved in 1989 from its original home in the magnificent Opéra de Paris Garnier to the new Opéra Bastille, and was hanging where every opera-goer was bound to see it. Holly stood for a long time drinking it in. Taylor was so maddeningly, infuriatingly right, of course. It was a girl's picture. Lohengrin stood, the knight in white shining armour, his sword in his mailed hands. How young he looked and how vulnerable. He had suffered, oh, how he had suffered, but he would fight for right.

No, thought Holly, I am reading things here that I want to read. It was a chocolate-box cover. The handsome prince was just too good to be true.

She made her way back to the little hotel near the Sorbonne where she had arranged to stay and got ready for her dinner with Taylor.

Chandler drove her to a small inn on the way to Versailles, where Taylor was waiting for her.

'You know me, Holly, always looking for places where the food is great. I hope it meets with your approval, and selfishly I hope Marin will be content not to expand.'

'It's more elegant inside than I had expected,' said Holly, looking at the snowy tablecloths and crystal glasses.

Taylor smiled and called the waiter, and Holly sat half hearing his faultless French and wondering what she could tell him about the portrait of his uncle. Should she admit that it disturbed her almost as much as the *des Grieux* had done?

'She painted them at approximately the same time, in the same year anyway, and the *Lohengrin* is painted with so much . . .'

'Adoration?' Taylor suggested, almost with a simper.

'Understanding,' said Holly crossly. But she had had no lunch and the warm, smooth wine had slipped easily down into an empty stomach so she smiled. 'No one stood up when you came in, Taylor.'

'I am a mere man, Holly,' he said indulgently, refusing to fight. 'All I have is money,'

'And good looks,' said Holly judiciously.

Taylor laughed and leaned back in his chair, elegant, soigné, sophisticated . . . amused. '*Merci mille fois*. You have had too much wine.'

Holly giggled. 'I know, but the paintings, Taylor. The *des Grieux* is almost as sad as the *Grief*.'

'No,' he said almost angrily. '*Grief* is a great painting; *des Grieux* is not. The artist was confused. When she painted *Grief* she knew what she was painting. Her personal grief is in it too.'

So he did know something about painting.

'I would like some coffee, please.'

He leaned towards her. 'Come back to my house, Holly. It's very pretty. Blaise left it to me and I'd like you to see it. It's probable that Tony was there.'

She looked at him steadily and knew that she wanted nothing so much as to return to his town house with him. She decided that was the effect of the wine. 'Not tonight, Taylor. I think I'm a bit squiffy.'

He leaned forward again. 'You are absolutely adorable when you're squiffy. We're having fun together. Isn't that pleasant?'

'Please take me back to my hotel.'

He did not argue.

She was now very, very sober.

Next morning, having paid her bill, she left and took an expensive taxi to the airport. It was as if she feared that he would stop her.

I In the ensuing weeks it was as if Scotland was trying Holly's mettle. She had forgotten that a day of showers was, alas, often followed by a day of showers. Holly stayed closeted in the cottage, reading, thinking and looking out at the bay. Then the postman cycled down the hill and brought her a letter from Taylor.

Why do we always fight, Holly? Maybe you should try to get along with me for Tony's sake. Running away was so childish. What in God's name did you think I intended to do to you?

Holly blushed when she read that. She decided not to think about Paris. Remembering Paris made her remember Taylor and those few moments in the restaurant when she had been so sure they were becoming . . . friends. Stupid Holly, to think that a man who has had the world given to him as a birthright might like Holly Noble. She picked up one of the photographs of the paintings and stared at it, at the absurdity of it: the tall elegant man, the skinny little girl. She willed it to surrender its secrets. She tried and tried, but her memories of Blaise Fougère existed only in the paintings.

SOMEDAY, SOMEWHERE

She went upstairs to take a hot bath in the huge, deep, old cast-iron tub. There was a lovely memory there; why had she not noticed that the great iron feet on which the tub stood above the floor had had their toenails painted quite recently?

Did he laugh too, Tony?

If I sell the cottage will I stipulate that the successful buyer must paint the bath's toenails?

Holly laughed at her absurdity. Anyone who bought the cottage would no doubt put in modern plumbing.

It was late so she pulled on a long-sleeved nightgown that she had found among Tony's clothes. She pulled the letter out and read it again.

Why do we always fight?

Because we don't like one another, that's why, Boy Genius.

She stood up and stretched and Taylor's letter fell into the fireplace. She reached down for it and then threw it onto the embers; for a few seconds it sat there turning red and then it burned quite satisfactorily.

Spring-cleaning, that's the answer. And improvements.

She began next day to clean the cottage from top to bottom. The ghosts who sometimes accompanied her up the stairs and into the studio were friendly and she did not fear them. She would be pleased to have their company. She was halfway up the stairs when she remembered. A ring. That was what Tony had always worn, not the lovely jewels reposing in stately isolation in Henry Gilbert's safe. Jeans, a man's shirt and round her neck a gold chain with a heavy ring suspended from it. But, oh, how many years was it since she had seen that ring?

Her memory was playing tricks with her because she seemed to have seen the ring recently, but Tony had not worn it in the past twenty years. Blaise must be wearing it in one of the portraits. She would look at them again carefully when she returned to London.

She cleaned until hunger drove her downstairs. She made tea and a cheese sandwich and sat in the chair at the window looking at the view.

How unusual. There was a car coming down the hill towards the bay. Who could it be at this time of night? Poachers would hardly be so bold. She went swiftly to the door and locked it, feeling slightly silly. Then she turned off the lamp and went to the window. The car had come into the driveway. Something had to be wrong. It must be the police.

But it wasn't. The car stopped. The lights went out. The door opened. Taylor. It was Taylor.

A million feelings, thoughts, sensations, chased one another around in her head and for some inexplicable reason in the pit of her stomach.

'Holly, open up. Damn it all, I saw the light.'

Exultate. She tried unsuccessfully to stifle her excitement. Yes, indeed, Taylor Hartman. Who else would travel thousands of miles and then swear at the person he had come to see?

Holly hurried to the door and tried to open it, but she had forgotten she had locked it and struggled with it.

'Goddamn it, Holly, I need the bathroom and a cup of coffee.'

'Stop shouting. There, I forgot I locked it.'

'How can you forget?' he muttered angrily as he pushed past her. When he came downstairs again, she looked at his face and saw lines of strain and fatigue. Where had he been? Had he come from Tokyo, or from Rio, just to speak to her? 'I'll make some coffee.'

She went into the kitchen. On the marble shelf in the pantry were two beautiful venison sausages that she decided to cook for him. She put on the kettle and prepared the coffee. No doubt he would complain about instant. But when she went through to the living room, he said nothing, for he had fallen asleep. She stood holding the tray, looking down at him. How vulnerable he looked when he was asleep. She put the tray down with a thump. John had also been able to look vulnerable and put-upon when it suited him.

'I cooked some of those venison sausages you like; they're not burned this time,' she added diffidently.

He sat up, rubbing his eyes like a little boy, and it was then that she saw the ring. Tony's ring. Blaise's ring. Taylor was wearing it.

'You're wearing Blaise's ring.'

He looked casually at his hand. 'He gave it to me for luck when I went to college. I always wear it now.'

She sat drinking her coffee while Taylor demolished the sausages and the toast she had made to accompany them. At last he sat back with a sigh. 'I remember this room as having a spectacular view,' he said.

She opened the curtains and he stared out into the night.

Had Blaise said something like that each time he returned to Torry Bay? Had Tony sat in the window watching him eat?

Holly got up abruptly. She was not Tony and he was certainly not Blaise. 'It's late, Taylor. Perhaps you could tell me why you are here.'

'And then you'll turf me out?'

'Oh, don't be ridiculous. There is nowhere for you to go. You can have the big room. I've never been able to sleep there.'

'Thank you.'

Was that all he was going to say? He had flown thousands of miles—why? She would not ask.

'I'm tired, Holly, and I'm not at my best when I'm tired so please don't fight me. That's all you ever want to do, fight, fight, fight.'

'Me? Me fight? Taylor Hartman——'

'See,' he challenged. 'I open my mouth and you're shouting at me.'

She stared angrily back at him and then capitulated. 'You're right. I'm sorry. Would you like to go to bed, Taylor?'

Hearing what she had just said she coloured violently, but he merely smiled. 'Is there water for a shower?'

'There's plenty of scalding water but no shower.'

'No big deal. Good night—and thanks, Holly.'

She did not move from her chair. 'Good night.'

A few minutes later she heard the sound of water cascading into the deep bathtub, and then Taylor's voice. 'Hey, that's neat—toenails!'

Holly was so aware of every move he made. When he was safely in the tiny bathroom she hurried up to her room and sat on the edge of her bed. She tried hard not to listen and even harder not to picture him. Eventually she heard him enter the room next door and then nothing until the early summer sun played on her eyelids and woke her. 'Well, Achahoish, are you not determined to let our visitor see you at your best,' she said as the soft purply blue that was the Argyll landscape spread itself out for her admiration.

Taylor was already in the tiny kitchen and he handed her a mug of coffee when she went down. 'Thanks. Taylor, why are you here?'

'I don't know,' he said simply. 'I always seem to do something wrong around you.'

'Like closing the exhibition.'

'It's temporary; Otto's lawyers are in there slugging too. I wish I could make you . . . never mind. If you have no plans for the day I thought you could show me Edinburgh. The art gallery there, at someplace called the Mound, has some of Tony's paintings.'

She looked at him. What was going on behind that surely deceptively friendly façade? 'Well, looking at my aunt's wonderful paintings beats spring-cleaning. To be honest it never occurred to me that there would be paintings of hers hanging there.'

He waited without complaining while she changed, and then he drove as fast as the law allowed towards Edinburgh.

'I had a girlfriend in college,' he said as they stood looking at the majesty of the city, 'who came to Edinburgh for the arts festival. She told me she walked around poking all those buildings; she was convinced Disney put them up the night before, just for her.'

'They're real all right. Taylor, how did you know there are paintings by Tony here?'

'Chandler,' he answered simply.

As they entered the National Gallery of Scotland Holly found that she was almost holding her breath.

The huge landscape dominated a wall of one of the galleries. It was the view from the point and captured a winter squall. The waves had been whipped up by fierce winds and such was the skill of the artist that the viewer stepped back from the painting as if afraid of the power of the elements. 'Powerful work,' Taylor said.

'You interested in Tony Noble?' The custodian's voice startled them.

'Yes,' said Taylor. 'We were told there is another painting.'

'Aye. We have two. Priceless, I think, especially now the poor woman's dead. There was a lecturer round the other day with some students. A great artist, was what he said. Well known just after the war, but she produced less and less and rarely exhibited. The professor said he'd read that some paintings were discovered in America. But you're an American, sir, you'll know.'

'No,' said Taylor, his eyes very carefully studying *Storm at Achahoish*. 'They were found right here in Scotland. Where is the other painting?'

'Through there. It's an old man, nicest face you ever saw in your life.'

They knew the painting immediately. It was of a tall stooped figure with an almost ethereal quality to the lined aesthetic face. He was standing, fork in hand, beside a small cairn of stones that he had removed from the obviously infertile soil. The painting was called *Vision*.

'Why that title?'

Holly remembered. 'He scratched a few old cabbages out of that inhospitable plot and yet he always hoped for roses.'

'That's the canon, then?'

Holly nodded. 'He was quite old when I met him,' she informed Taylor. 'He had retired and lived in a monastery near Oban.'

'Catholic, I guess.'

'Oh, yes. Roman Catholic. Like Blaise? I suppose he didn't believe in divorce.'

She could sense his tension. He seemed to draw inside himself.

'Look, she can paint. OK. We knew that before.'

They spent just over an hour in the gallery, and three hours later they had walked up to the castle, taken a guided tour, gone into the Camera Obscura, next to the castle, and had walked back down the Royal Mile to the palace, stopping to see several historic buildings on the way.

'Know what I'd like?' said Taylor. 'Lasagne. Let's find an Italian restaurant and then I'll drive you home.'

She tensed as she made quick calculations and he laughed. 'This isn't a seduction, Holly. We'll eat, I'll drive you home and then I'll find a hotel. Maybe I'll come back here.'

Holly hardly knew whether to be annoyed or relieved. Yet Achahoish was a long way—even for a driver like Taylor—and she did not want him in the cottage. Not tonight, not after a lovely day when they had been so relaxed and at ease, with the spectre of the exhibition and Taylor's court orders so far away. Neither did she want to stay at a hotel with him. Damn him. 'I'll get a car. Please. That'll be easiest.'

'Your thoughts are written all over your face, Holly. I will drive you home. One, I'm starving and so must you be. Two, I like driving. Three, what would my mother say if I abandoned my date?'

'This isn't a date.'

'Explain that to my mother.'

Better to say nothing.

He hailed a cab and asked the driver to recommend a good Italian restaurant. Less than fifteen minutes later, Holly found herself sitting with a large glass of wine in her hand.

By the time the waiter brought their coffee, she was relaxed again, and it was not so late as she had thought it might be when they left Edinburgh for Argyll. They talked little. Holly's mind was too full of conflicting thoughts and opinions and she was content to look out of the window and watch Scotland flash past. At last they were well out of civilisation and heading into the artist's palette that was the west coast.

'No wonder they loved it so much,' she said at one point, but Taylor said nothing and Holly decided not to provoke him.

There was still light when they reached Torry Bay but nevertheless she felt he should not drive all the way back to Edinburgh.

'Taylor . . .' Holly began.

'You know what they say about opera, Holly? It's not over till the fat lady sings. Good night.'

She stood at the door and watched until the rear lights of the car had disappeared into the blue-black night.

Flowers in the Stream
TORRY BAY, 1957. LONDON, 1957

Tony hardly left the cottage for weeks after Blaise had left; she ate very little and she slept less. She did not paint and she did not listen to music. She existed. She was numb. She had cried and railed against life so much when she had had the pregnancy terminated that she felt there were no tears, no grief left. There was a bottle of wine in the kitchen and she wondered what would happen if she opened it, drank it all, and then walked out into the sea. But she left the wine inviolate, and that decision began the healing, if healing there was.

One day when she woke up she was hungry and when she looked in the mirror she was ashamed. She bathed and dressed in clean clothes and walked to the village for groceries.

Chrissie looked at her and her old face crumpled. 'Ach, lassie, I'll no' ask you a thing but I'm here.'

Tony hugged her friend. 'I know,' she said.

She bought sausages and fish, bread, coffee and an apple. She hurried home, pricked the sausages all over and when they were squealing happily in an iron frying pan on the stove, walked up to her letterbox to see if anyone had written to her.

There were several letters, and as she looked through them it was only the smell of burning sausages that alerted her to near disaster in her kitchen. She ran back just in time to throw the frying pan into the sink and to pull down the curtains at the window in an attempt to douse the fire.

Blast! Blast! Blast! I've burned my hands. She was a painter and she had burnt her hands! She would have to go back to the village to see Simon.

'You look awful,' he told her kindly as he bandaged her hands.

'Well, it was either my hands or my home,' she said and he laughed.

'They are just burns on your hands, Tony. It's the rest of what ails you that really troubles me.'

'I've been busy,' she lied. 'When I'm painting I forget to eat.'

'With a new invisible paint? This postwar era is truly remarkable. Tony, old friend, even at Major Cunningham's elegant drinks party last Christmas there was paint ingrained on your hands . . . It's over, isn't it?' She said nothing but dropped her gaze from his face to his hands. They were hands she should paint.

'Would he have divorced his wife?'

She shook her head violently. 'No. Yes. I don't know. Maybe. All of the above. But I couldn't win him that way, Simon. He would have grown to hate me, perhaps more than he hates me now, and he would have loathed the scandal, and so would I.' She stood up. 'Thanks for this,' she said and walked out.

When she reached home she thought about starting a painting of Simon's hands. But memories of other hands came into her mind and the tears started again.

She crept into the little room at the top of the stairs and cried herself to sleep on the horsehair mattress.

SOMEDAY, SOMEWHERE

Morning came. Tony got out of bed and went to the window. Outside stretched a painting that was more beautiful than anything she could ever achieve. The rising sun on the sea, the sea as it caressed the shore, the mist that hovered almost lovingly over everything . . . they spoke of life. For the first time, it was all horrifyingly obvious.

I should have had my child and this should have been his room. He should have woken here every morning. She knew it would have been a boy. She could see him down there on the shore, dancing in and out of the waves, her baby sprite, his limbs strong and brown like his . . . Pain, worse than the pains of the abortion itself, gripped her again until she crouched down below the window and prayed to die.

But she did not die and eventually she got up and went outside to let the morning sun begin to heal her. I'll paint my grief, she decided. She climbed the hill behind the cottage and stood looking out to sea. Somewhere away over there, that's where he was. How long had it taken him to tear Toinette from his heart for the second time? Was it easier because she had murdered his baby?

My baby. My baby too. My son. My little son.

There were little blue flowers growing on the headland, pale blue petals, so lovely, so delicate. Forget-me-nots.

'Forget me not,' she cried desperately and threw the flower from her into the stream. It danced along. If it goes to the sea, it will reach him and he will remember and come back. Feverishly she pulled more flowers, and then she knelt down by the water and patiently tore each perfect little flower from the parent stem. One by one the tiny blue flowers tumbled bravely into the turbulent water. Oh, to have the courage to throw the husk that was Tony Noble in after them, to end this purgatory. She pulled herself to her feet and stumbled back to the cottage. They were upstairs, her unborn babies, her precious little cherubs.

Tony felt cold, so cold as she picked up her palette knife, colder still as she hacked her unborn babies from their fluffy clouds. Then she set fire to the pieces.

'Stupid. Idiot.' She started forward in dismay. 'No! No! My babies!' She reached for the burning pieces of the singing babies but she was too late. She had murdered her babies twice.

Simon found her and put out the fire before the other paintings, the cottage, and the painter herself went up in flames.

She tried to explain that she had not meant to burn the cottage down, that she had changed her mind and tried to rescue the painting. Her paintings were her children conceived in delight, born in mingled ecstasy and agony, but such talk embarrassed him.

Tony waited patiently for her hands to heal and then she painted Simon's hands and gave him the picture for Christmas. At dinner on Christmas Day he asked her to marry him.

'I've loved you for a long time, Tony, and I want to take care of you.' She had expected the question but not quite so soon. 'I still love him, Simon.'

'I know, but this can't be mended, Tony. He wants it broken. Think about it. It wouldn't be as it was with him but it would be peaceful, Tony, and perhaps we could have a child.'

'You deserve better, Simon. I can't marry you. I've always thought of myself as married to the baby's father . . .' She stood up. 'I must go, Simon. I have work waiting.'

He did not argue but walked her down to the cottage and waited until she was inside.

She began to work on *Flowers in the Stream*. It took her three years to finish it almost to her satisfaction and still it was not right, but then they never were. Nothing was ever perfect, not now, not without Blaise.

Frederick wrote. He had met a nurse, Gilda, in the mission station in Africa. They were going to be married. She must come to the wedding. Freddie the sexless, married. You bet I'll come, Frederick, just to see what humourless individual would take you on.

Her letter of acceptance was couched in more acceptable language. The wedding was to be in London in June. As the date grew nearer Tony found herself becoming quite excited. When had she last been in London? Three years, four? How ridiculous. She must visit the old galleries. One or two of them still kept in touch, and Klaus and his new partner, his son, Otto, had asked her to remember them. Perhaps she'd take *Flowers in the Stream* or *Lohengrin*.

Tony went to Frederick's wedding and said all the right things, and then when the happy couple were off on their honeymoon she found herself strangely reluctant to go back to Torry Bay.

She telephoned Otto.

'Tony, my dear, we thought you were dead. Lunch? Dinner? Breakfast? You name it.'

She laughed. He had not changed. 'A chat would be fine.'

'We have a new gallery. I did tell you you've never visited, never sent us anything.'

'Otto, I will come and I will talk about paintings.'

The new gallery in Bond Street was almost as elegant as Otto himself but much more masculine. Solicitously he helped her to a seat but as usual he made sure that she did not clash with his cushions. 'You have been ill and I have harboured such negative thoughts. I have looked, Tony, yes, I am compelled to confess, and I have looked, but you're not selling with anyone.'

'I haven't been painting.' She did not deny that she had been ill. 'My brother was married on Saturday and I came down for the wedding.'

'And the opera? Fougère is guesting with the Royal Opera. You painted him just after the war, didn't you? I could get you another commission there, my dear.'

She could hardly breathe for the pain in her heart. To hear him spoken of so casually . . . to pretend that the name meant nothing . . .

'I thought landscapes, seascapes.' She looked at the paintings on the walls with disdain. 'You're stealing from the illiterate, Otto.'

'Can you still paint better than any of them, Tony?'

She said nothing. Of course she could, with her eyes shut.

'Go home and paint me some pictures, Tony. Welcome home.'

Home to the world of paint and canvas and brushes and heartbreak or possibly immortality.

She was excited. She thought the excitement had gone but it was still there. She sat on the train and her mind saw blues and green and yellows and reds that sang clearly and defiantly.

I haven't lost everything if this has not deserted me.

CHAPTER ELEVEN
TORRY BAY, 1999. LONDON, 1999

THIS WAS WHERE SHE WAS going to live; ergo, she must make it more comfortable. She was not Tony who dealt cheerfully with an open fire and almost primitive plumbing. Holly put on a jacket and walked up to the village. The plumber was out on a call but would be sure to drop in on his way home. She returned to the cottage, got out the Yellow Pages and soon a very cheery voice was telling her of the advantages to be had from the use of a British Telecom land line.

'Just a telephone is fine, thank you.'

'We put in the line, missus, and points where you want them. You have to buy your own phones at a shop.'

'But you'll come as quickly as you can?'

'Oh, aye, I've put you down. A few weeks, no more.'

'A few weeks?' repeated Holly to herself as a loud knocking at the front door startled her.

'Hello, missus. We're Reid the plumbers.'

The men measured all the rooms, consulted her about the size and positioning of radiators, and were gone with a promise that they would drop in a catalogue for the latest in showers.

She went off to buy her telephones and settled on a dark green one for the living room and a red extension for the upstairs hall. Less than a week later she was surprised by a visit from the telephone company.

'Well, if you aren't the luckiest woman to be where you are. Another hundred metres down the coast and the cost of installing a land line would be ridiculous.'

Holly smiled. Yes, she was the luckiest woman to be where she was. The next few days were fine and dry and she spent them walking along the coast collecting driftwood. She could hardly believe how contented she was. She was not cut off, for now she had her beautiful new telephones. There was a radio but no television and so in the evenings Holly either listened to the radio or read a book. Most of the time, however, she thought. One day there was a note from Mr Reid to say that 'the bits are coming in soon.' She would be delighted to see them, bits and all. Soon Torry Bay would be a cottage to be reckoned with. She wondered what its inhabitants felt about the renovations.

Darling girl. Hollyberry.

She told herself that she was not talking to ghosts but merely clearing her mind of what had been happening as she prepared for the upheaval of the renovations. Why am I dusting? Have you any idea the amount of dust there is going to be in here over the next few weeks?

She decided to go for a long walk to clear her lungs. She did not expect her lovely new phones to ring because she had given no one the number, but she switched her mobile to answering service. When she returned she burnt herself some sausages but assured herself that that was how she liked them.

I wonder where Taylor is dining? What if I had gone to his house? Would I have felt Blaise's presence? Were you ever there, Tony?

Hollyberry.

I don't know what to do. I don't know what I want to do. Yes, I do. I want to make love to Taylor Hartman.

Damn it, I'm depraved or desperate or both. I'm certainly out of my mind. He is the most pig-headed, egotistical, conceited . . .

Hollyberry.

Oh, shut up.

Was there censure in the sigh, *Darling girl?*

Wonders of technology—she had messages, and Sod's Law prevailed. After weeks of silence someone had chosen to ring when she was out. She accessed her messages. John: 'Holly, you've punished me enough, don't you think? We need to talk . . .'

The fellow lived in Glasgow and could not bring himself to drive for two hours to petition her. Taylor Hartman flew thousands . . . Enough, enough. I don't love John any more. I do not love John.

Otto: 'Holly? Have you seen the German papers?'

Sure, Otto, they sell them on every street corner in Achahoish, she thought flippantly and then, Oh, God, why would he think I might want to read a German-language paper?

Shaky fingers managed to punch his number on her lovely red telephone. 'Otto, what German paper?'

'Good evening, Holly, how are you?'

'Fine.' Enough courtesy. 'What German papers?'

'I assume all of them. Someone has been doing some investigations. Now new publicity—and this morning, so many offers.'

'It's been weeks. How can they cover an exhibition that wasn't?'

'Oh, you know newspaper people,' he said vaguely. 'Somehow they get a seed and the seed germinates. They can't say anything when they know nothing; they are running some old stories and awakening interest, that's all. Not just in Blaise, of course, but whatever they can find on Taylor and the Hartman Corporation, and old press pieces on Tony.'

She didn't want to ask. 'Is there speculation about Eleanor?'

He was quiet, hesitant. 'She is mentioned, Holly, but the Hartman machine is powerful.'

'Otto, if you have leaked any of this I will never deal with you again.'

'Holly, I am going to make you rich.'

She hung up and went to sit, almost shaking, on the edge of her bed. Taylor will be furious and rightly. Oh, damn. Tony, you were wrong; how could you have thought he wouldn't care? Did you forget Blaise's sister was still alive? Had grief impaired your judgment?

It's just imagination that Taylor could care for me. In Paris, in Edinburgh, he seemed . . . I don't know, approachable, nicer. I wish he were here now. Love or lust? I lust all right. I wish he was here. I don't give a hoohah if there's a difference between love and lust. I want him here. I have no pride, no shame.

Les Bébés qui Chantent, Hollyberry.

133

I want a baby, Tony, but not for you.

Oh, damn, this is so sad.

She undressed, pulled a cotton nightshirt over her head and climbed into bed. Then she climbed out again, padded across to the red telephone and dialled John's number.

'You have reached John Robertson . . .' Damn all answering services.

'John. I'm sorry. There is no nice way of saying it. I meant what I said. It's over. I'm sorry but please don't contact me again. Good luck with the election. I'm sure you'll win.'

It was hours before she slept.

The plumbers arrived just before eight the next morning. The only way to avoid the constant hammering was to walk for miles along the shore and the only thing to do while walking was to think about wasted lives and wasted opportunities and to resolve for the millionth time that 'It's not going to happen again.'

The plumbers were leaving as she got back to the cottage. 'That wee phone thing has fair been ringing.'

I just bet it has. John must have been stunned.

It was Taylor. Taylor? Of course. She had forgotten she had given him her mobile number.

'I called last night but you had it switched off.'

'Yes.'

'I wanted to know if Otto von Emler has been in touch.' Damn, damn, damn. 'I was out of your hair, Holly, but you had to let the papers have these stories. Mother and I are returning to London next week. She says there is something she wants to tell you.'

'Then you had better have my new number. Long calls on mobiles are so ridiculously expensive, Taylor.'

She heard him suck in his breath. 'Thank you,' he said when he had noted her brand-new number. 'She'll be in touch. I will stay well away but I am toying with the idea of breaking Otto's neck.'

'Don't be silly.'

'One last chance. I give you personally five million dollars and you allow me to keep the paintings in a vault for twenty years. The Hartman Corporation will show them.'

'To whom? A few of your sycophantic, rich friends? You can't buy your way out of this one, Taylor.'

This time Taylor was the one who disconnected.

She sat down. The gentle beauty of the hills and the terrifying awesome beauty of the sea calmed her and focused her mind. First things first. Tony's paintings would be exhibited, and not after they had lain in some storage vault for another twenty years. She would go to London to see Mrs Hartman again and she would ask Otto to show her the articles in the foreign press.

'**D**ear Holly. How lovely to see you. I take it this means Taylor is in town?'

'I would like to see the papers, Otto.'

Otto altered the position of an orchid on his desk a fraction of an inch. 'I have them here. Shall I read them to you? British education is so lacking.'

'I can manage the French. You read me the German.'

'It is no fun teasing someone who refuses to react, Holly.' He saw that she was in no mood for idle chatter. 'Very well. Here we are.'

He handed Holly some cuttings from various European papers and she trusted him to translate the German ones correctly. The French she stumbled through but refused to ask his help. All in all, there was more of the pap that had been printed at the time of the exhibition.

'Taylor is going to . . . "break your neck", I think were his words.'

'So violent, and it is nothing to do with me. I am sitting here, working hard for all my clients. I have given no interviews that I have not discussed with you, Holly, and remember that I have been in New York. I cannot starve to death while I wait for busy judges to lift the injunction.'

Holly looked at him with equal measures of annoyance and affection. 'You're an old fraud, Otto. I'm off. Nicole Hartman has something important she wants to share. Why didn't you tell me she was a client?'

He did not even look abashed. Otto, too, had his ideas about loyalty. 'But my clients' names are not mine to bandy about, Holly, not without permission.'

She had arranged to meet Nicole for lunch at the Royal Overseas Club. They ordered from the menu and sat quietly among the other diners, and it was as if Nicole had no idea how to bring up what she wanted to discuss. Eventually Holly asked, 'Madame, there is a break in the dates of the paintings. Have you any idea why there are so few paintings from the 1950s?'

'I believe you have no children, Holly,' was the strange answer. 'I managed, with enormous effort, to produce one. I think I would kill for him,' said Nicole simply. 'Tony probably felt for you as I do for my son, especially since . . .'

Holly went cold. 'Yes, madame.'

'Holly, do the words, *Les Bébés qui Chantent* mean anything to you?'

'I can translate them, madame.'

'It was a painting. Blaise said it was a masterpiece, like one of those Italian masters, the naked cherubs on the clouds. Tony started to paint it before the war but either she destroyed it or painted over it.'

'Why?' The question was barely a whisper.

'She had an abortion.'

Although she had already known the answer to her question, the confirmation made Holly feel desperately ill. She was cold and clammy and fought to control her heaving stomach. 'Why?' she managed to hiss. '*je ne sais pas*—I don't know. All I know is that Blaise came home and could not sing; he cancelled performances—something he did very rarely—but his voice, it was gone. He did not see her again for years. She had killed his Tosca, he said, his singing baby.'

Holly could bear no more. 'Excuse me.'

She managed to walk in a dignified manner through the tables of happy people and then rushed to the Ladies' room. Luckily it was empty. Nicole joined her there ten minutes later.

'I'm sorry, Holly. I was almost sure that you did not know and I deliberated about whether to tell you or not.'

Holly raised her tear-stained face. 'His baby, his Tosca. My God, what arrogance, what conceit. What about Tony's baby, Tony's pain?' She shook her head wildly. 'I can't handle how cruel your family is.'

Tentatively Nicole put her arms round the sobbing woman. '*Chérie*, we each look after our own. Of course I felt for Tony but at the time I had to succour my brother. Quite frankly I believed, and still do, that to nurture his voice for the world was my duty.'

'Everything Tony did was for your precious brother and his voice.'

'You cannot believe that she thought to abort would help his voice?'

Holly deflated like a little birthday balloon and she sagged against the smaller woman. 'I don't know. The answers are in the paintings.'

'Could you bear to go again?'

'Where is Taylor?'

Nicole looked surprised by the question. 'At this moment? I have no idea.'

'It's just that I would prefer him not to know that I am here; we parted . . . I don't know,' we didn't fight but . . . and then we tend to hang up on one another.'

'You thought he might want to sleep with you? You are afraid of him. He told me. He was hurt, Holly. I think I raised a gentleman.'

For a moment, Holly could say nothing. Her feelings for Taylor were so confused. 'I am not afraid of him,' she said at last, but did not add, 'I am afraid of myself.'

Nicole smiled. 'Let us have another private view. You are well again?'

Holly, who felt that she would never be well again, acquiesced. This time they looked at the dates of the paintings. It appeared that one had been produced almost every year from the time the pair had met in 1937 till Fougère's death when the last painting had been dated. There were two large gaps: the last years of the war and the years between 1957 and 1962, which Holly now so painfully understood. Invisible and inescapable magnets drew them to a large painting. Holly felt her stomach revolt again as she read the title. *Grief*, 1957. Blaise's sister and Tony's niece viewed the painting of the bowed figure in the rowing boat with deeper understanding.

'So much waste; so much tragedy. I cannot bear to look at it.'

'What about this one, madame? Tony worked on it for three years, between 1957 and 1960. Is that why it is so different, a new style? And it's not Blaise.'

It was a landscape and had been painted up on the hill behind the cottage. There was the cottage or a suggestion of the cottage and a figure kneeling by the stream with outstretched arms, and on the surface of the water, twisting in the currents, flowers, tiny blue flowers.

'It is, I believe, a companion to *Grief*, Holly, and they should go together. Look, it is Tony's grief. The flowers are forget-me-nots. Those years were hell for him and her . . . look at her pain. Men and their stupid pride: their honour. I tried, please, Holly, believe that I tried.'

'I can't take any more, madame.'

Having seen Nicole Hartman into her car, Holly walked back to her hotel. Her mind was fully engaged with the story of her beloved Tony and the abortion and the knowledge that Blaise Fougère had told his sister of his grief.

Taylor had the audacity to talk to his mother about me. What a family for sharing their woes.

She blushed again as she replayed the scenario of Taylor saying quite baldly, 'She thought I wanted to sleep with her.' The thought of them discussing her, perhaps laughing at her, made her squirm.

Once again the immediate necessity was for flight. She checked out and rushed to Euston Station as if something dreadful were pursuing her. Ten hours, two trains and a taxi ride later and she had reached her sanctuary.

At the front door she found Taylor asleep on the back seat of a rather small car.

137

Refuge from the Storm

NEW YORK, 1963. LONDON, 1963. TORRY BAY, 1963

'Blaise, why do you put yourself through this?'

He did not answer. He sat on the chair beside Eleanor's bed and he watched her sleep. Asleep she looked almost normal. Her husband could almost forget that she had just tried to kill herself, that it wasn't the first time, and that it was all his fault. He had loved Eleanor because they had told him Tony was dead, and then Tony—so alive, so desirable, so part of his skin, part of his blood, part of his breath—she had murdered his baby and so was dead again to him. And all that was left was the great tenor and this shell who occasionally roused herself enough to try to end it all.

'How amazingly fragile is a human being,' Blaise said, and his sister, Nicole, so French, so practical, had looked down at the exquisitely nightgowned form of her sister-in-law and had said, '*Au contraire, mon brave*, as tough as old boots. If she didn't hold on so hard you would be free to marry Toinette.'

He had pushed away her loving hand, had turned his face away.

'Divorce her, Blaise,' Nicole hissed at the broad back that was all she could see. 'She doesn't know. She doesn't care.'

'It's my fault. She feels she failed me by not giving me a child. I will never desert her.'

Eventually Blaise heard the tap-tap of his sister's expensive highheeled shoes as she gave up and left the private hospital room. He smoothed the lace ruffles on the nightdress. He had them copied in Paris from her wedding trousseau. To dress Eleanor in the gowns that had made her feel pretty was a small thing to do.

The nurse was there. 'She'll sleep for a while, Mr Fougère. We could call you if there's a change.'

He did not look up. 'I'll stay.'

Tomorrow he had to go to London. He was going to sing *Otello* there for the first time.

On the plane Blaise studied the score. He did not need to, for he had been studying it for years, but if he thought about *Otello* his mind would not be free to think about . . . anything else.

London. He had sung in every major opera house in the world. The Met owned part of his heart, the Paris Opera House another part, but Covent Garden owned his soul, the only opera house where he kissed the floor the first time he entered it again.

He liked walking around London, though it was more difficult now that television was making singers part of popular culture. He went to Bond Street and looked in the windows of the exclusive shops and galleries. Outside one gallery, he began to tremble and had to lean against the plate glass for support. The window held one painting: *Flowers in the Stream.*

He recognised the hill behind the cottage where he had been so often with Tony, and he recognised the stream. He knew the artist, even without looking at the signature. He could see her, a cigarette that she never drew on hanging from her lip, her hair a mess and covered in paint as stress made her constantly touch it. He recognised the tiny figure on the hill and only he in the world knew that he had dealt the blows from which the frail figure cowered as she tossed her little flowers into the stream. He could not enter the gallery. He hailed a taxi and went back to his hotel from where he sent Stefan to buy the painting.

Stefan had been almost afraid to return.

'It's not for sale. It's a come-on. Really quite unfair. You may commission from it and there are some nice landscapes.'

'You bought them?'

'No, sir. I thought—'

'I don't pay you to think. Buy them. Use cash. Try again for the *Flowers.* Think of a number, Stefan, and double it. I rely on you.'

Stefan was ready to weep when he returned. He had managed to buy one small view of Torry Bay. The others had been sold almost as soon as they had been hung in the gallery.

'When may I have the painting?'

'Saturday, Monsieur. The show ends then.'

He would send Stefan for the painting. No, he would go himself. No, Toinette would be there. He no longer loved her, but there was no point in exposing old wounds.

He had a rehearsal on Saturday. It did not go well. It was the first time he had worn the armour breastplate and it constricted his chest; he could not breathe, never mind sing.

'There is room there for his chest expansion,' fumed the costume designer to the director. 'Chaliapin could get into it.'

'I know it and you know it but he doesn't know it.'

She took it away to adjust it. He tried again. He felt strangled.

'I can't sing in this breastplate.' He tried to remain calm. He hated fuss of any kind and especially when he was causing it. 'Maybe it's the neckline. Can we lower the neckline?'

'I can lower it all the way to your damned diaphragm and you'll still complain that it can't expand.'

'You wear it yourself and sing Otello,' he shouted at her and stalked off the stage.

Blaise Fougère was not known for his tenor angst but now he had walked off and Hilary Stewart, one of the best designers in the business, was in tears.

The director looked at his Desdemona who was world famous for her tantrums. She smiled at him sweetly. 'Tenors,' she said demurely. 'Well, I can't make love to the pot plants, darling. Shall we have lunch?'

'Lunch for the principals,' shouted the director and went off in search of his Otello, who was in a rehearsal room with a répétiteur. The 'Exultate', Otello's proud boast as he jumps ashore from his ship, was ringing out again and again and again perfectly.

'You see,' he said, turning to the director, who had entered the room. 'I am not difficult. That must be perfect and it is so difficult to get right with no build-up. It's the armour.'

'Absolutely. Let's go across to the pub for a beer and a sandwich.'

Blaise took the young pianist's hand and kissed it. 'Thank you, Marian. I was so worried.'

'It's the armour,' she said.

'It's his head,' mouthed the director as he ushered his star out.

'Blaise, we'll relax, have a beer, come back and try again. Shoots the hell out of the afternoon schedule but heck.'

Blaise sat back in an alcove in the pub and realised that he had managed to avoid having a free afternoon. Had he been free he might just have gone to Otto's gallery to pick up Toinette's painting . . . No, ridiculous, it was the armour that constricted his chest expansion. He had proved it was the armour. He sat forward, smiling, and refused the offer of a beer. 'Do they have avocados? I had the best sandwich in San Francisco last season: avocado, bean sprouts, tomato.' He kissed his fingers.

'You'll have to go back to California, *mon ami*,' said the director, and they both laughed. 'I hate English bread though, don't you?'

Mrs Lumsden and her home-baked bread. Mrs Lumsden dead in the war. 'Some is fine,' he said quietly. 'When I've finished I'll buy flowers for Hilary. She had my measurements wrong, but it will be perfect now. *Pauvre petite*, I am sure she is, at this very moment, working hard.'

The director, Yannis, smiled. No way would he tell the tenor that Hilary was spending her lunch break eating yoghurt while she stuck pins in a full-length picture of Blaise Fougère. No prizes for where most of them were going.

That afternoon, the soprano walked off the stage. 'Your tenor is deliberately upstaging me and, in the love duet, which is so crucial for me, so important, he's making sure the audience can't see my face.'

She refused to come back unless Blaise apologised.

Blaise was intransigent. '*Non*. Call any soprano in the world, they'll say I never upstage. Besides, I'm not hiding her pretty little face. How can I when I'm beside her? Get her cover in. That will bring her out here *rapidement*.'

The strategy served merely to have the soprano's manager call in her lawyers.

'Please, Blaise. I'm on my knees,' begged Yannis.

'Then get off them. This is ridiculous. I shall sing *"Gia Nella Notte"* with little Miss Sofrani, and I shall sing full voice. I may even kiss her, gently yet lingeringly, as we walk off stage to Otello's "Paradise". Yes, I will. I will then walk past Madama's dressing room telling the world how exquisite is the Sofrani and how thrilled I am that she is to have this chance. Then I am going to the gym.'

Hilary showed how grateful she was for his apology by slipping into the weeping soprano's dressing room and managing to suggest that 'your bloody tenor has the hots for Sofrani, Madama. Don't let him get away with chasing you off.'

Capitulation, not one hundred per cent gracious, but capitulation.

Then the rehearsal was over and it was still only four fifteen and he had forgotten to tell Stefan to pick up the picture. He wanted to go to the gym. He needed the exercise.

He walked to the gallery. The flowers painting was gone from the window and a new group of canvases were up on the pale wall.

'May I help you, sir?' He had not heard the gallery owner approach across the miles of deep carpeting.

'I bought a painting,' he began.

Otto von Emler clapped his hands together reverently. 'Monsieur Fougère, what an incredible honour.' The young, very effeminate man spoke perfect French. 'So you are the real Mr Lazlo. I wondered—'

'Stefan Lazlo is my secretary. May I have the painting?'

'Of course and . . . yes, I hoped so.' He broke off as he looked over Blaise's shoulder. 'Tony, my dear, one of your admirers.'

Tony was standing in the doorway. When Blaise turned, she went quite white and grabbed the door handle as if for support.

Blaise took a step forward. 'Toinette,' he said.

Otto looked from one to the other and many things became quite clear to him. 'I'll just wrap your picture, Mr Fougère,' he said, but he knew that his customer neither knew nor cared what he was saying.

'*Flowers in the Stream*,' Blaise said. 'I saw it. Oh, God, forgive me, Toinette, forgive me.'

'Please,' she whispered, 'please don't do this to me. Take your picture and go.'

'I saw the picture, Tony. It's you. I know what it means.'

'It means you hurt me six years ago. Almost as much, I suppose, as I hurt you. But the girl in the painting no longer exists. You don't have to feel sorry for her. She's fine.'

'But I'm not, Toinette. I feel sorry for me.'

'That's good,' she said coldly. 'The catch in the voice . . . use that in *Otello*.' She turned away from him and ran out, and he was too stunned to follow her.

Otto, who had watched everything through the glass walls of his office, came out, essaying a smile. 'I've wrapped the painting, monsieur. A little gem. I wish she would sell *Flowers in the Stream* or other work like it, but it's just the landscapes she does for sales, and her swans.'

His distinguished customer said nothing.

'I have one of the swans in my private office, monsieur.'

Blaise put up his hand. Otto had seen it raised like that so often on the stage, a graceful gesture. 'Don't intrude,' it said.

He intruded. 'I don't want to sell it to you, monsieur, but I do think you should look at it. Please.'

Blaise looked at him and Otto saw the desolation in his eyes. 'You really ought to see it, sir.'

Blaise went with him.

The painting was small. Blaise recognised the bay and the headland. In the bay, but heading for the shore, was a swan, a magnificent and very beautiful bird. There was a tiny blur of gold just above its proud head. Did the artist mean it? His heart, which had seemed to stop beating when Tony had left, began to race. He leaned forward and laughed. How did she do it? Close up, the little blur became a crown. He looked at Otto and smiled.

'Once she called it Lohengrin,' Otto said. 'When I asked her she said, "It's just a swan." But I don't think it's just a swan. *Au revoir*, Monsieur Fougère. Enjoy your painting.'

Blaise picked up his picture and tucked it under his left arm. Then he held out his hand and Otto shook it.

'It's an honour, monsieur,' he said, and Blaise knew that he was not referring to the sale of the painting.

In the street Blaise looked for Tony but he knew that he would not find her. He knew where she would be. Not tonight, and he could not get there anyway, but one day soon . . . he almost skipped to the edge of the pavement to hail a taxi. When he got back to his hotel he took the little painting and propped it up on his dressing table. He touched the headland delicately.

Don't touch, don't touch. There's oil on your fingers.
I know, ma mie, I know.
Forgive me Toinette.

Otello was a triumph. It had to be recorded. It had to be televised for future showing. His work was always his number one priority, but he had to get away. At last Blaise looked at his schedule, so carefully crossed and recrossed by the meticulous Stefan, and there were two whole days.

'I'm going to Scotland.'
'Very good, sir.'

On the plane he fretted. He must not read anything into her painting of the swan as the legendary Lohengrin. It was an artist's joke, no more. It did not mean that she hoped one day to see her love arrive on the wings of a princely swan to save her from all evil. She hated him. But then she had known he was to sing *Otello.* If she hated him, would she still be aware of his schedule? She liked music. No doubt she had asked the Garden for a schedule of their forthcoming productions. He would arrive in Torry Bay and she would not be there.

He arrived in Torry Bay and she was not there.

Until the moment he saw the cottage he had believed deep down that she would be waiting for him, ready to listen, to allow him to beg, and then to give him another chance. It was raining slightly and the cottage looked forlorn, unloved. How foolish to come all this way. He turned off the engine and got out of the car. One last look from the headland.

Dear God, it was beautiful. Until this moment he had not understood that Torry Bay as well as Toinette had become a part of him. At least he had the little picture. He would carry it everywhere with him. He looked at the hollow.

Love me, Toinette, love me.
We are so near the cottage.
I can't wait.

He had to get away from here. In another second he would be sobbing like a child. He held up his hand, as he had done countless times on stages all over the world. *Goodbye,* was what that graceful gesture said, and the fans knew he would not return, no matter how they clapped.

143

She was standing beside his car, an overnight bag at her feet. She looked up and saw him. He began to walk towards her, slowly, fearful of rejection. When he was closer he saw the expression in her eyes and he began to run.

He did not deserve her. He did not deserve her love, her compassion, her giving. She gave and gave and gave and never seemed to resent the unfairness of the giving. He knew it, he understood it, but he could not find the words in any of his languages.

'Toinette. Toinette.' He could not go on. All he could do was hold her, kiss her cheeks, her hair, her lips.

'It's all right,' she said. 'I understand. *Je comprends, ma mie. Ma mie.*'

He held her, looked deep into her eyes and on the pebbled path he fell to his knees, his hands sliding down her painfully thin body until he was clasping her around the knees. He pushed his head against her belly, against the womb from which she had in physical and mental agony expelled his child, their baby, their singing cherub, and he wept. As always, she lifted him up, and comforted him.

'It's all right. I understand. *Je comprends. Je t'aime*, Blaise. I have never stopped loving you.'

'A baby,' he began. 'It was so . . . I was wrong, Toinette, so wrong, and I have paid.'

'It's over and you're here. I was wrong too and I have paid. If you love me, we can go on.'

'I am nothing without you, Toinette. I perform, but I am a man without a heart, Toinette. I left it here.'

'But you had mine, my dear. You always had mine.'

They turned, arm in arm, and walked slowly towards the cottage. She said nothing but held his hand more tightly as they reached their old room and turned towards each other, their flesh burning as it had burned with unfulfilled longing when they were younger.

Tony began to paint *Refuge from the Storm* while Blaise was driving back to London. She painted their beloved headland: she painted the sky, glowering and lowering. She painted the seas, grey and whipped up, and she painted Lohengrin and his family as they returned for shelter to the bay.

But on the headland she painted two figures. The man held the woman in his arms, his broad shoulders protecting her frail figure from the winds that raced in from the sea. He was her refuge. She lost herself in him and she never appreciated that hers was the strength that allowed him to be what he was. Only towards the ends of their lives did she understand exactly what she meant to him.

CHAPTER TWELVE
TORRY BAY, 1999

HE WAS THE LAST PERSON in the world she wanted to see. She had cried long despairing tears on the journey from London, and now when she needed two aspirin and a hot bath, there was Taylor, come to say what?

'Would you like to have dinner with me, Holly?'

Someone around here is crazy. 'How did you get here, you lunatic? Are you stalking me?'

He laughed. 'This new thing, invented by an American; it's called the airplane.'

She was seeing three of him. None of them looked good. 'I really don't think I can face you tonight, Taylor.' She turned and walked away from him towards the cottage. She reached the cool, dark haven of her single room and lay down, fully clothed, on the bed. She was just drifting off to sleep when someone knocked on the door.

He couldn't. He wouldn't. Surely he doesn't think he's so irresistible.

'Go away,' she said furiously.

'Room service.'

She got up and opened the door. Taylor stood there with a tray. On it there was a cup of something that steamed and a small foil-wrapped packet. Silently she stood aside to let him enter the room and put the tray down. He said nothing but left as quietly as he had come.

I don't want to like Taylor.

Hours later her new telephone rang. She was conscious of a warm glow of expectation. 'We have to talk, Holly.'

'Where are you?'

'In that little inn where we had lunch.'

'All I want to know is when you are going to have the court order lifted?'

'I can't.'

'Today—yesterday—I found out that your precious uncle was a first-class bastard who put my aunt through hell. You knew about the abortion, didn't you?'

She heard him gasp. 'Abortion? I can't believe it. He was—'

'So full of his career and his image that he let my aunt abort their baby and then he dumped her. Goodbye, Taylor.' She slammed the receiver down, stood silently for a moment and then opened the door to let the peace of Achahoish permeate the cottage. She went out and walked up to the point and looked at the bay that still lay wrapped in night. She turned and looked back at the cottage and saw the moon reach up behind the stone walls, setting fire to the roof, the chimney stacks, the rhododendron bushes. How unruly they were becoming, Tony had always kept them well cut back.

Suddenly exhaustion so intense it was almost tangible wrapped her in its folds and she struggled back to the cottage, climbed the stairs and fell face down on her little-girl bed. She woke six hours later.

The front door stood wide open and two sheep were in the living room. One black face stared at her unconcernedly from where she was demolishing the rug before the fire, and the other presented a fine rear view as she stood with front hoofs up on the table. She had eaten a sizeable piece of the red-and-white gingham tablecloth and would no doubt have eaten the rest of it had her hostess not disturbed her. She dropped down, whirled round and skittered out of the door, scattering black droppings widely in her wake.

'Oh, damn you, sheep,' yelled Holly, and the other ewe jumped up and galloped after her sister.

'Not a job I relish on an empty stomach,' complained Holly as she seized the broom and swept the sheep's gift out of the door. But by the time she had finished and had made some coffee, she was laughing. She picked up her coffee cup and, locking the door behind her, walked up to the point. On her way back, refreshed and reinvigorated, she saw the little red van belonging to the local postman turn off the road and crawl down to Torry Bay.

There were letters from London, Glasgow and Edinburgh. Mr Gilbert had sold several pieces for her and told her she needed to speak to a financial consultant about the best way to handle the money. The people who were buying her flat wanted it complete with furniture. Otto wanted to know her feelings about holding the paintings in storage.

Holly telephoned him in his office.

'I lunched with Mrs Hartman before she flew back to New York,' he told her. 'She says her son is still adamant about refusing to allow us to sell. Wants to compromise, I believe.'

'Yes. He wants to hide the paintings for twenty years. I should have told you. After that they can be exhibited. But I've decided I'm not prepared to wait. I want to see Tony's name in lights.'

SOMEDAY, SOMEWHERE

'Even if it means completely alienating Taylor?'

'Why on earth should you think that his opinion matters to me at all?'

He laughed. 'Dear Holly,' he said, and hung up.

Later, Holly took her favourite long walk along the coast. After a while, she turned and looked back at the cottage. The light from the lamp she had left on in the living room shone with a friendly welcome. Her heart filled with emotion.

I'm happy.

Life was not perfect but it was damned good. Was it the cottage that had seen deep love, appalling tragedy and grief? The echoes of the tragedies were long since gone. All that remained in the old stone walls was the memory of all-encompassing love. Did its ghosts welcome her return as the little light did?

Darling girl.

I can manage. Mr Right would be nice but I can manage.

She would paint the cottage and when she was bored she would walk on the beach and collect shells. She would light a fire and sit before its flickering warmth, reading. She could almost smell security.

A car was parked outside the cottage.

It was Taylor.

'Go away.'

He stood waiting for her to open the cottage. For a few minutes she stood looking at him. 'I'm not leaving, Holly, not till you explain. I called my mother. "Holly's right," she says. My uncle wanted children. Open the door or do we stand and yell at one another right here?'

It was no use. She gave in. She unlocked the door and walked before him into the cottage.

Hollyberry. Darling girl.

She smiled. 'Open the shutters while I make some coffee,' she said.

He did as he was bid and then sat looking out of the window at the sea. Idly he played with the stones. Holly 1964, Holly 1972. 'Cute,' he said and he smiled, but his eyes were sad.

She put two mugs of coffee on the table. 'There's nothing to eat,' she said ungraciously and this time he smiled with his eyes too.

'I know your erratic housekeeping. I brought your supper, the one you wouldn't have with me last night. I even brought the wine.'

'I'm not having supper with you.'

'Why ever not?' he asked. 'Even the condemned man gets a last meal. Holly, my mother says you are right but I know my uncle would never have encouraged abortion. I know it.'

147

He turned. His posture reminded her . . . Blaise, of course. 'Whether he spelt it out or wrote the cheque for the doctor's bill or did nothing doesn't matter. He let it happen.'

He sank down into the chair by the window. 'He didn't know, Holly. If he knew, why *Grief*? Why Tony's masterpiece?'

That thought had not occurred to her. 'All right. He did not tell Tony to abort but it looks like she was so crazy about him that she dared not tell him. The great tenor's career must not be disturbed. She loved him so much that . . .' She was crying again, great choking tears that tore at her throat. 'I hate him,' she sobbed. 'I hate him.'

Hollyberry, Hollyberry.

He was holding her like a father holding a child, and she lay against him until her sobbing dropped to an occasional hiccup. 'I hate him,' she said on a sigh.

'It doesn't matter what you feel, it's what Tony felt.'

'I know but sometimes I feel . . . oh, I feel sometimes as if I'm experiencing her pain.' She looked up at him. His eyes did not mock or taunt but were calm and clear and gentle. 'Damn it, it's so hard to explain. It was 1957, Taylor. God only knows how appalling it must have been, how dangerous. Why did he let it happen, Taylor? Why did Tony believe it was what he would want?'

He seemed to draw inwards inside himself and it was almost as if he were no longer standing there with her. Had his uncle used this phenomenal self-control in his work? 'We can only learn so much by looking at the paintings. I thought I knew Blaise: you thought you knew Tony. We did and we didn't. Let it go. We're not going to find out all the truths. You're reading things into the paintings that aren't there, things you want to see to support your belief in this great love affair.'

'Which you believe in, deep down, and your bruised little ego and family pride won't let you admit to.'

'For God's sake, Holly. OK, I admit she was a great painter. Now, let's walk along the beach.' He let her go and she was almost embarrassed that she had stayed in his arms so long. What must he be thinking?

'You won't think much of this beach; there's very little sand.'

'This is neat,' he said ten minutes or so later. 'Shall I pick up a stone and write Taylor, 1999, or wouldn't your John like that?'

'It's not his business any more.' She avoided his eyes and walked quickly. 'There was a painting, *Les Bébés qui Chantent*.'

He looked down at her, puzzled. 'Singing babies?'

'She painted their babies waiting on clouds to be born. They were all singing and painting but we can't find it.'

SOMEDAY, SOMEWHERE

'Maybe she painted over it. Maybe Otto will be able to tell— But look, they're not dead. They just haven't been born yet. See that cloud?'

She looked up. There were clouds in the sky, pale grey just kissed by the pale pink light from the evening summer sun.

There were no seraphim.

'See,' he said, pointing. 'There, on the pink cloud, that sassy little one is painting streaks on her brother's arse.'

This was an unexpected side to Taylor Fougère Hartman and his silliness allowed Holly to pull herself together. 'Do you usually go crazy on Scottish beaches?'

'Only when there's no sand.'

They walked on quietly for a few minutes.

'Holly, my mother says Blaise lost his voice completely in 1957. He only regained it when I was born in 1959. Maybe it was the abortion; maybe he was ashamed of leaving Tony, if he did leave her. There's that painting *Grief*. If he was gone, how could she have painted him?'

'Memory. She saw him sitting in the rowing boat. You're trying to make me say *Grief* wasn't painted from life so the other paintings are made up.' She turned away from him and began to hurry back down the beach towards the point. Shit. Every time she thought he was human he said or did something to prove her wrong.

His legs were so long he didn't even need to break into a trot to catch up with her. 'Holly. Pax, please. Let's eat and then we'll sleep on it and talk again in the morning.'

'Eat. Sleep. You're unreal, Taylor. Go away.'

'Pax, Taylor. We'll eat and then I am going to bed and when I wake up, you will be gone.'

'Fine. White wine or red?'

'I don't care.' Her voice was shriller than she meant it to be.

'Then let's have red.'

The food looked delicious. Holly thanked Taylor. He cut into his quiche. 'Hot food is great, don't you think?'

She laughed. 'Do you hate cold quiche? I have an oven, you know.'

He followed her into the tiny kitchen. 'I was scared to suggest it.'

'I bet.'

She walked on and could hear him, almost feel him, following on behind. They arrived at the cottage together.

'You should put geraniums in those window boxes. Look great all summer.'

'Doesn't start here till about July.'

'Heck, that should give you two whole months of flowers.'

149

Once again the atmosphere had changed. If she could forget Tony and her sorrow she could like Taylor.

Hollyberry.

You stay out of it.

They ate warm quiche washed down by a delicious claret. They talked only about Holly's plans for the cottage and Taylor's years at Oxford University, but stayed at the table long after the light had faded.

At last Holly stood up. 'I'll wash up.'

'You heated the quiche.'

She laughed and looked at him. Mistake, Holly. She felt herself swaying. No, impossible. Two glasses of wine. What else could intoxicate?

His fingers very lightly stroked her cheek. 'I'll clear up.'

Still she stood, unable to move, and his hand slipped from her cheek and she was in his arms. His lips, warm, soft, were on hers, and his arms were around her. She responded to him and his tongue parted her lips; she felt her whole body melt.

He let her go so abruptly that she almost stumbled. 'Forgive me. You go up first. I'll wash up.' And so that she was left in no doubt that he did not intend to join her he said, 'Good night, Holly.'

She stumbled up the stairs and hid herself in her room.

Had she thrown herself at him?

No, we were in that together, weren't we?

'Tony.'

I'm here, darling girl.

Comforted, Holly undressed and crept into bed. She lay there and listened. At last the sounds she had dreaded. He was coming up the stairs.

'Holly?'

What should she do, say?

'I want you very much, Holly. Downstairs I was so ready to seduce you.' He laughed a little. 'There's no place big enough in that room for seduction. The thing is, Holly . . . it's this damned cottage; there's some strange kind of atmosphere. Probably damp. I don't know whether you're sweetly asleep but I'm taking a raincheck. *Le cœur a ses raisons que la raison ne connaît pas.* That's Blaise, but Blaise Pascal this time. Whatever is between us is not over. Remember what I said: "It's not over till the fat lady sings." Good night.'

He was gone and she heard nothing until the morning light forced her awake and she got up and went downstairs.

She would pretend it had never happened.

'I hope my plumbers turn up today,' she said. 'Plumbers never come when you're waiting for them.'

'Serves you right for hiding yourself out here,' Taylor said with a smile.

The exhibition. There had to be an exhibition . . .

'Taylor . . .? The exhibition?'

'Sell me the paintings. I'll double my offer. You can build a house someplace with big enough walls for the ones you want to keep.'

'They want them exhibited now.'

'God, you're talking to those ghosts again.'

How could she ever have imagined that she might . . . yes, admit it, Holly, love him. Holly, the genius, has done it again. Backed a loser and this time with eyes wide open so there was no excuse.

'You'd better go.'

He got up immediately. 'Don't throw out the bath with the painted toes, will you. I have plans for that bath.'

She looked up at him tremulously but he was smiling. He bent swiftly and kissed her fiercely on the lips and then he turned and walked out of the cottage.

Clover
TORRY BAY, 1965

'Come on, Blaise, just a little further.'

'What do you want me to see?' He was laughing. Always she wanted to see what there was to see from the top of the next hill. Water, more hills, strawberry clover and common clover, some of its heads already turning pinkish, and rosebay willowherb. That was a new one; she did not remember it from her childhood. Blaise had seen it in Europe.

'It came here in the bombs, I think.'

'Don't be silly. Nothing nice ever came out of a bomb.'

'Then, Mam'selle So Clever, tell me why it is all over ruined streets?'

She had no answer and so ignored the question and walked on, and he smiled quietly and followed. 'My favourite role,' he said to himself, 'to follow my Toinette wherever she leads.'

They had been together for two glorious days and still he found his heart contracting at the sound and sight and smell of her.

Already she was over the top of the next hill, standing in the midst of a sea of flowers. 'Stand here,' she ordered. 'If I can capture the blues . . . look around you, Blaise. It's so beautiful, it hurts.'

So it is, he agreed silently. But he was looking at Tony.

Tony swiftly sketched the lines that would later become one of her most sought-after paintings, and Blaise stood and enjoyed the picture

151

of concentration. She is so like me in the way she works, he decided. The concentration is total; she is aware of nothing but her art.

He was having trouble holding his pose because he could feel something crawling up his right leg, and it's drive me crazy.'

'In a second,' she began. 'Oh, you have ruined it.'

'Merde,' swore Blaise and he began to claw at his trouser leg. 'I'm sorry, Toinette, but it's bitten me.' He hauled his trouser leg up as far as he could but was unable to get it past his knee.

Tony was laughing. 'Poor little boy,' she teased. 'Bitten by a little creepy-crawly. Will I kiss it better for you? Try to get back into that position, sweetheart.'

He tried but: 'Je regrette,' he began formally and then switched to English. She said she would learn French as she had said she would learn to drive, but she forgot everything when she was painting. 'I feel strange, Tony. I'm sorry about the picture and the light and your blues but I want to go home.'

She looked at him. She did not like what she saw. 'Blaise.' She ran to him across the clover. 'What is it? Let's look at the bite.' She eased his jeans down over his hips. 'It's just a little sting, darling. Look, can you see? It's on the back of your knee and it is a little red, maybe an inch, not much, nothing to worry about.'

'Bien.' He tried to smile. 'A little bite and I am a baby but I can't pose.'

'No, we'll go home, Blaise, and it will be fine.' She put her slim arm round his waist and he leaned on her as they began to walk back to the cottage. She could see that the sweet-smelling clover was alive with bees. A bee must have stung him. She did not dare ask if he knew whether he was allergic; surely if he was there would be a much more livid swelling of the entry wound. Of course there would be.

He was leaning on her more and more heavily. 'I feel dizzy,' Toinette and with nerve, like before I sing.' He clutched at his chest and then he let go of her and began to scratch his arms, his chest, his face. 'It's so itchy and my chest. It's tight, and my neck . . .'

Tony turned to him and she suppressed a gasp as she saw that his face and neck were beginning to swell. 'Can't breathe,' he gasped.

What on earth was she to do? They were miles from the village. 'Blaise, try to keep calm.' 'Dear God, he was sweating and he was beginning to tremble as if he were cold. How could he be hot and cold at the same time? 'We are almost there. You'll be safe at the cottage while I go for the doctor. Look, look, ma mie, hold on, ma mie, we are home.'

They stumbled together across the shore and into the cottage and he half fell onto the settee. She ran upstairs and pulled the bedcover off her bed and carried it downstairs. 'Sing *Fidelio*,' she ordered as she wrapped him up. 'All the parts. Go through it all very calmly. I will be back with Simon long before you get to Florestan's aria. I promise.'

He tried to smile but she could see the terror in his eyes and she knew its cause. 'There's no poison in your throat, believe me.'

She kissed him quickly and then ran outside. There was Blaise's car. This year I'll learn to drive. She stumbled back into the cottage and took the keys from the nail at the door. She had never driven before. But it had to be easy, didn't it? She turned on the engine. So far, so good. The brake . . . And this knob thing. I have to move the knob thing . . .

She pushed the knob and the car lurched forward and then stalled. She wanted to scream and cry with vexation. 'Shit, shit, shit. St Blaise help me. St Cecilia help me.'

She turned the key again and then somehow found the clutch pedal. The expensive car jumped, with the most alarming sounds of grinding and squealing and affronted protest, up the path to the road. 'Dear God, don't let him die. I'll give him up if you don't let him die. I promise.'

At last she was in the village. She parked the car by the simple expedient of stalling in the middle of the road directly in front of Simon's surgery and she threw herself out of the car and into the house.

Simon had seen the erratic approach of the car, which had been watched by all the villagers who were anywhere near the street.

'It's the artist lady from the bay,' a customer informed Chrissie, who was weighing cheese, and Chrissie pulled off her apron and ran out into the street. She was just in time to see Tony running into the surgery and she followed. She and Simon reached Tony together.

'Simon, it's Blaise. Help me, help me,' Tony sobbed as she collapsed into Chrissie's strong old arms. 'A friend, Simon, he's at the cottage. A bee sting, I think. An allergic reaction.'

'I'll get my bag. Chrissie, get someone to move that car off the road. Then ring the cottage hospital for me. We'll take him straight there.'

Tony's energy had returned. 'It was the meadow beside the stream. I was sketching. Oh, Simon, his throat is swelling.'

'We'll be in time, Tony.' He did not ask anything. His mind was telling him that a man, the man whom Tony had always loved, was in her cottage, dying. He forced his old car faster. Idiot, he chastised himself. You should have taken his fancy car. Goes three times as fast as this old heap. Too late to think of that now.

They reached the cottage. Even from outside they could hear the choking sounds. Tony threw open the door and Simon saw a tall man.

His face was turned almost black and his eyes were popping from his skull. He gave another gasp and fell from the settee.

Tony screamed. It was a sound that Simon prayed he would never hear again. 'He's dead, Simon. He's dead.'

He pushed her out of the way and knelt down. The patient's grossly swollen tongue had blocked the airways. Simon pushed the head back and the chin down and then put two fingers of each strong hand under the jawbone just below the ears and thrust the jaw forward. Blaise gave a cough and then lay still.

'It worked,' Simon told Tony. 'The mandible thrust.' He reached for his bag and prepared a syringe. 'Adrenaline.' He smiled up at her.

Tony burst into tears. 'His chest, Simon,' she whispered. 'It's moving.'

'We medical men call that breathing.'

She was half laughing, half crying. 'I will honour you all my life,' she said. Together they looked at Blaise. Already the face was almost back to normal, the swelling was going down, and the breathing was regular.

'You know who he is,' said Tony.

He nodded. He could not look at her. 'I heard him sing at the Edinburgh Festival. You will have to help me get him to the car, Tony. We need to get him to hospital.'

'Hospital? Oh, Simon, must he? Can't I nurse him here?'

'He was within seconds of death, Tony. He should be checked out thoroughly, watched overnight at least.'

'You could tell me what to do. I'll watch him. Please, Simon. His world must never know about us.'

He was not there to judge. For years he had hoped, but now Simon saw that Tony would never love him.

'I can't force you. He's over the crisis. I'll do everything I can to help, but he should be in the cottage hospital.'

'Doctor.' The famous voice was very low. 'You are a good man and I owe you my life but I cannot go. There are others to consider. Please.'

'Newspapers,' said Tony.

'Please, Doctor, for Tony's sake also.'

Simon looked down at his patient. 'I can't force you to accept hospital treatment but you are unwise.' He closed his bag. 'You must tell your own doctor. No doubt he'll arrange for you to have a syringe with you.' His tone was curt, professional. Then he relented and smiled. 'And keep out of fields of clover.'

Blaise shook his hand. 'Thank you.'

Tony walked with Simon to the car but did not wait to see him drive up the hill.

Blaise had pushed himself up and was more comfortable. He held out his arms and she ran to him. They did not speak. They did not kiss. He held her and she put her head against his chest and listened to his heart beat. Most precious of sounds. How close. How close.

'You saved my life, Toinette.'

'Simon did.' She put her arms round him. 'I will learn to drive and I will see about a telephone.'

Later, Simon drove Blaise's car down to the cottage and Tony persuaded him to stay for supper. 'I came really to get another look at my patient. Heartbeat, pulse, everything is normal. You will see your doctor?'

Blaise had no chance to answer, for they heard a car and looked out to see an old black Hillman coasting down the hill. Tony ran to the door.

'It's the canon, saving petrol again. I hope he stops before he reaches the sea . . .' Tony had not seen Canon Gemmell for some weeks. She walked down to where the car had finally stopped.

'Canon, how lovely to see you.'

'Hello, my dear. A party? I won't intrude now. They said Simon was here and I wanted a word.'

'You could never intrude, Canon,' she lied. Of course he was intruding. He was a Catholic priest and he lived and breathed his vows. She did not want to lose his respect, his friendship, and surely she must. 'Simon's here—in a professional capacity, I suppose, seeing a friend who was staying with me. We're having omelettes and salad. You are welcome to join us.'

They had reached the door.

'Simon, the canon . . .' began Tony, but the old man had walked past the local doctor, his eyes on the man who sat wrapped in blankets on the settee.

'Monsieur Fougère, this is a great honour, sir.' He pushed Blaise, who was trying to rise, back on to the seat. 'Now I understand *Lohengrin*. I will take a little supper after all, Tony, if I may.' He turned back to Blaise. 'I trust you are not ill, Mr Fougère?'

'Bee sting,' filled in Simon.

'Canon, Blaise has been staying with me here,' said Tony and Blaise and the priest smiled at one another. She was so honest. She could not bear it that the canon might not understand.

'What a lovely place to escape to, Tony my dear.'

Later, after they had eaten, Tony walked with the priest out to his car.

'Tony, whatever did you do with *Sea Sprite*?'

She started. 'You could not have known then?'

'No, I had never seen him nor heard him sing. I remember the painting sometimes. Now I know why.'

'It's upstairs in the attic.'

'What a waste. It should be in a gallery.' He eased his old body into the driver's seat. 'The first time we met I told you I was always here, Tony. I *am* always here.'

'Thank you,' she whispered as he waved and drove away, and then she turned as Simon joined her.

'I was sure he would disapprove.'

'I'm sure he does. But it doesn't change his affection for you.' He kissed her lightly on the cheek as he had done once or twice a year for over twenty years. 'He's fine, Tony,' and he was not talking about the canon. 'The constitution of an ox. He will be well enough to travel.' He started off towards the road into the village. 'I'm here if you need me.'

She said nothing but stood watching him until he reached the brow of the hill. He was 'here' and the canon was 'here' and for one more day so was the man she loved more than life itself.

'*Ma mie?*' The voice was questioning.

'I'm here, my darling, here.'

CHAPTER THIRTEEN

TORRY BAY, 1999, NEW YORK, 1999

EVERY MORNING HOLLY made coffee, real coffee, and every morning, except when it was raining heavily, she took a mug out to the point. She felt close to Tony on the point. Tony had painted from here often.

She thought about Tony a lot too when she was painting the living room. Twice a week she phoned Otto or was contacted by him, but Taylor had returned, as she had known he would, to his world of high finance. His lawyers and Otto's lawyers argued with each other and still Tony's magnificent portraits hung with no one to admire them. Holly sighed. Everything was drifting like the swans in the bay.

She had had enough. She would bend her stiff neck and ring Taylor. As usual: 'Mr Hartman is unavailable.'

'Chandler, tell Mr Hartman that if he does not ring me back within the next two hours I am personally going to stand in Otto's gallery and sell the paintings to the first person who comes in off the street.'

'You would be breaking the law, Miss Noble.'

'Then he can visit me in jail,' she said.

Taylor rang four hours later. 'The thought of visiting you in Wormwood Scrubs, or wherever hardened criminals are sent, Holly, is unbelievably appealing, but I'll do a deal with you. I'm not in the States at the moment. Could you please meet me in New York and we'll talk?'

'New York?' Holly had never visited the United States. It was always one of the things she was going to do when . . . 'Why can't you talk now?'

'Trust me. We need to meet in New York.'

This is stupid. New York? She would think twice about agreeing to meet someone in Glasgow. 'Fine. I'll meet you in New York.' The plumbers would certainly be finished by the time she got back.

New York? I am out of my tiny mind. Why am I doing this? Why?

When the call was finished she put down the receiver and sat down shakily in the big armchair. Through the open window she could hear the sea and gulls calling and far overhead the sound of an aeroplane. She was as excited as she used to be as a child when she knew that soon a plane would take her to Aunt Tony and the freedom of Torry Bay.

Two days later, sitting in a hotel in New York, waiting for Taylor, her excitement had gone, to be replaced by nausea.

What does he want? What do I want?

'Coffee, please, and . . . a toasted muffin.'

That was why she felt sick. She was starving and the smell of hot coffee, hot toast and melted butter from the next table was activating all her glands. Was there a more comforting smell anywhere?

Expensive cologne is not comforting.

Taylor had somehow materialised before her. 'I'll wait,' he said by way of greeting. Breakfast arrived. 'Another cup, please.' He smiled at the waitress, then he sat down across from Holly and waited patiently while she poured.

'I've been doing a lot of thinking, Holly, and I have never been absolutely straight with you. I deliberately lied about one point.'

'Good heavens,' said Holly.

'I want you to come with me to visit my aunt.'

She dropped her muffin. 'Your aunt is dead.'

'To the world, yes. Will you come with me?'

With shaking hands she reached for her cup. 'Taylor . . .' she began.

'Have your breakfast. Don't fuss, Holly,' Taylor said, standing up. 'I'll wait for you outside.'

She watched him walk away. Other people were looking at him too. Hands still shaking, Holly gulped her coffee down and then poured another cup. It was a sick joke . . . but Taylor was not into sick jokes . . . so it had to be true. But he had said Eleanor was dead, hadn't he? That then was the lie to which he admitted. Tony had believed that Eleanor was dead, or had she merely assumed that by the time Holly read the note Blaise's wife would have died? *No one is alive now who cares one way or the other.* Oh, Tony, dearest aunt, how wrong you were.

Once she had finished her coffee, Holly went upstairs to fetch a jacket. When she reached the foyer, Taylor was there. As usual a car was waiting outside. Holly was too upset to be even vaguely impressed.

'Take a look at the Hartford papers,' said Taylor curtly.

Holly took the newspaper he handed her. EXCLUSIVE: ELEANOR RIDGEWAY FOUGÈRE IN A SANATORIUM. An 'intrepid reporter' had tracked Eleanor Fougère to a sanatorium in Connecticut.

Last night our reporter uncovered the mystery that has baffled the gossip columns of America for nearly fifty years. Eleanor Ridgeway Fougère, wife of the tenor, Blaise Fougère, who died in an air crash— some say on the way to his paramour Antonia Noble, the British painter—is alive and living in an exclusive sanatorium in Connecticut.

'She trusted me, and I promised her, and him, his memory, but you had to show the paintings. The money wasn't enough, was it?'

'If you even think that I sanctioned any salacious gossip, Taylor, there is no point in us going any further.'

He did not look at her. 'Isn't this fun, Holly? I really love this part, sneaking around avoiding the press. Great fun.'

'I don't understand.'

'This is not one of my cars. Chandler is in my car heading for Madison. We are going in the opposite direction.'

Holly said nothing as Taylor drove. She watched Connecticut, its trees, its lovely towns and villages sweep by, but did not see them, for she was seeing the end of her newly born dreams. The reporter had destroyed whatever there might have been between Tony's niece and Blaise's nephew. At last they came to great iron gates set in a tall, stone wall. The house was beautiful. A country house of great charm.

'The Fougère Foundation pays for this,' said Taylor tersely as they waited for admittance at the beautiful carved oak doors.

The door opened. 'How bad is it?' he asked.

'We are so very sorry, Mr Hartman. I don't know what more we could have done.'

He brushed everything aside. 'How is she?'

The doctor, if it was a doctor, smiled. 'The same.'

Holly went, with Taylor, along a corridor to a suite of rooms. Taylor did not knock but opened the main door softly and walked in, almost dragging Holly behind him.

The room was beautiful. The furniture was French provincial, and the yellow upholstery was full of the promise of spring. Huge vases of specially grown spring flowers stood on every table.

A young girl sat in a chair by the window. Her hair was as pale as the gold of the fabric that covered her chair and her peignoir was a master-piece of the dressmaker's art.

She turned as the door opened. 'Blaise, my dearest one, I knew you would come. I have been waiting; I knew you would come.'

'Of course I'm here, Eleanor.'

He stepped forward and Holly started, almost with horror. The hair and the clothes were those of a young girl but it was no child who held Taylor's hands, now babbling away in words that made no sense at all.

Taylor continued to hold her hands, making soothing noises, and Holly stood transfixed and watched him. An attendant was there and she stood for a few minutes and then stepped forward. 'Now, now, Madame Fougère, there's a performance in five minutes. We wouldn't want to hold him up now, would we?'

'No, oh no,' said the ghost of Eleanor. 'My Blaise must sing; he sings for me. Don't you, my dearest.'

'*Pour sûr, mon ange.* I sing for you.'

The attendant led the girl-woman out of the room and Taylor almost fell into a chair.

'I thought she was dead,' Holly whispered.

'Her body lives. She's eighty-two years old and has been diagnosed as legally insane for almost sixty years.'

Tragedy upon tragedy. 'Oh, Taylor, but I thought she didn't recognise Blaise.'

He lifted his head from his hands. 'She didn't and then, one day, maybe eight years ago, when I visited, for some reason—maybe my age at the time—she thought I was Blaise. We, the family, had promised that we would care for her always, protect her as he protected her.'

He got up and moved across to her so quickly that she was startled. 'I blew it, Holly, because of you, because of this damned mixed-up love-hate thing we have going. I knew the right thing was to close the exhibi-tion, not to let those damned sewer rats in to poke their sleek, cold little noses into my family, but I was too late.' He grabbed her and pulled her over to a window. 'Look out there. Look. See those cars? That's gutter press, Miss Noble. They'll wait and take photographs if she appears at a window, walks in the grounds. They'll talk to gardeners, boot boys, delivery men. They'll find out what she eats, what she wears. Goddamn you, Holly, why didn't you just take the money?'

Love-hate thing. Love-hate thing. So he felt something too or had felt something. Damn, damn, damn.

'It wasn't a question of money, ever,' she began desperately. 'You could have told me, Taylor. Tony thought everyone was dead.'

'We allowed the world to believe that.'

'What are you going to do? Move her?'

'Blaise built this house for her. I can't take it away from her. We'll see if Hannah can keep her away from the windows and out of the gardens for a while.' His great frame seemed to sag. 'Soon we will be yesterday's news. A sort of Connecticut Miss Havisham, in a peignoir, not a wedding gown.' He got up and walked to the door. 'They'll bring you coffee. I'm going to sit with her for a while.'

He left the room and Holly sat looking out at the line of cars outside the gates. What have I done? If I hadn't given Otto the right to exhibit the paintings maybe no one would have found out.

But they have found out so what difference will showing the paintings make now?

The prurient will come to gape. The prices will go sky-high because they will outbid one another to be part of this soap opera.

But it's not a soap opera; it's a tragedy . . . for everyone including me.

A cheery woman brought her a tray. Tea. He had had tea sent to her. A spark of hope lit in her belly and she felt tears start. Oh, Taylor.

'We'll go now.' She had not heard him enter. 'When we get in the car put your scarf over your face if you don't want to be famous tomorrow.'

She had never experienced anything like it.

Taylor drove like a maniac straight for the group of photographers waiting at the gates and they jumped out of the way, flashes exploding.

'Fun, Holly?' he asked angrily as they screeched out of the gates. 'That was what life was like for my uncle, who wanted only to sing, to bring joy and to look after his poor sad wife.'

She dared not mention Tony.

'They waited for him outside opera houses and restaurants. Sometimes he wore disguises. Why wasn't the world content just to hear his voice? They wanted everything. He used to ask me, "What good does it do them to know that I like raspberries more than strawberries?" He could not understand their interest in him. I had no idea how to comfort him.' He turned and looked at her. 'Do you know his voice, Holly?'

Hollyberry.

'I've heard him once or twice.'

'That's not enough. You have been abducted, Miss Noble.'

'Don't be ridiculous.'

'There's something else I want you to see; something you need to see. My beach house. It's near here. We can walk on the beach and talk, grill a couple of steaks, listen to a CD. You could stay over, there's a guest room. But if you prefer to go back to the city now, just say so.'

Holly looked at him, trying to work out what was going on inside that beautifully sculpted head. 'Why should I see this particular house?'

'When you see it, you'll know.'

T aylor's house stood on a point overlooking the Atlantic Ocean, where sighing waves rolled up onto a sandy shore. It was, she was surprised to see, a moderately sized wooden building, white, with blue doors and shutters. It was built on a little promontory and the rhododendron-lined driveway that led to the front door also meandered on down to a private beach. There was a sign on the gates: TORRY BAY.

Holly gasped.

Taylor stopped the car at the front door and switched off the engine. 'My uncle bought this house thirty years ago,' he said at last. 'He came quite often when he was at the Met. We could never understand why he had rhododendrons, although they were kept well cut back.' He looked at her white, still face. 'You must have noticed in Scotland: they're alive with bees in the summer and Blaise was allergic to bee stings.'

Holly could say nothing. Taylor had known all the time that there was truth in her story and yet he had pretended. She remembered his stunned comment when he had first seen Torry Bay. She had thought it was the location when all the time it was the name.

'Take me to New York; no, the nearest railway station.'

'Holly, please. He was my white knight. I was his page. Your paintings ruined my memories. I didn't want to believe he'd loved someone else, loved another child. I wanted to be special. Childish, I know.'

'You knew all the time.' The realisation hurt like a slap.

'No, of course I didn't. He said the bay reminded him of a friend's house. That's why he called it Torry Bay. He didn't say, "I'm calling the beach house after the place where I am happiest, where my heart is." I never lied to you about that. The lie was saying she was dead, *pauvre petite.* I promised, Holly. "I'll never let anyone hurt her," I said.'

161

There was silence in the car for some time, as they sat deliberately not looking at one another. The silence hung heavy, tense. 'No harm in taking a look,' Holly said at last.

It was at the same time like and unlike Torry Bay. It was bigger, more luxurious, and where Tony had had a wall of glass that slid away at the touch of a button, Blaise had had a wall of glass that looked out onto the bay. There were stones on a table to the right of the window. Taylor 1970, Taylor 1973. Above the mantel was a small painting that Holly recognised at once.

'She must have painted that for him.'

'I don't think so. There's an ancient sales receipt signed by Otto. Blaise took it everywhere with him. I'm surprised it wasn't on his plane the night they crashed. I hung it here after his funeral. Would you like to walk down to the bay? No swans, I'm afraid.'

She went with him out onto the terrace. Pots full of rioting flowers greeted her with their perfume. They were geraniums. 'Is there a lot of rain?'

At first he did not understand. 'Oh, the flowers. I grow tomatoes too. The people who look after the house water them. Blaise never left anything to die.'

No, he left nothing to die, except Tony. Holly began to cry and it seemed so right that Taylor should hold her in his arms.

'It's so sad,' sobbed Holly when she could speak.

'Yes, but wonderful too. They loved one another for more than fifty years, Holly. Isn't that something? I'd like that, wouldn't you?' His voice was intense and so were his eyes, those eyes so like Blaise's that stared into hers, forcing her to admit to feelings that she had tried not to acknowledge. 'Took me for ever to understand why you got under my skin so much, Holly. You're so unlike any woman I ever loved.'

She laughed shakily. 'I'm no oil painting, as the saying goes.'

He looked surprised. 'Everything's in the right place but there's something more important than surface beauty. It's you, Holly, just you. The Holly who went to Africa for a year and stayed for two; that Holly who's ready to take on the world and Taylor Hartman if she feels he's wrong. She shines right out of your lovely blue eyes.'

He tilted up her chin and bent down to kiss her lips and at his touch the pent-up fires exploded, consuming her.

How did they return to the house? She did not know.

They were in the bedroom and he was kissing her mouth while his hands found buttons, fastenings, and she was his equal. She unbuttoned his shirt as he removed her blouse and his lips found her breasts.

She gave herself up completely to sensation. He pushed her down and then his body was on hers. He slid into her as easily as if their knowledge of one another was primeval and she gasped as her body matched and responded to his rhythm.

Never had she experienced such a flood of sensations. Even her throat burned and tingled as feelings long tamped down exploded. They climaxed together and lay silent, exhausted and satisfied.

'I'm told everyone spoils you, Taylor.'

He laughed. 'I want you to spoil me atrociously every day for the rest of my life.'

Every day. She sat up and looked down at him. 'I didn't mean this to happen.'

'Nor me, it's all I have been able to think about for months. I want to make love to you again, Holly.' He took her hand. 'Feel how much I want you. Say, stop it, and I will stop.'

She wanted to say it. Her mouth desperately tried to form the syllables, but his hands. Oh, where had he learned how to work such magic? She had never experienced being loved like that; she had never dreamed that the act could be like that, so much giving, taking, and no false modesty. She felt beautiful, voluptuous, a woman.

At last they fell asleep and hours later she woke in the dark with his legs and his arms wrapped round her. She was cold and she was embarrassed. How was she to get out of his arms, his bedroom and his house? She was insane. He had said he wanted to make love to her. Well, he had. Indeed he had, but why? Because of whatever he thought he saw in her eyes? They should never have allowed themselves to get into this situation. How could they evaluate their feelings after a day in which their emotions had been beaten and battered? Eleanor, poor Eleanor. How many miles away was her gilded cage?

How quickly we forgot her in our passion, Holly admitted as she looked down at him. He was her Lohengrin, her knight and she loved him and would willingly wait for ever. But what was she to him? And had Tony's glorious portraits anything to do with what had just so beautifully, wonderfully happened?

He stirred. 'Dinner now, sweetheart, or is it breakfast?'

'Taylor, this is very awkward but I'm afraid this should never have happened. I'm not . . . looking for a relationship.'

He sat up and she was glad it was dark, only pale moonlight showing them as dark shapes in the pastel room. 'You sure as hell found one.'

'I'm sorry. I never meant . . .'

'Lie to me if you like, Holly, but don't lie to yourself. You could have

163

stopped me at any time and you didn't. Well, I hope I was a good lay. You were great. In fact, you were so good, I thought we might even have been made for one another.'

What was he saying? What had she done? Another Noble mistake?

'We don't even like one another.'

He pulled her round and for a moment she stiffened with fear. He was so strong, but no, it was Taylor, and she did not fear him. There was no reason to fear. She relaxed but it was too late.

'I never rape, Holly. I get it for nothing whenever I want it. Usually I send a little gift, just like my uncle. What will it be . . . diamonds, rubies; no—sapphires, I think, to match your innocent blue eyes.'

She slapped him as hard as she could and he got off the bed, stalked into the bathroom and slammed the door. She slid from the bed and searched frantically for her clothing.

He was dressed when he came out again. The clothes she had helped pull off him were still lying on the floor and he wore a tracksuit.

'The bathroom's all yours. I'll get the car.'

'Thank you,' she managed stiffly.

They said nothing on the way to the city and at the door of the hotel he leaned across her to open the door. She was conscious of his body, as she had never been conscious of a man's body before. She felt like a streetwalker.

She was weeping when she managed to get the little card to work so that she could enter her room.

The bathtub was as big as the one with the painted toes and she filled it and lay in the hot scented water, meaning to wash Taylor away.

'Oh, God, what have I done,' she sobbed and took her nailbrush and tried to scrub the memories away.

CHAPTER FOURTEEN

TORRY BAY, 1999, LONDON, 1999

THE NEXT FEW DAYS REMAINED for ever a blur. She got to the airport, how she could not remember. On the long flight she ate nothing, drank nothing, read nothing, and, when she arrived, found Scotland echoing her misery. It was raining in Glasgow.

The voice of the man beside her in the line for the shuttle bus did penetrate the pall of misery. 'Wouldn't you know it—bucketing?'

Sure. Somebody up there was chucking buckets of the stuff. He continued to pitch, bung and heave buckets of rain down on the beleaguered little island all the way from Glasgow to Torry Bay. Cascading rain and her own tears hid from her the scenery that Tony had delighted in exploring and painting.

She reached Achahoish safely and drove slowly down to the cottage beside a sea angrier than she had ever seen it. Holly buttoned up her coat, and ran, buffeted by the wind, her face stung from drops of rain sharp as needles, to the cottage door, but it was not shelter from the storm she was seeking, or was it? Tony had come back here bruised and beaten to seek shelter from the storm of life. She had found it too if the beautiful painting *Refuge from the Storm* was true. She opened the door.

Darling girl. Hollyberry.

She sat down in the chair by the window and wept, but she was comforted. The cottage was warm, too warm, and delightedly Holly ran from room to room exclaiming over her brand-new radiators. Then she swooped down on her little green telephone, lifted the receiver and held it to her ear. But there was no one to ring to tell about the dizzy heights of modernisation. 'Yes, there is,' she said defiantly. 'There's Otto and Mr Gilbert and the Reids; old friends in Glasgow who'll be wondering what I'm doing, and I may well ring painters and decorators.'

Anything to stop herself thinking of those magical hours with Taylor.

She felt tired, lethargic and, for two days, she stayed closeted in the cottage, hiding from the raging wind and making her telephone calls. Mr Reid was delighted and promised that their bill would 'be with you shortly'.

She rang Mr Gilbert and promised to make an appointment with a financial adviser, and then she dialled Otto's number. 'You will never guess where I have been.'

She was beginning to read the tone of his voice. 'How intriguing, do tell,' he said, but she was almost sure that he already knew.

'New York,' she said and she let herself remember. For just a moment her body felt as if it were wrapped in the finest silk. Oh God, why did I leave? What demon possessed me to take the gift I had been given and throw it back?

Back to reality.

'Taylor took me to a sanatorium in Connecticut. Eleanor is still alive.'

She heard him gasp. There was a heartbeat's pause. 'I know,' I rang you when the story broke but, of course, you didn't answer. Holly, every paper had something, even the better papers, but you were not mentioned. I had no idea that you were there.'

Sweet relief. He had not known. She was glad of that. He was Tony's friend and was selling her paintings: too cruel if he had known. 'Don't you see, Otto, it wasn't his mother he was thinking about when he asked me to hide the paintings for twenty years, it was his aunt.'

'Holly,' he began again; his voice sounded as old as his years. 'I, we, everyone thought her dead years ago; you must believe that.'

Holly felt cold. 'Of course I believe it, Otto. What are saying?'

'I knew.' It was her turn to gasp but he hurried on. 'Taylor's lawyers told me, or at least they told my lawyers. That was the only reason he got the temporary order.'

'You knew—and you didn't tell me?' She was fighting nausea now. Was there any man in the world she could trust? 'How could you lie to me, Otto?'

'I never lied. Look Holly, Miss Noble, I'm a businessman. I want to sell these wonderful paintings but I'm like the lawyers: I wanted an equitable remedy, the right to sell them, but I need the business of the Hartmans and all the clients they send, and so do you.'

She was crying now. 'You should have told me; it would have made everything different. I would have . . .' She stopped and blew her nose. What would she have done? Not fought so much with Taylor, for a start, but the paintings? Tony and her paintings; that was all that mattered. *No one is alive now who cares one way or the other. But there was something else in the letters, something she had overlooked. I never wanted to sell in my lifetime. I made a pact. A pact? Who with, Tony?*

Darling girl.

Oh God. Tony promised Blaise not to exhibit in Eleanor's lifetime.

Hollyberry.

'You should have told me. It was your duty to tell me.'

'I'm sorry, I didn't take the decision lightly, my dear, and if you hadn't stormed off and said you were taking them off the market we could have discussed it rationally.'

She wanted to hang up on him, never see him or speak to him again, hide away at Torry Bay from them all. No, she was through running.

'I'll have to think, Otto.'

'Madame Fougère doesn't understand anything, does she?'

'No.'

'Then what does it matter when you found out? Now that the story has broken, every city where there's a major opera house will run a story, and most will be perfectly sympathetic.' He was quiet for a moment and Holly could picture him gathering himself together to say something he knew she would not want to hear. 'I know you dislike any talk of filthy lucre but the telephone and Internet bids on the paintings will go through the proverbial roof.'

'This is unbelievably distasteful.'

'This is human nature.'

'Otto, I really have no energy at the moment and I have to think. I don't know what to do for the best. Besides, Taylor and I . . . we had a blazing row,' seemed like the best way of explaining.

'Oh, dear, I actually thought I saw a *tendresse* developing.'

A *tendresse*, tenderness. 'Pigs might fly.'

She remembered to give him her telephone number before hanging up, only to sit down and gaze into space. Get a grip, Holly. You blew it again—three strikes and you're out—so get on with life and stop feeling so damned sorry for yourself.

The outside, with its constant drizzle, was now more appealing than the cottage where Taylor had intruded. She walked towards the point. The world looked sorry for itself. The sheep in the field huddled together miserably and the sea was almost hidden by a cloud of grey rain. She had forgotten how mild Scottish rain can be and took off her scarf to allow it to bathe her hair and her face with its soft gentleness. She reached the point and stood looking out at the sea, but no voices called her, no murmurs told her of times past. There were no swans on the water, just one or two ducks bobbing along at the whim of the tide. Incongruous sight: two beer bottles bobbed along beside the ducks. Holly clambered down and fished them out of the water.

Did you deal with beer bottles in your refuge, Tony? It's so lovely here but it won't be enough for me. I'm not you. I can't paint and there is no one I love who will rush to me whenever he is free and I will not stand here day after day looking for a swan and finding a bloody beer bottle.

Her eyes filled with those so-ready tears and she sighed and turned back with the bottles to the cottage, where the strident ringing of her new telephone greeted her.

'We've done it, Holly. Taylor has given in.'

Otto was jubilant. After months of expensive litigation, Taylor Hartman had capitulated. No reason given. 'Miss Noble may sell her paintings. Mr Hartman sees no reason to continue the action and has withdrawn his suit.'

Holly did not feel the exhilaration that she had expected. In fact she felt even more bereft. She roused herself to pretend normality. 'Why, Otto?' Because the secret was a secret no longer or because he . . . Shut up, Holly.

She almost heard the shrug of expensive tailoring. 'Clearly, it doesn't matter now; the secret is out. He has given in. We've won. I shall ring all my friends in the media immediately.'

'Wait, Otto. Let me speak to Taylor first. I have to know why he gave in. The paintings have waited; they can wait a little longer.'

'Very unwise, Holly; the timing is perfect.'

Her mind was made up. 'Otto, make no plans until I have spoken to him.'

She was sick with tension. She nerved herself to dial Taylor's office. 'Mr Hartman has just left Switzerland for Japan, Miss Noble. May I ask him to call you?'

Holly had no choice but to wait.

She telephoned Otto again when it was obvious that she was not going to hear from Taylor that day. 'It's time zone, I think, Otto, but I won't authorise the sale until I hear from him.'

Suddenly she felt ravenously hungry and she went into the kitchen to scramble some eggs and make some toast and tea.

Why had Taylor resigned from the fray?

Is this my pay for services rendered? I can't bear it. Don't make me a whore, Taylor.

Much better than sapphires, but it was such an empty victory.

She had eaten too much too quickly. She felt absolutely dreadful and was violently sick. The last time she had been sick was when Nicole told her about the abortion so this, obviously, was a delayed reaction to her visit to the sanatorium. Her horror at the picture of poor Eleanor had been buried for a while by her passion for Taylor.

She felt much better in the morning. Then the postman cycled down the hill and brought her a packet. It was from the Hartman Corporation. She could not bring herself to open it. Obviously he had carried out his threat and had sent sapphires.

Pain grabbed at her insides. 'No, Taylor, please no,' she howled.

She stood with the parcel in her hands. She wanted to open it and, at the same time, she wanted to dispose of it. Thoughts went whirling round and round in her head and her fingers itched to tear open the brown paper. There was no reason for Taylor to send anything to her and this was square and hard. It was, therefore, not a letter. She stared at the label while something inside sighed and died. She had hoped and prayed and now she knew it had been futile. She could not bear to see what value he put on their glorious abandonment.

What was I worth, Taylor?

She dropped the package on the floor and almost recoiled from it.

A few minutes later she was standing on the headland and tears of the most abject despair were rolling, unchecked, down her cheeks.

If my tears fell into the sea would they make a difference? Oh, God, to whom, to what? I care only for Taylor and he has paid me what he thinks I'm worth.

Holly stood there for some time, aware of the swans at anchor, like ghostly galleons, on the waves.

Sweat beaded on her forehead. She felt hot and clammy and colder than she had ever felt in her life.

She sniffed loudly and drew her fingers across her face. 'Stuff you, Taylor,' she said, turned, and almost ran back to the cottage. She punched the button on the telephone that would give her Otto's number.

'I have changed my mind. Never mind Mr Hartman. Sell the paintings and to the highest bidder.'

'But Holly, what—' he began.

'Just do it.' She almost slammed the new receiver back on its rest, and then, calmly, but with the same violence, she kicked the offending package and watched it slide out of sight under the chest of drawers.

Uncle Fire

TORRY BAY, 1999. TORRY BAY, 1967–1972

Holly knelt in front of the fire looking at the photographs of Tony's paintings. Everything you have ever learned is buried in your subconscious, a lecturer had informed her during her university years. She dug deep. Of course, of course. She remembered now, Uncle Fire. She had met him twice, maybe three times. Tony must have taken great pains to see that they never met when she was older, when she was capable of recognising one of the world's most famous men, and, worse, telling her strait-laced parents all about him.

Holly sat back on her heels and looked at the picture. Blaise Fougère in a fur coat was walking out into the sea and he was holding by the hand a little girl dressed in nothing more than a minuscule bikini. The child was dancing beside him and it was obvious that she was ecstatically happy and not at all cold. Holly stared at her four-year-old self. And then at Blaise, his feet bare and his trousers rolled up around his calves under the folds of the fur coat. He was looking back at the artist and laughing. He looked young, carefree, and incredibly happy.

He had not been expected. She had been staying with Tony while her parents were away on yet one more evangelical crusade, and together aunt and niece were lining a path with lovely white shells that they had collected on the beach. Neither of them had heard the car but, all of a sudden, something big had blotted out the sun and Holly looked up to see him standing there.

Tony had, to a four-year-old mind, behaved very strangely. She had jumped up and thrown herself into the man's arms and they had kissed. A kiss that was very different from the chaste salutes exchanged by Holly's parents, a kiss that had gone on for a very long time; so long that she had lost patience and pulled at Tony's legs.

'The path,' she had demanded imperiously, and to her surprise the big man had squatted down beside her.

'Hello, Holly, I am your Uncle Blaise. Permit me to help.'

Immediately she had handed him a shell that he had arranged with gratifying care on the path; she had awarded him a smile.

In the morning she had not remembered his name and when he did not appear at the breakfast table she had cast around in her memory bank for his name so that she could question Tony. At last, when she was almost ready to explode with frustration, she had remembered. 'Where is he?' she had demanded. 'Uncle Fire.'

Uncle Fire he had remained. Funny how she had forgotten all about him and had never once found anything familiar about Blaise Fougère. She had heard his recordings; she had seen occasional broadcasts from Covent Garden or the Metropolitan Opera House in New York; but she doubted if she had ever heard his speaking voice. Surely she would have recognised Uncle Fire's voice? But Blaise Fougère was notorious for avoiding interviews and he appeared on no talk shows.

Holly looked at the painting with eyes bright with unshed tears. The child Holly had loved her Uncle Fire. It was obvious in the way she danced confidently beside him, her little toes barely touching the sand: the tall figure in the ridiculous fur coat was making no concession to the child's size.

How the child, now grown up, wished she could remember more.

Tony had looked up when his bulk had blotted out the sun and her heart had danced. She had forgotten Holly, the path, everything but her overwhelming love, and she had thrown herself into his strong, reaching, waiting, demanding arms.

Eventually little Holly had pulled on her legs with her small but equally demanding fingers. 'The path.'

Blaise had stooped down with his inexhaustible courtesy and begun to help and Tony had said nothing. He was here. Holly was here. The two people she loved most in the entire world, in her heart, and now here in her home. She thought her heart would choke her and he knew what she was thinking because he looked up and smiled.

'Now we are a family, *ma mie*,' he said. 'Does she sing, this little one?'

'No, but she makes lovely red paintings.'

'I will teach her to sing. All children can sing, *ma mie*. It is as easy as to breathe. Sing, Hollyberry.' He began. '*Sur le pont d'Avignon, l'on y danse, l'on y danse . . .*'

When Tony stood up to go into the cottage, Holly was lisping along in recognisable French and curtsying to the tall man who bowed to her in their song as if she were the greatest diva in the world.

'Don't fret, *ma mie*. I have our meal in the car.'

She blushed because she intended to change the sheets and he knew that too and smiled at her wickedly.

'But there are other things you have to do while Mam'selle and I complete our task.' He bent again to the little girl. 'Tell me, Hollyberry, do you prefer white chocolate or brown?'

'Bof,' she said and smiled at him with a smile that stole his heart away.

'You have a rival,' he told Tony later. They lay wrapped in one another's arms and scents. 'The parents must be better than you say.'

Tony sighed and twisted her fingers more tightly into the curling hairs on his broad chest. 'She likes you.'

'*Bien sûr*,' he agreed complacently. 'All women love me.'

She pulled the hair to punish him. 'When?' she whispered softly.

'I have tomorrow and the next day I must go. London for three weeks. You will come?'

'I can't.'

'Bring her. During the day you can show her all our favourite places, the park, the bandstand; and in the evenings . . . what can we do in the evenings, Toinette?'

'We can do nothing, my heart, because they love you too much in London. On the nights when you are not singing there will be parties and I cannot go to them.'

She did not mean to sound aggrieved. She tried so hard not to let her status rankle.

He propped himself up with pillows. He had no idea how flattering was the moonlight. He looked like a creature not quite of this earth, of air and water perhaps. His annoyance, however, was most assuredly worldly. 'I will not parade you before the world as a trophy, Tony.'

'I would hate that,' she mumbled into her pillow.

'Or even as a friend. The world would talk.'

His world, the world of the opera, and that other world, Eleanor's world. Tony's world was Chrissie, Simon, the canon and Holly.

'If you exhibited more, came to London more . . . New York . . . ,'

'I could not hide how I feel, Blaise. Could you?'

He looked down at her. Her face was hidden and he traced her spine with one finger and felt her tremble. His finger continued its voyage of discovery and when he reached her ankle he turned her over and began the journey up, up, until neither of them could bear more and he gathered her trembling to him. 'No, *ma mie,* I could not hide my love.'

When she climaxed she screamed his name and only when they were calm did they remember the child.

'I'll check her,' Tony said and slipped off the bed.

Holly was lying on top of her bed, one little leg bent. Her arms cradled her parents' sole concession to childhood, a toy cat. 'Tomorrow we will buy you a doll, Holly,' she whispered. 'I loathe cats.'

The morning brought another perfect day and after breakfast Tony took Holly down to the beach.

Instantly Tony wished she had said nothing. 'No, darling. They're very busy.'

'Like Uncle Fire?'

'Sort of.'

'He'll come. He works very hard, Holly, and so he was very tired last night. He came all the way from Australia to see you.'

The little girl looked up from her digging. 'Mummy and Daddy too?' she asked hopefully.

'Uncle Fire?'

'I'll check her,' Tony said.

She went on with her digging, singing to herself. '*Sur le pont . . .*'

Tony leaned back against a boulder and dozed.

'*Café,* mam'selle?' Blaise was bending over her with a mug of fragrant coffee. 'You have been snoring with your mouth open, *ma mie.* Hollyberry and I have been laughing.'

Tony squinted up at him. 'That's rather unkind,' she said as she took the mug. 'I got very little sleep last night.'

They sat quietly drinking their coffee and watching the little girl. This was how it should have been. If only, if only.

'You are cold, *ma mie?*' he whispered against her hair.

'No. I was just thinking . . .' She could not go on.

He singed me a new song. Does he sing hymns like Daddy?'

She was not comparing the voices but Tony smiled at the thought. 'I don't think so.'

'Good.'

His arms tightened around her. 'I too, but we have this time, this child. We must be grateful, Toinette. Hollyberry,' he called. 'Aunt Tony wishes to buy you a doll. What shall it be?'

The little girl put down her spade very carefully. She stood up and brushed the sand from her plump little knees and then she came and stood in front of him, looking straight into his eyes. 'A really truly doll?'

'*Ça va sans dire.* Whatever Hollyberry wishes.'

'A fairy princess with a beautiful frock and a magic wand.'

Tony was distressed. 'Blaise, Chrissie won't have a doll that looks anything like that.'

'Tomorrow I go to London, Hollyberry, and I will go to this wonderful store which is full of dolls of all kinds and I will find the most beautiful princess for you.'

Again the child examined his face and, as if she liked what she saw, she smiled. 'All right,' she said. 'Swimming now?'

He groaned—he found even the Pacific chilly—but he stood up.

'Blaise, the water is freezing. You will catch cold.'

'Let's get changed. Mam'selle Holly will swim and I will, what you call, paddle.'

When Tony had changed Holly into her little swimsuit they found Blaise in the living room. He was wearing the heavy fur coat he had left in the cottage at the end of his last winter visit. Holly saw nothing strange in his attire but Tony laughed. 'God, if your fans could see you now. You look so ridiculous; a fur coat and bare feet.'

He leaned over and kissed her. 'The sun is hot but the water is cold. Is that not so, Holly?'

Holly shrugged. She was four years old and accepted everything that adults did. Her touching innocence affected Blaise deeply and he tightened his grip on the little hand that pulled him towards the door. 'I have a nephew called Taylor, Holly. I love him as much as Aunt Tony loves you. You must meet him one day and play with him. You will be good friends.'

'Is he a little boy or a big boy? I don't like big boys.'

'One day you will.'

'How very French you are, Blaise Fougère. Now, if you are going to walk into the sea in a fur coat I must get my sketchbook.'

'Another chef-d'oeuvre. What is it to be called, *ma mie*? The fur coat . . . *Siegmund in the Sea*?'

She looked up at him as he grinned down at her. He was so happy with the child and his silly coat. Her stomach tightened with love. 'No,' she said slowly. 'It will be called *Uncle Fire*.'

Uncle Fire.

Holly stood up and jumped around to relieve the pins and needles in her legs. How long had she been sitting there lost in thought? *Uncle Fire.* Blaise Fougère was Uncle Fire. She remembered the doll. He had sent it but it had stayed at Torry Bay in its box for two years before she had been able to play with it. Her parents had returned to a church in Glasgow and so there were no visits to Torry Bay for a while. Tony had come though, that first Christmas, and she had tucked the little girl up in bed on Christmas Eve.

'Holly, do you remember the fairy princess, the one you wanted?'

Holly had looked at her and had remembered. 'He forgot,' she said.

'No, darling. She arrived the day you left and she's the most beautiful princess in the world.'

'With golden hair?'

'Of course, and blue eyes, and a white dress sparkled with stars.'

'And a wand.'

'Bien sûr,' Tony had said and buried her head in the pillow so that Holly would not see how close she was to crying.

'Bien sûr,' Holly had repeated. 'Tell her I'm coming as soon as I can.'

'She'll wait. We are very good at waiting in our family.'

The princess had waited for two years and Holly had played with her every holiday. Where is she now? the grown-up Holly wondered. I remember playing with her until . . .

Until what? She had absolutely no idea what had happened to the beautiful doll. Had her memory of Blaise Fougère and of the doll disappeared together? No point in trying. The memories would come back when they were ready. She looked at the painting again, saw the expression of mischievous delight on Blaise's face, and saw Tony so clearly, although her body was not in the painting. Her heart was.

How they loved each other. That's what I want: love that can withstand anything that life throws at it.

'I will keep this painting, Taylor,' she said and would have felt a great deal better if she had thought for one second that Taylor even cared.

Two weeks later, Holly, in a designer suit and an almost as expensive designer haircut, stood again in Otto's newly decorated salon nervously awaiting the hordes of socialites, international critics and buyers, and representatives of the world's media who had promised/threatened to attend. Many, unfortunately, were interested in more than the worth of the paintings. The painter, the subject and the subject's wife were all favourite topics of conjecture.

'How many years did the affair between artist and subject last?'

'All their lives.'

'Oh, how sad.'

'Oh, how sordid.'

'No, how stupid. What a waste.'

'His wife was in a sanatorium, for God's sake. I think it's lovely.'

Holly sighed and looked around. Already there was barely room to move among the paintings, so great had been the interest. Several carried NFS stickers; they were not for sale and were the ones that she and Nicole had decided to keep. Nicole's cheque, her donation to the Tony Noble Foundation for artistically talented but disadvantaged children, seemed to weigh heavily in Holly's ridiculous evening bag.

There was a stir among the great and the good, in other words, the wealthy. Taylor stood at the door, surely aware of his amazing looks, and the effect they were having on Otto's guests. Holly's stomach fluttered. So must his uncle have stood, allowing the masses to admire, while only the special few could get close enough to touch.

Taylor took his time looking around and then pretended that he had just seen Holly. She stared back at him. What she thought of his sapphires, still lying under her furniture, she would never tell him—unless he asked. She would hold up her head and, what was the expression, 'tough it out'.

He did not ask.

Followed by his satellites, both male and female, he ploughed his way through the crowds towards her. 'Miss Noble,' he began politely, coldly, as he reached her. He smiled thinly. 'I like the suit, and the new haircut. A new image?'

She ignored that. 'Why did you come?'

'My dear Miss Noble, I have every right to be here. Besides, have you been reading London's finest newspapers?' The words seemed to spit themselves out from between the oddly smiling lips. 'You don't think they're done with us, do you? Believe it or not'—for a moment his eyes softened and his face relaxed—'I am here to protect you, even though you have shown me that you don't give a damn what I do.'

She flushed. She was the one who had been paid in stones. 'The speculation was bound to be renewed. If you had only told me the truth—'

'I spent a great deal of money and an unbelievable amount of time hiding the truth that the scavengers wanted. My aunt's misery is now fodder for gossip columnists. I truly hope that you are strong enough to bear discovering that money can't buy happiness.'

'I'm giving it away.'

He looked down at her and smiled broadly now, that smile that turned her very bones to thistledown. 'Well done, *ma mie*.' He turned and was gone.

Holly stood, will-o'-the-wisp turned back to stone. *Ma mie*. It was, surely, a French endearment and she knew that she had heard it before. Not from Taylor. She was shaking from her confrontation with him and wished she was anywhere else. No, not anywhere. Torry Bay.

Then there was Nicole.

Holly had had some difficulty speaking to Taylor's mother. She had lied or at least been economical with the truth. She had known about Eleanor. When Holly had taxed her with deception she had said, as she had said once about Taylor, 'But, my dear, it was none of your business.' The French. So practical.

'Sometimes I wish Tony had painted some smaller canvases,' Holly said now, trying to smile.

'You must buy an apartment with lots of wall space.'

Holly shook her head. 'No, I've decided to stay at Torry Bay for the foreseeable future and the walls are really too small for such work.'

'Nicole. Darling.'

Holly had so far managed to avoid the celebrity journalist but knew from the gleam in this woman's eyes that she would not get away easily.

'Amy, how nice. Miss Noble, have you met Amy Rosenthal?'

'Miss Noble, how wonderful. Nicole, darling, you'll let me steal our little celebrity, won't you?'

Je vous en prie.' Nicole smiled and slipped away.

Amy watched her go. The eyes had stopped smiling and all at once the predator appeared. 'Now, Holly, I want you to know whatever anyone else has offered, we will beat it.'

'The paintings are priced, Miss Rosenthal. No negotiation.'

'You misunderstand me—Taylor, why don't you go away?'

Taylor, alone for once, had returned to Holly's side.

'Your wish is my command, Amy dear. But . . . forgive me . . . I must take Holly with me. We have an interview with a Japanese station. How's your Japanese, Holly darling?' He smiled into her eyes as he tucked his hand into her arm. 'What are you thinking of?' he hissed as he propelled her through the crowd, which parted like the Dead Sea before the wrath of God. 'That woman could make mischief if she was locked in an empty room.'

'Mrs Hartman left me with her.'

He stopped in mid-stride. 'Mother? Now what's her agenda?'

The next hour was a blur for Holly. She and Taylor smiled and posed for countless photographs and were asked innumerable questions in several languages. They answered the polite ones, which were mainly about the discovery of the paintings, and became adept at avoiding or deflecting those that probed too closely. Holly was grateful that Taylor made no attempt to deny the relationship that had existed between the artist and her subject.

'Miss Noble, when did you discover that there had been an affair between Blaise Fougère and Tony Noble?'

'All is speculation.'

'What documentation exists?'

Holly swept her hand around the vast room and said nothing.

'Mr Hartman, your aunt——'

'Has suffered enough in her life. Like Mr Fougère and Miss Noble she must be left in peace.'

'Since the evidence suggests a love affair, Miss Noble, can you tell us why Tony and Blaise never married? Did they make a pact to wait until Mrs Hartman passed away?'

'They are dead and their tragedies and sorrows should be allowed to die with them,' Holly managed bravely while her fists curled.

'Is it true, Mr Hartman, that the Ridgeway family refused to countenance divorce?'

Taylor was still smiling but Holly could feel the tension. 'My uncle loved my aunt until he died. No more questions, ladies and gentlemen. Go look at the paintings. They should be enjoyed as great works. The critics, the connoisseurs, are buying them up. See them while you can.'

He turned Holly round and pushed his way through the crowds into Otto's office. Nicole was there. 'Was that dreadful, darling?'

'You were clever to hide, Maman,' said Taylor. 'Did you buy the ones I wanted, with your permission of course, Miss Noble?'

'Clover and Les Dents de Lion, mon ange. Is that permissible, Holly?'

'Of course.' Holly was exhausted. She wanted to steal away like a wounded animal to lick her wounds. 'When will this be over?'

'It has been over for some time; they have all sold.'

Holly, feeling both drained and exhilarated, looked at him. 'How do you know?'

Taylor pointed to the gallery. 'You can see red dots from here, of course, but my secretaries are there; I am informed.'

Holly sat back and closed her eyes. Tony Noble had arrived in the world where she had always belonged. 'The buyers, Taylor?'

'Just as you wanted,' he said flatly and without emotion. 'Galleries all over the world as well as to private collectors. You have made millions.

That should make you happy. Good night, Maman.'

He said nothing to Holly but walked out. They sat and watched his progress through the room, attendants running along to keep up.

His mother stood up. 'Will you dine with me?'

Holly shook her head. 'I have an unbearable headache, madame.'

'Tension, my dear, but look at darling Otto. He's almost jumping up and down. We have a foundation, too, and all the money from the sales of Blaise's re-releases goes into it. I did tell you I authorised re-releases, didn't I? So sensible. Both our foundations have done well and, for you, the best thing, *ma belle*, Tony is acknowledged, *n'est-ce pas?*'

'I will wait to see what the papers have to say,'

Holly stood up, the world swam around her, and she knew no more.

Rainbows
TORRY BAY, 1978

'**I**t is extraordinary, Tony, you have no education.'

She turned round and laughed at him and the breath caught in his throat at the love and laughter in her eyes. 'I know wot I likes,' she teased.

He determined not to smile. 'I am serious, Antoinette. Do they teach nothing in these English schools for girls? You can read and write, and you can paint, but that you did not learn at this St Agnes.'

'I learned to love beauty there. Rainbows for instance. Every time I see a rainbow now, my heart fills with joy. Just think, Blaise, all the flowers that wither are gathered up together to form rainbows.'

She was teasing him. He knew it, but his practical French soul would not allow him a way out. 'Wait a moment. I have to translate that.' He closed his eyes and thought for a moment. 'A rainbow is an . . . arc, an arch with prismatic colours in order, the seven colours, you know, and it is cause by the reflection and . . .' he hesitated; what was the word in English? '*disperser* . . . the dispersion of the sun's rays in the drops of the falling rain.'

'Darling Blaise,' she said. 'How dull. I much prefer the withered roses theory and so we shall use that.'

They had reached the top of the hill and the sea disported itself wantonly in front of them, rushing in wildly and then drawing itself shyly back.

'It's so beautiful.'

'*C'est vrai*,' he agreed, but he was not looking at the sea.

Much later they brushed the grass from their clothes and wandered back down the hill, hand in hand.

That evening, he cooked dinner while she painted. Months later, when he saw the finished work and examined it closely, he saw that the rainbow over his head was composed of tiny flowers.

CHAPTER FIFTEEN
LONDON, 1999. TORRY BAY, 1999

WHEN SHE CAME TO she was half-lying on one of Otto's white sofas. It was so comfortable; she would stay there for ever. Holly sighed.

'Well, you did take centre stage for a moment there, *ma chérie*,' said a voice she vaguely remembered. Nicole Hartman.

She sighed again and lay back. Then she remembered where she was. Oh, my God, the exhibition. She started up, but a firm cool hand held her down.

'Only Otto and the catering staff are left, and me, of course. How professional of you to wait until the party was almost over.'

She sat up. 'I don't know what came over me; the heat and the crowd, I suppose.'

Older, wiser eyes smiled gently into hers. 'I think you know very well what came over you, Holly. It is the whites of the eyes, *mon enfant*; one can always tell.'

Holly sat up. 'It honestly never occurred to me. My age, I suppose. When I did think . . . I was afraid to hope.'

'*Et maintenant*, like Tony, you will—'

Holly put out her hand to stop the words. 'Oh, no, I won't'.

'Dear child, I meant like Tony you will go back to Torry Bay to wait. *Pauvre* Otto, I shall let him in? He was quite terrified.'

Holly nodded and watched Nicole walk across the seemingly miles of white carpeting to the glass door. When she returned with Otto, Holly was on her feet tidying her hair. 'I'm so sorry, the heat and all those people . . .'

Otto smiled at her. 'My dear girl, you quite frightened me but Taylor was so good.'

Holly felt a flush stealing up her neck. 'Taylor? But he had gone.'

'Luckily he had turned to say something to Chandler when you fell, Holly,' said Nicole. 'Taylor picked you up and put you on the sofa.'

Taylor had carried her in his arms. My God, did he know? Nicole seemed to read her mind. 'He would have stayed, Holly, but I explained about stress and heat.'

She felt light-headed again, but with relief this time. 'You are all so kind, and I have caused enough commotion. I think I'll go back to my club. I'll talk to everyone tomorrow.'

She had to get away; she had to be alone to digest this wonderful but rather terrifying news.

'Very well,' said Nicole, taking charge. 'I shall drop you there.'

Less than thirty minutes later, Holly was alone in her room. She had promised to meet Otto the next morning to read the reviews in the papers, but she had no intention of keeping her promise. He'll forgive me. She smiled to herself. And anyway, they'll be wonderful. We have done it, Tony. You are taking your rightful place in art history and there hasn't been too much damage done to anyone.

She put a hand gently on her stomach, frighteningly, breathlessly aware of the miracle. Now she understood the mood swings and the fatigue of the last few weeks. Will you be a singing baby or a painting baby? Both? Neither? I don't care, little treasure, little gift from God. She ordered a light meal from room service, rang the desk to reserve all the newspapers, bathed and got ready for bed.

The next morning she stuffed the newspapers into her weekend bag and took the train to Scotland. How different from her last journey when everything had been a dark mess. Even the sun echoed her happiness. When she reached Glasgow she got her car out of the long-term parking lot, stopped at the first supermarket she saw and filled the car with healthy foods, before driving north to Torry Bay.

No car sat in her driveway, but she had not expected one. There was no sense of disappointment, just security and overwhelming peace. The ghostly voices drifted out on sunbeams to meet her, to welcome her home.

Darling girl, Hollyberry.

She would not look under the chest of drawers.

'Works of a master discovered, Tony. The papers are full of your ability to paint light, to paint emotion, to suggest with a flick of your paintbrush. *Uncle Fire* and *Flowers in the Stream* are coming back here. I've changed my mind about *Sea Sprite* and let Nicole have it, especially as she bought *Grief* to donate to a Scottish gallery. She also has *Refuge from the Storm* and Taylor has *Clover* and *Les Dents de Lion*. Boy, did he have to pay for them. A ghastly woman kept begging some Marvin to get the dandelions for her.'

Suddenly she laughed out loud. 'I'm talking to myself but I don't care. From now on I can blame my wonderful, magnificent condition.' She sat down abruptly. Her wonderful condition? Was it wonderful? She had always wanted a child . . . but not like this. She had wanted to create a family . . . but not like this.

The telephone disturbed her thoughts. Don't let it be Taylor. Let it be Taylor.

It was Otto. 'Do you know that Taylor did say that you had an odd habit of running away. We had a date, remember?'

'Forgive me, Otto.'

'Holly, you mustn't lock yourself away up there. It's not healthy. Are you well this morning?'

'Never better.'

'And never richer.'

'It's all going to the foundation, Otto. You may be on the board.'

'Honoured, but how are you going to live?'

'Tony left me a substantial legacy, Otto, so much so that I need to see a financial adviser. I'll ring you in a few days. Bye.'

She felt more at ease in the kitchen and was singing as she unpacked her groceries. '*Sur le pont d'Avignon, l'on y danse, l'on y danse . . .*' From what layer of memory had that song come? She remembered a beach, and a tall man in a fur coat bowing to a little girl in a bikini . . . .

'All children can sing, *ma mie*. Sing, Hollyberry.'

Ma mie. Of course. Nicole had told her. Blaise called Tony *ma mie* and Taylor . . . why Taylor?

The light went out of the day, Taylor. She could not ignore him, could not ignore that he was the father of her unborn child. Did he have rights? Did the child have rights . . . to Taylor's love, to Nicole's? A family; but we're never going to be a family because he sent me sapphires to show me that he thinks no more of me than he does of a highly paid call girl.

Darling girl.

'Oh, you don't understand. He sent me sapphires to pay me. I kicked them under the chest in the living room. God, how childish.'

She went into the living room, got down on her knees and peered under the chest. There it lay, an innocuous-looking little package.

'Damn, damn, double damn. I should have taken them to the exhibition and thrown them at him.'

I'll go up to the village, buy a padded envelope and send them back; no need to explain.

Why didn't he ask me about them?

She answered herself. It would have been cruel, ungentlemanly. Oh, don't be so wet, Holly Noble.

She retrieved the package and blew off the accumulated dust.

'Oh, Tony, why did I let myself love him?' There was no answer. Of course there was no answer. She was alone, always alone.

She tore open the packet. Taylor had written a letter to accompany the gift. His writing was black and bold and very legible.

There was no excuse for the things I said. Forgive me but I hated you so much. I thought at last I had found someone who would be like Tony; a woman who would love me unconditionally; who wasn't impressed by my money, and you threw it in my face. Then I went to Switzerland because Mother asked me to check all the original recordings in Blaise's bank vault. She's quite a business-woman, my mother. She decided to make the publicity work for us. 'It's coming anyway,' she said, 'so milk it.'

We plan to re-release all of Blaise's recordings for the Fougère Mental Health Foundation. Blaise never recorded cross-overs although he could sing almost anything and so I was surprised to find this; he must have been working on it when he was killed. I admit it, Holly, and will no longer fight: Blaise loved Tony and these must have been letters to her. I send them to you. Please accept them, and with them—your Taylor.

The box did not contain sapphires. Inside was a compact disc. There was no company label. Instead there was a label bearing a few words: 'Pour ma mie.' Ma mie, the breath in my body.

Holly sat looking down at the note and the box. Stand up, genius of the month. If she had not been so quick to judge she would have opened the packet, found the letter, realised why Taylor had lifted his court order, greeted him with a warm smile instead of coldness. No wonder he had at first been frosty.

Please, God, don't let it be too late.

But first, what was on the disc? Tony? Tony had held technology at bay. She had conceded and put in electricity, but no telephone, and she would never have understood disc players.

Will I have to drive all the way to Glasgow to buy one?

The car! She rushed out. Thank God for yet another miracle of modern science. She sat in the driver's seat, turned on the engine and inserted the disc into the player. In a few moments the most flawless sound that Holly had ever heard enveloped her. The voice was at the same time beautiful and heroic, small in some passages and then robust and round in others. Everything was sung with exquisite style and outstanding musicianship and was of a highly individual timbre.

With tears running down her cheeks, Holly listened to the great tenor sing love songs in faintly accented English. He sang songs from musicals and he sang folk songs. Had they ever been sung more beautifully? It was as if he were playing: singing new things, snatches of this and that, occasionally a complete verse. The glorious voice sang accompanied at times only by a piano, at other times he sang *a capella*.

'You would have loved it, Tony.'

With shaking hands Holly took the CD out of the car player and went back to the cottage. She sat down at the table and picked up the telephone receiver.

'Mr Hartman is in Paris, Miss Noble.'

'Would you give Mr Hartman a message, please. Tell him I didn't open it; I thought it was sapphires.'

If his secretary's secretary was surprised she gave nothing away. She repeated the message carefully and Holly thanked her and hung up. Now there was nothing to do but to wait.

He came when she was sitting up at the point looking out to the bay where some swans floated serenely on the water. She heard the car, turned and smiled. Taylor was having trouble levering his frame out of the salmon-pink Mini. Her heart swelled with happiness. It must have been the only car left at the airport. Only a man very much in love . . . .

He managed eventually, turned and saw her, and began to run.

CHAPTER SIXTEEN
CONNECTICUT 1990. TORRY BAY, 1990

BLAISE SAT DOWN beside the woman who had been his lawfully wedded wife for forty-three years, and who had been a wife to him, in every accepted sense of the word, for only three of those years. He felt deep sorrow and overwhelming guilt.

'I'm tired, Eleanor. I'm almost seventy. I can't sing, not in the way I used to, and you know that when I was singing I could be oblivious of all

The milk boy brought a message. 'There's going to be a phone call—near to nine in the morning as he can get it.'

Tony as usual rose early to meet the demands of the light, but her heart was full as she hurried up to the village. In the shop she sat quietly for a minute or two, but at last the telephone rang.

'Hello.' His voice was dark with exhaustion.

'Blaise, why aren't you in bed at this time?'

Impatiently he brushed away the question. Fuss, fuss. '*Ma mie, ma mie*, will you marry me?'

'Marry you?'

'I looked in the mirror a few days ago and saw the world's greatest—'

'Tenor.'

'*Imbécile*, the ass,' he said and there was laughter in his voice, but then he added desperately, 'I did all I could, Toinette, didn't I?'

'You've been wonderful, my darling.'

She knew that he was smiling.

'Tony, you haven't answered me.'

Tony sighed. What difference would a few words and a piece of paper matter at this stage in their lives? They could be together though; that was something. 'I have been your wife all my life.'

'Will you marry me? I am on my knees.'

She laughed. 'Like Lohengrin?' she asked. 'Eyes raised to heaven, *Bien sûr*,' he said, 'but I am, as they say, fresh out of swords.'

'I will marry you.'

She heard his sigh of relief.

'There is much to do here, the divorce and cutting all the ties, legal

the problems in my life, all the worries, big and small. I could forget you and even Toinette. Sometimes I used to go almost mad with guilt about you and about her. Two women loved me and I ruined both their lives. I'm leaving, Eleanor. I want some peace and I know where to find it.'

His heart filled with an intense joy. 'Toinette, my darling Toinette.' His wife, except in the eyes of God, or was God kinder than man?

He decided not to contact her immediately. First he would take care of all the legal business in New York. He had not sung for years but there were so many teaching colleges, so many boards and opera houses, and he was leaving them all. His stomach churned and he felt like a boy on his first date: scared, full of anticipation. Fifty-three years. Over half a century of love and pain, sorrow and great joy, and soon, please God, if Tony agreed, he would be able to tell the world.

affairs, lawyers, wills, that kind of thing, and then, Toinette, we will marry before the eyes of God and man and we will never be apart again. I can't believe how stupid I have been. Forgive me, Toinette.'

'You have been the most decent man, Blaise.'

'For decency's sake I have wasted your life, and mine too. As soon as I sign the last damn piece of paper I am coming to you.'

'I shall watch for you sailing across the bay on the wings of your swan.'

He laughed. 'I am too old for swans,' he said, 'but not for love.'

Stefan died with him, of course, and so Tony read it in the papers like everyone else: BLAISE FOUGÈRE KILLED IN AIR CRASH. 'Blaise Fougère, arguably the finest tenor of his generation, and certainly the greatest singer ever produced by France, was killed this morning when his private plane exploded on take-off . . .'

She did not need to read further. He had been coming to her and he was dead. There was nothing else to know.

'Except, perhaps, why can't I die too?'

She went up to the headland and sat watching Lohengrin. Surely he would sail away now, abandoning her as Blaise had abandoned her. It was final this time. There would be no loving letters, and no sudden visits. How would she bear it? There was Holly, of course, but she could not write to her, not yet, because Holly would know that all was not well and the time was not right to reveal her secret. She would reveal it though—after poor Eleanor . . . one day.

She began to make her preparations. She took Blaise's clothes and wrapped a few old favourites in garment bags and hung them in the wardrobe. Holly would recognise them in the paintings. She opened all the boxes of jewels. She hoped Holly would wear them. Jewels would suit the girl as they had never suited her aunt. She sat for hours remembering each occasion on which he had given her a gift.

'Don't say no, *ma mie*. You let me do so little for you.'

'Let me buy you a ring, Toinette. You have only my old signet ring.'

She had persuaded him to take the ring back to give to his beloved nephew. Of course she had wanted to keep it, but Taylor was like the son she had stolen from him and the ring should be his.

'I feel that you are my husband, Blaise. I no longer need a ring to prove it to myself or to the world. See, I will wear my rubies.'

He had laughed at her. Oh, his laugh. It was like life-giving water tumbling down from the stream behind the cottage.

'Rubies with jeans, *ma mie*. You have set the trend.'

Now Holly should wear them and enjoy them, not with that rather stuffy young lawyer she was dating, but that was not for her aunt to say. That was for Holly's heart to decide. Can I write, 'Never settle for second best, Holly', or is she sensible enough? Shall I write and explain my relationship? No, Holly will understand. She will know he never ever meant to hurt me. Carefully and methodically, and very slowly, because the weight of a broken heart was dragging her down, Tony wrapped her jewels, and went upstairs to look at her paintings for the last time.

I cannot stand up in here, ma mie.

Had she known he would be there? She smiled at him. 'I was wondering whether to write Holly a long letter.'

Your life's work is a long letter. My Hollyberry will understand, and she will make Taylor understand too.

'Can you stay?'

I will always be with you, ma mie, while I wait as you waited.

EILEEN RAMSAY

Art and music are Eileen Ramsay's twin passions, and so it seemed appropriate that when I met her in London she had just been to see the Summer Exhibition at the Royal Academy of Arts in Piccadilly and was full of enthusiasm for it. 'You must go,' she told me. 'I just love art, although I don't paint at all.'

Born and brought up in the Southwest of Scotland, she did not know what she wanted to do with her life. 'As a little girl, my dream was to be a ballet dancer. Then, as I got older, it never occurred to me that I could be a real writer even though I wrote all the time, stories and poetry, all long lost, thank goodness! I took what seemed the only option to me and became a teacher.'

Eileen went to teach in America for a year and ended up staying for eighteen. 'My first job was at the Sacred Heart School in Washington, DC—a school of high-powered little people with famous parents—I was petrified of teaching them! It was a needless worry, for they were all delightful. Years later one was actually a bridesmaid at my wedding. They taught me a valuable lesson: all children, rich, poor, black, white, sick, well, are the same and deserve the best of what you can give them.'

One of the enduring gifts that Eileen passed on to her students was an appreciation of music. 'I remember one rainy day when I was a teacher and I was playing opera during a break. I suddenly turned round and noticed that some of the children had crept in and were listening and

186

loving what they heard. It was a Verdi opera. After that, every Tuesday at three o'clock, we would clean up the classroom and listen to each other's favourite music. Within two weeks the children stopped bringing in their music and just wanted to listen to my operas! Apart from my family, the great love of my life is opera. And you know, one of the things I love best about going to the opera is that you can be sitting with a duke on your left and a telephone engineer on your right and that's how it should be—classless.'

When Eileen married Ian, a Scottish scientist working on the first space missions to the moon, she was whisked away from Washington to life in sunny California. 'There I took two university degrees and had two children—my supreme accomplishment. I wrote stories for my boys and published them in small magazines and then began writing a Regency romance, while pretending to watch my sons swim. In fact a lot of my work was written while I pretended to watch cricket, rugby and riding.'

For the last eighteen years, home for Eileen and Ian has been in their native Angus, in a beautiful cottage in three acres of ground. It is here that Eileen writes and meticulously researches her novels. 'I love writing about my passions, art and music. But I hope that my reader doesn't realise that my knowledge of art and music is like a speck of sugar on a spoon. I just hope that in some small way I pass on some of the magic.'

Jane Eastgate

187

Brought up by a drunken mother who had a different boyfriend every week, Julie Barenson left home as soon as she could. But her life took an upward turn when she met and married Jim and learned for the first time what it was like to love and be loved in return. Then, all too soon, tragedy cuts Julie's happiness short and she finds herself alone again—only this time she has a guardian angel on her side . . .

PROLOGUE
Christmas Eve 1998

EXACTLY FORTY DAYS after she'd last held the hand of her husband, Julie Barenson sat looking through her window towards the quiet streets of Swansboro. It was cold; the sky had been angry for a week, and the rain made gentle tapping sounds against the window. Trees were barren, their cragged limbs curling in the frigid air like arthritic fingers.

She knew Jim would have wanted her to listen to music tonight; she could hear Bing Crosby singing 'White Christmas' in the background. She'd put up the tree for Jim as well, though by the time she'd made the decision, the only trees left were dried out and sparse, free for the taking outside the supermarket. It didn't matter. Even when she finished decorating it, she couldn't summon the energy to care. It had been hard to feel anything at all since the tumour in Jim's brain finally took his life.

At twenty-five, she was a widow, and she hated everything about the word—how it sounded, what it implied. If people asked how she was doing, she simply shrugged. But sometimes, just sometimes, she had the urge to answer. *You want to know what it was like to lose my husband?* she wanted to ask. *Here's what it's like: Jim's dead, and now that he's gone, I feel like I'm dead, too.*

Is that, Julie wondered, what people wanted to hear? Or did they want platitudes? *I'll be OK. It's hard, but I'll make it through this. Thank you for asking.* It was easier to simply shrug and say nothing

After all, she didn't feel as if she were going to be OK. Half the time, she didn't think she was going to make it through the day without breaking down. Especially on nights like tonight.

In the reflected glow of the Christmas-tree lights, Julie put her hand to the window, feeling the cold press of glass against her skin.

Mabel had asked if she'd wanted to have dinner tonight. So had Mike and Henry and Emma. But she'd turned to have dinner tonight. All of them understood. Or, rather, they pretended to understand, since it was obvious that none of them thought she should be alone. And maybe they were right. Everything in the house, everything she saw and smelt and touched, reminded her of Jim. His clothes took up half the wardrobe, his razor still sat next to the soap dish in the bathroom. There were still two bottles of Heineken, his favourite, in the refrigerator. Earlier that evening, when she'd seen them on the shelf, she'd whispered to herself, 'Jim is never going to drink those,' and she'd closed the door and leaned against it, crying in the kitchen for an hour.

The scene outside her window was out of focus. Lost in her thoughts, Julie gradually registered a faint thumping. It was a moment before she realised someone was knocking at the door.

Julie stood, her movements lethargic. At the door, she paused to run her hands through her hair, hoping to compose herself. When she finally opened the door, she was surprised to see a young man in a yellow slicker. In his hands was a large, wrapped box.

'Mrs Barenson?' he asked.

'Yes?'

The stranger took a hesitant step forward. 'I'm supposed to deliver this to you. My dad said it was important.'

'Your dad?'

'He wanted to make sure you got this tonight.'

'Do I know him?'

'I don't know. But he was pretty insistent about it. It's a gift from someone.'

'Who?'

'My father said you'd understand as soon as you opened it. Don't shake it, though. And keep this end up.' The young man pushed the box into Julie's arms, then turned to leave.

'Wait,' she said, 'I don't understand . . .'

The young man glanced over his shoulder. 'Merry Christmas,' he said. Julie stood in the doorway, watching as he climbed into his truck. Then, back inside, she set the box on the floor in front of the tree and knelt beside it. A quick peek confirmed the absence of a card, and there were no other clues about the sender. She loosened the ribbon, lifted the separately wrapped lid and found herself staring wordlessly at what she'd been given.

THE GUARDIAN

It was matted with fuzz and dwarflike, no more than a few pounds, and it was sitting on its haunches in the corner of the box, looking just about as ugly as she'd ever seen a puppy look. Its head was large, out of proportion to the rest of its body. Whimpering, it looked up at her.

Someone, she thought, bought me a puppy. An ugly puppy.

Taped to the inside of the box was an envelope. As she reached for it, it dawned on her that she recognised the handwriting. She paused. No, she thought, it can't be. She held the envelope in front of her, reading her name over and over. Then, with trembling hands, she took the letter out.

Dear Jules,

It was Jim's nickname for her. Julie closed her eyes. She forced herself to take a deep breath and started again.

Dear Jules,

I know that if you're reading this letter, I've already passed away. I don't know how long I've been gone, but I hope you've been able to begin healing. I know that if I were in your position, it would be hard for me, but you know I've always believed you were the stronger of the two of us.

I bought you a dog, as you can see. Harold Kuphaldt was a friend of my father's, and he's been raising Great Danes since I was a kid. I always wanted one when I was little, but since the house was so small, Mom always said no. They are big dogs, granted, but they're also just about the sweetest dogs in the world. I hope you enjoy him (or her).

I guess I always knew in the back of my mind that I wasn't going to make it. I didn't want to think about it, though, because I knew that you didn't have any family to help you get through something like this. It broke my heart to think that you would be all alone. Not knowing what else to do, I made arrangements to get you this dog.

If you don't like it, you don't have to keep it, of course. Harold said he'd take it back, no problem. (His number should be included.)

I hope you're doing all right. Since I got sick, I've worried nonstop about that. I love you, Jules, I really do. I was the luckiest guy in the world when you came into my life. It would break my heart if I thought you'd never be happy again. So please do that for me. Be happy again. Find someone who makes you happy. It might be hard, you might not think it's possible, but I'd like you to try. The world is a better place when you smile.

And don't worry. From wherever I am, I'll watch out for you. I'll be your guardian angel, sweetheart. You can count on me to keep you safe.

I love you,
Jim

193

Through her tears, Julie peeked over the lid of the box and reached in. The puppy, a male, curled into her hand. She lifted him out and held him close to her face. He really was an ugly thing, she thought. And he'd grow up to be the size of a small horse. What on earth would she do with a dog like this?

The puppy started to whine, a high-pitched cry that rose and fell like the echo of far-off train whistles.

'Shh. You'll be OK,' she whispered. 'I won't hurt you.'

She talked to the puppy in low tones, letting him get used to her, still getting used to the idea that Jim had done this for her. The puppy continued to cry, almost as if accompanying the tune on the stereo. Julie scratched beneath his chin.

'You singing to me?' she asked, smiling. 'That's what it sounds like.'

For a moment, the dog stopped crying and looked up at her, holding her gaze. Then he started to whine again, though this time he didn't seem as frightened.

'Singer,' she whispered. 'I think I'll call you Singer.'

ONE
Four Years Later

IN THE YEARS since Jim had died, Julie Barenson had somehow found a way to start living again. It hadn't happened right away. The first couple of years after his death had been difficult and lonely, but time had eventually worked its magic on Julie, changing her loss into something softer. Though part of her would always love Jim, the pain wasn't as sharp as it had once been. Now when she thought of Jim, she remembered him with a smile, thankful that he'd been part of her life.

She was thankful for Singer, too. Jim had done the right thing by getting her the dog. In a way, Singer had made it possible for her to go on.

But at this moment, while lying in bed on a cool spring morning in Swansboro, North Carolina, Julie wasn't thinking about what a wonderful support Singer had been during the past four years. Instead, she was mentally cursing his very existence while gasping for breath, thinking, I can't believe that this is the way I'm going to die. Squashed in bed by my very own dog.

THE GUARDIAN

With Singer splayed across her, pinning her to the mattress, she imagined her lips turning blue from oxygen deprivation.

'Get up, you lazy dog,' she wheezed. 'You're killing me here.'

Snoring soundly, Singer didn't hear her, and Julie began squirming, trying to bounce him from his slumber.

'I'm serious,' she forced out. 'I can't breathe.'

Singer finally lifted his massive head and blinked at her groggily.

'Get off!' Julie rasped out.

Singer yawned, then pushed his cold nose against her cheek.

'Yeah, yeah, good morning. Now scoot!'

With that, Singer snorted and found his legs, squashing her further as he got up. And up. And up. Towering over her with just a smudge of drool on his lips, he looked like something from a low-budget horror movie. Good Lord, she thought, he is *huge*. You'd think that I'd be used to it by now. She took a deep breath and looked up at him, frowning.

'Did I say you could get into bed with me?'

Singer usually slept in the corner of her room at night. The past two nights, however, he'd crawled in with her. Or, more accurately, on top of her. Crazy dog.

Singer lowered his head and licked her face.

'No, you're not forgiven,' she said, pushing him away. 'Don't even bother trying to get out of this. You could have killed me. You're almost twice as heavy as I am, you know. Now get off the bed.'

Singer whined like a pouting child before hopping down to the floor.

Julie sat up. 'C'mon,' she said, 'I'll let you out. But don't go sniffing around the neighbours' garbage cans again.'

Singer left the bedroom, heading towards the front door. Julie followed in her pink pyjamas.

A moment later, he was outside. Instead of heading towards the garbage cans, Singer wandered over to the vacant wooded lots that bordered one side of her house. Thank heaven for small favours, Julie thought. Singer had been driving her crazy for the last couple of days. He'd followed her everywhere, refusing to let her out of his sight for even a few minutes, except when she put him outside. He was even worse at night. Last night, he'd had a growling fit for an hour.

Not that Singer's behaviour had ever been . . . well, ordinary. The dog had always acted as if he thought he were human. He refused to eat out of a dog bowl, he'd never needed a leash, and when Julie watched television, he would crawl up on the couch and stare at the screen. And when she talked to him—whenever anyone talked to him, for that matter—Singer would stare intently, his head tilted to the side, as if he were following the conversation. And no matter what she told him to do, Singer would carry it out. *Could you go get my bag from the bedroom?* Singer would come trotting out with it a moment later. *Will you turn off the bedroom light?* He'd balance on two legs and flick it with his nose. Sure, other dogs were well trained, but not like this. Besides, Singer hadn't needed training. Not real training, anyway. All she'd had to do was show him something once and that was it. To others it seemed downright eerie, but since it made Julie feel like a modern-day Dr Dolittle, she kind of liked it.

Singer, though, had been acting strangely ever since she started dating again, and he hadn't liked any of the guys who'd shown up at the door in the last couple of months. Julie had expected that part. Since he'd been a puppy, Singer tended to growl at men when he first met them. She used to think that Singer had a sixth sense that enabled him to tell the good guys from the ones she should avoid, but lately she'd changed her mind. Now, she couldn't help but think that he was just a big, furry version of a jealous boyfriend.

Julie went into the bathroom to start getting ready for work. Standing over the basin, she grimaced at her reflection. Look at me, she thought, I'm twenty-nine and falling apart at the seams. During the day, her brown hair was long and straight, but after a night in bed, it looked as if it had been attacked by comb-teasing pillow gnomes. It was frazzled and puffed out, 'under siege', as Jim so kindly used to put it. The tip of her nose was red, and her green eyes were swollen from the springtime pollen.

Maybe, she thought, she wouldn't have to work so hard at discouraging Bob's interest after all. She'd been cutting Bob's hair, or rather what was left of it, for a year now. Two months ago, he had finally worked up the nerve to ask her out. He was balding, with a round face, and had the beginnings of a paunch—but he was single and successful, and Julie hadn't been on a date since Jim had died. She figured it would be a good way to get her feet wet in the world of dating again.

Wrong. There was a reason Bob was single. Bob wasn't only a triple bogey in the looks department, he'd been so boring on their date that even people at nearby tables in the restaurant had glanced her way in pity. His preferred topic of conversation on their date had been accounting. He'd shown no interest in anything else: not her, not the menu, not the weather, not sports. Only accounting. For three hours, she'd listened to Bob drone on about itemised deductions and capital gains distributions. By the end of the dinner, Julie's eyes were so glazed that they could have flavoured a dozen doughnuts.

It went without saying, of course, that Bob had had a wonderful time.

He'd been calling three times a week since then, asking 'if they could get together for a second consultation, hee hee hee'. He was persistent, that was for sure. Annoying as hell, but persistent.

Then there was Ross, the second guy she dated. Ross the doctor. Ross the good-looking guy. Ross the pervert. One date with him was enough, thank you very much.

And can't forget good old Adam. He worked for the county, he said. He enjoyed his work, he said. Just a regular guy, he said.

Adam, she found out, worked in the sewers. The relationship was doomed from the start.

Just when she was beginning to wonder whether normal people like Jim even existed any more, Richard had come into the picture.

And, miracle of miracles, even after a first date last Saturday, he still seemed normal. A consultant with J. D. Blanchard Engineering, Cleveland—the firm repairing the bridge over the Intracoastal Waterway—he had made her acquaintance when he came into the salon for a haircut. On their date, he'd opened doors for her, smiled at the right moments in the conversation, and not so much as even tried to kiss her when he'd dropped her off. Best of all, he was good-looking in an artistic sort of way, with sculpted cheekbones, emerald eyes, black hair and a moustache.

Singer wasn't quite as impressed. After she'd said good night to Richard, Singer had growled until Julie opened the front door.

'Oh, stop it,' she'd said. 'Don't be so hard on him.'

Singer did as he was told, but he'd pouted the rest of the night.

If my dog were any more bizarre, she thought, we could team up and work for a carnival, right next to the guy who eats light bulbs. But then, my life hasn't exactly been normal, either.

Julie stepped into the shower, trying to stem the tide of memories. What was the use of replaying hard times? Her mother had been attracted to two things: booze and toxic men. Her mom went through boyfriends the way kids go through paper towels, and some of them made Julie feel uncomfortable once she hit adolescence. The last one had actually tried to have his way with her, and when Julie told her mother, her mother, in a drunken, teary rage, had blamed *her* for coming on to *him*. It wasn't long before Julie found herself without a home.

Living on the street had been terrifying for the six months or so before Jim came along. Most everyone she met used drugs and begged or stole . . . or worse. Scared of becoming like the haunted runaways she saw every night at the shelters and in the doorways, she searched frantically for odd jobs that would keep her fed and out of sight. When she first met Jim at a diner in Daytona, she was nursing a cup of coffee with the last of her change. Jim bought her breakfast and on the way out of the door said he'd do the same the following day if she returned. She did, and when she challenged him about his motives, Jim denied any improper interest in her. At the end of the week, when he was getting ready to head for home, he made her a proposal: If she moved to Swansboro, he would help her get a full-time job and a place to stay. She remembered staring at him as though he had bugs crawling out of his ears.

But a month later, she showed up in Swansboro, thinking as she got off the bus, What in the world am I doing in this nowhere town? Nonetheless, she looked up Jim, who—despite her persistent scepticism—brought her over to the salon to meet his aunt Mabel. And sure enough, she found herself sweeping floors for an hourly wage and living in the room upstairs from the salon.

At first, Julie was relieved by Jim's lack of apparent interest. Then curious. Then annoyed. Finally, after running into Jim repeatedly and dropping what seemed to her quite shameless hints, she broke down and asked Mabel if she thought Jim found her unattractive. Only then did he seem to get the message. They went on a date, then another, and the hormones were surging after a month together. Real love came a short time later. He proposed, they walked the aisle in the church where Jim had been baptised, and Julie spent the first few years of their marriage drawing smiley faces every time she doodled by the phone. What more, she wondered when considering her life, could anyone want?

A lot, she soon realised. A few weeks after their fourth anniversary, Jim had a seizure and was rushed to the hospital. Two years later, the brain tumour took his life and, at the age of twenty-five, Julie found herself staring over once more.

Nowadays, she thought, it was the little things in life that mattered. Mabel had helped Julie get her licence so she could cut hair and earn a living. Henry and Emma, two good friends of Jim's, had remained close. And then there was Mike, Henry's younger brother and Jim's best friend.

In the shower, Julie smiled. Mike. There was a guy who would make some woman happy one day, even if he seemed a little lost sometimes.

A few minutes later, after towelling off, Julie put on some make-up and slipped into her clothes. Since her car was at the garage, she'd have to walk to work—it was about a mile up the street—and she put on a pair of comfortable shoes. She called Singer just as she was locking the door on her way out, nearly missing what had been left for her.

Out of the corner of her eye, she spied a card wedged under the mailbox lid, right next to the front door. She read it on the porch as Singer burst from the woods and trotted up to her. *Dear Julie, I had a wonderful time on Saturday. I can't stop thinking about you. Richard*

So that was the reason Singer went bonkers last night.

'See,' she said, holding out the card so Singer could see it. 'I told you he was a nice guy.'

Singer turned away.

'Don't give me that. I think you're just jealous.'

Singer nuzzled against her. 'Don't be jealous. Be happy for me. Now c'mon. We have to walk because Mike's still fixing the Jeep.'

At Mike's name, Singer's tail wagged.

Mike Harris's song lyrics left a lot to be desired, and his singing voice didn't exactly make recording executives beat a path to his door in Swansboro. He did play the guitar and he practised daily, hoping his big break was just round the corner. Like many people, Mike had the dream and desire to be a musician. He just didn't have the talent.

He could, however, fix practically anything. He was the consummate handyman, a veritable knight in shining armour when puddles formed beneath kitchen sinks or when garbage disposals went on the blink. But if he was a good handyman, he was a modern-day Merlin when it came to anything with four wheels and an engine. He and Henry owned the busiest garage in town, and while Henry handled the paperwork, Mike was in charge of the actual work. He could listen to an engine and figure out what was wrong, usually in a couple of minutes.

The traditional ladies' man reputation associated with mechanics and musicians had passed Mike by. He'd had two serious girlfriends in his life, and since one of those relationships had been in high school and the other, with Sarah, had ended three years ago, a case could be made that Mike wasn't looking for a long-term commitment. At thirty-four, Mike Harris was remarkably well versed in the tender art of embracing women in brotherly hugs while they cried on his shoulder about what a jerk their previous boyfriend had been. It wasn't that he was unattractive. With light brown hair, blue eyes and an easy smile to go with his trim build, he was good-looking in an all-American kind of way. Nor was it that women didn't enjoy his company, because they did. His lack of luck had more to do with the fact that women who dated Mike sensed that a relationship with them wasn't what Mike was looking for.

His brother, Henry, knew why they felt that way. So did Mike's sister-in-law, Emma. Mabel knew the reason as well, as did practically everyone who knew Mike Harris.

Mike, they all knew, was already in love with someone else.

'Hey, Julie—wait up.'

Having just reached the outskirts of Swansboro's old-fashioned business district, Julie turned when she heard Mike calling. Singer looked up at her, and she nodded. 'Go ahead,' she said.

Singer galloped off, meeting Mike halfway. Mike stroked his head then scratched behind his ears as they walked. A moment later, they reached Julie.

'Hey, Mike,' Julie said, smiling. 'What's going on?'

'Not much. I just wanted to let you know your Jeep is done.'

'What was wrong with it?'

'The alternator.'

'Did you have to replace it?'

'Yeah. Yours was dead. No big deal—the dealer had plenty in stock. I also fixed the oil leak.'

'There was an oil leak?'

'Didn't you notice the stains in your driveway?'

'Not really, but then I wasn't looking.'

Mike smiled. 'Well, like I said, that's fixed, too. Do you want me to grab your keys and bring them by?'

'No, I'll get 'em after work. I don't need 'em until later. I've got appointments all day. So how much were the repairs?'

Mike scratched his chin absently. 'Two haircuts should do it.'

'Come on. Let me pay this time. I do have money, you know.'

In the past year, the Jeep, an older-model CJ7, had been in the garage three times. 'You are paying,' he said. 'Even though my hair's getting a little thinner, it does need to be cut now and then.'

'Well, two haircuts doesn't sound like a fair trade.'

'It didn't take all that long to fix. And the parts weren't that much.'

Julie raised her chin. 'Does Henry know you're doing this?'

Mike spread his arms, looking innocent. 'Of course he knows. I'm his partner. And besides, it was his idea.'

Sure it was, she thought. 'Well, thanks, I appreciate it.'

'My pleasure.' Mike paused. Wanting to talk a little longer but not knowing exactly what to say, he glanced towards Singer. Singer was watching him closely, his head tilted to the side, as if urging, *Well, get on with it, Romeo. Both of us know the real reason you're talking to her.*

Mike swallowed. 'So how'd it go with, um . . .'

'Richard?'

'Yeah. Richard.'

'It was nice.'

'Oh.' Mike nodded. 'So . . . where'd you go?' he asked.

'The Slocum House.'

'Pretty fancy for a first date,' he offered.

'It was either that or Pizza Hut. He let me pick.'

Mike shifted from one foot to the other. Not good, he thought. Richard was definitely different from Bob, the romantic number cruncher. Or Ross, the sex maniac. Or Adam from the bowels of Swansboro. With guys like that as the competition, Mike thought he stood a chance. But Richard? The Slocum House?

'So . . . you had a good time?' he asked.

'Yeah. We had fun.'

Fun? How much fun? This, he thought, was not good at all.

'I'm glad,' he lied, doing his best to fake enthusiasm.

Julie reached for his arm. 'Don't worry, Mike. You know I'll always love you the most, right?'

'That's just because I fix your car,' he said.

'Don't sell yourself short. You patched my roof, too.'

'And repaired your washing machine.'

She leaned over and kissed him on the cheek, then gave his arm a squeeze. 'What can I say, Mike? You're just a good guy.'

Julie could feel Mike's eyes on her as she walked to the salon, though unlike the way she felt about some men's attention, she wasn't bothered at all. He was a good friend, she thought, then quickly changed her mind. No, Mike was a *really* good friend, the kind of friend who made life in Swansboro a whole lot easier simply because she knew he'd always be there for her. Friends like him were rare, and that's why she felt bad for keeping some of the more private aspects of her life—like her most recent date—off limits.

She didn't have the heart to go into detail about it, because Mike, well, Mike wasn't exactly Mr Mysterious when it came to how he felt about her, and she didn't want to hurt his feelings. She knew Mike wanted to date her, she'd known that for a couple of years now. But her feelings for Mike were complicated. Jim and Mike had been best friends. Mike had been best man at their wedding, and Mike had been the one she'd turned to for comfort after Jim had died. He was more like a brother, and it wasn't as if she could flip a switch and suddenly change the way she felt.

But it was more than just that. What would happen if they did go out, but for whatever reason it didn't work out? Things could change between them, and she couldn't bear losing him as a friend. It was easier if things just stayed the way they were.

She suspected that Mike knew all of this, and it was probably the reason he'd never so much as asked her out.

Sometimes, though, she got the feeling that he was working up the nerve to do it, and Mike was a little comical when those moods seemed to strike him. Instead of being Mr Happy-Go-Lucky—the first to laugh at jokes—Mike would get quiet, as if he suspected his whole problem with Julie arose from the fact that she didn't think he was being quite cool enough.

Later, having been unable to summon the courage to ask her, he would be back to his old self. Julie liked that version of Mike a whole lot better. She liked guys who laughed, and Mike laughed a lot. And she really liked the sound of his laugh.

As she mulled this over, Singer nudged against her. He looked up at her. 'Yeah—go on, you big mooch,' she said.

Singer trotted ahead, then turned at the propped-open door of Mabel's salon. Mabel had a biscuit for him every day.

'So how'd her date go?' Henry leaned against the door frame next to the coffeemaker, talking over the rim of a Styrofoam cup.

'I didn't ask her about that,' Mike answered, his tone implying the very thought was ridiculous. He stepped into his coveralls and pulled them up over his jeans.

'Why didn't you ask?'

'I didn't think about it.'

'Mmm,' Henry said. At thirty-eight, Henry was four years older than Mike. Henry was taller and heavier and coasting into middle age. With a twelve-year marriage to Emma and three young girls and a house instead of an apartment, he had more stability in his life. Like most older brothers, he felt that he had to watch out for his younger sibling. That this brotherly support included teasing and the occasional zinger to bring Mike back down to earth might have struck some as heartless. But how else was he supposed to do it? Henry smiled. Somebody had to watch out for Mike.

Mike shrugged as he zipped up the coveralls. 'I just wanted to tell her that her car was finished.'

Henry nodded. 'So what did you charge Julie for her car this time? Three pencils and a sandwich? A shiny rock?'

'No, the usual.'

Henry whistled. 'It's a good thing I run the books around here.' Mike tossed him an impatient glance. 'You know you would have given her a deal, too.'

'I know that.'

'So why are you bringing it up?'

'Because I want to know how her date went.'

'How does what I charge her have to do with her date?'

Henry smiled. 'I'm not sure, little brother. What do you think?'

'I think you had too much coffee this morning and you're not thinking straight.'

Henry finished his cup. 'You know, you're probably right. I'm sure you don't care at all about Julie's date.'

'Exactly.'

Henry reached for the coffeepot and poured another cup. 'Then you probably don't care what Mabel thinks, either.'

Mike looked up. 'Mabel?'

'Yeah, Mabel. She saw them out on Saturday night.'

'How do you know?'

'Because I talked to her after church yesterday, and she told me about it.' Henry turned and headed for the office, breaking into a grin. 'But like you said, you don't care, so I'll just drop it.'

TWO

THOUGH ANDREA RADLEY had been working for Mabel for nine months, she wasn't the best of employees. Not only did she have a tendency to take 'personal days' without warning, she was rarely punctual. Nor was she particularly adept at styling and cutting hair. In fact, Andrea cut everyone's hair exactly the same way. Not that it mattered. Andrea had the same number of clients that Julie did, though, not surprisingly, every one of them was a man.

Andrea was twenty-three, a long-legged blonde with a perpetual tan, who looked as if she'd come straight from the beaches of California rather than the small mountain town of Boone, North Carolina, where she'd been raised. She did her best to dress the part, too—no matter how cold the weather, she wore miniskirts to the salon. She called every client 'sugar', batted her long, mascara-enhanced lashes, and chewed gum incessantly.

Despite her outward appearance, Andrea was a bit naive about men. Oh, she knew what men wanted, and for the most part she was right about that. What Andrea didn't understand was how to keep a man afterwards. It never occurred to her that her appearance might attract a certain type of man at the expense of another. She had no trouble getting dates with tattooed men who drove Harleys, or guys on parole, but she was never able to get a date with men who had steady jobs. In the past three months, she'd been out with seven different men with zero jobs, and right now she was feeling a little sorry for herself. On Saturday, she'd had to pay for dinner and the movie because her date didn't have any money. And had he called this morning? No. Of course not.

But Richard had called the shop this morning, asking for Julie.

Why, Andrea wondered, did Julie get all the good guys? It wasn't as if she dressed well, what with her jeans and baggy sweaters. So why had Richard been so taken with Julie? They had both been in the salon when he walked in last week, and they had both looked and said 'Hi' at the same time. But Richard had asked Julie to cut his hair, and somehow that had led to a date. Andrea frowned just thinking about it.

'Ouch!'

Brought back to the present by the yelp, Andrea glanced at her customer's reflection in the mirror.

'What happened, sugar?'

'You jabbed my head with the scissors. It hurt.'

Andrea's lashes fluttered. 'I'm sorry, sugar. You're not mad at me, are you?'

'No . . . not really,' he said finally.

Across the room, near the window, Mabel looked up from her magazine. The man, she noticed, was practically melting into the chair. She shook her head as Andrea started cutting again.

Mabel saw Julie come through the door a minute after Singer had entered. She was about to say hello when Andrea spoke up.

'Richard called,' Andrea said, not bothering to hide her disgust.

'He did?' Julie asked. 'What did he want?'

'I didn't ask,' Andrea snapped. 'I'm not your secretary, you know.'

Mabel shook her head, as if telling Julie not to worry about it.

At sixty-three, Mabel was one of Julie's closest friends—that she had been Jim's aunt was almost beside the fact. Mabel had given Julie a job and a place to stay eleven years earlier and Julie would never forget that, but Julie knew she would have enjoyed Mabel's company had none of those things happened.

THE GUARDIAN

It didn't matter to Julie that Mabel was a little eccentric. In her time here, Julie had learned that practically everyone in town had rather colourful aspects to their personality. Mabel drove a moped to the salon unless it was raining, favoured clothing with polka dots, and viewed her Elvis collectibles as 'fine art'. But Julie adored everything about her. Even her tendency to pry.

'So how'd it go with Richard?' Mabel asked.

'Well, to be honest, I was a little worried about you the whole time,' Julie said. 'I thought you might pull a neck muscle if you craned your head any further trying to listen in.'

'Oh, don't worry about that,' Mabel said. 'A little Tylenol and I was good as new the next day. Did it go OK?'

'It went well, considering I just met him.'

'From where I was sitting, it almost looked like he knew you from somewhere.'

'Why do you say that?'

'I don't know. His expression, I guess, or maybe it was the way he kept staring at you all night.'

Julie laughed as she slipped into her smock.

'I guess I must have dazzled him.'

'I suppose.'

Something in her tone made Julie look up. 'You didn't like him?'

'I'm not saying that. I haven't even met him yet, remember? I was out when he came into the shop, and you didn't exactly introduce us on Saturday. You were too busy staring back.' Mabel winked.

Just then, the door swung open and a woman stepped in. Julie's first appointment for the day. Mabel's appointment, another woman, followed her a moment later.

'Are you going to go out with him again?' Mabel asked.

'I don't know if he'll ask, but I probably would.'

Mabel's eyes twinkled. 'So how'd Mike take it?'

From her seat by the window, Mabel had seen them talking.

Julie shrugged. 'OK.'

'He's a good guy, you know.'

'Yeah, he is.'

Mabel didn't press any further, knowing it wouldn't do any good. She'd already tried a few times, without results. But, in her mind, it was a shame that things hadn't worked out between them so far. Mike and Julie, she thought, would make a good couple. And despite what either of them imagined, she was sure that Jim wouldn't have minded at all.

She should know. After all, she was his aunt.

As the morning sun led an early-season heatwave, Mike's wrench got stuck on a bolt in the inner reaches of a car engine. Struggling to free the wrench, he pulled a little too hard, nicking the back of his hand. Cursing to himself, he pushed away from the car in frustration and stared at it, his expression cold, as if trying to intimidate the car into doing what he wanted. All morning long he'd made one stupid mistake after another. How was he supposed to concentrate on his work when he couldn't stop thinking about Julie's date?

Her *nice* date. Her *fun* date. What, he wondered, had been so *nice* about it? And what had she meant by *fun*?

Only one way to find out, he knew, though he dreaded the very thought of it. But what other choice did he have? It wasn't as if Julie had been all that forthcoming with him, and he couldn't exactly head over to the salon and ask Mabel in person, not with Julie standing right there. That left Henry as his only option.

Mike reached for a rag and began wiping his hands on his way through the garage. The challenge, he knew, was to not let Henry know why he was so interested. It would be best if the topic came up naturally or Henry would end up rubbing his nose in it. After taking a moment to formulate his plan, Mike poked his head into his brother's office.

Henry was sitting behind his cluttered desk, placing an order on the phone. Directly in front of him was a packet of miniature doughnuts. Henry waved him in, and Mike took a seat in the chair across from the desk just as he hung up.

'So what's on your mind, little brother?'

Of course, Henry already knew what Mike needed to talk about. The look on his brother's face made the topic plain, and though he could have come straight out with what Mabel had told him, he didn't. There was something about seeing Mike squirm that always left him feeling gleeful for the rest of the day.

'Well,' Mike said, 'I was thinking that maybe I should start going to church with you and the family again.'

'Oh, really?' he said, hiding a smile.

'Yeah. I haven't been in a while, but it would be good for me.'

'Mmm. You want to meet there, or do you want us to pick you up?'

Mike shifted in his seat. 'Before we get to that, I want to know what the new reverend is like. I mean, do people like what he says in his sermons? Do they talk about it after the services?'

'Sometimes.'

'But people do talk? After church, I mean.'

'Sure. But you'll find out this Sunday. We go at nine.'

'Nine. OK. Good.' Mike nodded. 'Well, just for example, what did people say after last Sunday?'

'Oh, well, let's see . . .' Henry tapped his finger in feigned concentration. 'I don't really know. I was talking to Mabel.'

Bingo, Mike thought. Just like I planned. I am a master of deception. 'Mabel, huh?' he asked.

Henry reached for the doughnuts. Taking a bite of one of them, he leaned back in his chair. 'Yeah. But we were just talking about Julie's date, and you've already told me you're not interested. So should we pick you up on Sunday or what?'

Realising his plan had just gone up in smoke, Mike vainly tried to recover. 'Uh . . . well . . .'

Henry laughed. 'Answer me a question, Mike,' he said. 'Why do you keep pretending you don't want to go out with Julie?'

Mike blinked. 'We're just friends.'

Henry ignored his answer. 'Is it because of Jim?'

When Mike didn't respond, Henry put the doughnut down. 'He's been gone for a long time now. It's not like you're trying to steal his wife.'

Put on the spot, Mike wasn't sure what to say. 'It's not that easy,' he finally answered.

'Of course it's not easy. Do you think that asking Emma out the first time was easy for me? There were a lot of guys who wanted to go out with her, but I figured the worst that could happen was that she'd say no.'

'But she wasn't married to your best friend.'

'No,' Henry said, 'she wasn't. But then, we weren't friends beforehand like you and Julie, either.'

'That's what makes it hard. What if things change between us?'

'They are already changing, little brother. Otherwise you wouldn't have had to ask me about the date, would you? Julie would have told you herself. She told you about Bob, didn't she?'

Mike had no answer to that, but when he left the office a minute later, he knew that Henry was right.

Singer's head rose as soon as Richard entered the salon, and though he growled, the sound was muted.

'Hey, sugar? Here for another haircut?' Andrea asked, smiling. He was wearing jeans, and his denim shirt was unbuttoned at the top, leaving just enough room to see the curly hair on his chest. And those eyes, she thought . . . 'I'll be done here in a minute.'

'No, thank you,' Richard said. 'Is Julie around?'

Andrea's smile faded. She snapped her chewing gum and nodded towards the rear of the salon. 'Yeah, she's in the back.'

Mabel had heard the bell on the door jingle, and she stepped out from behind the partition. 'Oh . . . Richard, right? How are you?'

Richard recognised her from the restaurant, and he knew she was evaluating him. Small towns were the same everywhere he'd been.

'Fine, ma'am, thanks. How are you?'

'Good. Julie will be out in a minute. She's setting someone up under the hair dryer. I'll tell her you're here.'

Though he didn't turn towards her, Richard knew that Andrea was still watching him. A knockout, that's what most people would say about her, but he liked women who looked wholesome, the way Julie did.

'Richard?' Julie asked a moment later. Singer stood up to follow her, but she held up a hand. He froze and stopped growling.

'Hey there,' Richard said as she approached. 'I guess he's getting used to me, huh?'

Julie glanced towards Singer. 'Him? Oh, we had a talk. I think he's fine now. He gets jealous.'

Richard raised an eyebrow, but he let the comment pass.

'So what are you doing here?' she asked.

'I thought I'd see how you were doing.'

'I'm fine, but I'm kind of busy right now. I've been swamped all morning. Why aren't you at work?'

'I am. Kind of, anyway. Being a consultant gives me a bit of freedom, and I decided to pop into town.'

'Just to see me?'

'I couldn't think of anything I'd rather do.'

She smiled. 'I had a good time on Saturday night,' she offered.

'So did I.' Richard's eyes darted from Mabel to Andrea, and though they both appeared to be occupied, he knew they were listening. 'Do you think we could talk outside? It won't take long. I promise. I know you're working.'

'I guess that's OK,' Julie said, walking towards the door.

Richard followed her outside. The door swung shut behind them.

'I found your card,' she said. 'You didn't have to do that.'

'I know I didn't. But I wanted to. I wanted to see if you'd like to go out again this Saturday.'

Saturday, Julie remembered with a pang, was supposed to be dinner at Emma's with Henry and Mike.

'I'd love to, but I can't. A couple of friends invited me over. Can we go on Friday instead? Or maybe sometime during the week?'

Richard shook his head. 'I wish I could, but I'm going to Cleveland this evening, and I won't be back until Saturday. And I just found out today that I might be out of town again the following weekend.' He paused. 'Are you sure you can't make it?'

'I really can't,' she said. 'They're good friends. I can't blow them off at the last minute.'

For an instant, an unreadable expression crossed Richard's face, but just as quickly as it had come, it was gone. 'OK,' he said.

'I'm sorry,' she said, hoping he knew she meant it.

'Don't worry about it. It's no big deal. But you won't mind if I give you a call in a couple of weeks? When I get back, I mean?'

A couple of weeks?

'Well, hold on,' Julie said. 'You could always come to the dinner with me. I'm sure my friends wouldn't mind.'

Richard shook his head. 'No. They're your friends, and I'm not real good at meeting new people—shy, I guess.' He smiled before nodding towards the salon. 'Listen, I promised not to keep you, and I'm the kind of guy who keeps his word. Besides, I've got to get back to work, too.' He smiled again. 'You look great, by the way.'

As he turned to leave, Julie called out, 'Wait!'

Richard stopped. 'Yes?'

'Well, if you're not going to be in town next week, maybe I can change my plans. I'll talk to Emma. I'm sure she won't mind.'

'I don't want you to have to break your date.'

'It's not that big a deal. We get together all the time.'

He met her eyes. 'That's great,' he said, and before she realised what was happening, he leaned in and kissed her. 'Thank you.'

Before Julie could think of anything to say, Richard turned and started down the sidewalk. All she could do was watch him go.

'Did I just see what I thought I saw?' Mabel asked, once Julie was back inside. 'Did you just kiss him?'

'Actually, he kissed me.'

'You don't look too happy about it.'

'I'm not sure whether "happy" is the word to describe it.'

'Why?'

'I don't know,' Julie said. 'It just seemed . . .'

'Unexpected?' Mabel offered.

Julie thought about that. Why did it feel as if he'd crossed a barrier without asking permission? She shrugged. 'I guess that's it.'

Mabel studied her for a moment. 'Well, I'd say that means he had just as good a time as you did,' she said.

Julie nodded. 'He also left a card on my porch.'

Mabel raised her eyebrows.

'You think it's too much?' Julie asked.

'Not necessarily. He might be the kind of guy who knows what he wants, and goes after it with gusto. You are a catch, you know.'

Julie smiled.

'Or then again,' Mabel said, 'he might be bonkers.'

It had been a long time since Richard had laughed aloud, and in the confines of his car, the sound seemed louder than it was. 'He gets jealous,' Julie had said about her dog. Cute.

Their evening together had been wonderful. He'd enjoyed her company, of course, but what he'd come to admire was her resilience. Her life had been hard, but he'd seen no traces of bitterness.

She was also lovely. The way she'd smiled at him with almost childlike excitement . . . he felt as if he could watch her for hours and never grow tired of it.

'I had a good time on Saturday night,' she had said.

He was almost certain that she had, but he'd had to see her today to make sure. But today, towards the end, maybe he shouldn't have kissed her. It wasn't as if he'd planned to, but he'd been so elated when she broke her plans, it just *happened*. A surprise for both of them. But was it too much, too soon?

Yes, he decided, it probably was. It would be better to take it easy the next time he saw her.

THREE

On Saturday night over dinner, Richard stared across the table at Julie, a faint smile playing over his lips.

'What are you smiling at?' Julie asked.

'Have I told you how lovely you look this evening?'

'About a dozen times.'

'Do you want me to stop?'

'No. Call me strange, but I sort of like life on the pedestal.'

Richard laughed. 'I'll do my best to keep you there.'

They were at Pagini's, a cosy restaurant in Morehead City that smelt of fresh spice and drawn butter. A bottle of Chardonnay sat in an ice bucket next to the table; a waiter had poured two glasses and they glowed yellow in the soft light. Earlier, Richard had shown up at the door dressed in a linen jacket, holding a bouquet of roses.

'So tell me about your week,' he said. 'What exciting things happened while I was gone?'

'You mean at work?'

'Work, life, whatever. I want to know it all.'

'I should probably be asking you that question.'

'Why?'

'Because,' she said, 'my life's not all that exciting. I work in a beauty salon in a small southern town, remember?' She spoke with good, brisk humour, as if to ward off sympathy. 'Besides, I just realised that I don't know much about you. You haven't told me much about yourself yet.'

'I think I told you I'm a consultant, didn't I?'

'Yeah, but you didn't go into a lot of detail.'

'Well, just think of me as the guy who, working behind the scenes, makes sure the bridge doesn't collapse.'

'Is that what the trip was about?'

'What trip?'

'The one to Cleveland.'

'Oh . . . no,' he said, shaking his head. 'There's another project the company is getting ready to bid on in Florida, and there's a lot of research to do. They have their own people, of course, but they bring in consultants like me to make sure everything will go through the government bidding system without a hitch.'

Julie observed him in the dim light of the restaurant. His angular face was at once rugged and boyish. 'What do you do in your spare time? Hobbies, I mean.'

'Not too much, really. Between work and trying to stay in shape, I don't have much time for anything else. I used to do a little photography, though. I took a few courses in college, and for a short time there, I actually considered making it my career. Even bought some equipment. But it's a tough way to pay the bills.'

'So you became an engineer instead.'

He nodded.

'And you're originally from Cleveland?' she asked.

'No. I haven't been in Cleveland all that long. Just a year or so. Actually, I grew up in Denver and spent most of my life there. Dad

worked at a chemical plant. And Mom was just a mom. In the beginning, anyway. But after my dad died, she had to take a job as a maid to
keep us going. To be honest, I don't know how she did it.'

'She sounds remarkable.'

'Was?'

'Is.' He looked down. 'She had a stroke a few years ago and . . . well,
it's not good. She doesn't remember me at all. I had to send her to a
place in Salt Lake City that specialises in her condition.'

Julie winced. Seeing her expression, Richard shook his head.

'It's not something I usually talk about. Kind of brings conversations
to an uncomfortable stop, especially when people hear my father died,
too. Makes them wonder what it must be like to be without family. But
you don't need me to explain that, I suppose.'

No, she thought, I don't. I know that territory well.

'So that's why you left Denver? Because of your mom?'

'That was only part of it.' He glanced at the table before looking up
again. 'I guess now's the time to tell you that I was married once. To a
woman named Jessica. I left because of her, too.'

'How long were you married?'

'Four years. I don't know what went wrong. I still haven't figured it
out. It just didn't work out.' He met her eyes across the table. 'Do you
really want to hear about this?'

'Not if you don't want to tell me.'

'Thank you,' he said, exhaling with a laugh. 'You have no idea how
glad I am that you said that.'

She smiled. 'So Cleveland, huh? Do you like it there?'

'It's all right, but I'm not there that much. Usually I'm on-site, like now.'

'I'll bet that's hard sometimes.'

'Yeah, especially when I'm stuck in hotels. This project is nice
because I'll be here for a while, and I was able to find a place to rent.
And, of course, I got the chance to meet you.'

As he was talking, Julie was struck by how much their lives seemed to
have in common, from being only children raised by single mothers to
their decisions to start over in someplace new. And though their mar-
riages had ended differently, something in his tone suggested he'd struggled with real feelings of loss. She felt an emerging kinship with him.

The evening wore on, and the sky deepened in colour, unveiling the
stars. Neither Julie nor Richard rushed through dinner. It was still warm
when they finally left. Expecting him to offer his hand or arm, she was
surprised when he did neither.

When they stopped at a crosswalk, Julie glanced at Richard. 'Do you like dancing?' she asked.

'Oh, I don't know. I'm not all that good.'

'C'mon,' she said, 'I know a great place. I promise I won't say a thing if you step on my feet.'

'OK,' he said, 'but I'll hold you to your promise.'

She laughed and nodded towards his car. 'Come on.'

The Sailing Clipper was a bar typical of small coastal towns. Dimly lit and smelling of cigarettes and booze, it was popular with blue-collar workers, who crowded around the bar. Along the far wall, the stage overlooked a slightly warped dance floor. A few dozen tables were arranged haphazardly, with chairs circling them.

The group on stage, Ocracoke Inlet, was something of a regular at the Clipper. The owner, a one-legged man people called Leaning Joe, liked the group because it played songs that put people in a good mood. They played nothing that couldn't be found in jukeboxes, which was exactly the reason why, Mike thought, everyone liked them so much. When they played, people came in droves. Never once, however, had they asked Mike to fill in, even though he was on a first-name basis with most of the group. Second-rate band or not, the thought was depressing.

But then, the whole evening had been depressing. The whole week had been depressing, for that matter. Ever since Monday, when Julie came by to pick up her keys and casually mentioned that she'd be going out with Richard on Saturday instead of spending tonight with them, Mike had been in a funk.

Sure, Henry and Emma were great, and he liked spending time with them. But on a night like this, Mike knew he was a third wheel. This was not the way things were supposed to be tonight. Julie was supposed to be here. Julie was supposed to be dancing with him, smiling over a drink, laughing and flirting. And she would have been if it wasn't for Richard.

Richard. He hated that guy. Simply thinking the name caused him to scowl, and he'd been scowling a lot, all evening long.

Watching his brother carefully, Henry finished the last of his beer. 'I think maybe you ought to cut back on that cheap brew you're drinking,' he said. 'Looks like it's giving you gas.'

Mike looked up. Henry was smirking as he reached for Emma's bottle of beer. She'd gone off to the rest room. 'I'm drinking the same stuff you are,' Mike said.

'True,' Henry said, 'but you have to realise that some men can handle it better than others.'

'Yeah, yeah . . . keep talking.'

'My, aren't we in a mood this evening,' Henry said. 'You've been riding me all night.'

'Considering the way you've been acting lately, you deserve it. We had a great dinner; I've been engaging you with my sparkling wit, and Emma's been making sure that you're not always sitting alone at the table like some loser whose date stood him up.'

Mike glared at him before turning away.

'All right, I'm sorry,' Henry said. 'But listen, just because she's out with Richard doesn't mean that you've lost your chance for ever. Instead of moping around, use it as a challenge. Ask her out.'

'I was planning on that. Tonight was supposed to be the night.'

Henry studied him. 'Good,' he said, 'I'm proud of you.'

Mike waited for more, but Henry stayed silent.

'What? No jokes this time?'

'No reason to make jokes.'

'Because you don't believe me?'

'No, I believe you. I have to, I guess. Because I'll get to see you do it.'

'Huh? What are you talking about?'

Henry raised his chin, nodding in the direction of the door. 'Guess who just walked in.'

Richard stood beside Julie just inside the door as she craned her neck, looking for a place to sit.

'I didn't realise it would be so crowded,' Richard shouted over the noise. 'Are you sure you want to stay?'

'C'mon—it'll be fun. You'll see.'

Though he flashed a quick smile of agreement, Richard was doubtful. He leaned in close to Julie. 'Let's get something to drink,' he said, 'before we find a place to sit down.'

Julie nodded. 'Sure. You lead the way. The bar's straight ahead.'

As Richard began squeezing between people, he reached back, offering his hand to Julie. Without hesitation, she took it. When they reached the bar, he held on to it as he raised his other hand to get the bartender's attention.

'**S**o that's him, huh?' Emma said.

Emma, thirty-eight, was a green-eyed blonde with a sunny disposition. Like Henry, Emma loved to tease, and when they got going, they seemed to feed off each other.

Henry nodded. 'That's him.'

Emma continued to stare. 'He's really something, isn't he?'

'I think Mabel used the word "sexy",' Henry offered.

Emma raised a finger. 'Yes, sexy. Very sexy. In a handsome stranger kind of way, I mean.'

Mike crossed his arms and sank lower in his seat.

'They do make a lovely couple,' Henry added.

'They certainly stand out in a crowd,' Emma agreed.

Mike glared at them.

Henry leaned towards Emma. 'I guess you should know my little brother's been having a hard time with all this. And from his expression, I don't think we're helping.'

'Oh, really?' Emma asked innocently.

'I'd be fine if you two would quit picking on me.'

'But you're such an easy target when you're this way,' Emma giggled. 'Pouting does that, you know. And it's not attractive. Take it from a woman who knows. Unless you want to lose out to a guy like that, you'd better change your tune before it's too late.'

Mike blinked at the honesty. 'So I should act like I don't care?'

'No, Mike. Act like you do care. Be her friend.'

'I am her friend.'

'Not right now, you're not. If you were her friend, you'd be happy for her.'

'Why should I be happy she's with him?'

'Because,' Emma said, 'it means she's ready to start looking for the guy who's right for her, and everyone knows who that is.' She smiled and touched his shoulder. 'Do you think we'd be giving you such a hard time if we didn't believe this was all going to work out for you two in the end?'

Julie and Richard's drinks arrived—bourbon for him, a Diet Coke for her. Her face lit up as soon as she saw Mike, Henry and Emma at a table near the dance floor. She reached for Richard's hand again. 'C'mon,' she said, 'I think I see someplace we can sit.'

They pushed their way through the crowd, crossed the edge of the dance floor, and reached the table. 'Hey, guys. I didn't expect to see you here,' Julie said. 'How are you?'

'We're doing well,' Henry said. 'We just thought we'd come by after dinner to see what was going on.'

Richard was standing behind Julie and she tugged on his hand. 'Richard, this is Henry and Emma. And my best friend, Mike.'

Henry held out his hand. 'Hey there,' he said.

Richard hesitated before grasping it. 'Hello,' he said simply.

Mike and Emma came next. When Julie glanced at Mike, he smiled pleasantly, though doing so practically killed him.

'Do you want to sit down?' Henry offered.

'No—we don't want to bother you,' Richard said.

'It's no bother. C'mon. Join us,' Emma chimed in.

Julie smiled and moved round the table to take a seat; Richard followed and did the same. Once they were comfortable, Emma leaned across the table.

'So, Richard,' she said, 'tell us about yourself.'

The conversation was stilted at first, because Richard didn't volunteer much more than was asked directly.

As he spoke, Mike did his best to appear interested. And he was, if only to see what he was up against. But as the minutes rolled on, he began to feel as if his future were that of a salmon swimming upstream. Even he could see why Julie was interested in Richard. He was intelligent and, unlike Mike, he was college educated and well travelled. Though he didn't laugh or joke much—or appreciate Emma or Henry when they did—it seemed that his discomfort stemmed more from shyness than arrogance. And the way he felt about Julie was obvious. Whenever she spoke, Richard's eyes never left her face. Through it all, Mike kept smiling and nodding, hating Richard's guts.

A little later, as Emma and Julie caught up on some of the latest news around town, Richard finished his drink. After asking if Julie wanted anything else, he excused himself to head for the bar. When Henry asked him if he wouldn't mind grabbing another couple of beers, Mike stood as well, volunteering to go with Richard.

'I'll help you carry them back.'

They reached the bar, and the bartender signalled that he'd get there as soon as he could. Richard reached for his wallet, and though Mike was right beside him, he stayed silent.

'She's a great lady,' Mike finally offered.

'Yes, she is,' he said simply.

Neither of them said another word to each other.

Once they were back at the table, Richard asked Julie if she'd like to dance and, after saying goodbye, they were gone.

Mike sat drumming his fingers on the table. Henry and Emma had gone to say hello to another couple they knew, and now that he was alone, Mike tried to figure out what it was exactly that he didn't like about Richard Franklin. Besides the obvious.

No, there was more to it than that. No matter what Julie seemed to think, Richard didn't strike Mike as a particularly nice guy. What happened at the bar made that plain. Once he'd said what he had about Julie, Richard had looked at him as if already recognising Mike's feelings for her, and his face clearly expressed what he thought about that. *You lose, so stay away.*

He leaned back in his chair, taking a deep breath as he scanned the room. During the band's break, Julie and Richard had left the dance floor and found a small table on the far side of the bar. Mike had been glancing their way ever since. He couldn't help it.

Slowly, Mike's eyes began to travel their way again. As he turned, he saw Julie rummaging through her bag. Richard's eyes, though, locked on his in a cool, confident appraisal. *Yes, Mike, I know you're staring.*

Mike froze; he wanted to turn away but couldn't seem to move until he heard a voice behind him. He glanced over his shoulder and saw Drew, the lead singer from the band, standing near the table.

'Hey, Mike,' Drew said, 'got a minute?'

Just past midnight, with the world glowing silver, Julie stood with Richard on the porch. Frogs and crickets were singing; a light breeze was moving the leaves.

'Thanks for tonight,' she said.

'You're welcome. I had a wonderful time.'

'Even at the Clipper?'

He shrugged. 'To be honest, I probably would have preferred something a bit more private. So you and I could be alone.'

'We were alone.'

'Not the whole time.'

She looked at him, a quizzical expression on her face.

Richard's eyes drifted to the porch light, then back to Julie. 'Hey . . . listen, I know I was kind of quiet with your friends. I'm sorry about that. I never seem to know what to say.'

'You were fine. I'm sure they liked you.'

'I'm not too sure that Mike did. He was watching us.'

She hadn't noticed. 'Mike and I have known each other for years,' she said. 'He watches out for me. That's all.'

Richard seemed to evaluate that. Finally, a small smile flickered across his face. 'OK,' he said. For a long moment neither of them said anything else. Then Richard moved towards her. This time, though she expected the kiss—and though she thought she wanted him to do it—she couldn't deny the feeling of relief when he turned to leave.

'There he goes,' Henry said, 'right on time.'

It was Tuesday morning, a few days after their evening at the Clipper. Henry was drinking Dr Pepper and watching Richard as he made his way down the street carrying a small box.

Hearing his brother, Mike emerged from beneath the hood of a car. After removing a rag tucked into his belt, he started wiping his hands. 'Must be nice being a consultant,' Mike said. 'Doesn't that guy ever have to work?' Then, almost immediately, Mike's face took on a startled expression. 'Is he bringing her a gift?'

'Yep.'

'What's the special occasion?'

'Maybe he wants to impress her.'

Mike wiped his hands again. 'Well, if that's the case, maybe I'll just swing by there a little later with a gift of my own.'

'Now you're talking,' Henry said, slapping his brother on the back. 'That's exactly what I wanted to hear you say. A little less whining, a little more action. But scrap the gift. That's his thing. It won't work for you.'

'But—'

'Trust me on this. It'll make you look desperate.'

'I am desperate.'

'You may be,' Henry agreed. 'But you can't let her know that.'

'Richard,' Julie said, staring down at an ornate, heart-shaped locket supported by a gold chain. 'It's beautiful.'

They were standing outside the door of the salon, unaware that Mike and Henry were watching from across the street and that Mabel and Singer were peeking through the window behind them. 'But . . . why? I mean, what's the occasion?'

'No occasion. I just saw it and knew you should have it.'

Julie's eyes flashed to the locket. It was obviously expensive. As if reading her mind, he held up his hands. 'Please—I want you to have it. If you have to, think of it as a birthday present.'

'My birthday's not until August.'

'So I'm a little early.' He paused. 'Please.'

'Richard . . . it's sweet, but I really shouldn't.'

'It's just a locket, not an engagement ring.'

Still a bit unsure, she gave in and kissed him. 'Thank you.'

Richard motioned towards the locket. 'Try it on.'

Julie slipped it round her neck. 'How does it look?'

He stared at the locket, an odd smile on his face. 'Perfect. It's exactly the way I remember it.'

'Remember?'

'From the jewellery store,' he said. 'But it looks better on you.'

Julie put one hand on her hip. 'People don't usually go around buying me gifts for no reason at all.'

'Then it's a good thing that I do.' He paused. 'So, are you up for doing something this Friday night?'

'I thought you were leaving town?'

'I was. But it turns out the trip got cancelled. Or rather, my part of it got cancelled. I'm free all weekend.'

'What did you have in mind?' she asked.

'Something special. I'd like to keep it a surprise, though.'

Julie didn't answer right away, and as if sensing her uncertainty, Richard reached for her hand. 'Trust me on this. But you'll have to get off a little early. I'd have to pick you up around four o'clock.'

'Why so early?'

'It takes a while to get where we're going. Can you make it?'

She smiled. 'I'll have to shuffle my schedule a bit, but I think I can make it. Should I wear something dressy or casual?'

'I'll be wearing a jacket and tie, if that helps. I'm sure you'll be beautiful no matter what you wear.' With that he kissed her, and when he left, Julie's fingers travelled to the locket. It opened with a click, and she saw that small photos could be placed inside. She was surprised to see that he'd already had it engraved with her initials, one on each side.

Hey, Julie,' Mike called, 'wait up!'

Julie turned to see Mike jogging towards her as she was heading to her car. Singer loped off in his direction, reaching him first. Lifting first one paw and then the other, he looked as if he were trying to grab Mike in preparation for a series of sloppy licks. Mike avoided that—as much as he liked Singer, it was a little disgusting to be drenched with dog saliva—but he did pet him. Like Julie, he also talked to Singer as if he were a person.

'Did you miss me, big guy? Yeah, I missed you, too.'

As Mike started towards Julie again, Singer spun and walked beside him. Nudging him playfully, he nearly sent Mike careening into a mailbox. 'I think you need to take your dog for a few more walks,' Mike said. 'He's all wound up.'

'He's just excited to see you. How are you? I haven't seen too much of you lately.'

'I'm good. Just busy, that's all.' He shrugged. 'I did get some good news, though. The band that was playing the other night? Ocracoke

Inlet? Drew asked me if I'd fill in for their guitarist. Their regular guy's got to go to a wedding in Chicago the next time they're supposed to be at the Clipper.'

'Wow—that's great. When is that?'

'In a couple of weeks. It should be fun. I know most of the songs, and the band's not all *that* bad.'

'That's not what you told me before.'

'They never asked me to play before.'

For a moment neither of them said anything. Mike shuffled his feet.

'So what have you been up to? Anything exciting going on?'

'Not much. Singer's been driving me nuts; that's about it. He's been so clingy recently. I keep stumbling over him every time I turn round.'

Mike laughed. 'I'd be glad to take him off your hands any time. I'll take him to the beach, and by the time he gets home, he won't have the energy to growl or bark or follow you.'

'I might just take you up on that.'

'I hope so. I love the big guy.' He reached out to Singer. 'Don't I?' Singer received Mike's affection with a friendly bark.

For Mike, the rest of the week passed torturously. Julie didn't call, and not only did Richard show up every single day, but on Friday Mike saw Julie leave the salon in midafternoon.

Richard, he thought.

He tried not to care. He told himself there was no reason to care. But he found out, from snippets of conversations around town over that weekend, where Richard and Julie had gone. Richard had picked Julie up in a limousine stocked with champagne. They'd gone to Raleigh for dinner. Afterwards, at the civic centre in front-row seats, they'd watched a performance of *Phantom of the Opera*. If that wasn't enough, it turned out that Richard and Julie had spent Saturday together as well. They'd taken a hot-air balloon ride before picnicking at the beach. How was he supposed to compete with a guy who did things like that?

Now that was a weekend, Julie thought to herself.

Staring at her reflection in the mirror on Sunday morning, she still found it hard to believe. She had never spent a weekend like it. The theatre was a new experience for her. She was entranced by it all. In the limousine on the way home, as champagne bubbles tickled her nose, she remembered thinking, I can see how people can get used to this.

The next day, too, had been a surprise. Though the balloon ride was fun, of all they did, from holding hands as they walked to posing playfully as Richard took a number of photographs of her, she enjoyed the picnic the most. That was more along the lines of something she was used to. After they'd finished with the food, Richard had offered to give her a foot rub. She'd initially laughed and said no, but when he'd gently reached for her foot, slipped off her sandal, and begun his massage, she couldn't help giving in and relaxing.

Strangely, at that moment, she thought of her mother. She remembered something her mother had said once when Julie had asked her why she'd stopped seeing a boyfriend.

'He didn't rock my boat.'

Staring at Richard, her foot in his hands, the expression came back to her. Did Richard rock her boat?

He should, she knew. He was the full package as far as eligible men went, but after four romantic dates she suddenly knew that he didn't. She just didn't feel the little tingles on her neck that she had when Jim first took her hand. She wondered if part of the problem was that she was trying to rush her feelings. While brushing her hair in front of the mirror, she considered it. Maybe. Then, laying down her brush, she thought, Yes, that's got to be it. Besides, it's partly my fault. I'm the one who's holding back.

Though she had talked for hours with Richard, most of their conversations had hovered over the surface. Whenever the past had come up, she'd found a way to avoid it.

Part of her was tempted to share it all with him, so he could really know who she was. But she didn't. For some reason, she couldn't. And he didn't tell her much about himself, either, she noticed. He had a way of avoiding the past as well.

Richard pushed open the door of the salon and held it as Julie's client made her way out.

'Oh, hey, Richard,' Julie said. 'Good timing. I just finished up.'

Though she wasn't any closer to sorting through her emotions, she was still glad he'd come by, if only to understand whether seeing him would make them any clearer.

'Yeah,' Julie said. 'My next appointment is in half an hour.'

'You look beautiful,' he said, leaning in to kiss her. 'Do you have a few minutes to grab a cup of coffee?'

Mabel had gone to the bank. Andrea was flipping through the National Enquirer in the corner, but Julie knew she was listening.

As she answered, Richard's eyes focused on the soft triangle of flesh beneath her chin. 'Where's the locket?' he asked.

Julie's hand travelled to her chest. 'Oh. I didn't wear it today. It kept getting snagged on my clothes when I was working.'

'Why didn't you just tuck it inside?'

'I tried, but it kept falling out.' She took a step towards the door. 'C'mon,' she said. 'I haven't been outside all morning.'

'Should I get you a shorter chain?'

'Don't be ridiculous. It's perfect just the way it is.'

'But you're not wearing it,' he persisted.

Julie didn't respond, and in the long silence that followed, she looked at him carefully. Though he was smiling, there was something plastic about his expression.

'Does it bother you that much that I didn't wear it?' she asked.

'It's just that I thought you liked it.'

'I do like it. I just don't want to wear it while I'm working,' Richard seemed to snap out of the spell he'd been under, and his smile suddenly became natural again. 'I'll get you a shorter chain,' he said. 'That way you can wear it whenever you want.'

'You don't have to do that.'

'I know,' he said. 'But I want to.'

Manipulated. That's how Julie was feeling now that Richard had gone back to work. Manipulated. As though he'd wanted her to promise that she'd start wearing the locket at work again. As though she should wear it *all the time*.

She didn't like that feeling, and she was trying to reconcile it with the man who'd taken her out over the weekend. Why was he so upset about something so insignificant?

Unless, of course, he was wondering if it was some sort of subconscious statement as to how she was feeling towards him.

Julie froze momentarily, wondering if that might be true, especially given the way she'd been feeling on Sunday.

No, Julie thought, shaking her head, that wasn't it. She'd known exactly what she was doing. The locket *did* get in the way.

Besides, this wasn't about her. It was about Richard and the way he'd reacted. Jim had never been like that. When Jim got mad—which wasn't all that often—he didn't try to manipulate her. Nor did he try to hide his anger behind a smile. Nor did Jim ever leave her with the impression that Richard had left her with, one she didn't like at all.

As long as we do it my way, everything will be fine, Richard seemed to imply. *We won't have this problem again.*

What, she wondered, was that all about?

FOUR

JAKE BLANSEN, THE FOREMAN from the bridge project, arrived a little after four to pick up his truck, and after settling the account in the office, he made his way towards Mike.

'The keys are in the ignition,' Mike said. 'And just to let you know, I adjusted the brakes so they're not so loose.'

Jake Blansen nodded. The consummate working man, Jake was beer-bellied and broad-shouldered, with a baseball cap and a toothpick wedged between his teeth. His jeans and boots were coated with concrete dust.

'I'll let 'em know,' Jake said. 'Though to be honest, I don't know why I got stuck with all this anyway. Maintenance was supposed to be handling all the vehicle stuff. But I guess you know how it goes. The bosses over there have everything screwed up.'

Mike nodded. 'How many guys you got out there these days?'

'A couple hundred, maybe. Why?'

'I met one of the engineers who consults on the bridge.'

'Which one?'

'Richard Franklin. Do you know him?'

Holding Mike's gaze, Jake removed the toothpick from his mouth.

'Yeah, I know him,' he said. 'You his friend?'

'No—like I said, I only met him once.'

'Keep it that way. You don't want to know him.'

'Why?'

After a long moment Jake shook his head, and though Mike tried to find out more, he said nothing. Instead, he turned the conversation back to the truck and left the garage a few minutes later, leaving Mike wondering what it was that Jake hadn't told him.

With her last customer of the day on her way out, Julie glanced around the salon. 'Have you seen Singer?' she asked Mabel.

'I let him out,' Mabel said. 'He was standing at the door.'

'How long ago was that?'

'I guess about an hour.'

Singer was curled up on an old blanket, as Mike adjusted the transmission of a Pontiac Sunbird.

'Hey, Mike,' Julie called out. 'You still here?'

Mike looked up at the sound of her voice and moved into the bay.

'Back here,' he called back. Singer raised his head.

'Have you seen Singer?'

'Yeah, he's right here.' Mike nodded to the side and grabbed a rag. As he wiped his hands, Singer rose and started towards her.

'There you are,' Julie said. When Singer reached her, she scratched his back. 'I was beginning to get worried about you.'

Mike smiled, thankful that Singer hadn't gone back.

She looked up. 'What's going on?'

'Nothing much. How are you?'

'I'm OK.'

'Just OK?'

'It's one of those days,' she said. 'You know how it is.'

'Yeah, I suppose I do,' he said, nodding. 'Especially today.'

'What happened today?'

'Oh—you know,' he said. 'The same old stuff.'

'Must have been good if you won't tell me.'

Mike paused and thought, A guy named Blansen came in and said some cryptic things about Richard. Want to hear about that?

No, now was not the time.

He shook his head. 'Not really. How about you?'

'Nothing.' She glanced at Singer. 'Except for this guy running away. For a little while there, I actually got scared that something had happened to him.'

'Singer? No car would stand a chance if it hit him. It would be crushed like a bug.'

'It still had me worried.'

'That's because you're a woman. Men like me—we don't worry. We're trained not to panic.'

Julie smiled. 'That's good to know. When the hurricane hits, you'll be the first one I call to board up the house.'

'You do that anyway. Don't you remember? You even bought me my own special hammer.'

'Well, you can't expect me to do it. I might panic or something.'

THE GUARDIAN

Mike chuckled, and for a moment silence settled in. 'So how're things going with Richard?' he asked, trying to sound casual.

'OK,' she answered. 'The weekend was all right, but . . .'

'But?'

'It's not important.'

He studied her. 'You sure?'

'Yeah, I'm sure.' She flashed a quick, forced smile.

Mike sensed her discomfort but let it go. 'Well, listen, if you need to talk about anything, I'm always around.'

'I know you are.' She put a friendly hand on his shoulder, trying to defuse the tension. 'Part of me thinks you should get out more. See the world, take exotic trips.'

'What? And miss reruns of *Baywatch*?'

'Exactly,' she said. 'Anything's better than television. But if travel's not your thing, you might consider something else. Like taking up a musical instrument or something.'

Mike pressed his lips together. 'Now that was a low blow.'

Her eyes gleamed. 'As good as Henry?'

'No,' he said. 'Henry's better. You're just a rookie.'

She smiled, then leaned back a little, as if taking a moment to evaluate him. 'You're pretty easy to get along with, you know?'

'Because I'm easy to tease?'

'No, because you're such a good sport about it.'

Mike took a moment to scrape a bit of grease from his fingernails. 'That's funny,' he said. 'Andrea said exactly the same thing to me just the other day.'

'Andrea?' Julie repeated, wondering if she'd heard him right.

'Yeah, this weekend. When we went out on our date. Which reminds me—I'm supposed to pick her up in a few minutes.'

He glanced at his watch, then his locker.

'But wait . . . Andrea?' Julie couldn't mask her bewilderment.

'Yeah—she's great. But listen, I've got to run.'

Julie reached for his arm. 'But . . . You and *Andrea?*'

Mike stared at her solemnly for a couple of beats, then winked. 'Had you going, didn't I?'

Julie crossed her arms. 'No,' she snapped.

'C'mon. Just a little?'

'No.'

'Admit it.'

'OK, fine. I admit it.'

Mike gave her a look of satisfaction. 'Good. Now we're even.'

225

Julie let the door swing closed behind her, still relishing her conversation with Mike. Mabel looked up from the desk.

'Were you supposed to meet Richard tonight?' she asked.

'No. Why?'

'He came by and asked for you. Didn't you see him? He just left a couple of minutes ago.'

'I was over at the garage with Mike,' she said. 'Did he say what he wanted?'

'Just that he was looking for you.' Mabel turned on the answering machine. 'I don't know about you,' she said, 'but I'm bushed. Everyone I worked on complained today. If it wasn't about their hair, it was their kids or their husbands.'

Julie was still thinking of Richard. 'Must be a full moon,' she muttered. 'Everyone was a little off today.'

'Even Mike?'

'No, not Mike.' Julie waved a hand in relief.

Mabel pulled open the bottom drawer of her desk and removed a flask of bourbon. 'Well, it's about time to shake off the cobwebs,' she announced. 'Join me?'

Mabel enjoyed shaking off the cobwebs regularly and, as a result, had fewer cobwebs than anyone Julie knew.

'Yeah, I'll join you. I'll lock the door.'

Mabel removed two plastic glasses from the bottom drawer and made herself comfortable on the couch. By the time Julie joined her, Mabel had kicked off her shoes and already taken a drink.

'So what's up with you and Richard?' she asked.

'It's going OK, I guess.'

'You guess?'

Julie took a drink, feeling the burn at the back of her throat.

'Do you remember the locket he got me?' she asked.

'How could I forget, J.B.?'

'Well,' Julie said, 'the problem was that I didn't wear it today. I think Richard was offended.'

Mabel swirled the bourbon in her glass. 'Maybe he was just having a bad day,' she said.

'So just let it go?'

'Not exactly. You shouldn't completely ignore it, either. Take it from a lady who's had too many dates and met too many men over the years. Everyone—you included—is on her best behaviour in the beginning of a relationship. Sometimes little quirks turn out to be big ones, and the big advantage that women have is their intuition.'

'So you *do* think it's a problem?'

'Honey, I'm just telling you not to simply shrug it off if it bothered you. But don't let it ruin a good thing, either.'

Richard was waiting for her when she got home.

His car was parked in the street in front of her house, and he was leaning against it, watching as she turned into the driveway.

After pulling to a stop, Julie looked towards Singer and unhooked her seat belt. 'Just stay in the Jeep until I say so, OK?' Singer pricked his ears up. 'And behave,' she added as she stepped out. By then, Richard was standing in the drive.

'Hi, Richard,' she said neutrally. 'What are you doing here?'

'I had a few minutes and thought I'd drop by. I tried to catch you at the salon, but I guess you'd taken off.'

'I had to go get Singer. He was over at the garage.'

Richard nodded. 'I just wanted to say I'm sorry about this morning. I think I went a little overboard.'

'Well,' she began, 'now that you mention it—'

Richard held up his hands to stop her. 'I know, I know. No excuses. I just wanted to say I'm sorry.'

'Were you really that upset that I didn't wear the locket?'

'No. It's just that I had such a good time on the weekend, and when I saw that you didn't have it on, I sort of thought that you didn't feel the same way. I guess I felt like I'd let you down somehow. I mean . . . Can you understand what I'm trying to say?'

Julie thought for a moment before nodding. 'Yeah.'

'I knew you'd understand,' he said. He glanced around. 'Well—I gotta head back into work.'

'OK,' Julie said simply. She forced a smile.

A moment later, he was gone.

In the darkness, under a sliver of moon, Richard approached the front door of the rented Victorian house he temporarily called home. It was on the outskirts of town, surrounded by farmland, set a hundred yards back from the main road.

The house was pale in the weak moonlight, half the height of the shadowed pines that surrounded it. Though neglected, it retained an old-fashioned charm. As he pushed his way inside, he flipped on the lights. The rented furniture was not to his taste, but in a small town like Swansboro, choices were limited.

Tonight, however, he didn't notice the decor. Tonight, there was only

Julie. And the locket. And the way she'd looked at him only moments before. Again, he'd pushed too hard, and again, she'd called him on it. She was becoming a challenge, but he liked that. He respected that, for what he despised above all was weakness.

Why on earth was she living in a small town like this?

Julie, he thought, belonged in the city. She was too sharp for a place like this. If Julie stayed, he knew she would grow weak, just as his mother had grown weak. And in time, there would be nothing to respect.

Just like his mother. The victim. Always the victim.

He closed his eyes, retreating to the past. It was 1974, and the image was always the same. With her left eye swollen shut and her cheek purple, his mother was loading a suitcase into the trunk of the car. The suitcase held clothes for both of them. In her bag she had thirty-seven dollars. It had taken almost a year to save that much; Vernon handled the finances and gave her just enough to do the shopping. She told herself she was leaving for good this time.

Richard thought of his mother on that day. How she had kept him home from school, how she'd told him to run inside and grab the loaf of bread and peanut butter, because they were going on a picnic. He was six years old and did as his mother told him, even though he knew she was lying.

He'd heard his mother screaming and crying the night before as he lay in bed. Heard the sharp crack as his father's hand connected with her cheek, heard her pleading for him to stop.

He hated his father. Hated the boozy way he smelt at night. Hated the way he beat his mother. Hated the way they always kept the curtains drawn, and how no one had ever been allowed to visit.

'Hurry,' his mother said, motioning with her arm. 'We want to find a good table at the park.'

He ran into the house. His father would be coming home for lunch in an hour. They should have left right away, right after his father had disappeared over the hill on his walk to the plant. But instead his mother had sat at the table for hours, smoking cigarettes, her hands shaking.

Now they were running out of time.

He came bursting through the door, carrying the bread and peanut butter, and ran towards the car. When he got in and closed the door to the Pontiac with a slam, she tried to put the key into the ignition, but missed. Her hands were still shaking. She took a deep breath and tried again. This time the engine turned over and she tried to smile. She put the car into reverse and backed out of the garage. In the road they idled for a moment, and she glanced at the dashboard. She gasped.

The gas gauge showed that the tank was nearly empty. So they stayed. Again.

That night, he heard his mother and father in the bedroom, but they weren't sounds of anger. Instead, he heard them laughing and kissing.

Richard opened his eyes. No, he thought, Julie couldn't stay here. Not if she wanted to lead the life she was meant to, the life she deserved. He would take her away from all this.

It was stupid of him to have said anything to her about the locket. Stupid. He wouldn't let it happen again.

Lost in thought, he barely heard the ringing of the phone, but he rose in time to answer before the machine picked it up.

Pausing for a moment, he recognised the Daytona area code on the caller ID and took a deep breath before he answered.

FIVE

IN THE DARKNESS of her bedroom, with an allergy headache raging, Julie threw her spare pillow at Singer.

'Would you please shut up!' she moaned.

Singer ignored the pillow. Instead, he stood near the bedroom door, panting and growling, wanting Julie to get up and let him outside. He'd been pacing through the house for the last hour.

She pulled a pillow over her head, but it wasn't enough to block out the sound, and the compression only made her head feel worse. 'There's nothing out there,' she muttered. 'It's the middle of the night, and my head hurts. I'm not getting out of bed.'

Singer continued growling.

She threw her last pillow at him. Singer retaliated by crossing the room silently and pushing his nose into her ear.

She sat up. 'That's it! That does it!'

Singer wagged his tail, looking satisfied. *Now we're getting somewhere. C'mon!* He trotted out of the room, leading the way.

'Fine! You want me to prove there's nothing outside?'

Julie got out of bed and staggered towards the living room. Singer was already standing at the front window. He had pushed aside the curtains with his nose and was looking from side to side. Julie peeked out as well. 'See? Nothing. Just like I told you.'

Singer wasn't placated. He moved to the door.

'If you go out, don't expect me to wait up for you. Once you're out, you're out. I'm going back to bed.'

She opened the door, expecting Singer to bolt towards the woods. Instead, he moved onto the porch and barked twice before lowering his nose to sniff. Satisfied, he turned and headed back inside.

'That's it? You got me out of bed for that?'

Singer looked up at her. *The coast is clear, he seemed to say. No reason to be worried. You can go back to sleep now.*

Julie scowled before heading back to the bedroom. Singer didn't follow. As she squinted over her shoulder on her way back to bed, Julie saw him sitting by the window, the curtains pushed aside.

'Whatever,' she mumbled.

The next morning, standing in the driveway beneath a sky so blue that it looked artificial, Julie wore sunglasses. Remnants of her headache lingered. Singer stood beside her as she read the note that had been tucked beneath the windshield wiper of her Jeep.

Julie,

I was called out of town for an emergency, so I won't be able to see you for a couple of days. I'll call as soon as I can. I won't stop thinking about you.

Richard

Julie glanced at Singer. 'So that's what all the noise was about. Richard?'

Singer looked smug as only he could. *See, I told you someone was here.* Julie wasn't in the mood for his superior attitude. 'Don't give me that. You kept me up for hours. And it's not like you don't know him, so get over it.'

Singer snorted and jumped into the Jeep.

Julie closed the back and slid into the front seat. In the rearview mirror, she saw Singer circle once, then sit with his back to her.

'Yeah, well, I'm mad at you, too.'

On the way to work, as she glanced in the mirror again, Singer still hadn't turned round. As soon as she parked the car, Singer hopped out. Even though she called to him, he continued on his way, crossing the street and heading towards the garage.

Dogs. Sometimes, she thought, they were as childish as men.

When she heard the door jingle behind her, Mabel turned and saw Julie come in alone. 'Where's Singer?' she asked.

Julie set her bag on a shelf beside her station. 'I guess he went to visit Mike. We had a fight.'

'A fight, huh?' Mabel said. 'What happened?'

Julie told Mabel about the night before.

'Richard left a note to apologise?' Mabel asked.

'No, he did that yesterday when I got home. The note was just to let me know he'd be out of town for a couple of days.'

Mabel glanced towards Singer's blanket in the corner.

'It looks sort of empty here without him,' she said.

'Oh, he'll be back in a little while. You know how he is.'

Eight hours later, however, Singer still hadn't returned.

I tried to bring him back,' Mike said, looking as perplexed as Julie felt. 'But he wouldn't follow me, no matter how much I called. I even tried bribing him with some beef jerky, but he wouldn't leave the garage.'

Julie looked at Singer. He was sitting beside Mike.

'You still mad at me, Singer?' she asked.

'Why would he be mad at you?'

'We had a fight.'

'Oh,' he said.

'You going to come over?' she asked.

Singer licked his lips but didn't move.

When she began to get upset, Mike flipped his hand.

'Go on, Singer. Before you get in bigger trouble.'

At Mike's command, Singer stood and, reluctantly, went to Julie's side. Julie sighed. 'I just don't know what's got into him lately.' Singer sat beside her and looked up. 'So what did he do here all day?'

'Snoozed, stole my turkey sandwich, went around back to do his business. It's sort of like he just moved in for the day.'

'Did he seem strange to you?'

'No. Not at all. Aside from being here, he seemed fine.'

'He wasn't angry?'

Mike scratched his head. 'Well, he didn't mention anything. Want me to go ask Henry? Maybe they talked while I was out.'

'Are you making fun of me?'

'No, never. You know I'd never do something like that.'

'Good. After almost losing my dog to someone else, I'm not exactly in the mood for joking right now.'

'You didn't almost lose him. He was with me.'

'Yeah. And now he likes you better.'

'Maybe he just misses me. I'm quite addictive, you know.'

Julie smiled. 'You are, huh?'

'What can I say? It's a curse.'

Julie laughed. 'It must be tough being you.'

Mike shook his head, thinking how beautiful Julie looked.

'You have no idea.'

An hour later, Julie was standing over the sink in her kitchen, holding on to the dishtowel she'd hastily wrapped around the broken faucet, doing her best to stem the flow of water that had exploded towards the ceiling like a domestic geyser.

'Could you get me the phone?' she shouted.

Singer traipsed to the living room; a moment later, with her free hand, Julie took the portable phone from his mouth. She hit the first number on her speed dial.

Mike was on the couch, munching on Doritos, his fingers frosted with orange powder, a can of beer wedged between his legs. When the phone on the table beside him blared like an alarm, Mike jumped, sending Doritos in all directions and spilling the beer into his lap.

'Crap,' he said, setting aside the empty can and bag. The phone rang again before he picked it up. 'Hello?'

'Hey, Mike,' Julie said, sounding stressed. 'You busy?'

The beer kept soaking through the fabric of his jeans and worked its way around to the seat of his trousers. 'Not really.'

'You sound distracted.'

'Just had a little accident here involving my dinner.'

'Excuse me?'

'It's nothing serious,' he said. 'I'll be OK. So what's up?'

'I need you.'

'You do?' His ego inflated momentarily.

'My faucet exploded.'

'Oh,' he said. 'How'd that happen?'

'How should I know? Can you come over or not?'

He made an instant decision. 'I'd have to change my trousers first.'

'Excuse me?'

'Never mind. I'll be there in a few minutes—I have to swing by the hardware store to get you a new faucet.'

'You won't be long, will you? I'm stuck holding a towel here.'

'I'm on my way.'

'Julie?' Mike called out as he entered the house.

Julie craned her neck, loosening her grip slightly on the towel.

'In here, Mike. It doesn't seem to be leaking any more.'

'I just shut off the water with the valve out front.'

Mike poked his head into the kitchen. Julie was soaked to the point that he could clearly see the outlines of her breasts. She looked as though she'd been in a wet T-shirt contest.

'You have no idea how much I appreciate you coming over like this,' Julie said. She unwrapped the faucet.

Mike barely heard her. Don't stare, he told himself, whatever you do. A gentleman wouldn't stare. A friend wouldn't stare. Squatting, he opened his toolbox. Singer sat beside him and sniffed the box, as if looking for goodies. 'No problem,' Mike mumbled.

Julie began to wring out the towel. 'I mean it. I hope I didn't drag you away from anything important.'

'Don't worry about it.'

Julie pulled her T-shirt away from her skin and looked at him. 'Are you OK?' she asked.

Mike began fishing around for the basin wrench—a long, thin plumbing tool used to reach bolts in difficult places.

'I'm fine. Why?'

'You're kind of acting like you're upset.'

'I'm not upset.'

'You won't even look at me.'

'Here it is!' he said, suddenly, thankful for the opportunity to change the subject. 'I was hoping I put this in here.'

Julie kept staring at him, puzzled. 'I think I'm going to go change,' she said finally.

'I think that's probably a good idea,' he muttered.

Mike spread some towels around and soaked up most of the water, then emptied the cupboard below the sink, stacking bottles and cans of cleansers on either side of the doors. By the time Julie got back, he was already working to replace the faucet—only his torso and lower body were visible.

Julie had slipped into a pair of jeans and a light sweatshirt. 'How's it going under there?' she asked.

'Good. I've just about got it done.'

'Already?'

'It's not that hard. I didn't know what kind of faucet you wanted, so I grabbed one that looks like your old one. I hope that's OK.'

She glanced at it. 'It's fine.'

She saw his arms start to crank the wrench again, and to her surprise, she caught herself eyeing the wiry muscles of his forearms as he worked.

A moment later, he slid out from under the sink. He stood and lifted the old faucet free, then handed it to her. 'You really destroyed that thing,' he said, pointing to the gaping hole at the top. 'What did you use to turn it on, a hammer?'

'No. Dynamite.'

'You might want to use a little less next time.'

She smiled. 'Can you tell what went wrong with it?'

'Just old, I guess. Give me another minute here, and I'll have every-thing up and running.' He put the new faucet in place, crawled back underneath, and hooked it up. Then, excusing himself from the kitchen, he vanished out of the door for a moment, Singer trailing close behind. After turning the water valve back on, he came back in and tried the faucet. 'Looks like you're good to go,' he said, squatting to put the cleansers back.

'Oh, no, you don't—let me get that,' she said, kneeling next to him. 'I can do something.'

As they were putting things away, Julie more than once felt his arm brush against her and wondered why she even noticed it at all. A minute later, the cupboard was closed and the towels were bundled up, still dripping. She left the kitchen for a moment to throw them in the laun-dry room while Mike put his tools away. When she came back, she headed straight for the refrigerator.

'I don't know about you, but I need a beer after all the excitement this evening. Do you want one?'

'I'd love one.'

Julie grabbed two bottles of Coors Light and handed one to Mike. After twisting off the cap, she clinked her bottle against his.

'Did you say you've already eaten dinner? When I called you earlier, I mean?' Julie asked.

'Why?'

'Because I'm starved. You up for sharing a pizza?'

Mike smiled. 'That sounds great.'

Julie started towards the phone, and as she moved away, Mike won-dered if the evening would somehow end up breaking his heart.

They sat in rockers on the porch, the heat of their skin escaping into the cool evening, cicadas humming and mosquitoes circling just outside the screen. The sun had finally dipped from sight.

Julie's home, which sat in half an acre, was bordered at the back and on one side by wooded lots, and when she wanted to be alone, this was the place she went. Singer was dozing on the porch near the steps. In the waning light, Julie's features took on a pale glow.

'This reminds me of the first time we met,' Mike said, smiling. 'Do you remember that? When Mabel invited all of us over to her place so we'd have a chance to meet you?

'It was one of the most terrifying moments of my life. You were all strangers to me. I had no idea what to expect.'

'Even with Jim?'

'Especially with Jim. It took me a long time to realise why he did what he did for me. I'd never known anyone like him, and I had a hard time believing that there were people out there who were good.' Julie paused for a long moment, then said, 'It's still hard for me to believe that I'm here sometimes.'

'Why?'

'Just the way things worked out. I'd never even heard of Swansboro until Jim mentioned it, and here I am, twelve years later.'

Mike looked at her. 'You sound like you want to leave.'

Julie tucked a leg beneath her. 'No. I like it here. After Jim died I thought I should start over someplace new, but where would I go? It's not like I wanted to live near my mom again.'

'Have you talked to her lately?'

'Not for a few months. She called me on Christmas and said she wanted to come up and visit, but I didn't want that. It would just open old wounds.'

'I know that's got to be hard.'

'It used to be. But I don't really allow myself to think about it much any more. She didn't show up for the wedding. She didn't show up for the funeral. After that, I just sort of gave up.'

Mike stared towards the darkening shadows near the trees. 'I don't know if I could make it on my own like you have.'

She looked at him. 'You'd make it. Besides, I'm not totally alone. I've got Singer, and I've got my friends. That's enough.'

Mike wanted to ask where Richard fitted into that equation but decided not to. He didn't want to ruin the mood.

'Can I ask you a question?' Julie said.

'Sure.'

'Whatever happened with Sarah? I thought you two had something special going. You've never told me why it ended.'

Mike adjusted himself in the chair. 'There wasn't much to tell.'

'That's what you always say. But what's the real story?'

Mike was quiet for a while before shaking his head. 'You don't want to know.'

'What'd she do? Cheat on you?'

When Mike didn't answer, Julie suddenly knew her guess was correct. 'Oh, Mike. I'm sorry.'

'Yeah, me too. Or I was, anyway. It was some guy from work. His car was at her house when I went by one morning.'

'What did you do?'

'You mean did I get angry? Of course. But it wasn't entirely her fault. I hadn't been the most attentive boyfriend at the end.' He sighed. 'I guess part of me knew it wasn't going to last.'

Neither said anything for a moment, and noticing he was almost empty, Julie pointed to his bottle. 'Need another one?'

'Probably,' he said.

She rose and Mike watched as the door slapped shut behind her. He couldn't help noticing how good she looked in jeans.

He shook his head, forcing the thought away. Now was not the time for that. If they were having wine and lobster, maybe, but pizza and beer? No, this was just a casual night. The way things used to be—before he'd done something as crazy as allowing himself to fall in love with her.

He still wasn't sure exactly when it had happened. After Jim had been gone for a while, he knew that. But he couldn't pin it down any more than that. It wasn't as if a light had suddenly blinked on; it was more like a sunrise, where the sun grows lighter and lighter, almost imperceptibly, before you realised it was morning.

When Julie came back out, she handed him the bottle and took her seat again. 'Jim used to say that, too, you know?'

'What?'

'"Probably." When I asked him if he wanted another beer. Did he get that from you?'

'Probably.'

She laughed. 'Do you still think about him?'

Mike nodded. 'All the time. He was a great guy. You couldn't have done any better. And he used to tell me that he couldn't have done any better, either.'

She leaned back in her seat. 'You're a good guy, too.'

'Yeah. Me and about a million others. I'm not like Jim was.'

'Sure you are. You two seemed more like brothers than you and Henry. Except, of course, for the fact that Jim could never have fixed that faucet. He couldn't fix anything.'

'Well, Henry couldn't have fixed it, either. He hates getting his hands dirty.'

'That's funny, considering you two own a garage.'

'Tell me about it. But I don't mind. I like what I do a whole lot more than his part of the job. I'm not a big fan of paperwork.'

'So I guess being a loan officer is out, huh?'

'Like Jim was? No way. I'd approve everybody who walked in the door. I'm not real good at saying no when someone really needs something.'

She reached over, touching his arm. 'Gee, really?'

He smiled, suddenly at a loss for words, wishing with all his heart that the touch would last for ever.

The pizza arrived a few minutes later. For the next hour they ate together, talking quietly in the familiar way they always did. As the evening slowly wound down, Julie found herself holding Mike's gaze a little longer than usual. It surprised her. It wasn't as if he'd done or said anything out of the ordinary. No, there was no reason for her to feel differently tonight, but she didn't seem able to control it. Nor, she realised, did she really want the feeling to stop, though that didn't make sense, either. In his sneakers and jeans, his legs propped up on the railing, his hair mussed, he was cute in an everyday guy kind of way. But then, she'd always known that, even before she'd started dating Jim.

Spending time with Mike wasn't like the dates she'd recently been on, including the past weekend with Richard. There was no pretension here, no hidden meanings in the phrases they spoke, no elaborate plans designed to impress the other. Though it had always been easy to spend time with Mike, she suddenly realised that in the whirlwind of the past couple of weeks, she'd almost forgotten how much she enjoyed it.

It was what she'd most enjoyed about being married to Jim: the lazy mornings they'd spent reading the newspaper in bed, or the cold December mornings they'd planted bulbs in the garden. Those were the moments when all seemed right with the world.

Remembering those things, Julie watched Mike eat. He was fighting long strings of cheese that ran from his mouth back to the slice, using his fingers to keep the toppings from sliding off or the tomato sauce from dripping. Then, laughing at himself, he would swipe at his face with a napkin, mumbling something along the lines of 'Almost ruined my shirt with that one.' That he didn't take himself too seriously, or mind when she didn't, either, made her warm towards him in a way that reminded her of how she imagined old couples felt as they sat on park benches, holding hands. It was still on her mind a few minutes later when she followed him into the kitchen, both of them carrying the remains from dinner, and watched him automatically reach for the garbage when he noticed it was full. There was a moment, just a moment, when the scene seemed as if it were taking place sometime in the future, just an ordinary evening in a long procession of evenings together.

'I think we've got it all,' Mike said, looking around the kitchen.

The sound of his voice brought Julie back, and she felt her cheeks redden slightly. 'Looks that way,' she agreed.

For a long moment neither of them spoke, and Julie heard the refrain she'd lived with the last couple of years start up. *A relationship with Mike? No way. Not a chance.*

Mike brought his hands together, interrupting the thought. 'I should get going. I have an early day tomorrow.'

She nodded. 'I figured. I should probably get to bed soon, too. Singer kept me up last night for hours.'

'Singer? What's going on?'

'Oh, Richard came by last night. You know how Singer gets around new people.'

'Richard was here last night?'

'No—not that way. He just came by to leave a note on my car to let me know he'd be out of town.'

'Oh,' Mike said. 'So what time was this?'

'I guess around two or so. Why?'

Mike pressed his lips together. 'I guess I was just wondering why he didn't leave the note before he left in the morning.'

Julie shrugged. 'I have no idea. Maybe he didn't have time.'

Mike nodded and reached for his toolbox. 'Well, thanks for calling me about this.' He held up the faucet he'd replaced. 'Believe it or not, I'm glad you did. I had a great time tonight.'

Their eyes met and held for a moment before Mike glanced away. After saying goodbye, Julie stood in the doorway watching as Mike went to his truck. She watched as the red taillights receded into the distance. For a minute, she stood on the porch, trying to make sense of her feelings. *Mike?* she thought. *Mike?* The whole thing was preposterous. A bunch of nonsense. Wasn't it?

In his office the following morning, Henry set a cup of coffee on his desk. 'So that's it?' he asked. 'You just left? Like that?'

Mike scratched the back of his head. 'That's it.'

'Let me make sure I've got this straight. You hear a bunch of cryptic stuff from Jake Blansen about Richard. Then you find out Richard is coming around Julie's place in the middle of the night, and you don't tell her that there might be something to be concerned about?'

'She might have thought I was just saying it because of how I feel about her.'

'Look, Mike,' Henry said, 'you're her friend, and you'll always be her friend. The same goes for me, and I don't like the thought of this guy hanging around her place in the middle of the night. Didn't you say that Singer kept her up for hours? What if that meant Richard was skulking around the whole time? And what if Blansen was trying to warn you somehow? Didn't you think of any of those things?'

'Of course I did. I didn't like it, either.'

'Then you should have said something.'

'You weren't there, Henry,' Mike said. 'And she didn't seem to think it was odd at all, so don't make this into something bigger than it is.'

'Look,' Henry said, 'I'm usually more than willing to let you do your own thing even when you screw up, but there's a time and place for everything. This isn't the time to start keeping secrets from her, especially about stuff like this. Does that make sense?'

After a moment, Mike's chin dropped to his chest.

'Yeah,' he said. 'That makes sense.'

Well, it sounds like you two had a good time,' Mabel said.

'We did,' Julie replied. 'You know how he is. He's always fun.'

Mabel swivelled in a salon chair as they were talking. No customers were scheduled for another few minutes, and they had the place to themselves. 'And your faucet's good to go?'

Julie was busy setting up her station, and she nodded. 'He put a new one in.'

'He sure is something, isn't he?'

Julie hesitated. From the corner of her eye, she saw Singer sitting by the front door wanting to be let out.

Though Mabel's question didn't require a response, there was an element of seriousness to the possible answer, one that Julie hadn't stopped thinking about since the night before. Her reply came effortlessly as she moved towards the door to let Singer out.

'Yes,' she said, 'he is.'

Mike,' Henry called out, 'you've got company.'

Mike poked his head out of the supply room. 'Who is it?'

'Take a wild guess.'

Before he could answer, Singer trotted up beside him.

It was late afternoon by the time Julie marched over to the garage. Hands on her hips, she glared at Singer. 'If I didn't know better, I'd think this was a plan to make sure I come over here.'

As soon as she said it, Mike did his best to project his thanks to Singer telepathically.

'Maybe he's trying to tell you that he hasn't been getting enough attention lately,' Mike said.

'Oh, he gets plenty of attention. He's spoilt rotten.'

Mike was unfastening the snaps of his coveralls as they were talking. 'I hope you don't mind,' he said, 'but this thing is driving me crazy. I got some transmission fluid on it and I've been breathing the fumes all day.'

Julie watched as he slipped off the coveralls. In jeans and a red T-shirt, she thought, he looked younger than he actually was.

'So what's on your agenda tonight?' she asked.

'Just the usual. Saving the world, fostering world peace.'

'It's amazing how much a person can do in a night if he puts his mind to it.'

'So true.' Mike gave a boyish grin. He caught sight of Henry leaning against the doorjamb, studying a stack of papers and making sure his presence was known so that Mike wouldn't forget what he'd said earlier. Mike pushed his hands into his pockets and took a deep breath. 'Hey, do you have a few minutes?' he asked. 'There's something I'd like to talk to you about.'

'Sure. What's up?' she asked.

'Would you mind going somewhere else? I need a beer first.'

Though puzzled by his sudden seriousness, Julie couldn't deny that she was pleased he'd asked. 'A beer sounds great,' she said.

A short walk up the street, Tizzy's was sandwiched between a pet shop and a dry-cleaner's. A television blared in the corner of the bar, and the windows were chalky with dirt. According to Tizzy Welborn, the owner, his bar was popular because it had 'character'. As Mike and Julie settled onto a pair of stools at the far end of the bar, Singer circled once before lying down.

Tizzy took their order before setting two beers in front of them.

Julie looked around. 'So what's so important that you felt the need to drag me here?'

'It's something that Henry said I should do. He thought I should have said something to you yesterday about Richard dropping off that note. He thought it sounded a little weird, you know, him coming by in the middle of the night.'

Julie looked at him sceptically. 'Why was Henry so worried? It's not as if Richard was peeking in the windows. Singer would have gone through the glass if that happened.'

'Well, there was something else, too.'

Mike told her what Jake Blansen had said. When he'd finished, Julie put her hand on Mike's shoulder and smiled. 'That's so sweet of Henry to worry about me like that.'

It took a moment for Mike to digest her response. 'Wait—you're not mad?'

'Of course I'm not mad. It makes me feel good to know that I've got friends like him who watch out for me.'

'But . . .'

Julie laughed, gently nudging Mike's shoulder. 'C'mon, admit it—you were worried, too. It wasn't just Henry, was it?'

Mike swallowed. 'No.'

'Then why didn't you just say that? Why put it all on Henry?'

'I didn't want you to think . . . well, I wasn't sure you'd—,'

'You didn't want me to think that you were just saying it so I'd stop seeing him?' Julie asked.

'Yeah.'

Julie studied him. 'Do you really have that little faith in our friendship? I don't think there's anything you could say to me that would lead me to believe that you're doing it to hurt me. If there's one thing I've come to know about you, it's that you're not even capable of something like that. Why do you think I like spending time with you so much? Because you're a good guy. A nice guy.'

Mike turned away. 'Nice guys finish last. Isn't that what people say?'

Julie used her finger to rotate his face back to hers and met his eyes. 'Some people. Not me, though.'

'And what about Richard? You've been spending a lot of time with him lately.'

She leaned back on her stool, as if trying to bring him into better focus. 'Why, if I didn't know better, I'd say you sound jealous,' she teased.

Mike took a drink of his beer, ignoring her comment.

'Don't be jealous. We went out on a few dates and had a few laughs. It's not like I'm planning on marrying the guy.'

'You're not?'

'You're kidding, right?' She paused. 'Well, I'm not. I'm not even sure I'd go out with him again. And it's not because of what you just told me, either. Last weekend was great, it was fun, but it just wasn't there, you know? And then Monday, he just seemed a little off somehow, and I decided it wasn't worth it.'

'Really?'

She smiled. 'Really.'

Mike felt his throat go dry. He took another drink of his beer. 'Well, maybe someone else will come along.'

'Maybe.' Julie rested her chin in her hand, holding his gaze.

'I'm sure there are a dozen guys just waiting to ask you out.'

'I only need one.' She smiled broadly.

'He's out there,' Mike declared. 'I wouldn't worry about it.'

'I'm not worried. Now that I've been out a few times, things are a little clearer. I want to find a good guy. A nice guy.'

'Well, you deserve one, that's for sure.'

Mike was sometimes as dense as marbles. She tried another tack. 'So what about you? You ever going to find someone special?'

'Who knows?'

'You will if you look. Sometimes they're right under your nose.'

'I hope you're right,' he said.

Julie exhaled. I guess this is going to be up to me, she thought. If I wait for this Casanova, I'll be so old that he'll have to escort me in my wheelchair. 'What are you doing tomorrow night?' she asked.

'I haven't thought about it.'

'I was thinking we might go out.'

'Go out?'

'Yeah. There's a place on the island that's really nice. It's right on the beach, and I hear the food's pretty good.'

'You and me?' He could feel his heart thumping.

'Sure. Why not? Unless you don't want to, of course.'

'No, I want to,' he said a little too quickly. Taking a deep breath, he forced himself to calm down. He gave her his James Dean look. 'I mean, I think I'll be able to work that out.'

Julie stifled a laugh. 'Gee,' she said, 'I appreciate that.'

J ulie unlocked the front door, carrying a bag of groceries and the mail, and staggered in the direction of the kitchen. Singer hadn't followed her in. He'd hopped out of the Jeep after it had stopped and taken off through the wooded lots that stretched to the Intracoastal Waterway. He wouldn't be back for a few minutes.

Julie popped a frozen lasagne in the oven, changed into shorts and a T-shirt in her bedroom, then headed back to the kitchen. As she thumbed through the mail, her eyes were drawn to the blinking light on the answering machine. She hit PLAY, and Emma's voice came on, asking if she'd like to go to lunch on Friday. Sounds good to me, Julie thought.

A moment later, the machine beeped and she heard Richard's voice. He sounded tired. 'Hey, Julie. Just calling to check in, but I guess you're not around, huh? I'll be out most of the evening, but I'll be home tomorrow.' He paused, and she could hear him take a long breath. 'You can't believe how much I miss you right now.'

Julie heard the click as he hung up the phone.

Oh boy, she thought suddenly, why do I get the feeling he's not going to take this very well?

SIX

MIKE SWUNG BY JULIE'S the following evening a little before seven, dressed in Dockers and a white linen shirt. After turning off the truck engine, he grabbed the box of chocolates and started up the walk, rehearsing his opening line. After hours of contemplation, he'd decided on 'What a great idea to go to the beach. It's beautiful tonight.'

Julie stepped outside just as Mike was approaching the door and said something friendly, but her voice, coupled with the staggering realisation that *the date was actually happening*, ruined his train of thought, and he forgot what he'd intended to say.

There were pretty women everywhere, he thought as he looked at her. There were women who made men turn their heads even if they had a date on their arm; there were women who could get off with a warning when a trooper pulled them over for speeding simply by batting their eyelashes. And then there was Julie.

Most people would consider her attractive. There were flaws, of course—a nose that upturned slightly, a few too many freckles, hair that more often than not seemed to do as it pleased. But as Mike watched her start down the steps, her sundress billowing slightly in the spring breeze, he knew he'd never seen anyone more beautiful.

'Mike?' Julie said. 'Are you OK? You look a little pale.'

Mike's mouth opened, then closed when he realised he didn't remember what he'd intended to say. He took a deep breath. 'I brought chocolate,' he said, holding out the box.

Julie looked at him. 'I see that. Thank you.'

243

The opening line . . . the opening line, he thought. 'You're beautiful at the beach tonight,' he blurted out.

Julie smiled. 'Thank you. But we're not there yet.'

Mike shoved his hands into his pockets. 'I'm sorry.'

'About what?'

'Not knowing what to say.'

'What are you talking about?'

Her expression was a curious blend of confusion and patience, and it was that, above all, that finally enabled Mike to figure out the right thing to say. 'I guess I'm just glad to be here.'

Julie sensed the sincerity of his words. 'So am I,' she said. 'Well, you ready to go?'

'Whenever you are.'

As he started towards the truck, Mike heard Singer bark from inside the house. 'Singer's not coming?'

'I wasn't sure you'd want him along.'

Mike stopped. 'He can come if you want. We'll be at the beach, and he'd love it.'

She smiled. A couple of minutes later, as they were driving over the bridge that led to Bogue Banks, Singer barked again. He was in the bed of the pick-up, his lips and tongue flapping in the wind, looking as pleased as a dog could look.

S Singer curled up in the warmth of the sand in front of the restaurant as Julie and Mike took their seats at a table on the first-floor balcony. Low-slung clouds were thinning out in the slowly darkening sky. The ocean breeze made the flaps of the table umbrella move in steady rhythm.

The restaurant was casual and pleasant. When the waiter came by, Julie ordered a glass of wine; Mike opted for beer.

During their first few minutes at the restaurant, Mike found it difficult to concentrate. After all, he'd thought of this moment pretty much every day for the last couple of years. Through their drinks, he kept up a stream of conversation and even made her laugh a couple of times, but by the time dinner came, his nerves were so jangled that he couldn't remember much of anything that was said. Get a hold of yourself, he thought.

Julie knew it would take a while for him to loosen up. She wasn't completely comfortable, either. She thought about Jim more than once as they were eating. By the time they finished their dinner, the moon had risen, leaving a fan of white over the darkened water.

'Would you like to take a walk?' Mike suggested.

'That sounds great,' she said.

Moments later, they were walking along the water's edge. They had taken off their shoes, and Mike had rolled up his trouser legs to midshin. Singer wandered ahead of them, his nose to the ground.

'You got kind of quiet towards the end of dinner,' Mike said.

'Just thinking,' Julie murmured.

Mike nodded. 'About Jim?'

She glanced at him. 'How did you know?'

'I've seen that expression lots of times. So what were you thinking?'

'It's not important. Besides, you don't want to know.'

'Why? Is it bad?'

'No.'

'Then tell me.'

'All right. I was thinking about his fingers.'

'His fingers?'

'Yeah. You have grease stains on your fingers. I was thinking that in all the time I was married to Jim, I never saw his fingers look like yours.'

Mike moved his hands self-consciously behind his back.

'Oh, I didn't mean it in a bad way,' she said. 'I kind of like it.'

'You do?'

'I guess I kind of have to. They come with the package.'

Mike's chest puffed out as they walked in silence for a few steps. 'So, do you think you'd like to go out tomorrow night? Maybe we could head into Beaufort.'

'That sounds like fun.'

'Is there any place in particular you like to go?'

'It's your turn to pick. I've done my duty.'

'And you did it well.' Mike reached for her hand. 'What a great idea to go to the beach. It's beautiful tonight.'

Julie smiled as his fingers interlocked with hers. 'Yes, it is.'

They left the beach a few minutes later when Julie started getting chilled. Neither of them said much on the way home, and when he walked her to the door, he hoped she would hesitate on the porch, before they said their goodbyes, giving him the chance to make sure his kiss was just right.

'I had a great time tonight,' he said.

'Me too.'

Mike nodded, feeling like a teenager. This was it, he thought, the big moment. It all comes down to this. 'So,' he said.

Julie smiled, reading his thoughts. She reached for his hand and squeezed it. 'Good night, Mike. I'll see you tomorrow.'

It took a second to process the rejection. 'Tomorrow?' he asked.

'Yeah. Our date, remember?'

She slipped her key into the lock, then looked up at him again. By then, Singer had joined them and she opened the door, letting him inside. 'And thanks again for a nice evening.'

Knowing she wouldn't be able to fall asleep, Julie flipped through a catalogue as she sat on the couch, replaying the evening with Mike. She was glad she hadn't kissed him when they'd said good night on the porch, though she wasn't sure why.

She picked up the remote and turned on the television. It was still early—not even ten o'clock yet. Twenty minutes later, she heard a knock at the door.

Singer rose quickly and bounded through the living room. He poked his head out of the curtains. Then he started growling.

'Richard,' Julie said as she opened the door.

'Hey, Julie.' He held out a bouquet of roses. 'I picked these up at the airport on the way home.'

Julie stood in the doorway, Singer by her side. He'd stopped growling as soon as she'd opened the door.

Julie hesitated before taking the flowers, wishing he hadn't brought them. 'Thank you,' she said.

'I'm sorry for coming by so late, but I wanted to say hi before heading back to my place.'

'It's OK,' she said.

'I called earlier to let you know, but I guess you weren't in.'

'Did you leave a message?'

'No. I didn't have time. They were announcing final boarding. I left you one yesterday, though.'

'Yeah'—she nodded—'I got that one.'

'So, were you in?' he asked. 'Earlier, I mean?'

She felt her shoulders give a little. She didn't want to do this now. 'I was out with a friend,' she said. 'You remember Mike?'

'Oh, yeah,' he said. 'The guy who works in the garage?'

'That's the one.'

'Oh,' he said. He glanced off to the side of the porch, then at her again. 'Can I come in? I was hoping we might talk.'

'I don't know,' she hedged. 'It's kind of late.'

'Oh,' he said, 'that's fine. I understand. Can I see you tomorrow, then? Maybe we can have dinner.'

Julie closed her eyes for an instant. 'I'm sorry,' she said, 'but I can't. I already made plans.'

'With Mike again?'

She nodded.

'So that's it, then? For us, I mean?'

Her expression answered for her.

'Did I do something wrong?' he asked.

'No,' she protested, 'it's not that.'

'Then . . . what is it? Didn't you have fun when we went out?'

Julie hesitated. 'It's not about you at all, really. It's about Mike and me. We just seem . . . Well, I don't know how to explain it.'

His jaw began to tighten. 'Must have been an exciting few days while I was gone, huh?' he said.

'Look, I'm sorry—'

'For what? For going behind my back as soon as I left? For using me to make Mike jealous?'

'I didn't use you.'

Richard ignored her, his tone becoming angrier. 'No? Then why are you ending this when we're still getting to know each other? And how did Mike suddenly get so interesting? I leave town for a few days, and the next thing I know, it's over between us and Mike has taken my place.' He stared at her, his lips beginning to turn white at the edges. 'It sure sounds to me like you planned this all along.'

His outburst was so startling, so unexpected, that the words came out before she could stop them. 'You're a jerk.'

Richard continued to look at her for a long moment before finally glancing away. His anger suddenly gave way to an expression of hurt.

'This isn't fair,' he said softly. 'Please, I just want to talk for a minute, OK?' he pleaded.

When Julie looked at him, she was amazed to see tears forming in his eyes. The man was an absolute roller coaster of emotions, she decided. 'Look, I'm sorry, Richard. But it's late and we're both tired. I think I better head in before either of us says anything else. OK?'

She took a step backwards and began to close the door. Richard suddenly thrust his hand out, stopping her.

'Julie! Wait!' he said. 'Please. I really need to talk to you.'

Before she fully realised that Richard had taken hold of the door, Singer had launched himself towards the hand, as if trying to catch a Frisbee in flight. Singer's jaw found its target and Richard howled in pain as he tumbled over the threshold.

'Singer!' Julie screamed.

Richard fell to his knees, one arm extended as Singer shook his head from side to side, snarling.

'Stop him!' Richard screamed. 'Get him off me!' Julie lunged towards Singer, grabbed his collar and tugged hard. 'Let him go!' she commanded. 'Let him go, now!'

Despite the fury of the moment, Singer fell back immediately and Richard drew his hand instinctively to his chest, wrapping his other hand round it.

Singer stood by Julie's side, fangs showing.

'Singer, no!' she cried. 'Is your hand OK?'

Richard moved his fingers, wincing. 'I don't think anything's broken.'

Singer's muscles were rigid, his eyes locked on Richard.

'I didn't even see him coming,' Richard said quietly. 'Remind me not to hold your door again when your dog's around.'

Though he spoke as if the incident were somewhat comedic, Julie didn't reply. Singer had acted instinctively to protect her, and she wasn't about to punish him for that.

Richard stood then. 'I'm sorry,' he said. 'I shouldn't have tried to stop you from going inside. That was wrong of me.'

You got that right, she thought.

'And I shouldn't have got angry with you.' He sighed. 'It's just that this came at the end of a really hard week. That's the reason I wanted to come by. I know it's no excuse, but—'

He sounded contrite, but she held up her hands. 'Richard . . .'

Richard's eyes darted to the side. He stared, seemingly at nothing. His eyes were missing. 'My mother died this week,' he whispered. 'I just came from her funeral.'

'That's why I had to leave the note on your Jeep that night,' Richard explained. 'I had to leave in the middle of the night.'

A few minutes had passed, and Richard was sitting on Julie's couch, staring at the ground. She couldn't help feeling a jolt of sympathy for him. She had allowed him into the house after putting Singer in the bedroom. Now she was sitting across from him in a chair, listening as he spoke.

'I know it doesn't change what you told me on the porch, but I didn't want us to end with a fight.' He cleared his throat. 'It just seemed so sudden, you know? I needed to talk to someone.'

Julie forced a wan smile. 'We can talk,' she said. 'We're still friends, aren't we?'

Richard rambled on for a couple of hours, bouncing from subject to subject: his memories of his mother, what he was thinking when he first walked into the hospital room, how it felt the following morning to know he was holding her hand for the last time.

Midnight came and went. By two, emotional exhaustion had taken its toll. When Julie went to the kitchen for a glass of water for herself, she noticed that Richard's eyes had closed. Wedged into the corner of the couch, his head was angled against the back cushion, his mouth open.

Holding the glass of water, she stood in place, thinking, Oh, this is just great. So what do I do now? She wasn't comfortable having him stay, but then again, he was already asleep, and if she woke him again, he might want to talk some more.

It's no big deal, she finally decided. He's fast asleep.

Julie turned out the lights and headed back into the bedroom, locking the door behind her. Singer was on the bed. He raised his head, watching as she slipped into her pyjamas.

Julie woke at dawn and glanced at the clock.

After crawling out of bed, she cracked open the door to peek out. Richard still appeared to be sleeping. She hopped into the shower and then dressed for work. By the time she entered the living room—with Singer moving warily beside her—Richard was sitting up on the couch, rubbing his face.

'Oh, hey,' he said. 'I guess I conked out. I'm sorry about that.'

'It was a long day,' she said. 'You gonna be OK?'

'I guess I have to be. Life goes on, right? His shirt was wrinkled, and he brushed at it with his hands. 'I'm sorry again for the way I acted last night. I don't know what got into me.'

'It's OK,' she said. 'And I know it must seem like it came out of the blue, but . . .'

He shook his head. 'No—it's fine. You don't have to explain—I understand. Mike seems like a nice guy.'

She hesitated. 'He is,' she said, 'but thank you.'

'I want you to be happy. That's all I ever wanted. You're a great person, and you deserve that.' Then he started towards the door. Opening it, he looked over his shoulder. 'Goodbye, Julie.'

When he finally got in the car, Julie felt herself exhale. At least it's over now.

Inside the Victorian house, Richard made his way upstairs to the corner room. He'd painted the walls black and covered the windows with duct tape and a light-blocking tarp; a red light dangled over a table along the far wall. His photography equipment was in the corner: four cameras, a dozen lenses, boxes of film. He turned on the lamp. Close by the shallow containers of chemicals he used to develop the film was a stack of photographs that he'd taken on his date with Julie. He reached for them.

He thumbed through the images. She'd looked happy that weekend, he thought, as if she'd known her life had suddenly changed for the better. And lovely, too. In studying her expressions, he couldn't find anything to explain what had happened last night.

He shook his head. No, he wouldn't hold her mistake against her. He knew quite a bit about Julie Barenson now. Her father was a drunk who lived in a trailer in Daytona. Her mother had left town when Julie was three years old. A different school every year until high school, she'd finally dropped out before graduation. He had no idea what Jim had done to entice her to Swansboro. She'd had a happy marriage, and a bland husband. Nice, but bland.

He'd also learned about Mike from one of the locals he'd met at the Clipper. Amazing how a few drinks can accomplish so much.

Mike was in love with Julie, but Richard had already known that. He hadn't known about the demise of his previous relationship, however, and Sarah's infidelity had opened up several possibilities.

He'd also learned that Mike had been best man at Julie's wedding, and their relationship began to make sense to him. Mike was comfortable, a link to her past, a link to Jim. He understood Julie's desire to hold on to that. But it was a desire born of fear—fear of ending up like her mother, fear of the unknown.

So careful, he thought. But there was no reason to live that way. Not any more. She could move forward, as he had. Their childhoods probably weren't that different. The drinking. The beatings. The cockroach-infested kitchen.

The memories of his father's death were still vivid: the cut of morning sunlight on the kitchen table; the vacant look on his mother's face; the officers as they spoke in hushed tones; the coroner who examined and removed the body.

And then, the wailing of his mother, once they were alone. 'What will we do without him?' she sobbed, shaking him by the shoulders. 'How could this have happened?'

This was how: his father had been drinking at a bar. He'd been laid off at the plant two months earlier, and by that time Vernon was beating both of them regularly. The night before he'd been particularly brutal. He left the bar a little past ten, stopped at the corner shop for a packet of cigarettes, and drove past the houses in the blue-collar neighbourhood where he lived. A neighbour, who was walking his dog, saw him as he was nearing home. The garage had been left open, and Vernon pulled the car into the small space.

This was where the speculation began, however. That he had closed the garage door, there was no doubt. But why, the coroner wondered, hadn't he turned the engine off first? And why did he get back into the car after closing the garage door? It looked like a suicide, though his friends insisted he wouldn't have done something like that.

The officers came back to the house two days later, asking open-ended questions and looking for answers. The mother wailed incoherently; the ten-year-old offered only his steady gaze. In the end, it was ruled an accident, and the death was attributed to alcohol.

A dozen people attended the funeral. His mother wore black and cried into a white handkerchief as he stood beside her. The son played his part well. He kept his eyes downcast; at times, he brought his finger to his cheek as if to swipe at a tear.

The next day, however, he returned to the grave and stood in front of the freshly turned earth. Then, he spat on it.

In the darkroom, Richard tacked one of the photographs to the wall, reminded that the past casts long shadows. It's easy to get confused, he thought. He knew she couldn't help it. He forgave her for what she had done. He stared at her image. How could he not forgive her?

Because she was already dressed by the time Richard left, Julie had enough time to stop at the garage before she had to be at work.

She didn't intend to tell Mike that Richard had ended up spending the night. Try as she might, she couldn't think of any way to tell him that wouldn't seem suspect, especially in light of what had happened with Sarah. He would always wonder about it, she felt, creating a stubborn splinter of doubt and hurt. Anyway, it wasn't important. It was over now. She crossed the street, Singer trotting ahead. By the time she walked past the cars waiting to be serviced, Mike was already making his way towards her.

'Hey, Julie,' he said. 'What a nice surprise.'

Though he had a streak of grease on his cheek, she couldn't help thinking, You look pretty darn good.

'Yeah, I'm happy to see you, too, big guy,' Mike added, reaching out to Singer.

It was while he was petting Singer that she noticed the Band-Aids. 'Hey, what happened to your fingers?'

'Oh, it's nothing. They're just a little sore this morning.'

'Why?'

'I guess I scrubbed 'em too hard last night after I got home.'

She frowned. 'Because of what I said on the beach?'

'No,' he said. Then, shrugging, he added, 'Well, I guess that was part of the reason.'

'So what did you use? Ajax?'

'Ajax. Lysol. I pretty much tried everything.'

She put her hands on her hips and studied him. 'I wonder what you'll be like when you grow up.'

'I don't think there'll be much chance of that.'

She laughed. 'Well, I just wanted to tell you I had a great time last night.'

'Me too,' he said. 'And I'm looking forward to tonight.'

'It should be fun.'

Their eyes met before Julie glanced at her watch. 'I should probably be going. I've got appointments all morning, and I'm supposed to have lunch with Emma, so I can't fall behind.'

They said goodbye, and a moment later Julie was crossing the street with a bounce in her step.

'It looks like your date went pretty well, huh?' In his hand, Henry held a half-eaten doughnut.

Mike hooked his thumb into his coveralls and sniffed. 'Oh yeah,' he said. 'It went *real* well.'

Henry waved the doughnut and shook his head. 'Will you cut the James Dean stuff, little brother? I'm telling you—it's not you. And it can't hide the cross-eyed goofy look in your eyes, either.'

'I don't look goofy.'

'Goofy. Love-struck. Whatever.'

'Hey, I can't help it if she likes me.'

'I know you can't. You're just irresistible, aren't you?'

'I thought you'd be happy for me.'

'I am happy,' Henry said. 'And I'm proud of you, too.'

'Why?'

'Because somehow, whatever your plan was, it looks like it worked.'

'So what happened with Richard?' Emma asked at lunch. 'The other night, it looked like you two were getting along great.'

'Oh, he was nice, but I just didn't feel anything for him.'

'I guess it was the way he looked, huh?'

'That part wasn't so bad,' Julie said, and Emma laughed.

They were having salads at the deli. Emma took a sip of her tea. 'So what's this I hear about Mike?'

Julie knew this was coming. 'That depends on what you heard.'

'I heard he asked you out and that you went to dinner.'

'Actually, I was the one who asked him out.'

'He couldn't do it?'

She looked over her glass. 'What do you think?'

'I think he probably froze up like a shallow pond in winter.'

Julie laughed. 'Pretty much.'

'So how was it? What did you do?'

Julie recounted their date. When she was finished, Emma leaned back in her seat. 'Sounds like it went well.'

'It did.'

She studied Julie's face for a moment. 'And, what about . . . Did you think about . . .' She trailed off, and Julie finished for her.

'Jim?'

Emma nodded, and Julie considered it. 'Not as much as I thought I would,' she said. 'And it didn't really bother me at all by the end. Mike and I . . . he makes me feel good about myself.'

'I'm glad. I always figured this was coming. I figured that you'd recognise the same things in Mike that I do when you were ready.'

'Like what?'

'That he'll never let you down. That boy's got a heart the size of Kentucky, and he loves you. That's important. Take it from someone who knows. Henry would risk his life for mine in a heartbeat.'

'And you think Mike's that way?'

'Honey, you can bet your bottom dollar on it.'

Julie was still thinking about her lunch with Emma when she left the salon at the end of the day.

She was thinking about a lot of things, actually. Especially Jim. That afternoon, she'd missed Jim more than she had in a long time. What will happen, she wondered, if I do fall in love with Mike? What would happen to her feelings for Jim? Her memories?

Julie reached her Jeep and got in. Singer hopped into the back, and Julie started the engine. She didn't head towards home. Instead, she followed the main street to the outskirts of town. A few minutes later, she reached Brookview Cemetery.

Jim's headstone was just off the main path, in the shade of a hickory tree. Julie made her way up the path. She reached the gravesite and stood over it, waiting for tears to come, but they didn't. She pictured Jim in her mind, recalling the happy times, and though a faint feeling of sadness and loss came with the memories, it was like hearing a clock tower chime in the distance, echoing softly before finally fading away. In its place, there was a numbness. She wasn't sure what it meant until she saw the winged angel etched above his name, the one that always reminded her of the letter that had come with Singer.

It would break my heart if I thought you'd never be happy again . . . Find someone who makes you happy . . . The world is a better place when you smile.

Standing by his grave, she realised that maybe *this* was what he'd meant by those words. And suddenly she knew Jim would be happy for her. No, she thought, I won't forget you. Ever. And neither will Mike.

A breath of wind shook the leaves above, sounding like the faint rattle of shaken pebbles in a jar. After a moment it stopped, as if someone had muted the sound. But then it wasn't quiet any more. From the road she heard a passing car. A child's voice carried from one of the distant houses. There was a faint brushing sound, something scraping the bark of a nearby tree. A bird broke from the branches. Glancing over her shoulder, Julie saw Singer swivel his head, his ears twitching. He remained rooted in place, however, and Julie saw nothing. She frowned slightly and crossed her arms. Turning from the headstone, she tucked her head down and began walking towards the car, goose pimples lifting the hairs on her arms.

SEVEN

MIKE APPEARED RIGHT ON TIME, and Julie stepped out, closing the door behind her before Singer had the chance to get out. Noticing that he was wearing a jacket and slacks, she smiled.

'Wow,' she said, 'that's two nights in a row that you're looking pretty spiffy. This is going to take a little while to get used to.'

Julie could have been talking about herself. Like the night before, tonight she was wearing a sundress that accentuated her figure. Small gold hoops dangled from each ear, and Mike caught a trace of perfume.

They ate dinner at the Landing, a waterfront restaurant in downtown Beaufort. As on the night before, they sat at an outside table from which they could watch the boats and the people on the boardwalk.

Julie put her napkin in her lap and leaned forward. 'Good choice, Mike,' she said. 'I love this place.'

'I'm glad,' he said, relieved. 'I like it, too.' Julie appeared relaxed and radiant to him, completely at ease in her surroundings.

They lingered over wine and dinner, talking and laughing, barely noticing the waiter scurrying about the table. By the time they were ready to go, the sky was filled with stars.

The boardwalk was still bustling; people leaned against the railings that overlooked the water and milled around the bars. As they left the restaurant, Mike offered his hand. Julie took it, and they began to stroll along the boardwalk.

They spent another hour in Beaufort. Lazy waves slapped against the sea wall, and the white glow of the reflected moon slipped across the water. They stopped at a patio restaurant and sat at a weathered table beneath the rotating blades of a creaky ceiling fan. The singer at the restaurant knew Mike and nodded towards him. Mike ordered a beer while Julie sipped a Diet Coke.

As they listened, Julie could feel Mike's eyes on her, and she marvelled at how much had changed in the past couple of days.

'Jim and I used to come here a lot,' he said. 'Before you moved to town. Did you know that?'

'He told me that you two used to come here to meet women.'

'We were here when he first told me about you. He said that you were pretty and that he promised you he'd find you a job and a place to live if you came up here.'

'Did you think he was crazy?'

'Without a doubt.'

'So what did you think when I took him up on it?'

'I thought you were crazy, too. But after that, I got to thinking you were brave. It takes guts to change your life like you did.'

'I didn't have any choice.'

'You always have a choice. It's just that some people make the wrong one.'

The music stopped then, and their conversation was interrupted when the singer put down his guitar and came over to their table. 'Sorry for interrupting. I'm taking a break and wanted to know if Mike would like to take over for a song or two,' he said.

Mike turned towards the set-up and stared before shaking his head. 'I would, but I'm on a date,' he said.

'Oh, go ahead,' Julie urged. 'I'll be fine.'

Mike grinned and put his bottle on the table; a minute later, the guitar strap was over one shoulder and he was plucking a couple of strings, tuning it. He glanced at Julie, then winked before strumming the first chords. It took only a moment before everyone recognised the song. He'd chosen a crowd pleaser, 'American Pie.'

His voice, she observed, was typically out of tune, but tonight, with this Friday-night crowd, it didn't matter. They sang and swayed in time. When Mike finished, he put down the guitar to a nice round of applause and started back towards the table. Julie watched him with a mixture of new-found admiration and pleasure.

Mike, she thought, had just made a really nice night even better.

At home, Mike walked her to the door, and when she turned to face him, she could see in his face that he was thinking about kissing her. Julie looked up at him, giving him the go-ahead. Then, taking Mike's hand, she pulled him towards her, tilting her head slightly as she leaned in. Mike tilted his head and closed his eyes, their faces drawing near.

On the porch, moths were fluttering around the light. An owl called from the nearby trees. Mike, however, heard nothing at all. Lost in her breathlike touch, he knew only one thing for sure: in the instant their lips first met, there was a flicker of something almost electrical that made him believe the feeling would last for ever.

That was nice, Julie thought as she closed and locked the front door. Even better than she'd thought it would be. She was still thinking about it after she'd heard him start his truck and then drive away down the street. She was smiling and had reached to turn off the porch light when she caught a glimpse of Singer. He was staring at her, his head angled and ears up, as if asking, *Did I just see what I thought I saw?*

'What?' she said. 'We kissed.' For some reason, it felt almost as if she were a teenager who'd been caught by a parent.

Singer kept staring.

'Would you stop staring at me like this?'

With that, Singer glanced away.

She headed back to the bedroom, her mind already replaying scenes from the evening. Lost in thought, she barely registered the sweep of headlights as a car rolled down her normally quiet street, slowing as it passed her house.

'You awake?' Julie asked into the receiver the following morning. Mike struggled with the sheet and sat up in bed as he recognised her voice. 'I am now.'

'So come on. The day's a-wastin',' she said. 'Up and at 'em, Private.'

Mike rubbed his eyes, thinking that she sounded as if she'd been up for hours. 'What are you talking about?'

'The weekend. What do you have planned?'

'Nothing, why?'

'Well, get up and get dressed. I was thinking we might head to the beach together. It's supposed to be a great day. I figured we could bring Singer and let him run around for a while. Does that sound good to you?'

They spent the day walking barefoot through the white sand, throwing a Frisbee for Singer, and sitting on towels as they watched foam curl atop the waves. They grabbed a pizza for lunch, stayed until the sky was purple with early dusk, and had dinner together as well. From there, they went to a movie; Mike let Julie choose the film and didn't complain when he realised that it was a chick flick. And when Julie had tears in her eyes halfway through and snuggled closer to him for the remaining hour, it more than cancelled out the scathing critical review he was preparing in his mind.

It was late by the time they made it back to her place, and again they kissed on the porch. It lasted a little longer this time. For Julie, that made it better; for Mike, being any better was neither possible nor necessary.

They spent Sunday at Julie's house. Mike mowed the lawn, trimmed the hedges, and helped her plant impatiens in the flower box. From there, he moved inside and began fixing those little things that tended to go undone in an older house—replacing the nails that had popped through a couple of boards in the hardwood floor, unsticking the locks, hanging the new light fixture she'd purchased for her bathroom months ago.

Julie watched him as he worked, noticing once again how good he looked in his jeans and how he was most confident when he was doing those types of things. When she kissed him once in the midst of hammering, the expression on his face told her exactly how he felt about her, and she realised that what had once been uncomfortable was now the response she craved.

When he left, she went inside and closed her eyes, leaning against the inside of the door. Wow, she thought, feeling exactly the way Mike had felt two nights before.

After work the following Tuesday, Julie was pushing a trolley down the grocery store aisle, grabbing what she needed for dinner. Mike had promised to cook for her, and though she wasn't thrilled with the list he'd provided, she was willing to give it a shot.

She was just about finished when her trolley suddenly bumped into someone. 'Oh, excuse me,' she said automatically.

'It's OK . . . I'm fine,' he said.

He turned round, and Julie's eyes widened. 'Richard?'

'Oh, hey, Julie,' he answered, his voice soft. 'How are you?'

'Fine. How are you doing?' Julie hadn't seen him since the morning he'd left, and he looked a little worse for wear.

'Getting by,' he said. 'It's been hard. There's a lot I have to take care of. But you know how it goes.'

'Yeah,' she said. 'I do know. How's the hand, by the way?'

'Better. Still bruised, but nothing to worry about.' He looked down.

'Listen, I want to thank you again for listening to me. Not a lot of people would have done what you did.'

'I didn't do much.'

'Yeah,' he insisted, 'you did. I don't know what I would have done without you. I was in pretty dire straits that night.'

She shrugged.

'Well,' he said as if trying to figure out what to say next. He adjusted the grocery basket on his arm. 'I feel like I owe you something. Maybe I could take you out to dinner?'

She looked off to the side, then back at him again. 'I don't think that I can do that,' she said. 'I'm sorry.'

'It's OK,' he said. 'I just thought I'd make the offer.' He smiled. 'So no hard feelings about the other night?'

'No hard feelings,' she repeated.

'So what exactly are these called again?' Julie asked.

Mike was standing over the stove in his apartment, the minced beef in the frying pan sizzling. 'Creole burgers.'

'So it's Cajun?'

'Yep,' he said. 'Why do you think I asked for these two cans of soup? That's what gives it the authentic flavour.'

Only Mike, she thought, would consider Campbell's chicken gumbo soup authentic Cajun cuisine.

When the meat was ready, he poured in the soup, then added a bit of ketchup and mustard before beginning to stir. Julie leaned against him to look at the concoction, an expression of distaste on her face.

'Remind me never to become a bachelor.'

'Yeah, yeah. You joke now, but in a little while you'll feel like you're eating in heaven's dining room.'

'I'm sure.'

'Did anyone ever tell you that you have an occasional tendency towards sarcasm?' he asked.

'Just a couple of times. But I think it was you that said it.'

'I always knew I was a smart guy.'

'So did I,' she said. 'It's your cooking I'm worried about.'

Fifteen minutes later they were sitting at the table, Julie staring at her plate. 'This is a sloppy Joe,' she announced.

'No,' he said, picking up the sandwich, 'this is a Creole burger. Sloppy Joes have a tomato flavour.'

'While you prefer the distinctive Louisiana flavour?'

'Exactly. And don't forget to eat your pickle as you go. Sort of adds to the whole experience.'

Julie glanced around the small apartment, stalling for time. Though the major pieces of furniture were passably tasteful, there were those touches that made it clear he lived in the style of single men everywhere. Like the gym shoes in the corner of the living room near his guitar. And the pile of unfolded clothes on his bed. And the giant-screen television, with a collection of imported beer bottles lining the top. And the dartboard mounted on the front door.

'So are you going to try it, or are you scared?'

'No. I'll try it. I'm just enjoying the anticipation.'

He nodded towards her plate. 'Good. Then you can figure out a nice way to apologise to the chef.'

Julie picked up the sandwich and took a bite. Mike watched her as she seemed to study the flavour.

'Not bad,' she said after swallowing.

'Not bad?'

She stared at the sandwich, faintly surprised. 'Actually, it's kind of tasty.'

'Told you,' he said. 'It's the chicken gumbo soup that does it.'

She picked up the pickle and winked. 'I'll try to remember that.'

On Wednesday, it was Julie's turn to make dinner. She prepared sole stuffed with crabmeat and sautéed vegetables, accompanied by a bottle of Sauvignon Blanc. (It's not Creole burgers, but I guess it'll do,' Mike teased.) On Thursday they met for lunch in Emerald Isle. Afterwards, while they were walking through the fine sand, Singer jabbed her in the leg with a stick he'd found. He dropped it in front of them, and when they ignored it, he grabbed the stick again, blocking their movement with his body. He looked up at Mike. *C'mon*, he seemed to be saying, *you know the drill*.

'I think he wants you to throw it,' Julie remarked. 'He doesn't think I throw it far enough.'

'That's because you're a girl.'

She elbowed him. 'Watch it, buster. There's a feminist lurking somewhere in here that takes offence at comments like that.'

'Feminists take offence at everything that men do better.'

He pulled away before she could elbow him again and grabbed the stick. He pulled off his shoes and socks, then rolled in just below the stick. He jogged towards the water and waded in, high enough for the waves to roll in just below his knees. He held the stick out in front of him. Singer stared at it as if it were a fresh-cut steak.

'Ready?' Mike asked.

He cocked his arm and threw the stick as far as he could. Singer charged into the waves.

Julie took a seat on the sand, pulling her knees up and wrapping her arms round them. It was cool out; the sky was broken with patches of white and the sun peeked through the clouds sporadically. Terns darted along the water's edge, looking for food, their heads bobbing.

Singer came bounding back with the stick and shook the water from his coat, soaking Mike in the process. Mike grabbed the stick, then threw it again before turning Julie's way, his shirt plastered against his skin. From where she was sitting, she could see the muscles in his arms and the way his chest tapered to his hips. Nice, she thought, very nice. Julie felt the breeze on her face as she watched them, wondering why she'd ever been worried.

I In a darkened bedroom of the rented Victorian house, Richard was sitting in bed, his back against the headboard. The room was illuminated only by a small candle on the bedside table. As he rolled a piece of wax between his fingers, he closed his eyes and thought about Julie.

She had been nice enough at the grocery store, but he knew she'd regretted running into him. He shook his head, wondering why she'd tried to hide it. It was pointless, he thought. He knew her better than she knew herself. He knew, for instance, that she was with Mike tonight. Didn't she see that if she stayed here, Mike would drag her down? He slowed his breathing, concentrating on Julie's image. He knew she was different from other people. She was special, better, like him.

It was that secret knowledge of his uniqueness that had sustained him in one foster home after the next. Aside from a few articles of clothing, the only items he'd brought with him were a camera he'd stolen and a box of photographs. The first people who took him in had seemed nice enough. But as in many foster homes, he was not the only child, and he shared a room with two older boys. It was these boys who had stolen his camera and sold it to buy cigarettes.

When Richard found them, they were playing in the vacant lot next door. On the ground was a baseball bat, and he reached for it. They laughed at first, since they were both taller and heavier. In the end, however, they were rushed to the hospital, their faces crushed. The foster-care caseworker wanted to send Richard to a juvenile detention centre. She'd come to the house with the police after his foster parents had reported him.

But Richard hadn't been afraid, just as he hadn't been afraid when the police had come to question him and his mother about his father. He looked down, then began to cry.

'I didn't want to do it,' he said quietly. 'But they took my camera, and I told them I would report it to the caseworker. I was scared. One of them attacked me—with a knife.'

With that, Richard opened his jacket and the police saw blood.

He'd been slashed across his stomach. The police found the knife on the warehouse roof, exactly where Richard said he'd seen one of the boys throw it. The two boys, not Richard, were sent to the juvenile detention facility.

Richard smiled, remembering with disdain the cut he'd so easily inflicted upon himself. He opened his eyes. Yes, he knew from experience that all hurdles could be overcome. Julie simply needed the right person to help her.

For Julie, the days began to acquire a new rhythm. Mike was becoming an exciting and important part of her life.

They were still inching their way through the relationship. Mike hadn't spent the night at Julie's, Julie hadn't spent the night at Mike's, and though there were a couple of nights when the opportunity had presented itself, neither of them seemed ready.

Walking Singer one day after work, Julie acknowledged that it was just a matter of time. It was Thursday, two weeks after they'd first gone out. Up ahead, Singer wandered into the vacant wooded lots that stretched to the Intracoastal Waterway, and Julie spotted the path the real-estate agents had been using. A month ago, signs had sprouted up all the way to the water. In a couple of years, she'd have a neighbourhood, which—though nice in the way of property values—was kind of a bummer, too. She liked the feeling of privacy the lots provided, and it was great for Singer. She walked for fifteen minutes before she reached the water and sat for a little while on a stump, watching the boats as they floated past. She couldn't see Singer but knew he was nearby; he'd come to check on her periodically.

As she approached the house an hour later, she heard the phone ringing. Hurrying inside, she let the screen door close with a bang behind her. Probably Emma, she thought.

She put the receiver to her ear. 'Hello?'

There was no reply.

'Hello?' she said again. Nothing. Julie put the phone back in its cradle and went to let Singer in. But as soon as she reached the door, the phone rang again, and again there was silence on the other end. Only this time, before she lowered the phone, she thought she heard a faint click as the caller hung up.

'I'm telling you, you're practically glowing these days,' Mabel said.

'I am not. I've just been in the sun lately,' Julie answered.

They were in the salon, enjoying a lull between clients. Andrea was cutting hair at her station.

'It ain't the sun I'm talking about, and you know it.'

Andrea's client soon left, leaving a big tip. All morning long, Mabel and Julie had been whispering to each other as if they were planning to rob the bank down the street, but Andrea understood they were talking about Julie's relationship with Mike. Andrea thought the thing with Mike was completely ridiculous. Mike's a nice guy, but he wasn't Richard. Richard had it all. Julie, however, was as blind as a bat when it came to men. If anything, Andrea thought, Julie should be talking to me. I could give her some serious pointers on how to fix the situation with Richard.

A short time later, the bell on the door jingled, and Andrea turned her head, thinking, Well, speak of the devil . . . .

For a long moment, the salon was silent. Mabel had slipped out for a few minutes, and Julie's most recent client was heading out, too. Richard held the door for her as she left. He was wearing sunglasses, and when he faced her, Julie felt an odd, sinking feeling in her stomach. Singer sat up on the blanket.

'Richard,' Julie said tentatively.

'Hello, Julie. How are you?' Richard slipped off his sunglasses and smiled. 'I was hoping that you had time to cut my hair.'

She scanned her appointment book and shook her head. 'I'm sorry. I don't think I can fit it in—I'm pretty busy today.'

'I see. I guess I should have made an appointment, huh? Well, maybe we could set something up. How about Monday?'

She flipped the page, again knowing what she'd find. 'I'm booked solid then, too. Mondays are always busy.'

'Tuesday?'

'I'm only working half a day.'

Sensing the tension between them, Andrea stepped back from her chair. 'I can do it, sugar,' she said. 'I've got a little time.'

After a moment, Richard took a small step backwards, still holding Julie's eyes. 'Yeah,' he said, 'that'll be fine.'

What was he doing there?' Mike asked. Mike had a tendency to stare in the salon's direction whenever he had a spare minute. As soon as he'd seen Richard leave the salon, he'd hurried over, and Julie went outside to meet him.

'He came in for a haircut.'

'Why?'

'Well, that's what we *do* in the salon.'

He gave her an impatient glance, and she went on. 'I barely talked to him. Andrea cut his hair, not me.'

'But he wanted you to do it, right? Even though you broke it off with him?'

'That I can't deny. But I think he got the message that I'd rather not see him any more, even at work.'

'Well . . . good. He does realise that you're seeing me, right?'

Instead of answering, she reached for his hand. 'You know, you're kind of cute when you're jealous.'

'I'm not jealous.'

'Of course you are. But don't worry, I think you're cute all the time. See you tonight?'

For the first time since he'd spotted Richard, Mike felt himself relax a little. 'I'll be there,' he said.

When Julie went back into the shop, Andrea was already working again, though her face was still flushed from her time with Richard. It was the first time, Julie realised, that she'd ever seen Andrea look nervous around a man.

Julie finished up with her work a little after five and began closing up. Andrea was already gone. Mabel was cleaning up in the back while Julie took care of the reception area. It was then that she noticed the sunglasses on the counter beside the potted plant.

She saw instantly that they were Richard's.

263

Julie had stopped at the store to pick up the makings for dinner and was walking in the front door of her house when she heard the phone ringing. She put the grocery bag on the table and answered.

'Hello.'

'Hello, Julie.' It was Richard. 'I'm glad I caught you. I missed not being able to talk to you today.'

Julie closed her eyes. 'Hi, Richard,' she said coolly.

'I was just wondering if you happened to come across a pair of sunglasses. I think I might have left them in the shop.'

'Yeah, they're there. You can pick them up on Monday.'

'Oh. You're not open on Saturdays?' He paused. 'Would it be possible for you to unlock the door for me tonight?'

Julie held the phone to her ear, thinking, You've got to be kidding. 'I think this has gone far enough,' she said. 'I know what you're doing, and it's time to stop.'

'What are you talking about? I just want my glasses.'

'Richard. I'm serious about this. I'm seeing someone else now. It's over. You can pick up your glasses on Monday.'

'Julie . . . wait—'

Julie pushed the button to cut off the call.

An hour later, Mike opened Julie's front door and poked his head in.

'Hey, I'm here,' he called out.

Julie was in the bathroom blow-drying her hair, and as soon as Singer heard Mike's voice, he trotted out to greet him.

'I thought we'd do steaks tonight,' Julie said as she emerged from the bathroom. In bare feet and faded jeans, she seemed the picture of grace to Mike. 'Does that sound OK?'

'Sounds great,' Mike said, adding, 'You look beautiful. As always.'

Julie brushed past him and reached for a wineglass from the cupboard. A moment later, she held out the glass and Mike poured the wine, then grabbed a beer for himself. They went out to the porch, and Julie held open the screen door so Singer could head out to the yard. Her blouse was sleeveless. Mike noticed the thin muscles of her upper arm and the swell of her chest and couldn't help but imagine what she might look like naked. He closed his eyes and took a deep breath. Please, he thought, don't let me make a fool of myself.

But it wasn't nearly as bad as he thought it might be. As usual, they settled into a light-hearted conversation while the evening breeze kicked in. Mike fired up the grill an hour later and cooked the steaks while Julie went inside to throw a salad together.

In the kitchen, she reflected on the fact that Mike had been staring at her all evening, and she knew exactly what he was thinking because, frankly, she had been thinking the same thing.

She diced cucumbers and tomatoes and added them to the bowl, then set the table with her good china. She found two candles, put them in the centre, and lit them. After turning off the overhead light, she nodded, satisfied. She went to the living room and slipped an Ella Fitzgerald CD into the stereo. She was putting the wine on the table when Mike came in, holding the steaks. He stopped just inside the door.

'It looks . . . wonderful,' he said.

She noticed that he was looking directly at her as he spoke, and for a long moment, they simply stared at each other. Mike looked away and set the steaks on the table. Instead of sitting, however, he moved towards Julie, and she felt her stomach tighten. Oh Lord, she thought, am I really ready for this?

Standing before her, Mike brought one hand up to her face, his palm open, as if asking permission to go on. In the background, the music played softly; the aroma of dinner filled the small kitchen. It was at that moment that Julie knew she'd fallen in love with him.

Mike gazed at her as if reading her mind, and Julie gave in. She pressed her face against his hand, closing her eyes and letting his touch become part of her. Mike moved closer until she could feel his chest against hers and the strength in his arms as he slipped them round her.

Mike kissed her then. It was soft, almost like the movement of air beneath a hummingbird's wings, and though they'd kissed many times, this one seemed more real than any before. He kissed her again, and as their tongues met, Julie embraced Mike, certain in the knowledge that their years of friendship had been moving them towards this moment.

When they pulled apart, Mike took Julie's hand and led her from the kitchen to the bedroom. They kissed again as Mike slowly began undoing the buttons on her blouse. She felt his fingers against her skin, then felt his hand move to the buttons of her jeans. He kissed her neck.

'I love you,' Mike whispered.

The room seemed to be nothing but shadows and the echo of Mike's words. Julie sighed.

'Oh, Mike,' she said, feeling his breath on her skin. 'I love you, too.'

It was past midnight, and they were still in bed. Julie was watching as Mike made small circular motions on her belly with his fingers. When she couldn't take it any more, she wiggled and laughed, reaching to stop his hand.

'That tickles,' she protested. She then rolled on her side, reached out and ran a finger over his cheek. 'I do love you, you know.'

'Yeah, I know.'

She pushed him away. 'And here I was trying to be serious for a change,' she said. 'The least you can do is tell me, too.'

Mike reached for her hand again and kissed each fingertip. 'If I had my way,' he said, 'I'd say it every day for the rest of my life.'

'Well, since you love me so much, would you mind getting us something to eat? I'm starved.'

'Sure.'

As he leaned over to grab his clothes, the phone started ringing on the bedside table beside him. On the third ring, Mike answered it.

'Hello?' he said. He paused. 'Hello?'

Julie closed her eyes, hoping he wouldn't say the word again.

'Hello?' He hung up the phone. 'No one was there,' he said. 'I guess it was a wrong number.' He looked at her. 'You OK?'

She forced herself to smile. 'Yeah,' she said. 'I'm fine.'

Julie crossed her arms. Though she told herself it probably meant nothing, she couldn't shake the same feeling she'd had when she'd visited Jim's grave.

Someone, she thought, was watching her.

EIGHT

THE CHANGES IN JULIE'S LIFE began that night.

Most of them were wonderful. Mike spent Saturday and Sunday with Julie. She was surprised—and thankful—that making love hadn't altered the friendship between them.

But as much as she wanted to deny it, what would stand out most in her mind in thinking back on that week were the phone calls. First, there was the call late on Friday night. On Saturday, there were two more calls. On Sunday the phone rang four times, and on Monday it was five. On Tuesday, after she'd gone to bed, there were four calls before she unplugged the phone. And on Wednesday, when she stepped into the kitchen after work, her answering machine was full. Twenty calls had been made to her machine that day, each lasting two minutes. In none did the caller say anything.

On Thursday and Friday, there were no calls at all.

'It sounds to me like everything's going great,' Emma said on Saturday. Earlier that day, Mike and Julie had met Henry and Emma at the boat launch on Harker's Island. They'd loaded a boat with cool boxes of food and beer, sunscreen, towels and hats, and enough fishing gear to hook anything that might happen to cross the stern. By midmorning, near Cape Lookout, Mike and Henry were standing next to each other, reels in hand. A tub was already filled with mackerel and flounder.

Julie and Emma were sitting in small deck chairs near the cabin.

'It is,' Julie agreed. 'Better than great, actually. This last week makes me wonder what I was so afraid of all this time.'

The way she said it made Emma pause. 'But?'

'But what?'

'There's something bothering you, isn't there?'

'Is it that obvious?'

'No. But I've known you long enough to recognise the signs.'

'I've been getting some strange phone calls lately.'

'From who?'

'I don't know. No one ever says anything on the other end.'

'Heavy breathers?'

'No, not even that. No sound at all. I dialled recall but the recording said it was a private number, so I called the phone company. All they can tell me is that the calls are coming from a cellphone. But the number isn't registered, so they can't trace it.'

'Do you have an idea who they might be from?'

Julie turned and watched Mike cast his line again. 'I think it might be Richard. I can't prove it, but it's just a feeling I get.'

Emma looked at her. 'What does Mike think?'

'I don't know. I haven't told him yet.'

'Why not?'

Julie shrugged. 'What's he going to do? Go after the guy? I don't even know for sure that Richard's the one who's calling.'

'Well, how many calls have there been?'

'On Wednesday, there were twenty messages on the machine.'

Emma sat up. 'Have you told the police about this?'

'No,' Julie said. 'I guess I was just hoping it would stop. And maybe it has. My phone hasn't rung at all the last two days.'

Emma reached out for Julie's hand. 'People like that don't stop. This is stalker kind of stuff. You do realise that, don't you?'

'Of course I do. But what am I going to say to the police? I can't prove it's Richard. He hasn't threatened me. He hasn't been anything but polite when we do run into each other, and even then, there have always been other people around.'

Emma frowned. 'So what are you going to do?'

Julie shook her head. 'I have no idea.'

An hour later, Julie was standing at the bow when she felt Mike slip his arms round her and nuzzle her neck.

'Hey there,' she said.

'You've been kind of quiet today,' Mike said, squeezing her.

'Just thinking.'

'About something Emma said?'

'No. Just the opposite. It's something I mentioned to her.'

'Do you want to talk about it?'

Julie took a deep breath and recounted the things she'd told Emma. When she had finished, he reached for her hand and turned her round. 'Why didn't you tell me about this before?'

'There wasn't anything to tell. Not until a couple of days ago, anyway.'

Mike glanced away, frowning, then looked back at Julie. 'Well, if it happens again, I'm gonna put a stop to it.' After a long moment, he put his arms round her again. 'Don't worry,' he said. 'I'm not going to let anything happen to you.'

By midafternoon, they'd lifted anchor and were passing Cape Lookout as they headed back towards Harker's Island. The boat was moving in rhythm with the gentle swells as Henry steered.

Mike was cleaning up at the stern, putting the tackle back in the box and making sure the reels were secured. Julie stood near the bow again, feeling the wind move her hair.

Mike had to be at the Clipper by eight to start setting up with the band. Julie didn't plan on heading in to see him play until around ten or so and she wanted to take a nap before then.

She went to her gear bag and threw on a shirt. As she glanced towards the beach, her eyes registered something wrong. Shielding her eyes from the sun, she scanned the water's edge, then the people on the shore. Someone wearing jeans and a dark blue shirt was standing near the dunes, pointing binoculars at the boat. Julie felt suddenly heavy as the man waved. I'm here, he seemed to be saying, I'm always here.

Richard.

She felt the blood drain from her face, and she inhaled sharply. But when she blinked, Richard was gone. She moved back to the bow and leaned forward. Nothing. It was as if he'd never been there at all.

Mike brought Julie home and was still in the driveway unloading her things when she went inside. Singer followed her, and when she put her bag on the kitchen counter, he balanced on his two back legs to greet her. She was trying to fend off his lapping tongue when she noticed the answering machine blinking with a single message. She pushed Singer away. For an instant, the floor seemed unsteady. Her stomach was knotted up. She reached the machine, brought her hand up, then hesitated.

Please, she thought, let me hear a voice. Any voice but his.

With a trembling hand, she pressed the button.

At first there was nothing. Then, faintly, came the sound of a whisper. She leaned closer to make out the voice. She listened, concentrating hard, and just as she was reaching for the delete button to erase it, her eyes grew wide as she recognised the chorus of a song she knew by heart. A tune from her evening in Beaufort with Mike two weeks ago.

'Bye, bye, Miss American Pie . . .'

Julie's cries brought Mike running inside.

She stood beside the answering machine, her face white as she hit the delete button over and over.

'What happened?' Mike demanded. 'Are you OK?'

Julie trembled as images raced through her mind. Richard had been at the beach today. It was Richard who'd been making the calls—there wasn't the slightest doubt about it. And Richard, she realised, had also been watching them in Beaufort. He'd been close enough to know the song that Mike had sung for her. And she knew with sinking certainty that he'd been watching her in the cemetery . . . He'd been everywhere.

This can't be happening, she thought, as her throat constricted. But it was. Everything seemed suddenly, terribly wrong.

'People like that don't stop,' Emma had said.

Julie buried her face in Mike's chest as the tears started to come. 'Julie? Tell me what happened,' Mike pleaded. 'What's going on?' Her voice was cracked and faint. 'I'm scared,' she said.

Julie was still shaking when she got in the car with Mike a few minutes later. There wasn't the remotest possibility that she was going to stay at her house alone while Mike went to the Clipper.

When Mike parked in the street in front of his place, she found herself looking over her shoulder and straining to hear anything out of the ordinary. The darkened spaces between the houses didn't do much for her nerves. What was Richard going to do next?

She wished she hadn't deleted the message. In fact, she wished she hadn't deleted any of the messages, since they were the only proof she had that something was actually happening. The police might have been able to do something with them.

Later, at the Clipper, Julie took a seat at the bar. Eight o'clock came and went. After the band had checked the amplifiers and tuned their instruments, they went backstage to relax. Mike joined Julie. They made a point of not talking about what had happened, but Julie could see the anger in Mike's eyes when he told her that he was needed onstage. 'I'll be watching,' he said.

By nine thirty, when the music started, there was a steady stream of people coming in the door. Julie turned reflexively towards the door whenever it opened.

Dozens of people entered, but Richard didn't.

The hours passed in a steady rhythm—ten, eleven, then midnight—and for the first time since that afternoon, Julie felt herself regaining a bit of control. And like Mike, with that feeling came anger. More than anything, she wanted to give Richard a verbal lashing in public. While she was envisioning her revenge, a group of young men wedged in next to her, ordering drinks. When they left, she glanced to the side. Halfway down the bar, she saw a familiar figure leaning towards the bartender.

Richard.

He was here. He'd followed her. Again.

Mike had seen Richard come in a minute earlier and wanted to jump off the stage to head him off, but he forced himself to keep playing. Richard had seen Mike as well. He nodded to him with a smirk before making his way to the middle of the bar, pretending not to notice Julie was there.

He did nothing. He neither looked Julie's way nor made any move towards her. Instead, he stood with his back to the bar, scanning the crowd with a drink in his hand.

The band started another song, and Julie glanced at Mike. He mouthed the words 'I'm almost done', and she nodded.

In the dim light, Richard's profile was shadowed. One leg crossed over the other, and for an instant, she thought she saw his mouth form an amused smile, as if she knew she was watching him.

It was time to end this. Without knowing where she found the guts to do what came next, Julie rose and started towards him.

Richard turned when she was close. 'Julie,' he said, 'I didn't know you'd be here. How are you?'

'What are you doing here, Richard?'

He shrugged. 'Just having a couple of drinks.'

'You followed me here!'

'What?'

'You know exactly what I'm talking about!'

People had turned to watch. From the stage, Mike was watching with frantic intensity, and the moment the song ended, he started towards them, letting his guitar fall to the stage.

'You think you can just follow me around and I'm just going to take it?' Julie demanded, her voice rising.

Richard held up his hands. 'Julie . . . hold on. I don't know what you're talking about.'

'You picked the wrong girl to try to scare, and if you keep this up, I'll call the police and have you locked up. You think you can call my house and leave messages——',

'I didn't leave any messages.'

'I'm not going to put up with this!'

Julie was screaming now, and people were looking from her to Richard and back again as the words sparked between them.

'Put up with what?'

'Just stop! It's over. Do you understand that?'

Mike pushed his way through the crowd. For an instant, Richard's eyes met his. Mike recognised the same smirk on Richard's face that he'd seen when he'd first walked into the bar.

That was all it took.

Mike ploughed into him, driving his head into Richard's chest. The momentum lifted Richard from the floor and sent him crashing into the bar. Bottles and glasses shattered on the ground.

Mike then grabbed Richard by the collar and cocked his arm. His first punch connected with Richard's cheek. When his head came up, Mike hit him again. Richard's head whipped sideways. He hit a stool and then bounced off, tumbling until he hit the floor. When he rolled over, blood was streaming from his mouth. Mike was set to lunge again when a few men reached out to restrain him.

The fight had lasted fifteen seconds. Mike struggled to free himself before he realised the people behind him were holding him because they were worried Richard might be hurt even further. As soon as they let him go, Julie took his hand and led him out of the door.

Once outside, Mike leaned against the tailgate of his truck, trying to collect himself. 'Give me just a minute,' he said.

'You OK?' Julie asked.

Mike brought his hands to his face and exhaled, speaking through his fingers. 'I'm fine. Just crashing a little.'

Julie moved closer. 'That's a side of you that I haven't seen before. You know, I was handling it OK on my own.'

'I could see that. But the look he gave me really set me off.'

'What look?'

Mike described it, and Julie shivered. 'I didn't see that.'

'I don't think you were meant to. But I guess it's over now.'

'I hope so,' Julie said. She smiled briefly, but she was clearly distracted. 'He said he wasn't the one making the calls.'

Mike reached for her hand. 'It was him. I saw it in his face. And if he does anything else, we'll go to the police and get a restraining order.'

I In the bar, Richard was finally able to get to his feet.

Among the first to reach him was Andrea. She had seen Mike jump from the stage. Though she was too far away to see the fight, she did see Julie leading Mike away by the hand while Richard used the lower rungs of the stool to pull himself up. As spectators rehashed what had happened, Andrea caught the gist of what went on.

'This guy was minding his own business when this lady started screaming at him, and then this other dude barged in.'

Andrea saw the gash on Richard's cheek and stopped chewing her gum. She couldn't believe it. She'd never heard Mike so much as raise his voice, let alone attack someone. But the proof was right here in front of her. *He's hurt! He needs me!* She cast off her date and practically lunged at Richard. 'Are you OK?'

Richard looked at her without answering, and Andrea reached out, slipping her arm round him. Not an ounce of fat on him, she noticed.

'What happened?' she asked, feeling flushed.

'He came up and hit me,' Richard said.

'But why?'

'I don't know.'

He wobbled, and Andrea felt him lean on her. His arm slipped over her shoulder. Muscles there, too, she noted.

'You need to sit down for a minute. Here—let me help.'

They took a tentative step, and the crowd started to part when Leaning Joe suddenly showed up to help Richard as well.

'C'mon,' he barked. 'I'm the owner here. We need to talk.'

He began leading Richard away, and Andrea was jostled to the side and forced to let go. A minute later, Leaning Joe and Richard were talking over a small table.

From across the bar, Andrea pouted as she watched them. By the time her date came back, she'd already decided what she had to do.

All in all, it was a day that Julie would rather not relive.

In the kitchen, Mike was tapping decaffeinated coffee grounds into the coffee filter. He'd been quiet in the car and was still quiet now. Julie sat at the table, Singer leaning against her.

The whole thing must have been planned. Richard had anticipated how she would react. His answers, his lies, had come too quickly, too naturally, too *smoothly*. And Richard had put up no fight at all.

Those things still bothered her. Especially the last one.

'You sure you're not dizzy? That's a nasty bump,' Leaning Joe said.

He and Richard were standing now just inside the door of the Clipper. Richard shook his head. 'I just want to go home.'

'I'd be happy to call an ambulance for you,' Leaning Joe offered.

'It's OK,' Richard said. He pushed through the door and stepped into the darkness. Scanning the parking lot, he noted that the police had already left.

As he approached his car, he saw someone leaning against it.

'Hi, Richard,' she said.

Richard hesitated before answering. 'Hello, Andrea.'

'You feeling any better?'

Richard shrugged.

After a moment, Andrea cleared her throat. 'I know this might sound odd considering what happened tonight, but would you mind giving me a lift home?'

Richard raised an eyebrow, saying nothing.

In the silence, Andrea took a step towards him. When she was close, she slowly raised her hand and touched the bruise on his cheek, her eyes never leaving his. 'Please?' she whispered.

'How about we go someplace else instead?'

She tilted her head, as if wondering what he meant.

He smiled. 'Trust me.'

In Julie's kitchen, the coffeemaker was gurgling as Mike sat at the table. 'What are you thinking?' he asked.

That everything that happened tonight seems wrong somehow, she thought. 'Just going through it all again. It keeps replaying in my mind.'

'Yeah, for me, too.'

The coffeemaker beeped, and Mike got up from the table and poured two cups. Singer's ears lifted, and Julie watched as Singer made his way through the living room. In their haste to leave earlier, she hadn't drawn the curtains, and she could tell a car was coming down the street.

Singer went to the window as the light outside began to intensify. But instead of seeing the sky fade to black again as the car whizzed by, Julie saw the beams from the headlights solidify; Singer began growling; the glow of headlights remained steady.

The car, she could tell, was idling in the road, and she sat up in the chair. Suddenly the lights switched off. A car door slammed.

He was here, Julie thought. Richard had come to the house.

Singer's growls grew louder. Mike put a hand on Julie's shoulder and took a step towards the door. Singer was barking and growling steadily now. Mike moved forward.

Someone knocked on the door. Mike peeked out of the window, and Julie saw his shoulders drop. When he glanced at her again, there was a look of relief on his face. He patted Singer's back and said, 'Shh, it's OK,' and Singer stopped growling. He followed Mike, however, as Mike reached for the door handle.

When he opened the door, Julie saw two police officers—Pete Gandy and Jennifer Romanello—standing on the porch.

NINE

'THEY TOOK HIM TO JAIL?' Mabel asked in disbelief.

It was Monday morning, and for the past ten minutes, Julie had filled Mabel in on everything that had happened. Andrea strained to listen in as she worked. She hadn't smiled since Julie had started talking, and the more she heard, the more she wanted to tell Julie that she didn't know what she was talking about.

Richard wasn't dangerous. Mike attacked him! Besides, Richard wasn't even interested in Julie any more. Richard, she felt sure, had finally seen the light. And talk about romantic! He'd taken her to the beach, and they'd talked—for hours! And he hadn't even made a pass at her. No guy had ever treated her with that kind of respect. And he was sweet, too. He'd asked her not to tell Julie because he didn't want to hurt her feelings. Did that sound like a stalker?

'Pete Gandy questioned him for an hour,' Julie said, 'and he was there until Henry bailed him out.'

Mabel looked baffled. 'Pete Gandy? Did you tell him what's been going on?'

'I tried, but he didn't think it was relevant to the assault charge.'

Mabel put her bag on a table. 'Is Mike going to be charged?'

'I have no idea. We'll find out today, I guess. He has an appointment with Steve Sides later.'

Steven Sides was a local defence attorney.

'So what are you going to do about Richard?'

'I'm changing my phone number today.'

'That's it?'

'I don't know what else I can do. Pete wouldn't listen to me, other than to say that if it kept happening, I should report it.'

'Did Richard call again on Sunday?'

'No. Thank God.'

Across the salon, Andrea frowned, thinking, That's because he was still thinking about me. Now quit badmouthing him.

'So you think he set that whole thing up, don't you?'

'I think he's been setting everything up, including Saturday night. Including me. I think he considers this whole thing a game.'

Mabel met her eyes. 'It's not a game, Julie,' she said.

It took a while for Julie to respond.

'I know,' she said.

Officer Jennifer Romanello was new in town, new on the job, and looking forward to the day she'd have her own squad car, if only to get away from the guy she was working with. After doing the majority of her police training in Jacksonville, she'd moved to Swansboro less than a month earlier. She'd been riding with Pete Gandy for two weeks now and had four weeks to go—all rookies had to work with an experienced officer during their first six weeks on the job to complete their training—and if she heard him mention 'the ropes' again, she thought she'd strangle him.

It was Monday morning. They'd been working together for only an hour, and Jennifer had already had her fill of Officer Pete. In the two weeks she'd been working with him, she hadn't learned anything about the job, other than the fact that Pete was an absolute moron when it came to interviewing people.

The other night was a prime example. She could see that Mike and Julie were scared of Richard Franklin, and if what they were saying was true, Jennifer figured they had every right to be.

'So what did you think of Mike Harris's story the other night?' Jennifer asked as they rode together in the squad car.

'Oh, well, . . . he was making excuses,' Pete said. 'Everybody who's charged blames the other guy.'

'But didn't you say you knew him and that he always seemed like a laid-back guy?'

'Doesn't matter. The law's the law; same for everybody.'

When she'd opened her mouth to ask Mike Harris a question, Pete had waved her off, commenting that 'the little lady is still learning the ropes about interrogation. Don't mind her.'

Had they been anywhere but the station, she would have put him in his place for that one. She'd almost done it anyway. *Little lady?* Once she was out of training, she vowed she'd make Pete Gandy pay for it.

Because of what Mike and Julie had said and the 'too smooth to be anything but squirrelly' way Richard had acted when they'd talked to him, she hadn't slept well after getting off her shift.

Richard, she had the feeling, was not the innocent victim in this. And neither Julie nor Mike struck her as liars.

'Don't you think we should still look into it, though? What if they were telling the truth?'

Pete sighed as if the topic bored him. 'Then they should have come down to the station to file a report. But they didn't. She didn't even know for sure that it was Franklin who was calling.'

Jennifer tried again. 'But what about her? Julie Barenson. She looked scared, don't you think?'

'Of course she was scared. Her little honey was just locked up. You'd probably be scared, too. Anyone would be.'

Jennifer shook her head. Imbecile. She wondered if maybe she should talk to them again, preferably when Pete wasn't around.

Henry was standing beside Mike in the office, listening in on the phone conversation with his lawyer. 'You've got to be kidding me' was followed by, 'I can't believe this!' Mike paced the small office, his heavy strides punctuated by looks of disbelief. At last, he hung up the phone.

'What was that all about?' Henry asked.

'He says he just heard from Franklin's attorney. They intend to file a temporary restraining order against me until the case gets sorted out. He also says they intend to file a civil suit against me.'

'You're kidding.'

'According to his lawyer, Richard is still dizzy from the other night. He's claiming that I gave him a concussion.'

Henry rocked back slightly. 'Did you tell him that Richard is lying? I mean, c'mon, a concussion?'

Mike shrugged. 'I've got to talk to Julie,' he announced, slamming the door on his way out.

By the time he reached the salon, Julie needed only a glance to surmise that Mike was just about as upset as she'd ever seen him.

'It's ridiculous,' he said. 'What good are the police if they won't do anything about him? I'm not the problem here, he is.'

'I know,' Julie said soothingly. 'And I'm sorry.'

'I am, too,' he said. 'Because of me, the police don't believe your story.'

Julie didn't want to think about that. The whole thing had worked out just the way Richard wanted. She was more certain than ever that he had planned it all.

A cross town, Richard stood above the tray of chemicals in his dark-room, his face glowing red, watching as the image on the photographic paper slowly took form. Becoming Julie.

He was still exhilarated from the other night. Julie's imagination was running wild, no doubt. Even now, she was probably wondering where he was, what he was thinking, what he would do next. And Mike, charging in like the cavalry at the bar. So utterly predictable.

Julie, though . . . So emotional. So brave.

So dive.

Studying the photograph in front of him, he again took note of the similarities between Julie and Jessica. Same eyes. Same hair. Same air of innocence. From the moment he'd walked into the salon, he'd thought they could be sisters.

Richard shook his head, feeling the memory of Jessica pull at him. They had rented a house in Bermuda for their honeymoon. It was quiet and romantic. There was a private beach where they could spend hours in the sun alone. Oh, how he'd been looking forward to that! He'd taken dozens of photographs of her during the first couple of days.

He loved her skin; it was soft and unlined. By the third day, it had darkened to bronze, and in her white cotton dress, she was dazzling. That night, he'd wanted nothing more than to take her in his arms and make love to her beneath the sky.

NICHOLAS SPARKS

But she'd wanted to go dancing. At the resort.

They went, and it was loud and filled with drunks, and Jessica was loud and kept drinking. Her words began to slur, and later, as she made her way to the rest room, she bumped into a young man. He touched her arm and laughed. Jessica laughed with him.

Richard seethed as he watched it happen. It embarrassed him. But he would forgive her, he told himself. She was young and immature. But she would have to promise not to do it again.

That evening, when they were back at the house, he tried to talk to her, but she wouldn't listen.

'I was just having fun,' she'd said. 'You could have tried to have fun, too.'

'How could I, with my new wife flirting with strangers?'

'I wasn't flirting. Stop acting crazy.'

'What did you say to me? What did you say?'

'Ow . . . let me go . . . you're hurting me.'

In the end, she'd disappointed him, Richard thought. And Julie had disappointed him, too. The grocery store, the salon, the way she'd hung up on him. He was beginning to lose faith, but she'd redeemed herself at the bar. She hadn't been able to ignore him, she'd had to talk to him, and though her words were spiteful, he knew what she was really feeling. Yes, he knew she cared for him, for weren't anger and love opposite sides of the same coin? Great anger wasn't possible without great love. And she'd been so angry.

The thought made him soar.

Richard left the darkroom and made his way to the bedroom. On the bed, amid the clutter of the cameras and lenses, he reached for the cellphone. He had to hear her voice tonight, even if it was only on the machine. He dialled the number, but instead of Julie's familiar voice, there was a recording from the phone company:

Richard stared at the phone. Oh, Julie, he wondered. Why?

After the tumult of the past month, the next week of Julie's life was startlingly quiet. She didn't see Richard anywhere during the week or the following weekend. Monday had been uneventful, and she kept her fingers crossed that today would be no different.

Her phone had been silent. Only four people—Mabel, Mike, Henry and Emma—knew her new number, and since she spent all day with Mabel and all night with Mike, neither one of them had reason to give her a call. Henry had never phoned in all the years she'd known him, which pretty much left Emma. But after hearing how the calls had rattled

278

Julie, Emma was giving her a break, not wanting to be responsible for peeling Julie off the ceiling.

On the legal front, there was mixed activity. Officer Romanello had come by the week before and talked to Julie and Mike. She got their story and said not to hesitate to call her if anything out of the ordinary happened again. The district attorney had declined to press charges. He'd done this, he said, because Richard hadn't shown up to give his formal statement. Nor had they been able to contact him.

Strange, she thought, when she heard about it.

Eight days of nothing, absolutely nothing, had emboldened Julie. So when Mike mentioned that his lawyer had left a message, asking him to swing by for a brief meeting after work, Julie told him that she was tired and was going to head on home alone. 'Just come over when you're done,' she said. 'And if you're going to be late, give me a call.'

As she parked at the house, Singer bounded out of the Jeep and circled the yard. When she called for him, he just looked at her. *C'mon*, he seemed to be saying. *Take me for a walk!*

Julie got out of the car. 'No, we can't go now,' she said. 'Maybe when Mike gets here.'

Singer stayed where he was. Julie crossed her arms and glanced around. She didn't see Richard's car, nor had she seen it while she was driving. The only car parked in her street bore the name of the real-estate company that was offering the lots for sale, along with the name of the agent who was selling them, Edna Farley.

Singer's tail moved back and forth. *Please?*

Julie didn't want to go, but she hadn't taken Singer for a walk in ages. Besides, all she had to do was yelp and he would come charging like a samurai warrior on steroids. 'OK,' she said. 'But we can't stay long. It looks like there might be a storm coming.'

Even before she finished speaking, Singer had turned and wandered into the woods, vanishing behind a clump of trees. Julie crept along the trail, pushing at overgrown branches. Because the sun was low and the clouds above were charcoal grey, the woods seemed unusually dark. She stopped to listen. She heard nothing except the call of a magpie. She looked up and down the trail and saw nothing unusual. 'Of course it's safe,' she whispered.

In the distance she heard Singer bark, and her heart hammered in her chest, instantly changing her mind. 'Singer! C'mon,' she shouted. 'Let's go back! Time to go!'

She waited, but Singer didn't come. Instead, he barked again. Julie took a step in the direction of the sound and stopped. She heard a voice.

Someone was talking to Singer and, when she recognised the voice, she heaved a sigh of relief. It was Edna Farley. Julie walked quickly, following the curving path until she could see the water of the Intracoastal. Here, the forest cleared, and she saw Edna patting Singer on the head. He was sitting on his haunches, his mouth open.

'Julie!' Edna called out. 'How are you?'

'Hey, Edna. I'm fine. Just taking a walk.'

'It's a nice day for it. Or it was when we got out here. But now it looks like it might start to rain in a little while.'

By then, Julie had drawn near. 'We?' she asked.

'Yeah, my client is looking over a couple of the far lots. He seems pretty interested, so keep your fingers crossed for me.'

As she was speaking, Singer stood and moved to Julie's side, the hair on the back of his neck bristling. He started to growl.

'Oh, here he is now,' Edna said.

Before Julie could move, Richard was standing beside Edna. 'You were right,' Richard said. 'Those lots were nice, too, but I think I like the ones on this side a little better.'

'Oh, yes. You're absolutely right,' Edna said. 'And the view of the water on this side is priceless. It's a wonderful investment.' She laughed. 'Where are my manners? I'd like you to meet a friend of mine.'

'Hello, Julie,' Richard said. 'What a nice surprise.'

Julie said nothing. Singer continued to growl.

'Oh, you two know each other?' Edna enquired.

'You could say that,' Richard said. 'Isn't that right, Julie?'

Julie tried to steady herself. Before she could answer, Richard glanced towards Edna. 'Edna—did you bring the information about the dimensions of the lots like I asked? And the prices?'

At the word prices, Edna's eyes lit up. 'Of course I did. It's all in the car. Let me go get it. I'll be back in just a few minutes.'

'Take your time,' he said. 'I'm in no hurry.'

When she was gone, Richard turned his smile on Julie. 'You look wonderful,' he said. 'I've missed you. How've you been?'

Julie took a step backwards. 'What are you doing here, Richard?'

Richard shrugged. 'I'm thinking that this might be a good place for me to put down some roots. A man needs a place to call home, and this way, we could be neighbours.'

Julie paled.

'Would you like that, Julie? Me living right next to you? No? Then maybe I just wanted to talk to you. You changed your phone number. You won't go anywhere alone. What else could I do?'

She backed away another step; Singer stayed in place, as if daring Richard to approach her, his rear legs shaking as if ready to pounce. 'I don't want to talk to you,' she said. 'Can't you get that through your head?'

'Don't you remember our dates?' Richard said. 'Our time together was special. Why don't you want to admit that?'

'There's nothing to admit.' She took another step away.

'Why are you acting this way?' He sounded wounded, puzzled.

Julie's eyes darted to the entrance of the path. Time to get out of here. 'If you make one move towards me or try to follow me, I'll scream—and this time, I won't pull Singer off.'

He offered a gentle smile. 'There's no reason to be scared. You know I'd never hurt you. I love you.'

She blinked. 'What the hell are you talking about?'

'I love you,' he said again. 'And we can start over now. We'll just chalk up this infatuation with Mike as a mistake, OK? I forgive you.'

As he spoke, Julie continued backing away, her eyes growing wider with every word. But it wasn't simply his words that scared her, it was the look of utter sincerity on his face.

He gave a sly smile. 'I'll bet that you haven't even told him that you let me spend the night at your house. How do you think he'd feel about that?'

His words struck her with almost physical force. Richard saw her reaction and, seeing that he was right, held out his hand.

'Now, come on, let's go someplace quiet and get a bite to eat.'

'I'm not going anywhere with you,' Julie hissed.

'Don't be this way. Please. I'll make you happy, Jessica.'

For a second, Julie wondered if she had heard Richard correctly, but then she knew she had. 'You . . . are . . . insane,' she spluttered.

This time, her words stopped him.

'You shouldn't say that,' Richard said, his voice acquiring an ugly edge. 'You shouldn't say things you don't mean.'

From the corner of her eye, Julie saw Edna entering the clearing.

'I'm coming,' she called out cheerfully. 'I'm coming!'

Richard was still staring at Julie when Edna reached them. She looked from one to the other. 'Something wrong?' she asked.

Richard turned away from Julie. 'No,' he said, 'not at all. We were trying to figure out how many homes there might be. Julie likes her privacy.'

Julie barely heard him answer. 'I've got to go,' she said.

Richard smiled. 'Bye, Julie. See you around.'

Julie turned and started out of the clearing. Singer stayed for a moment as if making sure Richard wouldn't follow, then went after her. Once out of sight, Julie ran. She crashed through branches along the path, her breath heavy and fast. She fell once and got up quickly, ignoring the pain in her knee. Almost there, she prayed, almost there . . .

Minutes later, she was choking back tears as Mike entered the house. He held her while she cried. After telling him what had happened, she gathered her senses enough to ask why he was home so soon. Mike's face had gone white.

'My lawyer wasn't the one who left the message.'

Officer Jennifer Romanello was seated at the kitchen table half an hour later, her eyes on Julie as she recounted her story.

'I don't like the sound of this,' she said when Julie was finished.

'What do we do?' Mike asked.

'I'm not sure yet,' Jennifer said. 'But can I go over a couple of things again, just to make certain I have them right?'

Julie was lost in thought, considering the one part of the story she'd left out. *I'll bet that you haven't even told him that you let me spend the night at your house.* She didn't realise at first that Jennifer had just asked a question.

'Do you have any idea how he knew you were out there?' Jennifer repeated.

'No,' she said.

Jennifer then turned to Mike. 'And you thought you had a meeting with your lawyer?' she asked.

'There was a message at the garage that I was supposed to meet him at five. When I got to the lawyer's office, he didn't know anything about a meeting, so I came straight to Julie's.'

Jennifer turned to Julie again. 'Can I ask why you went out there in the first place?'

She took a deep breath. 'I hadn't seen or heard from Richard in a week, and I guess I hoped it was over.'

'What do you know about Jessica?'

'Nothing, really. He said he was married to her for a few years and that it didn't work out. He didn't say any more than that.'

'And he's from Denver?'

'That's what he told me.'

'He didn't threaten you specifically?'

'No. But he didn't have to say anything. He's crazy.'

'And he's never suggested what he might do next?'

Julie shook her head. 'I just want it to stop,' she whispered.

'Are you going to arrest him?' Mike asked the police officer. 'Or bring him in for questioning?'

It took a moment for Jennifer to respond. 'I'll do what I can.'

Julie shook her head. 'So where does that leave us?'

'Look, I know you're worried. I know you're scared. And, believe me, I'm on your side, so don't think I'm going to leave here and forget about this. I'm going to look into Richard Franklin's past to see what I can come up with.' She reached across the table and squeezed Julie's hand. 'I give you my word we're going to do everything we can to help you.'

An hour after Jennifer Romanello had left, Julie and Mike were still sitting at the kitchen table. Mike was sipping on a beer, but Julie hadn't joined him. She couldn't stomach the glass of wine she'd poured earlier and had dumped it in the sink. She just stared ahead vacantly, saying little, and though she looked tired, Mike knew better than to suggest that she go to bed, since sleep was an impossibility for both of them.

'You hungry?' he finally asked.

'No.'

'You want to rent a movie?'

'Not really.'

'Well, I have an idea,' Mike said. 'Let's just sit around and stare at each other for a while. And maybe we can worry a little, just to break up the monotony. I mean, we need to find something to do to pass the time.'

With that, Julie finally smiled.

'You're right,' she said. She reached for his beer and took a sip. 'I'm getting tired of it, anyway. It doesn't seem to be doing me any good.'

'So what do you want to do?'

'Would you just hold me?' she asked as she stood and walked over to him. Mike got up and put his arms round her. He pulled her close.

'I'm so glad you're here,' she whispered.

Before Mike could say anything, the phone rang. Both he and Julie tensed at the sound. Mike let go of her.

'Don't,' Julie said, fear in her eyes.

Mike ignored her. He went to the living room and picked up the phone. 'Hello? Oh, hey, Emma,' he said. 'How are you?'

'I'm fine,' Emma said, her voice full of energy. 'But listen, I'm in Morehead City, and you're not going to believe who I just saw.'

'Who?'

'Andrea. With Richard. And get this: I just saw him kiss her.'

I have no idea what it means,' Julie said. 'It doesn't make sense.'

Mike had hung up the phone. They were sitting on the couch, a single light behind them. Singer was sleeping by the front door.

'Did she mention anything in the shop this week? About seeing him, I mean?'

Julie shook her head. 'Nothing. Not a single word. I know she cut his hair, but that's all I know about.'

'Didn't she hear the things you were saying about him?'

'She must have.'

'But she didn't care?'

'Who knows? But I'll talk to her tomorrow. Maybe I can talk some sense into her.'

Later, Richard brought Andrea to his house and they stood on the porch, staring towards the sky. Pressed against her, he wrapped his arms round her, moving his hands towards her breasts. Andrea leaned her head against him and sighed.

'For a while there, I wasn't sure you were going to call.'

Richard kissed her neck, and the warmth of his lips made her shiver.

The moon cast a silver shimmer on the trees.

'It's so beautiful out here,' she said. 'So quiet.'

'Shh. Don't say anything. Just listen.'

He didn't want to hear her voice, because it reminded him that she wasn't Julie. He was with another woman, a woman who meant nothing to him, but her body was soft and warm, and she desired him.

'And the moon . . .'

'Shhh,' he said again.

An hour later, when they were in bed together, Andrea moaned and dug her fingers into his back, but Richard had told her not to make any other sounds. No whispers, no talking. He had insisted on total darkness in the room as well.

He moved above her, feeling her breath on his skin. *Julie,* he wanted to whisper. *You can't keep running from me. Don't you see what we have? Don't you crave the completion that our union will bring?*

But then he remembered their meeting in the woods, the look of horror in her eyes. He saw her revulsion, heard her words of rejection. He felt her hatred. The memory wounded him, an assault on his senses. *Julie,* he wanted to whisper, *you were cruel to me today. You ignored my profession of love. You treated me as if I meant nothing . . .*

'Ow,' he heard in the darkness, '. . . you're hurting me. . . .'

The sound brought him back.

'Shh,' he whispered, but he didn't relax his hands. In the dim light from the window, he could just make out a shadow of fear in Andrea's eyes. He felt a surge of desire.

284

Though her shift started at eight, Jennifer was seated at the computer by six on Wednesday morning, the arrest report on Mike Harris beside her. At the top of the report were the basics: Richard Franklin's name, address, phone number, place of work.

She still wasn't sure where to begin, since the information was sketchy and the hours she had to look into him weren't exactly standard business hours. The night before, she had called Richard's landlord who had put her in touch with the real-estate company that managed the rental. After a bit of cajoling, a manager there faxed over the rental application. Richard's references listed his local employer and the head of personnel—no one from Ohio or Colorado. She managed to get his Social Security and driver's licence numbers, and as she sat at Pete Gandy's desk, she typed those into the computer.

She spent the next hour searching for information, beginning with North Carolina. Richard Franklin apparently had no criminal record in the state. Though his driver's licence had been issued in Ohio, it was too early to check with the Department of Motor Vehicles there. Ditto with Colorado. Was he really from Denver originally? Julie thought so, but who really knew?

Though it was illegal, Jennifer decided to check his credit record. She knew there were three major credit-reporting agencies, and most offered a free report annually. Using the rental application as a guideline, she typed in the information required—no doubt the same information that the management company had used when renting him the home. Name, Social Security number, latest address, previous address—she hit pay dirt. Richard Franklin's records were spelt out in plain detail over a number of pages. As she scrolled quickly through the record, it struck her that every account on the credit report had been closed.

Studying the record in more detail, she saw that there was one major default from a bank in Denver, four years earlier. There were a series of other late payments around that time. All were registered as delinquent for a year but were eventually paid off.

Jennifer leaned back in the chair, thinking about it. OK, she knew he'd lived in Denver at one point, and he'd run into some sort of financial trouble four years ago. He'd mentioned to Julie that he'd been divorced. Maybe that had something to do with it. Without a doubt, she had to find out more about Jessica. But without further information, there was nothing to go on.

Jennifer wondered what to do next. Her best bet, she decided, was to wait until the personnel office at the bridge project opened so she could talk to the people there. Not knowing what else to do, she scanned the arrest report again before focusing on his address and thinking, Why not? She wasn't even sure what she was looking for, exactly. She just wanted to see where he lived. She grabbed a cup of coffee on her way out of the door and got into her car.

A short time later, Jennifer turned onto the gravel road where Richard Franklin lived. She was struck by how remote these homes were. She wondered why an engineer from a major city would choose to live out this way. Jennifer slowed the car. She spotted his house through the trees. It was a two-storey home, set back from the road. The yard was horribly overgrown. People who lived out this way probably did so because it was family property or because they had no other choice. Why would he have chosen a place like this?

Because he wanted to hide.

She didn't stop. Instead, she drove past and made a U-turn half a mile up the road. The same questions cycled through her mind as she passed the house again and made her way back to the station.

Richard Franklin drew back from the curtains, frowning.

He had a visitor, but he didn't recognise the car. It wasn't Mike or Julie, he knew. Neither of them owned a Honda. Nor was it anyone who lived out this way. Someone had come to see where he lived. He'd watched the car creep up the road. The U-turn had confirmed his suspicions.

'What are you staring at?' Andrea asked.

Richard let the curtain fall back in place and turned. 'Nothing.'

He moved towards the bed and sat beside her. On her arms he could see bruises, and he ran a tender finger over them.

'Good morning,' he said. 'Did you sleep well?'

In the morning light, wearing only jeans, Richard looked exotic. Sensual. So what if he got a little rough last night? Andrea pushed aside a loose strand of hair that had fallen across her cheek. 'When we finally got around to sleeping, I did.'

'Are you hungry?'

'A little. But I have to go to the bathroom first. Where is it again? I was kind of tipsy last night.'

'It's the last door on the right.'

Andrea scooted from the bed, taking the sheet as she went. Richard watched her go, wishing she'd left the night before, then turned to the window again. He rubbed his forehead. Who was it, then? The police? Yes, he could imagine Julie calling them.

Richard's thoughts were interrupted by a scream coming from Andrea's direction. When he went into the hallway, Andrea was standing still, staring at him with wide eyes, her hand over her mouth.

She hadn't opened the door on the right, the one that led to the bathroom. She was staring into the room on the left. The darkroom.

She turned to look at Richard as if seeing him for the first time. 'Oh my God,' she said.

Richard brought his finger to his lips, his eyes locked on her. 'Shh . . .' When she saw the look on his face, Andrea took a step backwards. 'You shouldn't have opened that door,' he said. 'I told you where the bathroom was, but you didn't listen.'

'Richard? The pictures . . .'

He took a step towards her. 'This is so . . . *disappointing.*'

Jennifer made it back with a few minutes to spare. Pete Gandy hadn't arrived yet, and she went to her desk, knowing she didn't have much time. She dialled the number of the bridge project, and asked to speak to Jake Blansen, the man Mike had mentioned.

Blansen came on the line. Jennifer identified herself as an officer in Swansboro and went through a brief recap of the incident.

'I don't know how much I can help you,' Blansen said. 'I'm just the foreman. You probably need to talk to corporate. They're in Ohio, but the secretary can get you the number.'

'Oh, I see. Still, maybe you can help me. You've worked with Richard Franklin. What's he like?'

For a long moment, Jake Blansen was silent. Then he drew a deep breath. 'He's dangerous,' he said in a low voice. 'The company hired him because he keeps costs down, but he does it by scrimping on safety. I've had men hurt out here because of him.'

'How so?'

'He puts off maintenance, things break, people get hurt. I reported it to corporate. They promised to look into it. But I guess he found out and he came after me.'

'He attacked you?'

'No. But he threatened me. He told me how disappointed he was that I didn't trust him. And he put his arm over my shoulders and sort of mumbled that it would be a shame if there were any more accidents. The way he said it gave me the creeps and, to be honest, I was thrilled to see him go. So was everyone else on the project.'

'Wait . . . he left?'

'Yeah. He quit. Had some out-of-town emergency, and when he got back to town, he let us know he needed to take some time off for personal reasons. Haven't seen him since.'

Mike pulled his truck to a stop at the garage. Julie was looking towards the floor of the truck, and he followed her gaze, coming to rest on the tips of her shoes. They were coated with a layer of dew from the lawn, and when Julie realised what she was looking at, she gave a half-hearted shrug as if to say, *I guess we'll see what happens today.*

When they got out of the truck, Mike hugged Julie and offered to walk her across the street to work, but Julie declined. Singer, meanwhile, bounded down and headed towards the salon.

'I'll swing by in a little bit to see how you're doing,' Mike said.

'OK.'

As Mike headed into the garage, Julie took a deep breath and crossed the street. Downtown wasn't busy yet. It was early—the salon wouldn't be open for another hour or so, but she was sure Mabel was already in. Wednesdays were her days for taking inventory, and when Julie pushed open the door, she saw Mabel dutifully scanning the shelves of shampoos and conditioners. When Mabel glanced over her shoulder at Julie, her face assumed a look of concern. She set aside her clipboard.

'What happened?'

'I look that bad, huh?'

'Richard again?'

Julie bit her lip in answer, and Mabel immediately crossed the room and put her arms round her, squeezing tight. A moment later she was sobbing in Mabel's arms.

'There, there,' Mabel murmured, 'you're going to be OK.'

When Mabel finally let her go, Julie sniffed and reached for a tissue. She told Mabel about seeing Richard near her house. She told her everything he'd said and the way he'd looked; she recounted her conversation in the kitchen with Officer Romanello.

Mabel's face expressed sympathy, but she said nothing. When Julie told her about Emma's phone call, Mabel shivered. 'I'll give Andrea a call,' she said.

Julie watched Mabel cross the room and pick up the receiver. She offered a tentative smile that gradually gave way to a look of concern when it became obvious that Andrea wasn't answering.

'I'm sure she's already on her way in,' Mabel said. 'She'll probably be here in just a couple of minutes. Or maybe she's decided to take one of her "personal days". You know how she is.'

Pete Gandy entered the gym on his lunch break and saw Richard Franklin on the bench press.

Richard worked through six reps then put the weight back on the bench and sat up. 'Hey, Officer, how are you? Richard Franklin.'

Pete approached him. 'I'm fine. How are you feeling?'

'Getting better.' Richard smiled. 'I didn't know you worked out here.'

'I've been a member for years.'

'I was thinking of joining. I got a trial membership today.' He paused. 'You want to work in a set while I recover?'

'If you don't mind.'

'Not at all.'

A chance meeting, followed by small talk.

A few minutes later, Richard said, 'Hey, Officer Gandy . . .'

'Call me Pete.'

'Pete,' Richard said. 'I just realised there was something I forgot to tell you the other night. You probably should know about it. Just in case.'

That night at Julie's, Mike was standing in the doorway, waiting to let Singer out. Julie passed him on the way to the kitchen. She opened the refrigerator and pulled out a yoghurt and a couple of chocolate-chip cookies, then grabbed an apple on her way back out.

It was while passing through the living room that she saw the locket and froze. It was on the desk near her calendar, partially hidden by a stack of catalogues, and the sight of it made her queasy. She didn't want it in the house, but in all that had happened, she'd forgotten it was there. But then, if she'd just spotted it so easily, why hadn't she seen it there before now?

Behind her, she could hear the clock ticking. From the corner of her eye, she could see Mike leaning against the door. The locket was reflecting the light from the lamp on an end table, its glow somehow sinister. She realised her hands were shaking.

She put down what she was carrying and reached over and slid the locket out from under the catalogues. It's just a locket, she told herself. She considered throwing it in the garbage, but instead decided to sell it when all this was settled. She'd put the money into the church basket on Sunday. She carried the locket with her to the bedroom and glanced at it as she was opening a drawer. The locket itself was the same, but something was different. Something . . . Her breath caught in her throat. No, she thought. Please, no . . .

She unclasped the chain, knowing it was the only way to be certain. Moving towards the mirror in the bathroom, she drew both ends round her neck. The locket, which once nestled just above her breasts, now rested two inches higher.

'I'll get you a shorter chain,' he'd said. 'That way you can wear it whenever you want.'

Julie suddenly felt dizzy, and she let go of the chain as if it had scalded her fingers. The locket tumbled down her blouse before bouncing against the tiled floor with a metallic ping.

Still, she hadn't screamed.

No, the scream didn't come for another couple of seconds, when she looked down at the locket. It had popped open in the fall.

And from both sides, in pictures he'd chosen especially for her, Richard was smiling back at her.

This time, Jennifer Romanello wasn't alone when she came to Julie's home. Officer Pete Gandy was sitting at the kitchen table looking across at them, not bothering to hide the dubious expression on his face. The locket was on the table and Pete reached out to pick it up.

'So,' he said, 'you beat the guy up, and as payback, he gives Julie a couple of pictures of himself. I don't get it.'

Mike clenched his hands beneath the table. 'I told you already. He's been stalking her.'

Pete kept staring at the pictures. 'Yeah, you keep saying that, but I'm just trying to see if there are any other angles here.'

'Angles?' Mike asked. 'Can't you see that this is proof that he's been in the house? That's breaking and entering.'

'But there were no signs of a break-in. All the doors were locked and the windows were closed. You said so yourself.'

'I don't know how he did it, but he did. All you have to do is open your eyes!'

Pete held up his hands. 'Now take it easy, Mike. I'm just trying to get to the bottom of this.'

Both Jennifer and Julie were as steamed as Mike, but Pete had told Jennifer that he was going to handle this once and for all and that she shouldn't say a word. Her expression was a mixture of horror and morbid fascination, especially after her own investigation. Was it possible he could be this blind?

'Get to the bottom of this?'

'Yeah,' Pete said. He leaned forward and put the locket on the table again. 'Now, I'm not saying that this doesn't seem a little fishy, because it does. And if Julie's telling the truth, then Richard Franklin has a little problem that's gonna require a visit from me.'

Mike's face tightened. 'She's telling the truth,' he said through gritted teeth.

Pete ignored the comment and looked across the table at Julie. 'Are you sure about everything? You're certain that the only way Richard could have put these pictures in here is by breaking into your house?' She nodded.

'And you said you hadn't touched this necklace in the last few weeks?'

'It was buried under some magazines on the desk,' she said.

'C'mon, Pete,' Mike cut in. 'What's that got to do with anything?'

Pete ignored the comment, his sceptical gaze still focused on Julie.

'There's no other time that he could possibly have put those pictures in there?' he persisted. 'No other time at all?'

In the aftermath of his questions, the kitchen was strangely silent. Pete continued to stare, and under his knowing gaze, Julie finally realised what he knew. She felt her stomach clench.

'When did he tell you?' she asked.

'Tell him what?' Mike asked.

'Did he give you a call and tell you he forgot to mention something?' she asked. 'Or did he run into you somewhere and bring it up then?'

Pete said nothing.

Mike looked back and forth between Pete and Julie, trying to figure out what she was talking about.

'Could you please just answer the question?' Pete persisted.

Julie continued to lock eyes with Pete. 'Yes,' she said. 'There was one time he could have done it.'

Pete leaned back in his chair, his eyebrows raised. 'When he spent the night, you mean,' he said.

'What?' Jennifer cried, her jaw dropping.

'What?' Mike echoed.

Julie turned to face him. 'Nothing happened between us, Mike,' she said evenly. 'His mom died, and he was upset, and we talked. He fell asleep on the couch. That's what Pete is talking about.'

When she looked at Pete again, his expression confirmed that Richard had implied something different.

And Mike, Julie noticed, saw it, too.

Richard lowered the camera. Equipped with a telephoto lens, the camera served as a makeshift set of binoculars, and he'd been watching Mike and Julie since they'd come home that evening. Or rather, what he could see of them through the gauzy curtains.

This was the night she would find it. He'd had to move the locket into a better position after his meeting with Pete Gandy, of course, but he'd known she would see it on the desk.

It would be a nasty business, he knew, but there was no other way. It was time to end her little infatuation with Mike once and for all.

After Mike had closed the door behind the officers, he leaned against it, using both hands for support. His head was bowed and Julie could hear his long, deep breaths.

'Why didn't you tell me?' he said, raising his chin.

Still standing in the kitchen, Julie looked away. 'I knew it would hurt your feelings, and there was no reason to do that. I swear to you—all he did was talk.'

Mike stood up straighter, his expression angry. Hard. 'That was the night of our first date, wasn't it?'

Julie nodded. 'I didn't know he was going to stop by. I was watching television when he came. We had an argument because I told him I didn't want to see him any more. And then Singer . . .'

She paused. She didn't want to go into this.

'Singer what?'

'Singer bit him. When I tried to close the door, he stopped it with his hand and Singer went after him.'

Mike stared at her. 'So let me get this straight,' he said. 'He comes to the door. You have a fight. Singer goes after him, and then you invite him in to spend the night. Your story doesn't make a lot of sense.'

'Don't be like this, Mike. Please . . . Do you think I slept with him?'

'I don't know what to think.'

Suddenly, Julie knew that this, too, was part of Richard's plan. She forced herself to keep her voice steady, without anger. 'After all the years you've known me, do you really believe I'd do something like that?'

Mike stared at Julie. 'I don't know.'

The words stung, and Julie felt her eyes water. 'I didn't sleep with him.'

'Maybe not,' Mike said. 'But it still hurts to think you didn't trust me with this.'

'I do trust you. But I didn't want to hurt you.'

'You just did, Julie,' he said. 'You just did.'

With that, he reached for the door and opened it, and for the first time, Julie realised that he was going to leave.

'Wait—where are you going?'

Mike raised his hands. 'I need some time with this, OK?'

'Please,' she said. 'Don't go. I don't want to be alone tonight.'

Mike paused, but with a shake of his head, he was gone.

Richard watched Mike make his way down the walk and slam the door as he got in his truck. He smiled, knowing that Julie would finally understand that Mike wasn't worthy of her. That she deserved someone stronger, smarter—someone equal to her love.

In the tree, Richard couldn't wait for the moment until he led her out of this house, this town, this life she had let herself become trapped in. Raising the camera again, Richard watched Julie's shadow through the curtains in the living room.

Even her shadow was beautiful.

TEN

'SHE DID WHAT?' Henry asked.

'You heard me,' Mike answered. 'She let him spend the night.'

In the fifteen minutes it took to reach Henry's house, Mike had only grown angrier. They were standing in the front yard.

'She told you that?' Henry asked.

'Yeah, when the police were there.'

'Hold on,' Henry said, 'the police were there?'

'They just left.'

'Why were the police there?'

'Because of the locket. Richard put his pictures in there. What the hell am I supposed to do now?'

Henry tried to follow along but was only getting more and more confused. 'Maybe you better start from the beginning.'

'So how long are you going to keep up the silent treatment?' Pete Gandy asked.

They were cruising slowly through downtown in the squad car, and Jennifer hadn't said a word since they'd left Julie's house. She glanced at him with an expression of distaste. 'What was with that little comment you made in front of Mike?' she asked. 'There was no reason for that.'

'You mean about Richard staying over? It was true, wasn't it?'

'But you didn't have to say it in front of Mike. You could have taken Julie aside and asked her about it. She could have explained it to Mike.'

'What's the problem?'

Jennifer closed her eyes. 'The problem is that Richard is stalking Julie and she's scared to death. Why can't you see that?'

Pete shook his head. 'Look, Richard told me about the locket, OK?

He mentioned it in case something like this came up, and he told me that he put the pictures in there when he spent the night with her. And remember, even Julie admitted she hadn't looked at it since then, so who's to say he was lying?'

He was interrupted by the radio crackling to life. Glaring at Pete, Jennifer reached for the radio and picked up the mike.

A dispatcher spoke: 'We just got a call from a trucker heading down the highway. He said he saw something strange in a ditch and thought we might want to send a car over. He didn't say what it was. It's just off Highway 24, about a quarter-mile past the Amoco filling station on the north side of the road.'

'We'll check it out,' Jennifer responded.

Mike had been gone for half an hour, and the house was eerily quiet. Julie went through the house, making sure the windows and doors were locked, then paced the living room, Singer at her side.

She was certain that Richard hadn't put the photos in the locket on the night he'd stayed over. No, he'd been here, inside her house, looking around, opening drawers, rummaging through her things. Which meant he knew how to get inside. And could do so again. Julie's throat constricted at the thought. She hurried into the kitchen, grabbed a chair from the table and wedged it beneath the front-door knob. How could Mike have left her? With Andrea missing and Richard stalking her? How on earth could he have left her alone? Moving towards the couch, Julie began to cry.

'**D**o you believe her?' Henry asked.

Mike glanced down the street. 'I don't know.'

Henry stared at him. 'Sure you do.'

'No, I don't,' Mike snapped. 'How can I know if I wasn't even there?'

'Because you know Julie,' Henry offered. 'Better than anyone.'

After a long moment, Mike's shoulders relaxed slightly. 'No,' he finally said, 'I don't think she slept with him.'

'So what are you going to do?'

Mike took a long time before answering. 'I don't know.'

Richard could see Julie's shadowed image as she sat on the couch. He knew she was crying, and he wanted to hold her.

He'd never been moved by the sight of someone's tears before.

He hadn't felt this way after watching his mother cry in the months following his father's funeral. But then again, by the end, he'd come to hate her. He'd hoped that she would be stronger after his father's funeral. But instead, she'd begun to drink heavily. Then she'd become violent. The first time it happened, he'd been sleeping when he woke to a staggering pain.

His mother stood wild-eyed above the bed, his father's belt dangling from her hand. She'd used the buckle end of the belt against his skin. 'It was your fault!' she screamed at him. 'You always made him angry!'

She swung again and again. He cowered at each stroke, pleading with her to stop and trying to cover himself, but she continued to wield the belt until her arms were too exhausted to move.

The following night she'd done it again.

Nine months later, his back and legs scarred, he ground his mother's sleeping pills and slipped the contents into her vodka. After going to sleep that night, she never woke up.

In the morning, as he stood over the bed staring at her, he thought about her limited intelligence. Though she'd suspected he had something to do with his father's death, she couldn't believe the same thing could happen to her. She should have known that he was strong enough to do what he had to do.

Julie, too, had been strong enough to change her life. Julie was a fighter. He loved that about her. Now that the charade with Mike was over, there was no point in delaying the inevitable.

Slowly, Richard began climbing down from the tree.

Officers Jennifer Romanello and Pete Gandy drove past the Amoco station and pulled the squad car to the side of the highway. After retrieving their flashlights, they emerged from the car.

Jennifer could see the lights from the gas station, saw cars being filled at the pumps. On the highway, cars whizzed past. The side of the road was bathed in swirling blue and red lights, alerting motorists to their presence.

'You go that way,' Pete said, pointing towards the station. 'I'll head this way.'

Jennifer turned on her flashlight and started her search.

Julie was still crying on the couch when she heard the sound of movement outside her door. Singer's ears went up as he ran to the window. Her heart hammering, Julie looked around for a weapon.

When Singer barked, she jumped up from the couch with wide eyes, before she realised his tail was wagging.

'Julie?' she heard him call through the door. 'It's me, Mike.'

She moved to the door and quickly removed the chair, relief surging through her. As soon as she opened it, Mike looked at her before glancing towards the ground. 'I know you didn't sleep with him,' he said.

Julie nodded. 'I didn't want to hurt you. I should have told you anyway. I'm sorry.'

'I'm sorry, too. For saying what I did.'

Julie stepped forward, and when Mike didn't back away, she came closer and leaned into him. She felt his arms wrap around her.

Richard had climbed back into the tree as soon as he saw Mike pull up. Now he was watching them, his face growing hard.

As if living a nightmare, he saw her go into Mike's arms. He saw her fold into him. Why did she insist on repeating her mistakes?

He'd tried to be nice. He'd tried to be fair. His eyes narrowed. Didn't she have any idea what she was forcing him to do?

Jennifer swivelled the flashlight from side to side, looking for whatever it was the trucker had seen. The moon hung low in the sky below the tree line. The underbrush was thick, impossible for her light to penetrate. Cars continued to pass, but she barely registered them. She was beginning to wonder if she should turn round and help Pete look in the opposite direction when the flashlight illuminated something that her mind, at first, refused to identify.

When it finally did, she screamed.

Pete Gandy turned at the sound and started running towards Jennifer. He reached her in less than a minute and saw her hovering over a body. He froze.

'Get an ambulance here *now*!' Jennifer called out, and Pete turned and raced to the squad car.

Stifling her panic, Jennifer focused on the body below her. The face of the young woman was bloodied and misshapen. There was a sickening ring of purple round her neck. Jennifer had believed her dead until she'd reached down and registered a faint pulse.

When Julie arrived for work on Thursday morning, she found Officers Gandy and Romanello waiting for her. By the expressions on their faces, she knew at once why they were there.

'It's Andrea, isn't it?'

Mabel was standing behind them, her eyes red and swollen. 'Oh, honey,' she said, crossing the room and going to Julie.

'What happened?'

'He beat her,' Mabel said. 'He almost killed her. She's in a coma. They had to fly her to Wilmington last night.'

Julie's knees seemed to weaken. A moment later, Mike and Henry burst through the door. Mike saw Julie and Mabel before he locked eyes with the officers.

'What did he do to Andrea?' Mike demanded.

'It was bad,' Pete said. 'I've never seen anything like it.'

Jennifer turned to Julie. 'Mabel said that Emma had seen Richard and Andrea together at Morehead City, right?'

'Yes,' Julie answered. 'A couple of days ago. The day I saw him in the woods.'

'And she didn't come in yesterday. Didn't that strike you as odd?'

'Of course we were worried,' Mabel offered. 'But it wasn't the first time she hadn't shown up for work. She's like that.'

Jennifer glanced towards Mike and Julie. 'I want you both to know,' she said, 'that if it is Richard who did this, then he's capable of anything. Do what you have to do to stay safe. Both of you.'

On the way out, Jennifer walked alongside Pete, neither of them saying anything. She had to give him credit, not only for letting her handle the questioning inside, but because of the new resolve she noted in his grim expression.

After getting into the car, he slipped the keys into the ignition but leaned back in his seat without starting the engine. He stared through the windshield.

'She cuts my hair,' Pete finally offered.

'Andrea?'

'Yeah. That's how I knew who it was last night.'

Jennifer stayed silent, watching as Pete closed his eyes.

'She didn't deserve what happened to her. No one deserves that.'

Jennifer put a hand on his shoulder. 'I'm sorry,' she said.

He nodded, as if trying to forget what he'd seen the night before. He started the engine.

'I think it's time that we pay Richard Franklin a little visit at work,' he said quietly.

Jennifer brought her hands together in her lap. Outside the window, trees and buildings were blurry as the car headed towards the bridge.

'He's not going to be there,' she said. 'He quit a month back.'

Pete glanced quickly at her. There were dark circles under his eyes; in the shadowed interior of the car, he looked as worn as she felt.

'How do you know that?'

'I called the personnel department at J. D. Blanchard.'

Pete looked at her again. 'You've been investigating him?'

'Not officially.'

Pete turned his eyes back to the road and pulled over, bringing the car to a halt in the shade of a towering magnolia. 'Why don't you start from the beginning and let me know what you've been doing,' Jennifer took a deep breath and began.

After Pete and Jennifer left, Henry turned to Julie. 'The police are right about doing what you have to do,' he said. 'But you can't stay here. It's not safe here any more, for either of you.'

'Where should we go?'

'Anywhere. Just get out of town until they catch this guy.' He paused. 'You can use the beach house. He won't find you there.'

'What if he follows us?'

'Take my car,' Henry said. 'And leave right away. Get to the highway and stay on it. It's a straight shot, and you'll know if someone's following you. The important thing is that you get away before Richard realises you're gone.'

'What about the police? Shouldn't I tell them?'

'I'll handle that. Just go. And whatever you do, don't go home first.'

It took about ten minutes for Jennifer to cover everything she'd learned—the strange credit history, Richard's seeming desire to keep a low profile, Jake Blansen's comments about Richard being dangerous, and the fact that he no longer worked for J. D. Blanchard. Pete was tapping the steering wheel and nodding when she finished.

'I knew there was something fishy about that guy,' he said. 'Even in the gym, he seemed a little too slick, you know?' He tapped the steering wheel again. 'So if he's not working, where is he?' he asked.

'I don't know. We could try him at home.'

Peter nodded. 'Let's do it.'

Fifteen minutes later, the squad car pulled into the drive of the rented Victorian house. Once out of the car, the two officers unsnapped their holsters as they surveyed the area.

Up close, Jennifer thought the house looked seedier than it had from the road. Curtains were drawn in the windows. There was no sign of a car.

'Looks like our suspect might have run,' Pete whispered.

They made their way carefully to the front door, the porch creaking beneath them. Pete knocked. Jennifer stood off to the side, hand on her holster. Then, instinctively, she drew her gun.

Richard watched them from behind the trees. He'd been at the back, wiping down the interior of the car—he'd already scoured the house in an attempt to eliminate the most obvious signs of what had transpired. He'd expected them, of course, just not so soon.

He took a long, deep breath, then backed further into the trees, wondering how they'd connected Andrea to him so quickly.

No matter. He already knew that his time as Richard Franklin had come to an end. He wished he could have had another hour to collect his things. His cameras were inside the house. He regretted having to part with them. And the photographs, too, especially the ones of Jessica in his briefcase. He wasn't as concerned about the pictures of Julie. They'd have the rest of their lives to make up for the ones he'd left behind.

He wondered if Julie knew about Andrea yet. Yes, probably, he thought. More than likely the police had just left her. So what would she do?

She'd run. She'd try to hide and bring the fool with her. She was probably gone already. Another reason to get away from here.

Quietly, he began moving towards the squad car.

'Let's head round the back,' Jennifer whispered. 'I've got a funny feeling that he's still here.'

Pete nodded, and they left the porch.

Near the rear of the house, they paused. Jennifer was in front and, flattened against the side of the house, she peeked round the corner. Richard's car was parked there, the door on the passenger side open. She held her gun to her chest, barrel raised, and nodded in that direction. Slowly Pete drew his gun.

She peeked again, then nodded for Pete to follow. They crept round the back, trying to be as silent as possible. The rear door to the house, they saw, stood open. The car was close now.

Jennifer paused, looking from side to side. He's out there, she thought. And he's watching us now. Glancing over her shoulder, she saw Pete on the back porch, approaching the open door.

It was then that they heard the scream, a piercing wail, coming from the front of the house.

Pete scrambled down from the porch and began running back the way they'd come. Jennifer followed. But when they reached the front, they saw nothing. They split up then, Pete approaching the front of the house, Jennifer moving forward into the yard.

Her mouth was dry and she was breathing hard, trying to stay calm. A short distance away, she eyed a grove of low-growing trees. That's where he is, she thought. He's hiding, and he wants me to come and get him. Behind her, she could hear Pete moving across the gravel. Suddenly, from the back of the house came the sound of a car engine turning over. The engine whined as the accelerator was slammed to the floor, and the car was racing towards them from the other side of the house.

Pete stood frozen in the middle of the drive. He saw the car a moment before Jennifer did. It wasn't slowing down. In the last second, Pete dived out of the way as the car ripped past him.

Jennifer had only a split second to take the shot, but because of Pete's dive she opted against it.

The car roared down the driveway, veered round the bend and vanished from sight, leaving a trail of flying gravel in its wake.

Jennifer ran towards Pete. He was already getting up and they ran to the squad car without a word. Their doors slammed simultaneously. Instinctively, Pete reached for the ignition keys.

They were gone. And the radio had been torn from the dash.

'Damn!' Pete shouted, slamming the wheel hard.

Jennifer grabbed for her cellphone and called the station. She didn't hold out much hope that they would be able to catch Richard in time. When she hung up, Pete looked at her.

'Now what do we do?'

'I'm going inside.'

'Without a warrant?'

Jennifer opened the door and stepped out. 'He tried to run you down, and he's probably on his way to harm someone else. I think that qualifies as a legitimate reason for entry. Don't you?'

The kitchen was miraculously clean, the kitchen sink gleaming in the sunlight. Jennifer moved forward, passing through what was once a breakfast nook and into the living room. There's nothing personal here, she thought. No photographs, no magazines, no plants. Just a couch, some end tables and lamps.

Jennifer looked up the stairs. Behind her, Pete came in, his gun drawn. 'Kind of empty, huh?' he offered.

'I'm going up,' she said.

Pete followed her. At the top, they peeked down the hallway before starting towards the right. Opening the first door they came to, they found the darkroom and flicked the switch. Bathed by the reddish glow, Jennifer felt suddenly weak as she realised what Richard had been doing with his time since he'd quit work.

'Lord help us,' was all she could say.

Not wanting to draw attention to himself, Richard slowed the car once he reached the major roads. He knew he had to ditch the car, but he wanted to put as much distance as he could between Swansboro and himself. He turned onto the highway that led to Jacksonville. There, he'd park the car where it wouldn't be spotted right away, and he'd begin his search for Julie.

Jessica had tried to run once, too, he remembered, and she thought she'd been careful. She took a bus halfway across the country. But he'd tracked her down, and when he opened the door to the motel where she was staying and found her sitting on the bed, she wasn't even surprised to see him. The waiting had worn her down. When he handed her the locket, she slipped it round her neck. He helped her up from the bed.

'You didn't think I'd let you go that easily, did you?'

'Please,' she whispered. 'Don't hurt me. Please, not again.'

'But you tried to run away,' he said. 'That hurt me, Jessica.'

'Oh . . . please . . . no . . .'

Standing in the doorway of the darkroom, Pete Gandy blinked a few times, his head turning from side to side as he tried to take it all in. Taped to the walls were hundreds of photographs of Julie. Julie leaving the salon. Julie in the woods taking Singer for a walk. Julie at dinner. Julie reading the morning newspaper, Julie on the back porch, Julie in her bedroom.

Julie everywhere she'd been over the last month.

Jennifer felt something collapse inside her. She wanted to stay longer, but she knew it was important to check the house for signs that Andrea had been there. Pete was still frozen in place.

'I can't believe this guy,' he whispered as she brushed past him. Jennifer glanced in the bathroom, then, in another room, she found Richard's workout equipment. He'd hung a mirror in there, surrounded by more pictures. She moved to the final door, which she assumed was his bedroom. Pushing open the door, she saw a photo on the bedside table that held her attention.

At first, she thought it was Julie. The hair was the same, and her eyes were a similar mixture of blue and green; yet it wasn't Julie, Jennifer realised after a moment, just someone who closely resembled her. Holding a rose to her cheek, the woman in the photograph was younger than Julie by a few years, her smile almost childlike.

As she reached for the frame, Jennifer noticed the locket round the woman's neck. The same locket Julie had shown her in the kitchen.

Her foot then hit something heavy. Looking down, Jennifer saw the corner of a briefcase poking out from beneath the bed. She slid it out and set it on the bed. Inside were dozens of pictures of the woman in the frame.

Pete came in behind her. 'What is it?' he asked.

Jennifer shook her head.

'More photographs,' she said.

'Of Julie?'

'No,' Jennifer said, turning towards him. 'I don't know for sure, but I think it's Jessica.'

W ithin forty minutes, Richard Franklin's home was crowded with Swansboro police officers and Onslow County sheriffs. The forensics team from Jacksonville was inside collecting evidence.

Jennifer and Pete were standing outside the house with their captain, Russell Morrison, a gruff bulldozer of a man with thinning grey hair. 'He tried to kill an officer,' Morrison said, 'and that doesn't happen on my watch.' He glanced at Pete. 'You're the lead on this investigation. But I'm going to put everyone on it.'

Pete nodded as they were interrupted by a shout from one of the officers who'd been in the house. He was approaching them rapidly. 'Captain?' he called out. 'I think we've got something.'

'What is it?'

'Blood.'

H enry's beach house was on Topsail Island, a spit of land half a mile off-shore, about forty minutes from Swansboro. Covered by rolling dunes speckled with sedge grass and white sand, the island was popular with families during the summer, though few people lived there year-round. During spring, visitors seemed to have the island all to themselves.

Like all homes there, the main floor of the house had been built above the garage and storage areas because of storm surges. Steps led from the back porch to the beach, and the windows along the back offered an unobstructed view of the waves.

Julie stood at one of these windows. She and Mike had stopped along the way, buying enough food to last them a week. The curtains were drawn on every window but this one. Mike had parked Henry's car in the garage. No one had followed them; they were sure of that. Still, Julie felt that Richard would somehow find her.

'Maybe they've already caught him,' Mike offered.

Julie said nothing. Singer moved beside her and nuzzled her hip. Julie's hand went automatically to his head.

'We're safe here,' Mike said. 'You know that, right?'

'I know.'

But she wasn't so sure, and her fear was so strong that she found herself instinctively backing away from the window.

Like Julie and Mike, Richard Franklin stopped at the store. After pulling his car into the rear corner parking lot of the hospital—where it wouldn't draw attention by remaining parked in the same spot for a few days—he grabbed the plastic bags from the store and headed into a gas station rest room. He locked the door behind him. Staring into the grimy mirror above the sink, he became his methodical self again.

In the plastic bags were items necessary for the change he'd gone through once before: a razor, scissors, hair colouring, tanning cream and a pair of reading glasses. Not much, but enough to alter his appearance from a distance; enough to hide in plain view for the short term. Enough to find her.

There was, however, the problem of where she'd gone. And she was gone; of that he was now certain. No one had answered the phone at the salon, and when he'd called the garage, one of Henry's flunkies had said that Mike had left as well.

So she'd run, but where? Richard smiled, knowing he'd have his answer soon. Even when people tried to be careful, they made mistakes. And her mistake, he was certain, came down to this: someone knew where she was. Henry or Emma or Mabel knew. And the police would know as well. They'd want to talk to her, to tell her what they'd learned, to keep their eye on her.

One of these people, he was certain, would lead him to her doorstep.

He whistled softly under his breath as he began to alter his appearance. Thirty minutes later he emerged into the sunlight, blond, tanned, wearing glasses, and without a moustache. A new man. All that's left is to find another car, he thought, and he headed down the street to the mall across from the hospital.

Back at the station, Jennifer called the Denver Police Department, where she was passed to Detective Larry Cohen.

'We've got information on a few Richard Franklins,' he said. 'Tell me about him.'

Jennifer gave him a brief description—height and weight, hair colour and eyes, approximate age, race.

'OK, give me a just a second.' On the phone, she could hear him tapping information into the computer.

303

'Huh,' he finally said. 'I don't think we have any information for you. We have records of seven Richard Franklins. Four of those are African Americans, one is deceased, one is in his sixties.'

'What about the last one?'

'A typical druggie. He's about the same age, but nothing else about him matches up. I don't think he's your guy.'

Jennifer glanced at the photographs of Jessica from Richard's briefcase. After hesitating for a moment, she asked, 'Could you check for a possible murder victim named Jessica Franklin.'

'No problem,' he said.

She waited as he checked the records.

'No,' he said finally. 'No murder victims listed under the name of Jessica Franklin, no missing persons, either.'

As she was hanging up the phone, Pete came rushing to her desk.

'Daytona,' he said. 'The son of a bitch went to Daytona when he said he went to his mother's funeral—'

'Daytona? Isn't that where Julie is from?' Jennifer paled. 'He didn't go to see his mother. I'd bet my life he went there to learn about Julie.'

Julie sat on the couch with Singer by her side. Mike turned on the television and surfed through the channels, then turned it off. He wandered through the house, making sure the front door was locked, then looked through the window, up and down the street.

Quiet. Completely quiet.

'I think I'll call Henry,' he said. 'Let him know we made it.'

Julie nodded.

Jennifer absently twirled a strand of her hair as she finished up her conversation with Henry.

'Thanks for letting me know,' she said. 'I appreciate it.'

So they'd left town, she thought, hanging up. On the one hand, she probably would have done the same thing if she'd been in their situation. On the other, they were further away if they needed help. Though Topsail was still in the county, it was at the southern end—at least forty minutes from Swansboro.

Jennifer returned her focus to the photographs. Many of the images were striking. Richard Franklin, she decided, wasn't simply a weekend photographer, but someone who viewed photography as art. It made sense, considering the equipment they'd found in his house. Could that knowledge be helpful? She couldn't help feeling she was getting close to something important.

ELEVEN

'SWANSBORO POLICE DEPARTMENT,' Jennifer said, answering her phone.

'Officer Romanello speaking.'

'This is Detective Cohen from Denver.'

Jennifer sat up. 'Oh . . . hey. Did you find anything?'

'Sort of. After your call, I kept thinking how familiar the name Richard Franklin sounded, so I asked around the department before it finally hit me where I'd heard it before.' He paused. 'It concerned a missing person case about four years ago.'

Jennifer reached for her pen. 'Jessica Franklin?'

'No, not Jessica. Richard Franklin. He's the missing person.'

'But he's here.'

'I understand that. But four years ago, he vanished. He didn't show up at work one day, and after a week or so, his secretary contacted us. I talked to the detective in charge of the investigation. From all appearances, he said, it looked like the guy suddenly took off. Clothes were on the bed, and the drawers looked rifled through. Two suitcases were missing and his car was gone. He'd made an ATM withdrawal the last day that anyone saw him. From the interviews with Franklin's acquaintances, no one could figure it out. They said he wasn't the type who would simply take off.'

'There wasn't any legal trouble?'

'None. It's like he simply decided to start over.'

'Why didn't his family report it?'

'Well, that's the thing. There really wasn't any family to speak of. His father was deceased. He had no siblings, and his mother was in a nursing home and suffering from dementia.'

'Do you have any information you could fax me on the case?'

'It's a thick file,' he said. 'Give me your fax number.'

Russell Morrison left his office, striding towards Jennifer and Pete. 'It's Andrea Radley's blood all right,' he said. 'I just got off the phone with the lab and they confirmed it.'

Jennifer barely heard him; instead, she was staring at the first page that had come through the fax from Denver Police Department.

'And we found a witness,' Morrison went on. 'One of the bartenders at Mosquito Grove remembered Andrea from the other night. Gave a perfect description of Richard Franklin.'

'He's not Richard Franklin,' Jennifer said quietly.

Morrison and Pete looked at her.

'The suspect,' she said. 'His name isn't Richard Franklin. The real Richard Franklin has been missing for four years. Here,' she said, handing over the first page of the fax. It was a picture of a bald man with heavy features. 'This is the real Richard Franklin.'

Morrison met Jennifer's eyes. 'You're saying that our guy took over this man's identity?'

Jennifer nodded.

'Then who are we looking for?' Morrison asked.

Jennifer glanced towards the windows at the far end of the department. 'I have no idea.'

It took more time than he'd imagined to find a car, but Richard exited the parking lot of the mall in a green 1994 Pontiac Trans Am. Turning into traffic, he headed straight for the highway.

He drove two hours northeast and checked into a motel. Soon he was lying in bed and staring at the ceiling. They can look, he thought, but they won't find me.

He wondered if the police had learned that he wasn't really Richard Franklin. Even if they had, he knew they couldn't connect him to Franklin's disappearance or learn his former identity. The hard part had been finding the right kind of man, a man without a family. Culling the professional association lists by using the Internet had been tedious, but he'd stayed at it, looking for exactly the right person.

He'd driven to Denver and spent three weeks learning the man's routines. He'd watched Richard Franklin as he'd watched Julie. He'd learned that, occasionally, Franklin worked late at the office, and one night he watched Franklin moving towards his car in a darkened parking lot, head down as he sorted through his keys. Franklin didn't hear him as he placed a gun to his head.

'Do exactly what I say,' he whispered, 'and I'll let you live.'

It had been a lie, of course, but Franklin had done everything that he had asked him to do and had answered all of his questions. Franklin had gone to the ATM and had packed the suitcases. Franklin had even allowed himself to be tied and blindfolded.

He'd driven Franklin to the mountains and told him to lie down on the side of the road. He remembered the begging, the fear. He had almost laughed at the man's weakness, thinking how different they were. Three hours later, Franklin was buried in a grave that would never be discovered.

The identity had been easy to assume. Without anyone pressing the search, Franklin's file was buried in the pile of other missing persons and forgotten.

He took care of the real Richard Franklin just as he'd taken care of his mother and father. And the boys in the foster home. And Jessica.

His eyes narrowed. Now it was time to take care of Mike.

Throughout the evening, the Swansboro Police Department was a hive of activity. After pounding the phones, they'd come across twelve possible suspects who'd checked into hotels. With the help of the Onslow County Sheriff's Department, they investigated their leads one by one without luck.

J. D. Blanchard had a good photograph of the suspect, and the police made copies, distributing them to the television stations. The report ran at the top of each news broadcast and calls flooded in within minutes of the airings.

The entire department was on hand to answer them; notes were jotted down and names were taken; the crazies were weeded out.

By two in the morning, the department had talked to more than 200 people. But none had seen the suspect that day. Nor had anyone spotted the car.

The following morning, a light mist hovered over the Intracoastal Waterway, burning off slowly as the sun rose above the treetops. A prism of light cut through the window of the police station, zeroing in on Jennifer's third cup of coffee of the morning.

They were looking for a ghost, she thought.

The fingerprints they'd gathered hadn't helped. Though Morrison had decided to use the FBI database as well as state records, the Bureau was backlogged with cases from around the country, and he'd been informed it could take at least a week to process.

The only thing they had to go on were the photographs from the briefcase, and she still couldn't figure out why she was so transfixed by them. She'd gone through them a dozen times, but as soon as she put the stack aside, she felt the urge to reach for it again.

Thumbing through, she saw the same images. Jessica in the garden. Jessica on a patio. Jessica sitting. Jessica standing.

Richard woke and showered, then hopped back into the stolen Trans Am. Two hours later, after buying a cup of coffee and a newspaper, he pulled into Swansboro, feeling as if he'd come home.

He was dressed in Dockers and a polo shirt. With his light hair and glasses, even he didn't quite recognise himself when he peeked in the rearview mirror. He looked like any other family man heading to the beach for the weekend. He made his way to a small park, perched on a bench, and opened the newspaper.

His picture was on the front page of the paper, and he took his time reading the article. Then he scanned the rest of the paper, looking for anything about the stolen car. Nothing. Then he settled in to read the article again, his eyes glancing up every few minutes.

He would wait all day if he had to. He knew who he was looking for, the one who would lead him to Julie and Mike.

Jennifer finally spoke to Julie's mother, but the call told her nothing that she hadn't already assumed. Yes, the mother had said, a man who said he was an old friend of Julie's had come by. A week later, he'd brought a friend with him. The friend matched the description of the suspect.

The call to the private investigator had gone unanswered.

Without new information, she was back to where she'd been before, and she was frustrated. Was he still in town? She didn't know. What would he do next? She didn't know. Was he still after Julie? She thought so but wasn't absolutely sure. There was always the possibility that because the police were after him, he would simply leave town and start over, the way he'd done in the past.

The problem was that for all intents and purposes, the suspect had become Richard Franklin. There was nothing personal in the house whatsoever, with the exception of his clothing, his cameras, and the photographs. And the photographs told her nothing. They could have been taken anywhere, and because Richard developed them, there wasn't so much as a lab they could trace them back to.

Jennifer's thoughts suddenly froze as she felt the answer begin to click into place. Expensive camera gear? His own lab? She stared at the stack of photos on her desk. This is something he's been doing for a long time. Years, even. Which meant he might have been using the cameras *before* he became known as Richard Franklin.

'Pete,' she called out, 'are his cameras in the evidence room?'

'Franklin's? Yeah. We put them in yesterday.'

Jennifer jumped up from her chair and started towards the evidence room. 'I might know a way to find out who this guy is.'

A moment later, Pete was struggling to keep up with her as she made her way through the station. 'What's going on?'

Jennifer was signing out the photography gear at the counter as the officer in charge of the evidence locker watched her.

'The cameras,' she said, 'the lenses.'

'I don't get it. What?'

The officer placed a plastic container on the counter, and Julie reached for it and carried it back to her desk.

Pete Gandy watched in confused fascination as she studied the back of one of the cameras. Fifteen minutes later she had the list of serial numbers she needed. She called information and got the numbers for the camera manufacturers, then dialled the first one. After she explained that she needed to verify the name and address of the owner, the person on the other end typed in the number.

'It belongs to a Richard P. Franklin.'

Jennifer hung up and tried the next one. Then the next. On her fourth call, however, a different name was offered.

'The camera is registered to Robert Bonham of Boston, Massachusetts. Do you need the address?'

Jennifer's hands shook as she jotted down the information.

The first detective she reached in Boston gave her the information she needed. 'Robert Bonham is wanted for questioning in the disappearance of his wife, Jessica, four years ago,' he said.

After sorting through the information faxed from Boston on Robert Bonham, and making a few more calls, Jennifer and Pete went in to see Morrison. He looked up as Jennifer slid the pages towards him and then took a moment to peruse them. When he finished, he sat quietly for a moment, trying to absorb the seriousness of the situation.

'What do you want to do?'

Jennifer cleared her throat. 'Until we find him, I think it's best if Pete stays out at the beach house with Mike and Julie. If what we learned is true, you know what he's capable of doing.'

Morrison fixed her with a steady gaze. 'Do you think they'll agree to something like this?'

'Yes,' Jennifer said. 'Once they know what they're up against.'

'Are you going to call them?'

'No. I think it would be best if we talked to Julie in person.'

Morrison nodded. 'If she agrees, I'll authorise it.'

A few minutes later, Jennifer and Pete got in the car. Neither of them noticed the stolen Trans Am when it pulled into traffic behind them.

'His name is Robert Bonham,' Jennifer began. 'The real Richard Franklin has been missing for four years.'

'I don't understand,' Julie said.

They were in the kitchen of Henry's beach house. Mike and Julie sat at the table. Pete leaned against the counter.

Mike reached for Julie's hand and squeezed it.

Jennifer started at the beginning. When she was finished, Mike stared at her. 'You think Robert Bonham killed him.'

Jennifer paused. 'Yes, it seems likely.'

'So who's Robert Bonham?' Julie asked.

Jennifer glanced at her notes. 'He was raised outside Boston as an only child. The police had investigated half a dozen incidents of domestic abuse over the years—until his father passed away.' After explaining the circumstances behind his father's death, Jennifer tapped the file. 'I talked to one of the officers in that case. He's retired now, but he remembered it well. He said that nobody believed Vernon Bonham committed suicide. He suspected the kid had closed the garage door and turned the engine back on after Vernon had passed out.'

Julie felt her stomach doing flip-flops. 'And the mother?'

'Died of a drug overdose a year later. It was ruled a suicide.'

Jennifer let the unspoken accusation sink in before she went on. 'He spent the next few years in foster care, moving from one home to the next. His juvenile records are sealed, so we can't say what else he may have done in his teens. But in college, he was suspected in the assault and battery of his former room-mate. Robert graduated with a degree in engineering. After that, the next bit of information we have comes from 1994, when he married Jessica.'

'What happened to her?' Mike asked hesitantly.

'Jessica's been missing since 1998,' Jennifer said. 'She'd moved back in with her parents, and the last time anyone saw her was at the supermarket. A witness remembered seeing Robert Bonham's car in the parking lot that night, but no one saw what happened to her. He vanished the same night she did.'

Mike and Julie leaned back in their seats, both of them pale.

Jennifer went on slowly, 'I don't know if you're aware of it, but Robert Bonham—Richard—quit his job a month ago. In his house, we found hundreds of pictures of you, Julie. From what we can tell, he's been watching you pretty much around the clock since you first started dating. And he's also been checking up on your past.'

'What do you mean?' Julie asked.

'The week he said he was with his dying mother, he went to Daytona to learn more about you. A private investigator was checking into your history. He's been stalking you all along.'

'Why me?' Julie asked.

'I don't know,' Jennifer said. 'But let me show you what else we found.' Jennifer slid a photo across the table. 'This is Jessica. Here—', she pointed—'I wanted you to see this, too.'

Julie glanced at the photo and saw what Jennifer was pointing to. Hanging from the young woman's neck was the locket that Richard had given Julie. Jessica Bonham,' she said, 'J.B.'

'We'd like to have Officer Gandy stay with you for a few days,' Jennifer said. 'If that's OK.'

Mike glanced towards Pete. 'Yeah,' he said, 'I think that's a good idea.'

Pete went out to the car and was retrieving the suitcase he'd packed when he saw Jennifer scanning the homes along the beach.

Only a few had cars parked in the driveways, the usual SUVs and Camrys and a Trans Am as well, something a teenager might drive, the car she herself had wanted in high school. Less than a quarter of the homes were occupied. She wasn't comfortable with that, but it was better than staying in town.

'And you'll stay awake all night?' she asked Pete.

'Yeah,' he said, slamming the trunk. 'I'll catch a few hours of sleep in the mornings. Do you really think he's still around? Or do you think he's on the run again?'

'Honestly? Yeah, I think he's around.'

Pete's eyes followed hers up and down the street. 'So do I.'

TWELVE

THERE WAS A LANGUID FEEL to the night air the following evening. After dinner Singer was standing near the back door, his tail wagging slightly. Julie crossed the room and opened the door for him, watching as he descended the steps and vanished into the shadows.

She didn't like letting him out. Despite Mike's and Pete's presence, she felt safer when Singer was beside her.

She'd thought about going outside; no doubt Mike and Pete would have said no. Still, it would have been nice. In theory.

Both Emma and Mabel had called her, and Henry had called to talk to Mike. None of the phone calls had lasted more than a few minutes. None of them, it seemed, had anything much to say, except for Mabel, who'd called after speaking with Andrea's parents. Late last night, Andrea had emerged from her coma. She was going to be OK.

Julie turned from the door and walked through the living room into the kitchen, where Mike was washing dishes in the sink. Pete was at the table, playing solitaire.

Julie slipped her arms round Mike, and he turned his head at her touch. 'Almost done,' he said. 'Just a few more to wash. You still thinking about what Jennifer told us?'

'Thinking about that, thinking about what he did in the past, what he did to Andrea . . . where he is now.'

From his vantage point near the dune, Richard watched Julie let Singer out. With the light glowing from behind her, she appeared like a descending angel. Richard found himself growing aroused by the thought of what was going to happen next.

Yesterday, after he'd located them, he'd pulled his car into the driveway of a home that was plastered with real-estate signs. A quick check revealed an alarm system for the house but not for the garage, and he'd worked his way through the lock with a screwdriver he'd found in the glove compartment of the Trans Am. From the trunk, he'd removed the tyre wrench. He'd slept on a dusty air mattress he'd found on the shelves, and he'd spent an hour that afternoon purchasing what he needed.

Now, all he had to do was wait until Singer wandered down the beach. He knew Julie would let him out, as she'd done last night.

In the distance, he could no longer see Singer.

Beside him were the four hamburgers he'd picked up from a place near the hardware store he'd visited that afternoon. He'd already unwrapped them and crumbled the patties into pieces.

Taking the hamburger with him, he began crawling through the grass towards the back steps of the home. There, he scattered the beef onto the steps that led over the dune and back to the house.

He wasn't sure how much Singer weighed, so he had mixed in as much of the bitter powder as he thought he could, while preserving the aroma of beef. He didn't want Singer to sniff and then ignore it.

He crept to his hiding place in the sedge grass and settled in to wait.

Minutes passed before he saw movement in the shadows near the dunes. Singer moved into the moonlight and swung his head from side to side. He then turned and trotted towards the steps.

The dog slowed to a walk before stopping. His nose rose slightly as he seemed to study the steps.

C'mon, Richard thought, *what are you waiting for? Eat it.*

Finally, Singer moved forward as if, at last, he'd smelt it. He took another step until he was hovering over the hamburger.

He lowered his head and sniffed, then began to eat.

Though curtains covered most of the windows, the dining-room window was open, and Richard watched for shadows. Other than the sound of the waves, he could hear nothing.

Julie would be heading for the back door soon. Usually, she didn't let Singer stay out for more than twenty minutes or so, and he wanted to see her face when she called for him.

Staring at the house, he allowed himself to hope that she would forgive him for what he had done.

In Swansboro, Jennifer Romanello spent the evening poring over the documents from Boston, learning what she could about the elusive Robert Bonham. Suddenly, she heard one of the other officers growing animated as he was speaking on the phone, and she looked up. He was nodding furiously and jotting down information, then he hung up.

Standing, he grabbed for the piece of paper and made his way towards her. 'We just got a call,' he said. 'His car has been located in the parking lot at Onslow Hospital in Jacksonville.'

'But no one has seen him?'

'Not that we know of.'

It wasn't surprising that he'd abandoned it, of course, but he had to have some way to get around. Tapping the phone book with her finger, she saw Captain Morrison moving through the office.

She brought him up-to-date then asked, 'Do you think it's possible that he stole a car?'

The captain's eyebrows rose. 'Let me make a call.'

Jennifer nodded, her mind already going through the scenarios. She reached for the keys to the squad car.

'Where are you going?' Morrison asked.

'I am going to head over to the hospital to see if they found anything useful. If you hear anything about a stolen car, let me know, OK?'

'You got it.'

313

Julie wandered to the window and put her face to the glass, scanning the beach.

'Have you heard Singer bark yet?' she asked.

Mike came up beside her. 'No, not yet.'

Julie frowned. In the distance, she could see the faint lights from a trawler off the coast. Though the beach was dark, she thought she'd be able to see Singer. 'Maybe I should go call for him.'

'Do you want me to do it?'

'No, that's OK. I need a bit of fresh air anyway.'

Julie crossed to the door and called for nearly three minutes, moving from the doorway to both ends of the porch.

Mike joined her. 'Not back yet?' he asked.

Julie shook her head. 'No. I can't see him, either.'

Mike looked from side to side. 'Do you want me to go look for him? Maybe he can't hear you because of the waves.'

Julie smiled. 'Thanks.'

Mike walked down the steps. 'I'll be back in a few minutes.'

Jennifer Romanello squinted into the oncoming headlights. Lack of sleep in the last couple of days had taken its toll, and her eyes ached. She was wondering whether to stop for coffee when she heard the radio crackle to life.

'Looks like we might have something,' Morrison said. 'I just got off the phone with the department in Jacksonville. They had a report of a stolen car from the mall parking lot near the hospital on the same day Richard vanished. It's registered to a Shane Clinton, 412 Melody Lane, in Jacksonville.'

'What kind of car was it?'

'A 1994 Pontiac Trans Am. Green.' He recited the licence-plate number and offered, 'We've already got an APB out on it.'

Jennifer made a mental note. 'Have you talked to Clinton?'

'No, but he lives right near the hospital.'

Jennifer decided to head that way.

Mike's feet sank into the sand as he moved down the beach. Glancing over his shoulder, he could see Julie standing on the porch, her image growing smaller with each step he took.

'Singer!' he bellowed.

His eyes were gradually adjusting to the darkness, and he scanned the dunes, watching for the dog. He was cupping his hands to call again when he noticed a shadow off to his left, near a set of stairs. He

THE GUARDIAN

squinted, then recognised the shape in the sand. Turning round, he shouted in Julie's direction.

'Found him!' He took another couple of steps forward. 'What're you doing, Singer? Come on. Let's go back inside.'

Singer's tail moved slightly, and Mike heard what sounded like a low whine. The dog was panting hard, his tongue out.

Mike squatted down and put a hand on the dog's chest. 'You OK?' he asked. He could feel Singer's heart beating fast. Singer didn't respond to his touch, and it was then that he noticed that one of Singer's rear legs was quivering.

Pete Gandy joined Julie on the back porch.

'What's going on?' he asked.

'Just waiting for Mike and Singer to get back.'

Pete nodded, and they stood in silence watching the beach. Julie was just beginning to wonder where they were when she heard Mike calling. A moment later, he appeared on the sand below.

'It's Singer!' Mike shouted. 'Something's wrong! Come on!'

Her chest constricting, Julie started for the steps.

'Wait,' Pete said. He tried to grab her arm to stop her, but Julie was already past him. Watching her charge down the steps, he debated whether or not to follow them.

'Damn,' he mumbled, then headed towards the beach.

Richard watched the three of them as they began to run down the beach. As they moved further into the distance, he could feel the adrenaline race into his system. It had begun.

When they vanished from sight, he crept over the dune. Staying low in the shadows, he moved towards the house, tyre wrench in hand.

Breathing hard as she tried to keep up with Mike, Julie felt panic begin to take hold. Behind her, she could hear Pete calling her name, pleading with her to return to the house.

A moment later, they saw where Mike was heading—and saw Singer lying in the sand. Julie began to tremble as she ran to Singer. By the time Pete reached them, Julie and Mike were hovering over the dog.

'What's going on?' Pete panted.

'Singer? What's wrong, baby?' Julie crooned. No response.

'Why isn't he moving?' Pete asked.

'I don't know,' Mike mumbled. 'I just found him like this.'

'What's wrong with him?' Julie cried. 'Help him!'

315

Mike gently lifted Singer's head from the sand. 'C'mon, boy, get up.' Singer's neck was rigid, and his panting intensified.

'We've got to do something!' Julie screamed.

Her anguished wail forced Mike into action. 'Pete—go back to the house and see if you can find an emergency veterinarian.'

'I'm not supposed to leave you alone—'

'Just go!' Mike shouted. 'And hurry!'

'OK. OK,' he said. A moment later he was charging into the darkness, leaving Mike and Julie with Singer.

As Jennifer entered the Jacksonville city limits something was gnawing at her mind. She was missing something, she thought, something obvious, something just out of reach.

OK, she thought, Richard's car had been abandoned. A car was stolen around the time that Richard would have arrived in Jacksonville. Put those two facts together, and she suspected—no, she knew—that Richard had taken it.

What had the captain said?

'A 1994 Pontiac Trans Am. Green.'

She frowned, wondering why that seemed so familiar.

From the porch, Richard heard Julie screaming about her dog. For a moment, he stopped to listen. He didn't want Julie to be upset, and he wished there could have been some other way.

Maybe he would get her another dog after all this was behind them. They could pick out a dog together, and she would forget about Singer. Yes, that was it. Another dog. A *better* dog. That's what he would do for her when all this was over. It would make her happy, and that's all he'd ever wanted for her. Happiness.

On the beach, he saw a sudden movement. Knowing what it meant, Richard retreated to the shadows.

Pete Gandy rushed up the steps, across the porch, and through the back door, racing for the kitchen. He tore open a drawer beneath the phone and grabbed the directory.

'C'mon, c'mon,' he said as he began flipping through the pages. Moments later he reached the nearest veterinarian, who told him, 'I can be in my office in ten minutes. It's just down the street.'

'I can find it.'

Pete hung up the phone and raced for the back porch, slamming the door behind him. He wasn't sure what first made him turn. But he knew, even before he saw Richard, that someone was moving towards him, and he was instinctively already beginning to duck when he felt something hard crash against his skull.

Julie was stroking Singer lightly, her hands shaking.

'What's taking so long?' she pleaded. 'What's he doing?'

Mike tried to reassure her. 'Singer's going to be OK,' he whispered. Singer was panting harder now, his eyes wide.

'Hold on, baby,' Julie pleaded. 'Please . . . oh, God . . .'

'Maybe I should go check on Pete,' Mike offered.

Julie barely heard him, but she nodded, her lips pressed together. Mike turned and started back towards the house.

Richard stared at the fallen figure of Pete Gandy. Gruesome business, yes, but necessary and, in its own way, inevitable.

Then, of course, there was the fact that Pete had a gun. Makes the rest so much easier, he thought, after removing the gun from the holster. He turned and was heading for the stairs when he saw Mike coming up the beach, towards the house.

Glancing down at the body, he realised that Mike would see it immediately. His mind clicked through the problem, and he crouched down, waiting for Mike's heavy tread on the stairs.

Jennifer had stopped at a red light in the heart of Jacksonville. Though she was making her way to Melody Lane to talk with Shane Clinton, her mind was still sorting through the problem of the Trans Am.

The kind of car she'd wanted in high school. She'd had the same thought recently, but where?

The light turned green and Jennifer shook her head as the car started forward again. Where have I been recently? Only to talk to Julie and Mike, when I dropped Pete off.

Her hands tightened on the wheel. No, it couldn't be . . .

Reaching for her cellphone, she pressed the accelerator to the floor, knowing it would take twenty minutes to reach Topsail Beach—and the green Trans Am she'd seen parked up the road.

Mike looked up just as a shadowy figure launched itself from the top of the flight of stairs. The momentum of the attack sent him tumbling backwards. His head collided with the stairs as something crashed down on him, crushing his rib cage and driving the edges of the stairs into his lower back.

The pain was staggering. He felt himself sliding down the stairs on his back, headfirst, until his head hit the sand, and he suddenly stopped, his neck bent at an odd angle. Above him, he could feel someone reaching for his neck and taking hold.

The hands began to tighten. Opening his eyes was difficult, but when he saw the face of Richard Franklin, his thoughts suddenly came into focus. *Julie!* he wanted to scream. *Run!*

But he made no sound. Cut off from oxygen, he began to grow dizzy. As he struggled to draw breath, he reached for Richard's hands. But Richard's grip refused to weaken. Mike thrashed his legs, trying to throw Richard off, but Richard wouldn't budge.

Get air: It was all Mike could think about.

Panicked, he reached for Richard's hands again, prising and grabbing, but this time he found a thumb and was able to latch on to it. He jerked with every bit of strength he had left. He felt something snap. Richard loosened his grip.

That was all Mike needed. He felt a wisp of air pass through his throat. He grabbed Richard's hair and rammed his knees into Richard's back. Richard went over him, landing in the sand behind him.

Gasping for breath, Mike pushed off the stairs into the sand beside Richard, who was on his feet first. He kicked Mike savagely in the ribs, and Mike toppled over.

Staggering onto all fours, Mike lunged towards Richard. But Richard kicked at him again. Mike kept driving forward. A moment later, he was reaching for Richard's throat when he felt something hard wedged against his stomach and heard a pop. Then there was fire in his belly, pain shooting in all directions. Mike blinked in shock. His body weakened, and Richard shoved him off.

When Mike reached for his stomach, it was slippery, oozing. In the dim light, his blood looked like motor oil puddling beneath a car. He couldn't understand where the blood was coming from, but when Richard got to his feet, he saw the gun.

Need to get up . . . have to warn Julie . . .

He knew Richard would be going after her. He had to save Julie. 'Julie!' he screamed, but the sound came out as a wheeze.

Another kick to his head, and then there was nothing.

I gnoring the pain in his thumb, Richard turned and started down the beach. It was a beautiful night, he thought. In the shadows ahead, he could make out Julie's form, hovering over her dog.

He began to walk more quickly. Julie, no doubt, would be frightened when she saw him. She'd probably react the way Jessica had when she'd found him waiting in her car that night outside the supermarket. He'd tried to make her understand, but she'd struggled and he'd put his hands round her throat until her eyes rolled back in her head, knowing that she had forced him to do it.

But he would treat Julie with the patience she deserved. He would talk to her in quiet tones, and once she understood his love for her, she would acquiesce. She'd be upset about Singer, but eventually she would see why he'd had no other choice.

'He's coming, baby,' Julie whispered. 'He'll be here soon, and we'll take you to the doctor, OK?'

She could barely see Singer through her tears. He had closed his eyes, and his entire body quivered, straining to fight off death.

Julie knew that Singer wouldn't be able to keep fighting much longer. 'Singer, you can make it . . .'

She was just about to shout out for Pete and Mike when the words caught in her throat. At first, she refused to believe what her eyes were seeing, and she tried to blink the image away. But when she looked again, she knew she wasn't wrong. Though his hair was a different colour, though he wore glasses and the moustache was gone, she recognised him immediately.

'Hello, Julie,' Richard said.

He was here. He's done something to Singer. He's done something to Pete and Mike. And now he was here for her.

He was walking slowly towards her.

'You . . .' was all she could manage to say.

He stopped a few feet away, and his eyes drifted to Singer. 'I'm sorry about Singer. I know how much you cared for him.'

Julie felt as if she were about to vomit. 'Where's Mike?'

Richard looked down. 'That's over now.'

His words carried an almost physical impact, and all at once she felt her hands begin to shake.

'What did you do to him?' she choked.

'It doesn't matter.'

'What did you *do*?' she screamed, unable to control herself.

He took another step towards her. 'I didn't have a choice, Julie. You know that. He was controlling you, and I couldn't let that continue. But you're safe now. I'll take care of you.'

He's going to kill me, she thought. He killed Mike and Singer and Pete, and now he's going to kill me. Julie began to stand as Richard closed in. Something inside her screamed, *Run!* And she bolted, her feet slipping as she charged down the beach.

Richard didn't try to stop her. There was nowhere for her to go. He hooked the gun into his belt and began to jog after her.

Mike was drifting in and out of consciousness. Trapped somewhere between a world of reality and dreams, his mind latched on to the fact that he was bleeding heavily. And that Julie needed him.

Trembling, he slowly began to rise.

Julie ran towards the lights of the only beach house that seemed to be occupied. Her legs were growing weary, and she began to feel as though she were running on the spot. The lights looked close, but she couldn't seem to reach them.

Only terror kept her moving. She stole a glance over her shoulder. Despite the darkness, she could see Richard closing in on her.

I'm not going to make it, she realised. She was stumbling now. It was all she could do to keep upright. She veered towards the dunes, hoping that on the other side there might be a place to hide.

Climbing up the sand was almost too much for her. She had to use her hands for balance, and by the time she reached the top, her legs were buckling. That was when she felt Richard snare her feet, like a football player making a tackle. Losing her balance, she tumbled down the far side of the dunes.

When Richard reached her, he bent over and took her by the arm, helping her to her feet. Julie flailed in his grasp and felt his fingers dig into her arm. She struggled harder.

'Don't be this way, Julie,' he said. 'Can't you see this was always how it was going to turn out?'

Julie jerked her arm. 'Let me *go!*' she screamed.

Richard tightened his grip, making her wince. 'We should be going,' he suggested calmly.

'I'm not going anywhere with you!' She jerked again, breaking free from his grasp. She tried to run, but Richard suddenly reached for her hair and jerked it hard.

'Why are you making this so hard?' he asked.

On the beach, Mike was trying to stand, reaching for the stairs, fighting nausea, his thoughts random and fragmented. *Have to call the police . . . help Julie . . . but the pain . . . the pain . . . where am I? . . . Julie . . . have to help her . . .* He took a step. Then another.

Julie swung wildly, hitting Richard on the chest and on the face. He pulled her hair again, making her scream.

'Why do you keep fighting me?' Richard asked.

'Let me go!' she screamed. 'Stay away from me.'

'Think of all we can do together,' he said.

'We'll do nothing together. I hate you!'

He pulled savagely on her hair, bringing her to her knees. 'Don't say that. I know you're upset. I don't want to hurt you, Jessica.'

'I'm not Jessica!' she screamed.

Richard stared at her. He blinked. 'What did you say?'

'I'm not Jessica!' she screamed again.

Richard's free hand went behind his back. A moment later, she saw the gun.

With one hand holding his stomach, Mike reached for the railing and pulled himself up. Nearing the top now, he saw Pete face down on the deck, blood pooling round his head.

Another couple of steps and he reached the deck, making his way to the door. He reached the knob and turned it, feeling disembodied as the door swung open. The phone, he thought. Have to get to the phone. That was when he heard something crash through the front door. Raising his eyes, he felt a surge of relief.

'Julie needs help,' he rasped out. 'Down the beach . . .'

Shocked by Mike's condition, Jennifer quickly moved to his side and helped him to a chair. Then she grabbed the phone and dialled the emergency number. When it began ringing, she handed him the phone.

'Get an ambulance!' she said. 'Can you do that?'

Mike nodded. 'Pete . . . outside . . .'

Jennifer ran out to the deck. She first believed that Pete was dead. Blood was pouring from his head, but as she bent over to check on him, he moved his arm and moaned.

'Don't move,' she said. 'Ambulance is on the way.'

A moment later, she was charging down the steps.

Richard put the gun to her temple.

'I love you,' he said. 'I've always loved you. But you're not giving me a chance to show you.' He pulled her closer. 'Say you love me.'

Julie said nothing.

'Say it!' he screamed. 'I gave you a chance, and I even forgave you for what you've done to me! For what you forced me to do. Now *say it!*'

Fear was in her chest now. 'I love you,' she whimpered.

'Say it so I can hear it. Like you mean it.'

Beginning to cry, she uttered, 'I love you.'

'Say you want to come with me.'

From the corner of her eye she saw a vision, like a dream, cresting over the dune—her guardian charging through the darkness.

As the vision took shape, Julie watched as Singer launched himself at Richard, snarling, his jaw clamping down on the arm holding the gun. Singer didn't let go, and Julie and Richard toppled to the side, Richard trying to free himself.

Singer tugged and shook his head as Richard began to scream, the gun tumbling from his hand. He was on his back now, fighting to keep Singer from his throat.

His face contorting, Richard held back Singer with one hand and reached for the gun. The dog didn't stop his attack.

Behind her, Richard's fingers curled round the handle of the gun. It was the sound of the gun going off that made Julie suddenly freeze again. Singer yelped.

'Singer!' Julie screamed. 'Oh God . . . no!'

Another shot and another yelp.

Looking over her shoulder, Julie saw Richard get to his feet. She began to tremble uncontrollably.

Singer was on his side, struggling to get up.

In the distance came the sound of sirens.

'We have to go now,' Richard said. 'We're almost out of time.'

But all Julie could do was stare at Singer.

'Now!' Richard boomed. He grabbed her by the hair again and tugged. Julie fought him. She was kicking and screaming, when a voice called out from the top of the dune.

'Freeze!'

Richard and Julie saw Officer Jennifer Romanello at the same time. Richard pointed the gun at her and fired wildly. A moment later, there was a sharp, burning pain in his chest and a sound like a freight train in his ears. He fired again, missed, and felt another burning sensation in his throat, forcing him backwards. The gun slipped from his hands, and he dropped to his knees. He turned towards Julie and tried to speak, but his mouth couldn't form the words. Richard fell forward into the sand.

Julie stared at his body, then turned to Singer. He was panting hard, his mouth hanging open. Julie went to him, bending down.

He whimpered as she laid her hand on his head, and his tongue flicked at it. 'Oh . . . baby,' she wept.

He was bleeding from two deep wounds, the blood soaking into the sand beneath him. His eyes were wide, and when he tried to lift his head, he yelped, the sound nearly breaking her heart.

She could feel his breath on her skin, rapid and shallow. He licked her again, and she kissed him. 'You were so brave.'

His eyes were on her. He whimpered again, and Julie stifled her cry.

'I love you, Singer,' she murmured as the muscles in his body began to relax. 'It's OK, sweetheart. No more fighting. I'm safe now. You can go to sleep.'

EPILOGUE

SHE WOKE UP in the hospital. Pete was there as well, and Mike. Pete was up and around in a few days, but Mike was in a critical condition for a week. Once his condition stabilised and he began to improve, he stayed in the hospital for another three weeks. The entire time, Julie camped out in a chair by his bed, holding his hand.

The police had more questions and also more information about Richard's past, but she found she didn't care about any of it. Richard Franklin was dead—in her mind, he would never be remembered as Robert Bonham—and that's all that mattered.

And so, of course, was Singer. Later, she'd been told by a veterinarian that he'd been given rat poison, enough to kill six dogs. 'I don't understand it,' the vet said. 'It was a miracle he was able to move at all, let alone fight with a grown man.'

But he had, Julie thought. And he saved me.

On the day they buried Singer in Julie's back yard, a warm, soft rain fell round the small group of people who gathered to say goodbye to the Great Dane who had been Julie's companion in life and, at the end, her guardian.

Once Mike was out of the hospital, the next few weeks passed in a daze. For the most part, he had moved in and Julie was grateful. But nothing seemed right any more. The house was too empty, nothing snuggled against her feet.

One night, she dreamed of both Jim and Singer. They were walking together in an open field, their backs to her, as she was running and trying to catch them. In her dream, she called to them both, and they stopped and turned round. Jim smiled. Singer barked. She wanted to go to them, but she couldn't move. They stared at her with the same tilt of their heads, the same looks in their eyes. Jim put his hand on Singer's back, and Singer barked happily, letting her know this was the way it was meant to be. Instead of coming towards her, they turned again, and she watched them go, the outlines of their images fading into one.

When she woke, she picked up her bedside picture of Singer. Her heart still ached when she looked at it. In the back of the frame, she'd tucked the letter Jim had written, and now she slipped it out.

As the morning sun warmed the windows, she read it again, her eyes slowing as she reached the final paragraph.

And don't worry. From wherever I am, I'll watch out for you. I'll be your guardian angel, sweetheart. You can count on me to keep you safe.

Julie looked up, her eyes moist. Yes, she thought, you did.

NICHOLAS SPARKS

Nicholas Sparks is not afraid to draw on personal experiences and emotions in his writing. His first novel, *The Notebook*, was inspired by his wife's grandparents, who for sixty years were inseparable; *Message in a Bottle* owed much to his father's experience of grief when Sparks's mother died tragically young; *A Walk to Remember* was written as a result of his younger sister's battle with cancer; and *The Rescue* drew on his son Ryan's problems with understanding language. With *The Guardian*, however, the author decided to try something a little different. 'In the course of my life, I've probably read a couple of thousand thrillers—I'm an avid reader—and though many of them had characters fall in love within the story, I can't remember reading one where the thriller element was secondary to the relationship. The reason for this is simple—the scarier something is, the more it dominates the story. The challenge I had with *The Guardian* was to find the right balance between the two elements and to pace the story accordingly, so that the reader never lost sight of what the novel really was—a love story between two regular people who find that they've crossed paths with the wrong sort of person. Though it sounds easy, on my end it made for many sleepless nights.'

He also wanted to write a story that included a dog, inspired by the great animal classics such as *Old Yeller* by Fred Gipson, *To Dance with the White Dog* by Terry Kay, and *My Dog Skip* by Willie Morris, all of which have brought him such enjoyment over the years: and he loved creating Singer, the Great Dane in his novel.

Nicholas Sparks admits to being an old-fashioned romantic. When he first met his wife, Cathy, on a spring break in Florida, it was love at first sight. 'At least for me. I told her the day after we met that we would be married one day. She laughed and told me to get another beer!' But Nicholas was right and they married a year later.

Today, he is very much a family man and says that his five children— Miles, Ryan, Landon, Lexie and Savannah—are 'the greatest thing that has ever happened to me. Although I do my writing at home, they never distract me. I'm not one of those writers who need absolute solitude to work.' Amazingly, between his hectic writing schedule and family commitments, Nicholas Sparks also manages to find time to run daily, lift weights three times a week and compete as a black belt in Tae Kwon Do. 'Reading and exercising are the ways I reduce stress,' he explains.

Jane Eastgate

325

The Trouble With Ally

Sheila Norton

Almost every woman has told a
little white lie about her age at
some stage in her life.

But when Ally Bridgeman does
so, the lie spirals wildly out of
control and lands her in a
great deal of trouble . . . .

Chapter 1

RATED OUT OF TEN on a scale of awfulness, of horrendous happenings that ruin your life, I suppose the cat being sick was only about a two or a three. So it's hard to explain to anyone who didn't know me at the time, why it was the catalyst for a disaster of a magnitude that sent me off the rails, spinning out of control, into a nightmare I could never have imagined in my worst . . . well, in my normal nightmares. Come to think of it, it was hard enough to explain to the people who knew me best in the world, so why the hell should you be able to understand if you've never even met me? Still, I think maybe you will. I think maybe you'll read my story and think to yourself: there's the story of a poor, sad, worn-out old cow who'd come to the end of her tether.

Or perhaps you'll think: that's the result of too much freedom in the Sixties, the inevitable consequences of the pop culture and moral dissolution of our society, the breakdown of marriage and the traditional family . . .

Let me make it clear from the outset that I prefer the 'poor sad cow' theory. It doesn't offend me one bit, and I think it's pretty accurate. So don't be afraid to apply it at any point in the story that you feel appropriate. Starting on the day the cat was sick.

It was an unusually cold April day, two months before my fiftieth birthday. The central heating wasn't working but I wasn't letting that upset me. I was wearing gloves to eat my breakfast and had accepted with good grace the fact that the central-heating engineer couldn't manage to get out to fix it until the Monday of the next week at the earliest. *C'est la vie.* A bit of cold never hurt anyone.

'When I was a kid,' I was telling Lucy, my younger daughter, 'we didn't have central heating. Nobody did.'

'And people lived in caves and wore wild animal skins—'

'And we had to scrape the ice off the insides of the bedroom windows, and get dressed under the bedclothes . . .'

'Jesus! Are we getting all that Hard Times in the Dark Ages stuff again?' Victoria asked her sister mildly, ignoring me completely as she appeared in the kitchen wearing two dressing gowns over her pyjamas and grabbing two slices of toast that had just popped out of the toaster.

'That's my toast!' said Lucy.

'Put some more on.'

'Mum! Tell her!'

I'm invisible and not worth listening to, but I'm supposed to tell a twenty-one-year-old not to eat a nineteen-year-old's toast. *On your bike.*

'Load the dishwasher when you've finished,' I said instead. The cat flap rattled and Apple Pie galloped in as if all the hounds of hell were after him.

'Cold out there, isn't it, boy!' said Victoria brightly, sitting down at the table with Lucy's toast on a plate, dripping butter down the top dressing gown. Apple Pie jumped up on the table, looked at her as if considering his options for a minute, and then vomited all over the toast.

'He did that deliberately!' squawked Victoria, who had jumped out of her chair, her face screwed up in horror.

'Serves you right,' said Lucy.

Apple Pie was lying on his side by the pool of vomit, panting lightly.

'He's not well,' observed Victoria. 'You'd better take him to the vet, Mum.'

'Is anyone going to help me clear this up?' I asked tersely, looking at my watch. Concern about the cat was doing a fine balancing act in my mind with concern about my job.

Victoria crept back towards the table, looking at it with barely concealed disgust. I handed her a couple of pages of the previous day's newspaper and between us we scooped the contents of the cat's stomach into this and thence into a bin-bag.

'Poor old boy,' she said lovingly to Apple Pie, who watched her with a baleful eye. She picked him up, shushing his angry growl of protest, rocking him like a baby and carrying on a one-sided conversation with him about the possibilities of his having eaten a frog or a mouse that had disagreed with him. Just as I finished swabbing the table with two solutions of disinfectant, he threw up again, this time straight down Victoria's top dressing gown, marginally compromising the inner dressing gown, and finally regurgitating the last few mouthfuls onto the table again.

'Fucking hell!' shouted Victoria, dropping the cat.

'Victoria! Be careful with him . . .'

'Careful? Look at me!'

'It'll wash off. Come on, don't just stand there, help me clear . . .'

'Mum, why the hell are you bothering to clear up, when he's quite obviously going to puke again as soon as you've finished—'

'He's shaking, Mum!' interrupted Lucy, down on the floor beside Apple Pie, who was lying on his side again and looking distinctly miserable. 'He won't let me pick him up . . .'

'Don't try, then!' I snapped. 'Just leave him alone.'

'I'll get his basket,' said Lucy sadly, 'if you're going to take him to the vet.'

'I've got to get ready for work,' said Victoria, leaving her two dressing gowns in a stinking heap on the floor.

'I've got to get to college,' echoed Lucy, dumping the cat basket on the floor beside Apple Pie's limp form.

They disappeared upstairs to their cold bedrooms (but not so cold that there was ice on the insides of the windows, because I'd plugged in an electric radiator on the landing outside their doors), and I heard the *boom-thump-boom* of their conflicting CD stereo players rising above the noise of their two-speed two-heat volumising hairdryers, their nail varnish dryers and their leg shavers. I looked around the kitchen, at the unloaded dishwasher, the uncleared vomit, the discarded clothes and the general debris of tea bags, butter knives and toast crumbs, and I wished there was something I could plug in, something noisy and effective that would drown out the responsibilities and frustrations of my life, take them over, clear them up and leave me with nothing more pressing to do than to shave my legs and curl my eyelashes.

'Apple Pie?' echoed the vet, looking at me over the top of his glasses.

'It's his name,' I shrugged defensively. 'The children were young . . . they liked apple pie . . .'

He was new to the practice. The other vet was used to us. More to the point, Apple Pie was used to him. He dug his claws into this new one's arms as he tried to encourage him out of his basket.

'I think he's in pain,' I said, making reassuring noises to Apple Pie through the side of the basket. 'Come on, baby. Let the nice man—'

'Ouch!'

The nice man finally managed to lift Apple Pie onto the examination table at the expense of several centimetres of his flesh. The cat promptly lay down on his side, panting, watching me with accusing eyes.

'He's very swollen,' said the vet, pressing his fingers gently into Apple Pie's flank and being rewarded by a howl of pain. 'Has he urinated this morning?'

Urinated? How would I know? I mean, it's not a thing I normally watch out for.

'He goes in the garden.'

'I think it's his kidneys. He could be going into kidney failure.'

I hadn't been prepared for this. Something Serious. I thought we'd get some anti-sickness pills, an extortionate bill and some advice about keeping him away from frogs.

'I'll have to do some tests. He's dehydrating. He needs to be put on a drip straight away.'

'I'll need to leave him here? Now?'

'Absolutely. He's a very sick cat. We'll give you a call later. We should know the results of the—'

'Will he pull through?'

He was Victoria and Lucy's Christmas present when they were eight and ten years old. I know you're not supposed to give pets as presents, but they were sensible little girls, and they loved animals.

'He's so *lovely*!' they'd squealed with delight at their first sight of the little fluffy black and white kitten.

'I'll love him for ever and ever,' declared Victoria solemnly, almost crying with pleasure as she held him on her lap.

'I love him more than anything,' said Lucy, not to be outdone. 'I love him more than . . . more than even apple pie!'

The vet lifted the yowling cat gently back into his carrying basket and called for the nurse to take him through to the hospital area.

'We'll do all we can,' he told me with a sympathetic smile.

'Bye, Apple Pie,' I called after the departing basket. 'Be good.'

T The traffic had built up by the time I got into town. I phoned work from my mobile phone as I waited at the first red lights.

'We did wonder what had happened to you,' said Snotty-Nosed Nicola on the reception desk. The sarcasm in her tone was so palpable it felt like it was slapping me in the face with a wet flannel.

'Well, I'm sorry. I couldn't phone before I left for the vet's because it was only eight thirty. You wouldn't have been there.'

The lights turned green and I brought my foot off the clutch so sharply the car lurched forwards, making me drop the phone.

'Hello? Hello?' came Snotty-Nosed Nicola's voice tinnily from the floor by my feet. 'Ally? Are you there?'

No. I've jumped out of the car window, you silly cow.

'Yes, but I've dropped the phone!' I bellowed through my knees, swerving to change lanes at the last minute.

'Hello? Hello? Are you there?'

'Oh, shut up,' I muttered, kicking the phone under the seat.

Things were fighting for space in the part of my brain reserved for worrying. I had to keep a space for worrying so that the things building up in there didn't spill over into the part that was supposed to deal with holding down a job and keeping myself and various other people alive. The things squirming and wriggling in the worrying part were growing large and fat in a grotesque and obscene manner because they wanted to burst out and take over my whole brain, but I wouldn't allow it.

'I have to concentrate on the traffic,' I told the Worrying Things now as I pulled up at another red light. 'Lie down and go to sleep.'

But they wouldn't. For a start I kept seeing Apple Pie lying in his basket with his eyes full of pain. And I kept seeing the bill, or rather, imagining what it was going to look like. Tests, drugs, X-rays, putting on a drip. We were talking Serious Money now, Serious Money that I didn't have. Not that I didn't think Apple Pie was worth it, but where was the Serious Money going to be found when it was needed? Victoria had blown any money that she'd ever had on the love of her life (her car), and Lucy, of course, being a Poor Student, never had anything to do with money. The really Worrying Thing about it all was that I might have to ask Paul for money. Again.

The last time I'd asked him for money had been for my car. To bring it back to life after it died suddenly and gracefully on the M25 in a January snowstorm. It had needed what seemed to amount to a new heart, lungs and complete digestive system. Apparently I'd been cheerfully and ignorantly driving around in a death trap. The mechanic at the garage had shaken his head sadly in that irritating way they have of pretending not to want to impart bad news, while trying to hide the gleam in their eyes.

'Big end's gone, love, drive shaft's knackered, sump's got a hole in it, tyres are bald, wipers aren't wiping, indicators aren't indicating, lights aren't lighting . . .'

And the ashtray's fallen out.

I went to Paul with a heavy heart. It wasn't that he objected to helping me out. In fact since we'd split up he'd been so generous financially that I was tempted to think he was rewarding me for the privilege of being allowed to leave me. It was the asking that I hated. It felt demeaning. It felt as if I was saying I couldn't cope without him. I couldn't, of course;

cope without his salary, and that was what I hated. How do other women manage? I suppose they have decent jobs, careers, high-flying executive positions, or they go on the game. I'd considered that, but I was always too tired to go out at night. Anyway, Paul had coughed up the money for my car's lifesaving operation without a murmur. And, let's face it, the cat was his responsibility as much as mine. He'd even chosen him, the only black and white kitten out of a litter of black ones, when we were shopping for the Christmas-present pet all those years ago.

But still, he'd left him, hadn't he, ten years later, along with his two daughters, his home, his fishpond, and me.

I was going to be late for work. OK, even later for work than I'd already told Snotty-Nosed Nicola. I was caught up, now, in the Return of the School Run Mothers, or, nannies, in competing models of Range Rovers, one child per car, who wouldn't consider dropping off their precious cargo anywhere further than two yards from the school gate, in case the kid got rained on, suffered sunstroke, got carried off by an unexpected tornado or abducted by aliens. The result was a queue of Range Rovers circling St Nicholas's Academy in much the same way as jets circle Gatwick waiting to land.

Once the child had been deposited at the gate, of course, the Range Rover had to filter its way back into the traffic so that mum/nanny could head off home/to the hairdresser/golf course/gym. Not that I'm envious, not in the least, lucky cows. But now I was seriously late for work and I was stuck behind two Range Rovers whose drivers were graciously letting every other Range Rover into the line in front of them rather than sticking like glue to the rear bumper of the one in front, in the time-honoured way.

'Come on, come on!' I muttered through my teeth at the back of a blonde head in the car in front. 'Are you going to sit here all day?'

And then I got hit from behind by a taxi.

'Where were you trying to go?' I demanded melodramatically of the taxi driver. 'Up my exhaust? On to my roof?'

'Sorry, love.'

He slouched against his taxi door, looking anything but repentant, feeling in his jacket pockets for his insurance details.

'Here you are, love. Insurance'll sort it out. Don't worry.'

Worry? Worry—me? About a crumpled bumper and a registration plate hanging off? About a smashed rear light and a dented boot? Come on, now, I had far better things to worry about. My head was beginning to ache and I could feel that sneaky sort of tickly dry throat coming on that usually means you're going down with the flu. It was now half past nine and my job was probably on the line. You think I'm joking?

I got back in my car, pulled off the road onto the pavement, allowing the five-mile traffic jam behind me to start crawling forwards, staring at my damage as they passed, and fished around under the seat for my mobile phone. No signal. Bloody thing was sulking because I'd dropped it. Tried to start the car again to pull back onto the road. Wouldn't start. Sulking because of a little bump from behind. Resisting the urge to get out of the car, jump up and down and kick it after the style of John Cleese, I counted to ten, then calmly and sensibly, without any visible sign of panic, got out, locked the car, and walked through a timely shower of icy rain to the nearest phone box.

'We'd almost given you up,' said Snotty-Nosed Nicola.

'Yes, well. I'm just waiting for the AA and then I'll be on my way again. Hopefully. If it isn't anything too serious with the car.'

It had better not be. Bloody hell, it had really better not be.

'So would you pass on my apologies, please, Nicola? To Simon?'

'Of course,' she sighed, as if it was going to be a strain but she'd manage it somehow.

I spent the whole of the walk back to the car imagining the sheer pleasure of putting her in a black bin-bag and dropping her in the Thames. Snotty-Nosed Nicola was the whole problem, the whole reason my job might be on the line. You might wonder how it was possible for a receptionist to have so much power. You might, however, stop wondering and begin to see the scale of the problem when I explain that S.N. Nicola was having it off with Simon, the managing director. Simon's power was absolute, as the only person in the whole world he had to answer to was his father, who owned the joint but lived in Portugal, where he played a lot of golf under the guise of looking into other business ventures. If Nicola didn't like you, Simon also tended not to like you, and Nicola didn't like me. I probably reminded her of her mother. I didn't call her 'Nic' and we didn't giggle together. So I was on dangerous ground, and being late for work gave her ammunition to complain about me to Simon. Trouble was, you see, before you start getting all indignant and politically correct on my behalf, trouble was that I'd been late for work quite a few times.

There'd been the previous Tuesday when I'd had to wait in for the man to fix the washing machine, and the Wednesday when I'd had to wait in for him again because he didn't turn up on the Tuesday.

Then, of course, I was always having to take my mother to the hospital. My mother was one of the other Worrying Things that I kept trying to shove back into that special compartment of my brain. She was eighty and quite sharp mentally; but bits of her were starting to go wrong in a sort of rotation system. One week it would be her ears, then it would be her eyes. Then her teeth would play up, then there'd be something wrong with her chest. Next it would be her stomach, then her urinary system, and then her legs would give way. As soon as we'd sorted out her feet, it would be back up to the top of her head again. It felt like a constant battle, with doctors of every speciality trying to hold back her rapidly advancing tide of ailments. It would have been bad enough if she'd been a dear, sweet little old thing who never complained, but she'd become a bad-tempered, cantankerous old crab.

'Don't rush me!' she'd shout, pushing away the arm I provided for her to lean on as we made our way back to the hospital car park after her latest check-up with the opthalmologist or the rheumatologist or the geriatrician. And so we'd spend a leisurely twenty minutes walking to the car, while I sweated and fretted about my job and its fate in the hands of Snotty-Nosed Nicola and Simon . . .

The AA man arrived at a quarter to eleven and started the car at the first attempt, trying without success to make me feel better by assuring me that there certainly could be a problem with the plugs or the distributor, which could quite possibly strike again at any time, so it'd be best to get it looked at. Perhaps at the same time as the damage to the rear bumper and light? I wouldn't talk to the car all the rest of the way to work. It had made me look bloody stupid in front of the AA man, and if it thought I was going to spend out a whole lot of money on it for a new bumper now, it could think again. I slammed its door when I got out, to show it who was boss, and the number plate fell off into a puddle.

'So there you are,' said Nicola as I walked into reception.

'So here I am,' I agreed tersely.

'I explained to Simon,' she said loftily. 'He wants to see you. In his office.'

The smile was truly horrible. Drowning in a black sack would be too good for her. I redesigned the fantasy, leaning towards objects of torture. Simon barely looked up as I walked into his office.

'I was in an accident,' I blurted out. 'Hit from behind by a taxi.'

'Much damage?' he asked, still without looking up.

I wanted to shake the miserable little bastard. Couldn't even look up to see if I was all right. Much damage? As if he cared.

'Not really. Two broken legs, a dislocated shoulder, an amputated hand and concussion.'

He looked up now, slowly, puzzled.

'I meant the car.'

Yes, quite.

'Nothing I can't forgive eventually,' I said.

He still looked puzzled. Isn't it exasperating? Where's the fairness in life, when the Simons of this world sit at big empty polished desks feeling important and knowing damn-all about anything, and they can't even understand sarcasm or irony?

'Sit down, Alison,' he said, still not looking at me.

Here we go.

'I . . . er . . . it's not that there's anything wrong with your work.'

Yes, here we go. I held my breath.

'It's your time-keeping.'

'I know. I know, I'm sorry . . . ' I began, desperately, hating myself for the desperation. 'I've had a few problems, but hopefully, now . . . ,'

'The thing is,' he drawled, finally looking up and meeting my eyes with a cold stare. 'The thing is that the company really can't afford all these lost hours. Look at it from the company's point of view, Alison.'

Oh yes, silly me. And there was I worrying about my mortgage and my phone bill.

'But I always make up for any hours I miss,' I said, trying to sound less like grovelling appeasement and more like righteous indignation.

'No substitute for reliability,' said Simon, leaning back in his chair and repeating it slowly to himself as if it were a prayer.

'No . . . substitute . . . for . . . reliability.'

We looked at each other across the polished empty desk. He with the Pierre Cardin shirt and the father in Portugal and all the balls in his court. Me with a mortgage and a red phone bill to pay, a cat in hospital on a drip and a car with things hanging off it, and despair in my heart.

'Please,' I said. My voice came out wobbly. 'Please give me another chance. I'll be reliable. I'll think about the company. I'll . . . I'll tell my car not to break down . . . ,'

I considered offering him a quick shag but I didn't think he'd realise I was joking.

He got up and walked to the window. My fate hung limply, anxiously, in his hands.

'I'm not an unreasonable person,' he told the potted plant on the windowsill. 'Let's call this a Serious Warning, shall we, Alison?'

The plant didn't respond.

'That's very reasonable,' I heard a pathetic, obsequious voice saying. 'Thank you, Simon. I appreciate——'

'But this Serious Warning is going into your Personal File.'

The pathetic obsequious person nodded agreement. Of course, the Personal File. No more than I deserve. A public flogging would be more appropriate but please, the Personal File, by all means, absolutely.

'And if there's any repetition, Alison, any repetition whatsoever, I will make NO exceptions—'

'Of course. I understand.'

'Nobody likes to have to let an employee go.' The ultimate threat. It vibrated in the air between us, making me shudder.

'Thank you,' I said again, as I got up and scurried out, mouse-like, trailing my shame behind me.

'How did it go?' smirked Snotty-Nosed Nicola as I passed her desk.

'Lovely, thanks,' I smiled at her. 'He's a terrific lay, isn't he?'

The vet phoned,' said Lucy when I got home late after working two hours of detention to make up for Missing Time. 'Apple Pie's got to stay in for at least two nights to stabilise him and then he's got to be on drugs for ever.'

'For ever?' I stared at her, dazed. 'Stabilise? What's wrong with him?'

'Renal something or other. He said it was touch and go but he hopes to stabilise him.'

I phoned the surgery.

'I can't afford . . .' I tried to whisper into the phone without Lucy hearing me. 'I haven't got Pet Save Insurance.' I felt like the sad case in a TV advert for Pet Save. This family didn't take out insurance. This family did (camera switches to glowing, smarmy-smiling mother and father fondly watching perfectly groomed children playing with Happily Recovered pet). So guess which parents wish they'd never been born?

'There isn't any option,' said the vet in his serious, professional, I'm-getting-your-money-voice. 'Apple Pie will need these drugs to stay alive.'

'Is Apple Pie going to be all right?' Lucy asked me, studying my face anxiously as I hung up the phone.

I changed my face from worried sick to calm and reassuring as only a mother can, and gave her a hug.

'Yes, he'll be fine.'

It's only money, isn't it.

Is Paul there, please?'

Shit. As if it wasn't bad enough having to phone Paul to beg for money, bloody Lynnette had to answer the phone. If I hadn't needed the money so much, I'd have hung up. I'd have done almost anything rather than have to speak to Lynnette.

THE TROUBLE WITH ALLY

'Oh, *hello*, Ally!' she trilled gaily like a budgie having an orgasm. 'How are *you*? How are the girls?'

As if you gave a shit.

'Wonderful, thanks,' I said sourly.

'I'll get Paul for you. *Paul, darling!*'

I felt my teeth clenching together with irritation. *Paul, darling?*

Give me a break. This is my husband, remember? I've known him for longer than you've been out of nappies, and I know just how much he hates that sort of pretentious rubbish.

'Ally, darling!' said Paul when he picked up the phone. She's changing him. The bitch.

The thing about Lynnette—apart from the fact that she stole my husband and she was twenty years younger than me—the thing I really disliked about her was her snobbishness. I mean, who the hell did she think she was? She was nothing special. I had serious doubts that her name was even Lynnette really. I suspected it was Lynn, and she added the 'ette' to make herself sound little and cute.

'It's the cat,' I said now to Paul. 'He's ill.'

'Is it serious?'

Ridiculously, annoyingly, I felt my eyes welling up with tears. It was the same whenever I spoke to Paul about something like this.

When Lucy broke her wrist falling down the steps of a nightclub. When Victoria got rushed into hospital with appendicitis. I was fine, I coped, I didn't even consider going to pieces—not until I heard his voice. Calm, strong, reassuring as ever, sounding like he still cared. If you still care, I wanted to cry, I wanted to pummel his chest and yell—if you still care, why did you go? Why, why, why won't you come back?

But of course, it wasn't me he cared about. It was Lucy's broken wrist, it was Victoria's operation, it was the cat being ill. Nothing to do with me.

'It sounds serious,' I said now, swallowing back the tears. 'Something to do with his kidneys. The vet's kept him in, put him on a drip . . .'

'Poor Apple Pie. Poor old boy. The girls must be upset.'

So am I! So am I upset! Comfort me! Care about me! Come back to me!

'Yes. He's getting old, of course, but still . . .'

'Is the vet hopeful? Can they get him better?'

'He's talking about stabilising him. But it means drugs-for-the-rest-of-his-life.'

'Well, whatever it takes. We can't just let him die. Poor old boy.'

'I know. I wish I'd taken out Pet Save.'

The TV advert family with their smarmy-smiling children drew together in my mind, arms around their grinning healthy labrador.

'You'll need some help with the vet bills,' said Paul matter-of-factly.

I hated it. Hated the fact that he knew that was why I was phoning. Not to let him know the cat was ill, but because I needed money.

'Yes. Sorry, I know it's a bit soon after the money for the car.'

'Can't be helped.'

'And I had a prang today. Taxi went into the back of me.' I wasn't going to tell him that. Why the hell did I tell him that?

'Jesus, Ally! Were you all right?'

This time my eyes overflowed completely. I couldn't answer. I sniffed and gasped as the tears ran down my nose and into my mouth.

'Ally? What is it? Were you hurt?'

'No,' I managed to get out eventually with a lot of sniffing. 'No, I was fine. It wasn't anything much. Just . . . annoying . . .'

'God, you've had some bad luck lately. You poor thing. Listen, get the vet to send the bills to me, all right? And you take care of yourself.'

Take care. Oh, you bastard, why do you say it? Why sound as if you care about me when you don't. When you walked out on me for a girl of twenty-eight and ruined my life? And I want to hate you but I can't. I put down the phone, blew my nose, hard, and looked round to find Lucy and Victoria watching me.

'Cup of tea, Mum?' asked Victoria, putting an arm round me.

'I'll do the dinner,' said Lucy, giving me a quick kiss. 'Sit down and put your feet up, Mum.'

Made me bloody cry again! Who needs men, anyway? I had my daughters to care about me, didn't I? With their help I'd survive another crisis and live to tell the tale . . . wouldn't I?

With their help, and Paul's money.

Chapter 2

AT THIS STAGE in the proceedings, I didn't know anything about the surprise party for my fiftieth birthday that was being planned with great and elaborate subterfuge by my daughters, aided and abetted by my mother. I suppose I should sound more grateful, but actually I don't like surprises very much, on account of the fact that I tend to react all wrong. There were some strange things going on at home; things that I only understood the strangeness of in retrospect. The phone would ring and one of the daughters would dive on it, knocking me out of the way, and slam a door shut between me and the conversation. Furtive talk involving pieces of paper would stop when I entered a room, with the papers being shuffled out of sight. The date of the Saturday after my birthday was marked with a red ring on the calendar, and when I asked why, there were Strange Looks passed between the daughters before they explained that I was being taken out for a celebratory meal, and that I must keep the evening free. Keeping an evening free had never been a problem since about 1969, so I was able to reassure them that I wouldn't be getting any other offers and I'd look forward to the night out with them.

'What do you want for your birthday, Mum?' asked Victoria, perhaps to throw me off the scent, not that I'd even had a sniff of the scent.

'Drugs for the cat,' I said. 'And a bumper for the car.'

'Dad's doing that,' she replied briskly. 'I'll get you some flowers.'

We picked Apple Pie up from the vet on the Saturday morning. He was huddled in the corner of his basket looking lonely and miserable. Half of one paw had been shaved where the drip had gone in.

'Poor baby,' cooed Victoria, opening the basket and scooping him up into her arms.

He looked up at her in bewilderment, yowling faintly.

'He doesn't recognise us,' she said, alarmed.

'That'll be the drugs,' said Lucy authoritatively.

'I'm sure he'll be fine when you get him home,' smiled the veterinary nurse condescendingly.

Apple Pie turned his head to the sound of her voice and blinked lovingly at her. Lucy gave her a look of pure hatred.

'That'll be one-hundred-and-thirty-nine-pounds seventy-five pence,' she rattled off with a beaming smile.

'Could you send the bill to my husband, please?' I beamed back. Ex-husband. Separated husband. Husband who isn't really a husband any more. 'Mr Paul Bridgeman, 32a Tilehouse Mews . . .'

The beam had vanished abruptly from the condescending face. She put her hand over the cat basket as if to stop it leaving the premises.

'We insist on payment at the time of completion of treatment,' she said stiffly, pointing to a notice on the wall behind her, which obediently stated: 'We insist on payment at the time of completion of treatment.'

'His treatment isn't complete,' pointed out Victoria. 'You said he'll need the drugs for the rest of his life.'

'Each repeat prescription will be billed as a separate treatment,' chanted the white-coat wonder, pointing to another sign behind her stating —'guess what?' I wondered idly how many more signs she'd learned off by heart. I resisted the urge to test her on the adverts for Pet Save (complete with smarmy-smiling family and healthy labrador).

'So that's one-hundred-and-thirty-nine-pounds-seventy-five,' she repeated with slightly less of a beam. 'Please.'

'I haven't got it,' I whispered.

I looked round the waiting room, not wanting there to be anyone witnessing my shame. An elderly lady was sitting by the door with an elderly poodle on a lead, and two children were waiting with something small and scampery in a cardboard box.

'Pardon?' said the nurse.

'I said, I haven't got it. I haven't got any money.'

In my mind, the waiting room became a scene from a musical. The elderly lady and the two children leapt to their feet and struck poses of horrified indignation.

'She hasn't got the money! She hasn't got the money?
She hasn't got the money for the cat!'

The nurse danced into the middle of the floor clutching Apple Pie's basket and singing in the slow, growly voice of the villain:

'People say They Can't Pay!
I won't give them time of day.
I insist on PAYMENT ON COMPLETION!'

'Mum,' whispered Lucy urgently, shaking my arm, drowning out the music in my mind. 'Mum! What are we going to do?'

'What are we going to do? I repeated. 'We're going to phone your dad again, of course.'

And the hero comes striding onto the stage, sweeping aside the villain with a single sweeping aside of his velvet cloak, throwing the bags of gold onto the table with a contemptuous gesture.

'Money? Is that all you want? Here—take the lot. It means nothing to me. All I care about is that my Apple Pie should be set free . . .' And the music reaches a crescendo as he takes the heroine into his arms—

'Paul? Yes, it's me. Listen, we've got a bit of a problem. I hate to ask, but could you possibly . . . Are you sure you don't mind? See you in a while, then.'

We sat down to wait, while Apple Pie was put back in his basket and out of our reach in case of escape attempts, and while the elderly lady took the elderly poodle in to have his boils lanced, and while the two children took the cardboard box in to have its occupant checked for lice.

'Hi, Ally, *darling*! Sorry, I got here as quickly as I could!'

He'd sent Lynnette. How could he? I'd never forgive him. How could he humiliate me like this? I looked at the floor. The girls coughed and stood up and tried to be polite.

'Paul forgot,' she trilled sweetly. 'He had to go to a meeting.'

On a Saturday? What, a race meeting, a meeting of minds?

'So he asked me to come over with the chequebook. A little rescue mission!'

She giggled happily at this most insulting thing that had ever been said to me in my entire life. *The* chequebook? His and hers? To rescue *me*? From financial embarrassment? *She*, who'd inherited, without lifting a finger, the serious majority of the financial standing of the man whose career I'd helped to shape from the day he took his O levels? Whose chequebook she'd effectively stolen from me?

'Thank you, but I'll manage without it. Without the rescue mission,' I retorted coldly.

'Mum!' hissed Victoria, sitting down next to me. 'Come on, we have to. Apple Pie needs—'

'I'll get the money somehow,' I told her fiercely. 'I'll borrow it. I'll go to the bank.'

'But I'm more than happy to help,' said Lynnette.

I finally looked at her face, her so-much-younger-than-me face, with its absence of worry lines and wrinkles, with its perfect make-up even on a Saturday morning, with its frame of cascading wavy red hair, its oh-so-sincere grey-green eyes with their perfect long lashes. And I wanted to smack that smug smile off her face so badly I had to sit on my hands.

'I don't need your help,' I said, firmly, loudly. So loudly that Miss White Coat came out of the consulting room at an anxious trot.

'Everything all right?' she asked nervously.

'I want to see the vet,' I said, in my new Firm and Loud voice. 'Now. Please.'

The vet came out of the consulting room wiping his hands on a paper towel. 'Mrs Bridgeman,' he said cheerfully. 'How can I help you?'

'You can help me'—I told him in my no-nonsense, don't mess with me voice—'by *not* insisting on payment on completion.'

'Sorry?' He looked around the room for enlightenment. 'I don't think I understand.'

'I haven't got any money,' I said, in my not-beating-about-the-bush voice. 'But my husband will settle your bill. I'd just like you to send him the bill. Please.'

'Or you can give me the bill, and I'll settle it now,' smiled Lynnette.

'No, you can't. She can't settle it.'

'Mum,' whispered Lucy, 'don't be embarrassing.'

'Take her bloody cheque,' whispered Victoria. 'Who cares?'

'I care,' I returned. 'She's not paying for our cat, and that's that.'

'Be reasonable, Ally, darling,' said Lynnette through her teeth. 'It's the same chequebook that Paul would use if the bill was sent to us.'

'But I don't want you signing the cheque.'

'It's Dad's money,' said Victoria. 'You know it is. It's not her money.'

No. She probably spent all hers getting her eyelashes to look like that.

'If you can't pay now,' said the vet, looking exasperated, 'I'm afraid I can't allow the cat to leave the premises.'

'Oh, Mum!' howled Lucy. 'That's not fair on Apple Pie, is it?'

'You can't keep him here, if he's better,' I told the vet coldly.

'But you can't take him home without his drugs.'

Trump card. Ace of spades. The drugs. There they were, on the counter. I could see them. As I watched, Miss White Coat picked them up and put them in her pocket. Thanks, bitch.

'If we pay for the drugs now,' I said, my voice having somehow slipped back to its normal Quiet and Timid, 'will you agree to bill my husband for the rest of the fees? Please?' The vet stared at me, stared at Lynnette with her perfect smile, holding the pen poised over the cheque-book, looked at White Coat, shook his head and shrugged.

'I don't see why . . . I don't understand the difference . . .'

'Nor do I,' muttered Lucy.

So perhaps I was deranged. Perhaps I was teetering on the edge of a nervous breakdown. Perhaps they ought to watch out in case I went berserk. But Victoria suddenly spoke up in a new firm-and-loud voice which she must have mysteriously inherited from me:

'It matters to my mum. It matters more than the actual money. My dad will send you the cheque straight away. So please just let us take the drugs and take our cat home.'

It was dignified. It was calm and impressive. I was impressed, anyway, and, as nobody else spoke, I can only assume that they were all too choked with emotion. Lynnette wrote the cheque for the drugs, handed it over, and the package reappeared from the pocket of the white coat. Apple Pie was released into our custody.

The balance of power had been retained.

'Just be careful,' warned the vet as we turned to go, 'about letting him out. Watch where he goes.'

What was this? A kidnap threat?

'Didn't my nurse explain to you?'

His nurse looked suitably shamefaced, studying her nails.

'This type of kidney failure is often caused by poisoning.'

'*Poisoning?*'

'Probably slug pellets. They're the worst. Gardeners don't realise cats pick them up. They're lethal. He's lucky he didn't succumb.'

Succumb. Such a deceptive word. It sounds soft and sleepy, like suckle and snuggle and slumber, and it lures you unsuspectingly to a dark and dreadful death, courtesy of a slug pellet.

'I wish I knew where I could get some,' I said viciously, looking meaningfully at Lynnette as she put her chequebook—Paul's chequebook—carefully away in her handbag. Even Apple Pie shrank away from the tone of my voice.

Well, you say things like that, don't you? You don't necessarily mean them.

'There was no need for that, Ally,' Lynnette reproached me in a hurt After-All-I've-Done-For-You whine as we left the premises and headed for our separate cars.

'Joke,' I said, sourly.

I had a couple of good friends at work. They weren't all like Snotty-Nosed Nicola and her admiring posse of hangers-on, thank God. Liz, who worked in the same office as me, was only a couple of years younger than me, and Mary, who worked in accounts and usually had lunch with us, had celebrated her own half-century a few years previously. So it was inevitable that conversation occasionally turned towards the ageing process and its effect on our physical and emotional health. Whether we'd survive to see our pensions and whether they'd be worth anything by the time we did. The usual cheerful, life-enhancing sort of discussions you have to cheer you up during a depressing day at work.

'When I had my fiftieth,' said Mary over lasagne and chips a few days later, 'Derek took me to New York.'

'Lovely.'

'And we saw Michael Bolton in concert.'

Ah well. Can't win 'em all.

'I'd like that,' I mused, toying with my chips. 'I'd like to jet off somewhere, with someone, and never come back,' I said, smiling triumphantly as if I'd just made a serious decision.

'What about your kids?' asked Liz.

'They wouldn't miss me,' I sighed.

'Not till the money ran out!' laughed Mary.

'Then they'd have to cope.'

Was this really me talking? Being so harsh and uncaring? But it was true, wasn't it? At their age, I was Fending For Myself, Standing On My Own Two Feet. My home was obviously too comfortable for them, with its stereo CD-players and volumising hairdryers and no ice on the insides of the windows. Why would they want to go and stand on their own two feet somewhere less comfortable? Why would they want to learn to cook, or load a dishwasher? No, the obvious solution would be for me to leave them where they were, and jet off somewhere myself.

'What are you grinning about?' asked Liz.

'The more I think about it, the better it sounds,' I said, sauce dripping off the chip which hung, forgotten, from my fork. 'I could come back and see them whenever I wanted. By private jet.'

'Or helicopter,' smiled Mary, getting into the game.

'And I'd invite them out there whenever I had a big party.'

'Banquet,' Mary corrected me.

'Ball,' I said firmly. 'I always fancied a ball. A ball with a banquet.'

'Never mind, Ally,' said Liz in her usual gentle way. 'I'm sure your party will be just as nice.'

There was a silence that lasted probably only about ten seconds. For about as long as it takes for a chip to fall off a fork. Roughly about as long as it takes for two people to gasp and look at each other in a way that very definitely says 'Oh shit!' without actually saying it.

'I'm not having a party,' I said.

'No. But if you did. If you did, it would be nice.'

'But I don't even want a party.'

'Well, then!' said Mary in a very hearty tone. 'Good job you're not having one, isn't it!'

'Yes,' I said, looking at her suspiciously, resentfully. I had this unhappy, niggly feeling that I was being taken the piss out of.

'So what are you doing, for your fiftieth, then, Ally?' soothed Liz. 'Something nice?'

With all this niceness around, I was beginning to feel a little sick. I thought about the 'nice' birthday meal the girls were supposedly organising for me and something suddenly came over me. Whose bloody birthday was this, after all?

'Nothing,' I said, firmly and cheerfully. 'I'm not doing anything.'

'Oh, really?' said Liz. 'Why? Why nothing at all?'

'Because,' I said, suddenly finding an interest in my chips again, 'I'm not going to be fifty. Not till next year. I'm only forty-nine this birthday!'

And that was the first lie.

THE TROUBLE WITH ALLY

I read somewhere once that the first lie is the hardest; after that it gets easier. *I didn't mean to fall in love with another woman. I didn't want it to happen. I didn't intend to have sex with her, even though she was twenty years younger than you and had beautiful red wavy hair and grey-green eyes and was offering herself to me on a plate like a cheap tart. I tried to stop it. I tried to say no. I tried to think of you and the children, the cat, the fishpond. I didn't want to leave you. I didn't mean . . . I didn't want . . . I loved you . . .*

Lies, lies, lies. So easy. I didn't find the first lie hard at all, because I just said it without thinking about it. It didn't seem such a terrible thing to say. It didn't really matter at all. Who cared whether I was fifty, or forty-nine, or a hundred and one that birthday, that June the fifth?

It just made the next lie a little bit easier, that was all.

In the backstage of my life, people were tearing around like blue-arsed flies, making phone calls, exchanging gasps and exclamations, cancelling things. Cancelling parties. Me, I sailed on blissfully unaware, well perhaps not blissfully but you get the picture. Giving the cat his drugs and trying to watch where he went in case he picked up slug pellets from some inconsiderate gardener's vegetable patch, feeding people and listening to their problems, tying the number plate on to the rear bumper of the car and tying it back again when it fell off, and so on, and so on. And it was getting warmer again, and there was less wearing of double layers of dressing gowns and more opening of windows, and April drifted into May with sunshine and short sleeves and diets in the house in order to get into bikinis for the summer, and it was at least a couple of weeks before I got the phone call from Paul.

'Ally, what the bloody hell's going on?'

'About what, in particular?'

'Your birthday. What are you playing at? You're fifty this year.'

'I know. I can't help it.' Well, he made it sound like an accusation. 'You were fifty, three years ago.'

'We're not disputing my age, here. What is it? Are you afraid of admitting it, or something? Have you got a problem with it?'

'Of course I haven't. What do you take me for? I don't have to try to compete with your young——'

'Don't start that.'

I didn't. I didn't start it, actually. You did, when you went off with her.

'You've been saying you're not fifty till next year.'

Oh. The Lie had caught up with me. But how?

'How? How did you hear that?'

'Never mind. The fact is——

347

'No, I do mind. I don't understand. It was only two girls at work, going on and on about fiftieth birthdays, and I decided to shut them up by telling them I wasn't going to be fifty. I was bored with the conversation. Who the hell told you?'

'Victoria did. She's worried about you.'

Could have fooled me. She'd been out in her car with her latest boyfriend every night for the past week.

'How did she know?'

'Doesn't matter. The fact is, Ally, people turn fifty every day. It's no big deal. It's not old, nowadays, in fact it's the beginning of a whole new era.'

'Who do you think you're talking to, you patronising git?!'

Well, honestly! The cheek!

'The girls and I are worried about you. Seriously. You seem to be in denial.'

'No I'm not!'

'See what I mean? Now, listen. We've cancelled the party. Fine, if you didn't want the party, in the frame of mind you're in, it's better if it's cancelled, but . . .'

'Party?' I said in a small voice.

'But you do really need to face up to this. This birthday. You can't spend the rest of your life running away, pretending . . .'

'I wasn't. I didn't know—'

'And while I'm at it: I know you're under a bit of a strain, but there was no need to speak to Lynnette the way you did.'

'Sorry?'

'The other weekend. At the vet's. She very generously offered to come and help you out with the cat . . .'

With your chequebook.

'And you caused a scene in the waiting room, apparently. Embarrassed everyone. And threatened to get some slug pellets to poison her.'

'It was a joke,' I said, still in my little, dazed voice. Like a child being unexpectedly told off despite being good all day. I could feel tears pricking at my eyes. Were you supposed to cry when you were told off when you were nearly fifty?

'Not funny, Ally. Remember what we used to tell the children? It's only a joke if everybody's laughing. Lynnette wasn't laughing.'

No, well. She's a miserable, boring cow with no sense of humour, but I didn't choose her as a mistress, did I?

'I'm not going to apologise,' I said, suddenly shaking myself out of my role of the naughty child and stamping my foot to match. 'It's about time she learned to take a joke. And stopped using your chequebook.'

'It's *our* chequebook,' he said, coldly. 'And it's about time you stopped being so jealous and spiteful, and tried to accept Lynnette as a friend. I really think you need some counselling, or something. You're fifty, Ally. Face it.'

And he hung up.

He hung up!

I stared at the phone. It was such a surprise.

We never argued, normally, not even since we'd separated. We'd been Amicable. Reasonable. Sensible. We'd agreed it was Better Like That. But was it? Who was I trying to fool? What hidden anger and hatred lurked beneath the surface of that reasonableness, that sensibleness? Perhaps I did need some counselling. Perhaps I really was cracking up. And anyway. What was all that about a party?

Chapter 3

'WHAT'S ALL THIS about a party?' I asked Lucy when she sloped downstairs to refuel with more crisps and Coke for some serious revision.

'It was supposed to be a surprise,' she shrugged.

'Sorry,' I said. 'I didn't realise . . . you must have gone to a lot of trouble.'

'Doesn't matter, Mum,' she shrugged again, looking in the fridge as if for inspiration. Then she turned to look at me. 'But are you all right?'

'All right, how?'

'Dad thinks you're in denial and you need counselling.'

'Oh. Nice of him to tell you. I suppose the whole world thinks I've flipped my lid, just because I didn't want everyone going on and on and on about being fifty?'

'Well, women are supposed to start getting a bit strange at your age, aren't they?' she replied affably, turning her attention back to the fridge with the lack of concern it's only possible to display about such a statement at the age of nineteen.

'**S**elfish, I call it,' declared my mother, filling up my kettle from my sink to make herself a cup of my tea. Without offering me one.

'I'm sorry that's how you see it,' I sighed. It wasn't worth arguing with her. I'd learned that much, if nothing else in my life since I left school.

'Everyone was looking forward to it,' she said, slamming down the kettle and plugging it in with vicious energy. Amazing how a bit of temper improved the arthritis in her hands.

'I'll have a cup of tea, too, please, while you're at it,' I said, trying to balance the washing basket on one hip while putting the Sunday joint in the oven on the way to the washing machine.

'Expect me to do it all,' tutted my mother irritably, slamming another mug on to the table and manhandling the kettle again. 'At my age.' Perhaps I'd rather be nearly eighty than nearly fifty (in denial)?

It was over Sunday lunch that she announced she was going away. It was done at the moment of everyone's first mouthful, for maximum effect. Well, get stuck in everybody; mmm, looks lovely doesn't it; got enough mint sauce, Nan? What's that you say? You're going where?

'Majorca.'

'Who are you going with, Nan?' asked Lucy brightly.

'A friend,' said my mother enigmatically.

She stuffed a huge piece of roast lamb into her mouth and chewed quickly, concentrating on her plate.

'What friend?' persisted Lucy.

'Never you mind.'

The girls and I looked at each other across the table. My mother continued to chew her lamb, looking at her plate. Lucy raised her eyebrows and Victoria stifled a giggle. I threw down my knife and fork. I couldn't help it. It was such a shock.

'It's a man, isn't it?'

'So? So why shouldn't it be? So what's wrong with a person having a holiday with a friend?' she gabbled, spitting gravy all over the tablecloth. 'Unless of course you want to deprive me of every last little pleasure I'm likely to get in this life . . .'

Lucy and Victoria were by now convulsed.

'Of course there's nothing wrong with it,' I soothed. 'Nobody's trying to spoil your . . . pleasure . . .'

I hadn't even realised I was going to start laughing. It was the girls, falling off their chairs giggling like that, setting me off. It was the word 'pleasure'. It suddenly reminded me of giving Victoria The Lecture, the first time she went away with a boyfriend. Should I be talking to my mother about Safe Sex? Should I ask her whether she'd booked single rooms, the way she used to ask me when I went away with Paul?

'I'm sure I don't know what's so funny,' she snapped, red in the face.

Lucy was almost crying, holding her sides, gasping for breath. 'Nan's getting more nooky than I am!' she said eventually.

'Lucy!' I hissed at her nervously, trying not to start laughing again myself. 'Nobody's talking about nooky.'

'His name's *not* Nicky,' declared my mother, laying down her knife and fork and sitting up straight, looking at us all severely over her glasses. 'It's Ted.'

Lucy pretended to need the toilet, but didn't manage to get there before the scream of manic laughter burst out of her. Victoria calmly collected the lunch plates (not finished) and made it into the kitchen before giving into spluttering noises which she tried to drown by running the taps.

'So how long have you known this . . . Ted?' I asked Mother in the dignified silence that followed.

'A year or so,' she replied defensively.

'And how old is he?'

And what are his prospects? And what do his parents do?

'He's sixty-six, if it's got anything to do with you.'

A toy boy!

'Well, good for you,' I said, meaning it, really meaning it. Good for her. Why the hell not? 'When are you going?'

'Friday. And we'll be needing a lift to the airport. Ted can't drive. He's got cataracts.'

I nearly found myself thinking that that explained a lot. But I couldn't be so nasty as to think that, could I?

On the Tuesday night, Apple Pie went missing.

'He hasn't had his evening tablet,' said Victoria, staring dismally out of the back door.

'Apple Pie!' I shouted in the middle of the garden at midnight, prowling around the shrubbery with a torch. 'Apple Pie! Come on, Apple Pie, where are you?' There comes a time in your life when you really, really wish you hadn't given your cat a silly name.

'Good boy, Appley! Come on, Apples, good boy!' echoed Lucy.

When two o'clock struck with no sign of the cat, I announced that I was calling off the search until first light and going to get some sleep.

'Mum, how *could* you?' accused Victoria, close to tears. 'He could be anywhere . . .'

'He's probably asleep,' I yawned. 'Asleep somewhere nice and snug and warm, and can't even hear us shouting. When we get up in the morning he'll be lying in his bed large as life——'

'And going into kidney failure,' moaned Lucy. 'He hasn't had his tablet.'

'Missing one dose isn't going to hurt him,' I said with more confidence than I felt. 'Now come on, we'll all be better able to help him when we're not so tired.'

Still moaning and sniffing back tears, the girls allowed themselves to be shepherded up to bed as if they were still eight and ten years old. I tucked them in and kissed them good night as if they were still eight and ten years old. They protested that they'd never be able to sleep a wink, and then they both fell immediately into a deep and untroubled sleep—as if they were still eight and ten years old.

I, meanwhile, lay on top of my bed in my clothes (just in case I should hear him meowing or crying in the garden), and tossed and turned, and turned and tossed, and drifted once or twice into a fitful doze. At seven o'clock, I got up and went downstairs to reassure myself that Apple Pie was indeed curled up in his bed large as life. But he wasn't. No cat, curled up or otherwise. No cat at all.

'Perhaps we should search the pond,' I said at breakfast.

'Oh, Mum!' howled Lucy. 'What are you saying?'

'I'm not *saying* anything,' I tried to pacify her. She shook off my pacifying arm. 'I just think we should reassure ourselves.'

'Mum's right,' said Victoria stoutly. 'We shouldn't leave any stone unturned, Lucy. Come on, Luce!' She tried a bit of pacifying herself. 'We'll find him!'

'What, at the bottom of the pond?' shuddered Lucy.

I shuddered myself. I swallowed a lump of tears down quickly with my coffee. I loved the damned cat too, you know.

By the time we'd got all of the water out of the pond, we'd blamed everyone. It was Paul's fault for having a fishpond. It was my fault for not filling it in after he moved out. It was the fishes' fault for living so long, for needing a pond to carry on their lives in. It was Lucy's fault for not calling Apple Pie in for his evening tablet before it got dark. It was Victoria's fault for going out for the evening when it was supposed to be her turn to call him in for his evening tablet.

'Turn?' I asked in amazement, emptying another bucket of slimy water. 'You have *turns* at calling in the cat?'

I tell you, you don't even know what goes on in your own house.

'I think,' said Victoria, stepping gingerly down into the weedy shallows remaining at the bottom of the pond, 'we can see now, can't we?'

We all followed her gaze as she stirred the water uneasily from side to side with a net.

'Nothing,' she said, and her voice came out squeakily with relief.

We all fell silent as we contemplated the empty pond (now needing a fast refill) and, more to the point, we contemplated, without any of us wanting to voice it to the others, the fact that it was now midmorning and if Apple Pie wasn't in the pond then where was he?

And then the phone rang, and we all became aware that midmorning on a Wednesday, we were supposed to be elsewhere.

'That'll be my work!' exclaimed Victoria as I went to answer it. 'Tell them I'm sick!'

But, of course, it wasn't her work. It was mine. It was Snotty-Nosed Simon, Simon who controlled my life, who had entered my Serious Warning on to my Personal Record, who would never understand about draining a pond to look for a cat, never in a million years.

'I'm sorry, Simon,' I said. 'I'm sick.'

That was the second lie. It was amazing how easy it was. Like I'd been born to it, like I was lying every day of my life. I didn't even feel any shame, any regret. Oh, I don't doubt Victoria did it, probably every time she fancied a lie-in, she had the flu or an upset stomach. But let me tell you, she hadn't been brought up to it, and no, neither had I. Much less had I! But, the fact is, I seemed almost overnight to have become an accomplished liar.

'Oh, dear,' said Simon, sounding unconvinced and not a little bored. 'What seems to be the trouble?'

'Sickness,' I said, vaguely. 'Bad, really bad sickness. I'd better go, I think I'm going to be sick again.'

'Well, I hope you feel better—'

I hung up, doing a good impression of someone just about to be sick again.

We all went sick that day. Victoria invented a sore throat and Lucy, who was only supposed to be in college for the morning anyway, said she'd think of her excuse when she went back the next day. We searched the shed. We searched the house, opening cupboard doors and throwing their contents onto the floor. We crawled under beds, we peered up chimneys. We walked the streets, calling out 'Apple Pie' dismally and gloomily and ignoring the looks we got from passers-by, who probably thought we were homeless and hungry.

Finally, Victoria said she'd drive around in her car with the windows down and Lucy said she'd go with her and lean out of the windows, looking. They went to the car and discovered the windows to be already open. And Apple Pie asleep on the back seat.

'You must have left the windows open when you got home last night!'

Lucy shouted at her sister, inexplicably bursting into tears as she lunged at the surprised cat and grasped him fiercely to her chest. He hung awkwardly in her arms, half strangled by the tightness of her embrace. 'Poor baby,' she moaned, burying her face in his fur.

'Poor baby, nothing!' I retorted, suddenly tired and exasperated by the whole episode now that he'd turned up safe. 'He hasn't been shut in there against his will. He probably crept in there during the night when it was cold and he's been lying there all the time we've been calling for him. He's just bloody ignored us! All that work draining the pond.'

'Mum,' rebuked Victoria. 'Suppose he *had* been in there?'

'I'd been supposing it all the time we were emptying it, thanks very much. To say nothing of supposing him lying in a ditch somewhere, or having been hit by a car, or having swallowed some more slug pellets.

'Yes. Well. He wasn't, was he?' I snapped.

It was late in the afternoon and not worth going back to work. I cleaned the oven.

The car didn't want to start the next morning. I reminded it, firmly but kindly, of all I'd done for it recently. All Paul had spent on it. How it had embarrassed me in front of the AA man and I'd still loved it. I promised it faithfully that if it would stop sulking, I'd get its bumper fixed as soon as I had time, and money, and furthermore I would get its rear number plate fitted on properly. I just needed it to start today. Please. *Please.* When it still wouldn't start, I got out, slammed its door and swore at it. It could wear its number plate tied on with bits of string for the rest of its life for all I cared. Bloody thing.

'What's up, Mum?' asked Victoria sweetly, tottering out to her own car in some high heels that it was impossible to imagine her driving in. How could you put your foot down on a pedal when your foot was six inches above the floor?

'Bloody car won't start. Again,' I muttered. 'And if I call out the AA it'll make a fool of me. I just know it. And it'll probably be the same guy.'

'What was he like? Nice?' she asked, hesitating. You could see the antennae coming out. Man alert! Was it worth her hanging around to do some chatting up?

'Old. At least fifty,' I smiled.

She pulled a face and opened the car door.

'Give me a lift to work?' I asked.

'All right. Hurry up.'

I grabbed my jacket and rushed to get into the car before she changed her mind.

'Although . . .'

Here we go. I've got to go the other way. I've got to pick up five friends.

'Why don't you stay off work and get it sorted out, while you've got the chance?'

'Stay off work? You must be joking.' I tried to keep the hysteria out of my voice. 'I might as well phone up Simon and ask him to sack me. I might as well say I've decided I don't need a job any more.'

'But he thinks you're sick.'

So he did.

'You could still be sick.'

So I could.

I paused, halfway to sitting down in Victoria's car.

'Make up your mind, Mum. I've got to get to work.'

I got out and waved her goodbye. And in a way, that was the third lie, although I didn't actually say anything. I just pretended, inside my head, that I was still sick. And I called AA Home Start (it was a different guy, and he was actually about twenty-five and very good-looking. Eat your heart out, Victoria!), and he jump-started the bastard and we got it to a garage. And they said We'll See What We Can Do (with much head-scratching and wiping of hands on oily rags) about having it ready for tomorrow morning—'Can't promise, love, depends what we find when we get under the bonnet, know what I mean, love?—And I walked home from the garage and thought about everyone at work, managing without me, and I felt as if I were on holiday. I swung my arms, I held my head back to feel the sunshine on my face, and I laughed out loud. An elderly woman shook her head and said something about drug addicts, which made me laugh even more. Her scowl reminded me of my mum.

My mum.

Shit, shit and thrice shit. She needed a lift to the airport tomorrow. She and her half-blind toy boy and their baggage for Majorca. I stopped dead in the street, upsetting a few more pedestrians, and wondered about going back to the garage and telling them I had to have the bastard car back for the morning, working or not. Then I told myself to calm down and talk sense. What good would it be if it wasn't working? There was only one thing for it.

'Victoria? Yes, it's Mum. No, nothing's wrong. Yes, the AA man came. No, he wasn't fifty, he was young and gorgeous and I've got a date with him for tomorrow night. I don't know why, he must just like older women. Listen, Victoria, darling . . . What do you mean, what am I after? Look, can you get the day off work tomorrow?'

Oh, typical, I see. Just bloody typical. Tomorrow is the day she happens to have booked a day off anyway, to go out for the day with the
new Darren in her life.

'Why tomorrow?' I pleaded. 'Can't you do that another day?'

It had to be tomorrow, apparently, because it was the second anniversary of Victoria and the new Darren going out together.

Second anniversary as in two weeks.

'Can't you go for a nice drive together to Gatwick Airport? With Nan
and her boyfriend?'

'I *like* Darren,' said Victoria pointedly.

'Can't you go out in his car?' (and I can borrow yours).

'He hasn't got one.'

'Don't you ever wonder whether some of these boys are only after you
for your car?'

'Why do you think I love my car so much?'

Can't argue with that one, can you?

I phoned Paul in the evening, after I'd checked with the garage about
the state of my car.

'They say it might be ready,' I explained to him after we'd got over the
initial slight coldness in the conversation caused by him hanging up on
me last time we talked. We got over it by me being very pathetic and
creepy and apologetic. Blaming it all on hormones, which I hate to do.
But the thing was, I was after something, wasn't I. 'But I have to leave at
nine thirty to get Mum to the airport. And it's *not* ready . . .'

'She'll kill you.'

'You know her well.'

'Ally, I don't know. I don't know if I can take the time off work at such
short notice.'

Work? Work! Bloody hell, I'd forgotten about that. Two days off, two
unofficial, lying days off, and I was acting as if I'd retired. What was the
matter with me? Did I *want* to get the sack? I felt weak and jittery at the
thought of it. Perhaps I really *was* ill.

'I'm ill!' I told Paul, interrupting him in the middle of his long spiel
about why it was difficult for him to take time off work at short notice,
particularly on a Friday.

'What?' He sounded alarmed, to be fair to him. I was quite pleased to
think he would sound alarmed about me being ill.

'It's not anything serious,' I added quickly. I was going to go on to add
that it was so *not* serious, it was non-existent, a made-up illness, an illness of the fictitious kind. But something came over me. Something to

do with the gratification it gave me to hear him sounding alarmed.

'It's probably just . . . some virus or other . . .' I said vaguely, trying to make my voice sound weak.

'Have you been to the doctor?'

'No . . . no need for that. I don't want to make a fuss.' Oh, it sounded weak now all right. I knew it did. I was getting into the part. And well into the Fourth Lie, of course, although I hadn't even stopped to think about it.

'Well, I think you should. I really do think—'

'I'll see how it goes,' I said.

'You should have said. You should have said you were ill. You can't possibly drive your mother to the airport, car or no car!'

Bit difficult without the car, actually.

'You're not to even consider it.'

Yes! Result! He'd take the day off, even if it was a Friday near the end of May.

'I'll ask Lynnette. She won't mind. She's only part-time.'

Lynnette? Lynnette, driving my mother and her heart-throb to the airport? Could I inflict that on her? Could I, come to think of it, inflict them on each other? Could I?! By Christ, I was going to enjoy it! I almost wished I was going with them to watch. But I was ill, wasn't I?

I don't think it's anything serious,' I told Snotty-Nosed Nicola, who was answering Simon's calls as he was probably too busy practising his golf swings in his office. 'Probably some sort of virus.'

Not really Lie Number Five. Just a repetition of Lie Number Four, to a different person. Actually it was beginning to feel as if it were true. I was beginning to sort-of grow into it.

'Perhaps it's your hormones,' said Snotty Bloody Cow Nicola, with a sneer in her voice.

'I don't think so,' I returned coldly.

'But that's what happens, isn't it,' she persisted. 'Women of your age . . . when you get to fifty . . . start having problems . . .'

'I'm not getting to be fifty,' I said, wanting to smack her one. 'I'm getting to be forty-nine, actually.'

Not really another lie. This one was just a repetition of Lie Number One, and necessary if I wasn't to lose face among my colleagues. If you're going to lie, you have to be consistent. Ask me, I was beginning to be an expert.

'Well, whatever,' said Nicola, sounding flustered, or perhaps she just had another call waiting, 'Whatever, you need to get a certificate.'

'Sorry?' A certificate proving my age? My birth certificate?
'Sickness. Sickness certificate. You've had three days off.'
So I had. Bloody hell, I really must be ill.
'Get your certificate, send it in, or you won't get paid.'
End of conversation. End of joke. This wasn't funny any more. I'd
have to lie to the doctor now.

'Paul says you must go to the doctor. Today.'
'I know, I know. I'm going.'
I'd made an appointment for five o'clock. Only because of the
wretched certificate. And I'd only invited wretched Lynnette into my
house because I wanted to hear how it went with my mother.
'Sit down, Ally. You're not well.'
'It's all right. I'll make you a coffee,' I said ungraciously. 'How did it go
with my mother?'

She sat down at the kitchen table. I was pleased to say she looked
worn out. Ha! The old girl must have given her a bad time.
'Fine,' she said. 'She's a dear, isn't she?'
A dear? That wasn't exactly the first word that sprang to mind when I
came to describe her, no.
'And Ted.' She smiled. 'Such a sweetie. So funny. They're so cute
together. All the way to Gatwick they were snuggled up together in the
back of my car, holding hands, laughing at little jokes together—'
Now I really did feel sick.
'Laughing?' I echoed bleakly. 'My mother, laughing?'
'It must be love,' she smiled knowingly, taking the mug of coffee I
passed her and stirring it thoughtfully. 'They looked . . . just the way
Paul and I look when we look at each other.'

I watched her stirring the coffee and took great comfort from imagining I'd dropped a couple of slug pellets into it.
'I've put poison in that,' I said viciously. 'So perhaps you'd better go
now. Before you start throwing up. I've just washed the floor.'
'Ally!' she spluttered, spraying coffee over the table. And some specks
fell on her little-girl-pink blouse. What a shame. 'Ally, I wish you
wouldn't be like this. It isn't funny. It's hurtful.'

Don't talk to me about hurtful. I know hurtful. I live hurtful.
Hurtful is when someone who regularly screws your husband sits
opposite you in your own kitchen, looks at you with big cow-like eyes
and talks about love. Being threatened with a poisoned coffee is a mere
little headache, a little graze on the skin of life compared with my hurt.
'I never mind helping you out . . . doing you little favours like this . . .

and all I get in return—' Her eyes were sparkling with tears. Why didn't she look a mess? If I so much as thought about crying, I became a red-faced, swollen, dribbling wreck.

'It has to be said, Ally,' she went on in a whimpering voice, wiping her nose prettily on a pretty pink tissue that matched her blouse, 'I think you're the one with the problem.'

'Of course I am!' I replied. Was that my voice? Was I shouting? How did that happen? 'I've got *all* the bloody problems! I'm the one whose husband walked out, remember? I'm the one with the house, the bills, the girls, the cat, the crappy car and the crabby mother. You . . . *you*, you smug cow. All you've got to worry about is . . . is your lipstick.'

Which she was, unbelievably, studying in her handbag mirror even now while I was yelling at her like a madwoman. She patted her eyes dry with her pink tissue, snapped the mirror shut and got to her feet.

'I'm not staying to listen to any more of this,' she said, flicking her hair and her perfume at me. 'I'll put it down to your being ill, Ally. That, and your age.'

Thank you and good night. She shut the door quietly and I threw my shoe at it. I considered, just for a moment, going after her and showing her up in public by having a shouting match out in the street. Then I suddenly decided I couldn't be bothered. I was too tired. And anyway, I needed some quiet time to get my head together to work out my next lie. I'd had no trouble with the lies up till now, but I had a nervous feeling that Lying To The Doctor was going to be a whole new ball game.

Chapter 4

DR LEWIS HAD KNOWN me since we were both young and enthusiastic about life. He was enthusiastic about being the new and vibrant young doctor at the new and vibrant general practice that had just opened at the local health centre. I was enthusiastic about being newly pregnant with Victoria. We'd both calmed down somewhat over the years, of course, what with putting up with ungrateful patients and NHS constraints in his case, morning sickness and nappy rash in my case, and newness and vibrancy wearing off generally.

It had been nice, over the years, to be able to consult a trusted family friend when there were problems like Paul's embarrassing rash and Victoria's sudden urgent need for the Pill. However, it wasn't quite so nice now, sitting in the waiting room outside the familiar door marked DR S LEWIS, MD, and practising in my head the lies I was going to tell him. I had the most illogical feeling that however convincing my story was going to sound, he'd look at me with a hurt but pitying look and ask why I didn't feel able to be honest with him.

'Because I'm skiving off work' probably wouldn't be the best response in the circumstances.

Would he be able to tell from my eyes that I was lying? There's no knowing what doctors can tell just from looking at you.

'Mrs Bridgeman?' called the receptionist, making me jump so sharply I dropped the magazine I'd been pretending to read.

'Yes!' I squeaked, as I jumped guiltily to my feet.

'Dr Holcombe will see you now, Mrs Bridgeman.'

Dr Holcombe? Who the hell was Dr Holcombe?

'Where's Dr Lewis?' I asked the receptionist in a slightly trembly voice, knowing even as I asked that he must have seen me through the waiting-room window on his way into his surgery, noticed from my eyes and the backs of my hands that I was skiving off work and had refused to see me. Dr Holcombe was probably the psychiatrist, brought in to treat people with Skiving Off Work disorders and Lying problems.

'Dr Lewis is on holiday,' smiled the receptionist. 'Dr Holcombe is his locum.'

New vet, new doctor, what next? With a bit of luck when I went back to work I'd find Simon gone and a locum boss in his place. I pushed open the door of the consulting room.

'Hello, Mrs Bridgeman. Come in and sit down.'

A girl who looked considerably younger than Lucy and couldn't have been more than four foot six inches tall appeared from behind the filing cabinet, slinging my medical notes onto the desk before leaping into the chair in a way that I'd only ever seen cats and very agile small dogs doing. I sat down, wondering nervously whether she might be the doctor's young and exuberant daughter who was playing in the surgery while he went for a pee.

'I'm Dr Holcombe. How are you?' she beamed at me. Hope died a nasty death. How could a sweet young doctor of about fifteen years of age be expected to listen to a pack of lies from an old malingerer so early in her career? It was more than anyone could expect of her.

'I'm fine, actually,' I said, looking at my watch. 'Actually, I feel much better and I don't think I'll take up any more of your . . .'

'Wait!' she said in a surprisingly commanding tone as I stood up and turned towards the door. 'Let's just have a quick chat about why you came. Since you're here now. Even if you do feel better.'

'Oh, well . . .' I hesitated, hand on the doorknob. 'I was thinking of asking you for a certificate for work. Sickness certificate.' What the hell. It was easier lying to a stranger. It wouldn't feel like lying in quite the way it would if it were Dr Lewis. 'I've been feeling ill for the past few days.'

'Have you?' She sounded so sympathetic, I let go of the doorknob and returned to her side of the room. 'Please, do sit back down. Just tell me a little about how you've been feeling.'

'Sick. Really badly sick. Not vomiting, just . . .'

'Nauseous?'

'Yes! And headaches. And . . . just generally . . . yuck. You know.'

'Feverish? Aches and pains?'

'Yes!' I looked at her with a new respect. She was even better at inventing symptoms than I was. 'Sort of shaky. Sweaty. I suppose it's a virus?' I added hopefully.

'Off your food?'

'Definitely.'

'Not sleeping?'

'Not a wink.'

I was beginning to forget I was lying. I watched as she jotted something indecipherable on my notes and then suddenly she was on her feet (not that it made much difference to her height) and advancing towards me with a thermometer, a digital thing, which she stuck in my ear. My *ear*! I flinched and stared at her in amazement.

'You think it's an ear infection?'

'No,' she laughed. 'This is the way we do it now.'

Before I'd had time to express surprise, she'd taken my pulse, done the feeling around the throat and behind the ears bit, looked into my eyes and had the blood pressure gadget round my arm.

'Everything seems fine there,' she smiled.

So that was that. No sick note, just a ticking off for wasting time and malingering. I hung my head, waiting for the lecture.

'Are you worried about anything?' asked the very young, very small doctor in a very soft voice.

I looked up at her in amazement. 'Worried?' I repeated stupidly.

'Any family problems? Relationship problems? Money problems?'

What was this, a survey? Did I choose one, or tick all three?

She ran her finger over the details at the top of my file, and then stopped abruptly, tapping the page thoughtfully before looking up at me again. 'Worried about turning fifty?'

'My husband's been talking to you!' I gasped. 'He has, hasn't he? Or my children? For God's sake.'

'They haven't. Should they have?'

'No. It's just that they all seem to think I'm in denial about it.'

'Are you?'

'No, I'm not! It was just—I didn't want a party, so they cancelled it. Then everyone at work kept going on about being fifty, and it got on my nerves so I pretended to be forty-nine, and then . . .'

'Are you having problems at work?'

'No.'

I felt myself flush. I was cross, and I'd been caught off guard. I knew that she could tell that I was lying now.

'Well,' I amended, shrugging awkwardly. 'Not really. It's just that this Nicola doesn't like me, and she's going out with this Simon, the managing director, and he's given me a Serious Warning.'

'Do you like your job?'

'It pays the bills,' I muttered.

Apart from the car's drugs and the car's operation.

Dr Holcombe was scribbling frantically in my notes. She looked as if she was really enjoying herself. Glad somebody was.

'Well,' she said at last, putting down her pen and leaning back in the chair. She looked up at me and gave me that sweet angelic smile again. 'I don't think you've got a virus at all.'

Shit. Not such a good liar after all. I picked up my handbag ready to leave in shame, but out of the corner of my eye I noticed she'd picked up her pen again and was filling out a sick certificate.

Yes! She felt sorry for me. She wanted to give me a few days off even though I was a liar.

'You're suffering from stress,' she said, still smiling.

Stress? I was the least stressed person I knew!

'I've never felt stressed in my life,' I protested.

'You're internalising it—bottling it up.'

'I am?'

'That's what's causing all your symptoms. I want you to read this leaflet. And this one.' She pushed them into my hands.

'Coping with Stress in Middle Age' and 'Psychiatric Problems of the Menopausal Woman'. Oh, great. I came in feeling like a young lying troublemaker and I'm going out feeling like an old stressed-out nutter.

'And here's your certificate,' she added.

Oh well, whatever it takes. I grabbed it ungraciously and made for the door.

'Rest!' she called after me. 'And I want to see you again before you attempt to go back to work.'

Attempt? Was it going to be that difficult? Was there something she hadn't told me? I'd worked myself up into a panic by the time I got home. I fished the certificate out of my handbag and smoothed it out on the table. What was that she'd written? Why couldn't doctors ever manage to write properly?

Then the words suddenly leapt out at me, becoming horribly, sickeningly clear: *Suffering from work-related stress.*

Work-related stress.

Work-related stress.

The silly cow! Why the hell did she go and put *that* down?

How was I supposed to send *that* into work? How the bloody hell could I turn up back at work on Monday and hand it over to Simon? 'Here you are, here's my certificate explaining how I had to stay off work last week because, quite frankly, working for you has made me ill.' Oh yes, go down a bundle, that would!

And then I saw the next line. *Should refrain from work for a period of not less than . . . three weeks.*

I was lying on the sofa when Lucy came in from college. It was the shock. 'What's wrong, Mum?' she asked from inside the fridge, mouth already full of Jaffa cakes.

'Stress, apparently,' I said in the weak little voice of one suffering but trying to be brave.

'Stress?' she echoed in tones of hysteria. '*You?*'

'Apparently,' I repeated, huffily. Could be if I bloody wanted to be. 'Here. Look.' I pushed the doctor's certificate under her nose.

'Work-related stress,' she read, obediently. She sat down next to me and gulped loudly. 'Christ, Mum. I never realised you were stressed.'

'Nor did I,' I admitted.

'Would you like me to cook the dinner?' she asked solemnly.

There was a rushing in my head like I was going to faint. Partly from shock at Lucy offering to cook, partly from fear at what might end up on our plates.

'Hello? What's up?' called Victoria from the front door, seeing us both on the sofa looking solemn.

'Mum's ill,' said Lucy, jumping up at once and rushing to lead her sister out of earshot into the kitchen. I could, however, hear 'whisper

363

whisper whisper' from Lucy, and then 'Stress? You sure? Fucking hell!' from Victoria.

After which they both approached me again, cautiously, as if unsure how I was going to behave, and Victoria announced gravely: 'Me and Lucy. We'll cook the tea and we'll wash up.'

'Yeah. You're not to worry, Mum, we'll do it all,' agreed Lucy. 'Till you're better.'

'Well, till tomorrow, at least,' amended Victoria, giving Lucy a filthy look. 'I'm seeing Darren tomorrow.'

'We're going to make a curry tonight,' went on Lucy, ignoring her. 'So you just . . . lie there.'

It's a despicable thing to lie to your own children. It's probably the worst kind of lie of all. In self-defence, all I can say is that I didn't actually intend to lie. I was on the point of telling them—laughing, jumping up from the sofa and shrieking at them: 'Ha! Not really. The doctor's an idiot. There's nothing the matter with me.'

But then something came over me. Something that had a little bit to do with how nice it felt to lie on the sofa and be told to stay there. Something about a curry being cooked that didn't need any input from me. It wouldn't hurt, I persuaded my protesting conscience, just to go along with it for a very short while, an hour or so, just as long as it took to cook the curry and wash up. They'd probably both kill me afterwards but it'd be worth it. They'd understand one day, when they were running a household and a family themselves and feeling worn out and wanting to close their eyes . . . just for a few minutes . . .

I dreamt I was on the back seat of my car with the young AA man, talking to him about the symptoms of stress in middle-aged women. Just my bloody luck. Anyone else, if they dreamt about being on the back seat of a car with a good-looking young man, would at least get to snog him in the dream. Me, I have to dream I'm boring him to tears. Quite honestly it was a relief to be woken up by the smell of burnt curry.

'Eat it all up, Mum,' Lucy was saying earnestly. 'We scraped the worst of the black off, and the saucepan's in soak.'

She'd make some man such a lovely wife one day.

I waited till the worst of the indigestion had worn off before I broached the subject of the Lie.

'I was only joking,' I said, putting my arms round both the daughters' shoulders simultaneously and giving them a hug.

'Mum. We're watching EastEnders,' said Victoria, pushing me off. 'Joking about what?' asked Lucy without the faintest interest.

And then the phone rang. Explanations would have to wait, as no one else was going to answer the phone while *EastEnders* was on.

'Ally?' Paul's voice was deep with concern. 'How are you feeling?'

'Fine,' I muttered vaguely. 'Why would I not be?'

'Ally, you must have realised the girls would tell me. Obviously, they're worried about you. Well, we're *all* worried about you, Ally.'

The next most despicable lie, after lying to your children, must be lying to the husband who used to be the closest person to you in the whole world, before he walked out of your life into the bed of a young tart. Again, in my defence, I can only plead that I didn't *mean* to do it. It was on the tip of my tongue to say that the whole thing was just a joke. Ask the kids, I'd just been on the point of explaining to them how it was all a joke to get them to cook the curry, never mind the burning, and I'd have admitted it by now if it wasn't for *EastEnders* . . .

But it was something about the way he said that bit about being worried. 'We're *all* worried about you, Ally.' It sounded so caring, so sincere, I could almost believe he still thought of me as a person, as Ally, his wife, the girl he'd loved from the age of fourteen when we first kissed in the sports-equipment cupboard, and not just some nuisance who asked for money for the cat and threatened his girlfriend with slug pellets.

'You mustn't worry about me,' I said, softly, gently. Do, do. Worry, worry like hell. I want you to, I like it. Say it again.

'But you're obviously very poorly. We had no idea, any of us. Of course, we knew you weren't quite right.'

'What do you mean? Not quite right in what way?' I snapped.

'Well. One thing and another. The retreating from reality . . .'

'*What?*' I almost shrieked. 'What reality?'

'You see?' he continued. 'You're beginning not to even recognise it.'

'Is this all about the fiftieth birthday business? Because if it is—'

'Not just that. You haven't . . . been acting . . . altogether . . . rationally,' said Paul slowly, picking his words carefully, weighing each one before he threw it at me. 'What with Lynnette . . . the party . . . the cat.'

'You think I've flipped my lid, don't you?' I said stonily.

I thought about Paul, sitting in his new home with Lynnette, telling her how worried he was about me, how out of touch I was with reality, how he'd suspected I hadn't been quite right in the head since I'd threatened to feed her slug pellets.

'Has the doctor prescribed you anything?'

I burst out laughing.

'Yes. Three weeks off work.'

'Good. Let me talk to the girls again, OK?'

'No. There's nothing you need to discuss with the girls. I'm perfectly all right. I'm not on any drugs, I'm not cracking up, I've just been given a certificate for three weeks off work because I pretended to have a virus.'

'Right.'

'Paul, I'm serious. I'm perfectly fine, I'm not suffering from stress, or anything else. It's all just a misunderstanding.'

'If you say so.'

And I knew then how it must feel to be buried alive. I was communicating, but I wasn't being heard. I was speaking English but being translated into Swahili. Nobody was going to take any notice of a word I said. And it was all my own fault for ever uttering the very first lie.

On the Monday morning, Victoria insisted on taking my sick certificate in to Snotty-Nosed Nicola for me on her way to work.

'I can post it. Or I could deliver it myself' I protested from the sofa, pushing up the lid of my coffin, glimpsing the movement of life beyond the grave.

'No. I'll take it straight there now. Or you won't get paid.'

Who was this strange girl, so thoughtful and caring, so kind and considerate? She looked like Victoria, she was wearing Victoria's clothes, but it must be an alien inhabiting her body. Or was she just nervous at the prospect of no maternal pay cheque?

'Now, don't you move,' ordered the alien Victoria as she left the house. 'Lucy will get you breakfast before she goes to college. You should have stayed in bed.'

Is that what people do when they suffer from stress? Lie in bed all day and feel like they're losing touch with reality, like their children are aliens and their sofas are coffins? Perhaps I really was going loopy. The alien Lucy brought me fruit juice and toast and made a great thing about me putting up my feet on cushions to rest my legs.

'I've got stress,' I snapped, 'not varicose veins.'

Then I remembered. I didn't have stress. I was suffocating in the grave of my own fabrications.

After they'd both gone, I got up from the sofa and sneaked round the house like a disobedient child, tidying things up at random, until it suddenly struck me that I didn't know what to do. I'd never had free time before, and now I'd got it I didn't know what to do with it.

The ironing was up-to-date. The dishwasher was stacked, nothing even looked dirty enough to clean. With a sinking heart I realised my life was so sad, I lost all sense of purpose after the washing bin was emptied. I might as well go back to work. Except that I couldn't, because by now S.N. Nicola would have shown my three-week certificate to Simon and Simon would, in all probability, have Got In A Temp.

The Getting In of A Temp was standard procedure for absences of more than about a week. I'd lived through many a Getting In of Temps in my time, and few of them had been pleasant experiences.

Some temps were as timid as mice, some couldn't type, some refused to make the tea or answer the phone, some never got off the phone to their boyfriends, mothers, best mates, hairdressers and personal beauty advisers. But the worst were the ones who wanted to run the joint the minute they set foot in the door, changing the absentee's log-in and the height of her chair, and clearing out her desk drawers as if she hadn't just gone off sick but left the country or died. By the time the poor sick colleague had returned from her dose of the flu, slipped disc or work-related stress, the temp had completely reorganised the work station, put a photo of her own children on the desk, entered her own personal data into the computer, and everyone was inviting her to their hen parties. The returnee felt like an interloper in her own office.

I sat in my kitchen and brooded. Would anyone miss me? Would anyone care if I never went back?

I might, on many occasions, have wished never to go back, but I did at least want to be missed. The phone rang, jolting me out of my fantasy of never going back and Simon telling everyone he never realised how much he'd miss me.

'Ally?' Liz sounded distraught. 'Ally, I never realised you were stressed.'

'Nor did I,' I admitted cheerfully, and then amended, 'I mean, I never realised that was what was wrong. Till the doctor explained everything.'

'You poor thing! Are you all right?'

'Not bad,' I said bravely. 'Bearing up.'

'Well, I mustn't keep you talking, and tire you out . . .'

'But I'm bored,' I admitted.

'Are you?'

She sounded surprised. Perhaps stressed people didn't normally get bored. I'd better read up on the symptoms if I was going to keep this up for three weeks. Three weeks! It stretched ahead of me like an endless desert, a silent, colourless desert of sofa-lying with feet up.

'I suppose it's part of the illness,' I guessed hopefully. 'The boredom.'

'Perhaps. Would you like some magazines? I could bring a few round tonight, if you like.'

'Oh. Yes. That'd be nice. It'd be nice to see you.' It felt as if I'd been away for months already. There must be some gossip or scandal to catch up on. I wasn't missing them all already, was I?

I must be even sicker than I was pretending.

Liz and Mary both turned up at about eight that evening, bearing gifts of chocolates and magazines. We sat in the kitchen so we didn't interrupt *EastEnders*, and ate the chocolates together and reminisced about when I used to be at work with them.

'Is there a temp?' I asked.

'Simon's talking about Getting In a Temp,' said Mary. 'But he hasn't done it yet.'

'Don't let her use my blue mug. And don't let her access my email.'

'She's not even there yet,' soothed Liz.

'And watch out for her getting too friendly with Snotty-Nosed Nicola. And another thing . . .'

'Ally,' said Liz, looking at me with big worried eyes, 'You shouldn't be thinking about these things. That's why you've been signed off work. Because it's been causing you stress.'

'But that's the funny thing,' I admitted, shoving four squares of Dairy Milk in my mouth at once. 'When I was there, I didn't feel it stressing me out. Only when I was being interrogated by Simon about my time-keeping, but not otherwise. Now I'm away from it, I keep thinking how I might be replaced. Someone might be better than me. You know, they might be younger or—'

'You see! It's this *age* thing. I knew that was behind all this stress business!' cried Mary triumphantly.

'No, it's not,' I returned forcefully, spitting chocolate everywhere. 'It's not age, it's everything else. It's the bills, and the car bumper, and the cat needing drugs for the rest of his life. It's my mother and her illnesses and her jetting off to Majorca with her boyfriend. It's Victoria spending her whole salary on her car so she can pull the lads, and Lucy doing her exams while she's worried about me being off work. It's Paul thinking I'm cracking up just because I joked about giving his girlfriend poison.'

'Poison?' queried Mary and Liz together, their mouths both dropping open wide, teeth glinting horribly with undigested Dairy Milk.

'It was a joke,' I sighed, feeling suddenly tired and depressed. Nobody laughed.

'I think you ought to get away,' said Liz suddenly.

'Oh, very funny. The private yacht's in for repair at the moment,' I said sourly.

'No, really, I mean it. Remember what you were saying that day at work? That lunchtime when I . . . when we let slip about your surprise party?' She smiled a guilty little smile. 'How you were saying you'd like to swan off somewhere and leave everyone to get on with it?'

'Well, of course I *say* that. Everybody *says* that.'

'It'd do you good,' agreed Mary. 'Take your mind off work. As long as you sit around here, fretting, you're not going to get better.'

Especially as there's nothing wrong with me in the first place. Or is there?

'There must be a way you can manage just a few days away,' persisted Mary. 'A mini-break of some sort. A late booking, or . . .'

'Phone for you, Mum!' shouted Lucy, backing into the kitchen with her eyes still on the TV screen, where someone in Albert Square was having hysterics over someone else having an affair. 'It's Auntie Bev.'

'Beverly!' I exclaimed with genuine pleasure. My older sister and I were very fond of each other but didn't get round to communicating often. 'How are you?'

'More to the point,' cried my sister across the miles from Cornwall, 'how are *you*, and what the bloody hell is all this nonsense about being stressed? What do you expect if you will insist on being cooped up there in London all summer? For Christ's sake, get yourself down here and get some sea air into your lungs, girl. When are you coming? I'll get Thomas out of the spare room and wash the duvet.'

So I had to go, didn't I? If only to find out who Thomas was, and what he'd been doing on the duvet.

Chapter 5

HOW DO PEOPLE manage to pack everything they need for a couple of weeks into one little suitcase? Victoria had been on a back-packing holiday the previous year. I remember looking at that one bag on her back and thinking: What about the hairdryer? What about the four different pairs of shoes and the nail varnish collection? How she managed without so many of the little luxuries that usually make up her life I will never know. Now here I was, contemplating not a backpack around Southern Asia but a swift jaunt down to Cornwall, and I couldn't do up my suitcase for sleeves and plugs hanging out of the edge of it.

'It's hopeless!' I said, sitting back on my heels and staring at the pile of stuff still needing to be packed. 'I need a bigger case.'

'Then you'd never be able to carry it,' pointed out Victoria.

'Take the car,' said Lucy. 'I don't know why you want to go on the train.'

'I don't want to, Lucy. I just don't want to spend most of my holiday on the motorway waiting for an AA man.'

'Take my car, then,' said Victoria.

The silence was so startled and so electric with shock, I thought she'd immediately retract—'No, no, I didn't mean it!'

But she looked from me to Lucy and back again, returning our stares, and merely said, 'What?'

'Well!' I swallowed my amazement and tried again. 'Well, I mean, Victoria, you can't be serious. Your car is your life, your baby, your most treasured possession. If I take it away from you, you'll cease to exist in the eyes of everyone you care about.'

'Darren thinks that, too. He thinks I'm selfish and uncaring and all I think about is my car.'

The bastard!

'So I've got to show him, haven't I?'

Aha. The ulterior motive rears its ugly head. Thank God for that. I was beginning to worry that she was becoming a nice mature person.

'And you think it'll impress him if you tell him you've offered your car to your poor ageing mother to drive down to Cornwall?'

'Something like that,' she admitted.

'Thanks, Victoria!' I planted a big kiss on her cheek, which she wiped off with a look of grave anxiety. 'I'd love to accept your kind offer, and I'll tell Darren myself what a thoughtful, caring person you are.'

'Oh.'

She looked at the carpet intently for a few minutes before leaving the room very silently. Lucy looked at me expectantly. I knew that expectant look. She was waiting for me to call Victoria back, laugh and hug her and say of course I wouldn't dream of taking her car. Victoria's slow progress towards her bedroom told me that she was waiting for the same call, laugh and hug. So perhaps I should have felt a bit guilty, carrying on with my packing, putting back the extra pair of jeans now that I knew anything spilling out of the suitcase could go in a black bin-bag in the boot of the car. Victoria's car. Victoria's car, paid for out of her own earnings. Her own earnings of which she'd agreed to give me 20 per cent as housekeeping, of which I rarely saw a penny.

She lived with me rent- and board-free in order to run her car, and I let her get away with it because she was my daughter and I loved her—but I shouldn't have done. It wasn't right for her, and it certainly wasn't right for me. I juggled with the bills for the gas and the electricity and the cat's drugs, so that she could enjoy that car—and if she was offering it to me, even if it was only to make Darren fall in love with her, then I was going to take it. Without any guilt. Or hardly any.

'Look after it,' she said in a sorrowful voice, stroking its roof gently as I packed my things into the boot the next morning. *Five pairs of shoes.* Well, why not? And two jackets, just in case it was cold in the evenings . . .

'Sure you've got enough stuff?' asked Lucy sarcastically.

'The weather's unpredictable in Cornwall.'

'Don't forget to use fifth gear,' said Victoria, still caressing her car. 'Only I know you're not used to it.'

Used to it? They hadn't invented it when my car was made.

'I'll drive perfectly,' I reassured her, getting in and starting the car. First time! That would take some getting used to.

'No need to give it any throttle,' warned Victoria too late as I hurtled out of the driveway. I pulled up sharply and nearly flew through the windscreen. No need to stamp on the brake, either, apparently.

'It'll only take a minute to adjust to the controls,' I smiled at her. 'And anyway, *you* be careful with *mine!*'

'Huh!' was all she could manage to say. I don't think she was planning to go out on the pull much in that old wreck. Wouldn't do much for her street cred.

'See you in a couple of weeks, Mum,' called Lucy. 'Have an excellent time.'

'I will!' I waved and drove off—very smoothly, I thought—to start my holiday. I was two miles down the road before I remembered it wasn't supposed to be a holiday. I was supposed to be ill. I was supposed to be recuperating. Then I did start to feel guilty. But only a little bit.

There's something very pretentious about driving a sports car. Victoria carried it off because of her youth, her sunglasses and her short shiny skirts. The first few looks I got from other drivers passing me on the motorway, I felt slightly ridiculous, imagining their disappointment on seeing a middle-aged woman in a cardigan at the wheel. But after a while I got into the game. Why not? I knew it was the car and not my hairstyle they were admiring, but it sure as hell beat the looks I got when anyone overtook me in the Metro. They were usually trying to attract my attention to point out the bumper hanging off or the lights not working. It made you feel good driving this thing. I was beginning to understand my daughter a little better and wondered if she'd lend me the car on a more regular basis, perhaps to do the Tesco run on a Friday night. See if I could pick up more than a bag of potatoes.

I smiled a mixture of pity and pure white-hot lech at a lovely young man driving a red Fiesta as he overtook me once, and I overtook him twice, and I laughed out loud to myself at the fun of being able to behave outrageously. I continued to smile to myself for the rest of the journey. And it felt more like a holiday than ever.

'What are you smiling about?' asked my sister almost as soon as I'd got through the door.

'The pleasure of seeing you,' I said, giving her a hug.

'You look unnaturally happy for someone suffering from depression.'

'Not depression. Stress.'

'Whatever. I was expecting you to look worn out and anorexic.'

'Sorry to disappoint you. Perhaps I feel better now I've got away from it all.'

'Good. Now, listen.'

Always a bit brusque, was Bev. A bit of the bossy big sister, still.

'I've put you in the back bedroom. Thomas has been warned. If he does come in at night, shout loudly. He's a bit deaf. Anything you need, just let me know. OK?'

'OK,' I agreed meekly. 'Who's Thomas?'

'Oh, sorry. Next-door's rabbit.'

Rabbit? Thomas the *rabbit*?

'He has the run of the house. It's a long story. He's clean—reasonably—considering his age. But he does like the back bedroom. I've told him you're coming, and I've moved his stuff into the little room, so he shouldn't be a problem. But shut the door at night. Just in case.'

Consider it shut. Nocturnal visits from an elderly, semi-house-trained rabbit I could do without.

'I've got some marking to do,' said Bev, handing me a mug of coffee and pointing out the biscuit tin. 'Can you get yourself settled in?'

Of course, I hadn't expected a fuss. Bev wasn't the type, and anyway it would have been embarrassing in view of the fabricated nature of my illness. I lugged my suitcase, black bin-bag full of shoes, curling tongs and a bag of novels up to the back bedroom, opened the window and stared out over the rooftops to the sea. I'd only been here once before. Beverly invited me in with the girls when Paul left. She'd just moved here from London and made Newquay sound like the Promised Land. I think she was a bit put out that I didn't immediately start to feel better about the whole business of my life being ruined and my heart being broken. Newquay may be nice, especially in summer, but it doesn't have magical healing qualities. This time, I hadn't come here with any illusions about escaping from my problems. I just wanted time off from them, that was all. A couple of weeks of relaxation. Not thinking about anything in particular. Recharging my batteries. I sighed, smiling to myself in anticipation of the relaxing and recharging I was going to do, and turned back from the window just in time to witness a large white rabbit defecating on my pillow.

'He's been so good recently,' sighed Beverly, stroking Thomas's ears with one hand while she put the pillowcase in the sink to soak. 'I suppose it was the trauma of changing his room.'

She stroked Thomas's ears and he snuggled into her chest. Is this what happens to middle-aged women who haven't had children? They get a rabbit substitute?

'Just shout at him, that's the thing. Show him who's boss.'

Thanks. I'll bear that in mind next time he craps on the bed.

'We'll get a takeaway tonight, shall we?' proposed Bev, opening a bottle of white wine and passing it in my direction. 'Indian or Chinese?'

Sharing chicken korma and mushroom bhajis at the kitchen table with more wine felt companionable and sisterly.

'Are you seeing anyone at the moment?' I asked as I mopped my plate clean with a chapatti.

'One or two,' smiled Beverly enigmatically.

'At the same time?' I tried not to sound shocked.

'Listen, Ally,' retorted Bev, swaying towards me slightly as she poured out more wine. 'I'm fifty-two. I've got no ties, no responsibilities . . .'

'Fine, OK, I know . . .'

'And I'll do whatever I like. With whoever I well . . . want to do . . . whatever I want.'

She'd lost the thread somewhat but the gist was clear.

'Absolutely. I didn't mean you shouldn't—'

'And they all know the score. Anyone I see . . . they know there's no commitments. No relationships. No one gets hurt.'

'But it sounds . . . sort of lonely,' I said thoughtfully. 'Isn't it? Like screwing a series of strangers?'

'Nothing wrong with that!' she snapped, and then added, 'Anyway, they're not. Not strangers. Friends. My life is full of friends.' She waved her arms somewhat drunkenly around the room as if they were all hiding behind the chairs. 'Life should always be full of friends.'

'Mine isn't,' I said bleakly.

I thought of Paul, supposed to be my best friend, my soulmate and life partner, now defected to Cow Lynnette. I thought of the girls at work, even now probably making plans to go to the pub with the temp. I thought of Victoria and Lucy, rightly engaged in their own lives with their own friends. And I struggled against an onslaught of drunken self-pitying tears.

'All I've got is a sick cat who needs drugs for life, a sick car with no bumper and dodgy lights, and a boss who puts Serious Warnings in my Personal File. And our mother.'

'No wonder you're stressed,' said Bev without the slightest sign of sympathy. 'What you need to do, girl, is to take hold of life. Grab it by the bollocks and squeeze all you can out of it.'

The kitchen echoed with the force of her rhetoric. The pots and pans positively rang with it. I expected the plates and cups on the dresser to get up and dance to a clash of saucepan lids.

And we got a little drunker, and a little more sentimental, and we hugged a bit, and said how we didn't see enough of each other and should do, and I cried a bit about Paul and Lynnette, and Beverly said she'd never liked him anyway, in her opinion he was an arrogant, super-cilious git and now I'd got rid of him I could start to enjoy life.

Enjoy life? I lay on top of the bed in the back bedroom (checked for rabbits) watching the ceiling spin round in an inexplicable, nauseating fashion and thought about what she'd said—what I could remember of it. Grabbing life by the bollocks. I liked that, liked the aggressive sound of it. That was what I needed now, I decided, a bit of aggression. But as I disappeared over the edge of consciousness into a totally pissed obliv-ion, I was still crying inside. Crying without even knowing why. Always the worst kind, that.

I was woken up by a hammering at the door. Or was it a hammering inside my head? Ouch! It was both, one echoing the other like thunder-claps. I rolled off the bed and staggered downstairs with a pillow folded over my head, protecting my ears, which had suddenly become very delicate. Too late, as I flung open the front door in a desperate mission to stop the knocking before it killed me, too late by a fraction of a second, which was the time it took for my bleary, bloodshot eyes to focus and blink in recognition of the appearance on the doorstep of the most beautiful man I'd ever seen in my entire life—too late I remem-bered what I was wearing. Or more to the point, what I wasn't wearing.

Apart from the pillow over my head, not a lot.

A flicker of the most amazing chocolate-brown eyes I was ever likely to have the pleasure of staring into, registered amused acknowledgment of my position, which was standing naked on the doorstep apart from an old pair of pink knickers and (now) a pillow clutched against my boobs, swaying and gasping with the worst hangover it was possible to have without being dead.

'Sorry,' said the beautiful man, and his voice was like dark chocolate truffles dipped in honey, 'I didn't realise you'd be in bed.'

He smiled on the word 'bed' as if it were a wicked secret between the two of us. I felt my whole body go into a hot sweat, and didn't have enough brain cells functioning to decide whether it was the sudden onslaught of the menopause, sexual excitement, or a prelude to serious vomiting. I didn't dare speak, just in case.

'You must be Ally,' he went on.

I nodded thoughtfully, memory slowly returning. Ally, yes, that rang a bell. It probably was my name.

'Is Bev at work?'

'I . . . don't know. I've only just woken up.'

'I expect she's at work. It's nearly twelve o'clock.'

Nearly twelve . . . ? Twelve o'clock? How did that happen?

I looked around wildly for a clock. I never slept till lunchtime, never, and certainly never since going down with fake stress, the worry of which had added genuine insomnia to my list of invented symptoms.

'Can you give her a message for me?' asked the Beautiful One.

'Of course! Of course!' I stammered, flustered, embarrassed that I hadn't made this obvious suggestion. 'Anything else I can do to help?'

Fly to the moon on a paper aeroplane? Fall to your feet and kiss the ground you walk on?

'Just the message,' he smiled, this time a full, face-stretching smile that made his eyes dance and dimples deepen beside his mouth, and which would make most normal red-blooded women want to drop the pillow from their chests, tear off their knickers, fling themselves to the ground and shout 'Now! Take me now or lose me for ever!' Most normal women, I said, not me, of course. I just fantasised about it for a few minutes but it made my hangover feel worse.

'Just let her know I'll be here tonight, could you? I forgot to confirm.' He dropped the smile and looked me up and down before adding, 'That's all—for now. See you later,' and turning away.

Maybe I'd save the fantasy for later. When I was feeling better.

I can't believe I was so hung over I never even asked who he was!' I admitted ruefully to Beverly, recounting the incident when she got home from college a few hours later. She laughed.

'That's James. And I'm furious with him for spoiling the surprise.'

'What surprise?'

'I told him it was meant to be a surprise welcome do for you.'

'For *me*?' I blushed scarlet, feeling like a child being taken out for a treat I didn't deserve. 'Why?'

'Why not? Do you good, cheer you up, meet some of my friends.'

'Is James one of your "friends"?' I asked pointedly.

'If you mean have I screwed him, yes, of course I have, but years ago, and got it all out of my system. Took some doing!' she laughed dirtily.

'As you can probably imagine!'

I tried to shrug a nonchalant little shrug. Could I imagine? Did I even want to? Could I *help* imagining that smile, those eyes, that ripping off of the knickers fantasy . . .'

'Well, of course you fancy him—it's written all over your face!' pointed out Bev helpfully. 'He's gorgeous. Thinks he's God's gift to women, of course . . .'

With a certain amount of justification.

' . . . but a terrific shag.'

I didn't think about that at all while I got myself ready for Beverly's dinner party. Not once did it cross my mind, while I sprayed myself all over with my least old perfume and searched through the suitcase for some underwear that didn't look as if it belonged to an overweight, middle-aged matron. I might have run through the episode on the doorstep once or twice in my mind, or a couple of dozen or fifty times at the very most, and tried to de-hangover the whole thing and perhaps move it all on just a few steps in my imagination, so that he'd pushed me indoors, tossed the pillow to one side, ripped off his clothes and . . .

'Phone for you, Ally!' hollered Bev from downstairs. 'Victoria!'

'You haven't called to say you arrived,' said Victoria sulkily.

'Sorry. I've arrived.'

'Car OK?'

Oh, I see. Now I understand the concern.

'No, I crashed it. I was racing this gorgeous man in a red Fiesta . . .'

'Very funny, Mum.'

She didn't believe me. If I'd told her I'd chatted to the most beautiful man in the world on the doorstep in my pink knickers she'd only sigh 'Mum!' in that tone that implied complete disbelief in the sexuality of anyone over thirty.

'And I was chatting on the doorstep this morning . . .' I began.

'Mum, please. I didn't phone to hear about your gossips with Beverly's neighbours,' she complained.

See what I mean?

'What's wrong, then?' I asked, suddenly alarmed by the edge of anxiety in her voice. 'Has Apple Pie been sick again? Has the bumper come off my car?'

'No. Nan's phoned from Majorca. She's not coming back. Ever.'

Chapter 6

SEE HOW IT HAPPENS? You can pretend to yourself that you've got away from it all, that you've exchanged, within little more than twenty-four hours, a life of burdens and anxieties for one of cavorting naked on doorsteps with men too handsome for their own good, but the things you were running away from don't just disappear, they're still there, and they come running after you. They come running after you, all the way from home, all the way from bloody Majorca.

'She's doing it on purpose, to spite me,' I wailed into my coffee cup.

'Why?'

Beverly was completely useless. I wanted someone to sympathise, to agree with me that the whole world, and especially my mother, was against me, not to rationalise.

'What's wrong with her staying out in Majorca? I should have thought you'd be glad.'

'Glad? Glad?' I stormed. 'Glad that she's taken leave of her senses? Glad that she's now certifiably insane as well as going into a steady physical decline? Glad that she's shacked up with some . . . some . . . TED, who wants to run a British bar in Palma?'

'At least he's prepared to work,' she pointed out, pouring more coffee.

'There's nothing else for it,' I sighed with resignation, thinking about going back upstairs and repacking the things I'd just started unpacking. 'I'll have to go out there and sort it out.'

'Just listen to yourself!' snapped Beverly, sounding so genuinely angry I dropped the spoon in the coffee in surprise. 'You'll have to go out to Majorca and sort it out, will you? What's the matter with you? Can't you bear to let Mum be happy?'

'And what would you know about it?' I hissed. 'When have you ever done anything for Mum?'

'I send her flowers. I phone her. I care.'

'Oh, you *care*, do you? You think sending flowers and phoning once a week means caring? Perhaps you should try sitting in hospital waiting rooms for hours on end while she gets her various complaints sorted out? Perhaps you should try having her turn up unannounced at your home at all hours, expecting to have meals cooked for her.'

'You're so bitter and resentful!' shouted Beverly.

'And you're so fucking lazy! You never did anything to help . . .'

'She wouldn't let me! She only wanted you, the bloody favourite daughter, and God knows why, when all you do is complain.'

'You'd complain if you had my life . . .'

'And you're so sorry for yourself!'

'Hello! Am I too early?'

The first guest for the evening, having given up with knocking on the door, had stuck his head in at the kitchen window. Of course, it had to be James.

'W' e're making a habit of meeting like this.'

Beverly had bolted for the bathroom, leaving me little option but to let him in, wearing only slightly more than I'd been wearing that morning on the doorstep. OK, I'd got as far as sorting out the underwear, but despite being black and lacy it didn't do anything to disguise the over-weight, middle-aged bit and it certainly didn't disguise the absence of any more suitable top garment than a tea-towel wrapped hastily across me at nipple level.

'Sorry. Come in.' I flapped around, panic-stricken, trying to hold on to the towel. 'You wouldn't mind, would you, if I . . .'

I gestured wildly in the direction of my bedroom.

'Sure. Take your time. Sorry if I interrupted anything.'

'No. I mean, it doesn't matter. I'll . . . just be a minute. Sit down. Have a drink.'

Gabbling like an idiot, I ran upstairs two at a time, realising with horror that I shouldn't have offered him Beverly's drink, especially as I hated her and was about to pack my case and leave.

Or was I?

In the three or four minutes it took me to put on jeans and T-shirt and start throwing things into the suitcase, I calmed down and debated a few crucial considerations in my mind: 1. *There was chicken chasseur in the oven, which was my favourite.* 2. *Not much fun driving back to London now, what with it getting dark soon.* 3. *I'd told Victoria not to worry.* This third consideration was the most crucial of the Crucial

THE TROUBLE WITH ALLY

Considerations. Don't worry, I'd told Victoria, as mothers do, making space in the Worrying Things compartment of my brain, shifting the other Worrying Things over so they had to sit on top of each other. Welcome into my brain, new Worrying Thing, the Worry about Mum staying on in Majorca.

Now, if I went bolting back from Cornwall tonight like a bat out of hell, having fallen out with Bev after only one and a half days, how was that going to rate as a no-worry situation from Victoria and Lucy's point of view? No good: I'd promised to straighten things out from this end and that was what I'd have to do.

Also, there was the chicken chasseur.

Also, I'd quite like James to see me with my clothes on just once.

I quickly pulled off the jeans and T-shirt, pulled on my black dress and legged it down to the kitchen to be met by a delicious smell of chicken chasseur and an icy air of hostility, with a shortly clipped 'No thank you' when I offered to help serve up the food.

I took my place at the table and did my own introductions. Jane, a colleague of Bev's from college, was (apparently) thrilled to meet me at last in the flesh. I couldn't quite figure this out unless she'd already been living with a cardboard cut-out of me, which seemed unlikely, but I spent the eternity we waited for Bev to bring in the first course smiling back at her in response to her warm and effusive girl-chat. The other guests were a mature student of Bev's, called Michael, whose only topic of conversation seemed to be his thesis on the influence of ambient social and sexual attitudes on the writings of the metaphysical poets; and an even more mature post-hippy beatnik called Bo, a bearded and boring nerd who called everyone 'Man'.

And there was James. Over the prawn cocktail he talked to me, his voice dripping sex appeal like syrup into the sauce, about living in Newquay and being divorced, and working in conference management and having holidays in South Africa, and what it was like for me living in London with two daughters and working in insurance and holidaying with Beverly in Newquay, thus building up a mini-profile of each other which excluded only:

1. The fact that I was not on holiday but pretending to be ill;

2. Any suggestion that I might be suffering from delusional stress, menopausal psychosis or any type of behavioural problems associated with being nearly fifty;

3. My husband being shacked up with the tart from hell;

4. The sexy car on the drive outside the house being not mine but my twenty-one-year-old daughter's.

None of these counted as lies, you understand, just avoidance tactics. The lies started with the main course, roughly coinciding with the wine entering my bloodstream and taking it over, and James beginning to look at me across the table with looks that bore into my eyes, through my head, and straight into my soul. You know those kind of looks? I used to have a dog that did it, a spaniel. Except that when he looked at me like that, it didn't have the same effect on me. It didn't make my legs tremble and my heart race and it didn't make me keep dropping my knife and fork into my chicken chasseur.

'You don't look old enough to have two grown-up daughters,' he said, his voice caressing me with softness.

'I'm thirty-nine,' I giggled prettily.

Well, it probably wasn't pretty at all. It probably came out as a drunken cackle, but we can only try. We can only lie. I shot Beverly a furtive glance to make sure she wasn't listening, about to shout out: 'Ha! Listen to her, she's nearly fifty, as if you couldn't guess . . .'; but she was deep in debate with Michael about John Donne's use of sexual imagery in his religious poetry. Instead, I waited for James to smile back at me, a slow, easy smile of understanding that said, 'Of course, we both know you're no more thirty-nine than I'm the Queen of Sheba, but we won't discuss it any further.' But he didn't. He reached across the table, lifted my hand in his and pressed my fingers very gently.

'You look much younger,' he said.

Now, you have to remember that I'd lived like a nun since splitting with Paul, and that this was the most beautiful man I'd ever seen in my entire life. If that hadn't been the case, I would of course have thrown back my head, howled with laughter and told him to piss off.

'Thank you.' I smiled back sweetly.

The dessert course, which I could hardly eat for excitement, passed in a blur of burning looks across the table and nudged knees under it. Coffee grew cold in the cups while we tickled each other's fingers and stared into each other's eyes. Brandy was licked suggestively off lips. What was happening here? Within the space of a couple of hours I'd turned from nun to nympho. At about half past one, James leaned as close to me as our separate armchairs would allow and said: 'I think it's time to go.'

'Don't!' I responded before I had time to be shocked by my own daring. 'I don't want you to go!'

'I mean,' he whispered, 'it's time for us both to go.'

He said goodbye to Beverly. I didn't. In the circumstances of our mutual hatred I didn't see the point. While he was in the kitchen I was panicking with a new and urgent worry, which was: just what was one supposed to take with one when going back to someone's flat for sex? Nightie? Toothbrush? Condoms? Should I pack an overnight bag with clean underwear and my make-up remover?

I suddenly felt naive and unready for all this. I didn't know how to handle this sort of stuff. He'd know. I'd do it all wrong and mess it all up. He'd laugh at me and kick me out of bed. The effects of the brandy and the kiss started to wear off and I decided to shake hands with him politely, thank him for the offer but decline. I'd congratulate myself in the morning for staying calm in a potentially awkward situation.

'Come on, then,' he smiled, appearing back in the room. He took my hand and propelled me gently towards the front door.

'OK,' I said.

And so it was that the eve of my fiftieth birthday saw me waking up alongside the (even more beautiful without his clothes on) man in the world, having had wild, uninhibited sex, which I somehow seemed to know how to do after all, during much of the night and finishing off with an encore at dawn. I didn't realise it was the eve of my fiftieth birthday at the time. It wasn't exactly the first thing on my mind. Nor the second, nor the third nor . . . well, let's just say I'd forgotten about it completely. I'd forgotten about a lot of other things, too, but they all came flooding back with the morning light. The immediate anxieties were trivial ones, like how one decently takes leave of someone one hardly knows but has just shagged senseless. I mean, 'See you around, then,' sounds rather too casual. 'Thank you very much for having me,' too crudely obvious, but anything more intimate at this stage in the game could be construed presumptuous. I lay in bed, watching James sleeping quietly next to me, and contemplated these issues. But before long, the Other Worries came sneaking back up; intruders slipping into my mind by the back door when it was unguarded, bashing me over the head with their cudgels of panic.

Bash! Take that! That's to remind you about your sister Beverly, who's probably chucked all your clothes out onto the pavement.

Bang! Bash! That's just to make sure you don't forget about your mother who's done a runner to Majorca.

Crash! Wallop! Got you! Thought you could forget about your husband, did you? Yes, your husband, Paul, the man you promised to stay faithful to until the end of your life. One minute you're crying your eyes out over him deserting you, next minute you're cavorting in bed with this . . . this . . .

James turned and sighed in his sleep and the intruding worries vanished out of the window. I touched his face gently and traced the line of his smile as it deepened, and as he opened his eyes I had to stop myself from gasping out loud. He was gorgeous. I could hardly believe my luck. Why couldn't I just stop worrying for once and accept this moment of pure pleasure and be grateful for it?

Dear God, thank you for providing me with a lovely man to have a night of fantastic, uncomplicated sex with. Amen.

'What are you thinking?' he murmured, propping himself up on one elbow and studying me closely.

'Saying my prayers,' I smiled.

'And what were you praying for?'

More of the same, please. As soon as possible.

'Oh, you know. The usual stuff. World peace, kindness and love for little fluffy animals, a win on the lottery . . .'

He laughed gently and kissed me, very slowly, until my toes curled in the twists of the sheets.

'And more of the same, please. As soon as possible . . .'

I was half past nine when I let myself back into Beverly's house, and the silence told me she'd probably left for work already. These college lecturers seem to work almost as infrequently as their students. I crept up the stairs as stealthily as a thief, and into my own room, where I threw myself on the bed with a sigh of relief, telling myself I'd just have an hour or so to catch up on some of the sleep I'd missed during the night, before getting down to some serious consideration of my new anxieties, to say nothing of brooding on the old ones.

If I hadn't thrown myself onto the bed with such abandon, it wouldn't have come as such a shock when something big and furry jumped out from under my legs. I fell off the bed like I'd been shot, shrieking blue murder, trod on the big furry thing and finally tripped over him as he hopped away.

'Thomas! You bastard rabbit!' I shouted after his retreating tail as I lay in a heap on the floor. Beverly's bedroom door opened slowly and Beverly, completely naked, followed by Jane, completely naked, peered round the door at me as I stared back in surprise.

'Don't worry,' said Bev later over breakfast. Worry? Me? 'I'm not actually gay. Jane is, of course, and she's such a good friend. I just sleep with her occasionally, you know how it is.'

'Sure, whatever,' I said, trying to adopt the same casual tone.

The incident with Thomas seemed to have broken the ice on our frozen relationship and we'd been laughing together somewhat nervously over the breakfast preparations, unsure which of us was going to voice an awkward topic first.

'So, what about last night?' asked Bev, fixing me with a very knowing look as she spooned vast quantities of Shreddies into her mouth.

'Yeah! Great dinner! Thanks, Bev. Sorry I didn't say—'

'Cut the crap, Ally. Not the dinner. How did it go with James?'

Annoying how a smile will insist on taking over your face even when you try to fight it.

'That good, eh?' Bev smiled back.

Yeah. That good.

'**I**s that the Hotel Picador? Yes? Could I speak to . . . do you have a Mrs Dobson staying there, please? Or they might be booked in under Mr . . . er . . . his name's Ted,' I faltered. Didn't know the bugger's surname.

There was a pause during which I could hear a muttering of exasperated Spanish and then a clonking sound followed by the ringing tone.

'No reply,' I mouthed to Beverly.

'Well, at least they didn't say they've checked out.'

'No.' I hung up and stared grimly out of the window. 'Probably out looking at properties.'

'Ally—'

'I don't like it. It's too sudden, it's too rash, she hardly knows him.'

'So, when are you seeing James again?'

Ouch. I felt myself go a little red. Well, pinkish, anyway.

'Well, all right. But I'm not thinking of going into business with him, am I?'

So what *was* I thinking of getting into, exactly?

'He's not permanent relationship material, you know,' warned Beverly that evening as I was trying on the sixth or seventh outfit in a frenzy of desperation about what to wear for dinner with him.

'Jesus, Bev! What do you take me for? We're both adults here, right?'

'It's just that you seem . . . a little bit stressed out about it all.'

'Of course I'm stressed out,' I snapped, pulling off a pair of white trousers in disgust. Why the hell I ever bought them I can't imagine; they made my bum look so huge. 'I'm *allowed* to be stressed out, I'm suffering from stress, remember?'

'Calm down,' she said, a little more kindly. 'The black skirt looked nice. With that red top.'

'You think so?'

'He'll love it.'

'You're sure?'

'For Christ's sake! I thought you said you were an adult, not a thirteen-year-old on her first date.'

Well, now, there's the thing. It was my first date, actually, in a kind of way. You see, I'd known Paul virtually all my life so we never went through the same sort of dating stuff that other couples do. We just drifted into going out together as an extension of hanging around together. I always felt comfortable with Paul because we were mates. I never had to beat myself up over what I was going to wear when I went out with him. There was never this angst, this worry, this . . .

Shit. I was just about to say there was never this excitement. I didn't mean that, of course.

I didn't mean, did I? That there hadn't been any excitement in our relationship, not ever. Nothing but the comfortable, caring love of a couple of best friends. I couldn't have meant that. It would be unthinkable even to *think* it . . .

Horrified, I sat back on the bed, clutching the red top and staring at myself in the mirror.

'You OK?' asked Beverly, looking at me dubiously.

Fine, fine, never better. Just discovered my whole life up till now has been a complete sham, a framework of self-deception and pretence.

'I don't think I was ever really in love with Paul,' I whispered at the mirror. My reflection looked back at me, white with shock.

'Come on, now,' said Beverly, looking very anxious now. 'This thing with James . . .'

'No, no, it's nothing to do with James,' I shook my head impatiently. 'Of course it's not. I've just . . . realised. I loved Paul, but I wasn't *in love* with him.' I just assumed I was. Because I was supposed to be. We were married, we had sex, we had babies together. It was absolutely obscene to suddenly start thinking about never having been in love with him.

'Perhaps I really am losing my mind,' I conceded softly, still staring at my reflection, still holding on to the red top as if my life depended on it. 'Not losing your mind. Finding it, perhaps,' Beverly said, gently.

'So when are you going to be forty?' I frowned at James across the table of the restaurant. 'Forty?' I smiled politely.

'You're thirty-nine now . . . I just wondered when your birthday was, that's all? Does it bother you, the Big Four-O?'

THE TROUBLE WITH ALLY

'Oh . . . er . . . not at all, really.'

Well, it wouldn't, would it? It was so long ago I'd forgotten how it felt.

Shit, change the subject, quick, quick, quick . . .

'Only as old as you feel, eh?' he smiled.

'Absolutely.'

What a bloody stupid lie to tell. Why did I do that? Perhaps I should just tell him the truth now, quickly, while I had the opportunity. Oh, by the way, that thing about the Big Four-O, actually it's a few years out— well a whole decade out, in fact, but hey! what's a little decade or two between friends, ha ha? No, I couldn't do it.

'Forty's nothing to worry about, nowadays,' I smiled cheerfully, with complete honesty. 'It's merely the beginning of maturity.'

'You're right, of course. Fifty worries me a little more, though.'

I choked on my chocolate gateau.

'Still,' he added with a meaningful smile at me, 'We've got a while before we have to face that one, haven't we?'

'Yes,' I nodded, spitting chocolate crumbs discreetly into my napkin.

Coffee came as a welcome respite from any further discussion of age. I breathed a sigh of relief. All I had to do was keep the conversation on safer ground. Not a problem.

'How long have you got?' James asked me as he stirred his cappuccino.

'Well . . .' I looked at my watch. 'I expect Bev will be home about mid-night, so I suppose . . .'

'I didn't mean that!' He laughed, and the look he fixed me with as he added 'We've got all night if we go back to my place', was like having all my birthday and Christmas presents wrapped up in one. 'I meant, how long is your holiday?'

I must have stared a stare of total blank lack of comprehension, because he laughed again and persisted: 'Your holiday! With your sister! How long?'

'Oh!'

Holiday. As in sick leave. As in pretended sickness, invented sickness, sickness that was supposed to have me confined to the house in a state of nervous exhaustion, not hopping in and out of bed with Beautiful Men with Beautiful Smiles . . . not a *holiday* at all, for God's sake! I felt myself flush crimson with guilt.

'Well . . . probably just a couple of weeks,' I said, vaguely.

'Depends if they can manage without you at work?' he asked.

'Something like that.'

Something like whether they got a temp in who was better than me. Whether my Serious Warning in my Personal File had become any more

385

Serious. Whether there was still a job for me when I got back. He covered my hand with his as he called a waiter for the bill. 'Don't let the job stress you out,' he told me, gently. 'Take a tip from me. I know how it can be. Take your holiday. You deserve it.'

'Yes,' I squeaked miserably.

Deserve it? I wasn't even supposed to be having it. I was supposed to be stressed out. He didn't know the half of it.

I should have told him the truth, of course. It had to come out sooner or later, and I couldn't have known it was going to be sooner. Do you ever wonder how you might have done things differently if you'd only known what sneaky little tricks Fate had lined up for you?

Well, you shouldn't. You shouldn't waste time wondering about it, because you probably wouldn't have done anything differently, would you? No, be honest. You wouldn't. We all do what we want to do, at the time, and it's too easy to say afterwards 'If only I'd known . . .'

Well, if I'd known my daughters were going to be lying in wait for me back at Beverly's house when James and I let ourselves in the next morning, would I not have spent the night having sex with him? Well what do you think?

Perhaps I would have made a bit more effort with the look on my face, which was probably still glazed with postcoital satisfaction.

Or perhaps James and I would have entered the house a bit less entwined, a bit less smoochily, a bit less caressingly . . .

'Hi, Mum! Happy Birthday!'

'Happy Fiftieth, Mum! Oh . . .'

Oh.

They'd done well, really, bless them. The room was bedecked with flowers and 'Happy Birthday Nifty Fifty' balloons, and they'd only been there a very short time because Beverly had been in the kitchen trying to get hold of me on the phone to warn me. The look on her face told me that. It also told me she was terribly sorry but what could she do? She could hardly refuse her nieces entry to the house when they'd come all the way from London by train to see their mum on her birthday.

'This is James,' I said to their united stance of stony disapproval.

'A friend of mine,' explained Bev helpfully.

'My daughters,' I told James automatically. 'Victoria and Lucy.'

'Pleased to meet you,' he said quietly.

They nodded.

'I'll . . . be going, then,' he said, turning back to me. The twinkle had gone out of his eyes. The dimple had gone out of his cheeks. He didn't look impressed.

'OK.'

'Have a happy birthday,' he added, raising his eyebrows at the balloons.

'Have we interrupted anything?' demanded Victoria aggressively, mis-interpreting the embarrassed silence.

You know how sometimes people say things with the best of inten-tions, which turn out to be the worst possible thing they can say? 'You look marvellous, you've lost such a lot of weight' to an anorexic, or 'Give my regards to your husband' to someone who's just been widowed. They usually feel worse than the person they were talking to, don't they. So I didn't blame Beverly. She was only trying to help.

'James is just a friend of mine,' she repeated patiently to Victoria and Lucy as if they were slightly thick students who needed extra tuition. 'He's just been helping me look after your mum, that's all. You know. While she's not been well.'

It wasn't enough. I wasn't completely dead yet. I was still twitching with the occasional spasm of rigor mortis. Stick the knife in again, Beverly, go on, right up to the hilt.

'While she's suffering from this stress syndrome thing. This menopausal . . .'

Enough! Enough!

'Thank you, Beverly,' I said very quietly as James turned to go.

'What?' she asked the shocked and silent room as the door closed after him. 'Was it something I said?'

Chapter 7

'WE'RE NOT *STUPID*,' declared Victoria, taking the tone of an understand-ing but concerned parent. 'We did *realise* you were having a thing with him.'

'Were' being the crux of the matter. The past tense of the matter. Judging by the speed of his exit, it looked pretty unlikely that James was going to be reappearing in my present or future tenses, and who could blame the guy? Being propelled through a woman's life from the age of thirty-nine to fifty overnight could perhaps be a little disorientating, to say nothing of taking on board her menopausal neuroses.

'I didn't realise you had boyfriends,' admitted Lucy thoughtfully.

'I don't! I mean, I haven't, up till now.'

'So is this part of your syndrome, then? Needing to get a man? Part of your, you know, your condition?'

Even Victoria stared at Lucy as if she'd just stepped out of a spacecraft.

'Don't talk bollocks, Luce. It's nothing to do with Mum's illness. It's probably just her age.'

Well, thanks. That's reassuring.

'Or perhaps it's because of, well, you know. Because of not getting it, since Dad left.'

They nodded wisely together. Two beautiful young heads nodding together in sage contemplation of the possibility of sexual frustration in the older generation.

'Have you quite finished?' I snapped. 'Discussing me as if I'm not here? I'm sorry if I embarrassed you by coming home with my lover—'

'Embarrassed? Us?'

'But the fact of the matter is, I'm not old, I'm not ill, and I'm not frustrated. I just met someone I liked, and he liked me, so we went to bed together. OK?'

Shocked silence.

'So now we've cleared that up ...,' I went over to where they were sitting together on Beverly's sofa, scooped them both into my arms and gave them a group hug. 'It's lovely to see you both! Thank you for all this ...,' I waved at the room full of floral tributes and balloons. 'And thank you for coming all this way.'

'Couldn't miss seeing you on your Fiftieth!' smiled Lucy.

'Don't keep on about it, Luce!' hissed Victoria. 'It's just a birthday, isn't it, Mum, same as any other, but, you know, older.'

'It's all right,' I laughed. 'I haven't really got a problem with being fifty, honestly. It was just all the fuss I didn't want. The surprise party, and everything. Although I do appreciate all the trouble you must have gone to, organising it,' I added, feeling guilty. 'And cancelling it.'

'Never mind,' said Victoria stoutly.

'How did you get time off work to come down here?'

'I'd already booked a couple of days off. The party was going to be on Saturday ...'

'Oh yes.' More guilt. Heap it on, go on, don't spare me.

'... so I would have been doing stuff, today and tomorrow. You know, catering stuff.'

THE TROUBLE WITH ALLY

'Catering?' Now I *really* felt bad.

'Who's looking after the cat?' I asked. The words were hardly out of my mouth when I was aware of a sort of chill, a little *frisson* of wariness passing between the girls and wafting over to me on a current of cold, tense air. They exchanged looks and coughed.

'Well, we couldn't ask Nan,' began Lucy diplomatically.

'On account of her legging it to Majorca with Ted,' added Victoria unnecessarily.

'So?' I prompted in the ensuing silence.

'So Dad said he'd do it.'

'Oh. Good.'

'In a manner of speaking.'

I looked at Victoria sideways.

'What manner of speaking?'

'Well, as in: Dad's in charge of the situation, but—'

'Lynnette's doing it, isn't she!' I exclaimed. 'You've left that cow looking after my cat?'

'Our cat, Mum!'

'Dad's cat too, remember!'

'And she's coming into the house? My house? When I'm not there? Touching my things?'

'Only the cat's dishes and the tin-opener,' said Lucy miserably. 'Oh, Mum, we had to ask her! Dad works too late. Apple Pie would get hungry.'

'We couldn't have come to see you, otherwise,' pointed out Victoria. 'Sometimes, you just have to do what you have to do.'

I pictured Lynnette, letting herself into the house with my key. Going into my kitchen, opening my cupboards. Calling my cat, picking him up and cuddling him. I could feel my mouth turning down at the corners. The postcoital glow had gone cold.

'Don't worry, Mum,' said Lucy gently, slipping an arm through mine. 'Apple Pie hates her. He meows at her and digs in his claws when she picks him up. And she doesn't like getting his hairs all over her skirts.'

Perhaps there's a God up there after all.

We went shopping in Truro. The three of us, just like the old days when they were little and I used to take them out to buy their new outfits from Top Kids. Except this time it was my treat.

'I haven't got much money,' I admitted as we parked the MG in the multistorey and headed for the shopping centre.

'It's all right,' said Victoria, to my astonishment. 'I have.'

'But you've never got any money.'

'I've been staying in.'

Of course. Difficult to get out in London without a sports car.

'Darren doesn't like the Metro?'

'Darren who?' she retorted pointedly.

The bastard! How *dare* he dump my daughter just because she didn't have her car to take him out in. How dare he dump her when she'd only lent me the car to impress him with her kindness and generosity.

'I dumped him,' she went on, swinging her bag cheerfully onto her shoulder. 'Because of Reece.'

'Reece?'

Hang on, I'd lost the plot here. I was several pages short of a chapter. Where did Reece come into it?

'He's gorgeous,' sighed Victoria, looking soppy.

I think I love him, mouthed Lucy, putting two fingers to her mouth and pretending to puke.

'I think I love him,' smiled Victoria happily with no sign of puking.

'Oh. Well. That's nice, then,' I said, trying hard to sound impressed, more impressed than I'd sounded a few short weeks ago about Darren, and a little while before that about Adam, which was only a mere flicker of time after Nathan.

'Reece is definitely The One,' she said dreamily.

'She's looking at *Brides* magazine again,' Lucy warned me ominously.

'Lovely,' I muttered.

I wasn't too worried, though. Even if Victoria ever got as far as booking a wedding, by the time the banns had been called, Reece would have been unceremoniously dumped in favour of someone who was even more definitely The One.

Did you know about Dad as soon as you met him?' asked Lucy while we were trying on trousers in New Look.

'What about him?'

'Well, that he was . . . you know . . . The One.'

'Like Reece,' put in Victoria, with the soppy smile back on her face.

I sat down on the little stool in the changing room, with a pair of green combat trousers half on and half off.

'I don't know what I thought,' I said, feeling suddenly tired and sad, remembering the fright I'd given myself the previous night when I started thinking about not being in love with him. It wasn't the sort of thing you said to your daughters about their father, though.

'We knew each other when we were just kids, remember.'

'Yeah, childhood sweethearts,' said Lucy happily.

'Did you never have any doubts, Mum?' persisted Victoria. 'Did you never fancy anyone else? Didn't you ever look at other men and think: cor, I wouldn't mind giving *him* one . . .'

'No,' I said, speaking to the floor, looking at my bare feet where they stuck out of the too-tight combat trousers like little sausages bursting out of their skins. 'Not really, no. I never really looked.'

No, but if you *had* done . . . pointed out the uninvited little voice with irritating determination, if you *had* ever looked at anyone else, say you'd looked at someone like James, eh? Hmm?

Someone with those eyes, that smile, that line of chat that had you eating out of his hands, almost tearing off your clothes as soon as he touched you? Are you trying to tell me you'd have stayed faithful to good old Paul, then? You'd have concentrated on your marriage . . . your good, stable, nice, secure . . . *dull* marriage?

Answer me that now, if you can, if you dare and tell me you still don't understand how it happened with Paul and Lynnette?

I jumped up off the stool again, nearly falling over the trouser legs in my haste to get out of them.

On the whole, I think, uninvited little voices in one's head are best told to shut up.

'Nothing fits,' I told the girls crossly when I'd tried on most of the trousers in Truro. 'What's going on here? Have the sizes changed recently?'

There was an awkward silence. Lucy clutched her Miss Selfridge bag with its contents of assorted skimpy pastel-coloured summer tops and hummed a little tune to herself. Victoria pretended to be looking at shoes in a shop window.

'What?' I demanded of my own reflection in the glass.

I watched Victoria's reflection turn towards mine, look at me for a minute as if considering saying something, and then look back at the shoes again. In that instant, I recognised the awful truth of it.

'I've put on weight, haven't I?'

'Maybe just a little bit,' conceded Victoria.

'Not that much,' amended Lucy.

'I'm going on a diet!' I shouted, much to the amusement of a group of teenagers passing by. Hysteria wasn't far off. Well, can you blame me? This just wasn't fair. Anyone else, *anyone*, who got a dose of work-related stress, would LOSE weight, wouldn't they? They'd become pale and thin and fade away to within an inch of their lives. They'd have people fussing around them, telling them to drink up their nourishing soup and try, please try, to eat just one mouthful of lovely steamed fish and spinach. They wouldn't be going out to posh restaurants with gorgeous men and being bought four-course dinners with those little truffle things in paper cases to go with the coffee, nor would they be guzzling a bottle of Hungarian Rioja with the main course. This, then, is where life is so cruel. You try to be cheerful, try to keep going for the sake of everyone around you, despite the crap life throws at you from every direction (including Majorca). You get on with your life and try to make the best of it. And what happens? You get fat.

Fat and fifty.

'I am!' I shouted after the retreating group of teenagers. 'I'm going on a diet, and I'm going on it now! Right now!'

'Try some more clothes on, Mum,' soothed Victoria, taking my arm.

'Try a sarong.'

'Why?' I asked suspiciously.

'They're One Size Fits All. You can get into any. They're really fashionable this summer. And when you lose weight, it will still fit you.'

'All right, all right, point taken. I'll get one from Marks & Spencer's.'

So I went home happy with my sarong, and the girls went home ecstatic with their several carrier bags full of mix-and-match outfits, bikinis and things that looked small enough to be dolls' clothes.

We spent the afternoon giving each other a fashion show, the girls modelling their dolls' clothes, and me wearing my sarong with a fixed smile on my face that was beginning to hurt. It wasn't so much that I was thinking about James. It was just that I was making a determined effort not to think about him.

'Perhaps he'll come round. When he's had a chance to get over it,' said Bev when she got home from work and noticed the look on my face.

'I'm not bothered one way or the other.' I lied.

'Don't lie to me.'

'No. That's the problem, isn't it. I shouldn't have lied to *him*. I seem to keep doing it. I never used to tell lies, and now I can't seem to stop.'

'Don't beat yourself up over it, Ally. It's really not the end of the world that you're older than he thought. Or sicker than he thought!'

'Very funny.'

Not sick at all, actually. Lying again.

'I'm not really sick at all,' I told her, wanting to stop all the lies once and for all before they caused any more trouble. 'I only went to the doctor for a certificate because I needed a couple of days off work.'

'Doctors aren't stupid,' Bev told me sternly.

'This one was.'

'No. You just didn't like what she had to tell you. If you ask me, Ally, it was a bloody good thing you did go to the doctor, otherwise who knows how long this might have gone undiagnosed?'

'What? My malingering? My lying?'

'Your stress. You didn't even realise you had it.'

'I haven't. I'm trying to tell you . . .'

'And you're still in denial. You see?'

I gave up. People never seemed to believe me when I told the truth.

We had a birthday party in the evening, just the four of us, with sausage rolls, pizza cut into funny shapes, trifle and double chocolate gateau. I nibbled on bits of cheese and celery and felt sorry for myself.

'This is silly,' said Victoria eventually, shoving a piece of gateau in front of me and putting a fork in my hand. 'It's your birthday, and you're making yourself and everyone else feel miserable. Eat something, Mother, for God's sake, and think about the diet tomorrow if you must.'

I hate when they call me Mother. It sounds so exasperated.

'Sorry,' I said in a small voice, picking up the fork.

'Unless, of course, it's that MAN you're pining over!' she added in an even more exasperated tone.

'Don't be ridiculous!' I snapped.

I wasn't, actually, whatever you might be thinking. I wasn't pining in the least. I'd known perfectly well it wasn't going to last with James. I just felt sorry that it had to end like that, after so few days. And so few nights. In such an unfriendly way. While I still wanted him. I knew one day I'd probably laugh about it, about the look on his face when he saw the 'Nifty Fifty' balloons, about the way he turned heel and scarpered at the mention of my stress syndrome. It just could take a little time to reach that point, that's all.

I put a big forkful of chocolate gateau into my mouth, to a smile of satisfaction from Victoria, and nearly choked it all out again when the phone began to ring.

'You get it,' smiled Beverly. 'Told you he'd come round!'

'Hello, Alison, dear,' crackled my mother's voice over the line from Majorca. 'Just calling to wish you a Happy Fiftieth!'

'Mum!' I spat, spraying chocolate gateau into the phone. 'We've been trying to get you! What's all this nonsense about staying out there . . .'

'It isn't nonsense,' she said stiffly. 'We're going into business. We've taken over a little bar in the main square, by the seafront.'

'You haven't! For God's sake, Mum, please tell me you haven't signed anything yet . . .'

'Oh yes, we have. We'll be home for a couple of weeks at the end of the month, to sort out all our stuff there, get everything packed . . .'

'Mum!'

' . . . and we're having the bar redecorated and refurbished in cockney style . . .'

'Mum!'

' . . . and we'll be ready to open next month. Catch the best part of the season. There's living accommodation over the . . .'

'Mum, listen to me.'

Silence. I could hear myself breathing, heavily, into the phone.

'No need to shout,' she said, sulkily.

'I can't believe you're doing this,' I breathed. In, out, in, out, calm down. 'You don't know *anything* about running a bar.'

'Ted used to have a pub. The White Hart in Tottenham. You know where the bus pulls in round the back of Woolworths—'

'It's not the same as a bloody cockney bar in Majorca!' Breathe. In— one, two, three—out, one, two, three. Think calm thoughts . . .

'What's she say?' hissed Bev from across the room.

'They open for business next month,' I said, passing her the phone. 'You talk to her.'

'Mum?' Beverly was trying to sound bright and encouraging. 'How's it going? You've found yourself a little place, then?' Not a good idea to patronise my mother. I could hear the indignant mouthful Beverly was getting, as she ruefully lifted the phone away from her ear.

'Yes, of course we want it to go well for you, Mum. No, we're not being negative. We're just concerned . . . Yes, I know you've got Ted to look after you but we don't really know anything about him, do we, Mum? . . . Yes, I'm sure he is a lovely man . . . Yes, I expect he is a lot more interested in you than I've ever been . . . Oh, for Christ's sake!'

She threw the phone back at me, red in the face and beginning to shake slightly. 'I need a drink!'

I breathed steadily into the phone for a few more minutes before beginning again.

'Your health,' I said slowly, 'isn't good.'

'I'm much better out here. The sunshine. It agrees with me. I feel twenty years younger.'

Twenty years younger. Christ, that was something, wasn't it? And it had to be said, she sounded different. Animated, excited.

She had an interest in life, something to plan for. A hope. It's what we all need, isn't it, when it comes down to it. We need to wake up in the morning and think: Today could be good. It could be fun, it could be exciting!'—even if it turns out to be dull and boring. Otherwise, what is the point of it all? We might as well stay in bed every day.

My mother probably felt like staying in bed every day, up till now.

What did she have to get up for, when you think about it? She was fed up, bored and miserable. Every day she found another problem, another ache or pain or malfunction somewhere in her body.

Now she was out there in the sun with a man who loved her, excited about her life, feeling twenty years younger.

What was the matter with me? Was I jealous or something?

'I'm sorry, Mum,' I said quite gently.

'Sorry? What for?' she asked, obviously taken aback.

'Sorry I've been . . . yes, a bit negative about all this. I hope it all goes well for you. So does Beverly. Yes, she's nodding at me across the room, she hopes it does, too.' Beverly was lifting her wineglass at me with a glazed look of insouciance. 'And the girls are here, Mum! Victoria and Lucy—they're both saying they hope it goes well, too! Now, listen, this phone call's costing you a lot of money, so . . . Yes, I'm having a lovely birthday, thank you. And we'll see you . . . well. Whenever.'

Whenever it all goes wrong. Whenever you fall out of love with Ted. Whenever the holiday atmosphere wears off, the reality kicks in and the dream goes sour. When you start arguing and you suddenly wish you were back in England, with the old familiar worries and the old familiar miseries. When that happens, if that happens, we'll see you then, Mum, because that's what families are all about, aren't they?

I hung up and looked around the room, at my daughters in their new clothes with the remains of my birthday tea spread out on the table in front of them, and my sister slouched in the armchair with her glass of wine and her apron on. And the flowers and the birthday cards, and the balloons hanging from the curtain rail. And I felt so emotional about it all, I had to swallow a couple of times and pour myself out another drink.

'What else did she say?' asked Beverly with a slight slurring of the consonants.

'That she missed us all. And she'll see us in a few weeks when they come back to pack up their stuff.'

'If they haven't changed their minds by then!'

'I thought you were in favour of letting them get on with it.'

'Sure, yes, absolutely. I'm just a bit cynical about their long-term prospects.'

'So what?'

We all looked at each other for a minute. Victoria scraped the last of the trifle out of the bowl and licked her lips.

'Mum's right,' she declared. 'So what if it doesn't last? As long as they're happy for now. For a week, for a month, for a year. It's all a bonus, at their age, isn't it?'

'Being happy is a bonus at any age,' I reminded her. 'It's not an automatic state of affairs.'

'Then Nan's lucky, isn't she,' said Lucy earnestly. 'Because up till now she's never seemed all that happy, if you ask me.'

'Better late than never!' laughed Victoria.

'Yeah. And at least I won't have to take her for any hospital appointments for a while,' I said, feeling a huge black cloud suddenly lift off my shoulders. 'And if you want a holiday,' I added with a smile, 'she said any of us would be welcome out there any time.'

It was like I'd lit the touch paper of a volcano. Victoria leapt out of her chair shouting with excitement, Lucy whooped and danced around the room, Beverly tried to shout them both down with information about flights to Majorca and Did They Realise How Much It Cost? and the phone started ringing again.

'Hello?' yelled Beverly, trying to make herself heard above the mayhem. 'James? Yes, she's here, James, hang on . . .'

I grabbed the phone out of her hand so quickly, she claimed later to have blisters in her palm.

I didn't wish you a happy birthday properly,' he said. I'd taken the phone into my bedroom to get some peace. And shut the door. And laid on my bed.

'Well, in the circumstances I could hardly expect you to.'

'I just wish you'd been honest with me. Did you really think I'd care whether you were thirty-nine or fifty?'

'Not really. I said it as a joke, but it got more difficult to explain as we went on.'

'So you're not really on holiday. You're recuperating from . . . what? A nervous breakdown?'

I laughed. 'No! I'm not really ill at all. But no one believes me, even the doctor. I tried to skive off work, and I somehow got myself into this situation where everyone thinks I'm suffering from stress. Even my family, I've given up trying to convince them . . .'

I didn't like the silence.

'What?' I asked.

'There's nothing to be ashamed of. You shouldn't be embarrassed about suffering from a psychological illness, any more than you would be about suffering from a physical one.'

'But I'm not—'

'I mean, if someone's got the flu, or tonsillitis, or something, people feel sorry for them, but if they have a nervous breakdown—'

'I haven't—'

'. . . nobody wants to talk about it, not even the person with the problem. We all pretend it isn't happening, like it's a disgrace to admit to it—' *'James!'*

He was beginning to seriously get on my nerves. I could feel myself getting close to the brink of telling him to shut up.

'Suffering from stress is a consequence of our modern lifestyle. We all try to live our lives in the fast lane, taking on too much pressure, and never pausing to watch the flowers grow or . . .'

'James?'

'Yes?'

'Can I tell you something?'

'Of course.'

'You're the best-looking man I've ever met, but you already know that, don't you? I had a fantastic time in bed with you, and I'm really glad you made me realise it was still possible.' I could almost hear him smirking. 'But you don't half talk some crap,' I added calmly.

'What?'

'Thanks for phoning, James. I'm glad we could finish up as friends.'

'Yes, but—'

'Bye!'

Funny thing was, it felt *so good.*

Chapter 8

VICTORIA AND LUCY slept in Beverly's lounge and stayed for another two days. We went to the beach and watched the surfers, and Lucy chatted up a bronzed, blond young god of the surf called Neil, who snogged her in full view of the rest of the family (to say nothing of the whole of Newquay) and took her out to the pictures that evening.

'What was he like?' I asked her in the morning.

'Horny,' she said, with a smile of appreciation.

The sun shone, the sea sparkled and our skin turned slowly golden brown as we basked on the sand with our personal CD-players and our Ambre Solaire Factor Twelve.

On the Sunday morning we woke up to grey skies and the threat of rain. More than two days of sunshine in England and we start to get overexcited, don't we? Victoria moped around the house for an hour or so after breakfast and then announced that she was missing Reece and that as she had to go to work the next day, they might as well start heading for home. Lucy said she couldn't go without saying goodbye to Neil, so they had to wait for him to be contacted on his mobile phone and turn up at the house on his motorbike. He and Lucy then spent nearly an hour saying goodbye outside the front door.

Eventually Victoria couldn't stand it any more.

'Lucy! I'm going! Right now, whether you're coming or not!' she shouted at her sister, who gave Lover Boy a last lingering kiss, exchanged addresses, phone numbers and souvenirs of each other and waved goodbye to him until his motorbike was a speck in the distance.

'Bloody hell,' commented Victoria as she looked at Lucy's slightly glazed expression. 'You only met him yesterday.'

It happens, girl. It happens.

'I suppose you want to take the car back,' I said with a certain amount of resignation.

'Oh, Mum! We couldn't deprive you—' began Lucy.

'Are you sure you don't mind?' cut in Victoria. 'Only it would be easier, you know, to get home fast so I can get ready for work tomorrow . . .'

'And see Reece for a bit longer,' muttered Lucy under her breath.

'No, I don't mind,' I laughed. 'It's the least I can do, since you came all this way to see me for my birthday. But you'll have to take my black sack of clothes back with you.'

I'd hardly worn any of the clothes, anyway. Most of the time so far I'd either been in my swimming costume on the beach, or naked in bed with James.

'Got any plans for your second week?' asked Bev as we chilled out with a microwave supper and wine-box that evening.

'Not really. Got any suggestions for me?'

'Well. I daren't introduce you to any more of my male friends. You seem to want to tear their trousers off the minute my back's turned . . .'

'Not all of them,' I smiled. 'Didn't fancy Bo very much.'

She laughed. 'No. I think he's an acquired taste.'

We studied our plates thoughtfully.

'Actually,' I said, 'I wouldn't mind not doing very much at all. It's all been quite . . . unsettling . . . James, and everything. I could do with some time to think about things.'

'Paul?'

'Those sort of things, yes.'

'Well, it has been two years, Ally.'

What was that supposed to mean? It's been two years, so it's about time you got over it? Moved on? Made a new life for yourself?

'It's about time you accepted her . . . Lynnette.'

Oh, great! I have to accept *her*, do I? Perhaps she should have accepted *me*, when she decided to steal my husband—accepted that I was his wife, that he was married, spoken for, not available.

'I have no reason,' I said, frostily, 'to accept her.'

'But what would you say if they wanted to get married?'

Now, there's an interesting thought.

I thought about it that night in bed, tossing and turning and furious with Beverly for bringing it up, spoiling my night's sleep. I thought about it the next day, sitting indoors with a book because it rained again, but unable to read the book because my mind kept straying to the Paul and Lynnette Getting Married Thing. I was still thinking about it the day after that, when it stopped raining and I went back to the beach again. Paul and Lynnette getting married. They couldn't. They wouldn't, would they? It had never even crossed my mind before.

So am I stupid, or what? Why hadn't it crossed my mind?

I always consoled myself, whenever I thought about Lynnette (which I mostly tried not to do), with the fact that she might have him now, but I was still Paul's wife. Official. Certified.

So however long it took for him to come to his senses and dump her, I would always have the upper hand and he would come back to me eventually. Divorce had never been mentioned and it hadn't occurred to me because of the temporary nature I'd always ascribed to our separation.

Temporary, but well, you know. I was kind of getting used to it. Over the course of two years, you have to, don't you? You have to get used to it. Not that I didn't still want him back. Of course I did. That was obvious. Wasn't it?

'I'm not standing for it,' I told Beverly over dinner, feeling better now I'd made up my mind. 'She's not marrying Paul. He's still married to me.'

'He might want a divorce.'

'He would have said by now. He hasn't ever said he wanted one. He doesn't. He doesn't want to marry her. He wants to stay married to me. She's just a bit on the side.'

'Ally—'

'Don't look at me like that.'

'She probably loves him, Ally. She probably really loves him.'

Love, huh! I was beginning to wonder about the whole thing.

'No,' I said firmly. 'She doesn't love him. She just wanted to steal him from me and my children. Well, she can't. She won't *ever* be his wife. I'd rather see her dead!'

I'd got myself a bit worked up by now.

'Ally!' remonstrated Beverly again. 'You shouldn't say things like that. You don't really mean it.'

'Don't I?' I retorted grimly. 'You watch and see if I don't.'

I was actually asleep when Victoria phoned.

'Mum? You're not in bed already?'

'Well . . .' I'd been lying on top of the bed, fully dressed, contemplating a few things, like whether I should go on a diet and whether Lynnette should be allowed to live, when I'd dozed off. It was only half past nine. Funny how you could get exhausted doing nothing.

'Have you heard about Lynnette?' said Victoria, coming straight to the point without any preamble.

'What about her?'

'She's ill.'

'Oh dear. Nothing trivial, I hope?'

'Mum, that's awful.'

'Only joking,' I said hastily. I wasn't, of course, but I didn't want my own daughter thinking badly of me. 'So what is it? Flu? Measles? Work-related stress?' Perhaps it's catching, I don't know.

'No. Food poisoning.'

'Food poisoning?' Perhaps she should avoid eating her own cooking. 'Is Dad all right?'

'Yes, apart from being worried to death.'

'Oh, come on. Just a stomach upset—'

'No, it's been really bad. She's been in hospital.'

Oh. I sat up straight on the bed. This wasn't funny, after all. I'd spent the last couple of days thinking evil, nasty thoughts about the woman and there she goes, getting herself food poisoning and being taken to hospital. It was scary. I felt as if I'd wished it on her. I'd better be careful what I thought about in future.

'Is she all right now?' I asked a bit shakily.

'Recovering. But very weak, very poorly, really.'

'Well. I'm . . . er . . . sorry to hear . . .' I said, trying to sound sorry. 'It's just that . . .' Victoria hesitated.

'What?'

Paul's decided he wants to marry her? Because she's been ill, he feels he ought to suggest it. He feels sorry for her. Thinks it would cheer her up to get dressed up in white and . . .

'Dad thinks it's you,' she blurted out.

'Me? What's me?'

'He thinks you poisoned her. Lynnette,' she added unnecessarily.

I nearly laughed, but checked myself when I heard the tone of anxiety in Victoria's voice.

'He thinks you put slug pellets in her coffee,' she added, sounding close to tears.

'Oh, how ridiculous!' I exclaimed. 'For God's sake, Victoria, I hope you told him to grow up and get a life—

'He's serious, Mum. I'm surprised he hasn't phoned you himself. He says you threatened to do it—'

'I was joking!'

'And you made her a cup of coffee and told her you'd poisoned it!'

'Joking! What's the matter with him? Can't he take a . . .' Well, no, he obviously couldn't. I suppose he wouldn't, would he, with his girlfriend lying ill and feeble in a hospital bed. I began to feel a rising tide of alarm. Surely he wasn't serious?

'That cup of coffee was ages ago.' I said. 'And anyway, I don't even know what slug pellets look like. Or how to get hold of them.'

'So you did say it? You did tell her you'd poisoned her?'

'Victoria, you're not listening to this rubbish, are you?'

'No, Mum,' she said quietly. She sounded tearful.

Bugger Paul. I was furious with him. How dare he upset the girls with this nonsense. He was only trying to get back at me for teasing Lynnette. Hurting her precious little feelings.

'You and Lucy take no notice of this.' I ordered sternly. 'Understand? And tell your father . . .' I ran out of steam. What were they supposed to tell him? That he was a total prat? That he should stop causing trouble and get back to looking after his sick girlfriend, try to stop her eating anything else that upset her? 'Tell him I'm on my way home,' I finished with sudden determination. 'Tomorrow. I'll see you tomorrow. OK?'

'All right,' sniffed Victoria. 'I'll tell him.'

It wasn't much of a homecoming. My own daughters looked at me as if I was an axe-murderer and even the cat wouldn't come near me, presumably because he'd heard I was handing out slug pellets like Smarties.

'Dad's coming round,' said Lucy.

'Oh, goodie.'

'Wants to talk it over with you.'

'I bet he does,' I said grimly.

'How are you?' she added, switching on the kettle.

How was I? I stared at her for a minute without comprehension.

It was Lynnette that was supposed to be ill, wasn't it? Oh, hang on a minute. Of course. The work-related stress. I'd forgotten all about it.

'Fine, fine,' I said vaguely. 'Be back at work on Monday.'

'If the doctor signs you off,' she warned.

'Well, it shouldn't be a problem as long as no one tells her I'm a mass-poisoner, should it?'

'It's not really funny, Mum.'

I'm not laughing.

Paul sat down on the edge of the sofa, looking at me warily. How did I get to have such power? All the family tiptoeing around me, looking at me with respect mixed with fear. What I'd have given for that when the children were little and I needed them to do as they were told, and needed Paul to help me. Silly me. If only I'd realised all I had to do was start a rumour that I was a crazy woman with access to deadly poison.

'You've put on some weight,' he said.

'Thanks. You look good, too.'

A ghost of a smile. Perhaps he wasn't convinced, yet, that I was crazy.

'I mean, I'm surprised you don't look . . . you know. Ill. Thin. Drawn. Wan. Wasted . . .'

'All right, I get the picture. Instead, I look fit and fat. Could be because there's nothing wrong with me.'

He ignored this, like everyone did.

'Sorry to hear about Lynnette,' I said with a supreme effort.

'She's been very ill.'

'So I hear.'

We looked at each other. Your move. No, yours I think.

'Food poisoning,' he said, nodding at me.

'Awful.'

'Something she ate, they say.'

'Usually is. That's why they call it . . .'

'Ally!' he snapped. 'I'd appreciate you not being flippant!'

'Sorry.'

'It affected her kidneys.'

'Poor her. Nasty. But she's getting better?'

'Yes. The point I'm making, Ally, or trying to make, is . . .'

THE TROUBLE WITH ALLY

I looked at him with polite, concerned interest. The point is?

'The cat. He had the same symptoms. And it affected *his* kidneys.'

Actually, that was quite interesting, I had to admit. Quite a coincidence, that. What was the point he was making here?

Lynnette was like a cat? Or she'd caught a disease from Apple Pie? I frowned at him, concentrating, really quite caught up in it all.

'And the vet diagnosed poisoning with slug pellets.'

'The vet? Lynnette saw a *vet*?'

'Don't be obtuse, Ally. The vet you took Apple Pie to. He diagnosed . . .'

'Oh. Well, he said it *could* be slug pellets. He said cats often pick them up from gardens . . .'

I stared at him. 'You're saying I poisoned my own cat?'

My hands flew to my mouth. This was horrific. I couldn't believe it. Christ, it was one thing to suggest I'd try to do away with Lynnette, but my own cat? What sort of a maniac did he think I was?

'Did you want to find out how much it would take, Ally? How many slug pellets would kill a cat, before you put them in Lynnette's coffee?'

'Paul, you're not serious about all this, are you? Come on, I know you want to get back at me for upsetting Lynnette, but this isn't very funny—'

'No. It isn't.'

'I say these things. It's a sort of . . . outlet. For my feelings. For God's sake, you can't blame me for my feelings! I don't *mean* anything by them. Can you really imagine me trying to hurt anyone?'

'Not normally.'

'What's that supposed to mean?'

'Well, as everyone's been trying to point out to you, you're not exactly normal at the moment. Not exactly yourself, are you?'

I stared at my feet. They looked normal. My legs looked like mine. My hands and arms didn't look any different. I was *me*.

'You're not . . . going around saying these things to anyone else, are you?' I asked, quietly, hearing my voice wobble.

'Not yet,' said Paul.

Not yet. He made it sound like a threat. *Not yet, but I might.*

I shuddered. There'd be a knock on the door in the middle of the night. 'Mrs Bridgeman? Wife of Mr Bridgeman, now living with Lynnette? We're arresting you on suspicion of the attempted murder, by poison, of one black and white cat and one skinny red-haired woman. You're not obliged to say anything but—'

'I didn't do it!' I'd scream, as I was taken away in a Black Maria, with a huge ugly crowd pressing against the windows.

The Slug Pellet Poisoner! the tabloid headlines would scream. 'Woman

403

tested poison meant for husband's mistress on her own cat!'

And all the animal rights activists in the country would send me hate mail in prison, where I'd be kept in solitary confinement to protect me from the other prisoners, who wouldn't tolerate cruelty to cats. No one would mind about Lynnette, apart from Paul, who'd spend the rest of his life campaigning for my sentence to be increased. I'd languish in jail, calling out for Apple Pie, my only friend, the only one who could save me, if only he could talk.

'What?' snapped Paul.

'If only he could talk,' I repeated, realising with a start that I'd said it aloud. 'Apple Pie. He'd tell you I didn't give him any poison.'

'Sorry, Ally. Cat's *can't* talk,' he said brusquely, getting to his feet. 'Which is why you used him to test the stuff, wasn't it?'

'Paul! You don't *really* think—?'

'I'll see myself out,' he said.

Just when you think things can't get any worse, they inevitably get worse. I was running late for my doctor's appointment so I decided to take the car.

'Where's my car, Victoria?' I called out, staring blankly at the space where it was normally parked.

'Oh,' she smiled at me. 'I forgot to tell you.'

You may think it slightly strange that I'd been home from Cornwall for two days without noticing my car wasn't there, but when you consider that since I'd been home I'd been accused of two counts of attempted murder, you might begin to understand that my mind had been just a tad preoccupied elsewhere.

'What,' I asked Victoria very nervously, 'what have you forgotten to tell me?' I closed my eyes, waiting for the blow to be dealt.

'We decided to give you a surprise,' she smiled again, looking very pleased with herself. 'Lucy and me. We wanted to treat you.'

'So you gave the car away?'

I might have threatened to do it myself on occasions, but I didn't mean it. You should know by now that I don't mean half the things I threaten. Murders, poisonings, car abandonment—they're all just idle threats . . .

'No. We put it in for its MOT, Mum.'

'Oh.' I gave her a hug. Nice to know they still loved me, despite having doubts about my sanity. 'That was very sweet of you.'

'Yes. We paid for it. Between us. As a sort-of birthday present.'

'Well, I'm very grateful. That was a lovely thing to do.' I waited. She smiled back at me happily.

THE TROUBLE WITH ALLY

'So where is it?' I asked. 'The car. Where is it now?'

'Oh.' She looked down, the smile fading. 'Still in the garage. They're keeping it there. Till we decide what to do. Well, till you decide, really.' 'Sorry?'

'We could only afford the test fee, Mum. And it failed. It failed on six different things. It'll cost about three hundred and fifty pounds to get it through. I said you'd think about it.'

I walked to the surgery.

I was pleased it was Dr Lewis I was going to see this time. I'd liked the little girl locum, particularly after she seemed to know such a lot about my pretend symptoms, but at the end of the day she'd done nothing but get me into more trouble. Giving me a certificate for work-related stress had been a stupid move, and as for giving me three weeks off work, well, she might just as well have written to Snotty Simon and suggested that he give the job to the Temp whenever he liked. Dr Lewis knew me. He'd see straight away that whatever minor, temporary little touch of stress I might have had, it was certainly not enough to keep me off work.

'Hello, Alison,' he smiled warmly, stretching out his hand to me as soon as I walked into his surgery. 'Long time no see!'

You see? He knew I wasn't a sick person. Sick people are regular visitors to their doctors, aren't they?

'And how are you now?' he continued as I sat down. 'I see you've had a few problems recently?'

'Not really,' I smiled, trying to brush my few problems aside with a little toss of my head. 'Nothing that a little bit of rest couldn't take care of. You know how it is, Dr Lewis. Sometimes you just get a bit overtired, and things seem a bit worse than they really are . . .'

He was nodding at me with grave concern. 'And have you been able to sort out any of your anxieties now?' he asked me quietly, looking straight into my eyes as if he were trying to hypnotise me.

'Anxieties?' I laughed, flicking my hair back gaily. 'Oh, they weren't really *anxieties*, you know, just little niggles like we all have . . .'

'Worries about losing your job?' he asked, looking down at my notes and then back into my eyes. 'About your boss not liking you? Anxieties about your financial situation?'

Bloody hell, she'd told him the lot. What happened to patient confidentiality? I sat up a bit straighter in the chair.

'The anxieties are . . . sorting themselves out,' I said uneasily.

'And your age-related concerns?'

'Pardon?'

'Dr Holcombe thought you might have had a problem with approaching your fiftieth birthday?'

I smiled to myself, remembering the morning of my fiftieth birthday. I'd probably never have another orgasm like that as long as I lived.

'You coped with the occasion?' Dr Lewis prompted me.

'Oh, yes, I coped, thank you, Doctor,' I smiled.

He was approaching me with the blood pressure machine.

'And the rest from work has done you good?'

'Yes, thank you.'

We both waited in tense silence for the reading from my arteries, while he continued to look into my eyes as if he was examining them for specks of dirt. Just as I was beginning to feel uncomfortable with the scrutiny, he announced: 'It's higher than it should be. Your blood pressure. And I've got no doubt about the reason.'

I'm dying? I'm having a stroke? A heart attack? I'm on my last legs, not likely to last the night?

'Physically, you're in very good shape.'

So the blood pressure machine's on the blink?

'Psychologically, I think you're in trouble.'

The silence lasted for a good thirty seconds before I yelled at him, smiling and head-tossing having completely gone out of the window.

'Well, thank you very much! I thought at least you would stand by me! Everybody else thinks I'm raving mad . . . my kids, my husband. Even the bloke I screwed on holiday thought I was having a breakdown.'

'You had casual sex on holiday?' he asked me calmly.

'Yes! And it was great!' I retorted.

He looked back at me, his calm, caring eyes resting impassively on my face, waiting. He didn't have to wait long. I'd known this man since I was a new bride. He'd seen me, as I've said before, in every position known to man (or woman). He knew me inside out. Literally. Under his gaze, I suddenly felt overcome with something like shame.

'All right,' I said. 'I suppose it was pretty stupid.'

'You're an adult,' he replied.

'I hardly knew him.'

'It happens all the time. You're human. Don't be hard on yourself.'

'I'm not.' Am I?

'Then what else is wrong?'

'Nothing.'

'Nothing? I don't think many people could say that, Alison, and certainly not many single parents with financial difficulties and job pressures, to say nothing of the worry of caring for elderly parents . . .'

'I told you, my anxieties are resolving themselves. My mother's gone, for a start.'

'Gone?' He shot me a look of acute concern.

'Oh, no. Not gone as in . . . departed this life. Just departed this country. She's gone to Majorca with a toy boy to open a cockney bar.' I felt myself frowning. 'How the hell she hopes to survive out there, I just can't imagine. What on earth does she think she's doing, taking such a risk at her time in life? I don't even know this Ted—he could be after her money—not that she's got any . . .'

'But your anxiety about her has resolved?' he pointed out gently.

'Well. You know. Perhaps only partly,' I conceded.

'But the girls are well?'

'Fine. Victoria buys *Brides* magazine every time she meets a new boy and Lucy's taking her first-year exams. No worries there,' I said, feeling my jaw tense as I said it.

'And Paul?' He did that thing again, where he looked straight through my eyes so that he could tell if I was lying. 'You're getting used to being on your own, now, Alison? How long has it been?'

'Two years,' I said tetchily. 'But that's no reason to accept it.'

'No?' he prompted.

'No! And I wouldn't accept them wanting to get married, either, not ever. I'd rather see her dead.'

I nearly bit straight through my lip after I'd said it. Shit! Why did I keep on saying that? Me and my big mouth.

'But I didn't *mean* that!' I added hastily, watching him scribbling in my notes. 'Don't write that down!' He put down his pen and looked at me again. 'I'm not saying I'd want to actually . . . you know . . . murder her. Not with poison, not with anything else. I wouldn't even know where to get hold of slug pellets, for God's sake. And I love my bloody cat. It's not my fault he was ill.'

I was crying now. Blubbing out loud. I could actually hear myself, making these big sobbing noises while I was still trying to speak.

'I wouldn't hurt my cat. I love him. I wouldn't hurt anyone, not even Lynnette. She probably just ate some of her own cooking . . .'

A box of tissues appeared in front of me. I groped for one and blew my nose violently.

The strange sobbing noise carried on for a few more minutes, getting gradually quieter, while he wrote in the notes and I soaked a few more tissues. 'I'm sorry,' I muttered, sniffing. 'I don't know what came over me. I was perfectly all right until I walked in here.'

'I don't think so,' he replied, very seriously.

He passed two pieces of paper across the desk to me. I picked them up, shakily. One was a prescription for diazepam. The other was a certificate for a further three weeks off work.

I don't know why I didn't argue. I should have refused to accept the certificate, told him I wouldn't leave until he'd signed me back for work. Instead I listened meekly while he told me I was to rest completely, have no contact with work whatsoever, and if I wasn't feeling any different after these three weeks were up he'd refer me to 'one of his colleagues'.

'A psychiatrist,' I said dully.

'It probably won't be necessary. Maybe just a stress counsellor. In the meantime, Alison, there are some self-help steps you can try. You can think about your diet,' he went on, writing 'diet' on a piece of paper.

'You think I need to lose weight?'

'That's not the issue here. The objective is to achieve a healthy mind through a healthy body. Stay off the junk food, the alcohol, the caffeine, the chocolate—all stimulants . . .'

All the things that keep me bloody going.

'And exercise.'

He wrote 'exercise' under 'diet' on the paper.

Exercise? I might have no choice if I can't find the money to get the bastard car through its MOT.

'Something strenuous, Alison. Something that will get you really out of breath.'

Walking upstairs? Making the beds? Reaching for the remote control?

'Jogging, or swimming, or aerobics.'

'So that's it, then? I cut out all the pleasurable things I normally eat and drink, and put myself through physical torture, and then you'll let me go back to work?'

'I'm only suggesting things that might help,' he replied gently. 'And the other thing, of course, is breathing.'

Well, I hadn't been planning on stopping that.

'Learn some relaxation techniques. You can get tapes from the library. When you feel yourself getting tense and worked up, you can learn to cope by relaxation and deep breathing.'

He wrote 'relaxation' under 'diet' and 'exercise', and passed the piece of paper to me with a smile and a putting down of his pen that indicated my time was up.

'Thanks,' I said, putting the paper in my pocket with the prescription and the certificate, and leaving the room feeling a hundred times worse than I had when I'd gone in.

How did this happen? How had I gone from making up a few little, tiny, harmless lies about some trivial symptoms, to get a few days off work, to having a full-flung breakdown that required drugs, rest, diet, exercise, relaxation and possible psychiatric counselling? When did I cross the line from pretend to real?

Was it real? Or was I still pretending? Why couldn't I tell the difference any more? Was I really as mad as everyone seemed to think I was? Or was I the only sane one left around here?

Chapter 9

I WAS LYING on the floor when Lucy came home, listening to *Floating*. *Floating* was one of two tapes of relaxation music I'd got from the library while waiting for my prescription to be processed at Boots. The other one was *Drifting*, but I hadn't tried that yet. *Floating* had loads of floaty music interspersed with some bird with an irritating sleepy voice telling you how to relax each bit of you in turn. It reminded me of those awful childbirth classes where you had to tense and then relax muscles in your toes and face and buttocks and pretend they were the muscles of your cervix. As that was possibly the most stressful memory of my life, it wasn't doing a great deal to relax me, but I'm open to all suggestions so I had my eyes closed waiting for the next bit of advice.

'Are you asleep, Mum?' asked Lucy without much interest. She turned off *Floating* and replaced it with her new Boyzone CD.

'No,' I said, opening my eyes. 'I was relaxing,'

'What, listening to that shit?'

Boyzone began to sing out lustily that they loved the way I loved them. They should be so lucky. I closed my eyes again and tried relaxing to Ronan Keating's dulcet tones. Certainly no worse than *Floating*, and no insinuations about childbirth classes.

'The exam was crap,' said Lucy mildly, throwing herself down on the sofa and stuffing two chocolate digestives into her mouth at once.

I sat bolt upright, clasping my mouth in horror, all thoughts of relaxation shot to dust.

'Your exam! I didn't forget . . . I just . . . had a few other things . . .'

'Don't worry, Mum.' She wiped biscuit crumbs off her chin and swung her feet up onto the arm of the sofa. 'It was awful. I revised all the wrong things.'

'Oh, Lucy.'

'But never mind. Three more to go next week. As long as I do better in them.'

'How much better?'

'Brilliantly. I need to do brilliantly now, to make up for the rubbish I've done today. If I don't, I'll be redoing the whole year.'

She spoke with a shrug, nonchalantly swinging her legs in time to Boyzone, but she didn't fool me. She was staring straight ahead of her at the framed picture of herself and Victoria on the fireplace. I followed her gaze. Two little blonde toddlers, the elder's arm protectively round the younger's shoulders, turning her face towards the camera. I could hear her now, as if it were yesterday: 'Look at Mummy, Lucy. Look at the camera, Lucy. Smile like me, Lucy; like this. Come on, Lucy, do like I do.' *Do like I do.* It was hard to break out of the little sister thing, to *not* be in Victoria's shadow, to *not* do like Victoria did.

Victoria had got a job straight after doing her A levels. Lucy had gone to college. It wasn't that she had to be better than Victoria—she just had to be different. I could understand that. She had to succeed.

'You'll do it, Luce,' I told her gently, levering myself up off the floor to perch on the sofa arm next to her feet. 'You'll pass, I know you will.'

'You've got no idea,' she snapped suddenly, leaping to her feet, making the sofa tip up from my weight on its arm. 'You've got no *idea* how hard it is. I wish I'd never done this course. I'm no good at it. I can't do it. I'm going to fail all the exams. I might as well give up now.'

She stamped upstairs to her room in much the same way as she had when I'd refused to buy her another My Little Pony about fifteen years back.

'What's with *her*?' demanded Victoria, coming in the front door just as the house was shuddering from the slamming of the bedroom door.

'Exam nerves. Just leave her alone,' I snapped.

'I *am* leaving her alone.'

She looked at me bleakly, her lower lip wobbling, her eyes filling up with tears.

'What's the matter?' I asked, taking a step towards her.

'Oh, what do you *think* it is? It's just *men*. I hate them. All of them. I'm never going out with another one as long as I live. I'll be a nun. I'll be a lesbian. I'll be a virgin. They're all pigs!'

And she followed her sister's route upstairs, her bedroom door closing more quietly but with a kind of sustained misery. Reece, I presumed, had joined Darren and all the others in the 'ex' file.

I turned off Boyzone, who were by now singing some very inappropriate lyrics about love being for ever, no matter what, and went into the kitchen to peel some potatoes. *Floating* would have to wait. It seemed to me that everyone else around here was more stressed out than I was.

I started keeping a Relaxation, Diet and Exercise Diary, just to show I was serious about it all, and also to show Dr Lewis, when I went back, in case he thought I hadn't been trying.

MONDAY, JUNE 23, I wrote very neatly on the first page. Just like being at school. I always wrote very neatly on the first page.

Relaxation: managed five minutes of listening to Floating without thinking about childbirth. Lay in front of TV on cushions and practised breathing.

Diet: breakfast: grapefruit and muesli. Lunch: lettuce and tomato sandwich. Mid-afternoon: two Penguins. One chocolate digestive. Five Jaffa cakes. Dinner: chicken with salad. Later: a few chips off Victoria's plate. Later: the rest of the Jaffa cakes. Bedtime: corned beef and pickle sandwich.

Exercise: found on old pair of trainers and tried them on, with a view to starting a jogging regime.

All in all, not a bad start. Tomorrow would be even better. And as for the neatness of my first page—it was beyond reproach!

Things were definitely looking more cheerful in the Bridgeman household by the next day. Lucy had managed to answer all the questions on her exam paper that morning, and she didn't mention leaving college more than four times during the evening meal.

Victoria had been lent a book by a friend at work called *Nobody Needs A Man In Their Life*, and was eagerly quoting passages from it to anyone who'd listen, which basically meant me because Lucy plugged her CD Walkman into her ears as soon as she started.

'Listen to this, Mum. "The period of history during which men were looked up to as head of the household is coming to an end and will probably not last another decade." Do you think that's true?'

'Perhaps,' I conceded vaguely, trying to concentrate on the neat writing of page two of my diary.

'"Men are lost and confused," she went on.

Join the club.

'"They have no identity, no purpose, no place. They have become irrelevant to the majority of women in the civilised world.''

You could almost feel sorry for them.

'''Millions of years of patriarchy are being turned upside-down.''

'Victoria, do you think you could just read that to yourself?'

I'd come very close to writing a wonky 'D' on 'Diet' and I really, really, didn't want to spoil this page.

'But, Mum! It's absolutely amazing, don't you think?'

'I've heard it all before, to be honest,' I said wearily. 'We're supposed to be able to live happier, more fulfilled lives without men. Great! So why do we all sit glued to the TV when George Clooney's in ER, and gasp and sigh every time he smiles?'

'It's pathetic,' she agreed. 'Well, I for one refuse to be at the mercy of my hormones for the rest of my life.'

I looked at her in alarm. What was she considering?

'I'm giving them up!' she declared stoutly with the religious conviction of a saint. 'For life!'

'So what's it to be? The convent or lesbianism?'

She shot me a scathing glance. 'Self-control.'

I dropped the pen, smudged the word 'Diet' and tore the page.

'Sod it!' I exclaimed crossly. 'Now look what you've made me do!'

'Celibacy!' she went on cheerfully. 'It's gaining popularity. Take my word for it, Mum, in a few more generations, everyone will be doing it.'

Oh well. By the time she'd realised the difficulty there, she would have finished the damned book. And at least she was more cheerful again, even if it was going to be slightly wearing having a celibate in the house. When the doorbell rang, my only concern was that if it was a man, Victoria might treat him to one of her quotations.

I got to the door just ahead of her, in case.

It was Simon the Slime, from work. And he was carrying a basket of flowers. And smiling.

Perhaps celibacy had its points after all.

I said the first thing that came into my head, which tends not to be a good idea. 'What are you doing here? I'm not allowed to have any contact with you at work. My doctor said . . .'

'Sorry,' he said, and that was strange for a start—Simon saying sorry. He even looked it. He stood there on the doorstep, clutching the basket of flowers and looking sorry, while Victoria hovered behind me with almost tangible vibes of hostility radiating from her. I expected her at any moment to call him a superfluous remnant of defunct male superiority or a testosterone-charged genetic design fault.

THE TROUBLE WITH ALLY

'Go and . . . er . . . feed the cat, please, Victoria,' I said firmly. I felt the sigh of her disapproval on the back of my neck, but she went, and I heard her banging tins of cat food about in the kitchen.

'You'd better come in,' I told the superfluous remnant of defunct male superiority. 'Or my neighbours will talk.'

He stepped into the hall, looking even more uncomfortable.

'These are for you,' he said, not meeting my eyes, putting the flowers down on the hall table.

A Get Well present? Or a leaving present?

Why would Simon come round here? Simon who hated me, who held the power of work and unemployment over me. Simon the Slime-man, in my home, bearing flowers, looking shifty. Very shifty.

'You're getting rid of me,' I said, my voice shuddering on the edge of control. 'Aren't you? That's what this is about, isn't it—getting rid of me.' 'No!'

I was surprised by his vehemence. He almost stamped his foot.

'What?' I continued with the merest suggestion of sarcasm. 'No as in "Not Yet"? Or No as in "Not Ever"?'

'Can we . . . er . . . do you think we could sit down?' he said.

I led him into the kitchen, where Apple Pie was gulping Whiskas down with greedy self-absorption and Victoria was pretending to stack the dishwasher.

'Thank you, Victoria,' I said in my new firm voice.

She sidled out of the room without looking at Simon but giving me a reproachful glare as she passed.

'He's my boss,' I tried to mouth at her, but this obviously impressed her not at all. He was still the enemy, the endangered species, the out-dated relic of paternalistic society.

'The thing is . . .' said Simon nervously as he sat down on a stool. Nervously! How the tables had turned! How the worm had squirmed! If only I'd been able to foresee, that day he'd made me beg and plead for my job, facing him across his huge and shiny desk, that he'd be sitting here tonight in my kitchen, *squirming nervously!*

'The thing is, Alison, I need to talk to you about this business of work-related stress.'

'You can't stop my pay,' I said at once, with more confidence than I felt. Actually, I realised with some surprise that I probably *did* appear confident. For once in my life, I had the upper hand. I had a few definite advantages, such as:

1. *It was my house.*
2. *He was sitting down, I was standing up.*

413

3. *This was my kitchen. My domain, where I'd spent nearly all my life, peeling potatoes and feeding the cat, feeding babies and cleaning the sink, emptying bins and buttering bread, frying eggs and unpacking shopping, drinking coffee and . . . well, you get the picture. And:*

4. *This was where I kept the knives.*

Now, don't get me wrong. I wasn't anticipating needing one. I hadn't flipped so seriously that I was contemplating sticking the bread knife in his back or cutting his throat with the grapefruit knife. But . . . well, it was reassuring to know that this was where I kept them. I always used to be reassured by that thought, when I was sitting lonely in the kitchen drinking coffee when Paul used to be out at night and the babies were asleep in bed. There were enough sharp knives in that kitchen to defend myself against the Russian army, should they be planning an invasion.

'You can't stop my pay,' I repeated, calmly, folding my arms and staring at Simon across my kitchen table. 'I've been certified sick by the doctor.'

'I know,' he said. 'We have no intention of stopping your pay, believe me.'

I didn't like this new, nervous, squirming, oh-so-sincere and here's-a-basket-of-flowers Simon. I didn't like it at all. It made me very, very suspicious and very, very irritated. Just looking at him now, and remembering how he'd treated me that day in his office, so supercilious, so dismissive, so arrogant . . .

I took a knife out of the dishwasher, tested its blade against my finger, held it up to the light, put it back again. Not sharp enough.

'Are you . . . all right?' asked Simon.

'Fine, fine. Just testing the knives.'

'Listen,' he tried again, evidently anxious to move the conversation on. 'The point is, nobody at the office realised you were . . . ,'

Crazy? Such a superb worker, an asset to the company?

'. . . under stress.'

'I wasn't. I mean . . . not until recently,' I corrected myself quickly. I looked at him with increasing dislike and added: 'Only since the interview in your office when you issued me with my Serious Warning. You know, the one that was going to go on my Personal File.'

He blanched. He really did! He turned white, looked like he was going to throw up, then went abruptly pink, then had a coughing fit from which he began to have doubts that he would ever recover.

Save me a job with the knife.

'Want a glass of water?' I asked eventually out of mere politeness and to pass the time before he stopped breathing.

He nodded, eyes popping, tongue lolling in a most unattractive fashion. I'd seen healthier sights in geriatric wards.

'Consider it . . .' he choked over his glass of water. 'Consider it . . .'

'Done?' I prompted, bored.

'Consider it struck off !' he managed eventually, loosening his collar and spitting up the last mouthful of water. 'The Serious Warning. Struck off your Personal File. As from today.' I stared at him, suddenly not bored any more. This was, suddenly, interesting.

'Why?' I asked, simply.

'Because we want you back at work, fit and unstressed,' he said, unconvincingly.

'Why?' I persisted.

'Because you're . . . a good worker!' He was wriggling uncomfortably on his stool. He was hating this, hating every minute of it. What had forced him to come . . .? Or . . . who?

'Who made you come round here?' I demanded, already knowing the answer. 'And don't try to pretend you made the decision yourself, out of decency, humanity, or compassion, because I'd have no choice but to stab you.'

His eyes bulged again and I thought he was about to start another coughing fit.

'Well?'

'My father,' he admitted, looking at his shoes. 'My father was very concerned to hear about your work-related stress.'

'Yeah,' I smiled. 'Yes, I bet he bloody was. I bet he's hurrying back even as we speak from his golf course in Portugal, scared about the possibility of me taking the company to court for causing my illness.'

Simon continued to study his shoes.

'Isn't he?'

'Probably,' he admitted finally in a whisper.

'Well, you can tell your old man something from me,' I said, folding my arms again and giving him the most evil look I could manage.

Oh, this was lovely, this was! I could get used to having the upper hand. It was almost orgasmic. No wonder people get hooked on power.

'Tell him I *might* decide to sue the company, and I might *not*. It depends.'

'Depends on what?' he asked fearfully. He obviously had to get the message right, to report back to Dad.

'How I get treated when I come back to work, of course,' I replied scathingly.

'So what are your demands?' he said.

'Demands? Demands?' I retorted. 'What do you think I am? A black-mailer?' Honestly. My reputation was shot to pieces these days, what with accusations of poisoning and all.

'Of course not,' he said at once.

'All I'm saying is,' I continued, and I had to think about this to make sure I got it right, said exactly what I meant, because I'd never get another opportunity, 'I don't want it to be the same old thing when I come back. I want a bit of understanding if I need time off for my car, or my cat, or my mother, or any of those things we all can't help. If I make up the time by working late, or working my lunch-breaks, why can't you be reasonable about it? Why is it one law for Nicola, and another law for me? I expect to be treated the same as her. Except, of course, for the sex, because that would make me puke.'

A bit daring, that. In normal circumstances I'd never have gone that far, but we weren't in the workplace now, were we—we were in my kitchen. With the knives.

'I understand,' he said quietly.

I didn't really need to say any more, so I didn't bother. Quit while you're ahead. Simon left, hurriedly, still looking at his feet, promising things would be different. I shut the door after him, wondering if I'd just had an out-of-body experience in a time warp. The whole thing seemed so unreal. Nothing for it but to sit down with a glass of wine and a box of Jaffa cakes, and watch *Two Point Four Children*.

I went jogging the next day. Well, to be absolutely honest, I put on the trainers, went out, jogged to the end of the road, stopped for breath, walked round the corner, and then it started raining so I jogged halfway home. And walked the other half. When I got home I had to have a cup of tea and two slices of toast to get over it. But it was a start, wasn't it?

The next day I jogged to the bus-stop before getting the bus to Tesco, but that was a bad idea because I then felt too knackered to push the trolley round the shop. However, by the end of the week I was jogging for England. I could keep going all the way to the end of the road, round the corner and almost back again without dying.

My diary (apart from the smudge and tear on page two) was looking impressive. I'd cut down on chocolate to the point where I only ate one Jaffa cake at a time, and had started doing the relaxation exercises.

I came back from my morning jog on the Saturday morning to find a motorbike parked outside our house. I slowed down (well, I was slow-ing down by now anyway on account of the sweat dripping down my neck and the pains in my sides), and stared at it.

I didn't *know* anyone who drove a motorbike. I didn't even know anyone who knew anyone who drove one. Then I remembered, just at the same moment as the front door opened and he came out with all his limbs wrapped around my younger daughter. Neil.

'Morning, Ally!' he called out cheerfully from somewhere around Lucy's neck.

'Morning,' I puffed and wheezed. 'What are you doing here?'

It took me a few seconds to realise how ungracious that sounded, and I followed it up quickly with: 'I mean, all the way from Cornwall?'

'I drove down this morning. To see Lucy,' he explained with a wide grin as she gazed into his eyes with adoration.

'He's staying the weekend,' she smiled, stroking his hand.

'Where?'

'Here,' smiled Lucy again.

The smile was so soppy it made my stomach heave. Lucy had had boyfriends before, but so far she'd managed to avoid getting that look on her face. She'd always enjoyed making fun of Victoria whenever she'd fallen madly in love, and now . . . .

Victoria!

'Where's your sister?' I asked sharply.

'Sulking in her room,' said Lucy without taking her eyes away from Neil's. 'We're going out on the bike,' she added, putting both arms tightly around his waist.

I looked at the bike suspiciously.

'Be careful,' I warned with the automatic and irrepressible fear of a mother about to put her offspring into the hands of an unknown stranger and a dangerous machine.

'Don't worry, Ally,' said Neil with perfect seriousness, putting a helmet on Lucy's head and smiling at her as if it were the latest fashion and suited her more than any Paris model. 'I'll look after her better than anyone's ever looked after her in her life.'

She simpered and giggled and obviously thought it was the most romantic thing anyone had ever said to anyone in the whole history of the universe, while I fumed with annoyance at the implied insult that anyone could ever look after either of my babies better than I'd been doing for the past couple of decades. *And* I'd be the one to mop up the tears and soothe the heartache when he disappeared back to Cornwall on his bloody bike. But did she even give me so much as a backwards glance as she sailed off into the distance clutching him tightly from behind, with her face pressed against his leather-jacketed back?

Motherhood's a bastard at times.

Lucy and Neil roared back up to the house at somewhere round about feeding time. Love didn't seem to have dulled their appetites.

'Can we have chips?' shouted Lucy, taking off her crash helmet.

'Chips sound great,' grinned Neil, and they sat down together on the sofa and proceeded to stroke and tickle each other's necks.

'Oh, yuk!' exclaimed Victoria. 'Do you mind?'

'If you want chips, go and cook them,' I told Lucy in the no-nonsense tones of an in-control mother. A non-stressed, non-sick mother.

'Yeah, go on, go and cook them,' repeated Victoria.

'Mind your own business,' snapped Lucy.

'Thought you were stressed out over your exams?'

'Thought you were stressed out about being dumped.'

'Dumped? Huh! No man's gonna dump me! I'm never giving another one a chance! I'm not going to prostitute myself for—'

'You calling me a prostitute?' glared Lucy.

'You acting like one?'

'Hey, that's enough!' I decided to intervene, just as Lucy aimed the first swipe at Victoria.

Victoria squealed and lashed out blindly, knocking her cup of tea over the cat, who'd been dozing on her lap. Apple Pie ran yowling out of the room, closely followed by Neil, who was obviously embarrassed by the girls' fighting and pretended to need the toilet.

'Wimp,' muttered Victoria.

'Shut up,' returned Lucy.

The doorbell sounded. Probably the neighbours complaining about the noise or the RSPCA having heard reports of a scalded cat. I opened the door cautiously.

'Hello!' sung out my mother, who was leading by the hand a dapper little man in a blue suit. 'This is Ted! Can we come in?'

They made Lucy and Neil look like a rather reserved old married couple. Mum sat in an armchair and patted the seat next to her, shifting over so that Ted could squeeze in beside her. They held hands and smiled cheesily. Victoria was elected to go out and get a takeaway, which she did with obvious relief, muttering 'Yuk' viciously to herself.

'We got a taxi from the airport,' explained Mum, patting Ted's hand with every syllable. 'Didn't want to bother you.'

'So you're back to sort things out?' I asked.

'That's right, dear.'

Dear? My mother calling me 'dear'? Had she flipped? Too much Spanish sun?

THE TROUBLE WITH ALLY

'We've got a lot to do. Packing everything up, sorting out . . .'

'You're not selling your flat?'

'I'm not stupid!' she retorted with a flash of her old bad humour, softening again quickly as soon as Ted squeezed her hand. 'We're both keeping our properties here, just in case,' she smiled.

'Not that we expect any problems out there,' added Ted. It was the first time he'd spoken apart from 'Pleased to meet you'. 'British bars are big business in Majorca.'

'Good,' I said weakly, still having great difficulty imagining my mother behind the bar, pulling pints.

Had I ever really known her? I stared at this stranger sitting in my lounge with her boyfriend and her deep Majorca tan. She looked younger, slimmer and fitter than I remembered her. What had happened to the arthritis? The headaches, the bad chest, the skin conditions and the unmentionable problems with her bladder?

Only one possible explanation for it. Love. Love had changed her from a fearsome old biddy into a new and gentler person. Eat your heart out, Victoria!—and the author of *Nobody Needs A Man In Their Life!* Here was living evidence of your fallacy!

My mother ate her way through chicken tikka masala with onion bhaji and pilau rice without once complaining about her digestion—or complaining about anything else for that matter—and we talked about Majorca, and the British Bar Business, and the legalities and practicalities of starting up in it, and Ted came to life and opened up and told us about his years of running the White Hart pub in Tottenham, and the characters he had met there, and the wealth of experience he had built up. He told us without a trace of coyness or embarrassment how he had met my mother and fallen in love with her and how he'd throw himself into the pit of hell before he'd see any harm come to a single hair on her head.

Lucy and Neil looked at each other with dewy eyes and even Victoria swallowed back any sarcastic reply that might have been brewing and gazed at her wineglass in silence. The wine had no doubt helped towards the silence, but it was welcome in any case.

When their taxi arrived to take them back to stay at Mum's flat for a couple of nights ('We'll sort out my stuff first and then go on to Ted's'), I hugged her and said a few affectionate things that I'd probably never said before, and which owed less to the wine than to Ted's speech and, to be fair, the change in her own demeanour.

'It's a strange thing,' I admitted to Victoria as we scraped the curry plates and loaded the dishwasher, 'to suddenly start liking your mother at the age of fifty, and just as she's about to leave the country for good.'

And Victoria gave me a hug and said how lucky she was that she'd always liked her mother and didn't have to wait till she was fifty to find out. And I laughed and said she must be pissed, but I shed a tear or two when I went to bed, and whispered one of those rare little prayers that you say on these occasions, thanking God a thousandfold for letting me have two lovely daughters—one of whom was sleeping off her excess alcohol in front of the TV and the other of whom was sleeping with her new boyfriend (and hopefully adequate contraception) in the room next to mine—I put the pillow over my head and fell asleep.

I knew I had to make a decision about the car, but how? Where was the money going to come from to get it through its exam, and if I couldn't find the money, how was I going to manage without it when I went back to work? Two buses and a tube to get across London for the pleasure of working for Slimy Simon.

I jogged past the garage where the bastard car was languishing, and pulled faces at it behind its back. The bastard! I'd loved it, cherished it, cleaned it at least once every couple of months or so, bought it unleaded petrol and even put one of those little hanging things in the windscreen that smell of pine. And this was how it paid me back! It sat there, bloody sulking, and didn't even care that it had failed its test. Failed to the tune of three hundred and fifty quid. It didn't even have the decency to throw an exam-stress wobbly like Lucy did.

'You'll be sorry,' I told the car as I jogged past it for the second time, having now built my stamina up to the point where I could do two whole circuits without completely collapsing. 'You'll end up being sold to some maniac boy-racer who drives you through built-up areas screaming at sixty miles an hour on two wheels. Or a used-car dealer.' (I thought I noticed the car shudder at this, but it may have been a trick of the light, or the effect of the sweat dripping into my eyes.)

'And serve you bloody right!'

Actually, after saying it I felt sorry and wished I hadn't been so cruel. The car would never forgive me for that, and if I did manage to get it back, it would stall on hills and roll backwards into buses, and break down on dark winter mornings with no antifreeze in it, and . . .

I did a third circuit, which came close to killing me, and made parts of my legs ache that hadn't been used since I (once only, and never again) tried horse-riding; and on passing the garage this third and final time, I smiled sweetly at the car and reassured it that I'd either be back one day soon to liberate it from its forecourt purgatory, or I'd sell it to a good, kind, caring retired vicar who'd polish it every week and never drive it above the speed limit or swear at it when it dropped a bumper.

Picture me thus, if you will, jogging in a very slow and exhausted manner on my knees, sweat sticking my T-shirt nastily to my chest and running down my neck, conversing in frantic gasps with a car on a garage forecourt, when a shiny silver BMW passed me at a gentle cruise and the driver, leaning casually on the half-open window, caught my eye from above his dark glasses and smiled.

And for some reason I smiled back, although it hurt all my muscles to do so and made breathing even more difficult. And as he accelerated away at the green light, I stopped to recover from cramp in my side and found myself staring after him. And feeling like I knew him from somewhere, or that he reminded me of someone, which considering the dark glasses was a pretty unrealistic thought.

But for some reason or no particular reason at all, I memorised the number plate of the shiny silver BMW. It wasn't difficult to memorise. It was IOU 1.

Chapter 10

'MONDAY, JUNE 30.

Diet: excellent. Run out of Jaffa cakes. Too knackered from jogging to cook dinner. Lucy pining over Neil, Victoria moody about Lucy pining, so nobody eating much. Found an old tin of chicken soup in the cupboard, past its sell-by date but tasted OK.

Exercise: excellent ***. Did THREE circuits of usual route past the garage today and was admired by a BMW driver. Will borrow Lucy's sweatband tomorrow. Might get hair cut. Need to buy track suit.

Relaxation: given up. Two out of three's not bad. How can you relax when your car's glaring at you from a garage forecourt and your husband STILL hasn't phoned you since calling you a poisoner?'

The other thing I'd done, was to forget to take the diazepam.

Well, I couldn't really have needed it, could I, if I only took it for two days and then forgot it? I felt guilty about even having been given it on

'You're looking better, Mum,' said Lucy a few days later, having started to recover from Neil's visit to the extent where she could look around her again and notice other things in the world.

'Better than what?'

'Just better. You look . . . different.'

I looked at myself in the mirror. It was true. You really *are* the fairest of them all, Snow White! I'd lost a bit of weight already.

Some of my clothes were feeling more comfortable, and others, the ones that had already felt comfortable on account of their elastic waist-bands or huge baggy nature, were starting to look like maternity smocks. I'd had my hair cut shorter so it didn't fall all over my face when I was jogging, and my skin somehow looked better.

'You ought to go out and buy yourself some new clothes, Mum,' said Lucy generously.

'What with?' I smiled ruefully.

'Well, you're not spending anything on petrol at the minute, are you?' she pointed out.

And so it was that I was in Dorothy Perkins that Friday lunchtime, trying on skirts in a size I used to be before I started the normal expansion programme of middle age, when I met Liz. I turned round from the mirror to see her staring at me across the changing room.

'Ally! My God, I didn't think it was you at first! You look so *well*! Have you been to one of those . . . health farmyards?'

'No. One of the pigs came to see me, though.'

'Sorry?'

'Simon. Last week. Bearing flowers.'

'Oh. Yes. I heard about that.'

'You did?'

We stared at each other for a moment, me in my old baggy T-shirt with a smart blue Dorothy Perkins skirt (size twelve); Liz holding an armful of blouses she'd apparently already tried on; and then before I'd even realised I was going to do it, I was letting her have it, right there in the changing rooms in front of a line of mirrors and an assortment of semi-naked females of varying ages and shapes.

'You could have bloody well phoned me. After all the years we've worked together, I thought we were friends, Liz. Whatever happened to

the NHS when there were probably people out there, *really* stressed-out people, who needed it. I resolved to take the rest of the pills back to Boots next time I went shopping.

Dr Lewis would never know.

sticking by your friends, that's what I'd like to know. You and Mary, both of you! Since I got back from Cornwall it was like I had some contagious disease, not a single sod has come anywhere near me. Well, thanks very much, all of you, for your concern, and you can go back and tell them, all of them, that I think they're selfish and uncaring and I just hope nothing ever happens to THEM, because . . .'

I ran out of breath. It was very quiet in the changing room, embarrassingly quiet. People were doing up buttons and zips quickly, hanging things on hangers and getting out of there. I unzipped the blue skirt and stepped out of it.

'But you and Mary, most of all,' I added, quietly, not looking at her. 'I thought you'd have stuck by me, at least.'

I picked up my bags, and turned to go, still not looking at her.

'Don't just walk out,' Liz called after me.

'Why not?'

There was a silence. I turned my head back to look at her. I was glad I'd managed to say all that without losing my temper or crying. I could make a dignified exit now.

'Why not?' I repeated calmly.

'Because you're only wearing your knickers,' she replied.

We went to Burger King. It was supposed to be her lunch break, but she phoned Simon and told him she'd been stricken with a migraine and couldn't make it back to the office.

'He's so different,' she said, 'since his encounter with you. Even if I'd told him I just fancied the afternoon off he probably would have said, "Fine, fine, whatever you say, take as long as you need." What exactly did you do to him?'

'Not as much as I'd like to have done,' I said, thinking again about the knives in my kitchen drawer. 'So what have you heard?'

'What *haven't* we heard,' she said with relish. 'But I want to clear something up first,' she added more seriously, putting the burger down on her tray. 'We didn't phone you, or come to see you, because Simon told us not to.'

'He *what?*'

'The day after he came to see you, I asked him how you were, and whether you were well enough for me and Mary to visit you. As soon as I mentioned your name, he went pale and started trembling. "No way!" he shouted. "She's got to have complete rest, and no contact with anybody from work whatsoever! Her doctor has ordered her to have no contact! No one's to go round there or bother her on the phone!" It was really bad, like you'd scared the shit out of him.'

'I think I did! It's true my doctor did say all that about no contact with work, but I still would have liked the odd spark of concern from someone. But no,' I scowled. 'No, I guess you only had time for the bloody Temp, didn't you?'

'Her name was Tracey. She was awful,' Liz replied, bitterly.

'Was?' I repeated. 'Was, as in, she's not awful any more?'

'No. Was, as in She's Gone.'

'Gone for good?'

'Too bloody right. She was having it off with Simon.'

'Bloody hell,' I said. 'I have been missing some scandal, haven't I!'

You can't believe it, can you? Life goes on in the same dull, monotonous way for year after boring year, nothing more interesting ever happening than the occasional visit by a photocopier engineer or the appearance of an unusual stamp on a letter. And then, overnight, as soon as I take time off, all hell is let loose. The Temp catches Simon's eye and decides to make a play for him. 'She toyed with him like a cat with a mouse', was Liz's graphic description of the flirtation process. Except it ended up with the mouse getting the cat's knickers off across his desk, which may or may not have been a shock to Tracey, but was definitely a shock to Snotty-Nosed Nicola when she walked into the office and caught them in the act.

'Jesus!' I exclaimed, gobbling up chips with tomato ketchup. Nothing like a good bit of juicy gossip for improving the appetite. 'What did Nicola say?'

'Apparently she threw things around the office, stamped her feet, tore things up, and ended up telling Simon that if he didn't get rid of "that slag", she'd tell his father what he'd been doing during office hours . . .'

'On his nice polished desk!'

'. . . and with the phone switched over to answerphone . . .'

'Causing irritation to any possible clients trying to get through. Definitely not very good for business.'

'Exactly. Well, before she'd hardly had time to get her clothes back on, Tracey was hustled out of the door with Nicola snapping round her heels like a rabid terrier.'

'So all's well that ends well?'

'Oh, that wasn't the end of it. The next day, Ian Unwin himself turns up at the office!'

'Who?'

'Come on, Ally, how long have you been away?! Mr Unwin? The owner of the company? Simon's father?'

424

'Oh, Christ! I've never even met him!'

'Nor has anyone else, as far as I know—apart from Simon, of course, and that's not too often, from what I hear.'

'He spends all his time abroad.'

'In Portugal. He only comes back at Christmas, or when there's a problem with the business.'

'And there was a problem? He heard about Tracey being screwed on the desk?' I asked, my eyes popping with excitement.

'No, you idiot. The problem was you.'

I dropped a handful of chips in my surprise. Me? A problem?

'In what respect?' I almost whispered.

'You *know* in what respect. In respect of your work-related stress! Simon had told him about it on the phone, as soon as you sent in the certificate for your second lot of time off. He was worried enough about the first certificate, but the second one had him running to the toilet all day, I can tell you.'

'Good.' I smiled smugly.

'So Dad turns up in the office,' she continued, 'straight off the plane. He marched through reception, with Nicola running after him asking where he thought he was going! Can you imagine it?'

I could, and it was giving me great, great pleasure.

'Straight into Simon's office, where Simon was apparently sitting with his feet on his desk listening to a Tom Jones CD.'

Sad git.

'And he slammed the door behind him so hard, the CD jumped and kept playing the same line over and over: "My, my, my Delilah!", while the whole company and probably the whole bloody street could hear him shouting and swearing at Simon, calling him a Useless Lazy Bastard and a Pathetic Little Shit.'

Not a bad judge.

'And Simon started shouting back, saying his father had buggered off to Portugal leaving him to take all the responsibility, with staff who let him down and wouldn't do as they were told . . .'

'Bloody cheek!'

'Yeah, but do you know what Mr Unwin said?'

No, but I'm sure you're going to tell me . . .

'He said that if he treated staff with more consideration they'd repay him with more efficiency and loyalty, and wouldn't end up being signed off with work-related stress and be on the verge of possibly suing the company, and that if the company *did* get sued, it would be Simon standing up in court answering for it, and furthermore, if he insisted on shagging the receptionist he should be more discreet about it because it was perfectly obvious that everyone knew about it and he, personally, couldn't see what he saw in the cheap little tart anyway!'

'No!' I breathed, loving it.

'And then he flung open the door and Nicola fell in on to the floor at his feet!'

'She'd been listening to all that from outside?'

'Ally, I'm telling you, it was so loud we could hear it all from our office!' she insisted gleefully.

I finished off my chips and took a long, blissful drink of Coke. 'So what happened then? After Mr Unwin went?' I demanded eagerly.

'Simon came out of his office with his eyes downcast, got in his car and drove off. We all wondered if he'd gone to throw himself off a bridge. Tom Jones was still going "My, my, my, Delilah", and eventually someone went in there to turn it off because it was doing all our heads in, and discovered Nicola still lying on the floor, crying her eyes out.'

'Why? Because of Tom Jones?'

Understandable but somehow unlikely.

'No. Because Simon had dumped her.'

'Oh!'

I clapped my hand to my mouth with excitement. This was getting better and better. I hadn't had a Friday afternoon like this since I was a teenager and we used to swap diaries and read each other's secrets.

'He dumped her because his father disapproved?'

'I think he just wanted to take his anger out on someone because he'd been given a bollocking, and she literally fell at his feet at just the wrong moment. He told her he couldn't carry on with her any more knowing that everyone knew about them, even his father.'

'He must have known everybody knew about them! She practically hung her underwear on his door handle.'

'Yes, well, he obviously believed that was their little secret. Anyway,' went on Liz, enjoying herself as much as I was, 'next thing we know, Simon comes back carrying a huge basket of flowers.'

'For me!'

'As it turned out, yes. But Nicola obviously thought different. She jumped up from blubbing on the carpet, wiped her eyes with paper from the fax machine, and went running out to meet him. She thought she was forgiven. She had one hand on the basket of flowers and the other hand round the back of his neck before he'd had time to blink.'

'What did he do?' I gasped, my drink halfway to my mouth, suspended in horrified fascination.

THE TROUBLE WITH ALLY

'He put down the flowers, peeled her off him, sat her down on the nearest chair and said "I've told you already, Nicola— it's over."'

'What? In front of everyone?!'

'Everyone,' declared Liz solemnly

'Poor Nicola,' I said, and I *almost*, almost, meant it. 'She won't be able to look anyone in the eye for a while.'

'She won't have to. She's left.'

Wow. It was going to be fun going back!

We carried on shopping after we'd finished our lunch, and I spent the fifty pounds that didn't get spent on petrol, on a dress and jacket. Well, to be honest it came to just a little bit more than the fifty pounds but I borrowed the extra out of the following week's money that wouldn't be spent on petrol.

I was frowning to myself over the mental arithmetic involved in this, on the way home on the bus, when I saw the silver BMW again. Same driver, same dark glasses, same strange feeling of déjà vu about him. It bothered me just enough to make me forget about the business with the money, which was a relief, as I could then go home and show off my new clothes to the girls without feeling guilty.

'Where are you going to wear it, Mum?' asked Victoria.

'What do you mean—where?' I snapped. Anybody would think I never went anywhere where I could wear a nice dress and jacket.

'Well. I mean, it's very nice. Very, very nice!' she said tactfully. 'But, well, you never really go anywhere where you could wear it—do you?'

'Yes, I do. I go to places. I go out to places . . . all the time.'

I felt stupid. Annoyed and stupid. It was horrible to think that I was the type of person who never went anywhere to wear anything nice.

'I'm going out tomorrow night,' I lied. Anything to stop thinking of myself as that sort of sad person.

'Are you?' Victoria looked interested. 'Where? Who with?'

'With the girls from work. Up the West End.'

'Good for you,' she said approvingly, giving me a kiss. 'It'll do you good. Do you far more good than all those bloody pills.'

That reminded me. I still hadn't taken the bloody pills back to Boots.

'Liz,' I whispered into the phone so that Victoria couldn't hear me. 'Do you fancy going out tomorrow night? Up West? You, me and Mary?'

'Yeah, why not!' she agreed, to my relief. 'What's the occasion?'

'Nothing. I just need to wear my new outfits.'

We went to a wine bar just off Piccadilly. We bought a bottle of Italian red and managed to get the last free table.

'It looks very nice,' said Liz generously, indicating my dress.

'Thanks. Victoria said I'd never go anywhere to wear it.'

'Huh. What do they know? We ought to do this more often. Go and see a show or go out for a meal. It's stupid living in London and never going anywhere.'

'Derek and I go out quite a lot,' said Mary. 'We've seen *Les Misérables* four times.'

'Why? Didn't you understand it the first time?'

'Ally, you can be quite cutting at times,' Mary reproved me.

We sipped our wine in silence for a while, watching the people around us as the wine bar started to fill up. Snatches of conversation drifted through the cigarette smoke.

'. . . *awfully* difficult for her, now the au pair's gone . . .'

'. . . and where they live now in Hampstead, they've only got two bathrooms, and the master bedroom isn't even en suite . . .'

We raised our eyebrows at each other across the table.

'Awfully difficult for me,' I muttered. 'The Metro's failed its MOT so I have to use the tube.'

'Ally,' said Liz, looking past me towards the door. 'Isn't that Paul that's just walked in?'

He had his arm round Lynnette, shepherding her in through the crowd. She looked little and fragile, and people made way for her.

'Thanks, old chap,' I heard Paul say to some guy who'd got off a bar stool and let Lynnette sit down.

'Is she anorexic?' whispered Mary.

'No,' I whispered back. I wasn't whispering on purpose, it was just that my voice wouldn't come out properly. It felt shaky and sort of strangled. 'She's been ill.'

'Christ. Something serious? She looks . . .' Mary shook her head. She looked dreadful. She must have lost about two stone, and she hadn't been big to start with. She looked pale and tired, her cheeks were hollow and her eyes, those grey-green eyes that used to sparkle and twinkle, looked huge in her tiny, pinched face. Paul still had his arm protectively round her. He hadn't seen me yet, but as I stared at her, Lynnette looked up and caught my eye.

'Ally!' she mouthed, and whispered something to Paul. I looked away quickly as he turned in my direction, but it was too late.

'Oh God,' I said, as they made their way towards our table.

'Ally! This isn't one of your usual haunts, is it?' said Paul.

'I don't have any usual haunts,' I returned, not looking at him. 'Not being a ghost.'

THE TROUBLE WITH ALLY

'Still the same old sense of humour,' he said, without laughing.

'How are you, Ally?' asked Lynnette, in a sad little voice.

'I'm OK, thank you.' I made a huge effort. 'It's me who should be asking you, I think.'

'Oh, I'm much better,' she said bravely, leaning on Paul's arm for support. 'I've started going out for little walks and I think I've put a little bit of weight back on. The doctor says I'm over the worst now.'

'That's good,' I said politely.

This was hell. It was like a scene from a nightmare. Were they going to stand there all night, staring at me, thinking thoughts of poison and waiting for me to break down and confess? Yes, she looked awful. Yes, I was horrified to see how ill she must have been—yes, I felt sorry for her. I really did feel sorry for her. But it was nothing to do with me. Nothing! To! Do! With! Me! I felt myself shiver with fear.

They surely couldn't really believe I'd do anything like that?

'I think we'd better go, actually,' I said suddenly, in the middle of something Lynnette was saying about her employers at the private hospital being so understanding and paying her full sick pay.

Mary and Liz both looked at me uncertainly.

'We're going on to see a film,' I said, scrabbling on the floor for my handbag, desperate now to get as far away from there as I could.

'Yes, that's right,' said Liz, catching on at once. She stood up and put on her jacket. 'Come on, then, or we'll miss the start.'

'Which film are you—?' began Lynnette, but we were already walking away.

'Nice to see you,' I called back, without turning round.

It wasn't until much later that I realised I'd acted exactly like someone with a guilty conscience. And I didn't even have one.

'Paul must be worried sick about her,' said Mary, as we strolled up towards Leicester Square.

'Yes.'

'What exactly did you say was wrong with her? Food poisoning?'

'Yes.'

'Must have been bad.'

'Yes.'

'You can see he's obviously devoted to her.'

'Mary,' said Liz. 'I don't think Ally wants to discuss—'

'It's all right,' I said, sighing deeply. 'I don't mind talking about her. Or him. I need, really, to talk about him.'

I needed to hear myself saying out loud the things I knew in my heart to be true.

'I don't mind any more. About him and Lynnette.'

'That's good,' nodded Mary wisely.

'I don't want him back.'

When did that happen? When did I stop wanting him back? Or did I never really want him back, but just wouldn't admit it?

'I'm not even sure if I really loved him at all.'

'Love's a funny thing,' said Liz, slipping her arm through mine. 'Who really knows what it means? Who can really say when it starts, when it ends, whether it's real or not?'

I thought of Victoria, with her succession of 'The Real Thing's', who'd all now been contemptuously dismissed as hormonal blips, and smiled to myself.

'I assumed I still loved Paul, and I assumed I'd do anything to get him back,' I admitted. 'But I think it was just a habit, really. If I'd still been in love with him I wouldn't have jumped into bed with James—'

'*James*?' squealed Liz and Mary together. 'Who's James? And when did you jump into bed?'

'Let's find somewhere to have another drink,' I laughed. 'And you wait till I tell you about James! He was the best-looking thing I've ever seen in my life.'

'Y̲ou were late home last night,' commented Lucy as she buttered her toast the next morning.

'Yes,' I said, smiling.

'Have a good time?'

'Excellent, thanks.'

One drink had led to another, and another, and then to a curry. One shared secret had led to many more, and by the end of the evening the three of us had been laughing and giggling like schoolgirls.

'I think I'm going to enjoy being single,' I confided to Lucy. 'Now I've finally got used to the idea.'

She looked at me with a frown of disapproval. 'You're not even divorced yet.'

'No, but I think your dad and I ought to start discussing it.'

Lucy's eyes opened wide in surprise.

'He and Lynnette are a couple now, Luce,' I said gently. 'He's not going to leave her and come back to us. I've had to learn to accept it.'

'Accept it? It sounds as if you're *glad* about it!' she retorted.

I sighed.

'Would you prefer me to be miserable and pine for him for the rest of my life? I've got to pick myself up and start again, Lucy. It's all right for you and Victoria. You've got your own lives to live. You'll eventually be moving out and—'

'Actually, Mum . . .'

She suddenly put down her toast and wiped the crumbs from her mouth.

'Yes?'

Something about her manner startled me. Something about the look on her face. Serious, nervous, but excited. I didn't like it.

'What?'

'Well, I wasn't going to tell you yet. But I don't think I can wait. It's going to happen sooner than you think.'

'What is? What's going to happen?'

'Me moving out. We're planning it now. As soon as we've found somewhere.'

'We? We who?'

'Me and Neil, of course! Mum, you must have guessed! You must have realised how right we are for each other! As soon as Neil's found somewhere for us to live, I'll go down and look for a job and—'

'Down where?' I asked with a heavy heart.

'Cornwall, of course!' she laughed with excitement. 'I'm going to live in Cornwall with Neil. We'll probably get married. And we want loads of babies. Are you looking forward to it, Mum? Being a grandma?'

Chapter 11

'WHAT'S UP?'

Paul sounded slightly irritated, like he'd been disturbed while watching *Match of the Day.*

'Can you come round? Now? Please? It's Lucy.'

'What's wrong with her?'

Sharp with concern now, no doubt imagining appendicitis, or a car crash.

'Nothing, no, she's not ill, nothing like that. Sorry. I just . . . need you to talk to her. Come and talk to her, please, Paul.'

'Why?'

'Paul. I don't often ask for your help, do I.'
I was surprised by the tone of my voice. So, I think, was he, because
he immediately agreed.
'No. OK. I'll be there in half an hour.'
'Just you.'
'OK.'

His forehead was creased with anxiety. 'What's the problem?' he asked
as he stepped into the hall. 'Exams?'
'No. She doesn't get the results till next month, but I think they went
all right in the end. It's this new boyfriend. Neil. She met him in
Cornwall and—'
'Hey, Dad!' shouted Lucy, coming down the stairs. 'Didn't know you
were coming.'
'Hi, Dad!' echoed Victoria, leaning over the bannisters. 'You staying
for dinner?'
'No. I . . . came to . . . see you. Talk to you,' he said, frowning at me.
'She's not *pregnant*?' he added under his breath, walking ahead of me
into the kitchen.
'Pregnant?' said Lucy, whose hearing was better than her father obvi-
ously remembered. 'Who is?' She stood stock-still and stared at Paul.
'Lynnette?'
'No. Nobody,' he said. He sat down at the kitchen table and I put the
kettle on. 'So tell me,' he said to me at length, looking from me to Lucy,
to Victoria, and back to Lucy again.
'Tell your dad,' I said to Lucy, 'about Neil.'
Victoria bit into a biscuit, looking puzzled. 'What about him?'
'Oh, thanks, Mum!' exclaimed Lucy. 'I wanted to tell Dad myself, in
my own time, when I was ready—'
'Tell him what?' asked Victoria.
'Why did you need to tell him?' went on Lucy. 'You have to make a
drama out of it, don't you, and get everyone all worried.'
'Worried about what?' demanded Victoria, her mouth full of biscuit.
'Well, of course I'm worried,' I shot back. 'You're only nineteen, and
what about your college course? You're just going to give all that up?
After all the hard work . . .'
'I can go back to it later. After I've had my babies.'
There was a silence. Victoria started choking on biscuit crumbs.
Paul put his hand to his forehead and swayed slightly.
'My God,' he said softly. 'You are, aren't you? You're pregnant.'
'No!' she said crossly. 'Not yet!'

'What do you mean, "not yet"?' cried Victoria. 'Are you *trying* to get pregnant? For fuck's sake, Lucy!'

'Watch your language, Victoria,' said Paul unnecessarily. 'Lucy, what's all this about? Why are you leaving college? I thought it was going well?'

'I'm in love,' she declared with an expression of self-righteousness.

'For fuck's sake!' repeated Victoria under her breath.

'I'm going to live with him. In Cornwall.'

'I don't think so,' said Paul.

'Well, I *do* think so!' she returned. 'And I'm over eighteen, so I can make my own decisions.'

'Please,' I said, banging cups of coffee down in front of everyone. 'Let's not get angry. Let's try to discuss this calmly and sensibly, like adults.'

'There's nothing to discuss,' said Lucy flatly. 'I'm going to Cornwall to live with Neil.'

'You're out of your mind,' said Victoria.

'Shut up, Victoria. You're just jealous, because Reece dumped you.'

'Jealous! Do me a favour. I think you're pathetic. You need to learn how to live without a man in your life. They're an anachronism, a relic of paternalistic society——'

'Thank you, Victoria,' I said quietly.

'I love him,' asserted Lucy, pushing away her coffee.

'It's only your hormones.' said Victoria. 'Isn't it, Mum. Tell her.'

'Victoria, do you really expect Lucy to listen to a word I say?' I hissed at her. 'Any more than *you* would have done?'

'I wasn't so stupid as to want to live in Cornwall and have babies.'

'You weren't really in love,' threw back Lucy.

'And neither are you.' I retorted. 'You just think you are! It just feels like it.'

'And what would you know about it?' asked Lucy scathingly.

Paul looked at me with raised eyebrows.

'I just do,' I said, reddening slightly. 'Believe me.'

'You should listen to Mum,' Victoria told Lucy aggressively. 'She knows more about life than you do. She's old.'

Not that bloody old.

'Nobody knows how I feel,' returned Lucy dramatically. 'Neil's the only one who's ever understood me.'

Oh, spare me the violin music, please.

'Thank you very much,' I said in peevish, martyred tones.

'You know what I mean,' she sighed. '*You know*.'

Yes, of course I did know. And so, of course, did Victoria, despite her new and superior knowledge of the subject, and so, perhaps more than

433

any of us, did, Paul, who when all was said and done had walked out on a wife who'd been understanding him since he was little more than a child, to live with someone who'd infected him with just exactly the same sort of madness as his younger daughter was displaying.

Whether it was the result of following this same train of thought, or whether he'd just decided to try a different tactic, Paul suddenly took a deep breath, took a gulp of his coffee and began again: 'OK, Lucy. Fair enough. It's not that we don't understand your feelings . . .'

But before he got any further, the phone started ringing and Lucy was upon it with the speed and agility of a rugby tackle.

'Neil! Hello, darling!' we heard her gush, and then the door was shut hard behind her.

'I can't stand any more of this,' said Victoria. 'I'm going out. 'Bye, Dad.'

'Who does she go out with?' asked Paul, watching her from the window as she got into her car and drove off, 'now that she's given up men?'

'Her friend Hayley. They go out drinking and clubbing,' I smiled. 'I'm sure it's only a phase. The next good-looking lad that chats her up, I bet all this anti-men stuff goes straight out the window. But I think it's doing her good being single for a while.'

I paused, and looked at him pointedly.

'It can be fun, being a single girl.' I said. 'And it helps you sort yourself out. Who you are, without being part of a couple,' I said.

'Is that right?' he said, looking back at me equally pointedly.

'Yes.'

'You look different,' he said after a while. 'Better.'

'Everyone keeps saying that. Did I look so terrible before?'

'That's not what I meant. I just said you look better.'

'I've been exercising. And eating better. I couldn't cope with the relaxation. The tapes reminded me of childbirth classes.'

He laughed.

'What am I going to do about Lucy, Paul?' I said, a lump coming to my throat. The childbirth classes had been a nightmare, the childbirth itself had been worse than a nightmare, but look what it had produced. The best two things in my life. I couldn't lose her now, could I? But I couldn't stop her, either. 'She's nineteen! She's an adult. If she insists on going . . .'

'Listen.' Paul sat down next to me and took hold of my hand. I stared at it. It seemed odd, now, after all this time, to see his hand holding mine like that, as if he still cared about me. As if he'd never said all those things to me, terrible things about poisoning Lynnette and the cat. 'I don't think we should fight her too hard,' he said gently. 'She'll run to this guy all the faster if we do. And cling to him all the more.'

'So what do we do? Just let her go? She hardly knows him.'

'Let her go and stay with your sister. Bev wouldn't mind, would she? Then she can see as much of this Neil as she wants, without rushing to move in with him.'

'What about college?'

'By the start of term, I wouldn't mind betting the love affair will have run its course. If not, then it will deserve us taking it more seriously.'

I held onto his hand for a minute or two more, thinking this over, nodding slowly to myself as the sense of it sunk into my brain and calmed the panic that had been threatening a takeover bid.

'Why didn't I think of that?' I said eventually.

'Because you're here all the time, getting all the worry and all the crap, aren't you? I just get called in at times like this, on a . . . consultation basis. I can look at things more clearly, perhaps.'

'Will you always? Always come if I call you for a consultation? Even if . . . if we get divorced?'

There. I'd said it. I'd been the first one to suggest it. My heart was racing. It sounded such a desperate thing to say. He looked at me with surprise.

'If we do. Yes, of course. You know I'll always be there for the kids. And for you, Ally. I've always wanted us to stay friends.'

'But I didn't give anyone poison,' I said quickly. 'Not Lynnette, and not the cat. Especially not the cat.'

He shrugged. 'I don't suppose you did, really. But I didn't know what to think.'

'Think about what?' interrupted Lucy, coming back from her phone call with the pink excited flush of someone who's just been giggling and soppy for half an hour.

'We think this is what should happen,' I said firmly. 'I'm going to phone Auntie Bev tonight . . .'

It went surprisingly well, Lucy having stopped protesting the minute she realised she could be on her way to Cornwall and in her lover's arms within twenty-four hours if she played her cards right. Bev was unlikely to be a very serious chaperone.

'I'll start packing!' she announced, a little prematurely, bouncing up the stairs singing something yukky about love.

'Thanks,' I told Paul, going to see him out.

'Glad you're looking better,' he said again. 'What tablets did you say the doctor gave you?'

I didn't.

'I'm not taking them. Didn't need them. I wasn't really stressed, just needed a bit of rest and exercise . . . dia-zie something. Hang on, they're here in the kitchen. I'll tell you . . . I'm sure it was dia-zie something . . . Where are they, now?' I moved a pile of bills and yesterday's paper to one side. 'Sure I left them here, 'cos I kept saying I ought to take them back to Boots. Where the hell have they got to? Lucy, have you moved those tablets that were on the side here in the kitchen? Lucy?'

She was bounding back downstairs, looking worried.

'Mum! Have you seen Apple Pie? He's been on my bed, and he's been sick all over the duvet, and it's absolutely horrible . . . . What did you say about tablets?'

The first time you prowl around your garden for hours shouting out 'Apple Pie, where are you?', your neighbours might well assume you just have a temporary problem. The second time, they could be forgiven for calling the nearest mental health authority. And God knows I had enough people concerned about my mental health already.

'He might be lying dead somewhere!' I cried, peering under shrubs and staring into the murky depths of the fishpond once again. 'I can't believe it! I just can't believe he managed to get the top off the pill-bottle. It was a childproof top!'

'Don't jump to conclusions,' said Paul. We hadn't found the pill-bottle, and there hadn't been any definite evidence of pills in the vomit, although to be fair we hadn't done an in-depth study of it yet.

'Well, what else am I supposed to think? The pills are gone and the poor cat's been poisoned again. Paul, he's already got dodgy kidneys! He hasn't even had tonight's dose of his drug! I'll never forgive myself, never! How could I have been so stupid, leaving tablets lying around the house like that! Any little child could have got them.'

'We don't know any little children,' pointed out Lucy.

'Well, any little cat, then,' I said. 'Apple Pie! Apples, darling, come on, where are you? Come to Mummy! Please don't be dead!'

Please, God, please don't do this to me again. Please don't make us have to drain the fishpond, I really couldn't stand it, but on the other hand if we do have to do it, thank you for making Paul be here.

'You'll have to drain your fishpond,' I told him snappily.

'No, I won't,' he retorted.

'If we don't find him, you will. What do you care most about, Apple Pie or your silly fish?'

'They're not silly. They have feelings too. They're living, breathing creatures. They fall in love, and have babies, and get sick, and die—'

'Oh, please! Fishes don't fall in love!'

'Of course they do. Look at that bright orange one there. I bet he fancies the little silvery-pink one rotten.'

'Paul, you don't even know if it's male or female, so——'

'I can't believe you two!' protested Lucy. 'Poor Apple Pie is probably dying somewhere, and you're arguing about fishes fancying each other? Christ! It's almost like having you living together again.'

Despite everything, we looked at each other across the pond and we both smiled. It wasn't anything like living together again. But it was still nice, and comforting, to be arguing in that careless, jokey, married sort of way again. I had a strange flash of passing thought that, now I'd decided I didn't love him, I could really get to like Paul again. But then I went back to panicking about the cat and forgot about it. Just as well. Not a good idea to indulge too much in those sort of thoughts while you've still got a possible poisoning charge pending.

It was beginning to get dark when we finally heard it. A faint, very faint, very feeble meowing.

'Mum!' shouted Lucy. 'I heard him!'

'Where?'

'Ssh! Listen!'

We all crept quietly towards the house.

'Meow! Meow!'

It was plaintive and pitiful, and it seemed to be coming from . . . .

'The shed!' called Paul, running to the kitchen drawer, where he knew we still kept the key to the old potting shed.

'It's not locked!' I called after him.

He stopped in his tracks and stared at me. 'Why not?'

'Does it matter? Let's just get the door open . . . .'

It was stiff, so stiff it hadn't seemed worth bothering to lock it any more. Paul used to preside over its security with the rigour of a prison warder. You'd have thought he had the Crown Jewels in there, but in fact it was just the sort of stuff men like to play with out of doors: bags of compost, lawn fertiliser and peat; pots of creosote and varnish; flowerpots, seed trays, spades and shovels; jars of screws and nails . . . you know what I mean, don't you? Things they play with for hours while you're doing the housework, thinking they're fooling you that they're busy, when really we all know it's just an extension of infant-school play therapy: sorting and stacking, cutting and sticking, painting and modelling. Maybe that's why they're so secretive about it. Anyway, suffice it to say I hadn't seen any reason to keep the bolt, the chain or the padlock on the shed door since he'd moved out, since there hadn't been any reports of flowerpot thieves in the neighbourhood for quite a few years. I tended to leave the little window open, too, in the summer, because it got disgustingly hot and smelly in there.

'The window's open,' Paul said accusingly.

'Only a fraction . . .'

A big enough fraction, apparently, for a medium-sized elderly cat to squeeze through.

Apple Pie was lying on the floor of the shed, panting lightly and looking apologetic about the pool of vomit beside him.

'My poor baby!' squealed Lucy, rushing to pick him up.

'I'll get straight on the phone to the vet,' I said.

'It's Sunday night.'

'The emergency service, then. They'll have to see him, won't they? It looks like poisoning again.'

Paul was staring at the floor.

'What?' I asked sharply, following his gaze.

'Fishing bait,' he said, pointing.

'Sorry?'

'All over the floor, look. The cat must have knocked the jar over.'

'So what!'

'I didn't realise I'd left it there. It's been there for years. It must be absolutely rank by now.'

'I wondered why it smelt so awful in here.'

'Ally,' he said, very quietly, still looking at the mess on the floor of the shed as if he were hypnotised by it, 'Ally, I think this is what Apple Pie's been eating. I don't think it was slug pellets at all. I think we ought to take some of this to the vet and tell him it's probably what poisoned the cat.'

I **I**f you have to be in the position of tearing through the London suburbs in the dead of night with a retching cat on your lap, it's better to be doing it with your ex-husband driving you in his Vauxhall Primera than sitting alone on the District Line of the underground. Indirectly, Lucy had done us a favour by announcing her elopement plans and getting her father over that day, whether she saw it that way now or not. The reason I mention this was that she was now on the back seat of the Primera holding a sample jar of foul-smelling fishing bait on one side of her and a sample jar of cat vomit on the other.

'This is *disgusting*!' she cried for the fifteenth time as Paul turned right, then left at the traffic lights, then left again at the second roundabout after the pub, as per directions given to us on the phone. 'Hurry up! I can't *stand* it! It's . . . *eurggh*!'

'Meow!' cried Apple Pie, coughing weakly.

'Paul, hurry up, I think he's getting worse!' I said anxiously. 'Is it much further?'

'I don't think so. Stop nagging, both of you, and look out for Greenway Road on the right, will you?'

We got to the emergency vet at half past ten. By eleven o'clock he'd anaesthetised Apple Pie and washed out his stomach, examined the contents of both our sample jars and agreed that the decaying fishing bait was indeed responsible for his food poisoning, but that we'd found him soon enough this time, before any of it had been completely digested and had time to cause any serious damage.

'Thank God!' I breathed, tears not far away now as I looked at the life-less little form in his recovery cage.

'Will he be all right, then?' asked Lucy, reaching out to hold his paw through the wire.

'Hopefully. We'll keep him here overnight for observation . . .'

'We don't have Pet Save . . .' I began, shutting my eyes tight against any random images of supercilious know-it-all families with irritatingly healthy labradors and beaming, goody-goody children.

'It's all right,' interrupted Paul at once. 'How much is the bill?'

He handed over the cash with a strange expression in his eyes.

I didn't recognise it at first, but on the way home I suddenly knew what it reminded me of. Victoria, when she stole my box of Quality Street when she was about seven years old. She gave me back what was left of the chocolates and said she was sorry, but then she burst into tears and said, 'I should be giving you all of them back, but I can't! I ate them!'

It was guilt. Guilt and regret. Well, it served him bloody well right.

Y\ou can see what I'm getting at here, can't you? Even if I'd knocked the jar of fishing bait off the shelf myself, even if I'd taken Apple Pie out to the shed and put him on the floor and said, 'There you go, boy, lovely fishing bait! Come on, eat it all up!', even if I'd mashed it in with his dinner and spoonfed it to him . . . Well, it was hardly likely I'd been able to do the same to Lynnette, now was it? I'm pretty sure that even in his most irrational moments—and I have to add here to be strictly fair to him that he's normally a fairly rational man—even in his most delu-sional of moods, Paul could never have seriously imagined Lynnette consuming anything containing that revolting, putrid, vile, mess of slimy, mouldy, stinking rotten maggots. How the cat could stand to eat it was beyond me, but a human being?

Never. Never in your wildest nightmares, not even if it was baked in a champagne gravy and served with chocolate sauce. No way. So I was perfectly aware that the silence in the car on the way home owed more to guilt and regret than it did to concentration on the homeward directions, tiredness, or even anxiety about Apple Pie's condition.

'I'll pick him up tomorrow night and bring him home to you,' he said quietly as he turned back into our road. 'And don't worry about the rest of the fees. I'll take care of it.'

'If you're sure.'

'Of course.'

'Thanks, then. Do you . . . want to come in for a coffee or anything?'

'No. I'd better get back to Lynnette.'

'Yes.' I opened the car door and started to get out, then added. 'I'm glad you were here, Paul.'

'So am I. Glad we've sorted out . . . what the problem was.'

He couldn't meet my eyes. I'm not a vindictive person, but I have to say this: he *deserved* that guilt. Hope it was screwing him up.

There were two messages on the answerphone when Lucy and I let ourselves back into the house. I pressed 'play' half-heartedly while I waited for the kettle to boil. They were bound to be for Victoria or Lucy but you never know, it could always be the Lottery organisers telling me I was the missing winner of a million pounds, or it could be George Clooney's agent saying George had spotted me when he was in town and wanted to take me out for dinner.

'Hello, Ally, love. It's Mum. Just phoning to say goodbye.'

I stared at the phone as the long beep sounded at the end of the message. Goodbye? Was that *it*? She was going off to live in Majorca for the rest of her life and she couldn't even be bothered to say Take Care, Keep in Touch, Have a Nice Life? No mention of missing me? No regrets at leaving me behind, after all I'd done for her, with her corns and her hip and everything? After we'd finally managed to become friends—or so I thought? Didn't I even deserve a visit? Well, great! Wasn't that just great! Well, if she thought I was going to go running after her to Majorca . . .

'Message Two', said the annoying smarmy voice of the Answerphone Man, and then my mother's voice began again.

'Oh. Ally, you're still not home. Oh dear.'

Beeeeeep! went the answerphone.

Oh dear? Oh dear?! Is that all you can say?

I threw coffee into mugs and slopped boiling water onto it in a reckless and dangerous fashion, steaming with anger. What sort of mother leaves messages like that on her daughter's answerphone? It would have been better not to phone me at all. She could have just buggered off back to Majorca and let me find out in my own good time that she couldn't be bothered to say goodbye to me, instead of advertising the fact and rubbing my nose in it.

'Have you heard from Mum?' I demanded, phoning Beverly a few minutes later.

'Oh God,' said Beverly, yawning.

'What do you mean, *Oh God? Oh God?* Oh God, what?'

'I mean, "Oh God, not another phone call." I was in bed, Ally. Do you know what the time is?'

'Oh. I see. In bed with who? Whom?'

'Lorenzo. No one you know.'

I heard the smile in her voice, the smile that said that Lorenzo was nibbling her ear or nuzzling her neck or . . . whatever . . . right at that moment as she was speaking to me. And I felt cross, and frustrated, and jealous and left out. Inexplicably, suddenly, I wanted to be in bed, too, with someone who was doing things to me that made me smile like that on the phone.

'What do you want, Ally? I've got a lot on my mind right now . . .'

I could hear that smile in her voice again. I scowled to myself. Lucky bloody cow.

'I wanted to ask you if Lucy could come and stay for a while . . .'

'Can't tear herself away from the new boyfriend?'

'Yes, well. We'd better discuss Lucy when you haven't got . . . other things on your mind. Have you heard from Mum?'

'Yes. She phoned ten minutes ago.'

'While you were in bed.'

'Well, yes. But I mean to say! It is late . . .'

'And she said?'

'Oh, she said goodbye.'

'And that was it? Goodbye? Just like that? Nothing else? Just a measly goodbye, before she jets off to spend the rest of her days on foreign soil, cut off for ever from her family who've given up their lives for her? Just goodbye!'

'Well, no, not exactly.'

I sighed.

'What do you mean, "not exactly"?'

'Sorry. Yes. She said she'd been trying to phone you. She said . . .' I could almost hear her trying to concentrate. 'Yes, she said she'd planned on going to see you tonight, to say goodbye and do all the stuff, you know, have a drink and kiss you goodbye and all that. But you weren't in. And she said she couldn't talk any longer 'cos the taxi was just pulling up outside.'

'And that was it? That was all? That was her goodbye?'

'Oh, yes! And then she said she'd get the taxi to stop off en route to the airport, and . . .'

The doorbell rang just at the point where Lorenzo had obviously got fed up waiting and the phone was thrown on the floor amidst a wail of giggling.

Apparently they'd been on standby and had got flights back to Majorca at very short notice, so I suppose it was understandable that, after all, I only got time to wish Mum and Ted all the best, kiss her goodbye and exchange a few tears, while the taxi waited outside for them. Almost everything they possessed had been packed up and shipped off, and the whole thing felt final and permanent to the point of unreality. The trips to the hospital with a moaning, ungrateful old woman who seemed to enjoy her ailments and enjoy upsetting everyone, seemed now to have no connection whatsoever with this excited and sprightly lady. But it was a shock when the last thing she said to me was:

'You're much better now, Ally, dear. Much more bright and cheerful, and you look younger too. You should keep up this diet and jogging or whatever it is you're doing.'

Much better? How come everyone was saying that to me, when there hadn't been anything wrong with me in the first place? She was the one who looked better. She was probably just seeing me in a different light, now she felt happier herself.

Victoria came home just as they were getting back into their taxi, so both the girls were able to say their goodbyes to their grandma, and we then sat up together drinking tea and talking about Serious Issues.

'Lucy's going to stay with Beverly for a while,' I told Victoria.

She nodded. 'Good idea.'

I stared at her. 'You don't mind? It doesn't bother you?'

'Why should it bother me? I can phone her. She'll be home again by September.'

'I won't!' asserted Lucy. 'I'll stay down there and marry Neil.'

'If you say so,' shrugged Victoria, sounding bored.

'I do say so!' said Lucy, obviously spoiling for a fight.

'Well, Auntie Bev will soon sort you out. She's an arch feminist, isn't she, Mum?'

'In some ways,' I said evasively, thinking of Lorenzo and wondering if he was going to be wandering round the house much while Lucy was staying there.

'I bet *she* doesn't need a man in her life,' said Victoria.

No. She needs several. At the same time. The only way she was likely to 'sort Lucy out' might be to persuade her against settling down too soon with just one. And that, in my view, would be a good thing anyway.

'It's a temporary measure,' I warned Lucy. 'We'll see how the situation goes.'

'We'll be looking round for our own place while I'm down there,' insisted Lucy. 'I won't have to stay with Auntie Bev for too long.'

'We'll see,' I repeated. I was buying time, and I knew it.

'I can't understand *what* I did with those tablets,' I commented as I put the cups in the dishwasher before we went to bed.

'What tablets?' asked Victoria.

'Those diazie-things. The ones the doctor gave me, that I didn't need. I thought the cat must have got them, but . . .'

'No. I've got them.'

'You?' I stared at Victoria in horror.

'Yeah. They're in my bag. Look . . .'

I knew it. I always knew it would happen. I couldn't have been lucky enough to get both girls through to adulthood without one of them turning to drugs. Stealing pills from your own mother, admitting to it openly. I looked at her closely. Were her pupils dilated? Did her breath smell funny? Or was I just imagining it? Perhaps it was garlic?

'What are you staring at?' she asked me curiously.

'What other drugs have you been taking?' I asked, sighing.

'Taking? Drugs? What are you talking about?'

'The diazie-stuff. What else? How long have you been doing it?'

'Mum. I can't believe you're saying this. You know perfectly well I don't do drugs. For God's sake! I just put them in my handbag to take them back to Boots for you tomorrow, 'cos you said you kept forgetting,'

'Oh.' I looked at her helplessly. 'Well, thanks. Sorry.'

She raised her eyebrows and shook her head.

'Overreaction, or what!?' exclaimed Lucy. 'Is it all right if I take a paracetamol for my headache, or do you want to phone the Drugline?'

'All right, I said I was sorry,' I said, feeling absolutely ridiculous. 'I'm going to bed.'

'She's still behaving a bit weird, don't you think?' I heard Lucy saying in a low voice as I climbed the stairs.

'Yeah,' answered Victoria. 'I mean to say, as if I could get a high from diazepam anyway. It'd just send me to sleep.'

Chapter 12

MONDAY, JULY 7.

Diet: breakfast—stayed in bed and couldn't be bothered, so—

Lunch—bacon sandwich with tomato sauce.

Dinner—very, very good—cottage cheese salad with a jacket potato.

Later—used up the rest of the bacon and it looked kind of lonely on the plate so fried two eggs, two tomatoes and some mushrooms with it.

But no chocolate and no biscuits, all day!

Exercise: excellent. Jogged for miles and miles, past the park, down to the canal, back up past the garage (to pull faces at bastard car), round by the pub and back again. So impressed with myself, went out for another jog in the evening (to work off the egg and bacon).

Of course, I didn't mention in the diary about the BMW.

It was getting to be uncanny. I'd seen it several times now, and the driver always looked at me as if he knew me. Or fancied me?

It seemed unlikely. The weather had turned very hot and I was jogging in an old pair of blue and white striped shorts, a pink vest-top of Victoria's with a Union Jack on the front and skull and crossbones on the back, and a baseball cap. Add to this the fact that I was very red and sweaty and you can see why it was strange that anyone would look at me at all, but because of the unusual registration I noticed the BMW every time. And then, that Monday, when I came back from the morning jog, it was parked outside my house.

I slowed down as I came round the bend and saw it there. This was strange. This was very bloody strange. The driver was sitting in the car with the window right down, leaning out of it and smoking a cigar. 'I Want to Break Free' by Queen was playing very loud and he was tapping his hand in time to the music.

Funny, the little things you notice. As I got closer I noticed that his shirt was cream, short-sleeved and expensive-looking, and his arm, the arm outside the car window, was lean and tanned and that there was a big chunky gold ring on his right hand, the hand holding the cigar.

'God knows, God knows I want to break free . . .'

I walked, very slowly now, past the car, trying to resist the urge to stare in the window, and turned into my front path.

'I've fallen in love . . . I've fallen in love for the first time; this time I know it's for real . . . God knows . . .'

I fumbled in the pocket of my shorts for my door key. Wrong pocket. I was all fingers and thumbs, wanting desperately, out of curiosity, to turn round and look back at the car, see if he was looking at me.

'I can't get over how you love me like you do . . . I've got to be sure, when I walk out that door . . .'

Got it. Got the key now. Put it in the lock, come on, just open the door and go in. No need to look round. Just being bloody nosy, that's all. Nothing to do with you if he chooses to park his BMW outside your house, just coincidence.

'Oh how I want to be free! God knows I've got to . . .'

Clunk. The music went off. The silence was appalling in its abruptness. Key in my front-door lock, door half open, I swung round in surprise as I heard the door of the BMW slam shut. I stared in surprise as the BMW driver stood up, smoothed his smooth brown trousers and his smooth grey hair, took off his dark glasses and looked straight at me.

'Mrs Bridgeman? Alison Bridgeman?'

Quite a few possibilities went through my head in those next seconds. He could be the psychiatrist, sent by Dr Lewis to check up on me. Or an RSPCA inspector who'd heard about my cat-poisoning reputation. Or worse, a detective called in by Paul while he suspected me of poisoning Lynnette. Then again, it could always be someone from the National Lottery about that missing million-pound ticket . . . or George Clooney's agent . . .

'Who wants to know?' I asked cagily.

'Sorry,' he said, smiling and holding out his hand to me. 'I should have introduced myself. I'm Ian Unwin. I believe you work with my son Simon in my company?'

That's who he reminded me of. Slimy bloody Simon.

We went through to the kitchen, me in my shorts and sweaty pink Union Jack vest, him in his crisp, smooth slacks and cream shirt, and it reminded me so much of the episode with his son and the basket of flowers that I couldn't concentrate properly on what he was saying. As soon as I'd made some tea I suggested: 'Would you like to sit out in the garden?' in the tone of a duchess inviting someone for Pimm's on the terrace, remembering too late that I hadn't cut the grass for four weeks and that there was still the ghastly remains of a sparrow that Apple Pie had killed and then got bored with, lying on the patio.

'Lovely,' he said, nevertheless.

We carried tea and biscuits outside and I arranged our chairs either side of the sparrow corpse, which we both pretended not to notice.

'I've called round a few times,' he said. 'But you've always been out.'

'Jogging. I've been doing a lot of . . .'

'I've seen you. I didn't realise it was you, of course, but I noticed you. Jogging.'

'I noticed you, too.' My face flared with embarrassment. 'I mean, the car. The registration—IOU. It's . . . noticeable.'

'My initials,' he laughed. 'Ian Oswald. Awful names, but the initials are catchy.'

There was an awkward silence. What did he want? Perhaps he was going to reprimand me for threatening his son with a grapefruit knife?

'I could have phoned. But I really wanted to speak with you in person.'

Must be serious. Must be the grapefruit knife.

'Your son . . .' I began.

'Is a prat,' he said with a shrug.

Oh.

'My fault, of course. I shouldn't have left him in charge of the place. Too much responsibility for someone of his limited capabilities.'

Oh.

'But I had a hell of a lot to do, setting up the branch in Faro.'

Oh! There really was a branch in Faro?

'Despite all the rumours about it being a golf course,' he added with a broad smile.

What a nice smile that was. How the hell did a man like this manage to have a son like Simon? How unfair the laws of genetics could be.

'So how's it going?' I asked, out of politeness. 'The branch in Faro?'

'Getting off the ground now. I've left everything in the charge of a manager out there who seems to be a lot more capable than my own son,' he said ruefully.

I felt quite sorry for him. It wasn't his fault Simon was a prick.

'I've shaken things up a bit, at head office,' he added.

'I've heard,' I admitted.

He looked at me questioningly.

'Oh, come on, Mr Unwin,' I exclaimed. 'You must realise how people talk. I've got friends . . .'

'And they're saying?'

'Well.' I stirred my tea with my digestive biscuit, feeling uncomfortable. 'Well, just that you and Simon had a few words . . .' I smiled. 'No wonder he came round to see me bringing flowers and all . . . '

'Did he?' He looked surprised. 'He didn't tell me that!'

Not even about the knife?

'Well,' he added, 'I hope he expressed our concern. About your stress.'

'Oh, yes. Yes, he did,' I said into my teacup.

This was so embarrassing. He could surely see from looking at me that I wasn't remotely stressed. Stressed people don't jog around the streets, looking fit and tanned, in old shorts and pink vests. They don't go on jaunts to Cornwall and have passionate affairs with gorgeous men. They don't go on shopping sprees and buy new clothes that they have to go out to wine bars to wear. I suddenly knew with absolute certainty that I'd never been stressed in my life. It had all started off as a lie, but Dr Holcombe and Dr Lewis, between them, had done such a good job of diagnosing my symptoms that they'd begun to have even me convinced. It had been good to see Simon squirming in my kitchen, scared shitless that I was going to take him to court. It had served him right and it had made the whole thing worthwhile, but somehow it wasn't half so much fun doing the same thing to his father, who seemed like a nice guy. It was no good. I had to come clean.

'I haven't had stress at all,' I told him, putting down my cup and looking him in the eye.

'You haven't?'

He looked puzzled. He went to put his cup down too, but the dead sparrow was there.

'No. The doctors . . . I saw two different doctors. They both thought I was suffering from stress, and I believed them. But now, now I'm feeling better . . . '

I stopped, suddenly confused. If I was feeling better, then I must have had something wrong with me, mustn't I? So the whole thing couldn't have been a complete lie after all. I frowned, trying to understand.

'Perhaps it was something else?' he prompted me. 'Something . . . less serious? A virus?'

'Perhaps,' I agreed uncertainly.

'You hear a lot of stories,' he went on, quite earnestly, 'about people who have a virus, sometimes just an insignificant virus, not much worse than a cold or a minor flu, who then end up with a sort of fatigue . . . '

'Post-viral fatigue syndrome,' I nodded eagerly. 'I've read about it in the paper.'

'And it can last for months, even years in some cases.'

'Well, I certainly hope that's not what I've got . . . '

'No, no, I'm sure it isn't, but—'

'But perhaps something similar?' I wondered.

'You could have been tired. Run down. Overworked. Anxious.'

Oh yes. All of those, and more besides. Worried, frazzled, fed up and worn out were just a few that sprung to mind.

'But I really don't think it was stress,' I added more confidently. 'Not work-related, or any other related.'

'Well,' he said, and I could hear the relief in his voice. I could almost feel it coming out of his pores. 'Well, I'm so glad to hear that, Alison.'

'Thank you.'

'I came along, as you can probably guess, to apologise. Apologise on behalf of my stupid son, and his even more stupid girlfriend . . .'

'Ex-girlfriend, from what I hear!'

'Yes,' he smiled. 'Stupid bitch! I'm glad she's gone. Well, on their behalf, I want to apologise anyway, even if you're *not* suffering from work-related stress, for the awkwardness and unpleasantness they may have caused you . . .'

'It doesn't matter,' I told him. It really didn't, any more. 'It's all in the past, isn't it? He won't dare mess with me any more, Mr Unwin.'

'Call me Ian, please,' he said. 'Why won't he?'

'I think he's scared of me,' I smiled, remembering his face as I sorted out my knife drawer.

'I'm looking forward to you coming back to work, in that case,' he said. 'It would do Simon good to be scared of someone. Make him get off his ar . . . his backside and do some work.'

'I hardly think I'll ever have that sort of influence over him.'

'Perhaps not.'

He got to his feet, narrowly missing stepping on the sparrow.

'Would you like me to bury that for you?' he asked calmly.

'That's probably the nicest thing anyone's offered to do for me for a long time,' I laughed, and was amazed at myself afterwards.

Amazed at myself, and amazed at him. He got a shovel from the shed, he dug a hole in my garden, he buried my sparrow corpse, and for God's sake!—he was (a) almost a complete stranger and (b) my boss. And I stood by and watched him do it, laughing with him, having a chat about cats in general (he had one himself, apparently, called Captain), and Apple Pie in particular, and how ill he'd been and how we drained the fishpond for him and then found him in the car. And he told me about an old cat he used to have, who had a habit of climbing into the bath and falling asleep in there, and how he'd once terrified a house guest by rising up out of the bath as the old guy leaned over to turn on the taps.

THE TROUBLE WITH ALLY

And by the time the burial of the bird was complete we were pretty relaxed and I wasn't embarrassed about calling him Ian or walking back into the kitchen with him past my clothes line full of underwear.

'Well,' he said at the front door, 'I'm pleased to have finally met you, Alison.'

'You, too,' I said, meaning it.

'Now, you take care, and get yourself completely better before you come back to work, OK? Whatever it was you've had. Virus, flu, stress, strain or fatigue, whatever—we want you back fit.'

'OK.'

I held open the door. He hesitated, looking at his car from the doorway. Nice car, but no need to stand there looking at it. I waited. Couldn't very well shut the door while he stood there, and couldn't very well walk away with the door wide open, so I just had to stand there, holding the door, waiting for him.

Just one other thing,' he said at last after I'd begun to get pins and needles in the arm holding the door open.

'Yes?'

'Do you like Thai food?'

I looked at him with the sort of level of comprehension I'd have felt if he'd asked me to solve an algebraic equation in Japanese.

'Pardon?'

'Thai food. It's very nice. A bit spicy, but not quite like Indian. More like Chinese, but—'

'I know what it is. I just don't understand the question.'

'There's a nice little Thai restaurant out on the New Park Road. Next to the Gold Digger wine bar, opposite the . . .'

'I know. I know where it is. I still don't understand . . .'

'I wondered,' he said, still looking out at his car. Then he turned to look at me and added all in a rush, 'I wondered if you'd like to go there. One night. With me. Would you like to come out for a meal with me? Please?'

'I don't think so,' I said.

Oh no, I don't think so, do you?

This is the trick, you see.

Go round and see her. Be friendly, drink her tea, eat her biscuits, give her a load of sympathy about her so-called stress. Get her on your side by moaning about your son. Bury her sparrow cadaver and share a few jokes about cats jumping out of baths. Butter her up. Smile at her, tell her to call you Ian. Then go in for the kill. Let her really think she's special. The boss offering to take her out for a meal! Wow!

She won't believe her luck. She'll be the envy of all the other girls at work. She'll be no threat.

You'll never hear another word about work-related stress out of her.

Well, sorry, *Ian.* I may be dumb, but I ain't *that* dumb.

It put me in such a bad mood I *almost* dug up the sparrow again.

A pple Pie looked so much better, when Paul brought him home from the vet, it was hard to believe he'd been rushed into hospital with the blue light flashing. Well, almost. He yawned and stretched when we let him out of the cat basket, flicked his tail at us disdainfully and strolled straight over to the cat flap.

'Is he allowed out?' I asked Paul.

'The vet said he could go back to normal but keep him on a light diet for a few days.'

Apple Pie pushed open the cat flap and climbed out. We watched from the kitchen window, like fond parents watching a baby's first steps, as he strolled nonchalantly across the patio, stopped, sniffed the ground, turned round three times, sniffed again, and stared at us through the window.

'He looks a bit disorientated,' said Paul.

'No,' I smiled. 'He's wondering where his dead sparrow went.'

W e all went to the station on the Tuesday morning, to see Lucy off to Cornwall.

'Why have you taken the day off work?' she asked Victoria suspiciously.

'To say goodbye to you,' retorted her loving sister. 'In case you never come back.'

'Well, I might *not,*' declared Lucy. 'But that doesn't mean to say you can put any of your clothes in my wardrobe.'

'Girls!' exclaimed Paul, pulling Lucy's suitcase on wheels down the steps to the platform. 'Come on, try to be civil. You'll miss each other . . .'

'Yeah,' shrugged Lucy. 'Like you miss a spot after you've squeezed it.'

'You should know,' shot back Victoria.

It bothered me more that Paul had taken time off work than Victoria. Victoria would take a day off sick with the least provocation, but Paul was a different matter. It made it feel serious, like Lucy was really leaving home. Like he really thought he might not see her again. I felt tears prickling the backs of my eyes as I looked at her, bright-smiled and excited, clutching her train ticket and a magazine for the journey. Going off to be with the man she loved. Leaving us behind without a second's thought.

THE TROUBLE WITH ALLY

It was the natural order of things, the normal course of events. I looked at her sadly, remembering the little pink bundle I'd brought home from the hospital nineteen years before; the toddler in red velvet dungarees following her big sister adoringly around the house; the pretty girl with her long hair in pigtails and ribbons going to birthday parties in her best dress . . .

'What are you crying for?' Victoria suddenly asked me accusingly.

'Nothing. Just something in my eye.'

'Why do you think she's crying?' Paul snapped at her, to my complete surprise. 'Your mum's going to miss Lucy, and so will you, Victoria, even though you might not like to admit it.' He put his arm round my shoulders, making me jump in even greater surprise. 'She's not going to be very far away,' he said to me gently.

And I couldn't even reply, I was too surprised. And too choked up.

We didn't say much on the drive back from the station. Paul pulled up outside the house and Victoria jumped out.

'Cup of tea, then?' I asked him.

'No . . . no thanks.'

He was just sitting there, frowning, holding on to the handbrake.

'Well. Thanks for taking us to the station, and . . .'

'Wait. I need to tell you something.'

My mind reeled with possibilities.

I've decided to come back to you.

I've realised I never really loved Lynnette.

I want a divorce.

I haven't paid the vet's bill.

The vet told me something else was wrong with Apple Pie, something serious.

I've lost my job.

Each possibility was more worrying than the next.

'You're scaring me,' I told him, not liking his expression.

'No. It's nothing bad. It's just . . .'

I waited, trying to stop Worrying Possibilities flooding my brain and spilling out all over my body.

'It's just that we've found out how Lynnette got ill.'

Go on. Not fishing bait poisoning, then? I looked at him with sudden real interest. 'What was it? A dodgy pint?'

He laughed. I think it was what's called a rueful laugh.

'You're closer than you think. Not a dodgy drink—a dodgy meal. In a dodgy restaurant.'

'How did you find out?'

'The restaurant's been closed down. There's been a spate of food-poisoning cases and all of them had eaten there during the few days before they got ill. It was traced to their kitchens.'

'Not good for business.'

'No. Like I say, they've been closed down. You'll probably see it in the local paper.'

'Which restaurant?'

'The Thai one down the New Park Road. Next to the—'

'Gold Digger wine bar.'

'You know it?'

'No.' And not likely to, now.

'Lynnette loved Thai food,' said Paul. 'But I don't think she'll ever eat it again now.'

Me neither.

'Well, at least the mystery's solved,' I said.

'Yes.'

He looked wretched. Served him right. Suspecting his own wife of poisoning mistresses and cats.

'I owe you an apology. For the suspicions. It was out of order. Totally.'

'Apology accepted,' I said flatly.

'If you hadn't been acting so strangely . . .'

'I wasn't.'

'If you hadn't kept making threats to Lynnette . . .'

'I was joking.'

'Yes. Well, I'm sorry. We both are.'

'Good.'

So my reputation was saved. I was no longer a suspected poisoner. Well, great. He was sorry, Lynnette was sorry, we were all bloody sorry, but it didn't change the fact that he'd suspected it. If he could suspect me of doing something so hideous just because he thought I was acting a bit strange, just because I'd made a few jokes at Lynnette's expense, well then, it just showed what he thought of me, didn't it?

A bouquet of flowers was delivered during the afternoon. Yellow roses and blue irises. Lovely. Must be for Victoria from some poor young man trying to break down her resolve.

'They're for you!' she said indignantly, almost throwing them at me. She stared at the writing on the card. 'What does IOU mean?'

He phoned a few hours later.

'Did you get the flowers?'

'Yes. Thank you. Very nice.'

452

'You don't sound impressed,' he said.

Oh, don't I? Perhaps it's just that I have this funny side to me. This tendency not to want to be bought by bribery.

'I've got something in the oven,' I lied.

'All right. I'll talk to you again another time, then . . .'

Don't bother.

Chocolates arrived the next day, champagne the day after that. I threw them in the bin, I tipped it down the sink. I let the answerphone take the calls and didn't return them. You think I was overreacting? No, look! *He* was overreacting. Who sends flowers, chocolates and champagne to someone they hardly know? Only someone who's after something, and I don't mean something nice. Only someone who wants to be sure that they won't get taken to court. He was no better than his son, with his basket of flowers and his pathological fear of knives. No, no, let me get this straight. He was ten times *worse* than his son, because I disliked Simon anyway, whereas Ian . . . I could have liked him. That was what made me so angry. I felt a fool. I'd started to like him, in that very short time, sitting on my patio with the sparrow's rotting corpse between us and the tea and digestives. I'd thought to myself that he was a decent guy, a father who didn't deserve his son. And now I just felt stupid and naive, and I didn't want to speak to him any more. I didn't care what he sent me, it would get thrown in the bin. I didn't care how often he phoned, it would get picked up by the answerphone and ignored.

Why don't you answer the phone any more?' demanded Lucy crossly from Cornwall towards the end of the week.

'I've had some funny phone calls,' I said with some justification. 'How are you settling down?'

'OK.'

'Only OK?'

Alarm bells sounded in my head. She was homesick. She missed me. Or perhaps she missed Victoria. Or her bedroom. Her stereo system.

'No, fine. Everything's fine.'

She paused.

'Auntie Bev's got some strange friends, though, hasn't she?'

'You could say that, yes.' I smiled. 'But it takes all types . . .'

'And . . .'

'What?'

'Well, I don't think it's going to be so good here, with Neil, as it was when he stayed in London with us. He spends too much time surfing.'

453

Cracks in the beautiful relationship? After only these few days? My heart leapt with hope. It could be all over soon. She could be home to lick her wounds in time for the new term.

'But I think it'll be better once we've got our own place,' she went on cheerfully. 'And get married.'

Yeah. And have roses round the door for ever and ever. Dream on, my poor baby. Dream on.

I could ignore Ian as long as he kept phoning, but it wasn't so easy when he turned up on the doorstep. It was Friday morning and I was getting ready for my appointment with Dr Lewis. I'd made an effort with my appearance. I know you don't normally set out to impress your GP, but I wanted him to see me as a normal, relaxed, calm, pleasant person. Someone without an ounce of stress in their entire life. Someone whose daughter wasn't considering marriage to a beach bum in Cornwall, whose mother hadn't eloped to Spain with a toy boy, whose cat wasn't sitting outside a garage glaring at her and whose car wasn't survived traumatic poisoning. When the doorbell rang, I was in the middle of practising my prepared speech about how much better I felt now that I exercised regularly and ate no chocolate, and I'd opened the door before I had time to think. Or time to check through the window.

'Oh,' I said, politeness (only just) preventing me from shutting the door again in his face.

'Sorry,' he said, fidgeting with his car keys like a nervous schoolboy. 'But I've been trying to get you on the phone, and—'

'I've been out a lot,' I lied. 'And in fact I'm just going out now.'

'I see. Yes.' He managed to meet my eyes and added, 'You look very nice, too.'

Of course, this was all part of his buttering-up and bribery business so I took no notice whatsoever. It was, however, reassuring to know that the efforts I'd made for Dr Lewis seemed to have been worthwhile. I almost asked him if I looked like a calm, sensible, unstressed person, but then I remembered I didn't really want to talk to him.

'I've got to go now,' I said, pointedly, keeping him on the doorstep while I picked up my handbag.

'Of course. I'm sorry. I've called at a bad time.' Any time's a bad time, mate. Get the message.

'But please let me just tell you . . .'

Funny. People seem to keep doing this to me. 'Let me just say one thing': and then they seem to get struck dumb and it takes them half an hour to spell out the One Thing.

454

THE TROUBLE WITH ALLY

'It's about the Thai restaurant.'

And the One Thing always seems to be about the Thai restaurant!

'The one that's been shut down for food poisoning?'

'So you did know about it!' He struck his forehead in such a theatrical way that I almost laughed despite myself. 'No wonder you refused to come out with me. No wonder you haven't answered my calls. You must have been so insulted. What an idiot I am! How could I have been the only person in London not to know about it?'

'But . . .'

'Please believe me,' he went on earnestly. Well, it *looked* like earnestly, but I knew better, didn't I. 'I knew nothing about it. I wasn't trying to be funny, or cruel, when I asked you to come there with me—I happened to like the place. I didn't get ill when I ate there.'

'My husband's girlfriend did,' I commented.

'You see,' he said, slapping his forehead again as if to beat his brain into action. 'No wonder you were offended. Your own family affected by the food poisoning. Trust me to put my foot in it.'

'But I've only just found out about it.'

He was too busy berating himself to take this in. Instead, he continued at a rate of knots, as if he had to get this speech finished before he changed his mind, or more likely before I walked off down the path (which I was waiting to do).

'Now, I won't insult you again by suggesting another restaurant, and running the risk of finding out later it's infested with cockroaches or been demolished!'—He laughed uncomfortably here at his own joke. Good job one of us did—'So what I'm going to do is, ask you to do it.'

'Do what?' I asked, looking at my watch.

'Choose the restaurant.'

'What restaurant?'

'Any one. Anywhere you like. For whatever evening you like.'

'Mr Unwin,' I said, beginning to get really impatient. 'Ian. There isn't going to be a restaurant. There isn't going to be an evening. Now, if you'll please excuse me, I really am going to be late for an appointment.'

'Well, can I at least give you a lift somewhere?' he asked, a note of desperation in his voice. 'As I've made you late? And will you then at least *think* about the restaurant?'

I hesitated. Not about the restaurant, but about the lift. I *was* going to be late for Dr Lewis, by the time I'd walked round there, and this was very annoying as it would ruin all my good work at appearing non-stressed. I also quite fancied a quick ride in the BMW. Not that I'm a car snob or anything, but when your bastard Metro keeps glaring at you about its MOT failure, anything like this does appeal. I might even ask him to drive past the garage just so I can lean out of the window and put up two fingers at the Metro. Just as I was about to give in and agree to the lift, just as I had the word 'Well . . .' forming on my lips, my mouth pursed into a thoughtful and considered 'W', I looked up to see another familiar car turn the corner and pull up behind the BMW.

'There's no need for the lift, thank you!' I told Ian, almost elbowing him out of the way: 'My boyfriend's here! Hello, darling!'

I watched his face drop as I tripped down the path towards the other car. But it was nothing compared to the expression on Paul's face as I kissed him extravagantly and jumped uninvited into his passenger seat, cooing: 'Where are you taking me, darling?'

Lucky for me that Lynnette wasn't with him!

'Are we going anywhere in particular?' asked Paul, fairly calmly I think in the circumstances. 'Or are we just running away from Mr Flashy BMW?'

I looked at him sideways as he accelerated on to the main road. Did I detect a slight, ever so slight, hint of jealousy in his tone there? Something to do with the flashy BMW? Or (surely not) something to do with the fact that another man had been chatting to me on my doorstep?

'The doctor's, please,' I said. 'And sorry for all that. Calling you my boyfriend and kissing you and everything.'

'Was he harassing you or something? The guy in the flashy shirt?'

Oh, so it was a flashy shirt now, was it? Not only a flashy car but flashy clothes, too. I smiled to myself.

'No. Nothing I can't handle . . .'

'Look, Ally, we may not be together any more, but I don't want to think of you . . . well, you know . . .'

Having a life of my own? Having any fun? Seeing any other men?

'Getting yourself into any situations . . . ,'

'Paul, what are you trying to say?'

He pulled up outside the Health Centre and turned in the seat to face me properly.

'You're an attractive woman, Ally, and a lot of men . . . well, they see a woman on their own, and they think . . .'

An attractive woman? I pulled down the mirror and stared at the little bit of my reflection that it afforded. Was I attractive?

'If I was such an attractive woman,' I said dully, 'that men were going to start beating down my door to get to me, then you wouldn't have gone, would you? You wouldn't have gone to Lynnette.'

'Come on, Ally. Let's not start all that, all over again. These things just happen. I'm sorry, but they do. It's nothing to do with how attractive you are, or how nice, and good, and . . .'

'I know. I know that, really.'

'You do?' He looked at me in surprise.

'Yeah. I do. I understand. It's taken me a while, but . . .'

'Well, of course it has.' His voice was trembly with relief. 'It's only natural that it should have taken a long while. It was so hard on you. I didn't know how to make it any easier.'

'Don't worry, Paul. And don't worry about me, either. I don't have hordes of men fighting over me. That one . . . with the BMW . . . he's my boss. Slimy Simon's father.'

'Oh. I see.'

That made it all right, then, apparently.

'And he wanted to drive me somewhere out in the country and rip off all my clothes, tie me up, gag me, rape me, murder me and bundle my body into the boot of the car.'

'Ally! Sometimes, you know, I really do wonder about your sense of humour.'

So do I. I wonder where the hell I'd be without it.

Chapter 13

'ALISON,' DR LEWIS looked up with a beam. 'Well! You certainly look a lot better than last time I saw you.'

Thank God for those hours I spent in front of the mirror.

'Yes. I've followed all your advice about exercise and diet,' I gabbled. 'And I've lost some weight, and I go jogging every day. And . . .'

I'd forgotten it. I'd forgotten my carefully prepared speech.

With all the hassle of Ian Unwin turning up, and then the in-depth stuff with Paul in the car, my mind had gone a blank.

'And how are you *feeling*?' prompted Dr Lewis.

'Oh, fine. Yes. Much better,' I nodded brightly.

'Sleeping better?'

'Like a baby.'

'Still needing the diazepam?'

'Oh . . .' I blushed and bit my lip. Forgotten about those. 'No, I . . . didn't need them for very long.'

'And how are you coping now with your anxieties? About your job?'

'I can't wait to get back,' I told him earnestly. 'I think it's going to be fine. The Written Warning's been taken off my file and the temp's been kicked out.'

He smiled. 'There will always be other problems, though, Alison. Every day you'll have new problems to face. We all do. What I need to know is, are you ready to go back to facing them?'

'Well, I won't know till I get back in there, will I?' I retorted. 'No one ever solved any problems by lying at home on the couch listening to soppy relaxation tapes and eating celery, did they, Doctor?'

He leaned back in his chair and laughed.

'Yes, I think you're better,' he said, starting to write out the form that would certify me sane and safe to return to work. 'And I'm very pleased to see it.' He handed the certificate across the desk to me. 'But come back if you have any more problems. Remember, you should be looking after yourself now. You've spent years looking after other people. Be kind to yourself now, Alison. You're a nice woman. You deserve a bit of happiness. Go for it!'

'Oh. Thank you,' I stammered, completely confused. 'I will.'

What with Paul telling me I was attractive, and the doctor calling me a nice woman, this could all go to my head if I wasn't careful. I smiled to myself as I walked home. The sun was warm, I felt fit and relaxed and ready to take on the world. Go for it? I'd go out and grab it if I got the chance! If only I knew where it was and what it looked like.

Do you want to go out for a drink again, tomorrow night?' Liz asked when I phoned her with the good news about being signed back for work.

'Yeah. Yes, why not. That'd be great.'

'Anywhere in particular you want to go?'

'No. As long as it's not the Thai restaurant in the New Park Road!'

'Have you heard about that? It's been closed down.'

'I know. Paul's girlfriend ate there and nearly died.'

'Bloody hell. Did you send them a bouquet?'

And Paul thinks I've got a problem with my sense of humour!

It gave us the idea, though, of going to the Gold Digger wine bar, which was next door to the closed-down Thai restaurant. None of us had been in there before, but it looked all right from the outside and would save going all the way to the West End.

'You look nice, Mum,' Victoria commented, a bit grudgingly, I thought, as I was getting ready to go out.

Again, I looked in the mirror in surprise. So what had happened recently, apart from losing a bit of weight, to make me suddenly look nice and be called a nice woman? Had passing the milestone of the fiftieth birthday somehow worked some magic spell?

'Are you going out on the pull?' asked Victoria disapprovingly.

'I'm going out to have a few drinks and a chat with my friends,' I replied defensively, feeling like the child instead of the mother. 'But if there's anything out there worth pulling, that wants to be pulled, well . . . who knows?'

'Mother, honestly,' spoke in reproving tones my own child, the born-again virgin, the voice of celibacy. 'I really think—'

'Don't worry, Victoria,' I said, kissing her hastily as I heard a taxi pull up outside. 'I promise I won't do any drugs, I won't drink and drive, and I won't get pregnant. I might be late, though. Don't lock the door!'

Perhaps she might let me stay out all night when I get a bit older.

'I'm so glad you're coming back to work on Monday,' said Liz for probably the twentieth time. I was beginning to think she was trying to convince herself. It was getting a bit wearing. Mind you, she was pretty pissed. We'd shared a bottle of red wine already and were well into the second one. 'It's been no fun while you've been away.'

I don't remember it being much fun while I was there, but perhaps I missed it. Perhaps I blinked while the fun was going on, or it happened while I was in the toilet.

'I'm glad I'm coming back, too,' I said cheerfully. 'It's all very well being at home for a few days, but eventually you start feeling useless.'

'It's done you good, though, hasn't it,' said Mary. 'You look so much better.'

See? There it was again—this thing about looking better. What was wrong with me before? I must have looked terrible, and no one ever told me. Don't you think they should have told me? They were supposed to be my friends, after all.

'Talking about work,' said Liz suddenly, leaning across the table towards us with a sudden drunken lurch. 'Look who's over there, Mary!'

Mary turned to stare over her shoulder.

'Who?'

'You won't know him, Ally,' went on Liz in what she obviously believed to be a confidential whisper but which actually came out only a few decibels short of a bellow. 'It's Ian Unwin—Simon's father.'

You know I told you he was over from Portugal? Nothing like his son, is he?'

I froze in my seat. Literally froze. I had goose bumps all over me. I took a gulp of my drink. There was no way I was going to turn round. I didn't want him to see me. I could just sit here and pretend to be invisible and perhaps he'd go away.

'Actually I think he's quite good-looking,' went on Liz relentlessly.

She seemed, if anything, to be getting louder. 'Don't you think so, Mary? What do you think, Ally? Look, he's over there . . . what do you reckon? Not bad, is he?'

'Yeah, I'd give him one,' giggled Mary into her wine. 'What's the matter, Ally?'

'You all right, Ally?' echoed Liz. 'You look really red. Have you started getting hot flushes? You poor thing. Are you going to go on HRT?'

'Shut up, Liz!' I implored.

'Oh, look. He's coming over.' Mary whispered, barely containing her excitement. 'He's seen us.'

Heard us, more likely. So have most of the people in the wine bar, and probably half of those in the pub over the road.

'You can start HRT even while you're still having your periods, you know,' Liz was continuing, well into her stride. 'And it keeps you coming on regularly every month. But I think you're still supposed to use contraception. You'd better check that with your doctor, Ally. But I suppose there's not a lot of need for that, at our age, eh. Chance would be a fine thing, wouldn't it! Ha!' She chortled merrily and then looked up and nearly fell off her chair in surprise. 'Oh, hello, Mr Unwin! How nice to see you. Ally, this is Mr Unwin . . . Ally?'

Wishing only to die, preferably instantly and regardless of how painfully or messily, I was halfway under the table pretending to do something intricate and desperately important to my shoe.

'Ally, this is Mr Unwin,' she said again a little louder in case people drinking in Manchester hadn't quite caught it the first time.

'I heard you,' I replied, straightening up and glaring at her.

'We've already met,' he said. 'Hello again, Ally.'

Liz and Mary looked at me open-mouthed, their eyes full of accusation. You crafty cow, said their eyes. What's been going on here?

Later, I told their eyes. Later, I'll tell you, I promise. Just keep your conclusions to yourselves for a minute and don't say anything else to embarrass me, please.

'What's all this, then?' said Liz, ignoring everything my eyes had been trying to tell her eyes. 'You've already met?'

THE TROUBLE WITH ALLY

'Yes, we have,' I admitted in a miserable whisper. 'Hello, Ian.'

'*Ian!*' said Liz's eyes, wide open with shock. So it's Ian, is it?

He pulled up a chair. Why don't you join us, I thought, even more miserably. Liz and Mary were both stunned into silence, which, although a profound relief from the point of view of saving me from any further discussion of my periods, meant that I felt obliged to talk to him.

'How's your boyfriend?' he asked me politely, without meeting my eyes. Mary choked on a mouthful of wine and Liz had to go to the Ladies. By the time they'd both recovered, I'd managed to change the subject but neither of them could stop staring at me, as if I'd suddenly grown horns or developed an interesting rash.

'Did you get to your appointment on time the other day?' asked Ian.

'Yes, thank you. Sorry I had to rush off, but—'

'No, no, I quite understand. Inconsiderate of me, really, to turn up unannounced like that.'

I didn't dare look at Liz or Mary but I could tell from the continued unnatural silence that their eyes would be out on stalks by now.

'So I just wanted to apologise,' he went on. 'And buy you a drink. To show there's no hard feelings?'

'That's nice of you, but not necessary,' I said stiffly.

'Come on, let me treat all of you to a drink. Another bottle of red wine?' he insisted.

'That'd be lovely, thanks,' Liz got in quickly, recovering her power of speech.

'Yes, lovely, thanks!' agreed Mary.

'So how long have you been seeing your boyfriend?' he asked me very quietly as he stood up to go to the bar.

'Oh . . . quite some time,' I replied, looking at my problem shoe again.

'Well, if the situation should change . . .' he added meaningfully, hesitating, trying to make me look up at him. But my shoe was far more interesting and demanding of my attention.

He wandered off to get the drinks.

'What boyfriend?' yelled Liz as soon as he was half a yard away.

'What situation?' spluttered Mary, dribbling in anticipation of a really juicy bit of gossip.

'You lucky cow,' said Liz, looking at his departing rear with open admiration bordering on lasciviousness.

'You crafty mare,' added Mary. 'How many are you carrying on with?'

'None!' I said. 'Ssh! Keep your voices down, for God's sake. He'll be back in a minute.'

'How did you meet him?' persisted Liz.

'He only came to talk to me about my work-related stress. He only wanted to apologise about Simon, about the written warning. He only wants to make sure I don't sue the company. That's all.'

'It doesn't look like it to me,' retorted Mary.

'Doesn't look like what?' I asked nervously, stealing a look behind me and seeing him heading back with the bottle of wine and another glass. He saw me looking and smiled at me. I felt the heat rise in my face again.

'Doesn't look like that's all he wants,' she replied, watching him too. She turned back to look at me and added, 'And it doesn't look like that's all you want, either.'

'No. It doesn't,' agreed Liz, slurring slightly. 'It looks like you're both just about gagging for it . . . ,'

'Here's the wine, then,' said Ian softly at my shoulder.

'Cheers,' I said.

If all else fails, getting pissed often seems like the best solution.

He drove me home. Well, he drove all of us home, but he dropped me off last. I wasn't really in any fit state to argue by then, and I did fancy a ride in the BMW, anyway.

'Can you drive past the garage in Essex Road?' I asked him. 'I want my car to see me.'

'It's dark,' he pointed out, but nevertheless did so, and slowed down so that I could lean out of the window and blow raspberries at the Metro.

'I think that told it,' I said, sighing happily. 'Bloody thing.'

'What's it done?'

'Failed its bloody MOT. Wants me to take out a second mortgage to rescue it. Not that it even deserves it.'

I'd completely forgotten I wasn't supposed to be talking to Ian Unwin. I felt mellow and safe in the leather seat of the BMW, cocooned from the world and all its evils. I couldn't even remember what its evils were. We cruised gently home and he turned off the engine.

'I meant what I said,' he told me softly.

'What bit?' I asked, frowning, trying to remember.

'About your boyfriend. If the situation changes . . . ,'

'What situation?' I asked, still frowning, trying to remember.

'Is there really a boyfriend?' he asked, looking at me intently. 'Or was that guy just a friend?'

I tried hard to concentrate. I'd been off there in a dream for a few seconds, trying to imagine how it would feel if he kissed me. That's the only thing with being totally pissed. Your mind starts to play strange tricks and you forget what you're supposed to be talking about.

'Pardon?' I asked. 'You were saying?'

'Would you mind if I kissed you good night?'

Couldn't think of a damn reason why I should mind. Why should I mind? I leaned towards him and took hold of him round the neck. Yeah. Felt good. I kissed him long and hard and started to wish we were somewhere more comfortable than the front of his car.

'Wow,' he said very gently when we eventually paused for breath.

'Nice,' I smiled.

Then my head began to swim and I suddenly felt very, very sick.

'Thanks for the lift!' I muttered, struggling with the door handle. 'See you . . .'

Just made it to the bathroom in time.

'**So**?' demanded Liz as soon as I walked into the office on the Monday morning.

'So?' I repeated. 'What do you mean, "So"? What sort of a greeting is that for someone who's been off sick for the past six weeks? "Welcome back" might have been nicer!'

'So,' she repeated, ignoring me completely, 'what happened? After we got out of the car? Come on, come on, give, give! Did you have it off with him? Was it good?'

'Liz! No! Who? What do you mean?'

I sat down at my desk, not looking at her, readjusting the chair after its adjustment by Tracey who was apparently a short-arse. Switched on the computer, asked it to let me choose a new password. Rearranged the telephone, the mouse and the mouse-mat to suit my longer arms.

'Who?' laughed Liz. '*Who?* Don't give me all that crap! You and Ian Unwin. Come on, what's the score? You know you'll tell me eventually.'

'There's nothing to tell,' I said stiffly. 'I had a bit too much to drink, *as you know, as* we all did, and he very kindly drove us home . . .'

'And?'

And. And that kiss.

Wow.

Nice.

I moved the mouse, crossly, jerkily, familiarising myself again with the icons, finding my way around the screen once more. Don't think about it. The feel of the hair at the back of his neck, surprisingly soft and springy. The touch of his lips against mine, shockingly gentle but firm,

disturbingly passionate, but lingering and slow . . .
Click. Don't think about it. Click. Read email. Click. New messages.
Click. What's this?

Reintegration?
'What?' asked Liz, seeing the expression on my face. She got up from
her desk to come and look at my screen. I clicked the mouse button
quickly and told her. 'I've got to go to a meeting.'
'Meeting?' she echoed blankly. 'I don't know about any—'
It took me five minutes in the loo to do my hair and another five min-
utes to find out which office he'd taken over.
'What's all this?' I demanded, waving the print-out of his email at him
as I walked into his office. 'Meeting? Reintegration meeting?'
'Welcome back, Alison,' he said, getting out of his chair to close the
door behind me. He was smiling at me. 'Good to see you. Sit down.
Please.'

I sat. I watched him walk back to his side of the desk and I suddenly
felt nervous. Why? Well, there were a lot of things I'd have liked to say
to him. Things like: Cut the crap and let's get this straight. I was pissed
when I kissed you and I want to forget it happened. I don't know what
came over me. I don't have a boyfriend, I made that up to get rid of you,
but I don't want to go out with you and I resent you thinking I can be
bought off that easily.
Or that I need to be.
But at the end of the day, he was my employer, and this was my first
day back at work.
'About the other night,' he said suddenly, watching my reaction.
'Yes,' I said, not reacting.
'I'm sorry.'
'So am I. I was drunk.'
'Yes. Exactly.' He looked down at his desk, doodled on a pad, and
frowned to himself. 'I'm of the generation that was brought up to believe
that only an absolute cad, a filthy bounder, takes advantage of a lady
when she's drunk.'
I smiled, despite myself, which annoyed me. I smothered the smile,

To: Alison Bridgeman.
From: IOU.
Subject: Proposed meeting.
Proposed meeting? What proposed meeting?
A meeting is proposed this morning at 09.30 in my office to discuss your
reintegration into the company.

but admitted: 'I'm of the same generation, and I was brought up to believe that a lady doesn't get drunk in the first place. So let's just forget it, please.'

Forget the feel of that hair at the back of his neck. Look at it now, just where it meets the collar. Soft and springy.

'But I won't give up trying to make you change your mind,' he added.

'Well, you should do. I'm not interested.'

Not interested in those firm, passionate lips. Look at them now, remember how they felt. How difficult it was to stop . . .

'But I think you could be. Perhaps if it wasn't for the boyfriend?'

'Please, Mr Unwin. Ian. We have to work together, so I can't afford to be rude to you, but please don't waste your time . . .'

'You don't like mixing business with pleasure?'

I don't like being taken for a mug.

'Perhaps.'

'Well, I'll probably be going back to Portugal soon.'

So what was I supposed to do? Book his plane ticket? Wave him goodbye?

'OK,' I said.

'Perhaps just one night out together, then? Before I go?'

To safeguard the company? Bribe me into submission?

'No. I don't think so,' I said, again, getting up to go. 'Thank you for the meeting. I'll get back to my work now.'

'Yes. All right,' he said, opening the door for me.

I walked away, aware that he was watching me, and probably didn't breathe until I sat back down at my own desk.

'Tea?' asked Liz. 'Biscuits?'

Oh, yes. It was good to be back.

The roses were delivered at midday, red ones, a dozen of them.

This was not really on, was it? I mean, this was not really playing the game. Flowers arriving at home was one thing. Flowers arriving at work was a whole different matter. It got everyone talking, and it got Liz and Mary into an absolute frenzy.

They couldn't even eat their lunch they were so excited.

'They're from *him*, aren't they!'

'So are you going out with him? You *are*, aren't you?'

'I knew it! The meeting this morning . . .'

'It's no good you keep shaking your head at us, Ally. We're not stupid. We can see what's going on right under our noses.'

I sent an email after lunch.

To: IOU. From: Alison B.
Subject: Roses.
Please do not send any more flowers. People are talking. If I wanted flowers I would work in a cemetery.

The next day, two dozen roses were delivered, accompanied by a card which stated in very large writing: 'LET THEM TALK. PS: The cemetery has no staff vacancies.'

A basket of fruit was delivered on the Wednesday. I sent it, together with the four bottles of vintage port and the silk scarf, straight back to his office. This was getting ridiculous and would have to stop. If he carried on like this I'd be signed off with stress again by the end of the week. Nothing arrived on the Thursday, and I breathed a sigh of relief.

'I think he's finally got the message,' I said to Liz as we were clearing up to go home. 'Thank God for that. I was beginning to wonder what was going to turn up next.'

When I got home from work, there was a new white VW Golf parked outside the house. Tied up with a blue ribbon, with helium balloons sprouting from its door handles, it grinned at me in a challenging way as I stood staring at it from the corner of the road. It was raining, and I'd walked from the tube station because the buses were on strike. I looked at the Golf, and it looked straight back at me.

'Now what are you going to do?' it said. 'You and your principles?'

'Fucking hell,' I said.

Chapter 14

THE KEYS FOR THE CHALLENGING white Golf had been put through my letterbox in an envelope, together with (by the feel of it) the paperwork. Nothing written on the envelope, of course. People who delivered new cars with balloons and banners on them to other people's houses presumed, I suppose, that the recipient would know who they were. And of course, I knew who he was, all right. My legs were shaking as I sat down, next to the window where I could look at the car, with the envelope in my hands, and thought about it. My legs shook so much, even while I was sitting there, that I had to go and pour myself a brandy from the bottle I kept for emergencies. I sat there, sipping the brandy, feeling the keys in the envelope, and staring at the car, for about half an hour. Every few minutes I closed my eyes, counted to ten, and opened them again, expecting the car to have disappeared and a TV crew from *Beadle's About* to have jumped out from behind the bushes shouting:

'So, Mrs Bridgeman. What have you got to say to the friends who played that little trick on you? Is it true that you've never had a nice new car like that in your entire life? Well, there you go! You've still never had one! Ha! Ha! Isn't she a good sport, everyone?'

Victoria's car pulled up behind the Golf and she got out, slowly, eyes riveted to it. She approached the car cautiously and touched its bonnet very gently. Was it a mirage? Was it going to melt away before her eyes?

She turned and ran up the path, let herself in at the front door and screamed: 'Mum! Whose car? Where's it come from? Is it a present? Who's it from? Why . . . ? What . . . ? Can we go out in it? When . . . ?'

'No,' I said, dully, still staring at it from the window.

'But why . . . ? Why not? Who . . . ? What . . . ?'

'Because I'm sending it straight back,' I interrupted before we could get any further into the interrogation. 'It's not mine, and I don't want it.'

'But . . .' She gulped, lost for words. 'But . . .'

I stood up, put down the brandy glass with a decisive thump and went out to the kitchen to make tea.

'Forget it, Victoria,' I told her brusquely. 'Forget you've seen it. Pretend it's not there. It'll be gone by tomorrow.'

I peeled potatoes viciously and stabbed sausages with a red-hot anger. Now I'd got over the shock and the disbelief, I was so angry, if I could have seen him right now he'd be in there with the sausages, stabbed and fried. How dare he? How dare he think he can buy me like this? What did he take me for? What sort of person would send back wine, chocolates and flowers but be won over by a car? I would *not* be that sort of person, however much I wanted the car, however much it hurt to send it back, however much it smiled and winked at me out there while the old bastard Metro sulked and languished at the garage. My moral indignation grew and swelled as the sausages spat and shrivelled. Did he really imagine I was going to sign some sort of declaration now, to say I accepted his gift of a car and would undertake never to sue his company for my work-related stress? Then, I suppose, he could fly off back to Portugal with an easy mind, leaving his slimy son in charge again, and the minute his back was turned, Simon would sack me. And nobody could do a thing about it because I'd be driving around in the Golf, paid off and signed off, and out of a job. Well, if he thought I was falling for it, he had another think coming. I wouldn't drive that car, I wouldn't get into it, I wouldn't open its door or touch its door handle. I wouldn't even look at it. It was going straight back.

I didn't have his phone number. I had to wait until I got to work the next day (by tube, *not thinking about white Golf GTi's* at any stage of the journey, even when the tube stopped between stations for ten minutes due to signal failure), whereupon I went straight to his office and flung the envelope with the keys and documents in it, onto his desk. The gesture was spoilt somewhat by the fact that he wasn't there, but it would make its impact as soon as he came in and sat down. For good measure I sent a very curt email:

To: Mr I Unwin.
From: Mrs A Bridgeman.

This is not acceptable. I do not accept it. Please remove it from in front of my house at once. I will treat any further offerings as harassment and may have to consult my solicitor.

After I'd sent it, I felt a quiver of anxiety about the fact that he was, after all, still my employer. Also, I didn't actually have a solicitor. However, I was still too angry and offended to really worry about it and, when all was said and done, he wouldn't have a leg to stand on if this whole business came out, would he?

I worked like fury all morning, taking out my temper on the keyboard and refusing to answer Liz when she tried to find out what was wrong. It was nearly one o'clock, and I was just contemplating going to lunch, when Lucy phoned.

'Mum? Listen, I haven't got long . . .'

'What? Lucy, is that you?' It was a terrible line, sounded like someone was practising Morse code in an aviary.

'Yes. Can you hear me? I'm calling from a payphone, and I haven't got any more money, so . . .'

'Why? What do you mean, you haven't got any more money? Where are you? Why are you on a payphone . . .'

'Mum, just listen, or the money will run out! I'm coming home.'

'You're what? Coming home? Why? What's happened?'

'Neil and I are finished . . .'

I knew it. The bastard. I'll kill him.

'And I . . . er . . . need to get away quickly. So—'

'What do you mean, quickly? What's happened? Lucy, are you all right? Tell me.'

'Yes, I'm all right, but I'm coming straight home.'

'Where's Beverly? Let me talk to her.'

'She's not here. Look, the money's running out.'

'What's *happened*, Lucy?'

I was on my feet now, shouting into the phone. Liz was staring at me across the office, hand to her mouth, eyes wide.

'Has there been . . . any violence?' I demanded, beginning to shake ever so slightly.

Silence. And then, in a very quiet voice: 'Well . . . sort of . . .'

'My God!' I practically screamed. 'I'm coming to get you! Stay there! Don't move! Don't let anyone in! I'll be straight there! Lucy . . .?'

The line had gone dead.

I thought I'd been through some Worrying Things in my time, but believe me, at that moment I realised none of them had even been worth a moment's concern. They had been nothing but minor irritations, mere itches on the skin of my life. This was the Fear, the Dread so great and so awful in every mother's heart that it can't even be spoken about. The one that starts to bug you when you first get the result of the pregnancy test, and grows huge and desperate when you hold that newborn baby in your arms and understand for the first time the vulnerability of life and your role as protector. The real terror you feel as you watch your child cross the street, ride off on their bike, drive a car for the first time. It never goes away, it just lies there dormant, and then a phone call out of the blue brings all the monsters suddenly and horribly to life. My baby, hurt, crying, needing me, out of my reach. I had to get to her, now, instantly, and nothing else mattered. I couldn't think, I couldn't reason, I couldn't listen to Liz trying to calm me down, I just had to go. Now.

'Tell them . . .' I said, my voice trembling, waving an arm in the direction of the management offices. 'I had to go.'

Liz was trying, gently, to hold my arm, stop me from rushing headlong out of the office.

'You can't drive in that state. You'll have an accident. Let me . . .'

'No. I'll be OK. I'll . . . oh. Oh, shit.' I couldn't drive. Of course I couldn't drive. I didn't have a car.

'I'm sorry. Mr Bridgeman's out of the office at the moment, Mrs Bridgeman,' said his secretary sweetly. 'Can I give him a message?'

'Shit! Sorry. No. No message. Don't worry.'

I hung up and dialled Victoria's work number.

'No, sorry,' said a strange voice answering her phone. 'She's off sick today. Who's calling?'

Nobody. Nobody calling, and certainly not her mother, a mother who didn't even know her daughter was skiving off work. I phoned home. No reply. The crafty little minx had taken a day off to go out somewhere without even telling me. Great! Just great! Never mind about me, needing her, needing her car to go and save her sister's life. I felt tears threatening and blew my nose angrily. This was no time for self-pity. I had to think of something.

'Please. Let me drive you,' said Liz. 'I came by tube but I can pick up the car and come back for you, and . . .'

'No. It's all right. I'll get the train down there. It'll be quicker. Or I'll go and steal the Metro back from the garage . . .' I stopped, suddenly remembering. 'No I won't,' I said, more calmly. 'I know what I'll do.'

Ian Unwin looked up from his desk in surprise as I flung open the door. 'I want the keys back,' I said abruptly, holding out my hand. 'I haven't changed my mind. It's an emergency. I need to use the car.'

'What keys?' he asked.

The tears overflowed and started running down my face. He jumped to his feet, looking alarmed.

'Don't play games, not now!' I cried. 'My daughter's in trouble and I've got to go down there! I'm sorry about the email, if it was a bit rude, but I don't want to be bribed. I just want to borrow the car, please . . .'

Out of the corner of my eye, I saw the envelope, still sitting unopened on his desk where I'd left it. I reached out and grabbed it, almost knocking him out of the way.

'I'm sorry!' I said, ripping open the envelope and tipping the car keys out into my hand. 'But I've got to . . .'

I threw the envelope back on his desk and ran out of the office.

I ran out of the building. I ran to the taxi rank at the end of the road. I ran out of the cab straight to the lovely white Golf GTi, yanked off the ribbons and the helium balloons and jumped into the driving seat.

I ran out of petrol about a mile along the M4.

Well. It was the last thing on my mind, wasn't it—petrol. I suppose I assumed that new cars were delivered to their new supposed owners with a full tank. Or perhaps I didn't assume anything, the state I was in. Perhaps I just completely forgot about cars needing petrol. I was lucky, of course, not to have an accident, lucky that when I started to lose power I reacted instinctively enough to indicate and get onto the hard shoulder before I stopped dead.

'Fuck!' I shouted at the car, with complete justification, you must admit. 'Fuck, fuck, fuck!' I smacked it, hard, on the dashboard. I put my head on the steering wheel and moaned with despair. Then, while I was lying there, my head on the wheel, my arms flat out on the dash, I became aware of a sound coming from the floor of the car. From my handbag on the floor of the car. It was my phone! My mobile phone! Oh, yes! Thank you, God, thank you, thank you, for the wonder of modern communication! I almost kissed it as I took it out of my bag and pressed 'talk'.

'Mum?' Victoria's voice sounded odd and strained. 'Is everything OK? I just phoned your work to ask you about getting chops for dinner, and Liz said . . .'

'No!' I snapped. 'No, it's not OK. Lucy's in trouble and I'm bringing her home.'

'What? What trouble? Where are you?'

'Stuck on the M4. Where are you, when I need you? Why are you off sick? Why aren't you home? What are you doing?'

'I'm at Andrew's house,' she said in a very defensive tone.

Oh, I see. Andrew, is it, now? The Last Stand of the Celibate Army has fallen at the feet of an Andrew. Didn't take long, did it? No wonder she kept it quiet.

'Well, get yourself out of Andrew's house and down the M4 in that car of yours, right now, can you?' I said tetchily.

'But what's happened to Lucy? Why?'

'I'll tell you when you get here,' I returned, cutting her off.

Almost as soon as I put the phone down it began to ring again.

'Ally!' said Paul. 'My secretary said you phoned. She said you sounded upset.'

'I was! I am!' I swallowed hard, trying not to start crying again. 'Paul, I'm on the M4 and I've run out of petrol, and I've got to get Lucy back from Cornwall, she phoned this morning, and Neil's finished with her, and something's happened . . .'

'Hey, hey, slow down, calm down!'

I stopped, breathing heavily.

'Victoria's on her way,' I added. 'She just phoned. We'll go in her car.'

'Are you in the Golf?' he asked.

I stared at the phone. Something not quite right here. Had I missed something? A chapter of my life? Paul didn't know about the Golf.

'Has Victoria told you?' I asked. 'She's told you about the Golf?'

'No, she hasn't spoken to me about it. Nor have you, yet, but I guess you were going to get round to it. But I presume it's OK?'

'What?'

'I should have told them to fill up the tank. If you'd phoned and let me know it had arrived, I'd have warned you.'

'You?' I said. 'You?'

In my mirror, I saw a silver BMW coming up behind me, passing me slowly, indicating left and then pulling onto the hard shoulder just in front of me. IOU 1.

'You!' I said again, still weak with shock, as I watched Ian Unwin get out of the driver's seat and stride towards me.

'Ally?' said Paul. 'Are you all right?'

'I'll call you back,' I said, very ungraciously in the circumstances.

'What are you doing here?' I asked, getting out of the car. I couldn't seem to help the ungraciousness, it seemed to have become second nature to me all of a sudden; even now I was facing my boss on the hard shoulder of the motorway having just accused him of bribery. The Worry about Lucy, the awful, primal fear and need to rescue her, had done away with my own survival instinct and common sense.

'I was worried about you—' he began.

'Worried?' I retorted. 'Worried? *You're* worried? I'm scared shitless, me!'

See what I mean—completely ungracious.

'Sit down,' he said, pushing me back into the seat of the Golf.

He came round to the passenger side and sat down next to me.

'Now, take a deep breath. Come on, try and calm down. You've got yourself so worked up—'

'Worked up? Of course I'm worked up! My daughter's lying somewhere, battered and bruised for all I know, and that bastard—'

'It's all right, Ally.'

'All right? It's not bloody all right! She's hurt, and it's all my fault!'

At this, this admittance of what was bothering me, what was lurking in my subconscious underneath all the primal fear, and nagging away at me, I started actually crying out loud. Sitting there, in the front seat of a brand-new car bought for me by my husband, being comforted and—yes, now, cuddled too—by my boss, I blubbed and bawled all over his shirt until my throat hurt.

'It's all my fault!' (sob, sniff) 'If I hadn't pretended to be ill . . .' (blub, blub) '. . . I made it all up, I never had stress, I just wanted a day off work and Simon would have sacked me . . .' (sob, howl) '. . . And now you'll probably sack me anyway . . .' (sniff, snivel) '. . . I should never have told all those lies . . .' (gurgle, sob) '. . . I wouldn't have gone down to Cornwall in the first place . . .' (howl, moan) '. . . and Lucy would never have met that *bastard!*'

'Ally,' said Ian, taking a huge clean white hanky out of his pocket and wiping my face with it. So gentle. So bloody gentle and caring, when really all he wanted to do was get rid of me, sack me quickly now he knew all about my lies and malingering, to say nothing of my accusing him of bribery with a new car. 'Ally, please stop crying. Please, listen to me. Everything's all right.'

'No, it's *not*!' I raged. 'Don't you understand? I have to get going, *now*. I have to get down to Cornwall . . .'

'No, you don't,' he said firmly. 'Listen to me. Your daughter phoned again.'

She did? I hiccupped myself into silence and clung on to him for a minute, sniffing slightly, before I realised what I was doing and let go.

'Liz took the call, just after you left,' he went on.

'What did she say? How did you know?'

'I knew because I was in your office at the time. I was trying to find out from Liz what was wrong with you. I was worried about you.'

He looked at me. I looked at him. Thought about him being worried about me. Thought about him being there, listening, when Lucy phoned again.

'What did she say?' I asked quickly. 'Is she all right? Is she hurt? Did you tell her I was on my way?'

'She's not hurt at all, Ally. She's absolutely fine. She knew you were worried, that's why she got some more change and phoned again.'

'But she said he'd been violent! Neil! He's been hitting her, or . . .'

Ian shook his head, smiling. 'Mothers! Your imaginations run riot! You got completely the wrong end of the stick. He hasn't done anything to her at all. She wanted to get away quickly before he found out what *she's* done to *him*.'

I stared back at him, my tears drying quickly, my heartbeat slowly returning to normal.

She wasn't hurt. She wasn't in danger. I could breathe. It felt good. It felt wonderful. I inhaled. Lovely. Exhaled. Lovely.

'What *she's* done to *him*,' I repeated, slowly.

'She's cut off his hair,' he said, and his smile spread across his whole face. 'She found him with another girl. So she waited till he was asleep, dead drunk, and she cut off his hair. Then she packed her bags and left.'

Wow. I took another deep breath, and started to smile myself.

Wow, Lucy, what a way to go! What a girl! Serve the creep right, the two-timing little git.

'So where was she? Where was she phoning from?'

'At the station. She was phoning from the station. She's on the train now, on her way back to Paddington. You don't need to drive anywhere. That's why I came to find you.'

'But you didn't know . . . you didn't know I'd run out of petrol . . .'

'No. I was going to keep heading on down to Newquay till I passed you, I thought at first that you'd be driving your old Metro, the one you pulled faces at in the garage, so I was pretty sure I'd pass you sooner or later.'

'And I'm not. I'm not in the old Metro. I'm in this . . . this white Golf.' I looked down at my lap, almost too embarrassed to carry on. 'How did you know it was me, then?'

'When you took the car keys out of that envelope on my desk, I didn't have a clue what you were talking about. I hadn't even opened the envelope because I didn't know what it was and I'd been busy all morning. Just as I was leaving the office to come and look for you, I thought to have another look in it. And there was the registration document for a white Golf GTi, and a gift card from someone called Paul. I still don't have the slightest idea what it had to do with me, but at least it told me exactly what car to look out for!'

'You thought I'd bought it for you?'

'I'm so sorry, Ian. I've made the biggest prat of myself . . . Oh, and the email! I'm so sorry about the rude email!'

'I haven't read it yet,' he replied, laughing. 'How rude was it?'

'I threatened you with my solicitor. But don't worry!' I added quickly. 'I haven't even got one.'

'That's all right, then.'

'It's not funny. I feel so embarrassed.'

'Don't be. I didn't buy you the car, but I expect I would have got around to it sooner or later. I probably wouldn't have moved straight from wine and flowers to a car, but I'd have built up to it.'

'Why? I kept telling you not to. I kept sending them back to you. I didn't want . . .'

'You can't blame a guy for trying. I had to try. Despite the boyfriend, and everything.'

'He's not my boyfriend,' I interrupted impatiently. 'That was just another one of my lies.'

'I knew it!' he smiled triumphantly.

'He's my husband.'

'Oh.' His face dropped.

'Separated. Been separated for two years.'

'Oh!'

'It's him, apparently, who's bought me the car.'

'Oh.'

'Must be because he felt so guilty about calling me a poisoner.'

He frowned at this, as well he might, but was wise enough not to comment.

'Anyway,' I sighed, rubbing my eyes, feeling suddenly very, very tired and wanting to go home. To get home before Lucy arrived, have the kettle on ready for her. Tea and sympathy and a hot bath. Give it a few days and she'd be over it. We both would. 'Anyway, now I've told you about my lies, about my malingering, you can push off back to Portugal, and you won't have to worry any more about me and my so-called work-related stress. You won't have to bother any more about trying to keep me quiet, bribing me with flowers and stuff . . .'

'Bribing you?' he said, and his voice was louder than I'd ever heard it before. I looked up at him. There was something in his eyes that I couldn't look away from. 'Bribing you?'

The traffic on the motorway flew past us relentlessly, at seventy or eighty miles an hour. *Whoosh, whoosh, whoosh.* Past the window they went, a red car, a black car, a coach, a lorry, another red car, while we sat there, in the front of a brand-new Golf with no petrol in its tank, paid for by my husband for reasons I could only guess at, and stared at each other, and the whole world suddenly changed.

'You weren't?' I whispered. 'You weren't trying to bribe me?'

'No,' he said. His voice sounded sort-of choked and half strangled. 'What a ridiculous idea. What sort of books do you read, for God's sake, you absolutely ridiculous woman?' And he burst out laughing.

'I'm sorry!' I said, mortified, still staring at him.

'I suppose it's my own fault,' he said eventually, trying to control himself. 'I went a bit overboard with the gifts, didn't I?'

And he reached out and stroked the hair off my face where it had got wet with tears and stuck to my nose.

'I suppose you thought I was trying to bribe you when I offered to take you out for a meal?' he said softly.

I nodded. He kissed me, gently, right on the tip of my nose and laughed, gently, right into my eyes.

'And now? Would you think I was trying to bribe you if I suggested you get into my car and I drive you home?'

I shook my head.

'Or if, instead of driving you straight home, I drove you to a motel somewhere and booked us into a room, and ordered champagne, and took you to bed, and . . .'

I don't know who made the first move. We kissed as if our lives depended on it, as if we'd both been locked up somewhere for about a thousand years, where kissing hadn't been allowed, and been forced to watch videos of other people doing it. I thought it was going to kill me; that the feeling I'd had building up inside me, without acknowledging it, since the day I first met him, since the day I saw him sitting in his car outside my house with his arm hanging out of the window and his hand tapping to Queen . . . 'I'm falling in love . . .' —that this feeling was going to overwhelm me and drown me. Feelings like this didn't happen to real people, people outside of books and films and *EastEnders*. I must be dreaming.

'MUM!!'

'ALLY!'

The shouting, the knocking on the window, the faces staring through the glass . . .

This was real, all right. This was no dream.

Ian and I sprung apart like two guilty children, looking at each other in amazement. How did that happen? How did we get to feel like this about each other? And when? Before we were born? Or just now?

'Mum! For God's sake!'

I turned my gaze reluctantly to the car window. Victoria was pounding on it, and next to her, Paul was shaking the door handle as if it wasn't locked, just a little bit stiff, and he'd soon get it open. The car was rocking from side to side from their combined efforts.

'All right, all right!' I exclaimed, opening the door and letting them both fall in on top of me. 'No need to get excited!'

I looked back at Ian (well, it had been a full five seconds since I'd looked at him), and we smiled at each other soppily. I *knew*, I knew it was a soppy smile but I didn't mean it, it just happened on its own without my permission.

'Oh, yuk!' said Victoria. 'Mum! I can't believe you! Lucy's lying in some hospital or somewhere, injured, and . . .'

'No, she's not. She's fine,' I said, still smiling at Ian.

'She's fine?' echoed Paul. 'You're sure?'

'I panicked. I overreacted. She's on her way home by train. She cut off his hair,' I said, all in one breath. 'Sorry, everyone.'

'Sorry?' echoed Victoria, pretending to be resentful, but relief oozing out of her like perspiration. 'Is that all you can say?'

'Yes,' I said, cheerfully. 'Thanks for coming to find me. You can go back to Andrew now.'

She looked slightly abashed. 'I was going to tell you about him . . .'

'It's all right, Victoria,' I smiled. 'I knew you wouldn't make it as a nun. Black and white doesn't suit you.'

I got out of the car and walked with Paul back to the Primera.

'I brought you a can of petrol,' he said, getting it out of the boot, not looking at me.

'Thanks, Paul. How did you find me?'

'Phoned Victoria on her mobile. You didn't call me back, and you switched yours off.'

Did I? Bloody hell. The things you do when your train of thought's interrupted by seeing a silver BMW.

'I thought I might get here quicker than her,' Paul went on. 'In fact I passed her just as I turned onto the M4. Then we both found you . . . and the BMW.'

'He's my boss,' I said. 'Ian. Ian Unwin.'

'So you said before.'

'And I think I'm in love with him.'

There. I'd said it. It was out. I'm in love with him. This is it.

This is what it feels like, then, after all this time, at fifty years of age. This time I know it's for real . . . .

'Be careful, Ally. Don't get hurt . . .'

Hurt? Hurt? You dare to stand there and talk to me about not getting hurt, you, of all people? You, you who left me after all those years of marriage, left me for someone young and pretty, left me on my own with the girls and the cat and the bills and all the Worries?

I turned and watched as Ian got out of the car, my new car that Paul had bought me (for reasons of his own which weren't, after all, too very difficult to guess), and approached us. He was tall, and lean and smart. He was tanned and fit and gorgeous. And I loved him. He smiled at me. I smiled back.

'Do you want to poison him?' I said very quietly to Paul with a sudden flash of intuition.

'I suppose I do,' he admitted.

'I'll tell him to look out for slug pellets, then, shall I?'

'No. Fishing bait,' said Paul, managing a smile.

We were in Portugal by the time I finally admitted it. We flew out for a couple of weeks in September so Ian could see how the Faro branch was doing and we could spend some time relaxing together in the sun. I was able, by then, to look back and think about it all a bit more clearly. A bit more honestly.

'I think perhaps I might have had a breakdown of some sort, after all,'

I said, leaning back in my chair beside the pool. 'Do you think I did?'

'Maybe, maybe not. Who knows? Who's to say what's normal behaviour and what isn't? Perhaps it's not so very strange to fall apart a little when everything gets too much to cope with.'

'I did have a lot of worries all going on at once. And they all seemed to build up and sort of . . . take me over.'

'That's understandable. Completely normal.'

'And to threaten your husband's girlfriend with poison?'

He smiled. 'Completely normal.'

'And . . .' I dropped my voice to a whisper, 'To actually *do* it?'

He laughed and leaned over in his chair to plant a kiss on my face. 'Totally, utterly normal, I'd say. Can't understand anyone who disagrees!'

So that's OK, then.

Isn't it?

Totally, completely normal.

Even if it was only laxatives in her coffee.

Nothing to worry about there, then.

SHEILA NORTON

'I just have this terrible feeling that I might wake up and discover that this has all been a dream,' Sheila Norton confessed to me when I met her recently near her home in Stock, Essex. 'I have always enjoyed writing and it has been a life-long ambition to have a novel published—it's just such a fantastic feeling and I still can't quite believe it yet.' All her life Sheila has been 'scribbling bits and pieces', as she describes it, and for the last five years she has edited the unofficial newsletter of Broomfield Hospital, where she works full-time as a medical secretary. She has also won a couple of short story awards and some of her stories have been published in *Woman* and *My Weekly*.

'The idea for *The Trouble with Ally*,' she told me, with a smile, 'first took root when I was out walking the dog with my eldest daughter. I told her that I wanted to write about an older heroine, having the sorts of problems and anxieties that women like me and my friends have. I wanted to write a book that we could relate too and say, "That's my life." My daughter was very encouraging and told me that she thought that I had discovered a gap in the market.'

I had to ask Sheila whether or not she too had found turning fifty a difficult time, as Ally does in the novel. 'Goodness, no,' she laughed. 'I had the biggest party and the best birthday ever. Fifty is an enjoyable

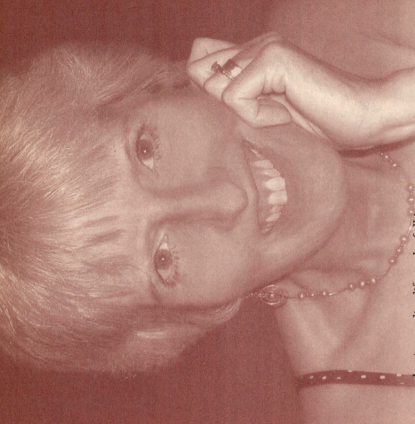

age and a time to live life to the full.'

Sheila, clearly, does exactly that; embracing new challenges such as taking piano lessons alongside her daughters and, recently, learning to swim. 'The one thing about getting older is that you start noticing that your body needs a little more attention,' she says, with a wry grin. 'A friend suggested that we swim to get fit and so we took swimming lessons at our local pool. It was great fun and the result was that I lost two stone!'

When Sheila had finished writing *The Trouble with Ally*, she sent it off to a number of publishers and sat back to wait for replies. 'I don't have an agent and so I was not too sure just how long it would take. Eventually, I had a positive reply by email from Piatkus and I remember sitting at the computer screen, tears flowing down my face. My husband came home and automatically thought it was bad news—it's amazing how we women cry when we are both happy and sad.'

Sheila has now written a second novel, *Other People's Lives*, and is currently working on her third, which is to be set in the kind of hospital environment in which she works. 'It's a tremendous privilege to be paid and offered a contract to do what I love doing,' she said. 'But I would do it anyway—I'd just have piles of unpublished manuscripts taking up every surface at home.'

Jane Eastgate

479

601-022-1